MIDSHIPMAN TOM

OR THE CRUISE OF THE WAR CLOUD

London: HOGARTH HOUSE, ST. BRIDE'S AVENUE, E.C.

THIS PLATE IS
GIVEN AWAY

"READY AYE READY."
With George Emmetts celebrated sea story

MIDSHIPMAN TOM

OR THE CRUISE OF THE WAR CLOUD

Ready at all Booksellers on Wednesday June 16. 1875.

London: Hogarth House. St Brides. E.C.

MIDSHIPMAN TOM.

BY

GEORGE EMMETT,

Author of "Sheet-Anchor Jack," "The War Cruise of the Mosca," &c.

PROFUSELY ILLUSTRATED

BY

EMINENT ARTISTS.

Publishing Office:

HOGARTH HOUSE, ST. BRIDE'S AVENUE,

LONDON, E.C.

CONTENTS.

MIDSHIPMAN TOM

OR,

THE CRUISE OF THE WAR CLOUD.

BY GEORGE EMMETT,

Author of "Tom Wildrake's Schooldays," etc., etc.

PREPARING TO ATTACK.

CHAPTER I.

THE COURT-MARTIAL.

THE most formidable sea robber that ever infested our coast was Derrick, or the Red Hand. No peaceful vessel was safe from the attack of his numerous horde of desperadoes, neither were the mansions of the wealthy that were situate near the coast more secure than the unarmed shipping, nor even the heavily-armed East Indiamen.

Red Hand's name was a terror; and to such an extent had his depredations been carried on that a ship of the line was ordered to be stationed on that part of the coast most frequented by the freebooter.

The man-of-war was furnished with an extra

number of large, swift boats, each armed with a gun in the bows, and it was to these boats the task of capturing the Red Hand devolved.

There had been many encounters between these armed boats and Red Hand's luggers; but up to the time our story opens, no advantage had been gained over the freebooters by the king's ship.

The officers were annoyed at this; for the admiralty had held out hopes of promotion to those on board the Hercules, should the freebooters be captured.

Several seamen were sent ashore, disguised as farm labourers or fishermen. Their duty was to keep a sharp look-out, and give timely notice to the line-of-battle ship of the movements of the freebooters.

One evening, just as the gun had fired from the bow of the huge vessel to announce the sunset, a fishing-boat shot alongside, and a man climbed swiftly to the deck.

He was garbed as a fisherman, but the sailors whom he met at the gangway received him as a messmate.

"What news, Ben?" asked one. "Any night-hunting afloat?"

"I think so," Ben replied. "Where's the officer of the watch? I see him. I must go and report."

* * * *

Night had thrown her mantle over the ocean; the moon was hidden by a bank of dark clouds, and, save for the pale gleam of the distant stars, there was nothing to guide the course of the four boats that, like dark shadows, were creeping, with muffled oars, from beneath the dark hull of the line-of-battle ship.

The leading boat was in charge of a midshipman, Tom Wilson by name. He had been reared, until he reached the age of fourteen, upon that part of the coast which lay within reach of the Hercules' heavy ordnance.

A bold, dashing fellow was this midshipman; one who had proved himself a young Briton in many a yardarm to yardarm engagement; yet, after four years' service, he had not advanced one step up the slippery ladder of promotion.

It was the opinion of his messmates that Tom was too independent to truckle to his superiors. Thus he was overlooked, when others less worthy, less brave, and less of a seaman were raised to a swab.*

But there was *one* on board who knew why Tom Wilson was so treated, and he kept that knowledge to himself.

It mattered but little to the light-hearted mid. He loved his profession too well to care for the rewards. So he fought and played practical jokes, did his duty manfully, with the assurance that the day would come when his true worth would be seen, and the prejudice so much against him would wear away.

* Swab, an epaulette.

It was not often he had an opportunity of distinguishing himself, and as he laughingly said to a brother mid when he was preparing to go with the boats—

"I should not have obtained this had it not been for my knowledge of the coast."

Twenty minutes' rowing brought the boats before a wide inlet. Here Tom Wilson ordered the blue jackets to pull swiftly in, while the other boats lay about a mile from the entrance.

The cutter had not gone halfway up the inlet, when Ben Bight, the look-out, whispered—

"Be careful, sir. I just caught the gleam of a lantern ahead; and if I ain't out of my reckoning that gleam means the robbers are getting their boats out, for we are close to the cave they hide in.'

"So much the better," said Midshipman Tom. "Pull away, my lads, and let's take the beggars before they are ready."

Scarcely had he spoken when the pistol he held in his hand went off, and a thousand echoes reverberated amongst the high rocks.

"Curse the pistol!" he said, "I did not know t was cocked. Bend your backs men, and dash at them. Concealment is no longer necessary."

The sailors replied with a shout, and the boat sped forward—no longer in darkness, for twenty rockets whizzed upwards from the cliffs, and their light revealed the position of the man-of-war's boat.

In an instant the sides of the inlet were alive with armed men, and volley after volley of musketry was poured in upon the unfortunate boat's crew.

"Give it them—muskets and pistols," said Tom; "ready with the gun for'ard, the boats are coming down upon us!"

It was too true—the dark outlines of six huge boats were seen coming from the shore, and the light guns in their bows began to throw charges of grape at the man-of-war'smen.

In a few minutes one-half of the rowers were struck down; and Tom, taking the stroke oar, called out—

"They are too many for us. Pull, men! pull, for your lives, and let us join our boats!"

It was a pull for life, for the freebooters were close upon them, and when they reached the entrance to the inlet the other boats from the man-of-war dashed up to Tom Wilson's assistance.

When the freebooters saw this, a blue light shot up from one of their boats; the firing ceased, and, like magic, the men disappeared from the rocks and the boats to a secret entrance that had hitherto baffled the man-of-war.

The lieutenant in charge of the boats would have saved the fearful slaughter that took place, but it was too late to escape the withering fire that came from the well-sheltered freebooters; and through this deadly storm of bullets he had to make his way from the inlet.

Angry and crestfallen, the party returned to the line-of-battle ship, and when the officer in command heard the story, a gleam of malignant joy shot across his features.

"Place Mr. Wilson under arrest," he said, "and tell him to prepare himself for a court-martial."

The lieutenant looked surprised at this command, but his duty to his superior kept him silent.

Midshipman Tom was placed under arrest; and until the court-martial assembled, all on board the Hercules, were puzzling their brains to make out the charge that would be brought against one of the best officers on the ship.

Tom Wilson had no suspicion of the enormity of the crime with which he was charged until the president of the court-martial read these words—

"Midshipman Thomas Wilson, of his Majesty's ship Hercules, you stand before this court charged with being in league with a band of desperate men who have defied their country's laws. The first charge against you is firing a pistol to give the pirates notice of the coming of the party under your orders. The second charge is for cowardice in retreating from the enemy when they opened fire upon your boat—such charges being against all good order and discipline, and unbecoming an officer and gentleman holding a position of trust under his Majesty's flag."

There was a pause, and Tom Wilson placed his hand upon his forehead like one in a dream. Poor fellow! he could not believe his senses.

"Midshipman Thomas Wilson," said the stern voice of the president, "are you guilty or not guilty of the charges preferred against you?"

The handsome youth drew his lithe form erect, and, looking his judges frankly in the face, proudly answered—

"Not guilty—so help me, Heaven!"

His answer was taken down in writing, and the trial proceeded—the sailors who were in the boat reluctantly giving their evidence about the explosion of the pistol, doing all they could to acquit Tom of any blame.

"Your honours," said Ben Bight, "the prisoner was a little narvous, like, and he had the pistol cocked, and his finger on the trigger; and when I saw the light he was excited and pulled "——

"That will do," said the president, "we do not require your explanation; your evidence is all we want."

One after the other the men were snubbed by their commander, and as each one left the state room, they gave Tom, their favourite, a pitying look.

The court-martial, as far as the evidence against the prisoner was concerned, ended, then Lieutenant Alton, a sinister-looking man, who, for some cause, bore Tom no good will, was called to give the prisoner a character.

"He's a good seaman," said Alton, "perhaps as good as we have on board in working a ship in calm or storm, a good fighting officer too, and, but for his connexions ashore, I have no doubt he would have "——

"His connexions ashore!" said the president, "pray explain, Mr. Alton."

"Well, gentlemen, he is the son of the once notorious smuggler, Philip Wilson; the man who, for some secret service has been forgiven his "——

"I am not Philip Wilson's son," said Tom, with startling vehemence. "This is but an invention of Lieutenant Alton's, who never bore me any good will."

"Silence, prisoner," said the president. "Now, Mr. Alton, please explain the connexion between the charges against the prisoner and the fact of his being the ci-devant smuggler's son."

"It's only an opinion I have formed, sir," was the crafty answer, "and as such I give it before this court. Since the affair took place I have thought it quite possible the prisoner's father is mixed up, more or less, with the pirate gang, and the prisoner, having become dissatisfied with the service, because he has not been promoted in his turn, may, for a bribe, have offered to give a signal that led to such fatal results. Of course, as I said before, this is merely a supposition, and I do not wish it to be as evidence against the prisoner."

The crafty villain knew full well the weight his words had with the members of the court, and when he retired, it was with the full knowledge that he had done more to damage the prisoner's cause than the charges he had to answer.

"What have you to say to this?" the president asked. "You have pleaded not guilty to the charges preferred against you."

"I have; and as far as Lieutenant Alton's accusations are concerned, they are a tissue of falsehoods from beginning to end."

"Your name is Wilson, is it not?"

"I bear that name."

"And you were brought up by Philip Wilson?"

"I was."

"Yet he is not your father?"

"He is not."

"Then your name is not Wilson, and Philip Wilson is not your father?"

"Such is the case."

"Then, may I ask what your name is, and who your parents are?"

Tom looked helplessly at the officers, and, his face reddening with shame and anger, answered—

"God help me! I do not know them!"

The president looked from one to the other of the assembled officers, and that look, as plainly as words, said—

"You see, gentlemen, he adds lies to the other crimes he is charged with."

"Take the prisoner away," he said, aloud, "and let a sentry be placed over his berth."

With bowed head and swelling heart, the boy was taken to the gun-room, there to await the sentence of the court-martial.

That sentence he knew would be—"DEATH."

———

CHAPTER II.

SNOWBALL'S PLOT.

THE sentry over Midshipman Tom was a gigantic African, called by his messmates, Snowball.

The dusky giant was particularly fond of the middy; and could he have swung at the yardarm in place of the gallant youth, he would gladly have made the sacrifice.

The African stood over his prisoner, his arms folded across his massive chest, his white teeth gleaming, and a tiger-like expression in his eyes; and when Tom raised his head he met the glaring orbs fixed full upon him.

"Well, Snowball," said our hero, "I suppose my end is pretty near?"

"Dat depends, Massa Tom. Snowball tink not. If you do what I tink you ought to do, you no die like mangy dog with a rope round um neck."

"What do you think I ought to do, Snowball?"

"Why, live."

"I should like to do so, my friend."

"You would?—dat good. Now listen, Massa Tom, and I tell you what dis infant, Billy Bight, Fo-castle Joe, and lot more talk about when you being tried, and we tink we do it, too."

"What is it, my dusky friend?"

"Just dis. You know me and lot more tired ob the king's service—very much tired, too much floggee; so we say, if Massa Tom like to be our leader, we go with him."

"Go with me where, and for what purpose?"

"Purpose, Massa Tom?" Why, to do as we like. You have ship—be captain. We stick to you, and King Sheorge and his service go to de debbil for all we care!"

"Well, but how is it to be done?" Tom asked, amused by Snowball's plot. "Where can we get a ship? How can I escape from here?"

"Both of dem easy enuff. I, your sentry, let you go, and go wid you. Den, as for ship, you know dat lubly schooner dat lay inshore, de one sent to help us cotch de pirates."

Tom's eyes had a momentary sparkle as he pictured himself upon the War Cloud's deck; but the light faded when he said—

"How are we to get possession of the schooner, supposing I consent and escape?"

"Dat easy enuff. Nearly all de crew hab come on board de Hercules, because we short-handed, and dey all say will go wid me and de rest, if you go wid us."

"But, Snowball, you forget we shall be guilty of piracy, and hanged as such, if we are caught."

"No, Massa Tom, we not pirates. De pirates hab been de cause ob you getting into dis trubble, and we cotch dem—dat more dan anybody else ean do."

"True. I begin to see your plan."

"Dat right. When we do dat, you go to de first man-ob-war, and say here de pirates; we cotch dem. Have your ship back again; have your sailors; and both de ship and de sailors ready to fight for you, if you forgive dem and me for de way which we prove we no friend to de robbers."

Midshipman Tom reflected for a few moments, and the more he thought over the plot to more it suited his bold nature.

"If carried out, Snowball," he said, "I do not despair of outwitting my enemies. But one thing you have overlooked—we shall be treated as outlaws until we can prove our true characters."

"Dat don't matter a bit; we soon do dat."

"Well, even so, we must live until then; I mean, we must have provisions and ammunition for the War Cloud."

"Dat true. And we get plenty, for dere is always lots ob de French ships in de Channel, and we must fight dem."

"So far you have answered every question: but there is another yet, Snowball."

"What dat?"

"Suppose we are chased by a vessel too big for us to fight—what are we to do then to save ourselves from being taken?"

"Ha! ha! Massa Tom, dat a good one, you know; and Bill Bight knows plenty ob caves in de rocks where we hide, and places where de sunken rocks are dat we get de War Cloud behind, and laugh at the king's cruisers."

"A good idea, Snowball."

"Den you say yes, Massa Tom?"

"I must have time for reflection, Snowball, for the step you propose is an important one, and the lives of many gallant fellows will be jeopardized by my consent."

"Berry well, Massa Tom. You 'flect as you call 'um, and when you 'flect enough, just go to de port; dere you will see a rope round de mouth of de gun, and at de end ob de rope you find a boat; if you go in dat boat, go to de Debbel's Rock and we come"——

"But"——

"Wait minit, Massa Tom. I go away now to talk to my mates; de captain say I could go when you fall sleep. Now, I come back in one little hour, and, if I find you gone, den I tell 'em, go and seize de schooner, and we meet you at the Debbil's Rock and take you on board, and den we show dem what we do. Don't forget, Massa Tom—if I find you gone, we go and do what I say."

Before Tom could reply, the African Colossus left the gun-room, and our hero began to consider well the dazzling offer made by the hardy, gallant sailors who so well loved him.

Snowball had not left the gun-room more than five minutes when one of the midshipmen came down from his watch on deck.

He was a friend of Tom's—a good natured brave young fellow, who felt deeply for his messmate's terrible position.

"Well, Tom, old boy," he said, placing his

hand upon the prisoner's shoulder, "keep up your spirits; all may yet be well."

"You don't believe what you say, Fred Ruddock: yet it is kind of you to try and cheer me a little."

"It is a serious matter, Tom; but I believe, had it not been for that snake, Alton, the charges would have broken down."

"You think so?"

"I do, and the opinion is shared by everyone on board, except your judges. What a pity it is, Tom, you could not have given him the lie."

"The lie?"

"Yes; told the court the name you ought to bear, and who your parents are; that would have set aside his story about old Philip Wilson. His son, indeed! Why, there's as much similarity between you as there is between Snowball and the captain's French poodle."

"I wish I could have done so, Fred,"

"I've been thinking," said young Ruddock, "of getting leave to-morrow, and visiting Old Philip. Perhaps he will throw a light upon the matter by at once disowning any relationship, and telling the captain who you are."

"He would not do so, Fred. He is a strange man."

"I know that, so fear my visit will be almost useless. Yet I can try."

"It would be waste of time. Would that I could see"——

"Ah! the very thing. Why can't you do so?"

"A prisoner! How is it possible?"

"Quite possible, I should think. There's a ball about to take place on deck. Don't you hear the band?"

"I do."

"Well, you are sure not to be visited by any of the officers until that is over, and you can easily get ashore and back before the morning."

"True. I had not thought of that. Thanks to Snowball, the means of doing so is at hand."

"What may the means be?"

"A rope attached to yonder gun, and a boat at the end of the rope."

"Good. Now, away with you."

Tom jumped to his feet, and when about half-way to the porthole, turned and said—

"Can I trust you, old fellow?"

"You ought to know best."

"True. I should not have asked the question. Well, listen. I have something to tell you, but never breathe a word to"——

"Damme—no proviso. If you don't know Fred Ruddock better than that, don't place any confidence in him."

Tom grasped the speaker's hand; then, in a low voice, told him the plot concocted by Snowball and his messmates.

"A wild plan," said Fred. "Just like sailors. They are as full of romance as schoolboys."

"You will tell them not to carry out their de-

signs. Tell them I shall soon return and possibly escape any punishment for the false charges brought against me."

"I will. Go on—good bye. Return as quickly as possible."

"Good-bye," said Tom, as he descended the rope. Good-bye."

Fred took off his watch coat, and arrayed himself in his best uniform to attend the ball, and thoughts of the approaching festivities quite drove all remembrance of Tom Wilson's message from his mind.

He put the last touch upon his natty tie, and looking at himself in the inch-and-a-half of glass, said—

"Not a bad-looking fellow, after all. So I suppose I shall stand a chance of getting a good partner for the dance."

"Mr. Ruddock," shouted the gun-room attendant, "the captain says you are to make haste, please. He wants all the gentlemen on deck."

"All right—I'm coming."

Away sped the mid to the quarterdeck, and, amid the sweet music of the ball and the charming society of the young ladies who had come aboard, he forgot all about Tom Wilson.

Half-an-hour later Snowball's woolly head appeared at the porthole where Tom had descended.

"Gone, by golly!" said the black giant. "Boat gone—Snowball and him mates go, too. Play up, you debbils on deck! Dance away, massa officers! You dance to a nudder tune to-morrow!"

Snowball put his thumb to his nose, and, with much inward satisfaction, moved his fingers insultingly in the direction of the quarterdeck.

Two hours after, Lieutenant Alton came to the gun-room. The prisoner had escaped, and the officer, with a bitter curse, went quickly to the captain of marines, and ordered him to send a party ashore and search for the fugitive.

"Do not bring him on board," he said. "Lodge him in prison. He will be safe there."

CHAPTER III.

A GALLANT DEFENCE.

PHILIP WILSON was rather astounded at the sudden appearance of gallant Tom, whose face was flushed with excitement and the dread that his absence might be discovered.

The meeting was not of a very cordial nature, for there was but little love between them.

There was something so repellant in the man's nature that totally chilled any affectionate feelings that would arise in Tom's breast for the man who reared him from his infancy.

It was not poverty that soured Philip's temper —far from it—for he lived in a style far above the country gentry.

Although he had become wealthy, his money seemed to have made him morose and sullen. His hair grew white long before its time, and those that had been near him when he slept spoke of strange mutterings falling from his lips.

Words that told of some heavy secret connected with the past, and a secret which had marked his face with deep furrows of care.

Though nothing definite could be gleaned from his dark mutterings beyond a few words respecting a ship that had foundered at sea, and all hands had perished.

In Philip's moments of frenzy he would shriek aloud—

"Keep off! keep off! I did not cut the hole below the water-line. Keep off!"

Before Philip had become wealthy, he brought to his home a child, a brave, handsome-looking boy, one of higher birth, from his appearance than Philip wished the world to believe.

"He is the son of an old mate of mine—a fisherman. He died, and left the boy to my care."

Such was Philip's story; but it seemed strange that he should so bitterly hate and illtreat his old friend's son, the gallant Tom Wilson. Yet he did hate him with an intensity peculiar to his nature; and oft as he saw the daring youngster climbing with fearless dexterity the dangerous rocks, he would mutter—

"Would that your neck were broken! for when I look at you it brings back the memory of that night! Ay, that night, when they all went down!"

Tom had reached the age of fourteen when the fact of his not being Philip's son was revealed to him. He was tall for his years, and with a frame as graceful as Apollo's, yet as muscular as a young gladiator.

Like all brave boys, he loved the ocean and its dangers, and much against Philip's wish he had gone to sea.

He had been away nearly four years, and Philip, when he scowled at the boy's noble form, inwardly muttered—

"He is like his father—very like him." And then, raising his voice, he said—"Well, Tom, what has brought you here to-night?"

"I have come," said a boy, with a quiet determination, "to have an explanation with you."

"What about?"

"My birth and parentage, Philip Wilson."

"Your devils! Don't you know you are my son?"

"It's not true."

"What do you mean by giving me the lie? I will horsewhip your carcase until"——

Philip jumped to his feet as though to put his threat into execution, and Tom, seizing a heavy chair by the back, swung it above his head.

"Keep back!" he cried, calmly, "or there will be mischief done."

"You murderous young wretch! Would you slay your father?"

In the same quite voice, Tom replied—

"Father, you lie, for a purpose of your own. You keep my birth a secret. I am not your son—

such being the case I defy you. But one thing I would ask before we proceed any further—that is, who are my parents?"

"Your parents—you—you cursed imp! I—I"——

"Liar!" was the quiet interruption.

Philip sprang to his feet, and clutched a decanter to hurl at the boy; but the sight of the heavy chair and the glitter in Tom's eyes caused him to replace it.

"It is well you have done so," said Tom. "I am in no humour to be trifled with! Again I ask you, who are my parents?"

"I don't know. Curse the hour ever I brought you into my house!"

"Are you speaking the truth?"

"You——Yes, I am."

"One thing more, Philip, before we part. Do you remember when I came to you? It may help me to discover who I am."

"No!" was Philip's savage answer.

"Yet," Tom continued, musingly, "you should do so; for your sudden prosperity, if people speak the truth, came about the time I first appeared under your roof."

Philip ground his teeth with rage.

"Unless for a sinister purpose," Tom went on, "you can have no interest in keeping the knowledge of my birthright from me. Answer this question, and I will be content: *Do you remember the night you brought me here?*"

Had a shell suddenly exploded under Philip's seat, he could not have sprung up quicker than he did when Tom used these words.

A moment he stood, as though suddenly rooted to the spot; his face, which had hitherto been pale with rage, was now livid and ghastly, the veins on his forehead stood out like thick cords.

Suddenly he clutched a heavy stool, and, with a howl such as a hungry tiger would have given, he yelled furiously—

"Remember the night! remember it! Ha! ha! ha! remember it!"

Then, sinking his voice to a whisper, he added fearfully—

"They all went down; not one—not one was saved!"

He ceased his low, terrible whisperings; his face paled, and his eyeballs starting as though suddenly encountering some unearthly vision; then, giving one wild shriek of fear, he fell senseless to the ground.

Tom, bold as he was, felt appalled at the terrible spectacle Philip presented, thus stricken down by the workings of an unquiet conscience.

With a long, steadfast gaze, Tom looked at the prostrate, guilt-stricken man, and he mused.

"There is some terrible secret connected with my birth—a secret that weighs heavily upon his mind, and one that it must be my task to discover."

The brave boy stood silent, as thought after thought rushed through his brain. Wild, convulsive thoughts, that sent the hot blood rushing in volumes to his face, and amidst these sudden conflicting emotions he saw a lovely, fairy-like form floating before his vision.

"Great heaven!" he murmured, bitterly, "my task to discover who I am? What shall I be in a few hours, that I should wish to know the secret of my parentage? Oh! why did we ever meet! Not one moment for a parting farewell! Yet, why should I wish it? What has the outcast boy who has dared to break his country's laws to do with the lovely heiress of yonder mansion?"

Philip here gave a low moan, and turned his wild, glaring eyes. A moment they rested upon Tom, then closed again as a shudder ran through his frame.

"Tom," he said, rising to his feet, and speaking in a thick, husky voice—"Tom, poor wronged, ill-used boy, do not be led away by the thought that my agitation has anything to do with the knowledge of your birth; it has not. But upon the night when I first saw you a dreadful affair happened; a terrible calamity, my boy, one that has haunted my brain ever since. But you have no connexion with it; it is the racking thought when I look at you and remember that night—that dreadful night when I carried you in my arms."

"Then you know nothing of those," said Tom, mournfully, "who so cruelly left me to the world?"

"Left you to the world, Tom? Your fate was far worse, had I not saved you. But I am ill, Tom, we will talk some other time. I have my suspicions, my boy—suspicions, should I but obtain the slightest proof, will elucidate a mystery that I have not yet fathomed."

"That mystery, Philip?"

"How you came where I found you. But hark! What is that?"

Tom listened attentively, and could plainly hear the measured tramp of armed men approaching the house.

Philip staggered more than walked to the window, and a cry of alarm escaped him as he beheld the glittering bayonets of a party of marines that were making for his door.

With a countenance expressive of alarm, he turned to Tom and said—

"What is the meaning of this?"

"It means," replied the boy, as he moodily folded his arms, "It means that I am wanted by those on board the Hercules."

"You, you! Why, what have you done?"

"I am a court-martial prisoner, and have broken my arrest to see you."

"My God!" ejaculated Philip, "it is all over with you, my poor boy! They will hang you at the yard arm."

Tom started and turned pale. Death he feared not, but a disgraceful termination like this to his existence caused his blood to curdle through his veins.

"A dog's death!" he muttered between his clenched teeth; "a doom they shall never inflict upon me."

"What would you do, rash boy?"

"This," replied Tom, taking a cutlass from the wall, "battle with those men until I fall pierced by ball or steel. That is the death of a hero! Not wait to be strung up like a dog."

As he spoke the brave boy's eyes flashed brightly, and drawing the cutlass, he hurled its sheath to the further corner of the room.

Simultaneous with this action, a heavy blow was delivered at the street door by the butt end of one of the soldier's muskets.

"Open the door," cried the officer in command, "open in the King's name!"

Pale and trembling, Philip went and opened the window, and, in an agitated voice, demanded—

"Who are you that would disturb peaceable subjects from their sleep?"

"It won't do, Philip," said the officer, gruffly. "You want to keep us in parley while the youngster escapes, but that won't do either. The house is surrounded with my men."

"What, in heaven's name, do you want with the boy?"

"Nothing, much. He has broken his arrest, for which little diversion he will swing from the yard arm to-morrow night. So come, open the door; we want Tom Wilson, and mean to have him."

Tom's blood boiled, and still grasping the cutlass, he flung the window wide open, and stepping upon the sill, said, in a loud voice—

"Tom Wilson is here to answer for himself, and those that want him will have to take him."

So saying, the boy closed the window, and rushed to the top of the stairs, there to await the coming of his captors.

With angry oaths they battered in the door, and, led by the officer, they came swiftly up the stairs.

About the centre of the flight they came to a halt, and gazed inquiringly upon that determined youthful figure, with his right arm bare, and clutching a shining blade.

"Drop that cutlass," said the officer, "and come quietly with me. It will be better for you."

Tom made no reply to this command, except by raising his weapon in a threatening manner.

"You young cub!" roared the officer. "Do you mean to defy me and six of King George's marines?"

"Ay, twenty, if they were here!" said Tom, scornfully.

"At him, men!" cried the infuriated officer. "Use your bayonets, but take him alive, if possible."

The officer drew his sword, and, setting his men the example, dashed up the stairs, and tried to knock the cutlass from Tom's sinewy grasp.

There was a sharp click as the blades met each

other, and Tom's assailant fell back with a loud scream of agony.

His cheek was cut open, and the blood pouring in a stream over his body.

In his haste to capture the gallant boy, he had overlooked the fact that from Tom's elevated position he could easily keep a dozen men at bay.

"Shoot him!" yelled the wounded man, "shoot the young fiend!"

Before the marines could pull back the hammers of their muskets, Tom dashed down the stairs, cutting and slashing his way to the door, which stood so invitingly open.

CHAPTER IV.

THE OUTLAWS' RETREAT.

SIXTY-FIVE strong-limbed seamen, with the African, left the Hercules during the time the officers were footing it merrily on the deck.

They left in small parties; for, although there was a fleet of shore boats that had brought the company on board made fast to the man-of-war, the men would not all go off at once, fearing they should be detected.

They pulled swiftly to the War Cloud, and the men in charge of the beautiful vessel, recognising their messmates, made no objection to their coming on board.

The midshipman in charge was surprised at so many men coming without an officer, so he turned to Snowball, who stood near, and said—

"What's the matter, Blackie, that so many men have come on board without an officer?"

"Dey hab do no such ting, de officers come wid em."

"Where are they?"

"Here one," said the African, striking his broad chest; "dare two more, and de commander he come soon."

Snowball pointed to Ben Bight and Forecastle Joe, as he spoke; and the mid, who had no suspicion of the true state of affairs, said—

"Look here, nigger, if you are not civil, I'll see what I can do to get you a couple of dozen before you have your breakfast to-morrow."

"You be dam," replied Snowball; "dere is no more floggee for de men who hab come on board dis ship."

"Hallo! mutiny! Here, seize this fellow and put him in irons."

No one stirred to obey this order, and Ben Bight came forward, and touched the mid on the shoulder.

"Look here, young shaver," he said; "we are no longer under the king's flag. Not to mince matters, we have deserted, and have, as you perceive, taken this vessel, which will soon be out of reach f the Hercules, or any force the Hercules can send against it."

"You mutinous scoundrel! What do you mean?"

"What I have said. That is, we are about to sail under the orders of Tom Wilson; so the sooner you leave the better. And harkee, my prying cock-of-the-walk, just tell the officers on board the liner to treat their seamen a little more like men, and less like brutes, or there will be a ship without any crew; for the lads are quite aware they can come to us, and join a ship where there will not be any cat-o'-nine tails hanging over them."

The midshipman was petrified with astonishment, and when he could speak he turned to the men who had been with him in charge of the brigantine, and said—

"Arm yourselves, my men, and drive these mutineers from the deck."

"Much obliged, cockey," said one, "but we have just joined 'em; so as you are the only one that is not wanted on board, the sooner you go the better."

He went down the companion, and Ben Bight called out—

"Perhaps you'll oblige us by taking the boat back. It belongs to some of the shore folk."

The middy would have preferred going in the War Cloud's light skiff; but fearing to ask for it —for there were many men on board he had been the cause of being punished—he seated himself in the heavy tub, and with the wind dead against him pulled for the Hercules.

"Now, my lads," said Ben Bight, "let's up with the anchor, for our young commander will be waiting for us at the Devil's Rock."

The swift vessel was soon skimming through the water, and when opposite the jutting rock, she was rounded-to and a boat lowered.

The men searched for Tom Wilson, and not finding him were about to return and ask Snowball if he had given the proper rendezvous.

They had pushed the boat out when Philip Wilson came to the water's edge and hailed them.

"Are you about to return to the Hercules?" he "if so, I will pay you well to take me aboard."

"The Hercules!" said Ben Bight. "We don't belong to her. You had better get a shore boat."

"I would," said Philip, "but they are all away with the people who have gone on board the man-of-war."

"Can't help it," said Ben. "Good night. Lay-to, lads."

Had they asked the old man one question, there would have been much less anxiety on board the War Cloud that night.

"Suffing's gone wrong," said Snowball. "Now, de best ting to be done is to run de brigantine through the sunken rocks; den we can look after Massa Tom. You know de Channel, Ben?—take de helm."

"All right, Snowy; and I know something else."

"What's dat?"

"Why, a secret cave, the entry of which is under

water; so that if we are followed we can get away. What do you think of that, Snowy?"

"Dat de berry ting, for dere will be a fine row when dey find out we hab gone; so brace up de yards, you lazy beggars."

The vessel was skilfully piloted through the reefs, and a small inlet, formed by a cleft in the rocks, totally hid her from the view of any passing craft.

"Now den for de cave," said Snowball; "let's see what sort ob a place it is. Den I go and seek for Massa Tom, and I don't come back till I find him."

"Be careful, Snowy," said Ben. "We must be like the owls, only go out at night; for there'll be a strong party on the look-out for us."

"I know dat," grinned Snowball; "so if I don't come to-morrow morning, you know I hiding somewhere in de rocks."

The cave was soon reached, and the men saw at once the extraordinary advantage it possessed either for retreat or defence, for it was un er one of the loftiest cliffs, and accessible from the sea, and then only at low water.

At other times, that is, when the sea was at its flood, the entrance was hidden by the waves.

It was an impossibility for the water to enter the cavern, as it was situated about the centre of the rock, and nearly fifty feet above the level of the ocean.

The outer entrance, which became full of water when the tide rose, led to a long flight of steps (beyond the second or third step the water never reached), and after ascending this rocky ladder, brought the outlaws to their secret retreat.

Upon the third night of Tom's imprisonment, the outlaws were assembled in their stronghold, and Snowball, who had been away, rushed into the cave, his countenance deeply agitated, and the seamen asked—

"What's up now, lad?"

"Seen a ghost, darkie?"

The African showed his white, gleaming teeth, and answered—

"Tom's taken."

"Who's taken him?"

"De sogers, de red coats, hab put him in de jail."

The outlaws bounded to their feet, and, grasping their weapons, rushed towards the entrance of their cave, shouting—

"Show us the place, Snowball, and if all King George's men were drawn up there, we would have him out."

"Stop! stop!" cried the African. "I have not told you all."

"Go on, then."

"Him young Tom was shot in de leg by a red coat, and when dey takes him to de prison dey put de irons on him and chains him up."

A growl of savage execration came from the throats of the outlaws.

"And when," said Snowball, "him get well dey is going to hang him up to ship's yard-arm."

Another growl of subdued ferocity followed this intelligence.

"Now, you not go," Snowball went on; "but me go first and give him file to take irons off, and at de night-time we all go and break prison!"

"Bravo, Snowball!" chimed a dozen voices. "You are quite an admiral."

Snowball smiled and said—

"You all agree to fetch him out of dat place?"

"We swear it, or to die in the attempt."

"To-night, then, I go with file," continued Snowball, "and to find out where him locked up. Den I come back and tell you."

"But the soldiers, Snowball?"

The black grinned, and tapped the hilt of a long knife that stuck in his belt.

A grim nod of approval greeted this act, and the outlaws reseated themselves, and drank success to the black's deadly mission.

That night the faithful fellow scaled the prison walls, but failed to discover the cell wherein his young favourite was confined.

The next night only ended in the same disapment.

Nothing daunted, Snowball made the third attempt—the result of which the reader is acquainted with.

Apprehensive that his visitor had fallen, Tom hid the file under his straw pallet; then, lying upon his pallet, he awaited the coming of his surly janitor.

Half an hour passed, and no visitor, and with a glad cry, Tom jumped from his bed, the new-born hope of life and liberty coursing like wild-fire through every vein.

Snowball's forethought had provided a small bottle of oil for Tom, and, pouring a little on the iron band that was locked round his ancle, he commenced noiselessly to cut it asunder.

How sweet to the boy's ears was the music of that sharp tool. Sweeter, ay, far sweeter to him than the dulcet strains—for that file sang the song of liberty to the hapless captive, who was to die upon the morrow.

Half-past ten chimed out from the prison clock, and found Tom plying his task.

Eleven pealed out, just as he had cut through one galling band.

"One hour more," thought Tom, as he commenced upon the second circlet of iron, "and my friends will be at the prison walls."

The clanking of keys disturbed Tom, and he had barely time to put his ancle in the severed hoop before the door opened, and the jailer thrust his head inside, and demanded—

"What—not asleep?"

"No," was Tom's reply,

"Well, seeing as how it's the last sleep you'll get this side of the gallows, you ought to make the most of it."

Tom felt very much inclined to hurl the stool at the fellow's grinning face. Restraining himself, he said carelessly—

"Is it? How do you know?"

"How do I know, my young shaver? I think I ought to know when I has the job to take you on board the ship, which is going to hang you at the stern."

Tom laughed a low, mocking laugh, yet buoyant and musical, as he asked—

"You going to take me alone?"

"Yes," said the jailer, "and very glad shall I be. When I see yer swing I shall be devilish glad!"

"Thank you, old bottle-nose."

This was an unkind allusion Tom invariably made, respecting the jailer's purple face.

"Don't taunt me, yer young cub. I'd a strung yer up long ago if I'd had my will!"

Tom laughingly answered him—

"You are very kind. I say"——

"What?" asked the jailer, putting his head further inside the door.

"Are you not afraid," continued Tom, "that face of yours will set your head on fire some day?"

The enraged jailer slammed the door violently, and Tom heard him go away muttering—

"Cheeky young imp! One thing, he'll dance upon nothing to-morrow.

Tom smiled at the old fellow's soliloquy, and when he had gone beyond hearing, recommenced the laborious task of cutting through his fetters.

Half-past eleven chimed. How sweet it sounded to the hopeful captive. With the echo of the bell Tom shook off his fetters.

"The first step to freedom," he murmured, "Oh! how bitter will be the change, should these brilliant hopes not be fulfilled!"

Slowly to and fro the narrow cell Tom walked. It was a relief thus to stretch his cramped limbs.

Another half-hour went, and then Tom took a sword from its hiding-place.

Standing at the grated window he listened breathlessly for the slightest sound.

As the time rolled onward, Tom's excitement increased, for his friends came not.

Maddening thought! Had Snowball fallen in his attempt to escape?

His limbs, now freed from the vile bonds, he panted to breathe the fresh air outside his musty prison—yearned once more to behold the glittering ocean.

All these things had Tom conjured up in his mind when working at the felon irons that fettered his limbs; and now to find those brilliant hopes dashed away, and death again awaiting him, struck horror to the gallant boy.

"One" pealed out from the clock-tower, and Tom listened with beating heart to a noise that followed its reverberations.

Could it be his friends? Yes. There was something more than the dying echo of the bell.

Nearer and nearer came that sound, like the rushing of the wind through a dense forest, and Tom's heart beat joyfully at the sound, for he recognised the tramp of men.

Leaving our young hero to endure the conflicting emotions of hope and fear, we will follow the movements of his brave but mutinous friends.

With a joyful visage Snowball hastened back to the cave, and told the outlaws of his success in discovering the gallant mid.

A glad shout greeted this intelligence, and the outlaws, collecting round Snowball, held a council of war.

The plan of the prison was chalked out upon the top of a barrel—also Tom's place of confinement. To reach this cell they found that two thick walls would have to be pierced, and a numerous body of well-armed and disciplined soldiers would have to be conquered.

It was a strange, wild scene this council, the bronzed countenances of the band giving a wild, fierce aspect to the group.

High above his fellows stood the African, listening, counselling, and calming the more hot-headed of the reckless, fiery natures, whose counsel would have entailed certain destruction to the enterprise.

"Let's take a couple of guns, and knock the place down," was their suggestion.

"No," said Snowball, placing his finger upon the spot that indicated the position of Tom's cell. "No, that never do!"

"Why won't it do?"

"'Cos, don't you see, dis place where Tom is, one side of it is joined by the inner wall.".

"Well, what of that?"

"Why, we send shot and knock down first wall; den, as you say, put guns in the de holes we is made, and knock down other wall. You see him shot that knock a hole in Massa Tom's prison kill him. Dat what we don't want—do we, men?"

"No, Snowball. We must not hurt a hair of his head," was the response. "Snowball is right. We should very likely kill him in our hasty endeavours. We must not use guns. Another plan must be carried out for making a breach in the walls, because get in the gate we never shall, even if we picked off the sentries."

"Dat is not all," Snowball continued; "agin taking de cannons, de noise would bring down de ship's crew from de Hercules and we'll have no chance agin so many."

"You are right, so haul in the slack. It is getting late, so if you have a good idea, pay it out."

He had a good plan. This was to take a heavy pole—portion of a ship's mast—and use it as a battering ram where the masonry had been loosened by the picks and crowbars.

The seamen divided into two parties when they came in sight of the prison.

Fifty were to attack the gate, the others to batter in the wall.

CHAPTER V,

THE ATTACK UPON THE PRISON.

MASSES of heavy clouds obscured the moon's pale light; thus the seamen were able to approach the prison unperceived by the unsuspecting sentries.

Ben Bight halted his party when they were within fifty yards of the gateway, and giving Snowball time to get in rear of the building, he raised his musket and sent a shot whistling past the soldier's ear.

The man, startled by the unpleasant whizzing of the bullet, cocked his piece, and peering out into the darkness, saw to his astonishment the glitter of the outlaws' weapons as they advanced upon the gate.

"Turn out the guard," he shouted, "here is Red Hand the pirate, and his gang."

The guard sprang up, and seizing their weapons, opened fire upon the seamen who returned the salute with interest, thus placing themselves beyond the pale of the law by taking up arms against the king's troops.

Unobserved by the prison defenders, who had quite enough to do to reply to the attacking forces, Snowball and his companions were at work in rear with pick and crowbar.

Soon one of the heavy stones was loosened, and the black called out—

"This way, lads, with the pole."

Twenty strong-limbed men were awaiting this order, and when they heard the African's voice they started at a swift pace, about a dozen yards from the loosened stone.

There was a crash when the heavy piece of timber struck the masonry, and the stone was hurled inside the wall, leaving sufficient space for the whole party to pass through.

The men dragged the battering-ram through the outer court, and began the attack upon the wall of Tom's cell.

The men worked with a will, and soon the brickwork was loosened, and the ram taken back for the final blow.

"Stand out of de way dere, Massa Tom," shouted Snowball, "we make big hole in one minute."

The middy stepped aside, and the heavy pole shattered the wall, and the outlaws were about to rush in when the door opened, and the jailer with a dozen soldiers at his back entered the cell.

"Hallo, my gallows bird," said the janitor, "you are not gone yet?"

Tom snatched up the sword Snowball had given him, and would have cut the prison official down, had not that worthy made his escape.

"Now," said Snowball, "dis way, Massa Tom. You soon be as free as de air."

"Don't be too certain," said a voice behind the captive. "You will swing yet."

Tom turned and saw the morose janitor and the soldiers had returned.

"Secure that boy," the official said to the soldiers, "or shoot him where he stands!"

Three of the men brought their pieces to the present, and would have fired upon the gallant mid, but for Snowball.

The black giant leaped into the cell, and, levelling a brace of pistols at the soldiers, thundered—

"De first man's finger dat touches a trigger will have dese bullets in um skull!"

The men were brave, but the certainty of one or more meeting death caused them to waver.

"Away wid you, Massa Tom!" whispered the black. "Me settle dese fellows."

"I shall not leave here," was the gallant youth's response, "until I leave with my friends."

"If dat de case," said Snowball, "we soon be off. Dis way, some ob you!"

A dozen sailors came through the hole in the prison wall.

"Shoot the first ob de redcoats dat touches deir muskets."

"Are you soldiers? Are you men?" roared the janitor. "Do your duty, and"——

He was seized by a powerful pair of arms, and flung against the redcoats.

Several were knocked down by the force of the concussion.

"Take dat!" said the black giant, "and learn to keep a quiet tongue. Now den, my lads, be off."

The sailors, exultant at the liberation of their young favourite, gave a mighty cheer.

The men who were engaged with the soldiers at the gate heard the shout, and gave a responsive "hurrah," and leaving the front of the prison met their companions, who were on the way to the cave.

There was no pursuit, for the troops were not strong enough to leave the prison, so the outlaws departed unmolested.

"My lads," said Snowball, "we not got on to de cave, but go on board de ship. I gib our young leader a proper salute."

The idea was quickly followed out.

The greater portion of the men ran to where the boats were hidden, and went on board the War Cloud.

The vessel was soon rigged out with gay flags, and the masts illuminated by battle lanterns.

"We'll give him a proper salute," said Ben Bight. "Stand to the guns, my Britons, and load with blank cartridge!"

It was done, and soon afterwards our hero stepped from the bulwark to the deck; and as he stood under the glare of the battle lanterns every inch the gallant fellow he was, a hearty "hurrah!" burst from the men's throats.

Then the guns roared out their loud welcome.

The crew again shouted with delight—

"Hurrah! hurrah! Welcome, gallant Tom! Welcome to the War Cloud!"

The youth's handsome face flushed with excitement and pride, and, removing his cap, he said—

"Thanks, my brave friends. For good or for evil our lot is henceforth cast together, and should we be driven from this coast, there are other climes, and a vast ocean for the cruise of the War Cloud and her gallant crew."

CHAPTER VI.

DERRICK OF THE RED HAND.

THE commander of the line-of-battle ship, the Hercules, made every effort in his power to capMidshipman Tom and the runaway sailors; but, failing in this, he had placards posted all over the town, offering £100 reward to anyone who brought in the boy or any of the band.

The placards stated that all the men and their young commander had been guilty of desertion and piracy, and henceforth they were to be treated accordingly, and anyone harbouring them would be guilty of an offence that would bring down the direst penalties of the law.

Not only had the young outlaw to contend against the powers he had defied, but he had a terrible foe in the pirate leader, Derrick of the Red Hand.

The boy had sworn to destroy the pirate gang, and Derrick had registered a fearful vow that he would annihilate the outlaw.

Many a fierce encounter had taken place between them, both on shore and out at sea, for it was Tom's intention not to sail upon his cruise until he had destroyed the gang of marauders.

It was during one of these encounters the young commodore rescued Laura Grey, a lovely golden-haired beauty, from the clutches of the pirates.

They had attacked a homeward-bound vessel, and were in the midst of their bloodthirsty work, when Tom and his outlawed band swept the merciless wretches from the deck; and the young girl having lost her father during the engagement, the gallant middy gave her a handsomely furnished chamber in the cave until she could discover her relatives.

A few weeks after her escape from the pirates, Laura Grey was carried off by Red Hand.

The young leader missed the gentle companion he was wont to meet at sundown on the bright yellow sands; so, ascending the cliff, he went in search of her.

Suddenly, Derrick and a dozen of his desperadoes started out from behind a rock, and confronted the young outlaw.

"Caught, by ——," said the pirate, fiercely, "and you shall pay for attempting to thwart the wishes of Derrick."

"Not yet," was the youth's reply. "Not yet, man of blood."

Tom stepped back, and his bright blade flashed from its scabbard—not a useless dirk, but a broad-bladed scimitar of Damascus steel.

"Cut the Jackanape down!" roared the pirate. "At him, my bullies!"

A matchless swordsman, Tom cut down all who approached him, until one of the gang crept behind the gallant boy, and stunned him with a mukset stock.

The young outlaw fell. It was at the very moment he felt confident of victory, for he had brought Red Hand to the ground with a blow from the pommell of his scimitar.

Gallant Tom would have been slain but for the pirate leader, who, springing to his feet, and spurning the senseless and bleeding form of the outlawed midshipman, said—

"Carry him off to the pit. Curse him! He shall see that damsel in my power—ay, in my arms. Then will I torture every drop of blood from his body, accursed, meddling young whelp!"

His ready band bore away the bleeding form of poor Tom, the pirate following, and with flashing eyes thinking over the rich banquet of revenge he should enjoy, hissed—

"Infernal young viper! Now, now, is my hour of triumph."

A turn in the winding rock hid them from view, and hardly had their forms disappeared when a body of the outlaws, with Snowball and a huge mastiff at their head, made their appearance at the opposite side.

The dog was some distance in advance, and when he came to the spot where Tom had fallen, he began to sniff the ground and bark angrily.

Suddenly he gave a low, savage growl, and bounded off in the direction taken by the pirates.

Snowball and his followers surveyed the scene of the conflict.

Five of the Red Hand's party lay weltering in their gore.

Close by was the young outlaw's well-known scimitar.

A cry of rage came from Snowball's lips when he saw the reeking weapon; picking it up, he muttered—

"Him gone, but dey have paid for it. Wish I'd a been here a little afore, den, by gar, dey no take him away."

"The chief, the chief! where is the chief?" were the words that came from the lips of the outlaws, as they gripped their weapons and gazed savagely around.

"Him taken away by dem debils," said Snowball sadly, "and him wounded too, or he no drop this blade. Cuss 'em! Cuss 'em!"

As the faithful African spoke, a large tear welled up from his heart, and rolled silently down his cheek.

THE MEANS OF RESCUE.

The men were scarcely less affected, and with savage cries they began to search about the rocks for any trace of their foe, for their hearts were filled with fury at the capture of their loved chief.

One of the pirates who had been wounded by the gallant boy, had crawled from the spot and endeavoured to follow his retreating companions.

But while doing so, the infuriated outlaws had burst upon the scene.

Creeping behind a large stone, he endeavoured to hide from them.

The attempt failed, for he was discovered, dragged from his hiding place, and in an instant a dozen weapons flashed before his eyes, whilst hoarse voices demanded—

"Where is your chief? Speak, or prepare to be cut in pieces!"

The poor wretch fell upon his knees, begging for mercy.

"Where is our chief?" was the repeated question, and bright weapons were placed against his breast.

"Mercy—mercy! I do not know," gasped the pirate.

"Liar!" was the gruff response. "Speak, and quickly, or you die."

The pirate cowed with fear.

"Where is he?" demanded Snowball, coming to the spot and speaking in low tones of suppressed passion. "Speak, you vile tief!"

The African showed his white teeth as he spoke, and looked at the kneeling pirate with an aspect so fierce that the trembling wretch's agony of fear caused big burning beads to ooze from his forehead.

"Where have they taken him?" demanded one of the band, placing the point of his weapon against the pirate's throat. "Answer me, you cut-throat?"

"Mercy! mercy! I do not know. Red Hand has taken him to the pit."

"The pit!" answered the angry listeners. "Where is that?"

The pirate saw all hope to save his life would be in vain unless he disclosed the secret haunt of the Red Hand.

Folding his arms, he replied, doggedly—

"I don't know."

A hoarse cry came from the lips of his captors, and the words—

"Kill him! Cut him in pieces if he does not tell!" came like a death warning upon his ears.

Snowball, the first stunning effects of his grief over, had now acquired his habitual calmness, and motioning the angry group aside, said—

"Me not want to kill you. Tell us where de place is, and you go away."

A gleam of hope lit the pirate's eyes at these words, and with affected reluctance, he answered—

"My oath forbids me telling you."

"Me take you to the place," said Snowball. "You no speak at all."

This was a plan that met with a shout of approval from the band, and twenty voices exclaimed—

"Will you do so?"

A cunning look for a moment passed over the pirate's countenance, and he answered—

"Yes."

From the beach he led them a little inland, through a tangled forest and down a steep valley that led to a thick, deep wood.

Here the watchful eyes of Snowball beheld the pirate, from time to time, cast furtive glances around him.

Snowball read his intention.

He was about to make an attempt to escape.

The African drew a pistol from his belt and never for a moment took his eyes off his guide.

It now commenced growing dark, and the outlaws, who were in no mood to be trifled with, suddenly inquired how much farther the place was.

Before the traitor could reply, one of the band

who had advanced a little, suddenly stopped and uttered a piercing cry.

The cry suddenly brought the whole party to a standstill, and caused the pirate to turn as pale as a corpse.

"What's the matter, Ben?" exclaimed Snowball.

"Secure that villain!" was Ben's answer. "Ha! he has escaped!"

There was a sudden report of a pistol, followed by a cry of death agony.

Not quick enough had been that sudden movement on the pirate's part.

When Ben turned and spoke, the doomed wretch suddenly dashed towards a clump of trees that stood near.

But before he had taken the second step, Snowball levelled his pistol and fired.

The outlaws moved forward to the spot where the pirate lay writhing in the pangs of death, and as his fast glazing eyes fell upon Ben, he rose himself upon his elbow, and while the lamp of life flickered for a few moments in his body, he faltered out—

"Curses—curses on you! In another moment you would all have been over the precipice, and I—I "——

He fell back; a gurgling sound came from his throat, the eyes became closed, his limps stretched themselves quiveringly out—then all became still.

He was dead.

"A just punishment," was Ben Bight's remark; "and only in time. Had I not happened to notice the faint gleam of a light a long distance ahead, and seemingly in the very bowels of the earth, we must have toppled over."

"How did you know we were so near?" asked one of the band.

"I know the spot well," replied Ben. "We are on Devil's Rock. That villain has led us a nice dance—hang him!"

"What's to be done, den?" said Snowball. "Dis not the pirate rendezvous."

Ben Bight reflected for a moment.

"No," said he, "It's somewhere near the coast, and we are inland. But where's the dog?"

Snowball turned, and the sudden recollection flashed to his mind that he had seen the dog bound off in a direction exactly opposite to that which they had come.

This knowledge he imparted to his followers, and a council was immediately held.

Many schemes were suggested, but Ben's seemed the most feasible, and was acted upon.

"The dog," he said, "has followed the scent of his master, and, from the fact of our chief's sword being found, he must be badly wounded. He would never drop his weapon while an inch of life remained in him. All we can do is to wait till daylight; possibly there may be a drop of blood or two on the road that will be a little help, and ten to one but the dog, who is a cunning one, will follow them to their haunt; then come back for some of us."

Snowball, who had paid great attention to Ben's words, now spoke.

"Yes," he said, "we must wait till de morning, and when de first little peep ob day come, Snowball go arter him chief."

"But not alone, Snowball?"

"Yes, Ben, by myself."

"What! and let us remain in the cave? No."

"Yes, Ben, and I'll tell why. I can follow de track same as Indian in de forest. You no understand dis. I tell you a little leaf of tree, a little piece of grass, all tell me where they hab gone."

"Well. But "—

"Be quiet, Ben. When I finds de place out"— fierce light gleamed in Snowball's eyes, and his huge hand played with a long, gleaming knife-hilt, as he slowly said these words—"when I finds it, I come and fetch you. But " added Snowball, mentally, " I bring de chief wid me, or no come back at all."

The African's savage nature, which had for a long time slumbered, was now aroused by the loss of his beloved leader, and he had resolved to restore him to freedom, or die in the attempt.

Better for Red Hand and his band had they never brought the inexorable anger of Snowball upon them.

The gigantic black, who had been a warrior in his own country, and well versed in the wars with the deadly tribes, would now exert that cunning and ferocity which had so long lain dormant within him.

And like the sleuth hound would he follow the pirates' track, so noiselessly, so stealthily and panther-like, that they would not know of his presence until his hand was upon their throat, his knife drinking their heart's blood.

A terrible foe had Red Hand, the pirate, raised in his path.

When the outlaws found Snowball's determination not to be shaken, they retired by a long and tedious way to the cave.

There was a short cut across the town, but in their present strait they cared not to risk an encounter with the soldiery or the king's officers.

They felt lost without their gallant young leader, and many were the deeply uttered vows of revenge against Red Hand, as they went on the lonesome path.

In vain Snowball tried to wile away the hours —in vain he tried to sleep.

Useless. He could not rest.

An ever-haunting fear that his beloved chief was being tortured kept his blood at fever heat, and, rising from his seat, he went forth upon the errand of revenge alone.

————

CHAPTER VII.

THE PIRATES OUTWITTED.

RED HAND, the fierce freebooter, had ordered a number of his band to pillage the houses of the wealthy inhabitants that lived near the coast, and, in accordance with his usual ferocity, his orders had been to slay all who stood in the way of the merciless villain.

Too well were these orders carried out by the murderous crew who sailed under his banner, and many were the deeds of rapine and violence committed on the undefended coast.

Old and young alike fell before the weapons of those merciless cut-throats. Maidens, after beholding their parents and brothers slain before their eyes, were carried off to meet a fate worse than death.

Upon this night a strong party of the Red Hand had found their way into Gordon Castle undiscovered, and the lady was alarmed by a sudden noise, and going to the door of her chamber beheld a horrid spectacle upon the very threshold.

Her two domestics, half naked, were lying lifeless on the floor.

The room was full of strange looking men. The unhappy chambermaid was kneeling before one of them vainly imploring for mercy; she received the fatal stroke.

What woman or even man on such an occasion would not have been struck with terror, and given up life and everything as lost?

A loud shriek of despair, a retreat of a few paces would probably have been the first act of most people. The Lady Blanche conducted herself in a very different manner.

"And you have come at last," she exclaimed, in a tone of heart-felt joy, and advancing towards her assailants with a haste that truly astonished them—they lowered their uplifted weapons.

"You have come at last, then," she repeated, "such visitors as you I have long desired to see."

"Whished!" muttered one of the assassins, "what do you mean by that? But stay, I'll"—

He had already uplifted his cutlass, but a comrade averted the stroke.

"Stay a moment," said he. "Let us first hear what our lady would have."

"Nothing but that which is your pleasure, my brave comrades. You are men after my own heart, and neither you nor I shall have reason to repent it, if you will listen to what I have to say."

"Speak! speak!" cried out the whole company.

"But be quick," replied the foremost of the group; "for we shall not make much ceremony."

"Nevertheless, that you will grant me a hearing I feel assured. Know, then, that although I am the wife of the richest gentleman in the country, yet the wife of the meanest beggar cannot be more unhappy. My husband is one of the most jealous and niggardly. I hate him as I hate the evil one:

and it has long been the wish of my heart to get out of his keeping. All my servants were spies, that woman whose business you have done so completely being the worst of them all. I am, I flatter myself, far from being ugly. If any one of you choose to release me from this, I will accompany you, be it either to the caves or to your ship; nor shall any of you repent having spared my life. You are in a well-stored mansion; with its secret corners I shall make you acquainted, and if I do not make you richer by twenty thousand pounds, then serve me the same as you did my chambermaid."

This inexplicable conduct on the part of Lady Blanche, coupled with the more than ordinary beauty which she possessed, produced a powerful effect indeed on the men whose hands were yet reeking with blood. They stepped aside and consulted in a low tone for some minutes.

Lady Blanche was thus left alone; but she betrayed not the slightest wish to escape.

"Let's despatch her, and the game will be all up," said one of the men.

Blanche, however, scarcely changed colour; there was one voice in that group spoke in opposition to that sentiment, and with her acute ear she had not failed to recognise it.

One, whom she thought was the leader of the pirates, now approached her.

He asked her twice or thrice whether he might rely on what she had said as truth—whether she did actually wish to be relieved from the tyranny of her husband and to join them; and whether she was willing to assign herself to one of them—to himself for instance—during the few peaceful days she could enjoy.

Having replied in the affirmative to all these questions, and having not only suffered the warm embrace of the robber, but returned it (for what will not necessity excuse?) he at length said—

"Come along, then, and lead us round. The devil trust you ladies of rank; but we'll venture for once. But let me tell you beforehand that if you were twice as handsome as you are, this weapon would cleave your skull the moment we saw the least disposition to betray us."

"Then it will be safe enough; and if this were the only condition of my being put to death, I would outlive you all, and even the Wandering Jew himself."

Lady Blanche, like a true crafty woman, smiled as she pronounced these words, and hastily caught up the nearest lamp, as though she had been as anxious as any of them to collect the plunder and be gone.

She then conducted the whole company through every apartment, opened every door, every drawer, and every chest; assisted packing up the valuables, looking with the utmost apparent indifference on the mangled bodies and aiding with the familiarity of an old acquaintance in the most laborious occupations.

Plate, money, jewels, and other valuables were now collated together, and the leader was giving the order for marching, when his appointed bride caught him by the shoulder.

"Did I not tell you," said she, "that you should not repent making a friend of me and sparing life? You may, indeed, have everything in places you find open. But it would be a pity that you should not come at the treasure which is concealed. What! do you suppose that among coffers so full there is no secret place? Look here, and be convinced to the contrary."

She pointed to a secret spring in the baron's desk. She pressed upon it, and out fell the sum of two hundred pounds.

"Zounds!" cried the leader of the outlaws. "Now I see you are an incomparable woman. I will treat you for this like a duchess."

"And, perhaps, better still," she replied, laughingly, "when I tell you one thing more. I am well aware you have spies, who informed you of the absence of my tyrant, but they did not tell you of the bags of gold he received yesterday."

"Not a syllable. Where are they?"

"Oh, safe enough! under half-a-dozen locks, and keys and bolts. But, like the iron chest, without me you would find them not. Still I will show you. Come along. Upstairs finished, we will see what is to be found below. Descend."

The robbers followed her with great precaution into a cellar. At the entrance of this a strong trap-door was provided, and a man was posted as sentinel.

Lady Blanche went on until she had conducted the whole troop to a vault at the further extremity of the cellar. She unlocked it, and in the corners of this recess stood the chest she had mentioned.

"Here," said she, giving the leader a bunch of keys—"here, unlock it, and take what you can, and as a wedding gift, if you can obtain the consent of your companion as readily as you have gained mine."

The robber tried one key, then another; but none would fit it. He grew more impatient, and Lady Blanche still more so.

"Lend me them," she said. "I shall find the way sooner. Indeed, if you don't make haste, the morn may overtake us. Ha! the reason why neither of us could unlock it is because I have the wrong bunch of keys. I'll obtain another."

She ran upstairs. Presently they heard her coming slowly down, as though out of breath with the haste she had made.

"I've found them!" she cried, at a distance.

She was within about three steps of the sentinel. One moment more she had made a spring at the man, who, not dreaming of such an attack, was thrust headlong down stairs from top to bottom. Another moment she had closed the trap door, bolted it, and secured the whole band in her cellar.

And as speedily did she carry out her plot. She flew across the court-yard, and with the candle set fire to a detached building. The watchman in the neighbouring village, perceiving the flames, instantly gave the alarm.

In a few minutes the inhabitants were out of their beds, and a crowd hastened to the mansion. Lady Blanche waited for them at the entrance of the court-yard.

"A few of you will be sufficient to put out the fire, and prevent it from spreading. You remaining will provide yourselves with arms, which you will find in abundance in my husband's armoury. Post yourselves at the avenues of the cellar, and suffer not one of the murderers and robbers shut in to escape."

The astonished crowd obeyed her orders, but not without some misgiving respecting an encounter with the fierce band.

CHAPTER VIII.

IN THE TIGER'S LAIR.

ABOUT three miles from the high rock, called Sampson's Head, existed, at the time of which we write, several caves of no great extent, but capable of affording shelter to that portion of Red Hand's band who, with their leader had taken up their abode ashore for the purpose of pillaging the large houses near the coast.

So precipitous were these rocks that none but men accustomed to a seafaring life could ascend them.

The entrance to the cavern was from a hole in the top of the rock, and then only by means of a knotted rope.

To this secret rendezvous the pirates carried Laura Grey and the wounded chieftain.

With brutal violence Red Hand kicked the young commodore, his eyes glaring maliciously as he muttered—

"Wake up, curse you, or I'll finish you outright."

A deep groan of anguish came from Tom's lips at the pirate's brutal treatment, and closing his eyes, he again swooned from exhaustion and loss of blood.

Laying Laura Grey upon a heap of dried rushes, the pirates lit a fire in the middle of the cave, and bringing out from the recess a large bottle of spirits, they were soon deep in their potations.

For a time their grim leader held away from their revelry. Sitting upon an empty powder barrel, he remained, his eyes fixed gloatingly upon the senseless forms of Laura and her lover.

"Ha! ha!" he laughed out. "Caged at last. Ha! ha! Little do you know the sight I have for you, my young whelp. Annihilate my band! Well, by all the imps of sulphurdom, I'll flay you alive before you are much older."

As he muttered these words he fixed his burning eyes upon Laura, and from the expression in them there could be no mistake as to his fell purpose.

Long he sat thus, until tired of awaiting a sign of returning animation in his prisoners, he turned to the noisy revellers, and quickly demanded—

"Has Pedro come back?"

"He has not, cap'n," said one of the band. The ruffian uttered a malediction, and rising from his seat, said—

"He has gone with twelve hands to sack a large house on the rocks."

"The cursed fool," said Red Hand, savagely.

A low whistle now sounded from above, and caused them to start.

One of the band went to where the knotted rope was dangling, and listened.

Again the signal was repeated. This time it was answered by the pirate from below, who, taking the rope in his hand, threw it up to the circular opening in the cave.

There it was caught and made fast, and soon a man descended.

One look at the nervous, agitated form told the ferocious bravo that something had gone amiss with his party of marauders, and not waiting for the affrighted pirate to speak, he vociferated—

"Well, what the —— is the matter?"

The pirate recoiled from the vicinity of Red Hand as he replied—

"Pedro and his party are taken, and the villagers are arming to destroy them."

"What!" yelled Red Hand, seizing the man by the throat. "What, you infernal wretch! Pedro taken?"

"Yes, captain," gasped the other, endeavouring to shake off Red Hand's grip. "They are caged in a vault."

"When?—where?" yelled again the pirate-chief.

"At Gordon Castle."

Red Hand's face became white with rage, and uttering a fearful malediction, inquired of the pirate how he managed to escape.

"It was left outside, captain, while Pedro and the others went in. I waited a long time, but instead of their coming back, a woman came out— the lady of the castle, I think, and set fire to some building in the court-yard."

"Curse her!"

"This fire brought the country people to the place, and I heard her tell them to arm themselves, as she had a band of robbers safely locked in one of the vaults."

"Well, don't hesitate."

"I did not wait to hear any more."

The pirates had sprung to their feet during this account of the misadventure of their comrades, and, in anticipation of the bravo's orders, had already armed themselves to the teeth.

Red Hand knashed his teeth with passion, and ordered Laura to be carried into a small apartment in the cavern which served him for a sleeping place.

He watched his follower as he bore the lovely

girl away. Then, turning to the expectant band, said, grimly—

"I'll finish them when we return. Up the rope with you as fast as you can."

The men obeyed his orders quickly, all but one, whom he motioned to stay behind and guard the cave.

The man, a swarthy Malay, when his companions had gone, seated himself by the smouldering fire, and began to imbibe the contents of the long stone bottle.

In this manner half an hour passed away, and the liquor began to operate on the sentinel.

Casting a savage look towards his prisoner, he saw he yet remained insensible, and muttering an oath, he stretched himself by the side of the fire, and was soon asleep.

No sound was audible in the cave except the half-broken snore of the sentry, and the low, deep breathing of the wounded young chief.

From the stunning effects of the blow he had received Tom now began to recover, and raising himself upon his elbow he glared wonderingly around.

By degrees, the truth of his position flashed to his mind; but with the exception of a little dizziness produced from the clubbed musket, he found himself but little injured.

Cautiously looking around for his enemies, he raised himself to a sitting posture.

The smoking embers of the fire threw out sufficient light to make everything visible in the cavern, and the young commander's heart beat gladly as he saw that, with the exception of the sleeping form by the fire, he was alone in the cave.

The first act was to feel for his sword, and a shade of disappointment passed over his face, when he found only the empty scabbard by his side.

Cautiously regaining his feet, the young chieftain picked up a cutlass that had been carelessly left in the place. Grasping it firmly, he crept towards the sleeper.

Once this blade was ready to strike, but the heart that beat within that breast was incapable of doing a cold-blooded murder.

He looked around for means to escape.

Joy! there hung the rope by which the pirates had ascended, and Tom, placing his weapon between his teeth, was about to ascend.

Suddenly he paused as the recollection of Laura came to his mind.

Cautiously he searched the cavern, and a bright hope arose within him that she had escaped capture.

So cunningly had the entrance to Red Hand's chamber been concealed that it escaped the eyes even of Midshipman Tom.

With this hope in his heart, he swiftly ascended the rope, and soon he felt the cool night wind playing upon his head.

Placing a mark near the entrance of the cavern,

he quickly descended the rock by clinging to the gnarled vegetation which grew upon its surface.

He had reached about halfway down when the sound of voices arrested his attention.

CHAPTER IX.

A PERILOUS POSITION.

Tom paused and listened attentively; for, in the voice of one of the speakers, he recognised that of his implacable foe, Red Hand.

The ruffian was unmistakably enraged at something, and Tom heard him say, in savage tones—

"Cursed fool to be led into a trap by a woman! But my revenge accomplished on that young whelp, we will burn that castle to the ground!"

"It would not be safe," another voice said; "the people are all up in arms, and a boat's crew was landed there from a man-of-war."

Red Hand replied to the intelligence with a fearful oath.

A noise, like the falling of some pebbles or pieces of dried earth, caused the young chief to pause ere he moved in his perilous position.

Attentively Tom listened for a repetition of the sound.

Again the pattering of small fragments of rocks could be heard.

Brave, even to rashness, as the young chieftain was by nature, yet when the cause of these sounds came to his mind, his face went a shade paler, and his heart beat quicker.

It was, indeed, a perilous position for the gallant young chief; for owing to the smooth face of the rock, he could obtain no foothold, and the weeds, to which he clung with both hands, were rapidly being loosened.

In this fearful position he hung—the cutlass clenched firmly between his teeth.

Yet of what avail was that weapon? He dared not remove his hand to take it.

Had he done so he would have been precipitated to the foot of the rock, and dashed into a shapeless mass.

These thoughts flashed with lighting swiftness through his brain, when he understood the cause of the falling earth and stones.

His foes were ascending the rocks just below his feet.

Nearer and nearer they came.

Their curses and oaths at the difficult ascent came plainer every moment.

And to add to the horrors of his critical position, the tufts of weeds which he had grasped with his right hand were gradually loosening.

Big drops of agony stood on the brave boy's forehead, but his presence of mind did not desert him,

In this moment of peril he placed his forehead against the rock, and to his joy, directly in front of his face, he felt a knotty shrub.

Quick as thought, his right hand quitted the yielding weeds and clutched it.

The young chieftain began to draw his breath freely. One imminent danger was passed, and, favoured by the darkness, he hoped to escape the notice of his foes.

To the right of where he hung by his hands he could hear the savage tones of Red Hand's voice urging his band to ascend more quickly.

And, to Tom's horror, he discovered that one of the band was below him.

Already had the pirate, in feeling for something to assist him in his ascent, touched the young seaman's foot.

There was but one course for him to pursue, and as quick as was consistent with his safety, he drew his legs up.

The pirate was slowly ascending.

Already had he reached the place where the young leader's foot had been.

There was no escape for him should the ruffian ascend another yard, and Tom, grasping the tough shrub lightly, swiftly extended his foot.

A scream followed this act; then was heard the noise of the pirate's body striking from point to point of the jagged rocks.

The heavy heel of the young outlaw's foot had descended upon the pirate's head with such stunning force that it dislodged him from the face of the rock, and hurled him below.

Red Hand uttered a fearful oath when the man's cry smote upon his ears, and bidding the others be more careful, resumed his ascent.

In a few minutes Tom's suspense was ended, for the pirates had reached the top of the rock, and were soon descending the knotted rope.

The fugitive, wasting all his strength, was quickly descending, when, having nearly reached the bottom, the heavy breathing of some on ascending the perilous rock caused him to suspend his descend.

Although the climber could not be more than ten yards from Tom, the darkness was so great he could not distinguish even the outline of any form. If he could have done so, he would have beheld his faithful follower. Snowball, tracking the pirates with a deadly knife between his set teeth.

Tom and Snowball had passed each other in the darkness, one to return to the cave and summon his band, the other to preserve a life that was menaced by the pirate leader.

When Red Hand led his men to the rescue of the ruffians so cleverly entrapped by Lady Blanche, he had determined to wreak summary vengeance upon the lovely lady and her surviving domestics.

There is no doubt but that a general massacre would have taken place at Gordon Castle, had not the pirates been met on their way by Pedro and a few survivors of the marauding expedition.

From the Frenchman, Red Hand learned that after they were fastened in the vault every outlet was surrounded by the people whom Lady Blanch had summoned to her assistance.

Escape was impossible, and the fierce pirates, not caring to stay and be killed like so many rats in a hole, broke open the door, and endeavoured to cut their way through the crowd.

In this endeavour, Pedro lost all but four of his band, and these were so badly wounded that one died on the road, and had to be left where he fell.

For the enraged peasantry pursued the discomfited gang so hotly that they had even to throw away their arms to escape.

Red Hand's rage was terrible; and vowing a fearful revenge upon the crafty woman, the whole party returned to the cave from whence they dared not move, for the tenantry were scouring the country in search of the marauders.

One thing alone filled the pirate leader's heart with joy, that was the rich banquet of revenge he was about to partake of, as he thought of the fearful death he would put his captive to.

Red Hand was the last to descend the rope, and looking around the cavern, he turned quickly to the man who had been left in charge of Tom, and demanded—

"Where is the prisoner?"

The pirate looked towards the spot where he had left Tom lying senseless: to his terror, he found the place vacant.

He rushed madly round the cave in search the midshipman.

The eyes of Red Hand blazed with fury, and. springing upon the unhappy wretch, he yelled huskily—

"Curse you! where is your prisoner?"

The man's face blanched, and, falling upon his knees, said, in an abject tone—

"He was here a few minutes since."

The cavern was again searched to no purpose. Red Hand's mouth foamed again as he felt assured his young foe had escaped, and, maddened as he was, he seized the sentry, and sent a bullet through his skull.

The prayer for mercy died upon the man's lips, as he fell a corpse at the pirate leader's feet.

By his order the bleeding form was raised by a rope, and hurled into the black abyss beneath.

The pirates stood appalled at this merciless act of their captain.

Suddenly he turned to the terror-stricken men, demanding whether a few drops of blood made them sick.

The men shrank from his furious gaze, and remained silent.

"Bring out a keg of spirits, you baby-hearted curs; see if that will take the white flesh from your cheeks," said Red Hand.

The ruffian crew required no second bidding, and bringing from a recess a small keg of the fiery liquor, they were soon seated round it, and the murder of their companion was forgotten.

Their brutal leader drank tumbler after tumbler,

until his fierce passion became more and more aroused. Then, staggering towards the couch where Laura lay trembling with fear, he caught hold of her long, streaming tresses, and pulled her from the couch.

The poor girl shrank in dismay, and clasping her hands in a supplicating manner, entreated him to have pity upon a poor, defenceless girl, and take her from that horrid place.

"Take you from here!" said he. "Ha! ha! ha! my little beauty. "You shall go when I am tired of you, not before."

Laura sank upon her knees. The brutal expression in the ruffian's bleared eyes caused her soul to sink within her.

Red Hand made a bound towards her, his drunken frenzy increasing every moment.

He ried to clutch the fair girl around the waist but the potent liquor was too much for the effort; for, missing his footing, he fell heavily forward, and striking his head against the wall, he rolled over, and lay motionless.

Laura crept from the drunken brute, and hiding herself in the farthest corner of the cavern, cowered in terror at the fearful looking monsters who were now growing uproarious and quarrelsome over their libations.

What an age to the poor girl seemed the few hours that intervened before the dull, grey light of morning began to gleam in through the aperture in the roof of the cavern!

Her heart sank within her as she heard the ribald jests of the lawless band, and her face and neck were covered with the crimson blushes of shame as she heard herself made the subject of their coarsest jests.

One by one the noisy revellers sank into repose held captive by the potent liquor they had taken.

A joyous feeling entered the heart of Laura. Above she could hear the notes of the feathered choristers, as they welcomed the new-born day.

In a moment her mind was made up. She would make an attempt to escape. So stepping quietly past the sleeping pirates, she feverishly clasped the knotted rope.

The new-born hope of freedom gave her strength, and she began to ascend the path that led to life and liberty.

The coarse, hard rope tore the skin from her delicate hands, but she heeded it not—liberty, sweet liberty, was before her.

Already the fresh morning air fanned her forehead. Another moment and she would be free from the den of villany and murder.

The top is gained at last. With a joyful cry she draws herself through the aperture and stands upon the summit of the rock.

Her heart throbs joyously as she gazes out upon the magnificent sight, and green fields and smiling hedgerows lay like a richly-tinted map at her feet.

CHAPTER X.

SNOWBALL TO THE RESCUE.

HERE and there, embedded among the trees, are the red-roofed houses; to her left, sparkling under the sun's rays, like a sheet of gold, lies the mighty ocean.

Can it be fancy?

No. There under the bluff headland, her sails furled, and riding at anchor, lies the beautiful craft of her gallant young preserver; while stretching out to sea are several vessels, their snow-white canvas gleaming in the morning sun.

So entranced is the lovely girl with the rich prospect before her, that she heard not a stealthy step slowly approaching.

Hapless maiden!

When she has feasted her eyes with nature's glorious beauties, she is about to turn away and seek a mode of descending the precipitous rock.

As she does so, a cry of alarm escapes her, for she is held fast by her dress.

The rosy colour which had risen to her cheeks in her first transport of joy now receded, and left her paler than marble.

She is too much terrified to turn and see what it is that then impedes her flight.

Alas! the cause is soon known; for, while she stands trembling, a harsh, grating voice sounds behind her, its tones of mocking triumph piercing the young girl's heart.

It was the voice of Red Hand.

"Ha! ha! my pretty bird!" said he. "Come back, you must have your wings clipped!"

Laura gave a scream of intense terror.

"Ay, howl away!" the ruffian continued. "It will do you no good."

Turning sharply round, Laura recognised the pirate.

With a withering look of contempt, and drawing herself up proudly, she said—

"Monster!—unmanly ruffian!"

Red Hand only laughed at her indignation, and, pulling her back by the dress, exclaimed—

"Very likely, my dear. Still, I mean to be very kind to you; so, come back."

Laura wrenched herself from his grasp, and ran forward to the edge of the rock.

"Attempt to lay your hand upon me, and I'll spring over the precipice!"

"Then if you do, my pretty one, you will kill yourself, and spoil that charming face."

"Better die," she replied, " than be in the power of so arrant a villian!"

Red Hand seemed to enjoy the poor girl's agony, and, with the greatest coolness, he replied—

"You think so, perhaps; but I may want you for a short time before you make the sacrifice. After I have grown tired of you, why, then, the sooner you go over, perhaps, the better."

Laura shuddered, and drew back from the dizzy height.

There was such a fearful look in the deep abyss that her brain reeled, and she put her hand over her eyes to shut out the sight.

Red Hand saw her hesitation, and with a cry like a wild beast, sprang upon her, and caught her in his arms.

"Ha! ha! ha!" he laughed. "Now jump over, my pretty bird!"

Laura struggled hard to free herself from him, until what little strength she had was exhausted.

Near to the spot where this struggle took place there was the trunk of a large tree.

Red Hand bore the fainting girl towards it. Human agony was to him a keen sport and enjoyment.

Placing Laura against the tree, he took a coil of thin rope from his pocket, and, despite her frantic struggles, bound her securely to the tree.

"Now," said the savage, "you can look at the country as long as you like."

Laura gave no other signs of noticing his words than a look of tearful agony.

Suddenly a gleam of passion shone in his fiendish eyes, and going close to the poor, helpless girl, he shouted—

"Do you want to live—eh?"

Laura turned away from his hot, pestilent breath, but made no reply.

"Do you hear?"

Laura's indignation at last got the better of her fear, and, looking the cold-blooded scoundrel full in the face, said—

"Inhuman brute! what pleasure can it be for you to torture me in this cruel manner?"

Red Hand gnashed his teeth with passion, repeating the question.

Laura remained silent; and the exasperated villian, drawing his pistols, cocked them, placing a muzzle of each opposite her eyes.

"You cursed, stubborn fool!" he growled; "if you do not answer me, I'll send the contents of these barrels into your head!"

Laura asked what he would have her say, and Red Hand lowered his weapons.

"I ask you if you wish to live, and if so, to do as I wish you."

The ruffian waited for her to reply, but the poor, frightened girl could only gaze piteously at the dark, savage, exultant face before her.

"Look here," he went on. "You know the secret entrance to the cave were that young whelp of an outlaw hides. Guide me to it, and you are free, or"——

The pirate was about raising his pistol when a heavy hand was laid upon his shoulder; turning, he beheld the giant form of Snowball.

"Drop dem," said the African, suiting the action to the word, by knocking the pistols from his hand, "hab been a long time coming, catch yer at last."

The suddenness of Snowball's attack took the pirate off his guard, and for a moment he was dumbfounded, and stood glaring upon the pistols which Snowball had knocked from his hands.

"You debbil!" muttered the African, "this chile only just in time."

Red Hand uttered an angry oath, and made an attempt to draw his sword.

In this he was frustrated by Snowball, who drew him from the spot where Laura, now in a swoon, was tied to the tree.

Red Hand, although a man of great physical power, was like a child in the hands of his assailant, and for a few paces he allowed himself to be dragged away by Snowball.

This submission did not last long, for making a sudden spring he wrenched himself away, and grasping his sword, said savagely—

"Curse you, for a meddling fool, but I'll——"

Before he could complete his sentence, Snowball again sprang upon him, and seizing his throat, forced the pirate to take his hand from his sword, and endeavour to push away the arm that held him. Snowball's eyes glared with rage; the ferocity of the negro, the untamed savage, was aroused, and giving his adversary's beard a wrench, he caused Red Hand to howl with pain.

"Where him Massa Tom?" said Snowball, still shaking his foe. "Where you put him?"

"—— him! he has escaped," yelled Red Hand.

"If not alive, where him? You tell quick."

And he accompanied each word with a tug at the long red beard which swept the pirates' breast.

Insensible as Derrick was to ordinary pain, he could not endure this, and he fairly howled with agony.

Again he repeated his statement, which was met by Snowball saying—

"You tell one great lie."

"Leave go my neck, you infernal nigger."

"See you hang first."

"Leave go."

"Tell me where Captain Tom, then."

"Curse you, he has escaped."

But Snowball would not believe the statement, he only gripped the tiger, and shook his foe the harder.

Red Hand was maddened with pain, and clenching his hand he dealt the African a blow upon the chest that would have felled two ordinary men.

But the negro only laughed at his puny effort, and hurling Red Hand from him he was about to cut the cord which tied Laura to the tree.

Before he could do so, the pirate, with a cry like a famished tiger, drew his sword and sprang upon Snowball.

The black caught his wrist ere he could deliver the blow, and almost wrenching his arm out of its socket, he took the sword from him and sent it whirling through the air.

Quick as thought the African drew his long

knife, and seizing Red Hand by the throat, held the shining blade aloft.

"You thief, you ! I two minds to cut your throat right round."

A stealthy footstep caught Snowball's ear, and he turned sharply.

Well for him he did, for one of Red Hand's gang stood with his musket grasped by the barrel, ready to smash the negro's head.

CHAPTER XI.

THE COMBAT.

SNOWBALL sprang nimbly aside, and the man, thus not meeting the resistance he expected to his weapon, staggered forward a few paces.

His last hour had come; for Snowball, raising him in his strong arms, sent the unfortunate wretch over the precipitous rock.

In a moment, Snowball and Red Hand, with open knives, bare arms, and clenched teeth, sprang towards each other.

An involuntary instinct caused them both to stand for a moment watching each other. Each felt certain it would be a struggle until death should end the conflict.

How could it be otherwise ? The surface of the rock upon which they stood did not cover an area of more than twenty yards, while on every side yawned a fearful precipice.

The assailants did not close on the instant; the long, keen blades glittering in their hands prevented an unguarded approach to each other.

Both were masters of their weapons.

It was a fearful scene this deadly encounter between two strong men, who stood face to face, hating each other with an intensity that blood alone could appease.

Big drops of perspiration stood upon their brows, as, with glaring eyes and compressed lips, they kept moving about in half circles from one side of the combat ground to the other, until, gradually closing, they stood knife to knife.

Snowball, whose veins now stood out like cords, uttered a savage cry—such as had been his wont when, as chief of his dusky tribe, he had gone upon the war path.

That cry was followed by a sudden rush upon his antagonist, and they closed together, the blades of each entering the fleshy part of the left arm of the other, which had been thrown up as a guard.

Then a deep, savage cry came from both, and they separated.

Blood once drawn, however, they forgot their former caution, and rushed savagely together.

In their deadly close encounter, excepting their heavy breathing, and the chink of the blades as they met, not a sound was heard.

Several random thrusts were given on both sides. With their left hands they vainly strove to grasp each other's throats.

Again they separated.

Regaining their breath, without a word they again closed. This time each caught the right arm of his adversary in his left hand, and, tightly holding the grip, continued to struggle.

The combat became now one of sheer strength. Both men knew that by releasing their hold they could clutch each other's throats ; but they knew, also, that the hand which held the knife would be set at liberty.

Thus the combatants held their grip.

Often on the very verge of the precipice did they sway too and fro, threatening to topple over.

Ultimately, Snowball showed his strength to be superior, whilst Derrick felt that unless he could, by a dexterous movement, throw off his assailant, his last hour had come.

So the struggle continued ; and the pirate's strength began to fail ; his breath came short and quick, until, with a last despairing effort to save his life, he suddenly stretched his head forward and seized Snowball's arm between his teeth.

The pain was horrible, yet the African did not suffer a cry to escape him ; but still held on, if possible, more tightly than before.

Snowball forced his antagonist backward, until Red Hand's limbs began to totter under him ; yet, with the energy of despair, he clung madly, with hands and teeth, to his foe.

Suddenly Snowball, by main strength, raised Derrick from the ground, and, by jerking him forwards and sideways, hurled the panting pirate from him, Red Hand carrying away a portion of the negro's arm in his teeth.

Before the pirate leader could gain a firm footing again, the negro, with a yell, dashed him to the earth, and, pressing one knee upon Red Hand's chest, he raised his knife to strike.

Vile as Red Hand was by nature, he was no coward ; yet he could not avoid closing his eyes when he beheld that glittering blade raised so menacingly over his breast, and the dusky savage's face that glared upon him.

The pirate had given up all hope, and lay powerless to avoid the death stroke.

But his hour was not yet come, for Snowball, at the moment he was about to plunge the deadly weapon into his antagonist's heart, suddenly paused, and, thinking of his young leader, said—

" I spare your life if you tell me one t'ing."

Receiving no answer, the giant shook his foe as a terrier would shake a rat, and repeated—

" I spare your life if you tell me one t'ing."

" What is it ?" gasped the pirate. Take your hand away from my windpipe. I cannot speak."

The long sinewy fingers were relaxed as the dark-skinned giant said—

" You tell me where Massa Tom is."

Red Hand unclosed his eyes, and with difficulty answered—

" I don't know."

" Dam lie !"

"It's the truth."

Snowball set his teeth, and would have rid the world of a monster; but the African's hand was seized—a heavy blow from the butt of a pistol fell upon his head, striking him to the earth.

Red Hand sprang to his feet as the negro's knee left his breast, when, to his surprise, he beheld several of his band coming towards them, and Pedro, who had come to his assistance at this critical moment, standing over the negro's prostrate form.

"We are surrounded!" cried Pedro; "the whole band are upon us!"

Red Hand ran to the edge of the rock, and espied the outlaws, with Midshipman Tom at their head, dispersing themselves round the rock.

Not a moment was to be lost; as it was, a volley was fired at him, one bullet grazing the skin of his shoulder.

Red Hand, in his haste to escape, thought not of the senseless negro, but picking up his knife, he rushed to Laura, and severing her bonds, bore her to the mouth of the cave.

"Quick!" he said, addressing his followers. "Down with you into the cave; collect the plunder, and leave by the secret passage. Then, hurrah for the open sea, our brave bark, and the black flag."

CHAPTER XII.

NEVILLE WIRELY.

"WIRELY AND SONS, SHIPBROKERS," gleamed out in large letters over a dingy suite of offices in King William-street, London-bridge.

The firm was regarded as one of the wealthiest in London, and their bills were considered as good to the commercial world as the newest bank notes or the brightest gold.

Had the portly merchants who placed such implicit faith in the firm of Wirely and Son known the conversation that took place one morning in the private office, they would not have felt very much impressed with the solvency of the eminent shipbrokers.

Wirely, senior, and his son, Neville, were seated at a table. The former looking over the shipping news in the various papers—the latter intently at work over a large ledger.

There was a strange contrast in the appearance of the two. The father was stout, below the middle height, of fresh complexion, and from his light blue eyes there beamed a seaming depth of honesty and love for his fellow-men.

His shining bald head and the few locks of silvery hair, aided by the semi-clerical character of his dress, added to his benign appearance, and deceived all who came in contact with him.

The son was tall and well-formed. His features could not be called handsome, yet they were not without a certain regularity, and those who looked at him wondered what it was that gave him such a forbidding appearance.

It was his dark, snake-like eyes. They were never raised except to his father's face; then only to meet a glance equally cunning.

Suddenly, Neville paused in his task and moodily said—

"There's no help for it, father. These infernal figures are too much. We have played our game out, and unless something extraordinary turns up, the firm of Wirely and Son will be no more."

"I expected it. How long do you think we can stand?"

"Three months at the utmost."

"Three months?"

"Not a day longer."

"Of course, you are calculating upon the restitution of the moneys we' have received from Colonel Grey's estate."

"Decidedly," said Neville, "and that must be met; for, by the colonel's last letter, I find he has taken a passage home in the Simoom."

"How long was that since?"

"Four months."

The elder partner jumped from his seat and said—

"He must be in England by this time. What a cursed fool I must have been."

"What for?"

"What for? for not leaving the country two months since, when we had possession of the forty thousand pounds belonging to the colonel."

"It was an oversight," said Neville; "so it is useless to dwell upon it. However, we are not sure that the vessel has escaped the dangers of the seas."

"True, and I have not looked over the *Seaman's News* lately. Hand me the file."

Neville did so. His father sat silent for some time, keenly searching paper after paper, until he had perused each sheet.

"Nothing," he said. "The Simoom spoken with, and all that sort of thing. What is the matter, Neville?"

The junior partner's eyes seemed ready to start from their sockets as he leaned forward with his elbows upon the table, his hands supporting his chin, and laying upon the table was a copy of the *Seaman's News.*

"Matter," he replied, "everything is right. Listen to every word, which is worth a thousand pounds to us at this moment."

The father leant forward, and his cheeks reddened with joy as Neville slowly read the following account from the newspaper—

"MASSACRE BY PIRATES.

"It is our painful duty to record another atrocity committed by the miscreants under Derrick, the pirate. The Simoom, homeward bound, and when in sight of England's white cliffs, was boarded by the pirates, and a terrible massacre took place, and there is no doubt but that every soul on board would have perished had it not been for the gallant attack made upon the murderous gang by the men who so lately deserted with Mr. Wilson, a midshipman, also of the Hercules, and whose strange story is yet fresh in the memory of our readers.

"The deserters or mutineers—whatever they may be termed—are still as much the foes of the murderous gang, as though they still served under the king's flag; for they not only cleared the vessel of the pirates, but took her safely into port, then retired to their secret retreat in the cliffs.

"For this gallant deed alone we feel assured the authorities will withdraw the proclamation of outlawry against the brave seamen and against this young officer.

"Among the passengers who fell before the arrival of the rescuers, we are informed is a gentleman of fortune, named Grey, who was returning to England with his daughter "——

Here Neville paused and said—

"This is sufficient for us. We have nothing to do with the list of names. Now, what's to be done?"

"Boldly claim the estates," said the elder Wirely. "We can easily do so by the virtue of the papers we hold."

"Suppose the girl is alive?"

"She will interfere with our scheme to a certain extent; but you must manage her."

"How?"

"Marry her, of course."

"Suppose other claimants should turn up?"

"The girl is first."

"I am supposing she is dead."

"Ah, true. Well, Neville, the estates are worth a struggle, and they must be ours at any cost; and as there is no time to be lost, the sooner you visit the editor of this paper, and find out from he obtained the news, the better."

A visitor was announced, and Neville left the room, and went on his way to the newspaper office.

"True," he thought, "the estates are worth a struggle, if even a little money be spent; but, what if, after all, this girl should be alive? It will certainly interfere with my father's scheme, unless I marry her."

Pondering deeply over this matter he reached the office of the *Seaman's News*, and inquired for the editor.

After a short delay, he was ushered into a little room where that gentleman was writing with lightning speed.

"Your business, sir," said the editor, without staying his flying quill, or taking his eyes from the paper. "Be seated, I shall be disengaged in one moment."

But that moment grew into an hour, as the little man kept to his task. Save the scratch, scratch of the pen, and the distant hum from busy workmen, not a sound was heard.

Neville began to be impatient. The very time he was wasting there might affect the plot, and he began to testify his restlessness by a slight cough, and moving his feet uneasily upon the floor.

Still the pen ran on its rapid flight, the writer's face varying in expression as his swift thoughts were transferred to the paper.

It is done at last. The pen is thrown aside, and the editor, passing his handkerchief over his heated brow, ran his eyes over the freshly-written sheets.

"Now, sir," looking towards Neville, "I shall be happy to attend upon you."

"You published an account of the piratical attack upon the Simoon," said Neville.

"We did, sir."

"Might I inquire the source of your information?"

"Certainly. But it is quite correct, I believe?"

"Quite so, unhappily."

"Dreadful affair; certainly very shocking; I trust you have no relatives on board?"

"Alas! yes. Mr. Grey and his daughters were relatives of mine."

"Very sad, very sad. I suppose, then, you would like to know for a certainty if this report of their fate be true?"

"I should."

"Very natural, very natural, indeed."

"Your informant was the only survivor, I believe, of the tragedy?"

"The only one, sir, the only one; although, I must confess, the account made, a capital column. Still the loss of life was very dreadful."

"It was, indeed; but, as my time is much occupied," said Neville, "and I am most anxious to see at once this person who beheld the last moment of my beloved relation, will you, sir, kindly tell me the seaman's address?"

Neville could play the hypocrite to perfection, and now he covered his white face with his cambric and got up a respectable shiver for the occasion.

"Poor young man!" thought the editor, as he wrote the seaman's address. "Poor fellow! he seems very much affected by their death."

It is a good thing for us sometimes that the secrets of our breasts are not laid open before the world, otherwise the editor would have felt anything but sympathy for the crafty dissembler before him.

Neville still kept his handkerchief up to his face as he read the slip of paper given him by the editor; and, in a voice of feigned emotion, he said—

"Thank you, sir, thank you. Should this report not have been correct I will call upon you."

"I shall be only too happy to make known to the world," readily interrupted the editor, "that any of your relatives have survived."

They shook hands at parting. The editor went back to his desk, and, amid his multifarious duties, soon forgot the visitor with the white pocket-handkerchief and the shaking voice.

Neville read the slip of paper—

ROBERT AMOS,
Goose and Gander,
Wapping.

RED HAND SHUDDERED AS THE BRIGHT BLADE GLEAMED ABOVE HIM.

CHAPTER XIII.

BOB AMOS TELLS HIS STORY.

WAPPING, although immortalised by Dibden in the famous song about the lady who was in the habit of washing her sailor lover's trousers, mixing his grog, and declaring she had never been false to him, was not a nice place, especially in the reign of the good (?) King George.

To that salubrious neighbourhood Neville made his way, not without some misgiving as to his personal safety, for Wapping, at the time we write, was infested by press-gangs.

England being engaged in a mighty struggle to keep her supremacy over the ocean, was com-pelled then to obtain men to defend her by any means.

Wapping at length he reached, and the Goose and Gander did not take long to find. A strong odour of bad rum and rank tobacco filled this well-known place of resort.

Repressing the strong feeling of disgust at the unsavoury effluvia, Neville passed inside, and went towards the open door, from which proceeded a tremendous cloud of tobacco-smoke, and the well-distended chorus of a highly popular naval song.

Neville had not ventured beyond the threshold of the door, when the landlord passed him with a tray of empty bottles.

3

He was a man of some bulk, possessing a countenance in which cunning and rapacity were strongly marked; the purple complexion of which plainly showed he was no stranger to the flavour of the liquors which he dispensed with such alacrity to the uninviting-looking company who thronged the place.

Before he could reach the bar, Neville inquired of him "If there was a seaman in there by name, Amos?"

"Perhaps there is, sir. I am sure I can't say exactly. What sort of a looking chap is he?"

"That I do not know myself, as I have never seen him."

The landlord eyed the questioner suspiciously, and a doubt seemed to cross his mind as to the respectability of Mr. Wirely.

"Perhaps he's a crimp,"* thought he. Anyhow, I'll keep my weather-eye upon him." Then he added, aloud—"Oh! you hain't never seen him?"

"No."

"Do you want him particular?"

"My business is important you may be sure, or should not have entered such a den as this."

"Well, den or not," said the landlord, angrily; "if you didn't want somebody here, it isn't the likes of you that would come."

"I meant not to offend you," said Neville, "so think no more of these hasty words; but mix a glass of your best—here's the money."

The landlord's anger soon evaporated at the sight of the half-guinea, which Neville threw upon the counter, at the same time desiring him to keep the change.

"I allers likes to do my best for a gentleman," said the obliging host, pocketing the cash. "I wants this chap there is a private room just behind—you can look into that ere room."

This private room mentioned by the rascally landlord was kept by him for the purpose of the press-gang overlooking the common room.

Through the little hole in the panel the leader of the press-gang could select his most likely-looking victims; and as they staggered from the house, under the influence of the villainous potations, they could easily be pounced upon.

The seamen were well aware of the landlord's little game in this respect; therefore, when he entered the tap-room and inquired for Robert Amos, that worthy kept himself quiet.

It was a strange scene, the interior of this place. Picture to yourself a long room, its walls black and begrimed with smoke and dirt.

The floor covered with coarse red sand, and earthenware spittoons.

A long deal table, running its entire length. Up each side of this, several wooden benches, which, by the way, were fixed to the ground. Of chairs and stools there were none; the frequenters of the Goose and Gridiron being too aptly given

* An agent who formerly decoyed men to enter into the Royal Navy.

to the breaking up of such articles, for the possession of their legs, as weapons of offence or defence in their frequent brawls.

Fill these benches with about twenty sailors and as many dissolute-looking women, always at hand to assist our tars in disbursing their hard-earned coin in such places; cover the table with glasses, pewter pots, "screws" of the "weed," short pipes, long ditto; broken stems and bowls out of counting; let the men be, with few exceptions, drinking incessantly, and the women all talking and straining their lungs to be heard above the general din, and you have just a well-drawn picture of the Goose and Gander in Wapping a century ago.

What Wapping is in one thousand eight hundred and sixty-nine, abler pens than mine have ere this told my readers.

The landlord had called upon Robert Amos several times; but that gentleman being too much taken up with the "attentions" of a lady who sat by his side, did not respond.

"Which is Bob Amos?" asked Boniface, in a shrill tone. "Why don't you answer the hail?"

Bob looked at the landlord, then at a pewter measure which stood before him. While his eyes were thus employed, he was weighing in his mind the penalties that were attached to flooring a noisy landlord with one of his own quart measures.

While he was thus debating, the landlord again spoke.

"Bob Amos, ahoy! Show yer figure-head."

Bob made a signal to the landlord of his being present.

"Come here, Bob; I want you."

Bob stuck his tongue in his cheek, and replied—

"You do? What, is there a trap on?"

"No, Bob, it's all square. It's a gem'man wants to know about the Simoon."

"Gammon!" says Bob.

"No; come on. It's all right."

Bob rose to follow the landlord; but before he could quit his seat, the lady who had been so attentive to him took offence at his wish to depart, and gave altogether a damper to any future expectation of her devotion, by throwing the dregs some half-and-half down Bob's back.

Bob told her to go to "Jericho."

Shaking himself, and cutting a fresh plug of pig-tail, he left the room after the landlord.

By the landlord he was ushered into the little room where Neville had been so long and impatiently waiting.

A fresh tumbler of steaming grog was ordered for Bob Amos, which having been brought in, and the landlord having retired, Neville commenced the conversation by saying—

"You were on board the Simoon at the time she was captured by the pirates?"

"I was, sir."

"And saw the death of Mr. Grey and his daughter?"

"Not his daughter, sir."

"Ah!" exclaimed Neville, almost jumping from his seat."

"But I saw the old man killed with a tomahawk."

"And his daughter," said Neville, feverishly, "what of her?"

"Well, just at the moment the old man was floored, I got one on the skull that kept me quiet for a few minutes, but I remember, just as I was falling, seeing a pirate take the poor girl up, and sling her over his shoulder. Here's good health, sir."

And Bob took a long pull at the glass.

Neville nodded, and asked, impatiently—

"Well, after that, what followed?"

Bob emptied the glass, and placing it down slowly, said—

"Ah, that was a scene, sir!—there's no mistake about it. You talk about"——

"To the point, man; I am dying with impatience."

"Talk of your battles, but this beat all as ever I seed or heard on."

"Speak, man, without so much circumlocution."

"I don't know anything about that ere; but what I know is, that ven the fellow was going off with the beautiful young lady in his arms, there was a shout and a rush, and up comes—but you ask"——

"Go on. Go on, pray, sir."

"And up comes a young chap all over gold tassels and finery, looking like a prince as we sees in the play."

"Do, for heaven's sake, bring your story to a close," exclaimed Neville.

"Look here, mister," said Bob, "if you don't let me spin my own yarn my own fashion, we shall never come to an anchor."

Neville fell back in his chair with a half groan. "Well, this young chap," continued Bob, "jumps aboard, and whipping out his sword, he cuts away at 'em right and left. Among the first he floors was the cove who had got the young lady over his shoulder; down he goes, and the young chap takes the gal, and puts her under the half hatch, and then rolls into them again."

"Who was this?"

"Wait a minnit, I aint done yet. You should have seen the beggars roll over the side when this young chap and his men comed on deck. My eye! didn't they make sail in no time; and them as didn't were soon laid on their beam ends. Never did I see sich beggars to fight as that young chap and his men."

"This does not interest me," Neville said; "I, wish for"——

Bob did not need the interruption; the subject was too pleasant to be cut short by Neville Wirely.

"When the varmints did get away to their ship," continued Bob, "the young chap was wounded in the head, but he binds it up, and says

to his men, 'lift me on your shoulders,' and they did lift him, and he points to the pirate ship and says, 'give them a salute.' So the gun as was on board was loaded, and fired slap at the reptiles, and they fired back again, and knocks over some of the young chap's men, but I warrant he'll pay 'em out for that."

"Have you finished your story?"

"Well, yes; but I'm awfully dry arter it."

Neville rang the bell, and ordered another glass for Bob.

"Now," he said, when Bob had poured about half the steaming decoction down his throat, and fished out the piece of lemon, "perhaps you will have the kindness to tell me who this hero was?"

"Well, you see," began Bob, "soon arter that a storm comes on"——

"Don't mind the storm, tell me who it was took the girl away."

Bob grinned at his interlocutor's impatience, and continued—

"Well they calls him"—

And Bob began scratching his head, as though invoking his memory.

Neville threw a guinea on the table.

Bob pocketed the coin, and it considerably refreshed his memory, for he immediately said—

"He is MIDSHIPMAN TOM!"

"And who is MIDSHIPMAN TOM?"

"I thought everybody knowed him."

"Perhaps everyone might; but I am, unfortunately, a solitary exception."

"That's just like you coves who lives all your life in London; you knows nothing."

The grog was beginning to operate on Bob.

"Very likely," replied Neville; "perhaps you will enlighten me?"

"In course I'll—hic—'lighten you."

"Come, out with it, man."

"Well, he's the—hic—outlaw chief."

"And he has possession of Miss Grey?"

"In course. I can tell you he's a regular young brick, and no mistake."

Neville's thin lip curled with scorn as he asked—

"Where does he live?"

"Eh? What, don't you know that either?

"No."

"Well, I'll tell you—on the West Coast."

"Ha! By Cornwall?"

"The wery identical—hic—'among the caves there."

Neville rose from his seat.

"Thank you for the information. Good day."

"I say," said Bob, as his visitor was about to open the door, "here!"

Neville paused.

"Look here," Bob went on, in drunken gravity, "if you means any mischief to'ards that young feller or the gal, you had better out."

"Pshaw!" growled Neville, as he opened the door and passed through, "you drunken idiot!"

Neville soon reached the street, and walking on

until he met a hackney coach, he hailed the driver, and was soon on his way home.

Bob sat gazing for a few minutes at the door by which his visitor had left, and then raising himself with difficulty from his chair, he staggered towards the tap-room, muttering—

"He's got a bad figger-head, that chap. I'm blowed if I don't go down to the cave and keep a look-out on him, for that's where he's going."

But poor Bob soon forgot all about his visitor and the newly formed resolution, for in less than half an hour afterwards he had rolled under the table in a state of helpless intoxication.

And the fair lady, whom he had told to go to Jericho, had helped herself to the change of the guinea Neville had given him.

CHAPTER XIV.

THE DEATH OF PEDRO.

RED HAND's miscreants took up their leader's cry, and defiantly shouted at the top of their voices—

"Hurrah for the black flag!"

And before their pursuers could gain the summit of the rock, they had reached the secret opening to the cave, and were soon hastily employed in collecting the riches they had accumulated in their various incursions in land.

On every side of the precipitous rock the outlaws now came up, and to the young sailor's inexpressible joy, he found Snowball, though stunned and bleeding, yet alive.

Leaving the negro to the care of some of his men, he drew his shining blade, and calling upon the remainder to follow him, dashed to the opening of the cave.

A wild hurrah greeted the middy as his men obeyed his command.

But when they reached the cave not a living being was there.

The young sailor's handsome face turned pale with rage when he thought of the probable fate awaiting the unfortunate Laura.

In a voice husky with emotion, he said—

"There must be some secret outlet. For God's sake, let us try and discover it!"

The outlawed seamen dispersed themselves about the cavern, seeking for the secret passage by which Red Hand and his associates had escaped.

But the mode of exit was too well concealed, and no trace of their foes could be discovered.

But one sad mememto was left in the cave.

Midshipman Tom picked up a ribbon which nad been worn by Laura, and, for the first time, since he had been acquainted with that fearless maiden, he felt an overpowering sensation fill his heart.

Agonizing thought! she was lost to him, and in the power of a ruffian!

His face reddened with passion as he twined the ribbon around the jewelled hilt of his sabre, and swore, as he kissed the precious token, never to sheath his blade until he had either released the maiden, or avenged any wrong she might have suffered.

Snowball, having recovered from the effects of the blow, now joined the young cheiftain.

"Dey hab gone, cuss 'em! but there will be the time, when dis knife do de work!" and he tapped the hilt of his weapon in a manner that boded ill for the Red Hands.

"We hab better leabe this cabe, or we nebber catch 'em," continued the nigger.

"True," said Midshipman Tom, clutching in the same breath the rope, and rapidly ascending. "Follow me now. Death to Red Hand's band!"

The cry was taken up by the outlaws as they followed their chief to the surface of the rock.

The morning had now fully dawned, and every object for miles was distinctly visible.

Calm as an inland river lay the majestic ocean, and, for a few moments, Tom's eyes rested upon his fairy-like vessel, which rode at anchor.

"Snowball," he said, turning to his lieutenant, "do you think it would be advisable to go a-board and wait for them?"

"I tink not, Massa Tom."

"Why?"

"Cause dey no gone far away from dis place, but like dem rats dey stops underground."

"But they may have an outlet somewhere near their vessel."

"Yes, dey hab; but dey no go dat way."

"You think not?"

"Dis child sure, because de only ship dey hab left am got big hole jist over the waterline, and dey not go out to sea like dat."

"Well?"

"Dat not all, you know. De king's cruisers are out in de Roads; so if de pirates did go in dere ship, de cruisers swallow dem up."

"Most excellent logic, Snowball; go on."

"Den, again, dey know de War Cloud catch 'em if dey 'tempts to go away, and dey sure no like our big gun, Massa Tom."

"What do you advise, then, Snowball?"

"Well, I tink best way be for us all to separate. You and I go one way, some ob de boys anoder, and some anoder. But all to meet dere," pointing to a rocky undulating space near the shore as he spoke.

"Perhaps your plan is best," said Tom, "but how would we know if either party gets on the trail of the villains?"

"We shall be close to one anoder, and when de trail is sprung, den him who find it fire one, two pistols, and we all go."

"Exactly so; but"——

"No but, Massa Tom. You see dis side ob de rock?"

"Yes."

"And dis?"

"Yes."

Snowball has pointed to the three sides of the rock, which was almost perpendicular. Extending his hand in the direction of the remaining side, he continued—

"You see, Massa Tom, them three sides not lead to anywhere?"

"I do."

"And dis one go a long way towards de sea?"

"Yes."

"Well, den, de 'retches are somewhere under dis part dat goes towards de sea."

"How foolish I must have been," said Tom. "Of course there can be no place else; for had any of them emerged from either of these sides, we must have seen them."

"Yes, Massa Tom, you hab it now. Well den, we separate. Me and you dis way; de boys in two lots dat way, and dat way, and all goes towards de place I mean."

"Excellent—most excellent!" cried Tom, his face brightening. "Your African warfare, Snowball, has given you a quick perception of the movements of an enemy."

The negro drew himself up proudly, and laying his hand upon his bare chest, declared himself "chief" in his own country, "where dem follow de trail ob an enemy for more dan a month, and then," he added fiercely, "kill him and take scalp!"

This colloquy ended, Tom proposed following the plan at once,

"Remember the signal. Two pistol shots when the trail is found."

The men lingered for a moment or two as Tom and his sable companion began to descend the rock.

Tom noticed this, and desired to know why it was they lingered.

An old grizzly outlaw doffed his cap and spoke—"Well, sir, we don't like the idea of you and the lieutenant going alone. Let some of us accompany you."

Tom declined the offer, and promising he would fire directly they got the scent, he swung himself down the edge of the rock.

The path chosen by Tom and Snowball lay through a wild and rocky path.

Behind every bush, every piece of fallen rock capable of hiding a foe, they searched.

Hour after hour passed, and still no sign of the pirates, or any report of firearms from their own party.

"I fancy," said Tom, as they descended a rocky defile, "these cowardly ruffians have burrowed in the earth, Snowball; but where," he added suddenly—"where is the dog?"

"Ah! What him!" almost yelled the black.

"Him good dog! Him on de track!"

"Are you sure?"

"Sartan, Massa Tom. When we follered that wretch, who tumble over precipice, we all go back to cave. You no dere; so de boys sits round de fire, and, by-and-by, goes sleep. Dis child no sleep; he gets up, and walks on de bank. When him dere, up comes big dog, and looks in him face, and makes funny noise."

"Whines, Snowball."

"Berry likely; I not understand what you call it. Den him take my trousers in him mouth, and pull—pull."

"Noble animal."

"Yes; den I says, dog know where Massa Tom am; so I goes, and dog runs on, and dat's how I find de place."

The young leader began to feel alarmed for the safety of his faithful hound!

"Where is the dog now?" he asked.

"Ah! where him now? I wish dis child know. Somebody lose hair."

"Have you seen him since we ascended the rock?"

Snowball rubbed his forehead, as it were to remember something.

"You bring him with you?" suddenly inquired Snowball.

"Yes, he was beside me, when I found you stunned on the ground."

"Ah!" said Snowball, rubbing the still aching place, where the butt of the pirate's musket had struck him, "I shall know that pusson agin, and if I cotch him—nebber mind—somebody lose scalp—not Snowball, p'r'aps; but de dog—just as I open my eyes agin, I see him go down de cave's mouth. Him all right, so am pretty lady. Me tinks him dog berry fond of her."

Relapsing into silence, they again pursued their way, descending the defile—too narrow for two to walk abreast.

Huge masses of loose rock were piled up in rugged grandeur around them, and Tom, who had walked some distance with downcast eyes, was suddenly aroused by Snowball stopping, and giving utterance to a loud—

"Waugh!"

Looking up, he beheld their further progress barred by large masses of loose stone.

And on the summit of the pile was seen the villanous face of Pedro, the pirate lieutenant.

Already had the ruffian loosed the ponderous mass, and was endeavouring to topple it over upon the heads of Tom and his companion.

"Waugh!" repeated Snowball. "You want to lose your hair."

The ruffian gave a yell of triumph, and applying his shoulder to the now moving mass, was about to hurl it upon the outlaw chief.

Already it began to oscillate, and in another moment they would have been crushed to atoms.

Before that brief space of time passed, Snowball levelled a pistol at Pedro's head and fired.

A death-scream answered the report, and the lieutenant's brains were scattered over the very stone he was about to crush his pursuers with.

"Him get dat," was Snowball's cool remark as

he replaced the discharged pistol, and, drawing his knife, scrambled up to where Pedro lay dead and quivering upon the rock.

"What are you going to do now?" asked Tom, as he followed his dark-skinned companion.

"Noting, only hab him wool—dat's all."

CHAPTER XV.

SNOWBALL MAKES A DISCOVERY.

"My faithful friend," said Tom, putting his hand on the giant's shoulder, "we are in a civilized country; you must not do that. The miscreant is dead—there let his body lie. He deserved his fate."

But Snowball's African blood was aroused; his forest instinct rekindled, and with a fearful war-whoop, he flourished his knife, and seized Red Hand's lieutenant by the hair.

Turning it round his fingers until he had drawn the skin tight enough for his purpose, he was about to tear the ghastly emblem of victory from the lieutenant's head.

But ere he could do so, the young outlaw was by his side; laying his hand upon the African's arm, he again said—

"Snowball, this must not be."

"Waugh!" cried the black, bringing the point of his keen knife to the quivering head. "Snowball hab him hair, anyhow."

Tom would not brook any contradiction not even from his most favoured officer, and, to end the dispute, he struck the knife from Snowball's grasp.

"It may be all very well," he remarked, as the weapon went flying through the air, "for the savage tribes in Africa, but no one, under my command, shall be guilty of such barbarity."

Snowball hung his head abashed at this rebuke, and gazing mournfully at the scalplock he had twisted, he muttered—

"Golly, it all berry well, Massa Tom; but dey would scalp you as soon as look."

"So much the worse for them, should I outlive it."

The African quickly asked—

"You would hab 'em all scalped, eh, Massa Tom?

The young sailor smiled at his follower's eagerness, and replied—

"We'll make that a matter for further consideration. But come—let us continue the search. I tremble to think of that poor girl's fate."

He turned from the spot, followed by Snowball, who kept glancing behind at the prostrate form of his enemy, and muttering, "Dis child like to hab him's hair, anyhow; p'r'aps he come back for it."

"We must be near the outlet of the cavern, Snowball," said Tom, thoughtfully, "or that miscreant would not have been there to bar our progress."

"Sartin, Massa Tom, sartin. You just stand still. Dis nigger listen."

The young leader watched his follower's movements curiously.

First, Snowball stretched himself at full length on the ground; then, picking up a feather, he held it between his thumb and forefinger for a moment, and in an upright position.

"De wind comes in from de sea—dat am bad," he said, as he watched the feather gently move to and fro; but nebber mind."

With Indian cunning, he dug a hole in the sand, and, plying his ear to the hollow, listened intently.

For several minutes he lay thus, neither speaking nor moving—his chief watching him with breathless interest.

Nearly a quarter of an hour passed; then Snowball uttered a loud "Waugh!"

"Can you hear anything, Snowball?" asked the middy, anxiously.

"A little someting, massa."

"What is it—a voice or footstep?"

"Not neider that you mean, but a pit-a-pat, pit-a-pat, like a lion coming down the grove."

Tom's face reddened with hope and excitement, and he ejaculated, "It is the dog! You say he followed the Red Hand."

"Golly! P'r'aps it am; den we right. Keep quiet a moment, Massa Tom—me listen."

Down went Snowball into the sand-hole again. Presently he spoke.

"Dat him little bark—werry angry one."

"In which direction does the noise proceed from?"

"Dat what puzzle dis chile, massa; it am not eider of de ways we hab come, and it ain't—yah!" he yelled suddenly, springing to his feet, "dis nigger am a fool, dat what me am."

Tom gazed upon him with astonishment.

What could Snowball's extraordinary actions mean, for he was now running about like a maniac, stamping the ground, and uttering short cries of delight.

"In heaven's name, Snowball, what is the matter?"

"Matter! dis nigger ought to hab a kick ob your right boot, and den one wid de left—that's what he ought."

"What for?"

"What for! Why you ask? when I hab been listening and listening, and all de while de sound underneff?"

"What?"

"Underneff us, Massa Tom, sure as we alive."

"Then we are upon the outlet to the passage?"

"Sartin. Dat's how dat dam wretch, whose scalp I hab not got—hab got out."

"But how?"

"Dat's it! How, Massa Tom? But I tink I find out."

Again he commenced his antics, stamping on

the ground, pushing heavy stones aside, and grumbling out sundry threats about the hair he would raise when he got at the pirate horde.

But to get at them was the chief affair.

It was evident the lieutenant had very carefully concealed the means of egress.

To obtain information from him was impossible, for Snowball's bullet had ended the ruffian's career for ever.

To be baffled in this manner made the African foam with passion.

The discovery he so ardently wished to make, was made in a sudden and ludicrous manner.

"Golly! Dam! Oh, yah! Here it am, and dis nigger stuck as fast as ship's mainmast!'

Tom laughed until the tears came from his eyes at the ludicrous sight, and as soon as he was able, he rushed to his follower's assistance.

"Pull me up a little bit, Massa Tom, 'case dey hab a fancy for dis chile's hansome legs."

Tom did as he was desired, and raised the captive black a little way.

Much to the captive black's delight, for every moment he expected to feel his ankles clutched by some of the earthed fraternity.

The young leader, though very powerful, found

TOM IN THE PIRATES' HAUNT.

Snowball was executing a war dance of the most savage description, and expressive of his rage and disappointment at being unable to find the secret outlet.

Gradually narrowing the circle he paced, he jumped on what appeared to be a heap of dried leaves.

Directly the black's foot touched the heap he disappeared save his shining face, and after trying for a few moments to extricate himself, he exclaimed, ruefully—

some difficulty in raising the gigantic form, for the orifice in the soil was not larger than to admit of the passage of an ordinary sized man.

First his brawny chest, then his waist became visible, and Snowball with the assurance that, "Tankee, Massa Tom, dat do fine!" prevailed upon the chief to release his hold.

He did so, and Snowball was about to extricate himself by raising his body by his hands.

This was worse than before, for the earth gave way under the tremendous pressure, and down went Snowball this time completely out of sight, several pieces of the dislodged earth and stones alighting on his head.

The young sailor dropped lightly down after him, and, to his amusement, beheld Snowball sitting on the ground, nearly covered by the *debris*, and rubbing his head in a most useful manner.

"Good job dis pimple hab a thick crust," he growled, "or dat big stone dat come so quick on him make a hole."

"Hush!" whispered Tom, warningly, "do not betray our presence to them before we reconnoitre."

"All berry fine to talk 'bout waiting wid tree great bumps on him head big as pumpkins."

Snowball scrambled slowly to his feet, and then feeling very carefully whether all his bones were sound, he muttered to himself, fiercely—

"Tree bumps, tree scalps, and as many more as him can get."

The place they now found themselves in was an arched passage of not more than sufficient height for a middle-sized person to stand upright in.

As for Snowball, he kept knocking his head at every step, each knock he received he added another scalp to the account.

There was no light save that from the aperture where Snowball had made his sudden descent, and, as they proceeded, Tom discovered that they were in the passage or gallery of a disused coal mine.

CHAPTER XVI.

IN THE PIRATES' HAUNT.

THE place was in utter darkness, and for a few moments, the adventurers stood and held a whispered consultation as to the best and least dangerous mode of proceeding.

They knew one of the galleries would lead to the haunt of the foe.

But the question was which to choose, for there were many, and it was too dark to gain anything by the appearance of the used track, which no doubt bore the footprints of the miscreants.

"Better foller our noses," suggested the black. "Dere no better way dat I can tink on. P'r'aps tink better, if dis nigger's head not ache so big."

The young outlaw knew the labyrinth they were likely to get into, unless the greatest caution was used in traversing these winding passages, now took the lead, and bidding the grumbling African follow him, groped his way in total darkness.

For nearly a hundred yards they proceeded in this manner, when, suddenly, they were brought to a standstill by the angry bark of a dog.

"By heavens, 'tis our dog!" ejaculated Tom. "I know his bark."

"Yes, Massa Tom, dat him; but where am him?"

"Hush! Listen."

Again the sharp, angry yelp—this time louder than before.

"Found!" whispered Tom, unsheathing his scimitar. "See you yon pale glimmering light?"

"Yass—go on. Dares some scalp for Snowball."

At first about the size of a sixpence; the light soon widened, and the hurrying outlaws soon found themselves at the extremity of the passage, the broad glare of day shining upon them.

They had reached the shaft, and, from the time-worn heaps of wood and iron that lay about, it was evident the pit had ceased working for some years.

The deep baying of the dog could now be plainly heard, and both starting a run in the direction of the sound, dashed through a small passage, and found themselves in the chamber which had evidently been used by the proprietor of the pit to keep horses in.

But a far different sight now met their gaze than a peaceful row of horses.

With his back towards them, and right in the entrance, stood Red Hand, his cutlass drawn, and his eyes rolling with fury, as he tried to keep at bay the huge dog, who, with bristling coat, and showing his long deadly fangs, stood before Laura Grey— a noble and fearless champion for the defenceless girl.

Little did the miscreant imagine, when he fled from the sudden attack of the outlaws, and bore Laura with him, that so determined a foe followed close upon his track.

Guided by that wondrous power of scent—a gift the noble animal possessed to a marvellous degreee—he had followed the villain abductor step by step, until he reached the old stable in the pit, just as Red Hand had remorselesssly hurled the young and beautiful girl upon a heap of decayed rubbish.

A few moments he stood gloating over her cowering form, and with an evil light in his eye, said, exultingly—

"Ha! ha! ha! Mine now, in spite of ten thousand devils!"

Laura sank on her knees, and said imploringly,

"Mercy! mercy! Oh, heaven! what have I done!"

"Done? Why you've won the heart of Red Hand, and I think you ought to be proud of it, instead of whimpering thus."

She covered her face with her hands, and shed bitter, scalding tears of agony.

"Come, don't hide your face!" he growled. "Look up and consent to be mine."

"Wretch! monster!" she exclaimed, as she sprang to her feet. "Heaven protect me against such a sacrifice!"

Her prayers were heard, for a loud angry bark rang through the chamber.

A fierce yell followed from the pirate's lips, as the dog sprang upon him, and dragged him to the earth.

Then they struggled, but the dog managed to hold the pirate down, and at length he shook him as we often see a puppy shake a young kitten in play.

"Call the dog off," gasped the wretch, "and you shall go free."

Well he knew that, should the dog shift his hold, the next grasp would be upon his throat; and the baffled monster cried in abject tones for Laura to call her protector off.

The maiden shuddered at the fierce contest, and bad as the wretch had served her, felt an emotion of pity in her breast, and did so.

The dog obeyed her instantly.

Giving Red Hand a parting shake, the dog went to Laura's side.

Red Hand was no sooner released, than he attempted to draw his sword, but the pain in his shoulder prevented him.

Laura now reminded him of his promise to set her free.

Red Hand laughed at her mockingly; and, by a great effort succeeded in drawing his cutlass, and threatened to settle the accursed brute!

He made a step forward.

As he did so, the watchful beast sprang to his feet and faced him.

Red Hand paused.

It was at this instant that Tom and Snowball came so suddenly and so noiselessly upon the scene.

And had it not been for Snowball's excited cry, "Yah! hab him hair now!" they would have secured the villain without a struggle.

The pirate turned suddenly and dashed past, dealing the luckless Snowball a terrific blow with his left hand upon that portion of the human frame denominated by the fancy his "bread basket."

Poor Snowball was nearly knocked double. The water streamed from his eyes, and he gasped for breath like a porpoise suddenly landed.

With every demonstration of canine delight, the dog began to leap and gambol around his master.

But the young chieftain scarce noticed the animal; he had flown to Laura, whom he enfolded to his heart.

"Thank heaven, Laura, you are saved!" said Tom; "saved, my darling."

Laura nestled closer to him; and, hiding her blushing face upon his shoulder, wept tears of joy; for, truth to tell, Laura's heart had long been the young chieftain's, and this act of noble disinterestedness on his part had told the trembling maiden she had not loved in vain.

Oh! that moment of ecstatic bliss—that elysium of pure celestial happiness which filled her soul when she clung so fondly, so confidingly to the idol of her young and faithful heart.

With the grace of the most polished cavalier,

the young outlaw uncovered his head, and bringing his face to hers, their lips met in one kiss of pure and holy love.

Thus was the love of Laura Grey and her brave young lover first spoken.

Snowball had very conveniently turned his head another way during this tender scene and smoothed the spot which yet smarted from Red Hand's fist, he thought—

"Golly! Massa Tom hab sweetheart now, dat am shame. And Snowball no get one. But he sure to have one ting—dat feller dat knock dis nigger's breff out of his body had better look for his scalp. Some fine day——Hallo! what's dat?"

Snowball leant forward, and beheld the pirate, followed by his band, creeping along passage.

"Not dis time catch us," muttered Snowball, as he drew his pistols and discharged them, one after the other, in the air.

The signal was immediately answered from above, and, to the African's great joy, he beheld the mouth of the pit surrounded by the well-known faces of his friends.

The firing brought the pirates to a sudden standstill; but, urged on by the powerful voice of their leader, they came towards the spot at run.

Snowball's pistols were rapidly reloaded.

Two of the leading pirates bit the dust at the the first discharge.

Tom started from his momentary trance of bliss, and came to the assistance of his sable lieutenant.

He asked no questions. The enemy were before them, and as quick as thought his beautifully embossed weapons were levelled and fired.

Another halt on the pirate side, followed by a wild volley, which did no harm, for both Snowball and Tom had retired out of range, to reload their weapons.

A hurried consultation took place among Red Hand's band, which ended in a retrograde movement.

They saw with dismay a circle of fierce faces and long, deadly tubes at the mouth of the pit.

And, to make matters worse for them, they could not advance only two abreast, in consequence of the narrowness of the passage.

"Dey is up to suffink," growled Snowball, "so we had better be hopping de twig."

"How are we to ascend?" asked Tom.

"Dat easy enuff. Hi! you up dere!"

"Hillo!"

"Send down a rope, and be quick, or we shall be cotched by dem varmints."

A stout rope was soon lowered, and Snowball, making a large noose, motioned Tom to advance with Laura.

The young chieftain did so, but disdaining to use the loop Snowball had made, he grasped the rope with his right hand.

Laura's arms were round his neck, and he held her close to him with his left arm.

Snowball then gave an imitation of a boatswain's whistle, and the young people were soon drawn to the surface.

The dog looked wistfully up at his master, then rubbing his head against Snowball, he seemed to ask how he should reach the top.

"All right, ole boy," said the African; "our turn soon. Master Tom and Miss Laura first, den you and me."

The dog wagged his tail, as though he understood him, and raising himself on his hind legs, placed his huge paws on the black giant's shoulders.

"Dat's just it," said Snowball, as he put his arm round the dog, in imitation of the manner in which Tom had supported Laura. "Come on dare wid dat rope."

The rope was again lowered, and Snowball, with his rude companion, was quickly hoisted up.

They had not gone far towards the outlaws' cave when Tom called his sable friend to his side.

The beauteous Laura had told her lover that she had been betrayed into the hands of the miscreant Red Hand, and when Tom told the black the name of the traitor, he grinned savagely, and said—

"By all the fetish gods of Snowball's country de 'retch die!"

CHAPTER XVII.

LADY MOUNTSTEVEN.

PHILIP WILSON, suspected by the revenue officers of aiding the free traders before his presumed son had become an outlaw, was subject to all kinds of surveillance by them after Tom had left the Royal Navy.

Morose and churlish before, Philip became more so when suffering from their espionage, as the officers were seldom out of sight of his house, for they hoped Tom would pay his father a visit, and thus fall into their hands.

Philip hated the boy more than ever, for he looked upon him as the cause of the annoyance, and would, had he been able, have given the gallant mid over to the authorities.

He had made up his mind to do this, and day after day, skulked about the rocks, trusting to an opportunity to carry his project into execution.

One day he had taken his post behind a heap of rugged stones that were banked up by the roadside, and had not been long there, when the sound of horses' hoofs caused him to look over his hiding-place.

The suddenness of his appearance caused the horse to swerve aside, and the lady who was in saddle had some difficulty in preventing the snorting brute from dashing over the cliff.

Philip knew the rider. She was Lady Mountsteven, mistress of a grim-looking old castle, that

had been the home of her husband's family many generations.

She was a dark-eyed, splendid woman of tween thirty and forty years of age, and time, place of detracting from her beauty, had given additional charms.

She was as haughty as she was beautiful, a as proud as Lucifer; so when she had restrain the dangerous curvettings of her steed, she r up to Philip, and, raising her whip, struck h across the face.

"Plebian hound!" she said, "have you thing better to do than endanger the life of lady?"

The cut stung not only Philip's flesh, but temper; and, with an oath, he sprang forwa and seized the horse's head.

He seemed about to back the spirited anin over the cliff, but controlling himself by an e traordinary effort, folded his arms, and sa fiercely—

"You shall pay for that blow, my lady, p very dearly"——

"Stand out of my path, hound!"

"Not until I have said what I have to s woman."

"Ah!" the cry was like an angry tigress, "d you speak thus? Do you know me? I am La Mountsteven."

"It's a lie!"

The proud woman went pale with passion, h he heeded it not, as he continued—

"It's a lie! Do you hear? You are no m Lady Mountsteven than your son who is away college heir to the lands of Mountsteven."

He must have spoken the truth, for she dropp from the saddle, and holding the horse by bridle, went straight up to Philip Wilson, a with a look upon her face that spoke, as plainly words could have spoken, her wish to annihil the speaker, said—

"Who are you that dare utter such words me?"

"Philip Wilson, madam. You knew me und a different name once, but that was nea eighteen years ago. Shall I tell you how we beca acquainted?"

She made no answer, although her lips mov as though she had not the power of speech left.

"You were a friend and companion to the La Mountsteven, and you loved her husband. Y need not grit your teeth. I am speaking t truth, and from here you do not move until I ha finished."

"Miscreant!"

"Keep your tongue quiet, and listen." Phil Wilson went on, speaking as coolly as though were an equal with the proud lady of the castl "There was an heir born to the house of Moun steven, and, before the child was an hour old, y stole it from the mother's side, and gave it to smuggler to take out to sea in his lugger, and throw it overboard."

She seemed like a stone figure now—so cold, so immovable—and from between her set teeth came the words—

"He did my bidding."

"He did not," replied Philip. "The boy lives. See you yonder vessel riding at anchor? He commands that ship, and people call him Tom Wilson; others, Midshipman Tom."

The woman, who had been so arrogant a few moments before, was now humbled and lowered to the dust, for she was in the power of a man she had long since deemed dead, and his terrible secret buried with him.

"You rid yourself of the child," the grim accuser said, "then you disposed of the mother "——

"She is dead, then?"

"I did not say so—thus your path was clear, and you became Lady Mountsteven; but—ha! ha! strike me again with your whip, and I will proclaim to the world "——

"Hush! for heaven's sake. Do you wish to ruin me? Do "——

"I want to repay the blow you "——

"Spare me! Here, on my knees, I ask your forgiveness for the blow I, in a moment of anger, gave you."

The haughty lady grovelled in the dust before the coarse, exultant plebeian. Her pride was humbled now. Through that simple cut with her riding-whip, she had found herself in the power of a man she loathed and despised.

Philip enjoyed his triumph. He could bear the tyranny of the king's officers better now he had some one to wreak his spite upon.

So he argued. But he knew little of the proud lady's nature; true, she grovelled before him, but even while she craved his forgiveness, her brain was dimly shadowing forth a plan whereby she could not only destroy the evidence of her crime, but the gallant boy she had robbed of his birth-right, and cast him upon the world.

"Get up, madam," said Philip, roughly, " and beware the next time that proud temper of yours makes you forget yourself."

"You will bear me no malice, Mr. Wilson? Come, give me your hand, and let us be friends —we know too much of each other to be foes."

"I have nothing to fear from you. Lady Mountsteven."

"You think not."

"I am sure of it."

"Listen," she said. "I am the wife of a peer, you are a man already more than suspected of breaking the laws of your country; and the crimes you can bring against me would be met and re"——

"Very likely," said Philip; "but I have in my possession proofs that Tom Wilson is the heir to the Mountsteven lands and title. I have also proofs that Lady Alicia did not perish in the foundering of the French ship I placed her on after taking her from the castle."

"She is alive then?"

Lady Mountsteven spoke calmly, but she writhed with suppressed passion.

"Alive, and can be produced if necessary; but I shall not move in the matter unless you give me leave."

"Will you assist me, as you assisted me so many years since?"

"If I am paid," said Philip; "for I want to leave this accursed country, and, as I bear the boy who has caused me so much misery but little good will, I should not care if he were hanging from the yardarm of the flagship to-morrow."

"What is the price of your assistance."

"Two thousand pounds, and an appointment under Government at one of the foreign ports; the money you can give me, the appointment your husband can obtain."

"Very well, both shall be yours; when will you give me a proof of your sincerity?"

"Between this and to-morrow's sunset the boy shall be either in the hands of the king's officers, or in the power of Derrick, the pirate."

"The latter will be the best," said the Lady, "for they are sworn foes; but how will you manage the matter."

"Very easily," said Philip; "there is a girl the boy rescued from Derrick; I know the place she frequents—it is under the cliffs; I will lead Derrick to the spot; he will capture her; then I will contrive to put the outlaws upon his scent, and the boy once in the pirates' haunt will be safe—for ever.

"A good plan; let this be done, then come to the castle, and the first part of the reward shall be yours."

They parted, and Philip, exulting in the prospect of gain muttered—

"Derrick will pay me for betraying the boy, for the young girl you, kind woman, will pay me, and I shall be avenged upon the lot; this has been a good morning's work."

CHAPTER XVIII.
PHILIP WILSON'S PROSPECTS CHANGE.

LAURA GREY had fallen into the pirate's hands, and Tom, the outlawed midshipman, had been conveyed to the secret haunt.

Philip's success had been greater than he had anticipated, as, with a joyful face, he went to report to Lady Mountsteven the success of his evil work.

But fate went against him while he stood before the proud lady, for at the very moment he was reciting the capture of Tom and the abduction of Laura, the young outlaw was on his way back from the rescue of the golden-haired beauty.

As Philip gleefully clutched a portion of the reward for his treachery, Tom had told Snowball the name of the traitor, and Snowball said—

"By all de fetish gods of Snowball's country, he dies."

Philip knew not of the change of affairs as he left the castle, nor did he dream of the danger until he was near his house.

There two of Tom's band seized the villain, and bore him to the cave.

There the outlaws were assembled, their young leader at their head, to try the captive, according to the laws of the band.

The finding was, that he had been guilty of endeavouring to encompass the death of the gallant mid.

Tom would have spared the guilty wretch, but it was beyond his power. The laws that held his band together were not to be broken by any member—not even the chief.

So the miscreant was sentenced to death, and the mode of carrying out the sentence was left to Snowball and the men, Tom retiring from the council.

But he soon returned, and confronting Philip, said—

"Wretched man! I am prepared to make every effort to save you, and will do so, if you confess the motive that caused you to doom to destruction two persons that never harmed you?"

Philip remained silent. There was a hope in his heart that Tom would not see him suffer,

"You do not answer me." said the brave youth. "I will give you another chance. Will you tell me here, before my gallant fellows, the secret of my birth"

A gleam of hope came to Philip's mind as he thought—"He'll not suffer me to die until that secret is divulged; but as it does not suit my purpose to divulge it, I will be silent, and thus save my life."

He made no answer to Tom's request; so the young outlaw asked—

"Who will carry the sentence into execution?"

The whole of the men, with Snowball at their head, responded to the call by stepping to the front.

Perceiving so many coming forward, who seemed desirous of fulfilling the office, the young chieftain suggested—

"You had better draw lots."

This being agreed upon, Snowball taking off his cap, stood ready to receive the articles deposited.

Some buttons cut from the jackets of the band, were now dropped into the cap. Then Snowball taking one out, made a cross upon it with his knife, remarking—

"Look, dis one, which ob us gets dis, has to do dis job."

The cap was then held out at arm's length, and one by one the outlaws approached, and drew out a button, none looking at it until every man should have drawn.

The African was the last to draw, and when he had done so, he placed the cap upon his head.

"Now den, open your hands," just see what you got in them."

One by one, until every man had shown, except Snowball, the buttons were turned up, but the one with the cross upon it, could not be seen.

Snowball gave a grin, and opening his dusky palm, showed the mark button to his companions, saying—

"Dis child hab got him."

In a soul-sickening state of suspense, the doomed wretch had observed their proceedings, and closing his eyes, as though to avoid seeing the African's preparations, he placed his head upon the block that had been placed in the centre of the cave.

Throwing off his jacket, and laying bare his right arm, Snowball placed his thumb on the keen edge of the scimitar.

Satisfied with it, he stepped backward to strike the fatal blow, but before he could raise his hand, Laura Grey had sprung among the group, and thrown herself upon her knees before the young chieftain.

The pleadings of the gentle voice evidently softened the heart of the stern judge, for the young midshipman turned to the band.

"My men," said he, "to you I leave the power of granting the maiden's prayer."

The men were silent; and Snowball, grasping his terrible instrument of destruction, raised it with a flourish above his head.

Laura saw the action, and clasping Tom's hand, she turned her sweet face to the shrinking traitors, and pleaded for his life in this touching language—

"Spare him, as you all hope for mercy hereafter. Spare! oh, spare the unhappy man!"

"Lady," said one of the band, coming forward, "there is not one amongst us but would give our lives to serve you, or alter anything you might wish, but, in such an instance as this, justice must be done."

Snowball grinned and muttered—

"Hab him scalp, head and all, anyhow, dis time."

Laura looked imploringly at the young chief.

"To you," she said, laying her soft hand upon his arm, "will I alone plead; for these men have steeled their hearts against the culprit."

"Laura," responded her lover," "why urge your plea so powerfully? Was it not by yonder trembling wretch you were delivered into the power of a brutal ruffian?"

"Yes, yes," she replied; "but the shedding of his blood will not recall the past."

"No," said a stern voice from the midst of the band; "but it can warn others not to disobey the outlaws' laws."

Philip's pallid face was turned towards the afflicted girl, as she so earnestly pleaded for his life—from her he turned to the rough-bearded band, as though appealing to them for a little mercy.

LADY BLANCHE BOLDLY CONFRONTED THE RUFFIANS.

Laura's intercession for the prisoner at length had its effect. The chief's stern resolution had given way to her supplications, and, as her warm hand still clasped his arm, he addressed his band—

"For once let our laws be broken. Unbind your prisoner; there are some secrets which he alone can tell, and which deeply affect our welfare."

Unwillingly, they obeyed their leader's order, and Philip Wilson, shivering as though suddenly stricken with palsy, stood in the midst of the angry outlaws.

"Bear him to the deep cave below."

While Philip was being conveyed to his prison the fingers of Snowball were playing with the handle of his knife, and he exclaimed—

"Dat am no fair—just as I tought I was to have him head and scalp."

After this the band soon dispersed to go about their various duties.

CHAPTER XIX.

THE FORTUNE TELLER.

NEVILLE WIRELY came from London to the only public-house near the outlaw's cave. He spent money freely while making inquiries about Tom and Laura Grey.

There was a red-nosed revenue officer in the house who was keel-hauled by Tom for prying about the entrance to the cave, and old Philip hearing him boast he could capture the outlaw at any moment, soon made himself agreeable to the man.

A few glasses of grog settled the business, and they parted for the night to meet early next morning and arrange matters.

Neville Wirely rose early, and, with cat-like caution, began to arrange his plot for the carrying off of Laura Grey.

"Once in London," he muttered, "she will be as safe as though in the grave."

The boasting revenue officer and Neville Wirely met before the day was many hours old, and in the quietude of Neville's chamber, at the Seaman's Retreat, the scheme was concocted.

As Neville shook the hand of his worthy friend when they were about to separate, he significantly remarked—

"You fully understand?"

"I do, sir."

"And, think you, we can manage the affair without assistance?"

"Yes, if we play cautiously. But there is one thing; who is to write the letter?"

"Ah! I had forgotten that. I will."

And Neville at once went to the table and penned a long note in a feigned hand.

"That will do, I think."

"Capitally, sir. Now I will prepare my disguise; and, whilst I do so, you stroll about St. Alban's Peak and select a spot for our work."

"I will, and shall meet you about two hours hence."

Neville Wirely walked to the beach, sat down upon a rock, his keen, grey eyes fixed in the direction of the outlaw's cave.

An open sketch-book was on his knees, and, to all appearance, he was trying to transfer the lovely view that lay out so gloriously in the distance.

An hour passed, still he moved not; nor did he notice the bent form of one in the garb of a gipsy woman until she stood before him.

"Let me tell you your fortune, sir," said the crone. "I can read the stars, and I will tell you even your most secret thoughts."

"No; go away, I want none of your juggling tricks."

The crone laughed mockingly as she retorted—

"Tricks, fine sir! Will you dare call my art by such a name?"

"Go away, foolish woman."

"Be convinced, sir."

"No—no!"

"But I can tell you the purpose that has brought you here, and even the name of one you wish to see."

The woman's confident manner somewhat struck Wirely, and, in a sneering manner, he said—

"Perhaps you can tell me also the issue of my adventure?"
"

"Absurd! Go and try your nonsense with the ignorant people here, not upon"———

"Neville Wirely, you would say," interrupted the old hag.

The man, for a moment, lost his habitual self-possession, and exclaimed—

"Ah, then, you know"———

"What I have told you before. Nothing lies hidden from my sight."

"Strange!" thought Wirely; "but probably she may have gleaned my name from the people at the inn."

Then, giving her a shilling, he said aloud—

"Come, after all, I will try your art. What is the name and sex of the person I want."

"There are two."

Wirely started, and the hag continued—

"One a youth, and the other a beautiful girl, whom you would carry off with you"

Neville Wirely sprang to his feet.

"——— You must have dealings with the devil!"

The old woman laughed, and drawing herself up, said—

"What, is my disguise so perfect that you do not even recognise me?"

The alteration of the voice, and the sudden assumption of his proper height, caused Wirely to start, as he beheld the form of the revenue officer before him.

"Admirable!" he said; "you are an adept in the art."

"I should be, sir, for I have been many years in the secret police."

"You have? I should have thought it a more desirable berth than the one you now fill."

"It was," said the man, with a sigh; "but I was discharged for no fault of my own."

"Indeed! how was that?"

"A few words will explain. Being on the track of a notorious criminal, a man of very high position, I had to assume for a time the livery of his house—in fact, to become his servant, and, while in that situation, to learn a secret that would fill up the only blank that existed in the chain of circumstantial evidence."

"And you succeeded?"

"Yes, too well."

"How do you mean, 'too well?'"

"You shall hear. This nobleman had succeeded in betraying a young girl of good family, and she poor thing, went one day to his house to upbraid him with his conduct."

"Yes. Go on. I feel greatly interested, I assure you."

"From that interview she never returned, and there is no doubt that he had quietly murdered her."

"Horrible!"

"Though we were morally convinced that such was the case, still there was no legal proof. Thi she was seen to enter the house, and no one saw her leave, was well known. To discover any trace of her body seemed impossible, until the chief of the secret police hit upon the plan of one of us being domesticated in his house."

"And you went?"

"I did, and watched diligently for weeks; but I could gain no futher intelligence—indeed, I was giving up all hope of doing so, when one day his lordship's valet suddenly left him, and I was appointed in his place."

"How strange!" said Wirely.

"Yes; nevertheless, it so occurred. Well, one day—I'm sure I can't tell you how it was; but while assisting his lordship to dress, my eyes became, as it were, fixed upon the strange make of a large black box that stood in one corner of the room, and a secret instinct led me to lift it up, as under it I should find all I needed to bring the wretch to justice."

"Was it unlocked, then?"

"No; but a key from a small bunch I always kept in my possession opened it."

"And you found"——

"Good heaven! yes. I shall never forget the sight! There lay the remains of the beautiful murdered girl, and the whole corpse covered with lime to cause it to decay.

"I must have been spell-bound with horror, for I did not hear the villain's stealthy step behind me, and not until his hand was upon my shoulder was I aware of his presence.

"Even then I had no time to make any defence; for, taken so unawares, he hurled me in the box and closed the lid down."

"With the dead lady?"

"Yes. And there was I kept for two long days, until I cut my way out with a knife. Good God! I wonder I did not go mad in the terrible captivity."

"Truly it must have been terrible."

"No words can pourtray it. But, to shorten the horrid story, when I did get clear I found myself alone in the house."

"Alone?"

"Yes; for the scoundrel had, during the time I was inside the box, discharged his domestics and gone, and I, when I had reported the case, received a reprimand and my dismissal for not capturing the murderer."

"It was unjust. But was he never taken?"

"Nothing has been heard of him since."

So interested had the listener and narrator been by the narration of this awful incident, that they did not notice Laura Grey and her young lover, Midshipman Tom, coming towards them.

Wirely gave a cry of mingled surprise and joy when he beheld the handscme pair; and the revenue officer, to keep up his assumed character, bent his body nearly double and hobbled towards them.

Wirely arose and, screening himself behind a arge stone, watched his companion.

"Bless those bright eyes, miss!" was the salute "Let me tell your future, and you rs, sir."

"Mine?" said Tom, good humouredly. think I already know my fate."

"Your hand," said the gipsy.

Tom, laughing, extended his hand, which the gipsy attentively scanned.

"There's a great danger menacing you."

"That's nothing unusual," said Tom, "for my enemies are always on the watch."

"But you will escape this, and many others; there is a bright destiny in store for you. You will marry a rich and beautiful young lady, and be the father of many children."

"A promising prospect," said Tom; "but, unfortunately, your fortune-telling always ends in the same way."

"Not always, young sir; for, if I mistake not, there is a very different future in store for beautiful young lady."

"Indeed! pray let us hear it."

"I must not—dare not; it would, perhaps, make her un"——

"Nonsense, my good woman! But come, before we go any further, tell me a little of the past—never mind the future."

"The past can afford no gratification," was the cunning reply; it is with the future that I alone have to do."

"Very well. Have you anything now for this lady's good or bad fortune?"

"That I must tell her out of the hearing of one of your sex."

With this remark the disguised officer drew Laura a few paces from her lover, and after startling the maiden with a few words, he slipped a note in her hand, saying, in a hushed voice—

"If you would learn more, meet me at the spot indicated in that slip of paper."

Then, releasing her hand, he hobbled away. Turning back, he again approached Laura, telling her—

"Not to breathe of the appointed meeting to a living soul, or the charm would be broken."

Laura put the paper in her breast and went to her lover's side, where she nestled fondly, and as though no harm could befall her.

So craftily had the whispered words of the disguised revenue officer been uttered, than she kept the existence of the note a secret from her lover.

Well for this poor girl had she told him. It would have saved them both much suffering and danger; but with that weakness so peculiar to the female mind, which seems to delight in mystery, she longed for the hour to come when she could open that slip of paper and peruse its contents.

And the time came, for the young outlaw, after wandering about for a short time with his beloved, returned to the cave, and Laura, as soon as she was alone, **drew the** paper from her breast, and read :—

"When the moon rises, be at the Imp's Dyke; there shall the hidden mysteries of the future be revealed. Come alone.

"SYBIL, THE GIPSY."

The superstitious feelings latent in the young girl's nature prevented that slip of paper being shown to the gallant mid.

Had he beheld it, his quick apprehension would have seen beneath the plausible surface, and prevented the accomplishment of Neville Wirely's base designs.

The place named in the note was a small valley close by the cave; and Laura, feeling sure that from the close proximity of the Imp's Dyke to the cave, no harm was intended her, made up her mind to meet the gipsy at the appointed hour.

In the meantime, the conspirators had completed their arrangements, in the carrying out of which a vehicle would be necessary; and to avoid suspicion, Wirely sent his ally to a distant village to engage a coach and four.

At the appointed hour, Laura, with beating heart, went out to hear the lying words of the supposed gipsy; and when she reached the Dyke, the old woman was there huddled upon the ground.

"Welcome, my beautiful girl!" said the gipsy, rising at Laura's approach. "And have you come alone?"

"I have," answered Laura.

Sybil took the unsuspecting girl's hand, and leading her further into the shadow of the weird-looking rocks, placed a small phial on her hand.

"This little bottle," she said, "contains a wondrous essence; it has the power of rendering the eyes capable of seeing at one glance the scenes that you will in after life take part in."

Laura took the bottle, and a dim sense of awe crept over her.

"Draw the stopper," continued the gipsy, "and inhale its rich perfumes."

The silly girl did so; but scarcely had she placed the fluid to her nostrils, than her senses began to leave her. Her head fell back, her limbs began to tremble, and she sank to the ground quite powerless.

Neville Wirely rushed from his hiding place, and, lifting the senseless form in his arms, bore her to the post-chaise.

He hastily gave the revenue officer his address, desired him to keep him well-informed of every movement made to discover the girl, placed a heavy purse in the fellow's hand, and desired the postilion to—

"Drive to London, sparing neither whip nor

The next minute Laura was alone with her abductor.

CHAPTER XX.
A COWARDLY DEED.

THE atrocious miscreant. Derrick, the freebooter, determined before he finally left the shores of England to be avenged upon the ready-witted Lady Blanche Gordon for the clever manner in which she had trapped so many of his gang.

He knew the castle was well defended by the armed servants and a number of the villagers; but he cared not for them. He had been foiled by the young outlaw, and his savage nature longed for vengeance; if not upon the gallant boy, he determined some one else should suffer.

His black-hulled ship was ready to sail at a moment's notice. Dividing his band, so as to keep up a communication between the shore and the vessel, he started upon his fell work.

"You must force the gate," he said to his men, "while I effect an entrance at one of the lower windows. Once in the corridor, I will fire the castle with this hand-grenade, then we can retreat to the boats."

The ruffians did their leader's bidding so far as to attack the gate, while he effected an entrance, and reached the corridor.

He was about to fire the hand-grenade when a stout-limbed young villager rushed upon him, and before the miscreant could draw a weapon, he was lifted from the ground and hurled through the window, the villager coolly remarking—

"He won't trouble us again."

Red Hand had left a strong party posted in a small hollow of the rock that looked seaward, his commands being that they were to repel the attack of any boats that might be drawn to the castle by the noise of the combat.

Great was the surprise of the gang when they saw their leader plunging through the air, and then disappear beneath the waves.

By the pale light of the moon they beheld him rise to the surface, and struggle with the water.

The noise of the attack upon the castle gate had aroused the sailors and their young leader; and the latter, with a youth's agility, was the first to reach the brow of the cliff.

He saw the miscreants beneath him; then, looking towards the sea, beheld Red Hand swimming towards the shore.

As quick as thought the middy drew a pistol from his belt and fired.

So true was his aim, that Red Hand gave a howl of pain and disappeared.

"Now," said Tom, turning from the cliff, "to exterminate the gang."

Rapidly descending the zigzag path, he blew a silver whistle to collect his men, and as he did so, Red Hand once more rose to the surface.

He had seen the young outlaw's form standing out beneath the moonbeams when the brave fellow levelled his pistol, and then followed the sting of the bullet as it went through the fleshy part of his shoulder.

The pirate gave himself up for lost, and dived beneath the surface, only to appear again to make another effort to reach the shore.

Though wounded by the bullet from Tom's pistol, the ruffian had strength enough left to remain himself in the water until two of his band plunged in and drew him to land.

"This is the third time," said he, "this cub has gained an advantage over me; but I'll be even with him yet."

By this time the outlaws were in close pursuit, so, crossing their muskets, the pirates made a litter to carry away their chief.

Pistol shots were now heard in front of them.

"To the beach!" said Red Hand, fiercely.

"But we have no boat."

"Find one."

They hurried round the base of the castle, and made for the shore, where, seeing an old fisherman and his son going out to sea, they seized the boat, which in a few minutes was dragged back to the beach by a dozen hands.

"Cut the rope, father!" shouted the boy, as he tried to cast loose the flying jib; "quick, and we shall escape."

The boy's words did not escape Red Hand's ear, and he saw the gleam of the fisherman's knife as he opened it.

With a fearful curse, he snatched a pistol from the belt of one of the men who were carrying him, and firing at the old fisherman, the ball went through his brain, and he fell dead on the deck.

The boy stood horrified for a few seconds, then smoothed the long silvery hair of his father, and imprinted one kiss upon his forehead, sprang to his feet.

The pirates by this time were scrambling over the vessel's side.

With a cry of agony and distress, the poor boy ran to the bowsprit; then turning, fixed his eyes on Red Hand, and exclaimed—

"Listen, miscreant that you are! From now do I devote myself to the task of avenging this diabolical murder of my father, and until that is accomplished, you shall have no safety from my vengeance!"

"Shoot the cub," said Red Hand, savagely, "and stop his patter!"

The boy gave them no time to fire, but springing into the sea, uttered the word—

"Vengeance!"

As he disappeared from those who would have taken his young life, little did the miscreants know of the implacable foe that merciless act had created.

An avenger that would, with unerring and bloodhound-like tenacity, follow inch by inch until their doom was consummated.

"Is that cub gone," asked the pirate, "or is he alive?"

"Can't live," was the reply; "I expect he is drawn under the boat."

"A good thing for him, the young reptile, as he threatened me with his vengeance. Ha! ha! ha! the vengeance of a whelp like that!"

Red Hand's ironical speech was cut short by a cry of—

"A sail! a sail!"

"Where?" asked Red Hand. "Near our vessel!"

"Yes, about half-a-mile off."

"Quick, then; push this crab-shell through the water."

"She will not carry more sail."

"How do you know her build? Curse you, do as I tell you."

"But"——

"Silence!" roared the ruffian, "or I'll put a bullet through your head."

The man became quiet, and turned away from the scowling visage of his leader.

Had that leader seen the lurking devil in the man's eyes as he shook out another sail, he would have been on his guard.

The fishing-smack now scudded swiftly along, sometimes dipping her short bowsprit beneath the foam, at other times running a considerable distance, gunwale flush with the water.

The greedy eyes of the crew were fixed upon a stately merchantman, as she came slowly through the water, her decks crowded with homeward-bound passengers, many of them ladies.

The pirates urged their boat onward, and when within a hundred fathoms of their own black-hulled, sombre-looking vessel, the fishing-boat, suddenly taken by a fearful gust of wind, heeled over, and left them all struggling in the water.

"I knew it," muttered the man who had ventured to raise an objection against putting so much sail on. "All I hope is, that he will be drowned—the surly brute!"

The accident was soon seen from the deck of the pirate ship, and the officer in charge immediately lowered a boat to their assistance.

Drenched to the skin, they were taken aboard, and by the time this was done, the merchantman was nearly two miles ahead.

"Set every sale," bawled Red Hand; "if we don't overhaul her before she gets any further, it will be no use."

The darkened canvas bellied out in the wind, and the pirate ship, moving through the water at double the speed of the heavily-freighted merchantman, started in pursuit.

Totally unsuspicious of the real character of the coming vessel, the captain of the merchantman continued on his course.

Nearer and nearer came the pirate ship, and not until she had ranged up alongside of her prey, did the unlucky passengers know the intentions of their pursuers.

"Up with the black flag!" yelled the pirate, "then board her, and carry off the women."

Like a death-knell his words struck upon the affrighted crowd.

The captain of the merchantman rushed down to his cabin, and clutching his pistols, darted to the deck.

He was an aged seaman—a man who had grown grey in the service of his country, and now, seeing that his career was ended—for he well knew the merciless character of those who were now coming on the deck—he calmly said to the crew—

" Men, you have knives, strike one blow for life and liberty !"

The words of the merchant captain roused the crew from the apathy which the sight of the yelling demons who were now pouring on the deck had caused.

Sending a bullet through the head of the foremost pirate, the gallant old captain set the example.

" Strike one blow," he cried, as he levelled his second pistol, " for those we have so long guarded from danger ! "

The clicking of the knife blades answered his appeal, as each seaman opened his knife.

" Look !" he continued, pointing to the group of trembling women, who were huddled in an agony of terror, on the poop. " Look at those helpless beings, and defend them, if you are men."

A cry came from the seamen's throats. Excited by their old commander's words, they felt ready to battle with the miscreant crew.

Each right hand grasped his knife as the demons came rushing towards them.

There was a short and fierce struggle as the pirates met their hardy opponents, and many fell under the long swords of the pirate's band.

But what could this handful of devoted men do against the overwhelming numbers that poured upon them ? and those who yet survived the steel were hurled to the deck and disarmed.

Long the grey-headed old captain struggled with two swarthy savages.

Grasping a handspike with both hands, he kept them at bay, until another miscreant, with a blow from a clubbed musket, struck him to the deck.

Among the passengers was an old Indian officer, who was, after a long service in India, returning to England with his two lovely daughters.

Standing on the quarter deck, and armed with his pistols, he had picked off several of the pirates.

But now, when he beheld the crew vanquished, the old soldier, with Spartan-like courage, carefully loaded his weapons. Then calling his daughters to him, he said, in a husky voice—

" Down on your knees, my beloved children, and commend your souls to your Maker; death or dishonour awaits you—let it be the former."

Then followed the sharp report of two pistols, and both lovely girls fell on the deck—dead.

Such an act checked the advance of the mis-
creants, and the old man, giving one faint cry of despair, sprang over the taffrail into the placid sea.

Then commenced a scene that baffled description, the young and handsome women being transferred to the pirate ship, the remainder thrown headlong into the sea.

CHAPTER XXI.

WALKING THE PLANK.

THE women in their possession were safely fastened in Red Hand's cabin when the plunder of the vessel began.

Bales of rich stuffs, boxes of ivory, rare skins, and other costly articles were transferred from the merchantman to the pirate ship.

Then the sanguinary monster ordered a strong cord, with a running noose, to be fastened under the old captain's armpits.

The poor old man was then hurried along the deck, and suspended from the point of the bowsprit, his feet within a foot of the water, and several hideous sharks playing round him.

The remainder of the crew were ranged near a plank placed across the bulwarks.

" And now, my hearties," said Red Hand, " you see your fate ; that narrow plank will speedily walk you into the other world ; but I'll give you a chance. If any of you like to join my crew, you can ; if not, over you goes."

The mate of the merchantman stepped forward, and, approaching the villain, said—

" Speaking for myself, and I may say for all my messmates, ten thousand deaths would be preferable to joining your miscreant band."

" Show him the way," replied the pirate leader.

And with that heroism which has ever distinguished the British tar, he walked up the death-plank with as firm a tread as though he was walking the deck of his vessel.

One step beyond the bulwarks, and the plank overbalanced.

There was a plunge, and the brave old seaman sank to rise no more.

The remainder of the crew, amid the jeers of the pirates, were made similar offers to ; but in vain the savage pirate leader tried to shake their resolution.

One by one they were consigned to a watery grave, until but four remained.

" Now," said Red Hand, passionately, for he was enraged at the stubborn defiance of the sailors, " now there are but four of you left, will you join us ?"

" Never !" was the stern reply.

" Then you follow the others."

One of the sailors stepped forward, and had placed his foot on the plank, when a sudden consternation seemed to seize on the whole of the pirates.

The sailors looked across the ocean's expanse,

and beheld a vessel bearing swiftly down upon them, her ports open, the guns run out, and the flag of England flying at her fore.

With a cry of rage, Red Hand ordered the remaining four to be cut down, and they were mercilessly butchered.

Then the miscreant crew and their leader rejoined their own vessel, and casting off the grappling irons, spread their sails and moved swiftly through the water.

The Osprey—for that was the name of the English man-of-war—spread every inch of canvas

beheld a human figure dangling from the bowsprit.

"'Bout ship !" sang out the officer.

Presently a boat was lowered, and the crew were on the deck of the merchantman.

What a fearful scene !

From stem to stern the deck was slippery with the blood of the pirate's victims, and so fearful had been the carnage that the spectators for several minutes were held spell-bound with horror—many of them feeling a chill enter their hearts, and their faculties for a time suspended.

THE ESCAPE FROM THE CAVE.

to come up in time; but, alas! as we have seen, too late to save life.

On her deck stood Peter, the murdered fisherman's son.

A bared cutlass in his hand, his features deadly pale, and as immovable as sculptured marble.

'Twas he who had apprised the commander of the Osprey of Red Hand's treacherous act in slaying his father, and the captain lost no time in starting in pursuit of the villain.

But for a time the pursuit was checked, for as they rounded the bows of the merchantman they

Here lay the stiffening forms of the Indian officer's lovely daughters—there the women slaughtered by the pirates; others, again, were lying where they had fallen under the blows of the pirates, numerous articles of female attire attesting the struggles that had been made.

The senseless form of the captain was sent on board the Osprey, and the officer, leaving a sufficient number of men to navigate the merchant vessel into port, reset his sails and started in pursuit of Red Hand.

A stern chase is always a long chase, and the

captain wishing to overtake the miscreants before the night set in, put on more canvas.

Like an avenging Nemesis, the young fisherman stood, with blazing eyes and compressed lips, watching the dark outline of the pirate ship, waiting the moment when he should spring on board, and confront his father's murderer.

The Osprey rapidly gained upon the pirate barque—so quickly, indeed, that Red Hand began to open fire with his stern-chaser.

The second shot came whistling through the Osprey's rigging.

The men on board ran to their bow-guns to reply to the salute; but the young captain, placing the speaking-trumpet to his lips, gave the word—

"Steady, there, forward! Every gun that is fired will impede our sailing. You shall give them plenty of it directly."

So it seemed, for the firing from the pirate ship had caused their speed to decrease, and the pursuers to gain upon them.

And, in spite of their guns, the Osprey came so close that those on the forecastle could see a number of men rushing about the decks. It needed no words to explain that the pirates were doing their best to escape the Osprey and her gallant crew.

CHAPTER XXII.

THE REVENUE OFFICER IN DANGER.

BUT for the sudden appearance of the Osprey, the young outlaw's swift vessel, the War Cloud, would have put to sea in pursuit of Red Hand.

The outlawed middy did not wish to provoke an encounter with any vessels belonging to the Royal navy. So he recalled the boats, and went towards the cave, leaving the pirate's punishment to the Osprey.

It was one of those soft, lovely nights, when the twinkling stars seem playing at hide-and-seek in their celestial home.

Gentle zephyr breezes came from the sea, which lay gently rippling under the pale starlight.

Tired with the noisy revelry of the carousing outlaws, Midshipman Tom left the cave, and strolled towards the beach.

In spite of the hard, stern life he led, his mind was not divested of those feelings of romance so peculiar to youth; and, after wandering for an hour by the quiet sea, thinking over the words of the gipsy, he suddenly bethought himself of his fair companion—his partner in his nightly rambles —the ideal of all his boyish dreams and aspirations.

Sorely he felt her absence on this calm night. So, quickly retracing his steps, he entered the cave, and went in search of Laura.

The first person he met was Ben Bight, who, in reply to his query, said—

"Miss Laura—is she not with you?"

"No."

"Great heavens! then my suspicions are confirmed. There has been some villainous means at work to carry her away."

The young sailor's hot blood rushed to his face, and he repeated—

"Suspicions, villainous means! Do I hear aright?"

"You do. Read this."

And he handed the piece of paper, which Laura had received from the gipsy, and which, in her haste, she had dropped on leaving the cave to keep the appointment.

Tom was stricken mute with amazement; he read and re-read the note, but only to come to one conclusion.

"This," said he, "is a man's handwriting, and if he is within reach of my arm, he shall pay with his life for this base treachery. Be comforted, Laura—you shall yet be restored!"

With these words lingering on his lips, he went into the cave, and holding out the small slip of paper, said to his astonished band—

"One hundred pounds reward for the man who can tell me the writer of this accursed note!"

The outlaws crowded round him.

"What is it, sir?" demanded several voices. "What is it?"

"Some villain has decoyed Miss Laura away by means of this note," was Tom's reply, as he handed the paper towards several outstretched hands.

It was a time of fearful suspense to the young midshipman, as the note went from hand to hand, and their only reply was a doleful shake of the head.

At last it came to the hands of Ben, who no sooner saw the handwriting, than he exclaimed,

"I know it!"

"Speak—speak!" said Tom, excitedly. "Whose is it?"

"Clark, the new exciseman's."

"Are you certain?"

"Quite."

"Before we proceed further," said Tom, "let me hear the grounds of your surmise."

"I will, sir," answered Ben. "Last night, when I was at the Seamen's Retreat, this Jack was bragging about how he would capture you if he had the chance."

A laugh greeted these words.

"And," continued Ben, "after he had been talking about you, I saw a stranger, who is, or was staying at the Retreat, edge himself in among the officers."

"Ah!"

"And he kept asking them all sorts of things about you and the young lady."

"Why didn't you put a knife in him?" asked one.

"So I would," said Ben, "had I known what he was up to."

"Go on with your story," said Tom, impatiently.

"Very well, sir. After a bit, I saw this stranger

and Jack in close conversation, and they each wrote something on a piece of paper."

"Go on, for heaven's sake! Every moment is precious."

"Well, the piece of paper the stranger got from Jack he put in his pocket; but I wanted to know all about it, so as he passed me I eased him of it."

Ben fumbled about in his pocket, then handing an envelope to Tom, he continued—

"And here it is!"

Tom compared the writing, and finding that Ben's statement was correct, he exclaimed—

"This scoundrel must be brought here, and the stranger you speak of."

"Yes," put in Snowball, whetting his knife upon his boot; "and then p'r'aps I'll hab a scalp—eh, Massa Tom?"

"Yes; his head, if you like."

Snowball grabbed the man who stood nearest to him by his hair, and, flourishing his knife, he yelled—

"Dis is how I'll do it!"

"Will you?" said the man, making a butt with his head at Snowball's stomach. "You will not practice on me, anyhow."

The head came in collision with Snowball's stomach.

A roar of laughter came from the band; but it was instantly checked by Tom, who said, sternly—

"Silence, all of you! We have other and far more serious matters to attend to than this mummery. I want two volunteers."

A dozen stepped forward, out of which Tom selected two, saying—

"To you I award the task of bringing this exciseman to the cave."

"It shall be done, sir," was the reply. And the men, arming themselves, soon left the cave.

The middy then, addressing the others, continued—

"You, Thistlewhite, and Tom Rogers go to the Seaman's Retreat, and bring the stranger here."

The men bowed, and silently left the cavern.

Jack Twist, the revenue officer, was seated upon a jutting piece of rock with his night glass in his hand, and, as he afterwards said, "Thinking of nothing at all in particular," when he was suddenly pounced upon by the two outlaws, who had silently crept upon him.

Before he could draw a pistol from his belt his arms were pinioned, and a gag fastened round his mouth.

Though his hands and tongue were tied, he kicked at the legs of his captors with might and main.

"Look—look here, my hearty!" said one, giving him a rap on the shin with the iron hilt of his cutlass; "if you don't be quiet you will get the other end of this."

The officer took the hint, and allowed his captors lead him quietly away.

They were not long in reaching the cave, and when the officer stood before the young chieftain a sense of dread began to creep over him.

Tom looked sternly at the trembling wretch for a moment, then addressing the men that had brought him in, said—

"Unbind him!"

When the revenue officer's hands were free, Tom held the envelope towards him, and said—

"Do you know these?"

The man, seeing at once his complicity in Laura's abduction was discovered, fell on his knees, and whined—

"Mercy—mercy, young sir!"

Snowball stood with folded arms surveying the prisoner's long hair, and in imagination feeling the delight of having such a goodly scalp lock.

"Hab him scalp," muttered the African, "and no mistake, dis time."

"Upon one condition alone will I grant you the least clemency," said Tom, "so beware how you answer me."

"Anything, sir—anything. I will confess all."

"Be it so," said Tom. "Speak, and that quickly; but beware how you attempt to trifle with me. The least attempt to mislead me shall be the signal for your death."

The calm, impressive tone of the midshipman's voice sank deeper into the man's mind than any blustering or fierce exclamation would have done.

With pallid face and quivering lips he told all he knew respecting the abduction of Laura.

"Is this all?" Tom asked.

"All I can tell you, sir."

"Can you form any idea of the motive that caused Neville Wirely to take the lady away?"

"I cannot, sir. He was too shrewd and too cautious to let me know his reason."

The man who had gone in search of Neville Wirely returned, and told them of the sudden departure of the ill-looking resident at the Seaman's Retreat.

"I know it," said Tom, quietly. "Now, Snowball, go on board the War Cloud at once, take as many of the band as possible, and go round the coast to the Thames; but before you enter among the shipping alter the War Cloud's rigging as much as possible, and drop anchor near the guardship, and wait until you either see or hear from me."

"Yes, Massa Tom; but what yar do?—yar want some of de gang."

"Four will be sufficient. I shall follow the same route as that taken by Miss Grey's abductor. But be careful you have a sufficient guard for the cave."

"Yes, Massa Tom; but what about the prisoner?"

"True. I had forgotten the doom of the traitor. Take him with you."

"And der one whose scalp I'm to hab?"

"**Let** him be locked up in the secret chamber **until** we return."

"Berry well, massa. We shall be in the Thames as soon as you a'most. Good-bye!"

CHAPTER XXIII.

PHILIP WILSON'S FATE.

THE saucy War Cloud tripped her anchor, and bowled along the coast at a spanking pace.

With the exception of Tom there was not a better seaman on board than Snowball; and under an easy press of canvas, and having no lights hoisted, slipped quickly past the king's cruisers.

Though, had she been attacked, she would have been found ready for any emergency. Every man was at his station; the guns were double-shotted; and the battle lanterns a light, but hidden under a piece of tarpaulin.

When out of danger they stood out to sea. Snowball, dropping the dignity of commander, mingled with his men: and after discussing the all-engrossing topic of their leader's expedition, turned their conversation upon Philip the traitor, whom they had brought with them.

"Well," said one burly fellow; "the chief said we were to do what we liked with him except take his life."

"Let's keel-haul him!"

"Hang him by the heels to the yardarm," said another.

"Have him over, and then fire at him," was third suggestion.

Snowball told them he had "a better way dan dat."

"What is it?"

"You all know that little island just to leeward?"

"Yes."

"And de big trunk of a tree that stands alone?"

"You mean the uninhabited island."

"Ob corse."

"Go on, Snowflake."

"What I thinks is, to put him ashore dar, and leab him to gnaw de tree for his breakfass!"

"But I think," said the first speaker, "I can suggest a better plan than that."

"Go on, den,"

"Take him ashore there, and tie him to the old leafless tree."

"Dat's the bery ting."

And Snowball slapped his ebony palms together with delight.

"We teach dam 'retch," he continued, "to put Red Hand on de scent. Ware ship, yer lubber at de wheel!"

"Ay, ay!"

"Now den, bring him up; for wid dis breeze we shall be dere in about half-an-hour."

Philip was dragged from the hold, and told by the exasperated outlaws of the fate in store for him.

Falling upon his knees, he yelled for mercy.

But the stern band were deaf to his cries, and mocked him with jeering expressions.

"He'll make a fine meal for the eagles," said one.

"I hope the snakes won't sting him!"

"Or the land crab bite his toes!"

So they went on until the vessel was rounded to, and a boat lowered, in which the unfortunate wretch was placed.

In an agony of terror, he fell on his knees in the boat; but the smart application of a rope's end brought him to.

Aided by the light of the battle lanterns, the outlaws found the massive trunk of a withered tree which stood alone on the small rocky isle.

Philip's back was placed against it, and the steady hands of the outlaws soon bound him fast to his place of doom.

This summary, but merited punishment having been concluded, they regained their boat and pulled for the ship.

How eternally long seemed the brief time that elapsed before the glorious morning broke to the doomed wretch.

And when the golden sun shone forth, lighting up the sea like a mirror of gold, he shrieked aloud in his agony.

Merciful heaven! What is it that causes him to look upwards, and yell with terror?

A huge bald-headed eagle, with distended jaws and open beak, is swooping around him uttering a succession of piercing cries, which sounds to the traitor like his death knell.

The voracious bird is but waiting for the moment when the hapless wretch shall have ceased to shout and struggle.

And then—but it is too horrible even to imagine —the fearful fate which now seems inevitable.

Shrieking, he looks towards the sea, and to increase his agony, he sees a vessel within a few cables' length of the barren isle.

Can it be imagination only?

Have they heard his cries of terror and agony!

No, the vessel swings round and sails slowly away; then the hoarse cry of the eagle causes him to look up, and to increase his miseries, it begins to narrow its circles round the tree.

Already has he felt the hum of his outstretched wings against his face, and seen the long keen black opened claws, as though about to seize upon him.

Nearer and nearer the bird wings its flight around the doomed wretch's head, then suddenly soaring high up in the air, it poises itself upon its wings, and uttering one shrill cry, and distending its sharp hungry-looking beak, makes a swift descent upon him.

Philip shrieked louder than ever in his soul's agony, and tried to break the bonds that held him.

But in vain. Practised hands tied that rope; and, closing his eyes with the calmness of despair, he became still, and awaited his fate.

That fate to feel the hungry bird tearing out his very vitals.

* * * * *

Without one thought for the helpless wretch whom they had consigned to such a fearful doom, the outlaws sailed away from the isle.

And as the day began to dawn, the War Cloud entered the mouth of the Thames.

But so altered, that it would have been impossible to recognise in the heavy, square-looking, lumbering craft that waddled about in the water, the graceful little War Cloud.

Her smart white sails were taken down, and in their place, old patched canvas was set.

The beautiful lines of her prow were covered by a false bulkhead, surmounted by a white figure of a very fat female, who held a bunch of something which resembled fruit in her hand.

Over the golden lettered name (the War Cloud) a board had been placed, which was decorated with white letters, nearly a foot long.

And these letters spelt—

The Phœbe of North Shields.

The dress of the band had undergone a great change.

In place of the smart costume, they now wore greasy old trousers. And Snowball, the usually glittering and gold-bedizened lieutenant, now ran about the deck in a ragged dirty-looking pair of trousers, his herculean body naked.

And to give greater character to his position (the cook) he, when passing the other vessels, kept running from the galley to the state-room with an old iron pot.

"Golly!" the African muttered, I dont tink Massa Tom eber know him craft again."

The guns were covered by all manner of rubbish that had been fished out of the hold, and altogether, the War Cloud looked as dirty and untidy a specimen of a coasting trader as could be imagined.

They dropped anchor just beneath the frowning guns of the gunship, and waited anxiously for the appearance of their chief.

Ere an hour had elapsed, two men, who had been sent to reconnoitre, returned in breathless haste with the startling intelligence that Tom and his companions were in the " lock up !"

An incautious officer had let it drop, that on the morrow they were to be taken to Newgate.

That night the band spent in concocting a scheme for the liberation of their friends.

It was a bold scheme, and one fraught with great danger.

CHAPTER XXIV.
CAPTURED BY THE CHARLEYS.

Tom shook hands with his gigantic lieutenant, took leave of the band, then left the cave, followed by Ben Bight, and three of his companions.

Bill Martin, the tapster, and owner of the Seaman's Retreat, procured for Tom and his companions a post-chaise and four, and in less than one hour from the capture of the exciseman, Tom was thundering upon the track of Laura's abductor, and the War Cloud was under sail, standing out for sea.

London being reached, the direction given to the revenue officer by Neville Wirely was shown to a hackney-coachman, who apprised Tom that the streets wern't altogether safe for people on foot nor coaches either.

"We'll risk the danger," said Tom. So, inside the musty old coach Tom and his three companions now entered, and as they were being jolted over the rough streets, Ben began to groan.

"What's the matter?" asked one.

"Matter!" replied Ben Bight. "Why, this is worser than being down in the hold of a vessel in a gale. Hi! You on the forecastle, heave to."

The coachman did not understand exactly the terms "forecastle" and "heave-to"; but seeing one of his fare's heads out of window, he pulled up.

"Want me, sir?"

"Yes. Is there no deck to this craft, for I'm stifled below."

"About a deck," answered Jehu, "I don't know anything; but here's the roof, if that'll do."

"Anywhere," said Ben, as he scrambled on to the roof, and desired the coachman to "make sail."

The Jehu made sail to some purpose, and Ben, after vainly trying to keep his seat upon the slippery top of the coach, was shot head foremost from the "deck" right into the cabin window of a craft that was at the moment sailing past.

The craft happened to be a gentleman's carriage, and Ben Bight's sudden appearance half way through the window was as unwelcome to the occupants as it was to Ben.

"Murder," yelled the owner of the carriage. "Help! Watch, watch, murder!"

Two ladies who were on the back seat helped with their voices, and Ben, finding he could not free himself from the window, kicked and swore most lustily.

The uproar was at its highest when a couple of watchmen ran to the rescue, and one trying to pull Ben down by the heel, received a kick in the face that sent him flying.

The second "Charley" at this sprang his rattle.

The signal was heard, and half-a-dozen of the guardians of the peace came upon the scene.

Tom and his companions had been convulsed with laughter at Ben's mishap. But when they heard the captive roar out to them to come to the rescue, they tumbled out of the coach.

Poor Ben's body being jammed in the windows, and his arms pinned close to his side. could not defend himself from the united attack of the occupants of the coach.

The old gentleman belaboured his skull with a heavy cane, one of the ladies tugged at his hair, and the other kept pricking him in the neck with a silver bodkin.

Ben craved mercy, but, finding he received none, he swore most mercilessly, and, as a reward, he was attacked with greater vigour by the trio.

The pain he endured caused him to kick out most fiercely, and this kicking kept his friends from helping him out of his misery.

At last they managed to seize him by the waist; a strong pull and a pull together, and down came Ben right in the embrace of a valiant watchman.

The outlaw was in too sweet a temper to suffer his captor to achieve a quiet victory, so over went the "Charley," seeing all sorts of stars and moons as Ben's fist left his nose.

Tom and the others were by this time engaged in a series of single combats, and, truth to tell, although they were good boxers, they received several taps from their opponents' staves that caused their eyes to water.

But inured to hard knocks, the outlaws cared little for a few blows of the wooden staves, and soon a dozen "Charleys" were placed *hors de combat.*

The four gallant fellows would, doubtless, have beaten the enemy, but as ill-luck would have it, another batch of the night guardians came to the rescue.

CHAPTER XXV.

AN OLD SAILOR'S STORY.

To escape from their dilemma without fighting was an impossibility, and bitterly regretting they were without any proper weapons of defence, Tom and his three companions went at it with a will; and the young mid, having possessed himself of a staff accidently dropped by one of the watch, battled bravely.

The "Charleys" had pressed down upon Tom, thinking he would be easier captured than his broad-shouldered companions, but they soon found out their mistake.

The middy's knowledge of the broadsword stood him in good stead, and many a "Charley" retreated with a broken pate.

But numbers soon decided the victory, and gallant Tom, after beating back his share of the foe, was assailed by a fresh detachment.

The watchmen had beaten Ben and one of his mates to the ground, and turning upon Tom and his companion, they, by the mere weight of their bodies, hemmed their antagonists in so that it was impossible for them to strike another blow.

The occupants of the carriage had watched the issue of the conflict, and the ladies caught sight of Tom's handsome face; one said—

"Papa, don't let them hurt that nice-looking young gentleman."

Papa stuck his head out of the carriage window, and to the surprise of the ladies, he roared out—

"Seize them! It's young Tom Wilson, the outlaw. Seize them!"

"Oh, papa! I'm"——

"Hold your tongue! I know the young rascal again. I saw him every day I was on board the Hercules."

This was the truth; for the old fellow was an admiral, and he had come home from a foreign station in the flag ship at the time Tom was on board.

So Tom and his companion with the senseless form of Ben and his messmate, were then bound hand and foot and taken into a secure room in the old lock-up at Eastcheap.

But though fastened hand and foot, he was revolving in his mind a plan to effect their escape.

Much to Ben's disgust when he recovered, he found himself in *durance vile.*

And cursing all watchmen and their staves, he went into a peaceful slumber.

To the hardy, roving outlaws, the confinement was only but pleasant.

Especially to Ben, who seemed to live on regret that he couldn't break the fellow's head who did his quietus make.

Tom bore his estrangement from the outer world tolerably. He could not believe his bright star had become lastingly darkened, and his exciting career so unceremoniously ended. Moreover, he was solaced by the impression that Laura was in safe keeping. Once on the deck of the War Cloud, he thought, while a shot is left, or a hand to wield a cutlass, she is guarded.

"But hark! here's some one coming."

The noise of the bolts being withdrawn could now be heard. The captives, who by this time began to feel hungry, were gladdened by the sight of a well-filled tray, borne by a benevolent looking old man.

It was the jailer, but without the repulsive characteristics so repulsive to his class.

Letting down the tray, he said jocularly—

"Now, my hearties, here's your breakfast—and a good one, too."

Ben eyed the viands keenly, and with a watering mouth asked—

"Do you always feed your prisoners like this?"

The jailer answered, he did not; but as he was once a sailor himself, the sight of their attire had warmed his old heart, and he hoped they would enjoy the meal.

Tom thanked him; and, at the same time, made the most rational inquiry "how they were to partake of his generous hospitality."

"By eating it."

"Impossible."

And the four showed their hands tied together by ropes.

"What!" ejaculated the old man, "did they leave you like this all night?"

OLD BILL TRIES A SHOT.

"Yes, hang 'em!" growled Ben.

The jailer soon freed them from their bondage.

"Now, my lads," said he, "I am an old man, and can do nothing against four such strong fellows; and, as you know I have exceeded my duty in cutting these ropes, you must promise me, on the words of sailors, you will not attempt to escape."

"We'd all be strung up masthead high first."

"I knew you were true to the backbone—I knew it."

The captives fell upon the good things contained on the tray: and Ben, between the act of swallowing his fourth egg and looking after the fifth, said—

"Did you say you were once a seaman?"

"I did."

"And brought to such a port as this at last?"

"Yes," said the old man, with a sigh. "And I once held the rank of captain."

Ben stopped short in the act of bolting a round of toast, and ejaculated—

"You did! then how was it you came to this pass?"

"Well, it will serve to pass a quarter of an hour away for you; so, if you like, I will tell you, and show you, too, the injustice a man can meet with in this world."

"Pay out the slack, I'm sure it is worth hearing."

"So am I."

5

"and I."

" But before I begin, I had better bring a little something to settle the breakfast."

" Yes," answered the three outlaws, who were always ready for " a glass," or a fight.

The old man left the cell, and returned bringing a bottle of real Jamaica and some glasses, and helping himself, commenced his thrilling story, by saying—

" In the year 17— I made a voyage to China by the way of Cape Horn. I had the command of the good ship Albatros, and was blessed with a good crew.

" Round the southern capes of America we had a rough time of it, certainly ; but when we entered the Pacific we had fine weather, and for some time went gliding on our way without trouble or hindrance.

" I stopped at Valparaiso, where I remained eight days, and then I set sail for New Zealand.

" Well, on the evening of the day after leaving Valparaiso, there was indication of a storm.

"'Shorten sail. Take in the topgallant sails, and double reef the topsails!' these were my orders.

" Nine in the evening it blue a gale from the eastward, by midnight forced to lay-to.

" In the morning when the sun rose, there was a lull, and it looked as if the storm had passed.

" At noon, I was able to get the sun, and found myself to be in longitude of 128° west, latitude, 32° 15 min. south ; wind light and baffling ; but with a heavy sea.

" In the middle of the afternoon, my mate, Spicer, asked what I thought of the weather.

"' Not settled by any means,' I replied.

"' No, and that's not the worst of it. We shall have a stinger, depend on it.'

"' Certainly, we shall have more gales,' said I, ' it is evident the storm is not all passed.'

"' Ay, ay, and we shall catch it this once, more southerly. I tell yer, capt'n, we're got to stand around sometime before we get clear of this place. I've been here afore.'

"' So have I,' I replied, ' several times ; but I never happened to get caught in a storm of any account in the Pacific yet.'

"' I have,' resumed Mr. Spicer, with a shudder. ' By my soul! they can get up some great blows here when they try. I rode out once here in an old hulk of a barque belonging to New York ; and for eight-and-forty hours, we expected every minute to have to say our prayers for the last time. I hope I may never see another such.'

" The mate then went forward to attend to the securing of the anchors, and having all ready for bending the sails.

" At five o'clock the wind was warm, seeming much like the fuming from a hot oven, and seemingly moving in round circles.

" It blew from no steady point, but was continually whirling and changing.

" Heavy clouds had come up to the northward and the westward, while in the southward and eastward there appeared to be a kind of lurid vapour rising and extending itself along the horizon.

" The clouds, after rising very fast, gradually descended until they actually rested upon the bosom of the sea, about as enveloping as in a thick, cold mist.

" This to me was a curious phenomenon.

" In half-an-hour the vapour swept away to the northward and westward again.

" As the sun sank into the vapours which rested upon the western, it had a blue, strange look, seeming like a huge lantern of blue glass. Suddenly my attention was called to the heavens to the southward and eastward, which had grown as black as night.

" Our ship lie in a dead calm, rising and falling like a lifeless monster upon the long heavy swell.

" Liking not the appearance, I immediately ordered the ship to be stripped of her canvas.

" Then I had life-lines rove. After this we waited for the storm.

" But we had not to wait long.

"' Do you hear that?' whispered Spicer, at the same time pointing off to the southward and eastward.

" I had seen it: it was a long line of white foam.

" In a moment more there came a rumbling sound, like the distant reverberations of a cannon.

" Our ship lay nearly stern-to, and I awaited the coming of the gale with almost breathless anxiety.

" And it came. It roared like thunder over the foaming waves, and the spray was rained upon us in torrents.

" The ship gave one plunge, and for a few moments I thought she would founder ; but she finally struggled up, and, throwing off her load of water, started on before the wind.

" I examined the compass, and found the wind had come from a point about south east by east.

" I had one source of comfort, and that was, plenty of sea room.

" I threw a log after the ship had got full headway, but it was impossible to make anything from it, for the mad sea that had leaped up before the gale ' brought the log home,' so that the reel would hardly turn, save by fits and starts.

" All night long the gale continued with unabated fury, and towards morning it became evident that we must either throw over most of our cargo, or else set some sail, for the seas were now very high, and they were beginning to run faster than the ship went, and I saw, should we be overtaken by some of the mountains of water, they would surely swamp us.

" I ordered the foresail to be set, it having been already double-reefed before it was furled.

" By care in casting away the buntlines and clew garnets, and in hauling down the sheets, we got the sail safely set, but this would not answer long.

"The seas were now so high, and it soon became evident that we must set one of the topsails.

"I felt sure the ship would scud the water under the fore topsail, and accordingly had that set.

"It was now morning, and the wind had not lost a whit of its fury.

"I tried many times to heave the log, but it would 'come home' with the seas.

"Once, however, I managed to run off seven fathoms, and I knew we were going faster than that: we were going ten at least.

"Noon came, and the gale was still up in all its power.

"I began to have some fears that we should not weather it, for the fore topsail had more strain upon it than I liked.

"I feared it would give way.

"I knew if it did go our chance of safety would be small. I had seen enough of the ship in gales to know that under the maintopsail she would be apt to yaw and broach-to.

"Our course was now north-west by west, and we had run nearly that for the last twenty-four hours, and yet I could not tell how far we had run.

"I could guess—that was all. I set it at two hundred miles; the mate said it was more.

"Night came again, and the gale was still raging furiously.

"At midnight I went on deck, but the mate would not go below.

"The men had become fear-stricken, for the ship now lay wrenched and loosened fearfully, pumps going all the time.

"At one I went back to my cabin, and sat down to my chart.

"I reckoned our sailing distance as well as I could, and I knew I had the course true. Then I placed my parallel on the chart, and at the first look my lips parted with an utterance of intense horror, and my eyes glared wildly.

"My rule struck the island of St. Beda.

"I called Spicer, and showed him the chart. He sat down, and in less than two minutes leaped up again.

"'Good heavens, captain!' he cried. 'St. Beda is right ahead, and surely not more than fifty miles off. We're gone as sure as fate.'

"'But may not the current set to the westward of it?' I said, hopefully.

"'No,' was the quick response.

"We went on deck, and after a few moments' consultation, I ordered the helmsman to keep the ship's head west-nor'-west, if possible.

"He tried it, but it was hard work, for ever and anon the seas washed him off like a cork, and the danger of being pooped by the huge water mountains was now threatening us.

"Yet I made the man at the wheel give her all the starboard helm she could bear. Towards morning the nature of the wind seemed to chang for the better.

"But the joy of this discovery was quickly damped.

"As the light of day came we witnessed the scene we had been so fearfully dreading.

"Not more than ten miles ahead was the shore of St. Beda.

"It was a coast of bold, sea-dashed rocks, and a cry of horror went up as we perceived it.

"Still blowing hard, we were being hurled at a fearful rate towards the rocks.

"What could be done?

"I went to my cabin and got my glass, and carefully surveying the shore ahead, a gleam of hope shot through my soul.

"'Mr. Spicer,' I said, 'that is the extreme western point of the island. That point to the left is the westerly cape of St. Beda. Clear away beyond I can just see the top of the next island.'

"'Well?' said my mate, interrogatively.

"'I am sure if we could clear that point we should be safe,' I added.

"'If we could clear it,' said Spicer; 'but that is impossible.'

"I hesitated a single moment, and then my mind was made up.

"'Boys!' I cried; 'if we run ashore upon these rocks, we are dead men. No power can save a soul of us; clearing that westerly bout, we may be saved. By the help of God, I shall make the trial.'

"'To clear that point you will have to put the ship's head due west.'

"'Certainly,' said Spicer.

"'I know it,' was my reply.

"'And she cannot be put there,' he said; 'she could not live a moment with her broadside thus exposed.'

"'I shall try it,' was my answer, therefore I ordered the men aloft to loose the maintopsail.

"It was already close-reefed.

"'Put the helm hard a star-board! haul the lee sheets home.'

"Next the weather clew came down, and the yard was hoisted clear of the cap in safety.

"Then the storm-mizen was set, and I soon found that the fore-staysail would be of benefit if it would hold.

"The mate said I was mad.

"I pointed towards the rocks, and asked him how he would like to run in there?

"I acknowledged my present course was one of extreme hazard; but was there one other plan within the range of possibility to be effected? I inquired.

"The ship was now heading due west.

"Every hatch was battened.

"I prayed then, and saw others pray, and there was need for it.

"Two stout men were lashed at the wheel, for they could not have stood without.

"I stood by the mizenmast, and hung upon a pin-rack.

"Six times did the lee-main yardarm dip into the water, and we were literally under water two thirds of the time.

"The masts groaned and cracked in their stoppings and chocks; the sheets strained and vibrated like the strings of a viol; the canvas swelled out till each particular thread seemed ready to snap, and the whole ship heeled over until her yards almost lay on the sea.

"No one could pull a rope; to have let go his hold, would have been to be washed, for a certainty, overboard.

"On we sped—on—on, and yet the ship was on her keel.

"The point we wished to clear was now under our lee-bow and not over a cable's length distant.

"Merciful heavens we are gone!

"A sea had struck us that moment, sweeping its crest high above our tops; the next instant we were engulphed.

"I felt the cold flood all about me; I had sense of a drownward motion, and I felt the dull gurgle of water above—yet I held on.

"It may have been for a minute—perhaps only a few seconds; but the time was an age to me, for thought of a thousand things the while.

"And then I found daylight again. The old ship had struggled up from the grasp of the ocean grave.

"My first glance was for my men.

"They were all safe—every one.

"But the sails had disappeared, excepting the fore staysail; all the rest had been torn from the bolt ropes in the struggle.

"I gave one timid, trembling look around me: we were safe.

"The point of rocks was under our star-board quarter; we were again before the wind, and all was clear for many a mile ahead.

"Four day's after we were in sight of land.

"But the vessel had received so much injury, we could not get her into port; and within twenty yards of it she foundered, barely giving us time to save ourselves by the boats.

"So far have you heard of the trials and dangers we went through, and how the hand of heaven was held over us; but man's hand "——

And here the old man paused.

"Man's hand," said he, "dealt me an unsparing blow. Would you believe it," and the old man's words rose to an impassioned ardour as he repeated it—"would you believe it, when I reached home I was deprived of my rank of captain, and nearly transported for carelessness, and dismissed the service with disgrace?

"Now, I ask you," he said in conclusion, "do you think I deserved to be so unkindly and so mercilessly dealt with?"

"No," replied Ben, emphatically, and thumping his fist upon the table, until the glasses nearly danced a set of quadrilles; "No. It was a burning shame, and, hang 'em, I'd like to punish 'em!" holding out his clenched fist after the manner of the best accomplished pugilist about "to try his strength."

The others, though in milder language, equally expressed their sympathy for the poor sailor, Tom adding thereto his determination to make this sympathy practical, for he had, he said, already resolved within his own mind, that so clever a seaman, as his language had proved him to be, should yet have another chance of treading the deck.

CHAPTER XXVI.

THE DOVE AND THE VULTURE.

So far Neville had played the winning card in this desperate game. Laura was in his power, and while on the road to London he contemplated putting her for ever out of his path to obtain the dead colonel's wealth.

But before the journey had ended, his sentiments changed. Her singular beauty inspired him, and as his wife he thought her father's riches would not only be his, but the beautiful heiress as well.

"Yes, yes," he muttered; "as my wife, and the rich dowry she brings, I can see a clear way to become not only rich, but a favoured guest in the halls of the proud nobility. They will receive her for her beauty, and me for our wealth."

He fed upon this idea until he imagined Laura had given her consent to become his bride. Poor girl, she had never raised her eyes since they started, and, after rising from one swoon, relapsed into another, and in this state they came upon the outskirts of London.

The jolting of the vehicle aroused him from his dream; but he soon returned to it, and as he gazed upon Laura's shrinking form, his eyes were ablaze with expectation.

"Mine! Mine!" he said, and his breath came hot and quick. "Mine for ever—mine!"

"Wake!" he cried frantically to the poor girl. "Let me hear your voice."

But her head dropped back, and her long golden curls fell in rolling masses round her neck.

Suddenly the motion and rumbling of the coach ceased. The coachman descended from the box, and laid his hand upon the door.

"Where are we to go, sir? This here's London."

Neville placed a guinea in the driver's hand, saying—

"King William-street. Two more of the same sort when you arrive."

The coachman closed the door, and mounted his box.

He jolted through the streets, and turned over London-bridge.

A faint cry from inside the coach caused him to turn his head.

"Poor little girl!" he muttered. "I hopes I shall see t'other young feller arter I gets back; for I don't think this one is much account. It's clear to me she ain't over partial to his company."

Wirely was a man whom Laura hated with a feverish hate; and when she found herself so immediately in his power, she shouted out—

"Monster! why am I here in your presence?"

A sinister laugh came from the lips of Wirely, as he said—

"Because I love you, Laura, and intend to call you wife ere many hours have passed."

The poor girl was frenzied at his words; and, before he had power to prevent it, she put her head out of the coach window, and uttered a piercing shriek for help.

But her cry was unheeded.

Wirely growled, and raised his clenched fist as though intending to strike her: but as Laura's large blue eyes fell fixedly upon him, he dropped his hand.

At this instant the coach again stopped.

They had reached their destination, and he looked upon Laura as beyond all reach of aid.

The coachman again descended from his box, knocked at the door of a portly-looking house, received his two guineas, and assisted Wirely to carry Laura, who had fainted, into the hall.

Up the broad oaken stairs he hurried with the unconscious maiden in his arms.

At the first landing he stopped, where from beneath one of the doors came the faint gleam of a light, which Wirely moved forward to open.

But before he could do so, a stealthy step behind him caused him to pause.

It was the confidential servant of Wirely.

The man bowed, opened the door of an elegantly furnished room, assisted in placing Laura on a luxurious ottoman that stood in the centre of it, and, lighting a large lamp, crept silently out of the room.

"Our journey is over for the present, pretty one," said Wirely. "Give me but one kiss, to repay me for the anxiety I have had in bringing you to the home over which I intend you to be the adorning mistress."

Laura answered him by a look of the profoundest indignation; and clasping her white hands together, sat, for a time, the very image of despair. But, suddenly arousing herself into an impulsiveness which started Wirely, she shrieked out—

"I care not! While life remains will I reject your proposal, and be true to him from whom you have so wantonly separated me."

"Well, then," said Wirely, coolly, "I may as well inform you that resistance would be useless, and that ere two days expire you must be mine."

She gave a low moan, and her head fell back. She was helpless.

There she lay for an hour, her pulse but feebly beating, and to all appearance sinking into death's icy realm.

Wirely chafed her little hands, and bathed her white temples, until a faint colour began at length to steal into her cheeks. When she revived, he thus addressed her—

"Laura, whatever I have done has been caused by your beauty. Believe me, I possess none other than a passionate and honourable fondness for you. Be mine, I repeat; let me but woo and win, and I shall be happy."

The ormolu clock on the mantle chimed the hour of four at this moment, and its low, silvery tone seemed to inspire Laura with a sudden thought.

"It will be light soon," was the swift reflection. "Can I but escape his importunities till then, some chance may yet free me."

This thought, like the lightning's flash, passed through her mind, and half averting her head, she murmured—

"Would you force me to do that at which my heart rebels?"

"I would not, sweet girl, were there any hope of your relenting."

He took her hand as she spoke. She suffered him to take it, loathsome as was the touch to her.

"Give me time to think," she said. "Leave me for a time."

"I will. In one hour I shall return."

Wirely left the room, his heart bounding at the blissful prospect of possessing Laura, and with her own consent.

Full of self-gratulation, he hurried out of the room, and without hearing Laura softly shoot the bolts into the sockets as he left it.

As the wild songster surveys its cage in mute bewilderment, and then beats its feathered breast against the bars of its prison, so did Laura survey this her gorgeous apartment, in which she was an unwilling captive.

With throbbing heart and heightened pulse she flew to her window, to see what chance there might be of escape.

Alas! there was none.

Laura felt sick at heart, her brain reeled, and sinking with clasped hands and tearful eyes upon a couch, she moaned in anguished accents—

"Is there no hope—no escape from this misery?"

A faint cry—so faint as almost to be unheard—answered the appeal.

Laura started from her suppliant position, and listened.

Again it sounded.

Swiftly the recollection came to her mind that she had left the window open.

She sprang to the open casement, and at right angles to where she stood was another window open, and by the mellow light of a large lamp Laura was enabled to behold the interior.

Concealed by heavy curtains stood a massive bedstead, and near it a female form who emerged cautiously and stood for a moment beneath the lamp light.

Laura was too terrified to speak, but stood with

parted lips and beating heart gazing upon the woman.

The stranger noted the poor girl's terror, and in voice low and musical she said—

"Be not alarmed, lady; I come to save, not to harm you. But"—pointing to the time-piece—"there are but twenty minutes remaining out of the hour's respite."

Laura started. There was something terrible in the pale woman's knowledge of the fearful trials to which she had been exposed.

"You seem surprised at my knowledge?" said the stranger, in a melancholy tone. "I will explain how I became possessed of this secret."

"See you this portrait?"

It was a life-sized picture of a cavalier.

Laura inclined her head.

The mystic woman placed her finger upon the brooch which adorned the cavalier's scarf, exclaiming—

"Through this I beheld the scene through which you have just passed."

She pressed the brooch as she spoke, and it disappeared, leaving a small circular orifice.

Laura uttered an exclamation of surprise.

The stranger gave a melancholy smile at the young girl's astonishment, and proceeded—

"And through this hole the long deadly tube of a pistol covered that villain's form, and had he proceeded further to coerce you, his corpse would be now lying upon this carpet!"

"Inexplicable being!" said Laura, "who and what are you that you should take such an interest in my fate?"

"I am called Maladine," said the stranger. "But we have not time for explanation. How can I serve you?"

"By taking me from hence."

"I cannot."

Laura looked up in bewilderment, and faltered—

"You cannot?"

"No; but I can serve you in another way. Quick! Ha! the time! We have but five minutes!"

Laura gave a terrified glance at the time-piece, and said—

"Then I am lost!"

"Not so. Have you no friends that could be informed of your position—father, brother?"

"Alas! neither."

"A lover, then?"

A rosy blush overspread Laura's cheeks as she tered—

"Yes, but he is too far away."

"You know not. I have messengers fleet of ot. Is he in London?"

Laura knew that her lover, when he discovered her abduction, would follow on her track, and his vessel would be moored in the river; and, feeling assured that even should he not be on board, there would be stout hearts and strong hands ready to

rescue her, "Yes," she replied, with drooping eyelids, "he is."

"Where? Quick, the address!"

"His vessel lies moored in the river."

"Its name?"

"The War"—— She recollected Tom would not sail under that name, and added, "I do not know the name."

"Here," said the mysterious woman, placing tablets and a pencil in Laura's hand, "write a few words on these. Inform him of your danger. The messenger will guide him hither."

"But," hesitated Laura, "he may not be"——

"You said a moment since his vessel had moored in the river."

"I did, madam; but it is merely a surmise, for—for"——

"Pray do not hesitate; time is precious. Tell me your grounds for the supposition that his vessel is near London."

"Only this," said Laura. "When we were together at the ca——in the country, he used to tell me, if ever I were carried off, he should come after me at once."

"Quite so. Well?"

"Once," continued Laura, "I asked him what he would do if I were taken to London, and he told me he should come by the road and send his vessel round the coast, so that I could, no matter where I might be, send word if I could find a messenger."

"You can find one. One moment. Is this gentleman to be depended upon."

"Midshipman Tom," said Laura, proudly, "never yet broke his word."

The stranger smiled at Laura's enthusiasm, and said—

"Enough. Write a few lines, and depend upon it I shall discover the vessel."

"How it seems to me"——

"Impossible, but it is quite easy to find the vessels that have lately arrived, and his will not have been here many hours."

"Not many."

"So much the better. Now, quick with the note, for the time is up."

With trembling hand she wrote about twenty words and gave the leaf to her companion.

"'Tis well. But hark!"

A gentle tapping at the door caused them both to start.

Laura clung to her companion, whispering—

"It is he—my abductor!"

A stern, determined expression came over the stranger's pale face as she drew from beneath her robe a small, delicately embossed pistol.

She handed the weapon to Laura, saying—

"You can use this?"

"I can," was the reply of the astonished girl, and as she spoke, a hasty summons at the door caused her to shudder.

"Be of good heart," said the strange woman

Keep up a conversation for a short time, while I send for your lover."

"Till then?"

"If he comes not in time, use that weapon, it is serviceable, and carries true."

"I will. But one word before you go."

"Quick—quick then!"

"Who, and what are you?"

the chamber, and before Laura could prevent him, he had clasped her in his arms.

She gently disengaged herself from his embrace, and closed the door.

Then in obedience to the mysterious woman's instructions to "keep him in conversation for a short time," Laura, guileless in her innermost soul as she was, suffered herself to dissemble with her

RED HAND PRESENTED A PISTOL AT THE HEAD OF THE TERRIFIED GIRL.

"*I am an agent of the police!* Some other time you shall know more. Farewell!"

The woman glided to the panel she had entered at, which slipped into its place as she leapt through.

Laura concealed her strangely acquired weapon: and as she made up her mind for the worst, her abductor opened the door.

Wirely uttered a cry of joy as he bounded into

unwelcome companion; charming him by the change in her demeanour, and making light of his overtures, until a considerable time had passed away.

Suddenly he returned to a display of his usual impulses, and endeavoured to clasp her in his arms.

But Laura gently repelled him, saying—

"You gave me an hour to decide."

"I did, sweet one; and your readiness to

re-admit me proves how much you value my for-bearance."

"It does; and trusting as you have trusted me, I have admitted you, that I may ask a further indulgence?"

"A what?" he said, abruptly. "A further indulgence?"

"Yes; for I find my mind the same as when you left me."

Wirely half rose from his seat, and catching her by the wrist, said, in a terrific voice—

"Then am I to understand all this condescension to be affected?"

The light in Laura's eyes became stronger as she replied quietly—

"Release my hands, and you shall know."

Wirely released his grasp upon her slender wrist.

"Speak, then," said he, "and quickly, or"——

"What?"

He thrust his hand into his breast, and drew a long, glittering knife.

"I have sworn to marry you! Refuse—by heaven!—and this knife!"——

He had thought to frighten her into compliance with his wishes; but to Wirely's surprise, she sprang from her seat, and levelling the pistol at his forehead, uttered boldly—

"And I have sworn you shall not! Move but a step, and I fire!"

CHAPTER XXVII.

BEN BIGHT'S STORY OF A WHALE.

"How long do you think we shall be here?"

This question was addressed by Tom Wilson to the old sailor when the latter had told the terrible story in connexion with his last voyage.

"It is impossible to say," was the reply, "for the cells of Newgate are so full of prisoners that you will have to wait until there is room."

"Newgate!" repeated Tom. "Surely they will not take us there?"

"Yes, my friend."

"Well," said Ben Bight, "I'd sooner be turned into a marine than go there."

"No doubt, but the charges against you cannot well be gone into at any other place."

"What is the charge?" Tom asked. "Not a very heavy one."

"Desertion from the Royal Navy," said the jailer, "piracy, and mutiny."

"Sufficient to hang us," said the mid. laughing; "but I hope we shall escape that fate."

"I hope so, too," said the jailer, "and I feel sure you will, for that gallant attack upon Derrick's band ought to alone obtain a pardon for your offences."

"Perhaps it may," said Tom; "so we will be of good heart, and while we are here, pass the time as well as we can."

"Let's spin yarns," suggested an outlaw. "Ben, spin us something."

"Not if I know it," said Ben.

Ben's messmates pressed him until he began.

"Well, I'm blowed if I can; this 'ere tarnation place ain't no place for a man to stretch his memory in, no more than 'tis his body. I'll give yer a short account of a cruise of mine in search of whales, if you like."

They nodded assent.

"'Thar they blows,' commenced Ben, "was sung out from the mast-head of our ship, while cruising in search of whales a few years since.

"'Thar again,' continued the voice.

"By this time the captain and all hands were on deck.

"'Where away?' demanded the captain.

"'About two points before the lee beam, a couple of miles off,' was the reply.

"'All right,' said the captain, 'I can see them; clear away the boats.'

"There was a considerable ripple on at the time, just enough to make a land-lubber comfortably sea-sick.

"The whales, for there were two of 'em, apparently a cow and a calf, were heading to wind-ward, going about three knots through the water.

"'We can cut them off,' said the captain address-ing the mate, 'and take them head-and-head.'

"'Now, lower away boys,' and down went the boats.

"'Pull, my hearties, pull. Thar they lay, like logs. D'ye see the white of their eyes? Five minutes more and we're on 'em. 'Pull, you lazy sinners, pull!'

"The whales were now very near to the boats, about eight or ten fathoms apart, taking it very leisurely.

"'Now,' cried the captain, addressing the boat-steerer, who pulled the bow oar, 'when you dart, be sure of your first iron. Don't be in a hurry to dart two and miss both. Thar, peak your oar—stand up! Hush! she sees the boat! Pull—pull another stroke with all your might—be wild for once, my lads—so—way, enough!'

"The boat had passed the whale's head, and was almost within ten feet of her side.

"She saw the boat, and seemed to quake with fear, before she made a dash to escape.

"It was too late.

"The boat bounded over the rising wave, and, quick as lightning, the two irons, one after the other, were plunged into the whale's quivering side.

"'Stern hard!' shouted the captain, at the top of his lungs; but, before he could repeat the order, the whale had breached entirely out of the water, and raised a cloud of whitened foam, that shrouded her from view, and nearly upset the boat.

"Away she dashes to windward, the line literally blazing around the loggerhead, and the sea coloured with her blood, curling and foaming over the side of the boat.

"'Bail—bail, my boys! Peak your oars, and now come aft,' said the captain."

"The last order was addressed to the boat-steerer, whose duty it was to steer the boat while the captain went forward to lance the whale.

"After running a mile or two to windward, the whale hove to, and commenced breaching and cutting about with her flukes in all directions, so as to render it impossible for the boat to approach her.

"In the mean time, the mate had fastened to the calf, which ran for shelter to its mother, and both lashed the water with uncommon fury.

"The captain approached the whale, and darted a lance into her, and she, in return, up with her flukes and knocked the bottom clean out of his boat.

"Of course the line was immediately cut, and away went the whale to windward, spouting and blowing like smoke.

"No one was hurt. The ship picked up the men and the wreck of the boat, and the mate killed the calf and secured it, which made about twenty barrels of oil."

Ben's account of his cruise ended, one of his mates, who had himself been whale-fishing, declared Ben's description to be both lively and stunning, and they, one and all, acknowledged that for once Ben had unquestionably presented them with a true story.

Ben had barely finished his narrative, when a good-sized stone, which had been dexterously flung through the window, came rattling at his feet. Ben stooped to pick it up.

"Hallo! what's this?" he said.

As he finished speaking, the outlaw removed a piece of paper; then looking at the superscription, he handed it to Tom, saying—

"It's for you, sir."

The young mid opened the paper, and read aloud—

"The band are near you—be prepared for anything."

Ben and his companions rubbed their hands in ecstasy.

"Is they?" said Ben. "Then we'll have a slap at the land sharks, and pretty quick!"

To which Mat added—

"I shall make one to take a few on 'em on board the little vessel called the War Cloud."

"So will I if we gets away, and especially that chap as dropped me one on the nob."

And Ben weighed his fist up and down, as if calculating how many pounds' weight it would fall on the watchman's nose.

The jailer, who had left the cell shortly after detailing his interesting story, now returned, and the outlaws could see by the sad expression of his countenance that he brought ill news.

Closing the door cautiously, he said, in a low voice,

"The officers have arrived to convey you to Newgate."

At the mention of this gloomy prison, Ben Bight's face became considerably elongated.

Turning to Mat, he said, ruefully—

"Shiver me from keel to truck, if that ain't a treat!"

"I am not of your opinion, Ben. I have no desire to visit the interior of his saintly majesty's stone jug."

"No more have I."

"Why, you said it was a treat!"

"I don't mean it, though."

The young mid. had been holding a short conference with the friendly jailer; at the conclusion, he turned to his followers, and said—

"Our friend has brought us bad intelligence."

The men became all attention.

"But still there is a faint hope yet that we may obtain our liberty."

Ben's face became much shorter. He had a marked dislike to visiting Newgate at government expense.

The mid continued—

"He informs me that, to prevent any suspicion, we must again be bound."

The countenances of Tom's companions did not express pleasure at this injunction.

Ben suggested, "As we have our arms unlashed, let's have a go in at 'em when they come to take us."

"The attempt would be useless," said Tom; "they are many, and well armed."

Ben felt sorry for this.

"But," continued the young leader, "it will be an easy matter for us to bind each other in such a manner that the least strain upon the ropes will relieve our arms."

Ben could have yelled with delight at the idea.

"And how are we to do that—the last one that is bound is not able to bind himself?"

"Easy enough," said Tom, smiling. "Our friend the jailer will bind the last one. He can tie the sort of knot we require."

"That will I, cheerfully," said the ex-captain; "but you must be quick, gentlemen. The land-sharks are mustering."

A few minutes sufficed to pinion their arms in such a manner that the knots of the rope were held by a loose end, which each prisoner held in his hand, ready at the proper time to give a pull that would untie them, though when that time would come, was a matter of future consideration.

These preliminaries were scarcely adjusted, when a man of forbidding countenance was thrust in the cell.

It was the visage of Grub, a famous runner of that period.

"Now then," he said, "are you ready, my lads, for the jug?"

Ben scowled; Mat looked at the toe of his boot; Tom, graceful and noble-looking as ever, turned upon his heel. But not one of them answered Grub's polite inquiry.

"Well," he muttered, "my kids, you shall, silent or not, have a night's lodging for nothing, and then a ride for nil, while we collers a hundred pounds for taking you."

Ben could keep quiet no longer. With a flushed face he retorted—

"You hav'n't got us there yet, you goat of iniquity?"

"Ha! ha! ha! ha! ain't we?" he affectedly sneered out. "Ain't we? Perhaps twelve on us won't take you—that's all!"

Ben was waxing furious.

"Look here, you beautiful imitation of an ugly beak."

"Vill, I is looking, and a pretty object you are to look at. Has the old woman got any more like yer?"

Ben foamed at the mouth as he answered—

"You bottle-nose thief! untie my arms, and bring five more like yourself in here, and I'll polish yer off!"

"You're very kind, young flamer. Is there anything else you take a fancy to?"

"Yes!" said Ben.

"Vat is it, 'cos I 'spects you will dance on nothing very soon?"

"I should like to bruise your varmint head!"

"You are very kind, but we hav'n't time to oblige you."

"I'll make you," thought Ben, "if the boys come up in time, my beauty!"

The officer's head now disappeared. He had, as he thought, tormented his prisoners quite enough, and shown off his wit too. So he went to assemble his brother myrmidons, who, with their bludgeons balanced in their hands, entered the cell.

And one of them, thinking he could play off a little joke upon Mat, gave the outlaw a push in the stomach with his truncheon.

Mat was not the sort of man to put up with this tamely, and before the officer could get out of the way, he lowered his head, and charged full tilt at him.

There was a laugh when Mat's head came in contact with the other's stomach, making the officer perform a back fall, much to his own astonishment and disgust.

CHAPTER XXVIII.
THE RESCUE.

THE majesty of the law had no terrors for the middy outlaw, or he would not have laughed so boldly at the appearance of the extended officer.

With the water streaming from his eyes, and his hand placed upon that part of his anatomy saluted by Mat, he gasped out—

"Ha! oh! ha! knocked the wi-win-wind out of me. Give him a nob-nob-nobbler."

The officers would have given Matt a "nob-nob-

nobbler," had not the calm, majestic voice of the young midshipman restrained them.

With uplifted bludgeons they had crowded round Mat, when Tom said—

"Shame on you! would you strike a man bound and helpless as he is?"

The officers drew back, abashed; and Grub, the chief of the pack, growled to the fallen one—

"Why didn't yer let him alone? Get up and foller on."

The discomfited joker did as his superior requested him, and the whole posse, with the outlaws in the centre, marched from the lock-up.

The facetious gentleman who had tried his little joke with Mat was observed to keep well in the rear, and look with anything but an eye of affection at Mat's round, hard head.

During their progress from the lock-up to the prison, much curiosity was manifested by the Londoners at the appearance of the stalwart-looking outlaws and their handsome young leader.

The constables and their charge had proceeded without interruption as far as as Holborn Hill.

A grin was on every constable's face, as the capture would be something to talk about.

But while their glee was at its height, and they were exchanging jokes, a party of sailors, one of whom was a gigantic negro, came rolling down the street.

"My eyes," exclaimed one, "here's a go! A lot of tars grabbed."

The captives' eyes sparkled with delight, for they instantly recognised their friends.

"What's up, my hearties?" hailed another. "We'll stand bail for ye all."

The chief constable drew his men closer round the captives, for he did not like the appearance of these rollicking tars, especially the negro, who carried a formidable axe under his arm.

"Avast there, yer swabs!" said the first speaker. "We wants to know what's up, and where ye going?"

"Look here, my fine fellows," said Grub.

They were getting very near the gates of Newgate, and he began to feel a little more confidence.

"Look here," he repeated.

"Well, we are looking."

"Do you see this place?"

He pointed with his bludgeon towards the frowning walls of Newgate.

"In course we does."

"Very well. Then sheer yourselves off, or you may find yourself inside very soon."

"What for?"

"Why, for interfering with the law."

"The law be hanged, and you too." Then addressing Ben, he said, "What's up, shipmates?"

The sailors had quietly surrounded the whole party while this colloquy took place, and Ben answered—

"Why, we're nabbed, that's what's up."

"And don't yer want to go in this craft?"

"It ain't likely."

"Forward," shouted Grub; "they will attempt a rescue."

"By gar, yes," yelled Snowball, flourishing his axe. "We hab 'em, too."

Like magic the cords fell from the outlaw's arms, and in less time than is consumed by reading this the prisoners had each wrested a bludgeon from the officers.

Ben, who had been savagely waiting this movement, no sooner had a bludgeon in his hand than he paid the chief constable in full.

Never, in the whole course of their career, did they receive such a sudden thrashing.

Although Snowball had brought but six of the band with him, to avoid suspicion, the constables were all sprawling on the ground in a very few minutes.

This was partly owing to the unexpected manner in which the prisoners attacked them in their very midst—a circumstance for which they were not prepared.

It was marvellous to behold the manner in which they went down; for, as they retreated from Snowball and his companions, the prisoners saluted them with well-directed blows on the backs of their craniums.

"Free once more!" shouted the young chieftain, as he shook hands with his deliverers.

But they had not much time to waste in congratulations, for the gate of the prison was thrown open, and a crowd of constables rushed forth.

"Go it, yer debils—run!" said Snowball, showing the example. "Follow dis child. Me show you where a boat is waiting."

The colossal African was well able to keep the lead, for in his native forests he had, barefooted, chased the fleet beasts of the chase.

To do the outlaws justice, they did their best to follow him.

A couple of carmen tried to stop the fugitives by placing themselves in their way.

One, the driver of a mud-cart, had better have looked after his own business, for the African seized him by collar and waist, and threw him crash through an apothecary's window.

The other received a domino from Ben which made his face ache for a week afterwards.

The young chieftain began to tire, and he lagged a little behind.

The negro noticed this immediately, and said—

"Get tired, Massa Tom? Me carry you."

"No, thank you, Snowball; I can manage the remainder of the distance. I can see the water."

The active outlaws had out-distanced their pursuers, whose shouts could be heard in the streets they had just emerged from.

They were upon the banks of the Thames.

A few yards further they would be safe in the boat that awaited them—the men lying on their oars.

But at this moment, to the astonishment of all, Snowball stopped.

"By gar," he said, "dat nebber do!"

"What, what?" was the eager query.

"Why, to go on de water."

"Why not?

"Why not—dam!—don't you see, we nebber get War Cloud clear ob de ships here, and the guns ob de Tower right ober head."

At this moment the pursuers came puffing and blowing round the corner.

Immediately they saw the outlaws they set up a shout of—

"There they are! there they are!"

"Yes," muttered Snowball; "but we not stop long."

The negro glanced quickly around; then, giving the boat's crew a signal for them to rejoin the boat, he said—

"Foller me, Massa Tom; come on, all ob you."

A black vaulted arch stood near; the light of day failing to illumine its murking interior.

Down this the outlaws rushed; the officers, with a cry ran after them.

But at the entrance they were stopped by Snowball's uplifted weapon.

CHAPTER XXIX.

A HOT PURSUIT.

THE herculean form, the glittering blade and the dusky fire that flashed from the negro's eyes, kept the officers at bay.

They withdrew with great unanimity of purpose, and, much to the detriment of each others toes, and, as usual among men, many of them had corns.

After a smart discharge of nautical compliments the officers held a hurried consultation.

It was the old fable of bell the cat.

Every one decided that the weapon should be taken away from Snowball, but no one attempted to do it.

Snowball watched them closely, and quickly guessed the purport of their conversation, and he called out—

"Now din, you lubbers, this chile am waiting for you."

As far as the constables were concerned he seemed likely to wait.

But a sudden change in the aspect of affairs caused a move quite unexpected.

The mob which had assembled, like all other mobs, when anything unusual takes place, always give notice of the appearance of any fresh object on the scene.

And so it was in this instance. When they heard the clatter of horses' hoofs and the ring of troopers' swords, they shouted, as with one voice—

"The soldiers—the soldiers are coming!"

This fact was of course heard with dismay by

the outlaws; and Snowball, showing his teeth, growled.

"Dam red coats! What we do, Massa Tom?"

Tom looked very grave, for capture seemed certain.

He knew it would be quite impossible to contend successfully against a body of well-armed, disciplined men, with their weakened hands.

But even then his heart did not fail him, and with a proud smile, he said—

"We must either fight or surrender."

"Fight, the debbil! How we fight, and only dis axe among all ob us?"

Ben Bight, who had a habit of prowling about in a strange place, now approached the young chieftain, and whispered a few words in his ear.

Midshipman Tom transmitted them in the same tone to Snowball.

They must have been very pleasing, for the negro grinned and put his thumb up to his nose and worked his remaining fingers in a most disrespectful manner towards the officers.

The dragoons had now halted, and were drawn up in front of the arch, and the officer in command, said, in a voice that seems peculiar to officers in general—

"Prepare to dismount."

The word was followed by—

"Dismount."

The troops sprang lightly to the ground.

"With ball cartridge load!"

The men unslung their carbines, and the rattle of the light ramrods, as they drove their charge to the bottom of the pieces, soon followed.

"Surrender in the name of the king!" Grub called out.

The captain of the troopers drew his sabre, and shouted to his men—

"Forward!"

And forward they went.

But, like a prudent general, he halted within a few feet of the archway to reconnoitre.

"Seize 'em!" shouted Grub from behind the troops.

The officer then flourished his sword, and chorused—

"Come out, my fine fellows! It's no use hiding in there."

No reply was made.

In lively remembrance of a large axe he had seen Snowball wielding a few moments before, Grub, feeling the necessity of appearing brave, took a very few steps inside, and said, persuasively and coaxingly—

"Now then, come out!"

But "now then" did not come out, as the officer requested; and so Grub and his comrades were ordered in.

When they had entered a few yards, they found the place was empty.

They were gone, to a certainty. But how?

The first gleam of light, no larger than a man' hand it seemed in the distance, told how.

For Grub gave a very surprising yell, and shouted—

"Cuss 'em! This arch leads to Thames-street, and they are off towards London Bridge."

"Are they, by George?" exclaimed the officer, savagely.

Then, turning to his men, he shouted—

"Prepare to mount—mount!"

The troopers were soon in the saddle.

"Threes, right—trot!"

Away the soldiers went, at a spanking pace, towards London Bridge, the officers close behind.

Ben, as we have said before, had been prying about, while Snowball guarded the entrance.

In his rambles he had found that the arch which they stood under led into a street parallel with the Thames.

This interesting fact he had communicated to Tom, and while the guardsmen were loading their carbines, the outlaws had made the necessary retrograde movement, and were going up the street at a headlong pace.

And while Grub was desiring them to "come out," Snowball was hailing the boat he had sent back to the vessel.

The rowers had recognised their messmates, and were now pulling swiftly for the shore. A hundred yards, and they would reach it.

The outlaws yelled to them to pull faster, for the white plumes of the dragoons could be seen streaming in the wind as they came galloping up the lane.

In the whole course of Midshipman Tom's wild career he had never been in greater peril.

It was a thrilling moment.

The horses' hoofs sending up a myriad of bright fiery sparks as they struck the jagged stones to arrest the outlaws.

The stout ashen blades bending like reeds under the brawny arms of the outlaws in the War Cloud's pinnace to be in time to release them.

Three boats' length was all that intervened between them and liberty, and not more than a hundred yards between them and the foremost horseman.

Tom's head was thrown back, his nostrils dilated as the peril increased, and now and then his hand wandered to the empty belt where his scimitar usually hung.

And now, when his breath was all but suspended, in the excitement of the moment Tom turned to his followers, and said, calmly—

"The boat will reach as at the same moment as our foes. Spring on board at once!"

"And you, Massa Tom?"

"I shall be last to enter."

At this moment the coal-black charger of the leading trooper dashed up to the spot where the young chieftain stood.

THE OFFICERS RUSHED IN WITH A YELL.

In a moment he was drawn sharply up, and the rider, raising his sabre, bellowed—

"Surrender! or I cut you down."

His words were answered by a glad shout that rose from the outlaws as they sprang into the boat, which, by this time, had reached the shore.

Tom heard the joyous shout his men gave; and stepping back to avoid the swift descending blow of the guardsman, he said fiercely—

"It is not to you that I would surrender."

The heavy sabre cleaved the air, and the trooper, enraged at missing his first blow, muttered an angry oath, and drove his spurs into the horse's sides.

The powerful animal snorted and plunged for-

ward, and would have crushed our hero, had he not, with wonderful presence of mind, seized the horse's bridle.

By the bottom bar of the bit he held him in check, and forced him back upon his haunches; then, with a sudden wrench, he caused the horse to rear up.

One moment he pawed the air.

The next he came down, crushing his rider with his ponderous weight.

Too late were his companions to seize the daring Tom; for, as they dashed up to the spot, he sprang into the boat, uttering a clear, silvery laugh of defiance.

The captain of the Life Guards, furious at the

escape of his prey, and hoarse with passion, yelled—

"Unsling your carbines. Shoot him! shoot him!"

A dozen tubes were cocked at the young chieftain, who stood in the prow of the boat; but ere a finger could contract upon a trigger, Tom roared—

"Hold!"

The men looked towards the speaker, and, to their amazement, they beheld each of the outlaws grasping a pair of pistols.

Those pistols levelled at their heads.

"Hold!" repeated Tom, "for, by heaven! I swear that the first man who moves so much as a finger, dies!"

There was something in the daring boy's voice and his appearance that caused a sensation, akin to awe, to creep over them.

And like statues they sat silently awaiting their commander's orders.

But before he could speak, the young chieftain said, as he pointed a long-barrelled pistol full at the officer's face—

"Move but one inch—dare even to open your mouth, and you die."

Then, lowering his voice, he called to his men—

"Give way, and move for the centre of the stream."

The men began to pull slowly, and when a few yards away from the shore, they bent to their work and sent the light boat flying through the water.

Statuesque and calm, the young chieftain had stood during the boat's progress, his eyes fixed upon the disordered soldiery.

An exclamation from Snowball now caused him to look ahead.

"Dam officers in front, Massa Tom!" growled the black. "Two boats full ob 'em."

It was so; the runners had pulled off in their wherries, and were bearing down upon them.

Ben recognised the fellow who had annoyed him in the police cell, and carefully ramming home a good charge of powder, he muttered—

"That swab will get a pill yet."

"Without any directions for taking it," said Mat.

"You can stow your funnyosity as soon as you like, Mat."

"I would rather stow myself in the fo'castle of the War Cloud."

The young chieftain waved his hand for them to be quiet, and suddenly gave the order—

"Down on your backs, all of you."

They were barely in time to escape a volley from the troopers, who had dismounted, and, falling on one knee, had fired point blank at the outlaws.

CHAPTER XXX.
ON THE VULTURE'S TRACK.

ONE of the rowers was hit by this discharge, and fell into the bottom of the boat.

With an angry cry, his companions levelled their pistols to return the fire, but Midshipman Tom's voice restrained them.

"Hold!" he said. "Are you mad? Would you have your pieces empty and those boats so close upon us?"

His dark, dashing eyes swept the river as he spoke; and, with a defiant laugh, he continued—

"Heed not the soldiery, we are out of range now, but pull with all your strength, Snowball."

"Yes, Massa Tom."

"Take the tiller, and run down the nearest boat."

"Ay, ay, sir!"

"And when we foul the first boat, send a volley into the second."

The outlaws smiled grimly.

"Do not shed needless blood," said Tom; "fire low—among their legs."

"Ay, ay, sir!"

The officers would have much sooner closed with the outlaws had they equally well understood the art of rowing.

Occasionally a pair of heels was suddenly elevated in the air, and once an oar drifted away—a hearty guffaw coming from the outlaws at the mishap.

All this time the outlaws were pulling with all their soul towards the centre arch of the bridge.

"There they come!" yelled Grub. "Pull! pull! or they will get past."

The officers tried to pull on; but, one side pulling stronger than the other, the boat turned sideways, and lay across the outlaw's bow.

Grub chuckled when he saw this; and more so as he saw the pinnace spanking down upon them.

"Ha! ha! ha!" he sniggered; "they can't get away this time."

"Blessed good job!" said a companion, looking, with rueful visage, at his blistered hands. "All the skin is off my hands pulling this beastly tub."

"Never mind," said Grub, cocking his pistols; "we've nabbed 'em now—our boat is right in their way."

So he found a minute afterwards, as he stood up, calling upon the outlaws to surrender.

Crash came the pinnace's sharp bow against their bulwarks.

Grub uttered an oath, as he went headlong into the water.

His companions gave another, as the boat, half cut in two, sank under them.

"Fire!" said Tom, at this moment. "Aim low."

The sharp report of half-a-dozen pistols rang out, and the bullets, to the dismay of the officers, came rattling among their legs.

In the confusion, the outlaws pulled swiftly away, their defiant cries mocking the hapless officers, who were plunging in the water.

Grub, in his agony and fright, had clutched Snowball by his woolly hair, the black having laid down in the stern to indulge in a hearty laugh.

Snowball yelled with pain.

But Grub held on.

"Dam wretch!" howled Snowball, "take dat."

This was to Grub, as the black sent his huge fist into that luckless officer's face.

Grub let go instantly, to feel whether his nose was flattened, and the boat shot onwards.

Once under the ledge they were safe; and, concealing their weapons under their seats, they quickly regained the vessel.

In a few minutes the War Cloud, with a spanking breeze, was moving gracefully down the stream.

Scarcely had her prow begun to divide the water ere the young chieftain, who had gone below, hastily ran on deck.

Making straight to Snowball, he said, excitedly—

"Snowball, we must rescue Miss Laura."

"Yes, massa, Snowball do dat."

"Yes, it must be so," Tom said. "Let me go ashore, or I shall be driven mad with thought."

"You not go by yourself?"

"I must, Snowball."

"Den you don't; for if you go, I go to. Haul in dat jib dere, you at de bow! Steady cutter's crew to de side."

The vessel was brought up, and while the boat was being loosened, Snowball went below.

He soon returned, armed with cutlass and pistol; his favourite weapon—the long, deadly African knife—hidden in his breast.

Tom pressed his faithful friend's hand in silent gratitude.

The boatswain's whistle sounded, and the boat fell gently upon the waters.

"Ben," said the young chief, as he passed to the boat, "keep the War Cloud ready to start when I return."

Ben touched his cap, and the young chief and his ebony follower went on the track for Neville Wirely.

CHAPTER XXXI.
PURSUING THE PIRATE.

The Osprey dashed madly through the foaming billows, as though conscious of the momentous chaise; but swift as the gallant vessel divided the foam, it did not prevent the hellish scene from taking place on board the pirate's deck.

The seamen were crowded upon the forecastle, their honest faces expressive of the deep horror that filled their hearts.

Many were the lowly breathed vows of vengeance that passed their lips, and, cutlass and pistol were gripped with more than ordinary determination.

Captain D'Arville, with the officers of the ship, were grouped upon the poop, and when the young officer took the glass from his eye, his handsome face was pale with horror.

"Great heaven!" he said, "they are murdering those defenceless people under the very guns of our ship."

The master-at-arms appeared, and touching his cap, said—

"Sir, let the bow-guns loose at them."

"Impossible; we shall lose time."

A shade of disappointment crossed the sailor's face, as, turning away, he muttered—

"Be it so."

"We'll try and hull the cursed craft, sir, an not touch the wimmen."

Captain D'Arville sighed as he said—

"An almost impossible task, I fear."

"We'll try, yer honour, anyhow."

To the delight of the seamen, the welcome order was passed for them to cast loose the bow guns.

An order which was complied with, with great satisfaction by the gallant seamen.

"Cuss 'em!" growled one grizzled tar, as he rammed home a round shot; "I hopes this will do 'em good."

The captain of the gun took careful elevation as he said, feelingly—

"So do I, Bill—the cursed varmint! But I say."

"What?"

"I wouldn't like to be that 'ere pirate cove."

"No, nor more should I."

"I don't mean 'cose we are arter him, 'xactly."

"What does yer mean, then?"

"Why I mean that 'ere young cove whose father that was killed."

"You're right, he does look awful savage."

Savage was perhaps the most expressive word the honest tar could have used; for the brave boy still stood a model of savage grandeur.

From the depths of his dark eyes there beamed a look of swift and appalling vengeance.

The angry tiger, crouching in his native jungle, could not have formed a more striking or terrible spectacle.

He saw before him the death-stricken face of his sire, and through that film of blood, the swarthy malignant pirate.

Once only he stirred, and this was when the boom of the Osprey's guns filled the air with mimic thunder.

The gallant young captain looked at the sad-hearted boy pityingly, and, addressing the first captain of marines, said—

"By heaven, Maltby, that boy is to be pitied!"

The marine turned with difficulty, and gazing at Peter, said—

"I don't know—I think his foe is."

"Do you—why?"

"Because he will not have long to say his prayers, should that youngster get him by the throat."

"I trust he may. Ha! Look!"

The marine followed the direction of Captain D'Arville's finger, and beheld the pirate ship lurching on her side.

"Your fellows have hulled her,' he remarked.

Captain D'Arville looked through his glass, and said—

"You are mistaken; she has been struck by squall."

So it was.

A mass of white vapoury clouds had suddenly burst; and, whirling down upon the pirate vessel, there came a sudden gust of wind.

Captain D'Arville seized his trumpet.

He knew the danger in which his vessel would be placed should the squall strike her with every sail unfurled.

"Forward there!" he cried; "leave those guns, and stand by to shorten sail."

Much to the disgust of the seamen, who were doing all in their power to disable the black-hulled pirate, they were obliged to leave their guns.

Again the trumpet was placed to his lips, and he asked—

"All ready for'ard?"

"Ay, ay, sir."

The boatswain's shrill whistle was heard; the men pulled with a will, and in a few minutes every inch of canvas was taken in.

But not one moment too soon.

Scarcely had the men been stationed at the tops when, striking the vessel on the larboard side, the squall was upon them, causing the stout masts to quiver, and the loose ends of the ropes to crack like so many whip-thongs.

As suddenly as it came it left them; not a cord —not a spar injured.

"Forewarned is forearmed," said the captain, closing his glass. "Stand by to unfurl."

"Yes," interposed the marine; "but our friends in front do not seem to have escaped so easily."

Captain D'Arville looked towards the pirate vessel, and saw the ship had righted, but many of her black sails were hanging against the masts.

The gear had been snapped by the violence of the gale.

A flush of joy passed over the young midshipman's face at this sight; and, gripping his cutlass, he muttered, fiercely—

"Revenge! miscreant—revenge!"

The poor boy's hopes were seemingly about to be crowned with success, as the gallant ship plunged forward on her dismantled prey.

The order to cease firing had been given, and every heart beat high in anticipation of the terrible revenge they would exact from the crime-stained monsters.

"More sail! more sail!"

Rang out the captain's voice, loud and clear, and his too ready crew obeyed his excited words.

Faster, faster through the blue waters sped the gallant ship.

"Hurrah!"

Another mile and they would be grappling with the foe.

That spontaneous cry of joy was repeated.

"Hurrah! hurrah! hurrah!"

And their noble craft seemed to plunge suddenly forward at the cry.

Sword in hand stood her gallant commander, and his trumpet-like voice rang out—

"Stand by the boarders! Stand by the larboard battery!"

There was a rush of feet as the men sprang to their stations.

Another wild cry as they cast loose their guns.

But ere a ramrod could be inserted in the mouth of one deadly tube, a sudden crash caused every man to stand appalled.

One glance upwards told the tale.

Terrible misfortune!

The mizen-mast had snapped in the centre.

One moment it swayed to and fro, held only by a few strands.

A sudden snapping and they gave way, and the tottering mast, sails—everything went, with a sudden plunge into the sea.

A confused cry of rage and disappointment came from the excited crew.

One moment Captain D'Arville gazed upon the broken stump of the mast; then, stamping upon the deck, he said—

"Let the guns loose! Never mind the mast."

In the excitement of the moment the men were so hurried in levelling the guns, that every ball passed wide of the dark-hulled pirate.

Captain D'Arville bit his lips, yet not a murmur of reproach escaped him.

CHAPTER XXXII.

THE ANSWER TO LAURA'S PRAYER.

THE long deadly tube was pointed full on the clammy face of the miscreant Neville Wirely.

"Move," repeated the brave girl, "but a finger —but a step, and I fire."

The ruffian recoiled.

He saw the deadly determined glitter in the angry girl's eyes, and his craven heart sank within him.

Step by step she forced him back, until the opposite side of the room was reached.

Then her eyes fell upon the portrait, and through the hole where the brooch was painted she beheld the muzzle of a pistol.

Could it be fancy? No.

The eyes of the cavalier moved, and, basilisk-like, followed every movement of the discomfited ruffian.

Laura had no difficulty in recognising those dark flashing orbs as those of Maladine, the strange visitor.

Lowering her pistol, she regarded Neville Wirely with a withering look of scorn.

"Ruffian!" said the noble maiden, and her bosom heaved with indignation as she spoke, "I could shoot you as easily as though you were a beast of prey."

The sound of her musical voice broke the spell which had held him silent, and as his eyes blazed with passion, he said—

"Do so, if you will; but, believe me, all that I have done has been from the unconquerable emotions with which you have inspired me."

"And do you sully the name of love with such conduct?"

Laura looked so superb—so queen-like, that he fell upon his knees and said—

"Laura, hear me! I love you—love you as man never loved human being before! I swear, by the heavens above, I will not harm you! Deign but to listen to my prayer, and I will make you my lawful wife."

A smile of scorn crossed her lovely face as she replied—

"Your wife! Sooner would I beg my bread from door to door than suffer you to support me."

He had crept closer to her as he spoke.

His eyes, tiger-like, watched the little hand which hung by her side.

The hand contained the pistol that had so well served her in her deadly peril.

She noticed not his snake-like approach, and a withering expression of contempt was on her lips. But before she could speak, Wirely gave a cry of rage, and sprang upon her.

With the hilt of his knife he struck her wrist a sharp and heavy blow; and Laura, uttering a cry of pain, let fall the pistol.

With a savage expression, he picked it up; and, grasping her by the sunny flowing tresses, laughed, satirically—

"Ha! ha! ha! my turn now!"

She struggled to release herself from his grasp, but, with devilish ferocity, he clung to her hair.

"Mine!" he yelled, triumphantly, as he dragged her head back and kissed her—"mine, in spite of all!"

Laura's blood curdled in her veins at this sound, and a prayer for mercy escaped her lips.

"Mercy?" he said, brutally. "Now who will aid you in"——

A sepulchral voice, seemingly at his very side, said—

"I will."

Neville Wirely sprang to his feet.

His finger was upon the trigger of the pistol he had taken from Laura, and his left hand clutched the long-bladed knife.

Wildly he glanced around, but nothing was visible.

The ruffian saw not a pair of dark eyes glaring upon him from the painted canvas.

Everything in and around the chamber was quiet; and, with a harsh, grating laugh he muttered—

"It was fancy. Fool that I am to think that it could be anything else."

A gentle rustling sound caused him to start, just as the last words left his lips.

The ruffian turned sharply round and demanded—

"Speak, whoever you are."

But no answer came, and again stooping over Laura, who had swooned, he was about placing the knife and pistol on a chair.

"The wind," he thought, "must have made the noise. I must be growing nervous."

Had he looked at the life-size picture, he would have seen the barrel of a pistol protruding through the breast, and in a line with his head.

Unconscious of Laura's invisible protector, he raised her sweet pale face, and soliloquised—

"I am sorry to have hurt her; but she shall be mine by fair means or foul."

"Liar!" said the same hollow voice that had before alarmed him. "She will never be yours!"

Wirely was thunderstricken, he let Laura's head fall to the ground, and snatching up the pistol, he glared around him in savage dismay.

"This is no fancy," he said; "speak, that I may know where this bullet may find you."

He raised the pistol as he spoke.

A mocking laugh caused him to turn quickly. Then again all became still.

The big drops of fear stood out upon his forehead, and his lips grew dry and hot.

Again came that terribly distinct word, causing him to tremble with unknown fear.

"Fool!" it said; "reserve your bullets for earthly foes. I am proof against mortal hands!"

Wirely trembled violently; but his presence of mind did not for a moment desert him.

He believed not in the supernatural, though the singular interruption would have tried a strong man's nerves.

He knew also the house they were in had many secret modes of entry, and when he had ascertained the direction from whence the voice came, he began to scan the apartment.

A subtle smile overspread his face when he beheld the life-sized picture.

Through the breast he beheld a pistol muzzle levelled at his head.

His peril he knew was imminent.

But a glance at the form of Laura made him desperate.

Raising his pistol swiftly, in line with the picture, he pulled the trigger, saying—

"We'll try a mortal bullet, my invisible friend."

The report of the pistol was followed by a suppressed cry of pain.

Wirely laughed.

"Hit, for a meddling fool," he said, as he heard a heavy fall. "Now for"——

Before he could finish his sentence, Laura awoke, and observing Wirely beside her, she gave a demoniacal look, and cried wildly—

"Tom! Tom! protect me now!"

Her prayer was answered.

For at that moment an appalling crash caused Neville Wirely to look round, and through the shattered window he beheld the lithe form of Midshipman Tom and the black giant about to spring into the chamber.

CHAPTER XXXIII.

OLD BILL TRIES A SHOT.

CAPTAIN D'ARVILLE knew that his men, in their eagerness to maim the pirate, who was rapidly rigging jury-masts to escape from their pertinacious pursuers, had caused them to waste powder and shot.

"Steady, my boys," he said, "steady! Be careful of your aim next time."

An angry word would have evoked deep, but silent curses from the tars; but these words went deep into their hearts, and every man ceased his occupation for a moment, and gave a loud 'hurrah '

"Another!" said the captain of the foretop, "another for the Osprey and her captain! Hip! hip! hurrah!"

The very vessel shook with the cries that came from their throats; and the captain taking off his hat, bowed in acknowledgement.

A bright spot gleamed on his cheeks; and the finely chiselled lips quivered with emotion.

The marine saw it, and said—

"A glorious salute that, D'Arville, one that is better than a few stereotyped words from the Admiralty."

"One I value more," said D'Arville; "for I love my crew, and should not feel happy away from them."

"Would that all could say that who wear an epaulette," half soliloquised the marine.

"It would be better for our navy," said Captain D'Arville; "the accursed system of press-gangs would be extinct. Ha!—by heavens! they are edging away from us!"

"You are right. There they go — curse them!"

The marine shook his fist in the direction of the pirate vessel, which was now slipping quietly away.

"I would give my chance of promotion for the next ten years," said Captain D'Arville, bitterly, "had I but a mainmast rig-gear."

Gun after gun was fired from the disabled Osprey; and when the smoke had blown away, the seamen beheld one of the masts swaying to and fro.

A cry of joy escaped Captain D'Arville, and rushing towards the forecastle, he said—

"Five guineas for the man that brings that mast down!"

An old tar, weather-beaten and grey, looked wistfully at the injured mast and then at the captain.

"Yer honour," he said, "I'd do it without the money! but it ain't stuck low enough."

"Try, you are an excellent gunner."

The old fellow carefully watched his ready messmates load the gun, then glaring at the pirate ship, he uttered an exclamation of rage

Every man looked ahead for an explanation of the old tar's anger.

They found it.

A dozen pirates were seen climbing up the rigging.

Two of the number carried a square piece of sheet-iron to fasten round the wounded spar.

"Now, mates," said one of the men, "give them a dose before they clench that piece of iron."

The old tar's eyes twinkled mischievously as he curtly answered—

"I'll try."

To the slightest shade he levelled the gun; and aiming beside the shot-hole, already visible, he fired.

Every neck was strained forward to watch the effects of the shot, and a murmur of approbation followed.

True to its aim, the missile flew; but the pirate vessel rolling a little to leeward, saved them from the old tar's shot.

As it was, one of the miscreants, who was busily engaged hammering the piece of iron to fit round the mast, was struck by the flying missile.

As clean as though severed by the guillotine, his head was whisked off, and the bloody trunk, bespattering his companions, fell into the sea.

"Well aimed!" said the captain. "You shall have the money."

"I ain't earnt it yet, yer honour."

"You have."

"Axes yer pardon, captain; but you said it was to hit the mast down: and them beggars is splicin' it."

"Minus one," said the marine, with intense satisfaction.

"Had she not rolled," said Captain D'Arville, "you would have done it, so no more scruples."

"May I have another try, your honour?"

"Certainly."

With the same care as before the gun was loaded; but, to the astonishment of all, old Bill depressed the muzzle of his piece.

"What are you up to?"

This was asked by the man who had rammed home the shot.

"I'll tell yer, mate. That last shot was nigh short. We are too far off for the mast."

"What's the use of trying, then?"

"Plenty," said old Bill. "They has a wheel on that ship; and if I don't smash it, I hope the cap'n 'ull stop my grog for a month."

"I'll give you a guinea," said the marine, and he dived for the coin in his pocket—"two, if you do it."

Old Bill grinned; and, taking a careful squint along the gun, fired.

Again the same anxiety was evinced by the

crew of seamen; and before the report had died away, a loud shout arose.

"He's done it!"

"You shall all have double allowance when we capture this fellow; in fact, whether or not. But see; what the devil are they up to?—curse them! Sweeps, as I live!

Captain D'Arville was right.

Red Hand, finding the wheel smashed, and several of his band slain by the broken fragments of wood and iron, ordered out the long sweeps that were kept ready for use.

"We can do no more. They have escaped by one of those unforeseen accidents which will mar the best project."

"Cuss 'em!" growled old Bill. "I didn't 'spect they had them outlandish things, or I'd done a little damage to his mizen, —— 'em!"

"Never mind; fasten the guns, and see what we can rig to supply this confounded mast.

Peter, the fisherman's son, had hitherto stood, with blazing eyes, noting the efforts made by his friends to overtake Red Hand.

But now, judging all was at an end for the

AT THE SEAMAN'S RETREAT.

And while they set up a fresh wheel, the broad-bladed sweeps impelled the vessel swiftly onward.

The pirates worked with a will.

For the miscreant band knew they had but little mercy to expect from the British man-of-war.

The blue-jackets had done all in their power to overtake the foe; and now, when they beheld them moving so swiftly out of range, many a hearty curse came from the sailors' lips.

The Osprey made but little progress through the waters; and her gallant captain, looking at his men, said, with a sigh—

present, he approached Captain D'Arville, and taking off his cap, said—

"Thanks, sir, for what you and your gallant crew have done to overtake my father's murderer; but your good intentions have been frustrated by an unforeseen circumstance. I, sir, cannot stay, but must leave your ship."

The captain laid his hands kindly on the boy's shoulders, saying—

"Leave my ship, my poor boy?"

"Yes, sir, and to-night."

"Sorrow has unnerved you; we are far from land. Such a course would be death."

A bright glow shone upon the boy's handsome face, as he replied—

"To you, sir, it may seem so; but to me, who have a father's cold-blooded murder to avenge, it is different."

Captain D'Arville looked at the poor boy pityingly, and, taking his hand, said—

"Stay with us. A few hours will complete repairs; then we'll track this monster to the furthest corner of the world."

Peter shook his head sorrowfully, and replied—

"Your words are kindly meant, and I thank you; but, ere I know any rest, that miscreant must die."

"What would you do by yourself?"

Peter pondered a moment, and then he answered—

"I would not, as you imagine, attempt to meet the miscreant on his own deck. But hate will find a way more terrible to him than instant death."

"You speak in enigmas."

"It may appear so, sir; but I will render it clearly. I promise, this moment," and he upturned his pale face to heaven as he spoke, "to devote my life to revenge for that pitiless deed. I will be as a shadow to this villain—ever marring his most favourable plots, or else bringing him to situations of deadly peril. And when I have gloated over his misfortune, than shall this hand wipe out my parent's murder."

Captain D'Arville regarded the speaker as one labouring under a wild dream; but that night a report was spread that Peter, the fisherman's son, had disappeared.

The ship was searched, but no trace of him could be found.

The watch were questioned, but none had heard the boy leave the vessel.

But he had left.

Left, to become a terrible unsuspected foe to that pitiless miscreant, Red Hand, the shedder of his father's blood.

Left, to work out his plans in secrecy and silence; ever-near the crime-stained monster, and dooming him to a living torture.

CHAPTER XXXIV.
SNOWBALL PREPARES FOR ACTION.

WHEN Snowball left the War Cloud with his gallant young leader, he seated himself in the stern of the boat, and glancing wistfully at Tom, he began rubbing his knuckles against the gunwale.

Several minutes passed in this manner, until the young chieftain happened to look at his trusty follower.

Seeing him thus employed, he asked—

"What are you doing, Snowball?"

"Me, Massa Tom?"

"Yes."

"Not'ing; only putting a little edge on him knuckles."

"What for, Snowball?"

The African grinningly answered—

"Some debil take away Miss Laura, Massa Tom."

"Too true."

"Well, we find dat somebody."

"I hope so."

"Hope so! By Gar, I say yes; and when we catch him—he! he!"

"You seem merry under the circumstances."

The young sailor's voice was slightly tinged with bitterness as he spoke.

Snowball noticed it, and looking affectionately at his chief, he replied, sadly—

"I no merry, Massa Tom, 'cos of lily lady being taken away."

Tom saw he had hurt his faithful follower's feelings, and extending his hand kindly, he grasped the other's huge fist, saying—

"Forgive me, most faithful friend, for I meant not to wound your feelings."

Snowball kissed the small white hand with as much reverence as ever courtier kissed that of a mighty monarch, and said—

"I know it, massa, and I feel you no tink me forget dear lily lady. Shall I tell you what dis child larf at?"

"Yes, Snowball."

"I say Massa Tom, when I tink how somebody's face get dis bunch of fives right on him nose!"

"That somebody, I presume, is Miss Laura's abductor."

"It am 'xactly de person I'm sharpening my fingers for beating."

Had Neville Wirely seen the white teeth and dusky gleaming eyes of the speaker, he would have thought so too.

The keel of the boat grated on the shore as Snowball finished speaking, and wrapping their boat cloaks around them, Tom and his lieutenant stepped ashore.

Tom turned to the boat's crew, and said—

"Remain there for a few hours; if we do not return, rejoin the ship, and look out for our signal."

"Ay, ay, sir—we understand; and we hope you will return with the lady."

"Thanks; that hope finds an echo in my heart."

The raw damp fog of early morn hung like a pall over the dingy warehouses and silent docks, as they emerged into the narrow streets that lined the water side.

Snowball gave a slight shiver, and said—

"Golly, it am cold, anyhow."

"It is," said Tom; "and quiet."

"Dat am true, and so am anoder ting."

"What is that?"

"Why dat dere will be a row presently."

"How?"

"When we find de place where Miss Laura am gone—den somebody's windows get broke."

"When we find it, Snowball."

"We shall, Massa Tom; but who de debil am dis coming?"

The outlaw and his companion drew back and watched a man pass them swiftly, and turn towards the water side.

"What am him up to?" said Snowball. "Let's foller him."

Before Tom could answer they heard the cry of an owl come from the direction of the river.

Both paused and listened attentively.

The cry was repeated,

Snowball grinned and said—

"What de debil up? Dat am de signal."

"It is," said Tom; "and one we must obey. Let us return."

"Golly, yes. Come on."

And with the swiftness of a hound suddenly loosened from the leash, the African started back.

Tom followed, and when they reached the boat they beheld the man who had passed them in close conversation with the rowers.

"This is our captain," was uttered by one of the outlaws as Tom and his companion came up.

The stranger turned, and eyeing Tom's noble form with a look of admiration, said, respectfully—

"You, sir, are the commander of the Phœbe?"

Tom's heart leapt within him as he replied—

"I am."

The stranger was a man of evident caution, for he said—

"Have you lost any friend, or one dear to you."

"I have."

"Male or female?"

"The latter."

"Old?"

"No; young and lovely."

The stranger handed the young leader a tablet, saying—

"This is for you."

Tom read aloud these words:—

"I am shut up in a room, and in the power of a ruffian."

A single scarlet spot glowed upon Tom's temple as he read these words; but, cooling his passion, he asked the stranger—

"Know you this place?"

"I do."

"And will lead us there?"

"I will."

Snowball's face exhibited the most intense joy, and rubbing his hands together, he said—

"Come on, den; somebody's nose hab a smeller yet."

The stranger was a splendid runner; but in the journey to the house, he found himself several times out-distanced by his eager companions.

"You run well," he remarked to Tom and his follower, as they slackened their speed to keep pace with him "I may say, as well as any man I ever competed with."

Tom smilingly answered—

"But never from a foe."

The stranger eyed his gallant bearing, and said—

"That requires no telling."

"While we are regaining our breath, will you answer me a question?"

"Willingly, sir."

"How came you by that tablet?"

The stranger replied with a quiet smile.

"Can you not tell me?" asked Tom.

"Not fully, sir."

"Why?"

"It is forbidden, sir."

Tom bit his lip, and said—

"Saw you the writer?"

"I did not, sir."

The young sailor gazed curiously at his strange guide. He could not understand his answer.

The stranger saw he was amazed, and said—

"My words surprise you, sir."

"They do."

"You would be more so, were I to tell you my vocation."

"Perhaps not. I feel interested."

"*I am an agent of the police!*"

"The debbil!" muttered Snowball. "Den I'd like to scalp yer, anyhow."

Possibly the stranger understood the ominous twinkle in Snowball's eyes, for he said—

"Be under no apprehensions, gentlemen. Your secret is safe."

"Our sec——"

"That the Phœbe is known by another name."

Snowball unconsciously began to finger his knife; but whatever intentions he had formed towards the stranger, they were dispelled by the latter stopping before a grand-looking house.

Their strange guide pointed to the window above, and said—

"In that chamber you will find the lady. Farewell."

Tom and Snowball turned quickly, but to their astonishment, their companion had gone.

"Queer fellow dat, Massa Tom."

"He is. But how are we to get in that room?"

Snowball took a careful survey of the place, and, sighting a pipe that conveyed the rain from the roof of the house to the ground, remarked—

"Easy enuff, up dis ting."

Tom drew his sword, and, placing it between his set teeth, began to ascend the waterspout.

Snowball was close behind, the long African knife held in the same manner as Tom's sword.

When about midway between the ground and the window a scream was heard.

Tom's heart leaped within him, for it was Laura's voice.

Snowball heard it, and recognised it, and through his clenched teeth he muttered—

"Go on, Massa Tom. By Gar you be too late!"

The noble-hearted boy needed no stimulant to urge him forward.

He would have faced a thousand weapons to rescue the object of his adoration.

The rough iron tore the skin from his hands, but he heeded it not.

With set teeth and glaring eyes he neared the window.

Another cry rang out.

The young mid's eyes blazed like burning coals.

Up! up! hand over hand, until the window sill is reached.

He waited not to try whether the window was fastened; but, drawing himself up by his hands, Tom hurled his lady against the window frame.

One crash, and a thousand fragments of wood and glass fell inwards.

Then Tom, with naked sword and gleaming eyes, followed, and a cry like a wounded panther escaped him when he saw the terrible scene within that chamber.

Neville Wirely had sprung up to face the intruder; but he shrank back appalled at the deadly glance in the young sailor's eyes.

Upon the ground lay Laura.

"Dog!" cried Tom, rushing upon Wirely, "die!"

His bright sword described a swift circle in the air, but, ere it could drink the ruffian's blood, the gallant boy stayed his arm.

He lowered the point of his sabre; and gazing upon the shrinking ruffian, said—

"I will not sully this bright blade with your foul blood. Snowball!"

The African sprang through the window.

"Here, Massa Tom."

CHAPTER XXXV.

SNOWBALL OBTAINS A SCALP.

"Hurl that dog from the room."

As he spoke, he stooped over his fair mistress, and raising her head, pressed his lips to her cold forehead.

He neither saw nor heard the dreadful tragedy that took place within a few yards of him, his whole attention being rivetted upon the hapless girl whose head was pillowed on his breast.

Snowball glared for a moment upon Wirely, and the brutal scoundrel crouched like a whipped spaniel from the gleam of those dusky orbs.

"Hab yer now, anyhow," said Snowball, showing his white teeth; "by Gar!" you soon know it."

The African was testing the edge of his knife.

Wirely shuddered visibly; but the purpose for which Snowball was trying his knife never for one moment entered his mind.

Seemingly satisfied with its keenness, Snowball suddenly stretched out his long arm.

Wirely tried to avoid him.

No use; for Snowball had him by the crown of his head, his dark fingers entwining in the unfortunate but brutal wretch's hair.

"Come dis way," said Snowball. "I teach you to touch Miss Laura, by Gar!"

The horrible agony of that moment to Wirely was indescribable.

Snowball had him suspended out of the window by the hair of his head, and Wirely yelled in his agony.

But his cries were mocked by Snowball; who, with a savage grin said—

"You tink Snowball and Massa Tom not come in."

"Mercy! mercy!"

"Den you do as you like with Miss Laura—eh?"

Snowball gave the agonised wretch a shake at every question.

"Mercy! Oh, spare me!"

"I spare you—hab your dam scalp!"

Snowball meant it, and, in spite of the terrible agony he endured, Wirely became all but voiceless.

The African's savage intention completely appalled him.

Twice the keen blade glittered before his eyes; then he felt its sharp point describing a circle upon the crown of his head.

One despairing cry of more than mortal anguish broke from his lips.

The next moment he was whirling through the air, his scalp in the African's dusky hand.

Snowball gave a loud war-whoop, as he looked at the sickening trophy.

That cry was answered by a shriek from below, for Wirely was impaled on the railings, hanging by one leg—the iron spike having passed through his thigh.

Snowball turned from the shattered window and returned to his chief.

Laura had by this time recovered; and, with her soft, white rounded arms entwined round her lover's neck, was telling him of the strange scenes she had gone through in the house where they were.

She extended her hand to Snowball, and the African passed the scalp into his left hand.

He did not wish Laura to see the sickening sight.

Tom shuddered as a mirror that stood opposite revealed the trophy that Snowball held.

The blood-stained knife was thrust in his belt, and Laura, pointing to it, said—

"Good heavens! you have not mur——"

"No, Miss Laura, him only punish a little; him no take you again."

It seemed not, for Neville Wirely was at that moment bleeding to death where he had fallen.

The young chieftain led Laura to a seat.

Then motioning Snowball to follow him, he held a short conversation with Laura, then went towards the secret panel through which the strange woman had passed to Laura on their first interview.

"Where you go, Massa Tom?" was Snowball's question, as he followed his leader across the room.

"I go to make myself acquainted with the mysteries of this house, Snowball."

He dragged Wirely to the open window, and thrust him through.

"I stick close to you, Massa Tom, 'case anybody want scalping. By Gar, dey soon get it."

They stood opposite the picture.

"Is this the spot?" asked Tom.

"A little to your left," said Laura, "you will find the panel; but pray be careful!"

"Him safe, Miss Laura; by Gar, dis chile not see one hair ob him head touched, if any try it," he added, a savage gleam lighting up his eyes; "it won't do 'em good."

Tom knew it, and when backed by his trusty associate, he felt no fear, however great the danger.

The panel was soon slid back, and Tom entered the aperture, thinking and hoping to come in contact with the kindly stranger who, at so fortuitous a moment had come to the relief of Laura.

Snowball tried to do likewise; but the opening was too small to admit his colossal shoulders.

Tom searched about, and examined the flooring, and every inch of the wall; but could find no outlet.

"What had become of the mystic woman?"

"Snowball," he called out.

"Yes, Massa Tom."

"Fetch a candle."

A light was handed through the aperture, and Tom found that he stood in a recess in the wall large enough to afford standing room for two men.

No mystic stranger was there.

Had she been spirited away, or was there some outlet which, in spite of Tom's close research, he had failed to discover.

Tom at length emerged from the room, and was greeted by Snowball with this question—

"Found de poor ting, Massa Tom?"

"No, Snowball, not any trace of the woman herself; but that she has been there is clear, as the name of Maladine is scratched on the wall of the recess.

Snowball rubbed his head reflectively, and at length said—

"I have a notion, Massa Tom."

"What is it?"

"Dat me go into de room where Miss Laura first saw this mystic woman out ob de window."

"I was thinking the same. Come on."

"Wait a minit, we must not leabe missey widout something to make noise."

"True; here Laura, take this pistol and sit with your finger on the trigger. On the slightest alarm, fire; we shall be near you."

"'Xactly—too near for somebody, if dey come."

The outlaws divested themselves of their boots and as silently as two shadows, they crept the room.

They had only time to pass through the panel, when a terrific noise at the door caused them both to run to the window.

"De debil!" muttered Snowball, cocking his pistols. "Dare am de officers; dey hab found dat fellow hanging like a plucked crow on de railings."

"We shall have to fight our way through the officers," said Tom."

"Dat am true," replied Snowball. "But we shall do it."

They went back to the room, where Laura sat awaiting their return.

She hailed the arrival of Tom and his follower with an exclamation of joy.

Then, noticing the sad expression on her lover's face, she said—

"You are sad. What is the matter?"

He drew her to his heart, and, kissing her cheek, said—

"Nothing of import, Laura."

"Your brow is not sad for nothing."

"It will pass away. But come, the bloodhounds are at the door, we must break through them."

He would have taken the pistol from Laura; but the brave girl retained it, saying—

"This danger has been incurred for me; I will keep the weapon; it may serve you."

They left the room, Snowball taking the lead, and went to the door.

The heavy bolts were slowly drawn back, and, with a yell, the officers rushed in.

They came to a sudden halt, and looked with blank dismay at the calm, silent, bold, and defiant-looking pair.

"The out"——

"This was all the officer could utter; for Snowball, lunging out his massive fist, struck him on the chest, and hurled him, doubled up like a ball, down the steps.

The fellow's companions stood dismayed, and made no attempt to advance.

Without the least quiver in his voice, the young sailor pointed with his sword to the open street, remarking—

"It appears you know us. So much the better—perhaps it will prevent a useless effusion of blood. You see that path; that is the spot we wish to reach, and I would advise you to let us pass.

The path alluded to by Tom was the open street.

The officers heard him quietly; then one more bold than the rest said—

"Suppose we don't, what then?"

Tom looked the speaker steadily in the face.

"We shall cut our way through you."

The officers held a whispered conversation When it was concluded, the same man who had before spoken said—

"We knows the reward as is offered for you; and, as we are six to two, we mean to try and get it."

"Have you done?"

"No; there is another thing yet."

"Speak it; and quickly, for we are in a hurry."

"We wants to know which of you threw this gentleman out of window?"

He pointed to the inanimate form of Neville Wirely as he spoke.

Snowball gave a peculiar grin; and, holding up the reeking scalp, answered—

"Dis chile done dat. Look, dis am him scalp."

The officers recoiled with horror.

CHAPTER XXXVI.
THE WAR CLOUD IN A FIX.

BEFORE the officers' horror subsided, Tom, placing Laura behind him, advanced to the threshold.

Snowball was by his side. The officers made a forward movement.

In an instant the outlaws' blades were levelled in line with the officers' throats.

Snowball, giving one wild whoop, wound his left arm around Laura, and, cutting right and left, made his way to the pavement.

This sudden action had astonished Tom as much as it did the officers; but, when he saw Snowball clear a passage through the pack, his own good sword was not idle.

At every whirl of the flashing blades a foe fell to the earth.

Four had bitten the dust in as many seconds; and the remaining two, thinking a couple of fiends had suddenly been let loose among them, dropped their bludgeons, and fled.

Snowball uttered a defiant yell, and would have chased the flying officers, but his leader restrained him.

"Snowball," he said, "are you mad? We shall have the whole pack, horse and foot, upon us. Away to the boat."

There was a muttering about "having their scalps and sheathing his blade," from Snowball as he followed his chieftain.

They were not long in reaching London-bridge: and, to Tom's surprise, as they were about to cross, one of his men issued from a recess.

"This way, sir," said the outlaw; "we have crossed the river."

Tom thanked him for his foresight, and followed down the steps.

Ten minutes' pulling brought them to the War Cloud, and for a short time their troubles seemed over.

A very short time, for scarcely had their swift little vessel gained the centre of the river, than a boat from a ship of war, carrying the royal pennant, hove-to across their bows.

"Heave-to!" said a voice from the ship; "we must overhaul you."

"We are only a coasting trader," answered Tom.

He thought by this ruse to avoid the search, for the brave youth knew that any attempt at open resistance would be followed by the destruction of the War Cloud.

As an addition to the ship's frowning battery, the guns of Tilbury Fort could be brought to bear upon them.

"Can't help it," replied the same voice; "we have orders to search all vessels that leave the Thames."

"It's the first time I have been stopped."

"Very likely; but this may not be the last. The admiral knows best, and if you lose anything by it, to him you must make complaint."

"May I ask the cause of this strange proceeding?"

"You may, and obtain a very explicit answer.

The fact is, we have received information that the outlaw, Midshipman Tom, is on the river, and any vessel we find with arms on board, our orders are to seize."

"Thanks for the information, I will heave to."

Then to Snowball he whispered—

"We shall escape."

"How de debbil? All the guns am on deck."

"Drop them quietly overboard."

"Oh de"——

"It cannot be helped; we shall soon get a fresh battery."

"And de small arms?"

"Hide them behind the galley."

The galley had a false locker capable of hiding all the swords, pistols, and muskets, wherever it might be found necessary to do so.

The numerous crew soon executed their leader's orders, and from the time the boat from the ship had pulled alongside, not only had the guns been all sent to the bottom of the Thames, but powder and shot as well.

They had to lower the guns by the strong ropes attached to the yardarm.

And when they were quietly lowered into the water, the ropes were cut.

The first lieutenant came on board, and made a rigid search all over the War Cloud.

He was baffled by the outlaws, who had rapidly changed their clothes, and looked as dirty as possible.

Tom had a huge pair of grizzly whiskers and a wig, which gave him the appearance of a man at least forty.

Snowball ran about as the cook, much to the royal officer's disgust, with a fryingpan full of fresh plaice.

He had given them a frizzle over the fire in rank oil, and while Tom was conversing with the officer, Snowball kept passing and repassing, wafting the nasty fume under the first lieutenant's nose.

The officer was in high dudgeon at having to get up so early to overhaul any outward bound vessel, and said all sorts of disagreeable things.

The smell of Snowball's plaice made his aristocratic stomach heave again, and he turned sharply to Tom, saying, with vast self-importance—

"Why the devil don't you teach your cook better manners?'

"What has he done?" inquired Tom, from behind his profuse whiskers.

THE GALLANT MID TOM WAVED HIS HAND IN DEFIANCE TO THE HORSEMEN.

"Done—demme! Why he has twice or thrice passed the odour of his filthy messes under my nose!"

"Sambo!" said Tom, in a gruff lingo.

"Yes, massa?" said the supposed Sambo. "Me come."

He did come; frying-pan, fish, and its accompanying smell, and, to make the matter worse, he was stirring them up all the time with a wooden spoon.

As close as possible without touching the horrified officer, Snowball whisked past, sending up such a disgusting odour that the lieutenant, in an awful passion, held his nose, and stepped back a few paces.

"You must not pass this gentleman with those fish," said Tom, as gravely as the knowledge of Snowball's waggery would let him.

"No, massa."

Snowball gave an extra lurch.

"Go away," said the officer; "you will make me sick as death, curse you! I wish I had you aboard my ship; I'd give you a dozen."

The back of Snowball's head was towards the officer when he said this.

Could he have seen the way in which the African stuck out his tongue, he would have felt his dignity awfully hurt.

"You have a large crew," observed the lieutenant, when Snowball had taken the objectionable fish away.

Tom was ready for him.

"Yes," he said, "they are not all mine. There is the crew of a foundered schooner among them."

"Oh, I see."

"Do you!" thought Tom; "you are clever."

"Who is that lady in the cabin?"

Tom began to feel his fingers closing, but he kept his temper, and replied—

"My niece."

"She is pretty.'

"Rather."

"Timid?"

"No."

"H'm!"

The first luff began to admire his figure with evident satisfaction.

"Ah!" he repeated. "H'm!"

"Nice girl!"

"Yes."

"Going to be"——

"Married?"

"Going to be what?"

"Can't say."

"H'm! Good morning."

The first luff went to his boat.

"Good morning," returned Tom.

Twenty grinning faces might be seen turned to the royal boat.

Twenty thumbs were placed against a like number of noses.

And the fingers were working backwards and forwards as the owners "took sights" at the first luff of his most gracious majesty's ship of war.

An hour later the gallant vessel was standing out to sea, her prow turned towards the western coast.

CHAPTER XXXVII.

A GOOD SHOT.

THE unlooked-for episode on the Thames had deprived the young outlaw of his guns, and, for a time, rendered his daring raids fruitless.

It was impossible to obtain guns in England, for that he knew would expose his weakness.

A swift vessel was sent to America, and to the extreme satisfaction of Tom and his band, the following message was brought back—

"A fast cutter, the Nelly, will bring you the battery and shot required. You will know her, she will have but four men on board. Be ready to give her any assistance she may require, for, I am given to understand, a couple of cruisers are on the scent.   F. L."

Mixed with the joy at the prospect of the coming armament of the War Cloud, the outlaw could not conceal his uneasiness at the chance of the schooner being captured by cruisers.

It was true two of the king's vessels had been waiting for Tom for some time past, both evidently bent upon capturing him and his ship.

Tom had watched them day after day manoeuvring about, and his fiery temper chafed at the thought of his vessel being powerless to give them battle.

He was safe while ashore, for the sunken reefs prevented any vessel approaching his haunt.

Time hung heavily with the band.

And great was Tom's joy when Snowball one day rushed in, saying—

"De cutter wid de guns, Massa Tom!"

There was a shout of satisfaction expressed.

But it was instantly checked, by Snowball adding—

"But de cruisers are arter de little vessel hang 'em!"

The band rapidly armed themselves; and, with Tom at their head, rushed to the mouth of the cave.

There the young leader and his band beheld one of the most exciting scenes they had ever witnessed.

Snowball's words were too true. The schooner had, seemingly, but a poor chance of escape.

Let us paint to the reader's mind the scene as it presented itself to the outlaws.

The sun was rising from the sea, throwing its fiery spears far across the sparkling waves, lighting up every object upon which they lit.

They were standing in towards the mouth of the inlet under top-gallant sails, with the wind free on the larboard quarter.

The vessels were half-a-mile apart, their course converging to a point.

The first was a cutter hugging the land, and endeavouring to make the entrance to the inlet.

Her broad mainsail was flung to the wind like a great white wing, and she was sweeping across the water like a gull flying before a storm.

She had been discovered by the enemy only a few minutes before, when they tacked together and pressed after her, making sail as they went.

Fifteen minutes more of the obscurity of the morning and the adventurous cutter would have got into the river, and under the guns of the cave unseen, or seen too late to be cut off.

It was a beautiful sight to behold the three vessels in motion.

The cutter was a mile in shore of the cruisers, and about three miles westward from the mouth of the inlet, being, when at first seen, just stealing round the point.

The cruisers stood on for about ten minutes after tacking in the same converging lines, when the corvette signalled the ship, which immediately luffed, and bore up four points eastward, while the former kept her first course.

The object had in view by this manœuvre of the ship was plainly evident to the outlaws, who, from the rocks upon which they were perched, were watching, with peculiar interest, the pursuing and pursued—was to intercept her, for they had quickly discovered that a direct chase would be useless, as the cutter showed himself to be a first-class sailer.

So the ship sailed straight towards the inlet's mouth, hoping to reach it in advance of the cutter, while the corvette kept on to capture her if she should attempt to run.

Accompany us now on board the little cutter, kind reader, and see how the miraculous escape was effected.

"We shall be tuk, darned if we ain't, cap'n," coolly remarked a tall, ungainly youth of eighteen, who, with a dipper fastened to a ten-foot handle, was beating up water from the sea, and throwing it upon the mainsail of the cutter to swell the threads of the canvas, and make it better hold the wind. As he spoke he paused in his work, and leaned upon his long dipper-handle, and, shutting one eye, took a deliberate survey of the cruisers.

"Not so long as two timbers of the Nelly hold together, Siah," responded the captain, who grasped the helm, and with one eye ahead and the other watching the enemy, directed the course of the little vessel towards the shelter he sought.

"If we'd only had another twenty minutes afore sun-up, we'd a got in. But the day ain't agoing to stop for any man, and I don't expect it tu. All we must do is to keep the Nelly out of the hands of the cruisers, now they've got their eyes on us."

"Wet the sails, Siah; keep wettin' 'em."

"I guess they'd kind o' guess what we've got on board, captain," said Siah, as he cast a shower of spray over the mainsail. "They seem to take all fired trouble to catch us. See how Nelly jumps. The way she tosses the water with her bows! I won't have to wet her jibs—she does that herself."

"If we don't get into the river, and them chaps overhaul us, what is to be done?" asked Job Twistle.

"It won't do to let them capture them six big guns, and two barrels of gunpowder, and ton o' shot that we've got, that's a fact, Siah," spoke very decidedly Captain Felix Podger, who owned or commanded the Nelly.

Shrewd, bold, and cool, the captain saw that by running only in the night, and hugging the shore, he could probably get into the river undiscovered, especially as the cruisers used to stand off from the shore at night a mile or two for an offing, and run in again at sunrise.

The agent, through whom the munition was sent, felt that a small coasting vessel, with so watchful a captain as Podger, would be quite as likely to get into the river as a large one, if not more so, and gave him the commission.

For the sum of three hundred dollars, the captain had bargained to take the munitions to the outlaws, and also bound himself that if there was any danger of being captured, to scuttle the cutter, and sink her.

The cannons were battery thirty-two's, six in number, and were laid athwart ship, side by side upon deck.

The shot were piled forward, and in the forecastle was stowed the powder in casks, and securely protected under canvas; tarpaulins also covered the guns.

"If we can only stand on ten minutes more, Siah," said he to his mate, "I don't fear them two cruisers a stick."

"One of them, you see, has luffed to try and cut us off. If 'twarn't for this plaguy heavy iron we've got in her, I'd show the enemy how to make a keel cut blue water through."

Captain Podger became silent for a few moments, as though he were figuring to himself the tactics he would pass through if he had such a chance. Then he continued—

"But we must get on, Job."

Job was a ragged old man, and looked like a weather-beaten fisherman, who comprised all his crew, and was now engaged tending the main-sheets, the slack of which he held in his iron fist.

"He's got in safely, cap'n," answered Job Twistle, gruffly; "and get three hundred dollars or sink the ship."

"That's a fact, Mr. Twistle," responded the American skipper, with emphasis.

And, shifting his tobacco from his larboard to his starboard cheek, he glanced under the main-boom to see how the fort and shore lay, and then hove his eyes to the windward, and took a deliberate inspection of the enemy.

"Give a small pull aft on the main-sheet, Mr. Twistle; Siah, haul aft the jib a bit, the Britisher is smoking his pipe," added the skipper, quietly, as he saw a jet of smoke belch forth from the bow of the corvette.

He had hardly got the words out of his mouth when the boom of a gun reached his ears, and almost simultaneously a shot passed whizzing over their heads.

"I don't stan' that one," said Siah, in a determined tone, which singularly contrasted with his awkward, rustic exterior; "give leave, cap'n, and I'll give 'em a shot back, darn me if I don't!"

"Your gun won't scare 'em, Siah. Ease off the main-sheet, Job. Be ready to dodge, for I guess there's another one o' them junks of wood this way. They ain't no pilot, or they wouldn't keep so near a porpoise rock ledge."

Cool and steady, the skipper stood at his post, and directed the course of his little craft.

All at once he gave a loud "hurrah!"

The corvette had struck upon a rock, barely below the water, under full sail, known as "Porpoise Ledge," and everything was taken aback, while her main-royal mast went over the side.

"That's for not taking a pilot on such a coast,"

said the skipper dryly, while his keen little eyes fairly glistened with pleasure.

But he made no further demonstrations of joy.

So, after taking a second glance at the vessel, and seeing that matters aboard of her were in too much confusion for them to trouble themselves further about him, he now gave his whole attention to the ship, which was about a mile from him, in a straight line, and about equal distance from the entry of the river.

Upon seeing the accident that had happened to her consort, the ship bore down a little, and hoisted a signal.

It was responded to on board the corvette, when the ship resumed her course.

"The corvette, I suppose, says she don't want any aid, so the ship is left at liberty to interrupt us," said the skipper. "It looks, too, as if she would be likely to get the entrance as soon as the Nelly, and then, I guess, it's all up with us. But I don't give up so long as a timber hangs to her, and I have a limb to hold on to the tiller by! But, what in natur' are you doing there, Siah?"

Well might the captain ask the question.

The ambitious young man has brought from the forecastle a keg of powder, and knocked the head in with a handspike, and was now tying about half a peck of it up in a handkerchief, which he had taken from his neck.

"Doin'! I'm going to give 'em a gun, darned if I ain't. If these 'ere guns have to go to Davy Jones's locker I'll have one fire out of 'em first, I guess, replied Siah.

As Siah spoke he threw down a movable section of the bulwarks amidships, leaving an open space to the sea before the muzzles of the enormous cannon that lay across the deck.

He then took up his huge cartridge, and thrusting it into the muzzle of one of them, began to ram it down with a handspike.

"What on 'arth is the crittur at," cried the captain.

Siah made no reply; but having rammed the cartridge home, he rolled a thirty-two pound shot towards it, and giving it a lift, shoved it into the muzzle after the powder.

"Now for primin' her, and then if I don't give 'em a Fourth of July salute, they never heard one."

As he spoke he poured a handful of powder into the vent, and then jumping to the caboose, he lighted a fire-knot, and, waving it to keep it bright, approached the gun.

Stop, Siah, stop!" shouted the skipper, at the top of his voice. "You'll blow the Nelly to t'other world at once, if you fire that 'are gun on board of her.

"I don't calculate I'll be tuk pris'ner by the Britishers, cap'n, and be put in Dartmoor, I guess. I don't mean to fire jist yet, but take a good chance for a good aim, and then give them saltpetre."

"It'll shake every bone out of the Nelly," said the captain in alarm.

As he spoke the ship fired a shot across her bows.

"That means heave-to, Job," said the skipper. "Siah, put out the fire-knot."

"I mean to, by-'em-by, cap'n. Wait till I get a good shot at 'em! I ain't afeard of hurting the Nelly a bit. You jist yaw her a morsel, and bring the muzzle of my artillery-piece right agin the ship, and if I don't show them how a Yankee can speak, I don't want to see t'other side of the old river agin."

A second report came from the ship, and the shot passed within ten feet of the captain's head, and made a rent a fathom long in his mainsail, and the shot caused his peak halyards to part, and let the peak of his mainsail down.

This caused the Nelly to fall off a point or two. and while the skipper unflinching, and with a quiet look, was trying to bring her to the wind again, Siah, taking advantage of a moment as she swung, in which his loaded gun bore upon the ship, instantly applied the torch to the vent.

The roar, the flame, and the concussion were terrible.

The little vessel reeled under the recoil of the vast gun, till the waves poured in under her bows and stern.

The skipper and Job were laid flat on the deck, while Siah found himself hanging by the heels on the lee-shrouds.

CHAPTER XXXVIII.
THE DETECTIVE.

FOR a few moments after the shot was fired the captain of the Nelly thought his little vessel would go down, she wallowed and plunged so,

But she soon steadied herself, though with her decks flooded and her jibboom blown away, and with her windlass unshipped.

"I guess if they get that shot 't'll settle 'em," said Siah, as he dropped, feet first, off the rigging into which he had been blown, upon deck, and tried to look through the smoke.

"You ought to be scuttled, you 'tarnal critter?" cried the captain, enraged. "You like to have sunk her, darn ye."

"Don't swear, cap'n. I want to see if the ship got it."

Got it, you fool! I guess you'll get it, if ever I see shore again."

As the smoke rolled slowly away, the ship was discovered no longer standing down, but knocking about at the mercy of the wind and waves; her foremast gone by the board, and dragged over her sides with all its yards and sails.

The shot had cut off the mast within two feet of the deck.

Siah was perfectly confounded, but manifested no surprise while the captain and Job set up a loud hurrah of triumph.

"Why! What's the matter? Why don't you hallo?" said the captain, taking breath.

"Coz it ain't nothin' morn'n I meant to do," replied Siah, with inimitable *sangfroid*. "I ain't surprised, if you be, cap'n."

The skipper had no need to ask the expectant outlaws to cheer, for, as the little cutter glided towards them, they rushed down to the beach, and set up a loud and oft-repeated hurrah.

The corvette lay upon the rock until the next tide, and, before sunset, both vessels steered away towards Portsmouth, to repair damages.

They made tracks only in time, for the War Cloud glided out into deep water, her ports open, and Midshipman Tom on her deck.

* * * * * *

Lord Mountsteven sat long over his breakfast. The food was untouched, for the nobleman's mind was full of thought.

An hour passed, and he moved not until he was disturbed from his reverie by a servant knocking at the door.

Twice the knocking was repeated before the word was given to enter.

"Enter."

The domestic entered, and, bowing to his master, said—

"My lord, a person desires to speak with you."

"A stranger?"

"Yes, my lord."

"Did he mention his business?"

"He did not, but wished me to state that it was of the utmost importance."

"Show him up."

The domestic retired, and soon re-appeared, ushering in a tall, dark-looking man, garbed as a fisherman.

The stranger bowed to Lord Mountsteven, and remained until the servant had retired before he spoke.

His lordship forestalled him by saying—

"You desired to see me on matters of importance?"

"Such is my desire. Are you alone?"

"Quite."

"Good. Then we will begin."

"Be seated," said Lord Mountsteven.

"Thanks, my lord. But do you not remember me?"

Lord Mountsteven looked hard at the speaker and shook his head.

The stranger smiled, and removing a pair of false whiskers, said—

"Do you know me?"

Lord Mountsteven started with surprise, and replied—

"I do; you are—are—a"——

"An agent of the police."

"Yes. Does your visit refer to the matter I placed in your hands?"

"It does.'

"Have you any hope?"

"Very great; and if my suspicions are correct the greatest caution will be necessary for the sake of—of"——

"Lady Mountsteven," said his lordship, catching and finishing the sentence for the stranger.

"Exactly, my lord; we must understand each other clearly."

"It is easy to do so. What do you wish to know?"

"A confirmation merely of my suspicions."

"Which are?"

The detective lowered his voice, and said—

"That you do not wish Lady Mountsteven's share in this dark work to appear?"

"Great heavens, no! Not for worlds!"

"Such has been my predominating thought. Now, my lord, prepare yourself for a surprise."

The wretched noble gave a ghastly smile, and uttered—

"Fear not for the effect of anything you have to say. My heart is too well schooled in misery to feel anything acutely."

"It is the reverse, my lord; my news is good —shall I say joyful?"

Lord Mountsteven clasped his emaciated hands together, and gazed in mute surprise at the speaker.

"Joyful in one sense, but in another most perplexing."

"Speak, speak."

Lord Mountsteven's cheeks were flushed, his tone of voice excited, as he uttered these words—

"I will. *Both mother and child are alive!*"

Lord Mountsteven had to suppress a scream at the overwhelming intelligence.

Then he sprang from his chair and wrung the the communicant's hands, exclaiming—

"Can this—is this true?"

"It is."

"Thank Heaven for its mercies!"

With these words his lordship's head drooped upon his breast, and a low sob escaped his lips.

"You are moved, by lord."

"I am," replied Lord Mountsteven, "and deeply, for this sudden lifting of a weight from my heart."

"Yet," began again the secret agent, "you"——

"I know what you would say—that my boy is left to the world, and his gentle mother discarded."

"Yet you were not to blame. You knew not, when your espoused Lady Mountsteven, that your former wife was alive."

"True. But the world. What will be their opinion?'

"That which is guided by the law."

"I know—I know. Terrible thought! That both must be set aside for his first wife's claim!"

"True, my lord. To prevent this, may I venture to make a suggestion?"

"Do anything to help me out of this embarrassing and strange position."

"Up to the present time," said the stranger, "neither the wronged lady nor her boy know of the discovery. I have guarded against such an unwise contingency."

"Thanks for that information. Your suggestion?"

"Simply not to enlighten them. For the present it is known only to ourselves."

"And you have gained this accurate knowledge without arousing their suspicion?"

"I have not even seen them?"

"You astonish me."

"It is easy to understand. When you saw me in London, and entrusted this delicate affair to me, I pondered long over it before I took a step."

"A wise precaution."

"So I found it. This was the effect of profoundly keeping the secret. Firstly, I knew I would do no good in London; therefore I came down here, and, by degrees obtained information. Here is the result."

He threw a roll of papers upon the table as he spoke, and continued—

"They will explain matters better than I can."

Lord Mountsteven clutched the papers.

"May I ask how you obtained these proofs?"

"Partly by threats, partly be persuasion. I became master of them; but I have every reason to believe the writer is dead."

"Dead!"

"Yes; for he disappeared suddenly some time since, and has not been heard of."

"Strange!"

"It is, very. But better for us, perhaps, for they were evidently intended for a purpose of his own."

"His?"

"Yes; it was a man—a fellow—part outlaw, part fisherman, but suddenly turned respectable."

"Do I know him?"

"You should; his dwelling is situate within a few rods of the castle."

"His name?"

"Philip Wilson."

"I remember; a sullen-looking fellow, who, from some unknown reason, Lady Mountsteven took under her protection."

The stranger smiled, when Mountsteven said—

"Unknown reason."

"Now, my lord," said the stranger, rising. "I must say farewell for a short time."

"I should like to know before you leave me how you come to fix upon this man, as a party in that dark mystery."

"You shall, my lord."

"Since my stay here I have made myself acquainted with the antecedents of the inhabitants. Philip Wilson's sudden prosperity aroused my suspicion. I was right, for in his desk I found these papers,"

"Thanks for your information. When am I to expect your return?"

"To-morrow night."

Lord Mountsteven bowed his visitor out, and then seating himself, he was about to read the documents.

Scarcely had he out the string that bound them than a distant shriek caused him to thrust them into his breast and rush into the corridor.

There was nothing visible from the door, and the amazed nobleman walked to the end of the long passage.

"There's nothing—no one."

He roused several domestics, but no one had heard the shriek which had so alarmed him.

Lord Mountsteven's cheek paled, and, with a grave countenance, he retired to his room.

More mystery.

The packet of papers had disappeared, but by whose hands the confounded nobleman knew not.

Everthing else remained on the table, just as he had left it.

But vain was his search for these precious records of crime.

He said nothing of his loss, but waited for the coming of the detective.

CHAPTER XXXIX.
MIDSHIPMAN TOM HEARS STRANGE WORDS.

IF the reader has not by this time discovered that gallant Tom, the outlawed midshipman, is the lost child alluded to by Lord Mountsteven in his conversation with the detective, all we can say is, the reader's penetration must be at fault.

Shortly after the interview at the castle, our hero was pacing to and fro on the soft golden sands in front of his stronghold.

The youth's heart filled with pride, as he gazed at the fairy-like rigging of his beautiful ship.

"Had I a fleet of vessels like that," he enthusiastically exclaimed, "and men as lion-hearted as my followers are to man them, I could conquer the world."

"A bold speech," said a shrill voice, "but in keeping with the spirit of the race from which you came."

Tom turned sharply, and beheld the bent form of Sybil, the gipsy fortune-teller. She was standing on the rocky ridge beyond the cave, her hands crossed upon the top of her stick.

The young outlaw looked upon the old woman with kindlier feelings than the fishermen who dwelt upon the coast, and thinking her words were but the emotions of a crazy brain, he said—

"Well, Sybil, do you want me?"

"I want you not," she replied. "It is destiny that causes me to seek you."

"My destiny, Sybil."

"Sneer not," she uttered in a mysterious manner. "What is written is written in the book of fate; and you, like all others, must obey its dictates."

"Oh, it is!" he said smilingly; "perhaps you will let me read a page of that wondrous book?"

"Your eyes," she replied, sharply, "are thick with worldly thoughts, to you it is closed."

"Oh, indeed; then how can I know its contents?"

"Not by scoffing, but by bright words, boy. Are you listening to me?"

"I am," said Tom, "and with tolerable patience, I think."

"But are you listening," she said, querulously, "listening with intent to hear—with less of the scoffing devil in your eyes?"

"I am listening."

"Woman!" exclaimed Tom, "what words are these?"

"Truths, boy—truths. I, and I alone know all you would wish to know."

"Ha! can this be true?"

"It is; a scion of a noble house and yet an outcast tyrant—yet a hunted felon—such you are, and such you will be, until"——

She paused to note the effect her words had upon the young sailor.

They had struck home. The kind solemn tone of her voice, the strange glare of her eyes, all told

LORD MOUNTSTEVEN GAZED IN MUTE SURPRISE AT THE SPEAKER.

"Tom Wilson," she began solemnly, "is that your name?"

Midshipman Tom looked up, and his reddening cheeks showed the gipsy's words had not been heard without their producing some effect.

"Tom Wilson," she went on, "is"——

"Silence, woman!" said the high spirited youth; "that is not my name! Think you that one drop of Wilson's plebeian blood courses through my veins?"

"I know your blood is free from such a taint, and know the purer stock from which you sprung."

upon her listener, who, with pallid face, clenched hands and dilated nostrils, stood drinking in with a strange fascination the woman's words.

"Until," she resumed, "you have courage to know who and what you are."

Sad, but stern was the youth's voice as he inquired—

"Is that some foolish jargon of your craft or do you speak from strangely acquired knowledge?"

She laughed a scornful mocking laugh, and then replied—

"Strangely acquired knowledge! Know you,

headstrong boy, that there are secrets known to my race, that from the remaining world are hidden?"

"The proof."

"You shall have it if you have courage to face the ordeal."

"Courage!" he said proudly; "in the smoke of the battle my hand and heart have never failed me—will they do so now?"

"I know not," said the hag, slowly. "I have seen strong men unnerved by the horror of my incantations."

"Mine will not fail me. But what shall I learn by seeking to pry into the book of futurity?"

"That," she answered, "that you would give the great wealth of your cave to know—your name, your birth, your parentage."

"And can you tell me them?"

"I can."

"When, and in what place?"

"At the Witches' Hollow at midnight. Have you courage to come?"

"I have."

"Then come and learn all! Farewell till midnight."

"Farewell!"

Tom looked up as he heard this word; but the Sybil was gone.

Pondering deeply over the words he had just heard, the young outlaw re-entered the cave; and when he had gone, Snowball's woolly head appeared from behind a large stone.

"Golly!" muttered the African. "I jist come in time to hear dat little bit."

He scrambled up to the piece of projecting rock, occupied by the gipsy during her conversation with Tom.

Standing on his toes, the black giant took a survey of the rocky road; but the gipsy had gone out of sight.

"Clean gone," muttered Snowball. "Dam de debil! she up to no good! Dis chile not be far out ob de way at the middle-night when Massa Tom go; anyhow, 'cos somebody want to lose dere hair."

So saying, Snowball came down from his perch and joined Tom in the cave.

*   *   *   *   *   *

The nobleman waited anxiously for the detective's return; but the days rolled on, and still no sign of the agent's reappearance.

His patient employer was anxious at first, for he became alarmed, and finding he could not curb his impatience he caused inquiries to be set on foot in every quarter as the last hope; but beyond the fact that the agent had been seen walking by the sea when he left Mountsteven Castle, nothing else could be gleaned.

And as the time went onwards on its dreary march, Lord Mountsteven became pale and more wretched every day.

The fearful mystery of that disappearance haunted him and added another pang to his sufferings.

He fully believed that no mortal hands had ever taken those papers; and the disappearance of the secret agent was a problem which time alone could solve.

Leaving him a prey to these reflections, let us visit the boudoir of the guilty Lady Mountsteven.

She was seated upon a chair; her dark eyes fixed upon a man who stood before her.

It was Pierre, a Frenchman, who had entered her service in France—a bold, sinister, crafty wretch, whose head and hands were ever at his mistress' bidding.

"You understand me, Pierre?" she said, "quite sure you understand me?"

The Frenchman bowed as he replied—

"I do, madam, perfectly. He dies to-night."

"And the other meddling fool?"

"He has paid for his folly."

"It is well. Leave me, and come when your task is done."

Pierre's eyes dwelt for a moment upon her voluptuous form, and bowing he left the room.

"Another link," he muttered.

And his dark eyes shone with triumph as he spoke—

"Another bond to make the servant master, and the mistress slave."

An hour later he stealthily left the castle and and went towards a cluster of small cottages which stood between the castle and the outlaw's cave.

The habitation was tenanted by a set of wreckers —men, who for the paltry gain of even a few pieces of a ship, would not hesitate to lure its crew to destruction.

Fit instruments for the subtle spirit who now sought their aid.

Pierre knocked at one of the doors.

It was soon opened by a scowling, half-savage-looking fellow, who remarked gruffly, as his visitor passed inside—

"You have come at last, then?"

"I have," said Pierre; "and brought you the reward for what you have done."

He laid a bag of gold upon the table as he spoke.

The ruffianly wrecker's eyes sparkled at its melodious chink, and clutching it greedily he placed it in a cupboard.

"I have more work for you," said the wily Frenchman, eyeing the wrecker, cautiously, "work that will be better paid for than the last."

"Have you?"

"I have; but you will require assistance."

"There is plenty to be got. What is it you require this time?"

The Frenchman rubbed his hands softly together, and pondered for a few moments before he answered.

CHAPTER XL.

THE WRECKERS AND THE FRENCHMAN.

"You know that young outlaw chief, Midshipman Tom?" queried the Frenchman.

"Yes, curse him."

"Curse him? Why, my friend, do you say that so angrily?"

"Say it!" said the wrecker. "Have I not reason to say it?"

"You know best, friend. Some injury he has done you, is it?"

"Injury! If you call depriving a man of his living an injury, he has done that; but he has done more than that."

"More than that?"

"Yes, more than that, for he has threatened to hang both my mates and myself if we do any more business."

"Business?"

"Well, call it what you like, it comes to the same end. I mean our getting a livelihood by picking up things from wrecked ships. Moreover, he has sworn to hang the first of us that sets a beacon on the cliff."

"A false light to guide ships, eh?

"Yes."

The subtle Frenchman had found a worthy instrument for his work—one whom he could depend upon, for, apart from the reward, his hate would b gratified by the death of the young outlaw.

"It is wrong," said the wily Frenchman, acknowledging the wrecker's words, "and his removal would benefit you."

"It would, and I would strike a good blow to effect it."

"You would?"

"Yes."

"Listen," began the Frenchman; "I will make you an offer. Five times the amount of your last reward will I give you if you rid the earth of your enemy."

The wrecker looked at Pierre before he said—

"I have a question to ask."

"What is it, friend?"

"Why do you take so much interest in his death?"

The Frenchman shrugged his shoulders, and replied—

"Personally, I take no interest; it is the interest of those whom I serve."

The wrecker smiled grimly.

"Well, it's no business of mine to inquire," said he. "When do you wish the attempt to be made?"

"As soon as possible. The sooner it is over, the more quickly will you obtain the reward."

"On the third night from this, then, the money will be mine. By that time he dies."

"Agreed."

Pierre soon after left the hut, and walked slowly towards the castle, his sinister face expressive of deep thought.

"His death," he muttered, "will form another link in my chain. Still I must be cautious. There is one thing yet requires finding out, and that is," he added, musing, "the cause of my mistress's dislike to the boy."

He slowly resumed his walk, his soul busy with some dark meditations.

Passion-inspired words fell from his lips, and his blue eyes sparkled in apparent triumph as he said aloud—

"To-night shall solve that mystery—to-night!"

He entered the castle's massive portals, and ascended a private staircase that led to his mistress' boudoir.

Here the wily villain placed his eye against a small hole in the wainscot, as he had often done before.

Suddenly he clenched his hands together, and muttered—

"The black box! Ha! there it lies then! In there is all I wish to know!"

* * * * * *

When Pierre left the wrecker's hut, the latter threw his cloak over his head, and went to a dirty-looking beer-house.

This house was known by the sign of the Mariner's Arms, and was the resort of every desperate fellow in the village.

There Swearing Jack, as he was called, found several of his boon companions.

The gang of wreckers, awed by the young outlaw's terrible menace, had not dared of late to pursue their pitiless calling; for they knew the character of the noble-hearted youth and the fidelity of the men who served him, and fear had kept them in check.

In return, his threats had inspired them with a most deadly hate against him; and there was not a man amongst them who—the opportunity offering of doing so without fear of certain detection—would not have plunged a knife into his heart.

Still, but for the tempting overtures of Pierre, in all probability they would have never thought of adopting the bold scheme that Swearing Jack had that night come to propose to them.

"Mates," he said, as he seated himself, "you don't look in high feather."

"High feather," returned one, "how—uttering a fearful oath—as, indeed, most of the wreckers did when they had, as they felt, occasion to give strong vent to their feelings—how should we, when we have not done a stroke of business so long?"

"You have no money, I suppose you mean?"

"Money, no! there is not as much as would jingle on a tombstone among us."

Swearing Jack laughed, and threw a guinea upon the table.

"Look there," he exultingly said, "do you see that?"

"Yes," was the gruff reply, "we are not blind."

"Would you like some like it?" asked Jack.

An uproar of voices bawled out—

"Rather!"

"Well, lads, I can put you on for a hundred of 'em a piece."

"You are making fools of us, Jack," said one.

"Stow that, Jack!" said another. Curse you! if you are in luck, you need not come to provoke us poor devils who have been out of it so long."

Jack replied to the last speaker by saying—

"I don't come to provoke you; but I repeat I can put you on for a hundred of them each."

"How? I'm your man, Jack, for half that sum."

"And I," said another; "and up to anything for it."

"Out with it?" they all shouted. "Let's hear the game!"

Jack put the coin in his pocket; and, jingling some more, he said—

"You know the outlaw, Tom Wilson?"

A volley of curses followed this question.

"He's the game," said Jack.

There was a silence. The bait was tempting, but the danger great.

Jack noticed the change in their demeanour, and said, with a sneer—

"What! seven of you afraid of a youngster like that?"

"Youngster!" said the former speaker, "we are not afraid of him, but his cursed gang."

"They are not always with him."

"No, but that brute of a dog and the nigger are never far away."

"That makes but two, then."

"Two! Why, hang it, that black devil would smash up a dozen of us."

"Aha! suppose I manage to get him by himself? What say you then?"

Several dirty hands touched the hilts of their knives.

Jack understood this suggestive action.

"Remain here until I return, then. Here's a guinea to spend in drink."

He left his accomplices deep in the consumption of the drink, and returned in a couple of hours.

"Good news, my bullies!" he said, gleefully; "we shall have the cub in our power to-night."

"How? Tell us how you managed it."

"That's soon done, my bullies. He goes at midnight to meet old Sybil, the fortune-teller, and goes alone to the hollow."

"Good!" said a black-muzzled ruffian; "to-night, when he is settled, we will hang out the false lights on the cliff."

"You shall, my bullies, you shall; and trade will flourish again as it did before that whelp deserted from the navy."

"I will get the lanterns ready," one began; but he was stopped by another saying—

"Don't be in a hurry, mate, in case it does not turn out all right."

The last speaker was sneered at as a croaking fool, and a fresh bowl of grog was call'd in, to drink success to the revival of the old trade.

CHAPTER XLI.
HOW THE WRECKERS SUCCEEDED.

It was near midnight when the young sailor with a heavy cloak drawn about him, left the cave to keep his appointment.

As a matter of precaution, his sabre hung at his hip, and in his belt were a brace of richly-mounted, hair-trigger pistols.

Ten minutes later, and Snowball emerged from the cave, followed by the mastiff.

Like the young outlaw, Snowball was wrapped in a large cloak, and well armed.

With Indian cunning, he tracked Tom's footsteps, and just before midnight he found himself in the Witches' Hollow.

Snowball paused, and looked around suddenly.

"Where de debil him gone to? P'raps me find it."

The night was murky, and lit only by a few pale stars, and while Snowball paused, looking around the black dog gave a loud growl.

Snowball felt for his cutlass.

"Dat not him," said Snowball, addressing himself to the dog. "You nebber growl at Massa Tom. S'pose I see who it am."

The negro laid flat on the ground, and listened attentively. In a few seconds he could hear the stealthy footsteps of two men coming towards him.

Snowball drew back into the shadow of a large tree, and overheard the conversation.

"Gone to the lone hut are they? Well, there could not be a better place for that job," said one.

"No," answered the other, "not at all bad; but I say"——

"What?"

"It is a lucky thing for us we face him alone."

"Rather."

They passed the spot were Snowball was standing.

He rolled up his sleeves with a very savage expression about his large dusky eyes.

"Well, I'm dam!" he growled, "you have suffink shortly."

It seemed so, for Snowball had laid aside his cloak, sabre, and pistols, and placing them by the trunk of the tree, he bared his scalping-knife, and went in search of the speakers.

The mastiff lay down quietly upon the cloak, as though confident that his sable friend was quite equal to the task he had undertaken.

Like a panther, so noiseless and cautious, Snowball followed on the trail, his long knife clasped in his right hand, his left hand shaded over his eyes, to aid his piercing the darkness.

"I know one ob dem," he thought; "it am a rascal ob a wrecker. By gum, he lose him scalp, anyhow, if I catch him."

The wreckers were still laughing and talking about the peril Tom was in, and close upon them came Snowball.

Nearer and nearer.

Then, giving a yell such as he had given when

at the head of his tribe, Snowball pounced upon them.

One blow of his fist sent one staggering to earth; the second he caught by the hair of the head, and throwing him backward, quietly remarked—

"Hab you now, by gum, you 'retch!"

The captured one gave a loud howl of terror, and tried to break from the African's grasp; the other as quickly as possible took to flight.

Snowball, though pretty well engaged with the fellow he had by the hair, soon saw his defeated friend making tracks.

A shrill whistle quickly brought the dog by his side. Snowball pointed in the direction the fugitive had gone, saying—

"After him, boy! fetch him back!"

The dog gave a short bark, and scampered away.

A moment after Snowball heard a loud howl of terror.

Snowball grinned tremendously, for he knew the dog had pinned the runaway, probably by the leg.

"You fust," he said, forcing his captive on his knees. "Fust you scalp; den de oder."

The wretch howled for mercy, as Snowball flourished his knife.

"Yes, I will gib you lots ob dat—lots ob mercy. At lone hut, eh? I go dere directly I hab your scalp, and take somebody else."

"Mercy! mercy! Do not kill me!" cried the fellow.

"Hold yer noise; gib it up quietly."

He placed the unfortunate wretch's head between his knees, and was about to whip off the scalp, when a loud cry, followed by a pistol shot, was heard.

"At it, 'ave 'em!"

Then giving the wrecker a blow on the head that felled him, he rushed off in the direction of the pistol shot.

He knew the way well. It was from the lone hut, he felt sure, that the pistol was fired.

The young chieftain, when he had reached the Witches' Hollow, found Sybil waiting for him.

"You are punctual," said the gipsy.

"I am. Now for your revelation."

Sybil glanced at him furtively, saying—

"Not here; let's go to the lone hut."

Tom inclined his head, and desired the old woman to—

"Lead on."

Like an evil spirit, the gipsy hobbled on before m, her tongue busy with strange mutterings.

Reaching the hut, she motioned him to enter. Tom did so. The hag closed the door.

"You would know your fate?" said she.

"I would know what you have to tell," was the answer.

"It is soon told. Thomas Wilson, your last hour is come!"

"Ha! is it for this you have lured me hither?"

She reeled upon a chair, and screeched—

"No; but your foes are here."

The door opened as she spoke, and Jack rushed in, followed by his six companions.

Tom did not hesitate, but threw aside his cloak and drew his sabre.

"Cowards!"

Jack, who had taken the lead of the party, made a fierce blow at him, saying—

"That will wipe out what I owe you!"

The brave fellow caught the other's blade upon his own, and replied—

"Fool! Do you measure swords with me?"

Jack's reply was a fierce lunge. This Tom parried, and setting his teeth said—

"Here's at you, then."

The conflict was but short, for the wrecker's blade was forced from his hand, and he found himself at the mercy of his foe.

The point of Tom's glittering steel was at his throat, and in another second he would have been pinned to the wall.

His companions, who had great faith in the prowess and skill of their leader, had been willing he should try his skill with the young outlaw; but when they saw the danger he was in, they rushed forward and assailed his antagonist.

Thus was Tom compelled to take his weapon from Jack's throat to defend himself.

The wrecker picked up his sword and joined in the combat.

Though Tom was perfectly hemmed in on every side, the gallant young hero's courage did not fail him; and placing his back against the wall, he fought resolutely and like a lion.

Severely wounded, two of his assailants had fallen; and Tom, who was growing weak from the wondrous swordsmanship displayed in this dreadful encounter, drew a pistol and fired.

The shot lodged in the shoulder of one of the wreckers, thus putting three of them *hors de combat*.

But, even yet, four to one. Tom's strength began to fail him.

He was bleeding severely, too, from a wound in the shoulder. Yet his face blanched not, although he felt that in one minute his life would be lost.

While parrying a fierce lunge and returning another blow, his failing strength was renewed by the distant sound of well-known cries—the war-whoop of Snowball and the bark of his faithful mastiff. Tom's strength revived. He, with desperate resolution, kept back his cowardly foes.

A fierce rush at the door, and Snowball, fo lowed by his dog, sprang in.

To seize the nearest to him by the neck, was bu the work of a moment for the dog. Snowball at the same time floored one of the wreckers by a back-handed blow of his giant fist; then placing himself beside his leader, he shouted at the top of his voice—

"Come on, yer debbils! come on!"

But they did not see exactly the force of Snowball's invitation, and dodging behind him they made their escape through the open door.

The huge mastiff went in pursuit, his white teeth gleaming in a manner that was suggestive of somebody's legs being attacked.

CHAPTER XLII.

SNOWBALL IN TROUBLE.

AMONG the strange friendships our hero formed during his eventful career, perhaps none was so true as that which existed between him and Herbert Beale, a young officer of the king's navy.

Captain Beale and Tom had met in a strange manner. The former had been sent to capture the gallant outlaw, and while in quest of the War Cloud, he had fallen in with Derrick's black-hulled vessel.

It was madness for the little sloop and her few men to attempt to cope with the horde of pirates and their large ship.

Herbert Beale was a Briton, so he thought it quite possible to do battle successfully with the villainous gang.

So he bore up, and opened his small battery against Red Hand's double tiers of heavy guns; and the result was that his Majesty's ship, the Saucy Jane, would have gone to the bottom but for the opportune arrival of another vessel.

A ship smaller than Red Hand's, but larger than the sloop; and this welcome vessel was the War Cloud.

Between them Red Hand was compelled to sheer off; and Herbert Beale, so far from attempting to capture or fight the outlaw, swore an eternal friendship with Tom.

"We are friends," he said, as they stood on the War Cloud's deck, "for as long as life does last!"

"Remember your commission," said Tom; "That will be "—

"Forfeited you would say. Well, let it be so. If the government does not acknowledge your bravery and good heart, I will."

They parted, and it was many months before the Saucy Jane came to anchor near the coast.

When she did so the gig was manned and Herbert was rowed ashore.

Leaving the gig and her crew at a remote spot from the outlaw's cave, he walked quickly along the sands, his object being to again clasp the gallant young outlaw by the hand.

Herbert had not forgotten his promise nor the terrible conflict they had both engaged in; the very remembrance of it strengthened the brotherly love that had existed between them.

He was well known to the sentinels who guarded the cave and the great wealth it contained, and he passed them easily.

At the entrance he saw Snowball standing with folded arms and moody brow, gazing at the sharp lines of the Saucy Jane.

At the African's feet the mastiff was crouching and Herbert, when he sighted the dusky hero, stood for a moment mute with admiration.

The negro's colossal form—his broad chest and well-knit limbs—the dog's massive head and strong limbs formed such a picture of savage strength and beauty that Herbert paused and muttered—

"Splendid, by Jove!"

The dog raised his head at the young captain's approach, and gave a loud growl, for strange enough the dog had a marked dislike for anyone wearing the royal uniform.

Snowball heard the dog and looked, and his sad-looking face broke into a quiet smile, as he extended his hand saying—

"Cap'n Beale, me nebber tink to see you again."

"I suppose not, Snowball; but I am worth two dead ones yet."

"Yes, Cap'n Beale, you am; and berry glad am Snowball to see yer like dis."

"Thanks, Snowball. Now, how is your chief? I suppose he his in the cave? I see the pretty little War Cloud at anchor."

The African ground his teeth savagely, as he answered—

"No, Cap'n Beale, he was here. I wish I knew how him is."

The heavy sigh that followed told Herbert something was amiss with the young leader, and acting upon his first thought, he asked—

"He's taken then?"

Snowball drew himself up proudly, as he replied to the captain's inquiry—

"If Massa Tom's taken, cap'n, neider Snowball, de dog, or one of de band be here now."

"Pardon me, Snowball," said the young officer. He saw that his question had wounded Snowball's feelings. "I mean't not to give offence. Full well I know that yourself and his trusty band would not let him linger long in captivity."

"No, Massa Beale," said Snowball, all traces of displeasure having left him. "You say right; but it am worse dan dat."

"Worse than being captured?"

Snowball's white teeth gnashed, as he said—

"Yes, worse—a great deal worse—den dat, cap'n; Tom am gone, and none of us know not where to look after him."

"That is strange. Have you no clue?"

"None; not a leetle."

"When was he here last?"

"De night afore last," said Snowball, "he come here; but dat was arter de dam wreckers try to kill him at the lone hut."

"The villains!"

"Dey is, cap'n; but by Gar!" Snowball looked unusually fierce as he said it, "dey get something for dere leetle trying."

Herbert asked the African for the details of the midnight attack on the lone hut."

"WE ARE ONLY A TRADER," TOM ANSWERED.

Snowball told him, as far as the reader knows. "Arter I come in," said he, in continuation, "de rascals run, but, by Gar, dis dog war soon arter dem, and ketches one ob de debils by the leg."

"Noble fellow!" said the captain, patting the dog's head. "He held him, did he not, Snowball!"

The mastiff permitted Herbert to stroke his head; he seemed to know the young officer was a friend.

"Hold him!" replied Snowball, his eyes dancing with delight. "Golly, yes, he did hold him till I come up, den him let him go, and go arter de oders. By golly, dey get suffink!"

Herbert saw, by Snowball's manner, that the wreckers had received a wholesome lesson; and, wishing to find the precise time at which his friend was last seen, remarked—

"You returned to the cave after that, I suppose?"

"Yes, cap'n, and he sleep till de sun had gon' eber so high. Den he hoist sail on de War Cloud, and overhaul a Frenchman."

"What, La Fleur?"

"Yes, cap'n, dat am de one; and, arter he takes what he wants out ob her, he comes to de cave, der it get near dark, and Massa Tom put him cloak on and go out."

"Have you on idea which path he took?"

"Yes, he go toward de castle; and since dat time me nebber see him."

"The dog did not go with him?"

"A leetle way, Cap'n Beale; but Massa Tom send him back agin."

Herbert mused for several minutes, then asked—

"Have you any idea of the object that led him to leave the cave?"

"I hab. But I no like to tell any ob de crew, 'cause dey might talk ob it, and Miss Laura get to hear."

"Ha! But you need not fear me, Snowball."

"No, cap'n. Wal, den, I tink he go to see de dark-eyed lady at de castle."

"Is Miss Laura here."

"Yes, cap'n. Why do you ask."

"Because," said Herbert, "Tom has plighted his faith to that young girl, and he is too honourable to clandestinely see another."

"You tink so?"

"I am sure of it, Snowball."

"Den I am 'feerd something happen to him."

"Does Miss Laura know of his absence."

"Yes, and been crying all day."

"Poor creature"——

Snowball interrupted Herbert by suddenly placing his hand upon his shoulder and saying—

"Cap'n Beale."

"Well, Snowball?"

"Do you tink it all right at de castle?"

"All right? I scarce understand you."

"I mean, suppose dey see Massa Tom dere, tink dey would gib him ober to de officers?"

"No, I think not; I am sure not."

"Den him not taken?"

"Well, no. If such was the case, it would be well known all over the fleet."

"Dat am true. Den, Cap'n Beale, Massa Tom keeping away. I no make out what you tink!"

"I almost dread to think. To me the matter is shrouded in mystery. But I have a plan, I think, whereby I may discover whether he has come in contact with persons belonging to the castle."

"You hab?"

"Yes, To-night I will visit them, and ascertain whether he has been seen by the lady."

"And den you come back here?"

"I will, immediately after. Hollo! what's that?"

One of the outlaws espied Snowball, and handing him a note, said—

"We found this between here and the castle; it looks as if it were meant for the chief."

Snowball handed a letter to Captain Herbert, who read—

"A friend wishes to speak with you upon matters of the most vital importance—one who can reveal the secret of your birth. Come alone."

Herbert put the paper in his breast, saying—

"You were right, Snowball; he has gone to the castle to keep this appointment; but stay, there was neither time nor place mentioned."

He opened the paper again, saying—

"Yes, here is a postscript."

"Be at the Willow Glen, by the castle's base, at midnight."

"Dat was yesterday," said Snowball, "dat de time he go, and not come back."

"To night shall unravel this mystery," said Herbert. "I will demand what has become of your chief."

The tears rose to Snowball's eyes, as he pressed the captain s hands, saying—

"If you find him, Cap'n Herbert, you hab nearly a hundred good friends who will fight for you while dey hab life."

Herbert soon after left the vicinity of the cave, and walked towards his boat.

———

CHAPTER XLIII.

PIERRE PLOTS AGAINST MIDSHIPMAN TOM.

PIERRE remained at his post of observation until his mistress had locked the black box and quitted the room.

Then, with stealthy, cat-like steps, he left the private way, and passing quickly down the corridor, entered the chamber.

There was a leer of triumph as he stood for a moment contemplating the depository of a secret which would so materially aid his plans, for the oily scoundrel expected to bring the haughty beauty to his feet, humbly, and suing for him to preserve her secret.

The crafty plotter knew not the fierce panther-like nature of the lady whom he served, or he would not perhaps have soared so high in the flights of his fancy.

Had he known that the faithless woman had twice imbued her hands in human blood, he would have been more been cautious, and less impatient of success.

His first movement when he found himself in front of the black box was to peer cautiously around, to ascertain if there was anyone in the chamber.

No, he was alone, as rubbing his hands softly together, he stood and apostrophized the box.

"*Diable cario meo!* how your great black eyes did shine when you lock dis box, but you did not know that your very faithful Pierre had a key that open every lock. No, no, not you; and your great black lids hold all inside, that shall make Pierre master here—yes, master."

He placed a long instrument in the lock when he ceased speaking, and began gently to probe the wards.

Taking it out he looked at the rust marks on the bright end of the steel, and muttered—

"You take number three key, my fine fellow, then, for the purpose."

Drawing a bunch of keys from his pocket, he selected one, and applied it to the lock.

For a few turns it resisted the skeleton key, so

Pierre drew it out and keenly regarded the slender, tongue-like projection at the end.

"It fit all right," he said, "but me mark again de key; there must be something else beside."

He carefully examined the box, and his face lighted up with joy when he saw a small ebony knob below the lock.

"Got you," he chuckled, "a spring as well."

Such was the case, for when he applied the skeleton key and pressed the knob, the box flew open.

Pierre clutched the papers he so much coveted, and carefully closing the box, placed them in his pocket, retired to his own room, chuckling with renewed glee.

With his sinister face bent over the written evidence of the lady's crime, and the writer's surmises, he became so absorbed that he did not hear a summons at the door.

The knock was repeated, this time louder than before.

Pierre started, and thrusting the papers into an open drawer, hastily closed and locked it.

Then schooling his passion-marked features to their usual coolness, he gave the word for the person outside to enter.

It was a page belonging to the castle.

"There is a person," the boy said, "in the hall that desires to see you."

"What can he want at this late hour, Joseph?"

"I do not know, but he said his business was important?"

"What sort of person?"

"From his dress, at least what little I can see of it, I should think he was a fisherman."

Pierre could not repress an involuntary start as he thought—

"What! so soon!"

Then to the page he added—

"Show him up here, there's a very good boy."

A few minutes after he returned, bringing a man Pierre well knew.

It was Jack, the wrecker, and when the boy had closed the door, Pierre said—

"Well, my good friend, is that little business managed?"

"No," was the gruff reply, as the wrecker threw his heavy hat upon the table, and disclosed his cheek, bound with white plaster.

"No," repeated the Frenchman, and you wounded?"

"No—and I am wounded."

"Has he escaped?"

"Yes, curse him! but not before that black giant and the dog had knocked over four of us."

The Frenchman lifted up his head in astonishment, exclaiming—

"He must be a fearful devil, eh, Master Jack?"

The wrecker made no reply, save by glaring upon the speaker in a savage manner.

Pierre saw the look, and said softly—

"Do not look so savage. We will have him yet, and you the money."

"Not for all the money in this place will we tackle him again."

"Yes, yes, my friend; but in a different way. Sit down and make yourself comfortable. Here is some wine. I will be back soon."

He opened a bottle of wine before the wrecker, and giving one furtive glance at the drawer to see if it was locked, he left the room.

To Lady Mounsteven's boudoir the rascally plotter went; but to his annoyance, he found she had retired for the night.

Knowing that her bed-chamber was far remote from Mountsteven's, he went there and knocked softly at the door.

The baroness was in bed, but not asleep, and in an angry tone she demanded—

"Who's there?"

"It is I—Pierre," he whispered, putting his mouth to the key-hole.

"Well."

"I have news for you, madame."

"What is it?"

"Ah, madame, I cannot speak; the walls they say have ears sometimes."

"Wait a few minutes then, if you must speak now."

"If you please, madame, now."

The baroness threw a dressing-gown over her regal figure, and turning up the lamp, admitted her confidant.

Pierre gazed in mute admiration at the outlines of her splendid form, while the loose wrapper tended to render her even more imposing and stately.

"Your communication, Pierre—speak!"

The Frenchman, recalled to himself by her haughty words, replied—

"Madame, the boy lives."

Lady Mountsteven started.

"What," said she, "were they afraid to undertake the affair?"

"No, madame; but he fought like a young lion,—killed four and wounded the remainder."

Lady Mountsteven tapped the floor impatiently with her slippered foot.

"Pierre."

"Madame."

"What is to be done?" You have a subtle brain—exercise it."

"I, madame? You do me so much honour—may I speak?"

"Yes."

"Then I advise, madame, that we bring him here."

"To the castle?"

"Yes, madame."

She reflected for a few moments, then nodded her head in the affirmative.

"Then," said Pierre, "the thing is easy. Your maid can write?"

"Ha! I see."

"Yes; and that will bring him."

"Then"——

"Madame will please leave the rest to me."

"Leave me now, Pierre. I will think over your plans."

The Frenchman bowed low, and was about to leave the room, but Lady Mountsteven called him back.

"Pierre," she said, "enter into no plan until you see me to-morrow morning."

"Then shall I not bespeak a little assistance?"

"Perhaps it will be as well, Pierre."

"And order them to "——

"Stay; I have a plan."

Pierre became all attention.

"Should the ruse," she said, "succeed, he must not be—be killed outside the castle."

"No, madame; that would bring a suspicion."

"I would have a strong party near the spot. You will be near, ready to gag and bear him to a dungeon below the castle. The rest you understand."

"I do—most excellent plan. Down there it would be easy—— He must die without food some day."

"Exactly. To-morrow, at ten, attend me."

Pierre again bowed, and left the chamber.

When he returned to his room he found the wrecker pacing impatiently to and fro.

He looked savagely at Pierre, and asked—

"What's the move now?"

"You are impatient, my friend."

"Impatient, yes; so would you be if you had as many cuts and gashes upon that lean body of yours as I have."

"Never mind; to-morrow night you shall have your revenge."

"My what?"

"Your revenge, my good friend."

"Look here, Mounseer Peer, or whatever your name is, do you take me for a fool?"

Rubbing his hands, as usually he did when his best strategy was called into requisition, he answered—

"No—no—no. Why do you ask?"

"Why? I will tell you—because I've had enough of meddling with that fire-eating young whelp."

"You say in this country that there are more ways of killing a dog than by hanging him."

"And what has that to do with this affair?"

"Plenty. Be patient. Sit down, and I will tell you."

The wrecker seated himself.

"To-morrow," began the Frenchman—"to-morrow night I shall want six of you."

"I'll be hanged if you get us!"

"Yes—yes, my friend. A little more patience."

"Go on."

"You'll have no more fighting, nor anything like the first affair."

"Do you think to take him without?" asked the wrecker.

"Yes, certainly I do. You'll see a woman wil be the best this time."

"A woman!"

"Yes, my friend—young and pretty. There will be an appointment. You and your men will be there."

"No. I will not "——

"Wait—wait one little minute now. The place where the meet will be—under a cliff. You see now?"

"No; I don't see 'now.'"

"I explain. One man will be on the cliff. There will be plenty of big stones."

"Ah! I begin "——

"Yes. One drop on his head, the others run out, tie his arms, and "——

"I'll knife him."

"No—no, my friend. Not there."

"What, do you think "——

"A little more patience. When he is tied, you take him to a dungeon, and do what you like. There nobody can find out. I think that will put an end to the fellow—eh, my friend?"

The wrecker's eyes glared savagely.

"Yes," he said, with grim ferocity, "that plan will do. I will be there."

"And some of your men?"

"If I can persuade any to come. They are rather chapfallen about it."

"Well, they shall come—if not for money, for revenge."

Pierre knew that the prospect of shedding the young chieftain's blood would, in the present state of mind of the wreckers, be more alluring to them than gold.

"At twelve to-morrow," he said, as he parted with his visitor at the castle-gate, "I will be at your house."

Jack turned away without a word, and his towering form was soon lost in the gloom.

CHAPTER XLIV.
IN THE PLOTTER'S POWER.

THE unquenchable desire felt by our young hero to solve the mystery that surrounded his birth, made him forget his habitual caution when there was a prospect of the secret being divulged. This was known by the astute Frenchman, when he arranged his plot with the cowardly wreckers.

Punctual to his appointment, Pierre attended his mistress at the hour she had named.

She was awaiting him, and her first inquiry was—

"Whom can we trust with this mission?"

"The page, madame, will be the best. I will tell him to take it."

"A good thought, Pierre. The rest is arranged."

"And will be privately carried out. He will not escape us this time."

The page, unsuspicious of the fell treachery of those by whom he was employed, went on his errand.

He found our hero, and delivered the note found by Snowball.

And when night's shadows began to darken the earth, Tom, wrapping his cloak around him, walked slowly towards the Willow Glen.

Pierre and his demon-like mistress had prepared for his arrival. A number of ruffianly wreckers were in ambush. Their leader, Jack, had taken a safe position upon a jutting piece of granite.

And, like a wolf, he watched his prey, as he sat in the gloom with a large stone between his hands, ready to hurl upon the brave young outlaw's head.

Pierre, he, too, was there, contemplating the reward he should have for his share in the transaction.

Not a sound broke the stillness of the hour, save the melancholy dirge of the sea as it washed the rocks.

Pierre began to grow impatient, and whispered to Jack—

"Diable! 'spose he not come?"

"He'll be here!" was the reply, in the same still voice.

"Is de stone ready to fall on his head?"

"Yes. I've got it to the edge, and the slightest push, down it goes."

"Good! Hush! hush! someone is coming!"

They listened attentively. It was the victim, who, unconscious, was silently advancing to the rock.

Step by step he came right beneath the very stone where Jack lay.

The wrecker trembled with excitement and savage joy, for the young outlaw halted beneath the crushing stone.

And Jack, no longer able to suppress his exultation, gave a savage cry, and sent the stone whirling through the air.

Taken by surprise, and struck to the earth Tom was rendered powerless. Then his foes sprang from their ambush, laughing derisively at the brave young fellow now in their power.

Though upon the ground and the savage wreckers round him, he strove to draw his blade.

But the numbing pain caused by the blow he had received, rendered his arm powerless.

The wreckers then bound him hand and foot, and tauntingly jeered the gallant fellow with his helpless position.

Pierre and Jack had by this time descended.

Grimly the wrecker gazed upon Tom's prostrate form, and, with a morose laugh, he said—

"Ah! at last, you rascally cub, I have you!"

Tom's reply was a scornful look of defiance.

"Ha! ah! ah!" laughed the wrecker, "now call upon your black giant and dog; you want them!"

"They'll come," answered Tom, quietly, "and wreak such vengeance on you for this outrage, that you had better never have been born!"

Pierre whispered a few words in Jack's ear.

The next moment Jack addressing his gang, said—"Blindfold him, and follow me."

A scarf was bound over the young outlaw's eyes, and, borne on the shoulders of four wreckers, he was taken to the rear of the castle.

Cunningly fashioned, so as to resemble part of the solid masonry, was a small door. This Pierre opened.

The men who carried the young chieftain followed the Frenchman down a spiral staircase which led to the dungeons beneath.

Near the foot of the stairs a long passage ran to the arched corridor under the sea.

At one of the doors Pierre stopped, saying—"In here."

The men followed, and placed their burden upon a heap of straw in the corner. Then they removed the scarf from his mouth, and the cord from his legs.

His hands were now coupled with a chain.

Tom, though he knew not where his enemies had brought him, felt resistance was useless, and reclined quietly on the straw, watching every movement.

With savage joy, Jack stood for a few moments contemplating the prisoner, and then broke into a scornful laugh.

"Ha! ha! ha! You have a comfortable bed, I see. Ho! ho! ho!"

Tom turned his face to the speaker.

"Don't you like it?" said Jack; then, addressing his companions, said, "What do you say, my lads? Suppose we trap his lady-love, and toss up for possession of her?"

These exasperating words stung Tom to the quick, and with a bound he sprang upon the ruffian, and dashing the fetters in his face, sent the wrecker stunned and bleeding to the earth.

The wreckers, in a body, drew their knives, and would have fallen upon the defenceless boy.

But Pierre prevented it by telling them to take up their senseless companion; the men were ordered from the dungeon, Pierre locking the door, and leaving Tom to solitude and his own reflections.

Sinking upon the straw, his head fell upon his hands, and he began to think.

In the midst of his reverie, he was aroused by the loathsome touch of a slimy reptile that had dropped from the roof; then large drops of water continued falling therefrom.

With an expression of disgust he sprang to his feet, and began to pace the narrow limits of his cell.

A troop of rats, disturbed by his tread, scrambled back to their hiding-places.

Suddenly Tom paused, and listened, and with an instinctive sense of coming danger grasped his manacles.

But the noise he heard continued its rumbling sound, and the youth remembered at last that he was imprisoned far below the level of the sea.

"Fool!" he said; "fool that I was to come alone to this meeting. The late attempt on my life should have warned me; but regret is too late now."

There was not a ray of light in the dungeon, and the gallant youth, striving to shake from himself the fearful truth that he was buried in a living tomb, began to sound the wall.

Vain hope! They were as solid as the gigantic rocks upon which the castle was built.

"Thus ends my life," thought Tom. "A fearful fate for one who has battled so long with the world."

He threw himself again upon the straw, and giving way to melancholy thoughts, in which Laura possessed a considerable share, he fell asleep.

CHAPTER XLV.
STRANGE SHADOWS.

HERBERT BEALE was deeply mystified by the inexplicable disappearance of his outlawed friend. A hundred causes came to his mind, but none could bear a moment's thought.

During his journey back to his vessel, he read the letter, but could not glean one atom of information from its contents.

"Strange!" he said, "if these lines were penned by a woman, surely some devilry is at work. These characters are too boldly written, and seem more like the handwriting of a man than a woman."

He folded the note, and placed it in his breast-pocket; then laying back in the stern-sheets, became lost in thought.

And from this state he was not aroused until the sailors peaked their oars, and the midshipman in charge jumped to the bow of the boat and fastened the guess warp.

A thin haze was over the water, when Herbert Beale left his vessel for the second time.

The regular sound of the oars soothed his mind, for the young commander's heart was full of dark forebodings at his friend's unaccountable disappearance.

Herbert stepped ashore, and bidding the men wait his return, he walked moodily towards the castle.

Although the hour was still early, not a light was visible from the windows of the dark pile of buildings.

Herbert, as is usual with mankind, looked at the dark side of the affair first. He gave himself no time to reflect whether one so proud and so beautiful as the Lady Mountsteven would aid or abet so black a deed.

He was about to move towards the gates of the towering edifice, when a sudden gleam of light from one of the lower windows fell across his path.

Herbert looked up and saw a small chamber window illumined by the mellow rays of a lamp.

Mentally wondering whether this could be the lady's room, or one of the domestic offices, his attention was attracted by a shadow on the blind.

At first faint and undefined, but growing soon into what seemed to be a tall and queenly woman.

He saw the figure stretch forth her hand in an imperious manner, then elevate it as though about to strike.

The young sailor's breath came quickly, for he saw that the uplifted hand held a long knife.

What could it mean?

Who was this female?

These were questions that now puzzled his brain, and feeling assured that there was another person in the room, whom this figure was threatening, he was about to run forward and climb the clinging ivy that bound the wall beneath the mansion.

He had scarcely taken a step forward, before his eyes were startled by a second shadowy form appearing upon the blind.

This time a man—tall, and apparently stout.

Herbert saw him bound forward and seize the uplifted hand, and, by the swaying to and fro of their bodies, it was evident a struggle was taking place.

Suddenly the room became dark.

As Herbert rightly conjectured, the lamp had been overturned in the struggle.

Drawing his sword to save the woman from what he well knew, from the nature of the struggle, must be a cowardly assault, he ran forward.

His sword-blade clenched between his teeth, and both hands clutching the ivy, he began his ascent.

He had not gone more than half-way, when a piercing shriek from below caused him to pause.

This he knew was a girl's voice, and, peering down into the semi-darkness, he saw a woman pass swiftly beneath him, followed by a man's form.

"She has escaped from the room," thought Captain Herbert.

He relinquished his hold upon the ivy, and dropped lightly to the ground.

Sword in hand, he rushed after the flying pair, and his speed increased when he saw the girl struggling in the arms of a swarthy-looking man, whose body was wrapped in a long cloak.

A dozen bounds brought him to the spot.

The stranger turned, and, releasing the lady, drew his sword.

Herbert was excited, and, without one thought for the consequences, he crossed his blade with the stranger.

CHAPTER XLVI.
IN THE PICTURE GALLERY.

THE combat was not of long duration, for Herbert catching the flat of his opponent's sword upon the edge of his weapon, the former snapped in two.

Just then the moon began to peep out from the murky clouds, and the gleam showed the captain a face and form he knew too well.

"Red Hand," he said, as he recognised the ruffian, "yield, or you die!"

He put the pointed sword against the monster's throat as he spoke, but, quick as thought, Red Hand drew a pistol, and levelling it at Herbert's head, fired.

"That's for you, you meddling fool!" said Red Hand, savagely.

The bullet grazed the young Captain's temple, and caused him to stagger back.

With a savage cry, Red Hand drew his knife, and was about to spring upon Herbert; but the young sailor quickly recovered from the dizziness

She was indeed exquisitely lovely—the reality far exceeding the idea created by the young captain's imagination—for Herbert Beale knew he looked upon the face of Lady Mountsteven.

Dazed by her wondrous loveliness, he for several minutes could do nothing but retain her in the same posture as when he first raised her head.

Wildly the young sailor's heart beat, and a sense of shame came to his mind when he thought of the baseness he had accused her of participating in.

"Beauteous lady," he muttered, "loath would I be to think that winged inhabitant of heaven would come on earth and commit so foul a deed as I have charged you with."

SHARK TAKEN BY AN INDIAN DIVER.

caused by the pirate's bullet, and, meeting his rush, drove his blade through the fleshy part of the arm.

It would have been through Red Hand's heart, had not Herbert's hand been rendered unsteady.

The pirate gave a howl of agony, and clapping his left hand to the bleeding wound, turned and fled.

For the moment Herbert was too confused to follow the pirate; and seeing the young girl whom he had saved lying in a huddled heap upon the ground, he returned his sword to its scabbard.

Then kneeling by the prostrate form, he gently raised her head, and as the white moonbeams quivered upon her beautiful face, a low cry of admiration left his lips.

His lowly-spoken words seemed to arouse the lady, and, opening her eyes, murmured—

"Save me—save me from this monster!"

"You are safe, lady," said Herbert, "let me assist you to rise."

She looked into his frank, handsome face, and seeing only kindness and manly beauty there portrayed, she placed her hand confidently upon his shoulder.

"Young sir," she said, "you have risked your life for mine. How can I reward you?"

"By not mentioning it again, madam."

"Reflect. I am rich, and, as you are a sailor, it may be in my power to advance you in your profession; and please heaven I live, it shall be done."

The young sailor scarcely heard these grateful acknowledgments. He was too much absorbed in contemplating the graceful form and faultless face of the lady.

There could be no deception. She was the original of the figure he had seen upon the blind.

And the young commander keenly scrutinized her dress and appearance, to try and find some traces of the struggle she had gone through.

He was more mystified than ever.

Her dress was faultless—not a fold, not a ribbon amiss—and her classic features were as still as though sculptured from marble.

Herbert did not notice the lurking fire that still burned in her eyes, or the alternate pallor and flushing of her cheeks. If he did, the cause was attributed to the late encounter she had had with Red Hand.

The patrician lady conducted her deliverer to the portrait-gallery, and then, pointing to a seat, said—

"Pray be seated. I will bring my husband to thank my gallant preserver for the service he has done."

She was gone before the young sailor could utter a word to prevent her. Then he rose and began to examine the family portraits of the noble house.

There were grim warriors armed from head to heel in steel, bishops in mitres, and seamen in the quaint costume of the Middle Ages.

Ladies there were in profusion; and Herbert, as he passed from generation to generation, could not help remarking the strong likeness that existed in the male line, and he fancied the features were familiar to him.

He came at last to the portrait of the existing head of the family. It was the picture of a youth garbed in a midshipman's dress—a bold, handsome fellow, the very *beau ideal* of what a sailor should be.

The portrait fascinated Herbert, for it was the exact counterpart of his friend, Midshipman Tom.

"There's something more than chance in this," thought Herbert. "Tom has more than once told there is a mystery about——Ha! can it be possible this splendid woman is the second wife of Lord Mountsteven! If so, the cause of my friend's dis"——

His thoughts were interrupted by the entrance of Lord and Lady Mountsteven; and the former approaching the young sailor with extended hands, thanked him for his manly gallantry.

"I served in the navy until my father's death," said his lordship in continuation, "and many of my former messmates now hold important positions, therefore I can do"——

"My lord," was the proud answer, "pardon me for interrupting you, but I prefer to win my way by my sword. What I have done is not worth mentioning. A lady was struggling with a ruffian, and I did as every Briton would have done under the circumstances."

Lord Mountsteven was pleased with the young commander's speech, and soon they were, with Lady Mountsteven, in a close and friendly conversation.

From this they were startled by the sudden opening of the door, which had been ajar, and, to their surprise, Tom's large dog entered the room.

"The master is not far off," thought the young sailor. "Should Tom be here, there will be a scene."

The dog stood for a few seconds near the door, sniffing the air; then he advanced to the centre of the portrait-gallery.

CHAPTER XLVII.

THE WRECKER'S REWARD.

AFTER the Frenchman and his associates had securely fastened Tom in the dungeon, the former led them to a private door in the castle wall.

He waited until they had passed through the doorway, then to the ruffianly leader he gave a small bag of gold.

The wrecker clutched it greedily.

"Thank you, master; take care of that cub."

"I will. For unless he eat up the rats, he'll not long be alive."

Jack went on some distance in advance of his party, towards the cluster of huts, his mind busy with a new idea.

That idea was how to cheat his companions of their share of the money.

Had he but known that his companions, at the same moment he was studying how to cheat them, were consulting in low whispers as to the best method of disposing of him and keeping the reward for themselves, he would have known only an unpleasant truth.

Upon the road back home, the wreckers were compelled to pass a narrow path, that only two could walk abreast.

Down upon either side was a ravine so deep that the jagged stones at the bottom were barely discernible.

Before entering the pass, the party in the rear came to a halt, and called upon Jack to join them.

Being disturbed, before he had satisfactorily determined which way he should settle the account with the wreckers, Jack answered very gruffly with a—

"Well, what do you want!"

"Come and see."

Jack strode towards his companions, and growled to the man who was speaking—

"You've got too much to say—a good deal too much."

"Have I? Well, don't you jaw; that will not stop it."

"Won't it?"

"No, and"——

"That'll do—no quarrelling," said another. "We want to speak to you, Jack."

"Speak on, then, and be hanged. What is it?"

"How much did you get for that job?"

"What?"

The question was repeated.

Jack's face became red with passion, and he stamped the ground with his foot.

"What is that to do with you?"

"Not to me altogether, but all of us."

"I don't know how much. There's the bag."

"Don't lie."

"I am not lying. And if you say so again, I'll smash you."

"Two can play at that."

"But only one can win."

"Perhaps you'd like to try it?"

"Stow that, both of you," was the general cry.

Jack seemed suddenly struck with a conviction that his companion intended mischief, for he plunged his hand inside his shirt, and clutched the hilt of his knife, saying—

"Look here, what is it you want, Sam?"

"We want to know how about dividing the coin."

"As I like."

"Perhaps; but how's that? Our bargain was, that the money was to be divided into nine shares; six for us, and two for you."

"Two shares!" exclaimed the wrecker.

"Yes," said Sam; "isn't that enough?"

"No; a'n't I wounded?"

"You should have kept your saucy tongue to yourself, then you would not have got it."

"But as I have got it, and done all the work as well, I intend to divide different."

"How? What—have more?"

"Yes; I'll take half—the other half can be divided among you."

Had Jack's greed not been stronger than his caution, he would have been warned by the angry expression of the lawless crew by which he was surrounded that there was danger threatening.

"Look here, Jack," said Sam; "if you tries on any of your tricks, it will be the worse for you. We want fair play, and we mean to have it."

"What do you call fair play?"

"For all to have an equal share of the swag."

"I'll see you all —— first."

"You will?"

"Yes."

"Then we'll take your share as well."

Jack stood upon his guard.

But too late; for with one simultaneous rush they threw themselves upon him, before he could use his knife.

He was a man of immense muscular power, and, though felled to the earth by his companions, he fought long and fiercely, several times catching his assailants' hands in his teeth, causing them to quit their hold.

At length he had bitten one of them completely through the hand, which had so enraged him that the next moment he plunged his knife up to the hilt in Jack's side.

The wrecker gave a roar of agony, and as the crimson tide began to gush forth, his struggles ceased.

To possess themselves of the wrecker's booty and search his pockets, was but a moment's work.

Then, hurling their leader's bleeding form into the ravine, they hurried from the spot.

CHAPTER XLVIII.
THE CAUSE OF THE STRANGE SHADOWS.

PIERRE, when the wreckers had gone a short distance from the castle, closed the side door and locked the gates.

Passing through the court-yard and long corridors, he went to Lady Mountsteven's room, and found her reclining upon a couch, her face pale, and evidently much troubled about the success of her schemes.

She rose when he entered.

"Have you succeeded?"

Pierre bowed low, and replied—

"I have, madame. Here is the key."

She took the key from him, and repeated—

"The key?"

"Yes, madame—of his dungeon."

Lady Mountsteven placed the key in a drawer, and said to Pierre—

"Is the youth wounded?"

"No, madame."

"He did not resist, then?"

"No, madame. We did not give him a chance."

"A surprise, then?"

"Yes, madame—a very clever one. I hope madame is satisfied?"

"Quite, Pierre."

"Pierre is grateful, madame."

Lady Mountsteven drew a ring from her finger and held it towards him desiring him to take it.

Pierre did so.

"Will madame," he asked, "allow me to kiss the hand that has given him so marked a proof of her favour?"

Lady Mountsteven, not for a moment presuming he had any bad intentions, held out her hand.

Pierre, by the masterly exercise of an unlimited natural cunning, had persuaded his mistress that his attention to her every behest was actuated only by duty and respect for her personally; nevertheless, the ruling passion, influencing his every thought and action, sprang from a thirst for gain—money—gold!

And it was this willingness to acquire riches, by any and every means which happened to fall within his reach, that led him to violate the sanctity of the black cabinet of his mistress, foreshadowing, as it did to him, that, one way or another, sooner or later it might bear him much rich fruit.

And now it was, also, that knowing his lady mistress really had not in her possession any sum, in hard cash, to meet his intended inordinate demands for the late service he had rendered her in capturing Midshipman Tom, his soul prompted him to try and seize the jewels, worth many hundreds of pounds sterling, from her ladyship's hand, as a far more substantial recompense than he otherwise could have secured.

At once, therefore, he seized the jewelled hand with the determination to dispossess it of the rubies, diamonds, and other precious stones with which the rings were set, and he held it in a vice-like grip.

The baroness was alarmed by his manner, and made an attempt to draw her hand away.

But Pierre maintained his grasp.

"Release my hand," she shouted. "Pierre, what means this insult?"

"Madame," said Pierre, very coolly, at the same time releasing her hand, "my answer is this. The possession of a secret, which gives me"——

"Fool!" she exclaimed, rising and going towards the bell, "we shall see."

"Stop," said Pierre. "Let madame listen to a few words before she would have her name coupled with murder."

It was then her white arm fell to her side, and she turned with pallid face, and repeated—

"Murder!"

"Yes, madame, murder."

Thinking he meant the young outlaw, she recovered herself, and said—

"Fool! I can have you whipped like a hound, and while your cries fill the room, I can release the young sailor."

"Madame can do this, but she cannot recal or deny that black deed written upon those papers she placed in the ebony cabinet."

The truth flashed across the mind of the lady, as she frantically uttered—

"Ha! and have you dared to"——

"Money will incite one to dare much," said Pierre coolly. "For that I became your slave, by that, which will produce it, I become your master."

Lady Mountsteven, in her trouble, scarcely noted these defiant words, but with one bound, she reached the cabinet, and found it open.

She clasped her hands together, and gave utterance to mingled cries of rage and despair, when she found that the papers had disappeared.

Pierre's malicious laugh stung her into madness, and, like a tigress, she pounced upon him.

Snatching a keen stiletto from the table, she exclaimed in a voice, rendered hoarse with passion—

"And think you, slave as you are, that you shall live with such a secret in your possession?"

Saying this, she sprang upon him and attempted to bury the keen blade in his heart.

But the Frenchman, well skilled in the use of the knife, at once closed upon her, and seized her right hand.

Not a word was spoken by either in the long struggle that ensued.

The baroness was a strong and resolute woman.

Pierre, though small of stature, was wiry, and capable of much endurance.

Nothing but their thick suppressed breathing told there was a battling for life in that room, until Pierre uttered a cry of triumph, and they fell to the ground together.

The room was now in darkness, and Pierre, having pinioned the baroness's arms, clutched her hands again, and, after some struggling, he forced every ring from her fingers, and eventually stripped her person of every golden adornment.

Pierre looked at the fallen and exhausted lady, and felt, for the moment, an abashment steal over him; but his avarice came to the rescue, and he was exulting over the cruel deed.

The next moment, he felt the stiletto buried to the hilt in his breast.

CHAPTER XLIX.

THE FISHERMAN'S SON ON HIS MISSION.

WHEN Red Hand received the thrust from Captain Beale's sword, he hurried swiftly back to the beach, where a boat from his vessel, the Black Snake, was awaiting him.

With a horrible imprecation, he ordered the men to give way and pull towards the vessel.

"Curse him!" muttered the miscreant, as he descended to his cabin; "but for his meddling, I should have possessed the lady."

He ground his teeth savagely as he thought of the baroness's beauty, and the goodly ransom he should have obtained for her release.

Striking a gong that hung from the roof of his cabin, he awaited impatiently an answer to the summons.

Duhouse, Red Hand's lieutenant, made his appearance.

The death of Pedro, by Snowball's hand, caused him to be promoted to that office.

Red Hand ordered the doctor to be sent for at once. All turned silently away, and in a few minutes the ship's doctor made his appearance.

"Wounded," he said briefly, as he entered the cabin. "Where?"

"A curse upon the fool that gave it me!"

"No harm done," said the surgeon, binding it up. "A few days' rest, and you will be right again."

"When I am," said Red Hand, "that pale-faced hound shall see my method of avenging it."

Red Hand forgot in his anger that Herbert Beale commanded a swift vessel, and a crew of hardy seamen.

The lieutenant, with cat-like stealth, glided into the cabin, and said—

"There is a sail upon the port bow."

"Well?"

"I thought it best to tell you, captain, for she looks suspicious."

"What do you mean?"

"From the light of their battle-lanterns, I can see the men at quarters."

"Is it a large vessel?"

"A frigate, from what I can make out."

Red Hand, by much effort, ascended the companion-ladder, and looked through his glass at the strange sail.

An angry oath passed his lips, as he made out the massive outlines of a magnificent frigate, with open ports, and her rigging illuminated with lanterns, was sweeping through the water.

Red Hand's first order was to have every light on board the Black Snake immediately extinguished.

His next to get under weigh.

Then like a black snaky-looking reptile, the pirate's ship, began to move through the water.

What the motive could be for the frigate's being at quarters at that hour of night puzzled Red Hand.

And while his ship was getting well under sail, he saw the frigate belch forth a sheet of fire.

He knew his own vessel could not be the object of attack, for the distance was too great.

Again and again the fire was seen, and the roar of the artillery rolled like distant thunder.

Then a rocket went up from the frigate's deck.

The blue light radiated the surrounding water for several seconds, disclosing to the pirates the cause of the frigate's firing.

For several fathoms around the noble ship the water was dotted with boats.

"A cutting out," muttered Red Hand.

"Yes," said the lieutenant, who had overheard the words, "but a failure."

"What do you know of the affair?"

"Much—I know both vessels."

"How did you learn so much?"

"Since you have been ashore," said Duhouse, "I have noticed both vessels come in from the Mediterranean. One is the English frigate, the Pomona Tiger; the other a French three-decker."

"The Frenchman then is trying to cut the frigate out from under the guns of the fort?"

"Yes—an' there they go."

As Duhouse spoke, the guns from the fort opened fire.

They could see the fuse of the shells like fiery meteors as they flew over the frigate, and landed with beautiful precision in the rigging of the French line-of-battle ship.

The frigate seemed to be hotly engaged, for her guns were at work on both sides, and during a lull the rattle of small arms could be heard.

They died away in a short time. Then the guns of the frigate ceased altogether.

"The French have struck," said Red Hand, savagely.

"Not yet," said the lieutenant.

To confirm his words, a dozen rockets were hissing up from the frigate.

And by the brilliant light the pirate captain and his lieutenant could see the Frenchman's boats pulling back to the ship as quickly as possible.

The three-decker shortly after this began to show her lights, and delivered broadside after broadside.

Then came a terrible roar, followed by sheets of flame leaping skyward.

The Frenchman had blown up.

Red Hand had watched the grave spectacle until the catastrophe had occurred; then pressing on all sail the masts could carry, he scudded away.

"That confounded frigate," he muttered, "might finish by an attack on us."

With her head before the wind, the Black Snake soon lost sight of the lights, both from the fort and the ship.

Then Red Hand lay-to, for he had not yet given up the idea of carrying off the beautiful baroness.

The morning had just dawned when the lookout on the foremast sang out—

"A boat on the starboard bow."

There was a rush of feet to the point indicated. And to the surprise of all on board, they beheld a small boat, seemingly a gig, coming towards them.

The boat was propelled by a single rower, a mere youth, who every few minutes turned to look at the Black Snake.

"Boat ahoy!" sang out one of the pirates.

"Ahoy!" came faintly over the intervening space of water.

The distance was soon lessened between the ship and the boat, as their heads were turned towards each other.

Red Hand stood on the quarter-deck, watching the coming boat, and listening to the colloquy between the man on the look-out and the solitary rower.

"Ship ahoy!" said the latter. "Heave to. I am nearly tired."

"Where from?"

"Bermuda."

"Our vessel went to pieces on the rocks. Will you take me on board?"

The man looked at Red Hand before he replied to the boy.

Red Hand answered, in token of assent.

"Pull to the side," said the look-out, "and catch the line."

The boy did as he was desired, and, making the line fast to his boat, he scrambled on deck.

He was a youth about eighteen, strongly built, and bold looking.

With a quick glance he scanned the bearded crew of ruffians, and when his eyes fell upon Red Hand, his cheeks became suffused with a crimson flush.

The pirate captain called him to the quarter-deck.

"What did you say—you were wrecked?"

"Yes, sir."

"What was the name of the vessel?"

"'The Avenger.'

"Nothing left of her?"

"Not a spar."

"I suppose if I let you stay on board you will, after a short time, want to go ashore?"

The boy's lips twitched as he answered—

"If you allow me to stay and become your servant, I will never leave unless you are no longer captain of the ship."

"Very well, be it so. I want an attendant. Go below and obtain instruction in your duties."

The boy bowed and was turning away.

"Here," said Red Hand, "do you know this vessel?"

"I do not."

"Her character?"

"Yes."

Red Hand looked keenly at him and inquired how he knew so much.

"By the size of the vessel, the appearance of your crew and your armament."

"Well?"

"I knew you were pirates."

"And I," said the pirate leader, "am Red Hand."

"I knew that," the boy muttered to himself as he went towards the aft hatch. "Miscreant, now for revenge!"

The ocean waif was *Peter, the fisherman's son.*

"At length," he thought, "I am safe upon the track of my father's murderer; and to avenge his death I swear a terrible and a binding oath to be the bane of Red Hand's existence."

And he had already marked out a slow but subtle plan wherewith to effect it.

"To sow seeds of dissension," thought he, "among the crew, and bring on mutiny and bloodshed; to thwart him in his dearest wishes, and mar his most favourite plans—these shall be my means for taking vengeance. Then, when my project's ripened, the hour has come, then will I execute my oath, and the pirate leader shall fall by the hands of Peter, the fisherman's son."

Red Hand, soon after Peter—or, as he now called himself, Giffard—had descended to his new duties, found the boy zealously arranging the cabin.

"What is your name?" inquired the pirate.

"Giffard."

"Very well, Giffard. Can I make a confidant of you?"

"You can, sir."

"I think I may; your face seems truthful."

The boy bowed.

"Did you notice the lieutenant when you came aboard?"

"Yes, I did, sir."

"Giffard, I mistrust that man, and want you to keep a watch over him."

Giffard's heart bounded with joy—he saw in this a speedy advancement of his plans.

"I will do so," he replied; "but may I be excused making a suggestion to you? It is a simple one, sir, and I think will aid your purpose."

"Let me hear it."

"You suspect this man of treachery, I suppose?"

"Yes, I do—the skulking hound!"

"Well, sir," continued Giffard, "my proposition would be, that you go ashore for a couple of days, remaining where I could give you hourly intelligence of what passes during your absence."

"Yes, I could do that certainly, but——"

"You would say, how will that assist you? Let that be my secret. You may, sir, have confidence; I never failed yet in anything I have seriously undertaken."

"Very well. I am going ashore to-night, and will remain there. You shall come with me to the cave."

That night the pirate, taking Giffard with him, went ashore, and Red Hand, showing him the secret entrance to the cave, said—

"Watch well, and bring me intelligence of anything that may transpire. You will find me here."

The boy returned to the vessel, his face burning with triumph."

The young fisherman soon found Red Hand's suspicions to be correct; for when he returned to the vessel he saw the lieutenant in close consultation with some of the men.

The voices were so low that he could not catch a word of their conversation, although he passed the group.

Duhouse was sitting near one of the open skylights over the captain's cabin, the men grouping around him.

By standing on a table below in the cabin, he was enabled to hear every word that passed.

"Then you think that the attempt had better be made at once?" said the lieutenant.

"Yes," answered one of the men, "for I do not think we shall get any more to join us."

"Why?"

"Because they stand in too much fear of Red Hand."

"The fools!" said the lieutenant. "I suppose they will stand by him."

"Just so."

"Then we must be sure and swift in our movements, for we are the smaller party."

"And how do you intend we shall act, Duhouse?"

"Remain quiet until he returns from the ship."

"Well?"

"And the first order he gives, do not take any notice of it."

"You forget he will shoot the first man who disobeys."

"I'll see to that. The bullets shall be drawn from his pistols."

"Very well—go on."

"'MOVE BUT A STEP AND I FIRE!'"

"He will get into a violent passion and, as usual, begin to bully and threaten."

"Yes."

"Then will be the time to tell him that his tyranny has come to an end, and you will no longer serve under him."

"You know the result of that?"

"I do; but will guard against his orders to place any of you in irons."

"How?"

"By having the irons out of the way."

"But suppose they who have not joined us should obey his orders?"

"They will not. It is only fear that keeps them from joining the mutiny. Once the attempt made, they will join us."

"And now let us disperse. We are attracting attention, and there may be a traitor among us who would sell us for gold."

The mutineers dispersed by Duhouse's advice, and Giffard, as he descended from his post, thought—"A nice hot-bed of villany that: but what matters—it may answer my purpose."

In the morning, Giffard went ashore, and described all that had passed.

9

Red Hand uttered a fearful oath, and foamed at the mouth with passion.

"Curse the fiend!" he yelled. "One by one shall they swing at the masthead; and as for that lieutenant—he shall die a horrible death for it!"

When Giffard returned to the ship he was met by one of the mutineers, who asked—

"Is the chief coming on board to-day?"

"In a few hours, I believe."

The mutineer's swarthy face lit up with triumph, and he went forward to report the intelligence to his fellows.

He came, as Giffard had foretold, and when he stepped upon the deck he glanced quickly around.

The mutineers were all standing apart in a body, and their leader, playing with the handle of his knife, was leaning against the taffrail, his dark eyes blazing with impatience as he thought of the near approach of the time when he should be the master of the Black Snake.

Red Hand gave a glance round and singled out the conspirators. Pointing to one, he said—

"Go up aloft and fasten the bunt."

The man did not attempt to move.

"Do you hear?" repeated Red Hand, "go up aloft and fasten the bunt."

The mutineer stepped forward and appeared about to speak, when Red Hand levelled a pistol at his head, the man instantly fell and expired.

"And now," thundered the pirate, "what do you mean? Are there any more mutinous dogs among you"

No one spoke, and the wily lieutenant, who had led the men to this step, bit his lip savagely at the unexpected turn affairs had taken.

"All hands aloft," said Red Hand. "the last up will have a dozen."

The men flew to obey his orders, each trying to be first up the shrouds.

Red Hand smiled grimly.

He could not put his threat into execution, as no one seemed last: like a swarm of bees they had ascended.

"Duhouse," said he, calling upon the lieutenant, "what is the meaning of all this?"

"I do not know, captain."

"You do not?"

"I do not."

"You are a double-dealing sycophant and liar."

He started and laid his hand upon his sword.

Red Hand levelled a pistol at him, saying—

"Take your hand from that weapon."

He obeyed.

"Duhouse," Red Hand resumed, "what fate do you deserve?"

"For what?"

"Crawling traitor as you are—do you dare ask for what?"

"I do."

"Then I'll tell you—for mutiny."

"What?"

"Mutiny—I say again."

"I have had nothing to do with these men."

"Ay! Did you not incite them?"

"No. I did not."

"Silence!" yelled the pirate leader. "Silence!"

"I will not be accused unjustly."

"Pitiful and cowardly dog!" began Red Hand. "So you wanted to command the Black Snake."

"I—wanted"——

"Yes, ingrate, and by——you shall."

The man cowered before the irascible pirate, and would have left the deck, but Red Hand's levelled pistol held him a prisoner where he stood.

Then came the command—

"All hands on deck!"

The men came down in a few minutes, and Red Hand harangued them there.

"There are several among you who have listened to the evil words of this black-hearted scoundrel. This man who aspires to command the Black Snake. Those who are dissatisfied, let them come forward."

Not a man moved.

"Such of you as were eager for a change, now speak out. (He paused.) Well, be it so; it is better for you. But, for this intriguing hound, he shall suffer!"

Duhouse drew his weapon, and, like a cat, crept, as he thought, unperceived towards Red Hand, with an unmistakable glare in his eyes telling his deadly hate towards the speaker.

Red Hand saw him coming, and he did not move, but cried out in a loud and peremptory voice—

"Seize him and, bring him forward!"

A dozen pirates sprang upon the lieutenant, some of them the very men who, only a few hours before, had been plotting the downfall of Red Hand.

Duhouse struggled wildly with the pirates, but numbers prevailed, and he was hurled to the deck stunned and bleeding.

"Bring the brute here," said Red Hand.

The men followed him to the forecastle, bearing the senseless body with them.

"Fasten a line round his feet."

It was immediately done.

"Run it through the ring at the point of the bowsprit, and throw him overboard; then leave him hanging by his heels," was his next command.

Dangling head downwards, his face within a couple of yards of the water, he hung hour after hour, hearing at times the maddening laugh of the pirate band, who stood at the bows watching his terrible agony.

Watching him as he swung to and fro, frantically yelling out for mercy.

Red Hand but laughed at his appeal.

"Mercy! mercy!" shrieked the mutineer; "this agony is worse than death. Shoot me!"

"That would be a death too rapid," sarcastically replied his captain; and he informed him there was a shark coming within his reach.

The ferocious monster turned upon his back, preparing to make short work of the poor lieutenant: and he certainly would have been cut in twain but for the vessel at that moment lurching over.

One of the pirates, moved to pity by the efforts of the miserable wretch to escape the fearful fate that awaited him, drew the line that was fastened round his ankles, thereby raising him several feet from the water.

He paid dearly for his kindness.

Red Hand treated it as a breach of discipline, and, his face purple with passion, he cried—

"Run him up to the yard-arm!"

The man turned pale, and faced the merciless wretch.

"Do so, if you are demons," said the victim; "you will not if you are men."

Red Hand declined to hear further expostulation, and ordered a group of pirates to "Reeve a line through the point of the yard-arm."

This order was obeyed, and the poor mutineer, who had shown by that one act he was not entirely without the bowels of compassion within him, was run up.

Red Hand, without displaying the slightest compunction of conscience, ordered the line to be cut.

It was done.

The cord whistled through the block, there was a sudden plunge, and the waters closed over the murdered pirate for ever.

The last eddying circle of the disturbed waters had dispersed itself, mingling again with the broad blue ocean, and the silent pirates turned from the appaling sight to behold the agonies of the wretched Duhouse; who, with distended eye-balls, was glaring at the shark, which gambolled about under the vessel's bow.

Inch by inch the fierce pirate lowered the line until the howling wretch's face touched the water.

Then a scene took place which made every soul on board the black craft sicken except Red Hand, who stood, fiend-like, upon the forecastle, smiling contentedly.

But let us pass quickly over the scene. One crunch, and then another, and the trunk was torn to pieces.

Then the line was cut, and the shark, taking the mangled remains of humanity in his mouth, disappeared beneath the surface.

There was something so demoniacal in the appearance of Red Hand in the eyes of his crew after he had caused such crimes to be perpetrated in their unwilling presence, that they shrank cowering from his path—as it were to avoid the touch of a thing so fearful.

The pirate leader went to the quarter-deck and called all hands aft.

The men obeyed; and Red Hand, surveying them sternly for a few seconds, said—

"You have seen how mutiny is punished on board a pirate ship—let it be a warning to you all.'

He passed down to his cabin when he ceased speaking, and the men silently withdrew.

In the cabin he found Giffard. The boy was sitting by the open port, gazing gloomily out upon the sea.

"Giffard," he said, "have you seen the end of those mutineers?"

The boy shuddered as he replied—

"I have."

"And you pity them?"

"No; I feel they deserve it."

"Right, boy. And now keep watch upon the crew in my absence."

"I will, sir; and you may rely on my fidelity."

CHAPTER L.
NEPTUNE, THE MASTIFF.

WHEN Herbert Beale saw the dog Neptune enter the room, a vague feeling of joy entered his heart.

He knew the mastiff's wondrous instinct, and hoped he would lead them to the spot where the young outlaw was confined.

For Captain Beale felt inwardly convinced that in some unknown manner the inhabitants of Mountsteven Castle had something to do with the young sailor's disappearance.

Lord Mountsteven noticed the dog, and remarked to Captain Beale—

"That is a fine animal of yours."

"It is not mine, my lord," the young sailor replied, "but the property of a friend."

Lady Mountsteven was sitting near her husband, and Neptune, who had made a careful inspection of every one in the chamber, suddenly stopped, passed directly in front of the astonished lady, and began to growl savagely.

This action startled the guilty woman, and, shrinking from the dog, she said to Herbert—

"For heaven's sake call the brute away! he seems as though about to spring upon me."

Herbert called—

"Neptune! Neptune!"

Save for the fierce curl of the lip, and a more angry flash of the eye, he seemed to take no notice.

"This is strange," said the captain; "the dog, usually so quiet, to show these symptoms."

Lady Mountsteven grew paler every moment, and would have left her seat; but the angry and quiet, determined look of the dog told her that the slightest movement on her part would be followed by the animal springing upon her.

Herbert began to feel alarmed, and, stealing quietly to the dog's side, he grasped him by the collar.

Neptune made no resistance, but lay quietly at Herbert's feet; his eyes fixed upon Lady Mountsteven, and occasionally a subdued growl coming from his lips.

"He is a noble animal," said Lord Mount-steven, "but dangerous."

"I have never seen him thus before."

"It is strange, is it not, he should show such hostility towards the baroness?"

"It is," responded Herbert—"it is strange—very strange."

"You say he does not belong to you?"

"True, my lord. He is devotedly attached to a friend of mine who has mysteriously disappeared; and, were not the idea groundless and ridiculous, I should certainly suppose her ladyship had something to do with his disappearance."

He looked at the baroness as he spoke.

Her features seemed immoveable. She met his gaze firmly and scornfully, and the proud lip curled with disdain.

Their conversation was interrupted by Neptune, who suddenly sprang to his feet, and began sniffing the air, and whining in a piteous manner.

There was something in this that alarmed both men, so they sprang to their feet; and as they did so, the dog gave a loud angry bark, and rushed through the open door, the two men followed him and Lady Mountsteven was left alone.

They were not gone long, but the time seemed to the guilty woman an age; and when her husband, followed by the naval officer, returned, the latter was pale and nervous, and gliding up to his wife he said, in a husky voice—

"Eleanor!"

She heard him not.

"Eleanor," he repeated, and a shiver went over his guilty wife's frame, "there has been a terrible deed committed in this place."

She looked up at him.

That look was hard and stony, and asked—

"A dreadful deed—what mean you?"

"Know you aught of it?"

"I? How should I, when I know not what you mean? Speak! let me hear, for your face speaks of horrible things."

"Ay, it does, for there has been murder done."

"Murder!" she repeated—"murder."

"Yes, murder, Eleanor. Saw you that dog when he sniffed the air?"

"I did."

"The taint of blood was in the atmosphere, and, true to his noble instinct, he led us into the room where lay the stricken man."

Eleanor bowed her head, as she asked—

"Where has it taken place?"

"In your boudoir."

"My boudoir! You are mad."

"I am not, Eleanor. Come, and you shall see for yourself."

A crowd of terrified domestics had by this time gathered at the door, and Lady Mountsteven, slowly rising, with head erect and dilated nostrils, followed her husband.

Herbert Beale had watched the scene, and was about to follow them, when his eyes fell upon a bloodstained handkerchief upon the floor.

In a moment he had taken it up and placed it inside his coat, then sped after the wretched pair.

He saw that stately woman calmly gazing on the body of Pierre, which lay lifeless, an ivory hilted stiletto driven the whole length of the blade in his heart.

Even as he looked in life so he looked in death—a cruel smile of triumph yet upon his features.

"Who can have done that?" asked the nobleman, in a low and anguished tone. "Great heavens! when will the miseries of this life cease?"

Lady Mountsteven looked at the domestics, who were gathered round the door tremblingly gazing on the dreadful spectacle, and sternly demanded—

"Know you aught of this, any of you?"

With the exception of Charley Phillips, the page, the affrighted creatures all shrank back at her words.

He alone looked fearlessly at his mistress, and replied—

"No, my lady."

The baroness fixed her eyes upon him, and demanded "why he answered?"

"I know not," said the boy, "unless it is that the others seem afraid to speak."

"The deed has been done by one of you, Charley Phillips."

"Yes, my lady."

"Were you not at enmity with the steward?"

"I was, my lady. But you do not"——

"Silence! Answer my questions."

The boy bit his lip.

"Have you not quarrelled with him this evening?"

"Yes, I have."

"And he struck you?"

"Yes, my lady."

"What words did you use as you went down the corridor?"

"Words—what—I"——

"No hesitation. What words did you make use of when you passed down the corridor?"

The boy threw back his head, and, in a fearless voice, answered—

"I said it would serve him right if a knife were driven into his heart."

"Anything else?"

"I do not remember that I said more."

"I will assist your memory. You added that if he ever struck you again you would stab him as soon as look."

"I might have said so. But surely madam, you do not think I—I could commit mur—murder?"

"It is not for me to think the deed has been done. And there is blood upon his clothes."

"Blood!" said the page, reeling back.

"Yes your breast is spotted with it. How came those marks there?"

The youth passed his hand over his forehead.

He was fearless by nature yet this sudden and awful charge nearly paralyzed him.

Again her ladyship spoke, her cold tones rousing the boy from his stupor.

"We await your answer," She said.

"You shall have it, my lady. About twenty minutes since I came into your boudoir to light the tapers as usual. It was dark at the time and when leaving the room I fell over something on the floor. It felt soft, and I thought it was a footstool, or one of the soft pillows; but, oh horror! it must have been the steward!"

"Well, what after?"

"I had forgotten to bring a light, and left the boudoir to fetch one. When I returned his lordship and that gentleman where here looking at the corps."

With a fiendish, triumphant look, Lady Mountsteven turned towards her husband saying—

"There, Mountsteven, I think the mystery is explained."

His lordship looked from one to the other.

He could not bring his mind to believe that the bold, handsome page could have committed the foul deed; still, with such damning evidence before him, there was but one course to pursue.

His lordship was the only magistrate on that part of the coast, and, being thus free to act as he thought proper, he said, after a minute's reflection

"You must be placed in security until this mystery is better explained. Take him away."

Two tall footmen seized the page and dragged him to the strong-room in the north-wing.

Then a sheet was thrown over the lifeless form of the wily plotter, whos avarice had cost him his life, and with silent tongues and fearful looks, the whole party left the chamber.

"Thou beautiful perfection of villany!" muttered Herbert, as he walked slowly after the group.

"So she would sacrifice that poor boy to save herself. But he shall escape or my name is not Herbert Beale."

The dog with drooped head and blazing eyes, followed the young seaman closely.

Captain Herbert stopped, and patting the brute's massive head, said—

Faithful fellow! I fear you have lost a master and I a friend."

Lord and Lady Mountsteven went to the library.

The domestics, frightened at their very shadows, and huddled together like a flock of sheep, went to the servants' hall.

Thus Herbert was left in the long ghastly looking corridor alone.

He passed by the open window and looked out upon the moonlit sea, and gazed upon the noble outlines of his vessel.

"There you are, my beauty," he soliloquized, "I would far sooner be the commonest seaman before your mast than lord of this stately mansion,"

How calm and beautiful the silver-lit waves looked, as the young captain thus soliloquized the tiny wavelets leaping over each other as if mimic playfulness.

And as he continued to watch his well-loved craft, her sharp dark hull and tapering graceful spars standing out in bold relief against the glorious firmament, how he mentally contrasted the quietude and happiness of his floating home with the crime-stained lordly towers where he was standing.

CHAPTER LI.
ONCE MORE FREE.

THE young sailor was startled by a sudden pull, and, turning, he saw Tom's dog holding him by the sling of his sword-belt.

Herbert saw the sagacious brute wished to lead him away, and he followed the mastiff until they reached the gloomy arches beneath the castle.

No sooner had the noble hound descended the steps, than he gave a short bark and bounded forward.

Herbert sprang after him, and tried to open the door; but his efforts were fruitless: it was locked.

He turned, and with a pained look on his handsome face, said, addressing the dog—

"I fear our efforts, my poor Neptune, are unavailing."

But a cry of joy suddenly escaped him, for accidentally, he beheld a key hanging upon a nail in the upper part of the door.

To snatch it down and to apply it to the lock was the work of a moment.

The next he thrust the door back and entered the cell.

There lay the object of his search—the young outlaw; but so pale—so emaciated, that he could scarcely rise to embrace his friend.

"Herbert!"

"Tom!"

"How came you here?" was Captain Beale's first inquiry when the greeting was over.

"It's a long story, Herbert; some other time you shall hear it."

Then, noticing the manacles on the young outlaw's hands, he uttered an exclamation.

"It's nothing," Tom replied. "By your assistance I can probably slip my wasted hands through these steel bracelets."

A suggestion that was soon carried out, and Tom was once more free.

The two left the dungeon, Tom trying to point out the secret means of egress to his companion.

"There is another act of mercy I would do before leaving this place," said Herbert.

"An act of mercy, Herbert! And what can that be?"

"Release the innocent from a foul, and as I know, a groundless charge of murder."

"Of murder!" replied Tom, in surprise.

"Where and when?"

"Not now, Tom; but you will know all shortly.",

"Pray enlighten me," said the young outlaw. "I hate mysteries, you know."

"There is no time for explanation now; we must do the work in hand at once, or it will be too late."

"I am with you, Herbert, let it be for good or for evil."

"It is for a good purpose."

The strong room, as it was called, was a circular chamber in the centre of one of the turrets that flanked the north wing, and it required the exercise of the greatest caution in approaching the door, lest they might disturb the groom, who lay across the entrance of it with a loaded gun in his hand.

The object of the two being to steal unawares upon him, then blindfold and gag the groom before he could either give an alarm or offer resistance.

And this they succeeded in doing; then they took the key from his pocket, and entered the chamber where the poor page, so unjustly charged by Lady Mountsteven, was lying fast asleep.

"The guilty could not sleep like that," thought Captain Beale, as he gently aroused the boy.

"Come," he said, when the lad had opened his eyes, "come; we will save you."

"I am not guilty." said the brave little fellow. "Why should I seek to escape?"

"Hush!" said Herbert, kindly. "I know it; I know you are innocent; but upon the evidence, although only circumstantial, you will be hanged."

Charley's cheeks paled at these words, and without further demur, he followed his rescuers, Herbert telling Tom the strange events that had taken place in the castle.

"I am," said the captain, in conclusion, "morally convinced that the murderer of Pierre was Lady Mountsteven; but from what I saw there is no doubt but that he deserved his punishment."

The young outlaw pondered deeply over his friend's words, nor did the gloom, which overhung his spirits, leave him until he had once more entered his cave.

Then his appearance was greeted by a shout of the greatest joy from the band, and Snowball cried like a child over his long-lost chieftain.

"Nebber t'ought to see you agin, Massa Tom," said the African, "nebber; but who done dis—who got yer away, Massa Tom?"

"Never mind, Snowball. I am safe here again; so let it pass."

"If you say so, Massa Tom; but, by Gar, dis chile would like to give him dis," fingering as usual the hilt of his long knife as he spoke.

Tom, having hastily shaken hands with every-one of the band, was about to pass into the inner chamber, where he knew Laura would be waiting for him, when the hoarse challenge of the sentry caused the outlaws to spring to their feet.

"Who comes there?"

Thrice this challenge was repeated, then a manly, yet musical voice responded.

"A friend. Do not fire, but give me protection."

Snowball went to the spot, and to the surprise of all, he returned with a princely-looking stranger.

The intruder was travel-stained and weary; yet in spite of his tattered garments the young outlaw recognised him as the unfortunate Prince Charles.

Midshipman Tom bent on his knee as he said—

"Charles Stuart, England's rightful king!"

"You know me then," said the fugitive, extending his hand.

"I do," replied Tom; "and I will protect you."

"Thanks, noble fellow! I need it, for I am sorely pressed."

"How came your highness here?" asked Tom, "and in such a plight? By the last account your troops were victorious."

"They were in the engagement with Sir John Cope and his dragoons, and also in some skirmishes; but the fatal field of Culloden has blasted my hopes for ever."

The outlaw gazed pityingly upon his visitor, and said—

"Fear nothing here; you shall be well treated."

"I do not fear for myself, but for you."

"For me?"

"Yes; for with a price of thirty thousand pounds upon my head, there are hundreds who will seek my capture."

"Let them begin it," said Tom, smiling.

As though in answer to his words, an outlaw came rushing into the cave, saying—

"We are surrounded by the king's soldiers."

A volley of musketry from the outside bore out the assertion.

CHAPTER LII.
A FRIEND IN NEED.

DURING the time Herbert was at the castle, a witness to the strange scenes there enacted, and an active agent in the liberation of his friend, the jolly-boat of his Majesty's ship, the Saucy Jane, was drawn up on the beach, awaiting his return.

The seamen, one and all, liked their commander too well not to feel some anxiety for his absence.

The coxwain of the boat, an original old fellow, was the first to notice it.

"Wal, messmates," he said, "I'd make one o' four to go arter him."

"That's no use," said another. "How does we know which way he's gone?"

The coxwain took the old quid from his mouth, and, tossing it into the sea, cut another and replaced it.

During this interesting operation he kept his eyes upon the speaker.

"Well, old gimlet eye," said the sailor, "what are you staring at?"

"At you," said the coxwain.

"What for?"

"Wal, I reckon I can tell you what for. I was just a-thinking what a gone 'coon you'd be among the Injuns."

"Among what?"

"The Injuns."

"Indians?"

"Wal, yes, if yer like; but I calls 'em Injuns, and I thinks I oughter know best, being as how I was so long with 'em."

"Well, s'pose you was, what's that 'ere to do with me being a gone 'coon?"

"What is it to do?"

"Yes, that's jest it, what I axed yer."

The coxwain solemnly turned his quid, and further proceeded—

"Wal, I'll tell yer. Do yer know what yer said about the cap'n?"

"Yes."

"What was it?"

"Why, I says, says I, what's the use of a-followin' of him when we don't know which way he's gone?"

"That's jest it."

"What is?"

"Why, that you shows up properly that you knows nothing about a trail."

"Do you?"

"Yaas. I reckon I oughter, seeing as how I was twenty years and more among them Injuns."

"But I don't see what that has to do with the cap'n."

"In course you don't—I'll tell yer. You say it's no use a-going arter him, 'cos we doesn't know which way he's gone. I tell yer it is."

"How?"

"How! yer son of a stumpy figger-head, this is how—by striking his trail."

The coxwain was called upon to give an elucidation of what he meant by striking the trail, but he declined; saying, angrily—"it was quite time they turned their 'tention to the matter of searching for the cap'n."

He was, however, soon relieved of any further anxiety on account of his master, as Captain Beale and Charley, the page, were discerned coming towards the boat, which they entered, and in a few minutes were cleaving the moonlit waters.

When they arrived on board, the young officer took Charley Phillips in his cabin, and pointing to a seat, he said—

"Now, my boy, we must think of what is best to be done for you. I cannot, as an officer, although I feel assured of your innocence, harbour a suspected criminal."

"You have been truly kind, sir, and I would not for worlds get you into trouble," was the reply of the poor boy.

"I know it," said Herbert. "But what can be done?"

"Anything you like to suggest."

"Would you like to go to sea?"

Charley's eyes lit up.

Go to sea! it had been the whole dream of his young life.

He had often looked with disgust at the menial livery his parents had compelled him to wear; and when from the castle windows his eyes had wandered over the free, dancing waters, how he envied the happy, careless, lucky seaman whose home was the blue main before him.

"Yes! yes!" he said, eagerly, to the captain's question, "I should, sir, very much like to do so."

Herbert smiled at the boy's eagerness and said—

"Very well, I will see what can be done. But, first, you must shift that suit—it will never do for you to go on board a vessel in that gear."

Ringing the bell as he spoke, the summons was immediately answered by his attendant.

"Send Mr. Churchill to me?"

The servant retired, and in a few minutes Mr. Churchill, a youth about Charley's age, entered.

He was one of the midshipmen on board the king's vessel.

"You wished to see me, sir?" he asked.

"Yes," said the captain. "Do you think you can find a suit of clothes for this youngster?"

"I'll try, sir."

He did try, and succeeded admirably; for, in less than five minutes, he returned with a complete rig out for Charley Phillips.

How proudly the boy's heart beat when he arrayed himself in the neat dress which young Churchill brought him.

He felt himself a sailor already.

During the time that he had been dressing, Captain Beale had written a letter to a friend of his.

The letter was handed to Charley, and the captain ordered a boat to be got ready.

When this was done, he accompanied his young charge to the side, and, directing the middy in care of the boat to pull for the Albion, he wished him a happy voyage.

Charley, while being rowed towards the whaling ship, began to build castles in the air.

"After all," he thought, "It has turned out a good thing for me that Pierre was killed; for I've now got my berth, and who knows what I may become now? What should I have been? Nothing. When I grew up I might have been a footman, perhaps. I should have got as high as a butler, but that's all. Now, I may be a captain —who knows?"

Before his soliloquy was well ended, the boat was pulled round to the gangway of a large full rigged ship.

"This is the Albion," said the middy. "Goodbye!"

"Good-bye!" said Charley, cheerily, as he ran up the side.

When he reached the deck he was met by the skipper, who gruffly, yet not rudely, asked him his business.

Charley handed him Captain Beale's letter for a reply, and when the bluff sailor had read the epistle, he looked at the boy and smiled.

"Ay, a likely-looking lad."

"May I stay, sir!" asked Charley, who began to fear from the captain's silence that he did not approve of him.

"Stay, yes, with such a letter. Tumble down below and get your name on the ship's books, then find something to do. We'll make a sailor of you. You'll find it rather rough at first, but you'll soon get used to it."

"I'll try and learn, sir."

"You'll learn quick enough. Now be off with you."

Charley did not tumble down, as the captain desired; but, not being used to the mode of descent to the purser's sanctum, he slipped down the last half-dozen steps, much to the amazement of some sailors.

The boy jumped up with a light laugh, and finding the important functionary he sought, he was soon entered on the register of the Albion's crew.

CHAPTER LIII.

BAFFLED.

WITH a baleful gleam in her cruel eyes, the crime-stained baroness ascended the steps that led to the north wing.

It was the midnight hour, and the solemn bell of the turret clock pealed out twelve.

The beautiful demon counted the strokes, and a wicked smile crossed her features.

"The witching hour when other spirits of evil are said to leave their haunts," said she. "So be it. I have companions, and they are fit ones for the occasion."

She paused in her stealthy walk and listened attentive.

Nothing disturbed the calm silence, save the sobbing gusts of wind, as they swept fitfully around the ancient building.

Lady Mountsteven paused again—this time near the deep recess of a window, and holding up a bottle of crystal fluid she muttered—

"Pierre gone! ah! by heaven that blow was well aimed. This boy too—it is hard for him to die, but my life is more precious than his. Yes, yes. Well, a few drops of this in the water he will drink; then death and inquest, and it will go forth to the world that the boy who murdered the Frenchman committed self-destruction to avoid the disgrace of being hanged."

Thus the hard-hearted ambitious woman soliloquised, as the deadly fluid danced and sparkled in its crystal phial.

But this time she reckoned without her host, for the bold, bright-eyed boy (as the reader already knows) had escaped from her fiend-like clutches.

Carefully replacing the bottle and its contents in her breast, she ascended the last flight of stairs, and stood before the door where young Philips had been confined.

The first thing she saw was the servant, bound and gagged, lying upon the landing.

A cry of rage escaped her; she guessed at once her intended victim had escaped, and freeing the man's mouth from the gag, she said vehemently—

"What is the meaning of this?"

The servant shrank from her blazing eye, and replied—

"I dunno, my lady, 'cept that the young chap is gone."

"Gone!" she repeated. "Gone! what do you mean, fellow?"

"It's no fault o' mine, my lady; there was two of 'em. The young mens comed up, and the two men knocked me down, and got inside."

"Fool! is this the way you keep watch over a prisoner, and that prisoner a murderer? Where was your gun?"

"The gun wasn't a bit of use. I was down'd before I had time to even bring 'm up."

"There were two, you say?"

"Yes, my lady."

"What were they like?"

"Well, one looked loike a sailor officer, and t'other was that young chap as the outlaws call Tom Wilson."

Lady Mountsteven reeled, and glaring upon the man savagely, she screamed—

"Are you mad?"

"I baint," he replied, surlily, "not a bit—it is all true, every word."

Lady Mountsteven ground her teeth, and muttered—

"That meddling fool who saved me from the pirate has released the boy. My curses be on him,"

The gamekeeper took up his gun, and descending the stairs, said—

"It be no use going on about it now, my lady. I'll go and see if I can find 'im."

"Do," she said. "Is your gun loaded?"

"It be."

"Then go at once, and if you get sight of him, fire, no matter whom you hit."

"I will, never fear, my lady. I'll make 'em pay for knocking I down."

His heavy footfall soon ceased to be heard, and Lady Mountsteven, with clenched hands, descended the stairs, saying—

"Perhaps after all the fool is mistaken; it is impossible the boy can have escaped from the dungeons beneath the castle."

With this hope in her breast, she went swiftly towards the cell where the young chieftan had been immured.

"Malediction! He also has escaped! But how?"

In a paroxysm of rage she dashed the phial to to the ground, and said through her set teeth—

"Lost—ruined! The blood I have spilled will have been uselessly shed if the boy be ever seen by my fool of a husband."

Slowly she ascended the steps, and with a deadly design against another's life, she reached her chamber.

The lady, absorbed as she was by her thoughts, did not notice two figures who were noiselessly coming down the corridor, and, who, as she approached, secreted themselves in the recess of one of the windows.

CHAPTER LIV.
ON THE TRAIL.

ONE of these men the reader has met before in the pages. He was Ned Hughes, the detective.

The other was a thick-set man, with piercing eyes, and of that restless aspect that denotes watchfulness of everything that comes under his notice.

He was also a detective—a man skilled above his fellows for his keenness in ferreting out hidden crime.

This man, Fred Baylis, had come from London to assist his friend Hughes.

His grey eyes followed her ladyship in her evening walks, and she already stood condemned in his estimation of being capable of daring the consequences of any crime she might herself commit, or cause to be committed by others, so that her own end be gained.

To his companion, Ned Hughes, had laconically summed her up thus—

"She seems devil enough for anything."

"And yet," said Hughes, "I can scarcely recognise her handiwork in that attempt upon my life. You do, I know, but I cannot."

Baylis laughed quietly, and said—

"You left the castle directly after giving the papers to the baronet, and walked by the cliffs towards your lodging, and—if I am rightly informed—you were suddenly set upon by two men, and tumbled into the sea."

"Yes; all this is true."

"And one of them you know well. His name was"——

"Jack Henson, the wrecker."

"Just so. And he it was whom the villagers found crushed to a shapeless mass in the ravine. Here is a link."

And he noted it down in his memorandum book.

"A link?" said Hughes. "I do not see any use in that fellow's death."

"I do," responded Fred Baylis; but I will let you know on another occasion. Let us now join Lord Mountsteven."

They emerged from their hiding-place, and went to the library, where they found his lordship, looking pale and more careworn than ever.

The mysterious murder of Pierre, the steward, had fallen heavily upon his mind.

He started when he saw Ned Hughes, and pressing his heated hand over his forehead, said—

"I never thought to see you again."

"Nor would you," said Hughes, "had it not been for the lucky chance that led me to fall on a mass of wet sea-weed instead of the hard rocks."

"Your life has been attempted, then?"

"It has."

The detective told the astonished nobleman of the attempt that had been made upon his life, giving a few more details than when speaking upon the subject to his brother officer.

Lord Mountsteven pondered over the narrative for a few minutes, then asked—

"Did any one see you leave the castle!"

This question seemed to bring a half-forgotten event to Ned Hughes's mind, for he said abruptly—

"Yes; now you mention it. I remember seeing that hang-dog Frenchman at the gate."

"Pierre?"

"The same."

"Did he follow you?"

"I cannot positively say; yet I have a dim remembrance of hearing stealthy steps as I walked from the castle."

His lordship groaned with anguish.

"Pierre," he said, hastily, "is dead."

"Dead!"

This was repeated by both detectives at the same moment.

"Yes," said his lordship, "found not three hours since weltering in his blood, a stiletto driven to the hilt in his heart."

Fred Baylis made another note in his book.

He then asked—

"Have you no clue to the perpetrator?"

"We have a boy confined upon the charge—a mere stripling."

"Have you any proofs, sir, of that boy's guilt?"

"None of a positive nature. The mere fact of his age, one would think, would preclude the idea of his having committed so foul a crime."

The gray-eyed-officer startled his lordship by the manner in which he put the next question—

"Where," he asked, "was the body found?"

Lord Mountsteven paused for a moment before he replied; then, turning his head to his interlocutor, he said, faintly—

"In Lady Mountsteven's boudoir."

The indefatigable Baylis had his note-book out in a moment.

"Yes, your lordship," he said, as he pencilled down a few words. "Yes; is that all?"

"Yes," replied his lordship.

Lord Mounsteven then addressed Hughes concerning the papers left with him when the detective left the castle on his last visit.

"They," said his lordship, "disappeared in a most mysterious manner, for when I was about to read them a piercing scream, which appeared to come from the corridor, caused me to leave the room, and when I returned the papers had disappeared.

"And have you not seen them since?"

"I have not."

Baylis was pencil in hand again.

He saw at a glance that some master hand, deeply skilled in cunning, was at work, and he determined to fill up the blanks before he had done with the mysterious affair.

"I should, if it would not be asking too much," said the man with the note-book, "like to see the chamber where the murder was committed."

His lordship lit a taper, and directed his visitors to follow him.

They did so.

And when the two stood in the room where Pierre was lying, Ned Baylis took the taper from his lordship's hand.

Then in a quick, business-like manner, he looked at the furniture.

Everything was in its place—not even a chair overturned.

He examined, more minutely, several articles of ornament and vertu about the room, and then passed to the dead body of the Frenchman, from whose rigid fingers he drew a small shred of lace, placing it between the leaves of his pocket book, muttered—

"A link!"

Then the detectives expressed themselves satisfied with the examination they had made, and proposed to return to the library.

When they were seated, he with the note-book said—

"Pardon me, my lord, but I am bound to tell you I see a distressing clue to these mysteries; but ere I acquaint you with the name of the one whom I suspect of being the assassin, I would search among the dead man's papers; other evidence might be found."

Lord Mountsteven, with a sad foreboding at his heart, replied—

"You have my permission to act as you think proper in the matter."

The officers left the room together, and the hapless noble was left alone with his wretched thoughts.

On the way to Pierre's chamber they encountered Lady Mounsteven emerging therefrom.

She had been there and recovered the papers Pierre had abstracted from the black cabinet.

"Mine, mine, again," she said to herself, "and I am now safe for a time—safe for ever. But the boy, or my poor, weak fool of a husband must be removed. One must die, and that speedily."

As these deadly thoughts passed through her mind, she was gliding towards her chamber.

Suddenly a slight but strange noise caused her to start and tremble; a deadly chill ran through her frame, and she clutched at the baluster for support.

Wildly her eyes gazed upon an object that stood silently pointing with outstretched finger towards her, and, as the large clammy drops of fear oozed from her forehead, she stood appalled by the terrible shadowy form   the late Lady Edith, Lord Mountsteven's first wife, and the mother of the gallant, outlawed boy—Tom Wilson.

CHAPTER LV.
OVERBOARD.

THE lad who, thanks to the kindness of Captain Herbert Beale, escaped from the clutches of the she-demon who would have destroyed him, found he had much to learn before he knew anything of sailing.

The captain of the vessel had the good sense to make the youngsters, who joined his crew, learn their duties properly.

"It will make good men of them," the old seaman was wont to remark, "and good officers too, for they will know how work should be done."

This custom was the cause of a misadventure to Charley, and one that nearly put an end to his existence, for when the vessel went out of harbour with a spanking breeze, she plunged her bows into the rough waves of the open sea.

Charley, while standing on the cat-head, looking straight before him, was absorbed in the romantic fancies exhibited by his novel situation.

These fancies, however, were soon very unpleasantly interrupted by the first mate, a short, stout matter-of-fact personage, wearing a little blue jumper, and a ponderous son'-wester.

"Ahoy there! Trying to shirk duty, are ye? This way at once, you young lubber, to help to h'ist these barrels of pork out of the hold."

Accordingly the lad hastened aft to the steerage hatch where the men were at work, and where he soon found himself so hastily employed in pulling upon a rope that, to say nothing of "castle building," he could hardly find time to breathe.

There was nothing very romantic in this kind of labour, and the hoarse voices of the seaman as they bawled out a rude chorus to the effect that a certain

"Billy at the tackle O !
Broke his backbone, Ho ! ho ! ho !
A pulling of the ship's ropes, O !"

were certainly not calculated to charm his fancy, or give relief to his aching spine.

At last, however, the business at the steerage hatch was completed, and as it was now late in the afternoon, the boy came to the conclusion that all work for the day was at and end.

He, therefore, walked forward ; seating himself upon the spritsail-yard, and fixing his eyes upon that distant part of the sea where the water seemed to wash the red face of the sinking sun, he began to reflect over his lucky escape.

"Hulloa! This way here, youngster!" roared

a voice at this juncture from the quarter-deck; and turning, the lad beheld the captain of the ship beckoning to him.

"Take that staging, and sling it over the stern; then get a scraper, and scrape that tar off the paint under the cabin windows!" were the quick, brief orders which saluted the ears of Charley, as he confronted the skipper.

"Ay, ay, sir," answered the boy, trying to imitate the gruff tone of his shipmates.

The next moment the captain had vanished through the companion-way, and, looking around him, Charley perceived that the quarter-deck was deserted by everybody except the man at the wheel.

This sailor was a Spaniard, with a dark hangdog visage, and but one eye.

He glanced wickedly and mischievously upon the lad, evidently much amused by the bewildered look of the boy as he raised the stage plank on its end, wholly ignorant of the manner in which he was to proceed to sling it over the stern, for the ropes had been taken out of the holes near the extremities of the board.

"He! he! he! laughed the weather-beaten helmsman, as the lad at length glanced towards him. "Why you no get another rope?"

"Where shall I get it?"

"We have plenty there," replied the Spaniard, pointing towards the starboard boat, while a mischievous twinkle made his one eye sparkle like a firefly upon an egg-plant. "Yees, yees, ye have plenty there!"

"It's all right, cried Charley, merrily, and with these words he sprang into the boat.

In the forward part of it he found a small coil of whaling line, which he believed was the rope to which the sailor had alluded.

Seizing the end, therefore, and disdaining to solicit further advice, he passed it through the holes of the stage-plank—in a very "lubberly" manner, and fastened it to the other part of the line with a clumsy "cow-hitch."

Then he lowered the plank astern, after having "taken a turn" with the line around one of the ratlins in the mizen shrouds.

"Now, that's what I call ship-shape'" muttered the lad, as, scraper in hand, he proceeded to descend by the rope to the plank.

As soon as his feet struck the board he went to work with a will.

But before he had more than half completed his task, the gloom of night, together with a thick fog, closed around him.

Thrusting the scraper in the belt about his waist, he was proceeding to mount to mount to the deck for the purpose of procuring a lantern, when a sudden terrible clattering noise saluted his ears, and the next moment he was precipitated with the plank into the water.

"Good heavens!" he gasped, as he straddled the floating board, "th rope—the rope has pa. and I am adrift."

A feeling of horror and desolation made the blood run cold in his veins.

He shouted several times with all the strength of his lungs, but no answering voice replied.

The booming of the ship still sounded in his ears, but her tall masks and dark hull were invisible in the fog and darkness.

CHAPTER LVI.
SAVED.

"Ay, ay," muttered Charley, "a gloomy presentiment tells me that I'll never see the decks of the Albion again. I am a castaway upon the wide ocean, and God only knows what will become of me."

At that moment the noise of the ship's bell sounding seven strokes was borne faintly upon the breeze, and it vibrated on the heart-strings of the boy like a knell of death.

He covered his face with his hands and shuddered.

"My doom is sealed," he moaned; "and yet, perhaps—yes, yes, perhaps I may yet be picked up by some outward-bound vessel. It is unmanly to give way to despair like this, for I have heard that a true sailor never gives up while there is a plank beneath him."

Then his heart bounded in his bosom with a thrill of exquisite pleasure as he said—

"This is just such an adventure as I have been longing for. Afloat upon the wide sea on a plank! It is glorious—glorious!"

Then he ran over in his mind all the accounts that he had read in books of shipwrecked mariners, and was pleased to compare his situation with that of a hero of one of the favourite nautical romances.

"What if I should be picked up by a pirate or a slaver," he thought. "Wouldn't that be a story to tell when I get home? That would be splendid! Just the thing that would suit me."

And the enthusiastic lad continued then to loosen the sails of his imagination, until it gained so much headway that his thoughts were carried far away from the reality of his situation.

But the fancy of Charley could not outstrip the long hours of that gloomy night. The cold sea, continually breaking over him, chilled his delicate form.

And hunger—for in his excitement at finding himself on ship board, he had forgotten to taste even a mouthful of food—began to crave for satisfaction.

These feelings, naturally enough, had the effect of damping his ardour, but not to subdue the beam of hope that still shone steadily and brightly in bosom.

He believed that the light of morning would reveal to him a sail—that he would be picked up soon afterwards, and have the pleasure of relating his singular adventure to groups of interested seaman.

When at last, therefore, after the lapse of many hours, the chilled, hungry, and wearied youth was enabled to catch glimpses of the vessels through the fog which began to be visible at different points through the receding darkness, his strained his eyes in every direction.

He expected every moment to behold the wished-for sail looming before him. While thus occupied he suddenly heard the creaking of yards; then the low hum of voices at no great distance ahead. Every nerve in his body thrilled with delight.

"Hooray! hoorray!" he shouted, unable to repress his enthusiasm. "I knew it would be so. I shall be picked up, and something tells me that the approaching vessel is a slaver. What a romantic adventure that would be! Hooray for such a life! Hooray! hooray!"

Even as he spoke he perceived, to his great joy, the weather was clearing.

He strained his eyes eagerly ahead, anxious to see the vessel which was to rescue him from his perilous situation.

The hum of voices sounded louder every moment.

And Charley now became aware for the first time that the board upon which he was seated kept shaking with a peculiar jerking motion that made it very difficult for him to maintain his position.

"Ay, ay," he muttered, with the assumed air of a thorough seaman, "these short chopping seas are playing their tricks with this plank, and I must hold on *hard*."

The jerking motion continued, seemingly increasing in violence every moment; so that at length the boy was obliged to use both hands to hold himself to the board.

He still kept his eyes riveted ahead of his frail support.

At length he was rewarded with the dim outlines of a vessel.

But the *stern*, instead of the *bow*, was turned towards him.

This circumstance surprised him not a little.

He could not imagine how a vessel with a stiff breeze and squared yards could approach stern foremost.

Presently, however, he was enabled to see above the quarter rail a number of grinning faces, which were turned towards him, and also a line which seemed to lead from the ship to the water, which kept swaying up and down as though busy hands were pulling upon it.

And then a familiar chorus broke upon his ear—

> "Billy at the tackle, O!
> Broke his backbone, Ho! ho! ho!
> A pulling of the ship's ropes, O!"

This charming ditty, roared out with so much gusto, caused a sudden suspicion to dart like lightning through the mind of our hero.

He thrust one of his hands into the water, and then his suspicions were confirmed; for his fingers came into contact with the same line upon which the men were pulling, and one of which was still fast to the board.

"So it seems that I have not been adrift after all!" he cried, in astonishment and much disappointment, as he clambered to the deck of the Albion after the plank had been drawn alongside.

This exclamation was greeted with a roar of hoarse laughter.

"D'ye see that?" cried the skipper, pointing to one of the thwarts of the starboard boat, around which one end of the line was fastened—"d'ye see that? Well, hang ye! how could ye get adrift with one end of the line fast to the boat and the other to the stage plank?"

"But I thought the rope broke."

"Break it, would ye? A young lubber like you break one of my lines that would almost hold a sperm whale! My eyes! Go for'ard at once and learn better manners. It was the rattlin'," continued the captain, "not the line that broke, mark ye that! and don't ever again use a whaling line for a staging. We'd have had you on board before, but it was too dark to see what had happened until near daylight. Now then, away with yer! Go for'ard and put on some dry clothes, and then I'll show you how to sling a stage plank.

This termination of affairs somewhat damped Charley's ardent taste for romantic adventures, and, in due course, he became a judge of the strength of the ropes on board.

CHAPTER LVII.
THE DETECTIVES TRAPPED.

The patrician lady seemed suddenly changed to a rigid statue, save for the tremulous twitching of her lips.

Had the dead returned? or was it the shade of the murdered lady that confronted her?

The first emotion of fear over, Lady Mountsteven rallied a little.

But though she trembled, and her mouth was parched with fear, she said—

"Spirit or mortal, what wouldst thou have?"

The figure fixed its sunken eyes upon the guilt-stricken woman, and replied in a sepulchral voice—

"Women of cruel and unrelenting heart, darest thou ask me? Has the memory of thy great and awful crime so soon died away?"

Lady Mountsteven could not reply; a sudden fit of ague seemed to have seized her, and she could not avert her startled gaze from the ghost-like face of the spectre.

But Lady Mountsteven was no ordinary woman; and nerving herself for the terrible *feat*, she sprang forward, crying—

"Whether spirit or mortal, I will see what thou art!"

"THOMAS WILSON, CRIED THE GIPSY, YOUR LAST HOUR HAS COME."

She tried to catch the mystic figure as she spoke; but the woman, bold as she was, recoiled with a shriek of the wildest terror when her hands grasped nothing.

The form, mortal or spirit, had passed away, and she stood alone in the corridor.

For some moments her strength failed her, and she was, for a time, unable to proceed to her chamber; but when there, her fear, in a measure, vanished; and snatching a crystal goblet of wine from the table, she drank it greedily.

And as the rich juice began to infuse new vigour into her head, she sat down to think and plot the commission of further crime.

By this time the detectives were in the murdered man's room, busily turning over the contents of every box and drawer in the apartment.

Baylis was intent on finding a secret-drawer in a curious-looking writing desk, which he had already emptied of its contents. A faint rustling of paper, as he shifted it from side to side, assuring him there was one to be found.

He was foiled in his efforts for a considerable time; and Hughes suggested the desk should be broken up; but Baylis, who, as he expressed himself, "took a fancy to outwit the clever fellow who made it," preferred continuing his search.

At length a smile broke over his features, and he called Hughes towards him.

'Here, Ned," he said, "here's a clue."

Ned looked, but saw nothing but a mass of grotesque little figures all over the desk, which was carved out of a solid piece of ebony, and evidently of rare antiquity.

"Do you see it, Ned?"

"No. I certainly do not."

The elder detective pointed to a figure rather more prominent than the rest.

"You see that little monk?"

"I do."

"Well, that key which is in his hand, it is my belief, represents a key having something to do with the secret drawer."

"I cannot see it," said Ned.

"I can. Look here."

Hughes held the figure between his thumb and fore-finger, saying—

"It's my opinion the gentleman is moveable—ha! so it is!"

A faint click was heard as he turned the monk, and a small hole became visible.

"There!" said Ned Hughes, triumphantly; "and here is the paper!"

He inserted his finger and thumb as he spoke, and drew out a folded sheet of note-paper.

Both men quickly read over its contents. It was—

"The papers will make me master of her ladyship."

"What inference do you draw from these words?" inquired Ned of his companion.

"This," replied Fred. "The fellow obtained possession of the papers either from Lord Mountsteven's desk, or after they had been taken therefrom; and he held them as a threat over his mistress. For what purpose you can guess. "Yes," continued the cute detective, "Lady Mountsteven had wealth. Pierre was grasping, avaricious, and selfish; the lady discovering the loss of her papers, had somehow—a secret, of course—at present that *somehow* traced their possession to Pierre. A scene took place—mind, we are only supposing these things—the steward either disowned any knowledge of them, or else determined to deliver them to her, and then, there came recriminations, followed naturally by violence, and she—"

"Stabs him. And supposing your surmise to be just, what has become of the papers?" inquired Ned. "Do you really think they were in Pierre's possession?

"I do," said Fred, "of course I do; for Pierre, disabled or dead, what more easy than by diligent search to recover them?"

The discovery in their own minds being thus effected, they retired to a room in the castle, placed at their disposal by the order of his lordship.

And until the small hours of morning, they sat planning how more effectually to solve the chain of mystery.

The following morning, after breakfast, the detectives were proceeding to the library at the summons of Lord Mountsteven, and as they passed the chamber of Lady Mountsteven they found the door open.

The detectives entered, and searching the room, their attention was particularly attracted to the black oak cabinet.

They were about to open it when the rustle of a dress was heard.

It was Lady Mountsteven who had returned to her chamber.

Ere she could place a foot inside the door, the detectives had quickly hidden themselves behind the heavy hangings that draped the windows.

From here they beheld her ladyship open a small pearl inlaid box, from which she took a couple of long cut-glass bottles of foreign make, both tightly stoppered, and full of a bright, rose-coloured liquid.

Lady Mountsteven took one and held it up to the light.

"A rare gift this," she said. "Truly, the women of the East understood the art of distilling these subtle drugs. One drop each day, and those who partake of it glide away from this world, leaving no trace for the most skilled physician to find out the cause of death!"

Lady Mountsteven, having thus improvised, was about to replace the crystal phial of death, when, as she bent her head, she saw something in the looking-glass that sent the blood rushing back to her heart.

But, unlike most women, Lady Mountsteven did not scream or faint.

And, as though nothing had occurred, she replaced the bottle.

Having secured the box, a wicked smile played over her lips as she said—

"Ha! I had forgotten my prisoner in the dungeons below."

The detectives started at her words; and as she left the apartment with a bunch of keys in her hand, they softly followed her.

She heard them; and as they descended the mildewed flight of stone steps the face of their guide brightened up with an unmistakable glow of self-satisfaction.

"Ho! ho!" she thought; "so the myrmidons of the law are creeping thus about the castle to ferret out my secret; they shall find it—ha! ha! ha!"

With devilish cunning she led them on until they had reached the further end of the stone passage, when, unlocking a door, she softly and, as it were, stealthily entered.

The detectives were both close upon her heels.

But when she placed the light outside the dungeon door they drew back.

This was precisely what the crafty woman wished.

She entered and placed the light behind the door, then quickly emerged.

The officers as quickly advanced.

Lady Mountsteven's cunning disposal of the lamp had put the doorway in darkness, therefore they did not see her emerge from the dungeon.

Scarce daring to breathe, they entered the place.

In the furthest corner the dim light indistinctly revealed a heap that looked like a human form.

The detectives went swiftly towards it, and had reached the centre of the chamber, when Lady Mountsteven, with a cry of triumph, closed the door violently.

Fred turned round to his companion, and in perfect dismay, said—

"Trapped, by heaven!"

The key was turned at the same moment; and her ladyship's voice of triumph sounded like a death knell upon the detectives' ears.

"Fools! fools! thus to be lured to a certain lingering death—ha! ha! You did not know I could see you in the mirror! When next you hide—if ever you have the chance—be careful that your feet are concealed, and that the toes of your boots are not visible from beneath when you hide behind window-curtains. Now stay and rot—die like yelping curs, that you are!"

While she, in mockery, was ringing these words into their ears, the lamp went out.

Another moment, and they were left to their horrible fate.

CHAPTER LVIII.
FIERCE BATTLE.

WHEN that volley of musketry was delivered into the entrance of the outlaws' cave, the band sprang to their arms, which were hanging round the walls.

A shudder of deep regret passed over the fine features of the prince when he beheld the men's eagerness for the fray.

Turning to Tom, who stood close beside him, he said—

"It is unjust that I should have brought you into this danger. Commence not to return their fire, rather surrender me into their hands."

"Never," said the young outlaw, "while these walls hang together, and I have a man to stand by me."

"Noble fellow," said the prince, "may you one day meet with a fitting reward."

Snowball here appeared before the outlaw, his dark face expressive of immense satisfaction.

The upper part of his body was completely naked, and, as he stood before Tom, Prince Charles was struck with admiration at his massive proportions.

"Well, Snowball," asked Tom, "are our foes numerous?"

"Dey are, Massa Tom, but I gib 'em somet'ing hot, by Jingo!"

Another shower of lead came pelting against the mouth of the cave.

"Man the embrasures!" said Tom, cocking his pistols; "and take steady aim."

The Stuart looked at the solid walls of the cave, and inwardly wondered what the young chief's words could mean.

He was not long kept in ignorance of the formidable defences of the young outlaw's cave.

A rope hung from the centre of the roof, and, one by one, the stalwart band swarmed up it, and disappeared apparently in the solid rock.

But close to where the rope was fastened in the jagged roof there was an aperture of sufficient size to allow a man to pass through.

This aperture had a gallery half circular in form, which ran round the front of the cave.

In the wall of this gallery a number of embrasures were hewn out, wide inside, but narrowing to a point, where they reached the outer wall.

This point was of sufficient size to admit the barrel of a musket, and, by the help of a small hole bored above the embrasures, the besieged were able to take aim.

Through these holes the outlaws reconnoitred the foe, who were still waiting against the entrance.

Snowball with a long-barrelled rifle took up his position in the centre.

"Cussed red coats," he growled, "you get suffink."

He thrust the muzzle of his piece through the embrasure, and, taking careful aim, fired.

"One!" he said, triumphantly, as he saw a soldier fall to the ground. "Go on dere wid de firing."

Puff after puff of white smoke curled up from the face of the rock, and the troopers looked up with dismay when they saw the disadvantage under which they fought.

They could see it was but waste of powder to return this galling fire, and, as their comrades began to fall around them, they clamoured to be ed to the assault.

Their commanding officer yielded to their shouts.

"Forward! Charge bayonets!" was the order.

Waving his bright sword above his head he led them to the cavern's mouth.

Here they were stricken down by sections; for the place, inaccessible by nature, was rendered more formidable by the encircled fire of twenty well-trained outlaws led on by Tom.

Baffled in this attempt, they hastily reformed, and returned to their original position.

There the fire of the men at the entrance was as deadly as ever.

Foaming with passion, the officer drew his men out of musket range, and held a council of war.

Under the very spot where they stood was one of the long passages that led from the cave to the sea.

Snowball grinned when he saw the position they

had taken up, and with the celerity of a monkey he scrambled down the rope.

"Massa Tom," he said, rushing to the young outlaw's side, "we hab 'em!"

"How?"

"Dey is jist above de ole passage. Hab I to make a mine, Massa Tom?"

"Yes, and quickly."

Snowball, with half-a-dozen men, went away, muttering—

"Golly! Dey go up directly, and no mistake."

From the magazine severals barrels of powder were soon brought to the place indicated by Snowball.

Then the heads were stove in, and a train laid to a safe distance from the anticipated explosion.

The soldiers, officers and men, were grouped together, each holding his own theory as to the best means of compelling the enemy to yield.

In the midst of their argument the train from the cave was fired.

It seemed as though the earth had suddenly been convulsed by a mighty earthquake.

The rocky soil parted, earth, stones, men and weapons were all hurled in the air with terrible violence.

Those who survived the explosion of the mine drew back appalled.

It seemed as though they were fighting against demons, not men, for no sooner had the smoke and dust caused by the explosion cleared away than a shower of firey missiles streamed from the rock.

The soldiers were not long permitted to remain in ignorance of this new weapon, for Snowball again mounted the embrasure; this time, in place of his rifle, having a long metal tube for the purpos of discharging rockets.

The deadly missile was soon hurling death among the surviving red coats, and soon a panic seized them, and with pallid faces they drew from the deadly spot.

"De coast am clear," said the dusky giant, as he rejoined his leader. "By gar! how dem debbils did run!"

"Clear, but at a fearful sacrifice," said the miserable Prince Charles. "The conflict has indee been short and deadly."

"It has," said Tom. "The fortune of war, Had they been conquerors and we the conquered I should have had the cord about my neck, and your highness the same."

"And a precious good thing too, as far as this fellow his concerned," muttered Ben Bight, "for the Stuarts were always a nuisance to England and no good only to hang by the neck, which I hope will happen to this one."

"Besides," added the young outlaw, "these men who have fallen are but hired assassins, who have sold themselves to do a tyrant's bidding for worse than a pauper'spay."

Ben was less chivalrous than his leader, or possibly he thought the risk they ran was not worthy of the object! and he was, or history lies, a better judge than Tom Wilson.

"There is truth in your words, my friend; but I will not lead you into any more danger. Let me depart."

"And where would your highness go?"

"A French privateer awaits me near the coast. Once on her deck, and I am safe."

"Then, outlaws as we are," said Tom, "your royal highness shall not leave us until we place you safe on that French deck."

"Place me aboard? It would be certain death to you. Are you aware that the whole of the coast is blockaded by men-of-war, all looking out to capture me?"

"I am."

"And yet you would attempt it?"

"I dare do all that may become a man," returned the young outlaw, "and I shall do that. Your highness shall leave the deck of my swift vessel when lying alongside of the privateer."

"Your words are incomprehensible. The very fact of the number of men-of-war which environs us would preclude the possibility of effecting it."

"Nevertheless," said Tom, "it shall be done."

Then, bidding his guest remain in the stronghold, the young outlaw wrapped his cloak around him, and, followed by the African giant, several of his men, and the huge dog, he left to prepare the War Cloud for sea; but, ere they reached the beach, a woman's scream of agony caused them to hurry towards the wrecker's cave.

CHAPTER LIX.
FROM BAD TO WORSE.

"LEFT to perish!" were the words uttered by Ned Hughes when Lady Mountsteven's voice died upon their ears.

His companion did not answer him; for while Hughes was speaking, the lamp, which had but partially gone out by the sudden gust of wind, began to rekindle.

Baylis clutched it eagerly and said—

"Ned, we have been had by that fiend in angel's form! and, by heaven! if ever we escape from this infernal dungeon she shall suffer for it!"

Ned looked at his companion, and said, in a short breath—

"She shall!"

They stood a moment regarding each other, then, with one instinct, they moved towards the table with outstretched hands to clutch the gleaming lantern.

"Hughes," said Baylis, quietly, "are we to be left to die and rot in this living tomb?"

"Try and escape, by all means," was the reply.

Baylis raised the lamp above his head, and its gleaming light revealed a heap of dried bones, which caused them both to shudder.

They turned from the sickening spectacle,

and then they began to examine the walls of their prison.

Baylis was in advance of his companion.

Suddenly he started back with a cry which caused the blood in Hughes's veins to curdle; after a moment he asked—

"What the deuce are you making that noise about?"

"Did you hear that voice?" said Baylis.

"Voice—no," was Hughes's curt rejoinder. "Did you?"

"Yes," was the frightened answer.

"What was it like?" asked Hughes.

Baylis shuddered as he answered—

"It was like the voice of a woman in distress."

Hughes looked at his companion and said—

"Well, if she is more in distress than we are, it——"

Ere he could finish his sentence they were both startled by a repetition of the shriek that had alarmed Baylis.

Ned Hughes's face paled.

"A woman's voice!" he said. "What infernal mystery is this?"

Here again the death cry rang out in the thick air, and before either could speak the light went out.

"The deuce!" said Hughes, "we are worse off than ever!"

"Yes," said Baylis, excitedly; "but that cry of distress has given me new life."

"Why?"

"Because," said Baylis, "there are others living besides us in this loathsome den."

"An undeniable fact," said Hughes. "We will try and make their acquaintance."

"We will."

They did; although Baylis was a man whom nothing in the light could appal, yet in the darkness he was prone to feel a sensation of timidity nearly akin to fear.

He missed his companion, and groping about the place to find him, he came in concussion with him.

They both fell to the ground.

The latter swearing, and in a most ungentlemanly manner, while Baylis was lying on his back, gasping on the ground and out of breath.

The corner of the table had struck him in the wind, so Hughes crawled away on his hands and knees.

Suddenly his head came in contact with something projecting from the wall.

The blow caused him to reel backwards, and at the same time he saw more stars in his eyes than he had the ability or time to count.

After recovering from the shock, he turned his head and shouted to Baylis with an exclamation that was not very becoming of a man immured in a dungeon, and who, for what he knew, might never be released therefrom.

"All right," answered Baylis, sulkily. "If you had all your wind knocked out of you, perhaps you would not be in such a hurry to move."

"Hang you for a fool!" answered Hughes. "Come and assist me!"

He had just discovered a large stone, projecting from the wall, "and it may be," said he, "that this stone has answered some special purpose, and been occasionally removed.

Baylis crawled towards Ned Hughes; and, while trying to raise himself by the before mentioned stone, he put his hand on something sharp.

He gave a loud exclamation of delight.

"Ned, there is something here. It feels like an iron chisel."

His companion groped out the place where it was to be found, and saying—

"Friend steel, come, let me clutch thee!"

Baylis got the supposed chisel, but on handling it more closely, he discovered it was but a rusty nail.

"Never mind," said Hughes. "It will answer the purpose for which we intend it."

He then set to work with a will and the use of his rusty nail, to try and move the stone.

By degrees he managed to pick out pieces of the mortar, by which it at first appeared to the inmates the stone had been fixed in its place.

But it turned out that a front casing only of mortar was placed round the stone, evidently intended to disguise its purpose of being removed when required.

The detectives adopted the idea at any rate, and their prospects of release brightened considerbly.

By degrees the face of the mortar crumbled away, and the stone began to loosen a little.

Baylis was then asked to take a turn at the work.

He did so; and with all the vigour of one in captivity, freshened up with the belief that on his own exertions alone depended a speedy liberty.

Suddenly he stopped.

His attention had been directed to a small streak of light which came beside the stone, and to which he called his companion's notice.

"Be careful!" said Hughes, "and don't let the stone fall so that it will make any noise, or it may draw the attention of somebody who may be there."

They crouched together, and came to the conclusion that if they could but withdraw the stone, it would lead to some other place.

Their conversation was interrupted by another agonizing shriek for help from a woman, but more plainly heard than the last one.

They both started.

Hughes was the first to break the silence.

"Ned." said he, "there is foul play going on hereabout! Let us set our hearts upon getting through this confounded wall. It may be we shall be in time for a rescue."

Baylis worked away with his nail again until he gave his companion a nudge to arrest him, as the stone appeared to be gently gliding out of the wall, and he saw a likely prospect of its lodging on his toes.

As Fred had had a bunion for no end of years, he shuddered at the weight of such a connexion.

The stone, however, suddenly fell, and Fred, only by limping back dexterously, managed to save his toe from that awful fate which he anticipated would befal it.

To the surprise of both the fall of the stone revealed a cave, with a large fire burning in one corner, and tenanted by at least a score of ill-looking men,

Some were quietly talking, others drinking, and a great portion of them smoking.

Greatly to the relief of the two detectives, they were not seen by the cut-throat-looking ruffians.

"Pleasant company," whispered Ned. "Rather decline than court the honour of their acquaintance."

"Ditto," said his companion. "Do you remember their faces—especially that mangy, dog-looking rascal over against those hogsheads?"

"I do, now you recall the circumstance. They are part of the band of murderers who infest the coast."

"They are. Hush! what is that noise?"

From the other side of the cave came the hoarse voices of a number of men, who were either quarrelling or trying to do for some poor devil.

The detectives looked eagerly towards the inlet to the cavern, and suddenly a piercing cry rang out. Then there was a few moments' silence.

Then another threat, followed by a gurgling sound, as though someone were being choked.

Then a shouting of rough voices, and the wreckers that were sitting around the fire arose.

There was a confused noise: the shrieks of women, mingled with blasphemous oaths and exclamations from the wreckers.

Now the noise grew more furious; and there came a rush of feet, and two beautiful girls were roughly brought in, led by four savage-looking men.

Behind them was a noble-looking youth, who struggled desparately with his captors.

"Well, mate," said one, who was smoking, addressing the leader, "where did you overhaul that prize? Not a bad craft."

"Well, you see as how there was a wreck, and a course we went to look after the booty, and the first thing my toplights catches a glimpse on was her; so I put my grappling irons on her, and tows her in land."

During this time the detectives had been looking on very interested with the scene.

"Spies, mates—spies!"

"Where?" inquired all the voices at once.

"Through there!"

And the speaker pointed with his finger to the hole through which Hughes and Baylis were looking.

When the detectives heard these words pronounced, they thought their fate was sealed.

Several of the wreckers rushed towards the hole, and dragged Baylis through by the neck and shoulders.

Hughes was served similarly. Then they were thrust into the middle of the cave.

"Well, yer lubberly-looking swabs," said a gruff voice, "what was yer sneaking game?"

Baylis looked at Hughes, and was about to speak, when he received a sudden jerk which nearly chocked him.

Hughes then attempted to speak, and was also nearly strangled by the collar.

"Avast heaving there!" said the same gruff voice; "and tell us what port you sailed from."

Baylis began to relate to them how they were put in the dungeon, and the way they tried to make their escape, and so found themseves in their present predicament; but before he could finish his story, one of the denizens of the cave savagely said—

"Stop yer jawing-tackle, and lay-to, yer lubber It's my opinion as how these sharks are perlice officers, and they came here to overhaul the place."

"Yes. Spies!" cried the leader.

"They must die!" echoed the band.

The detectives turned pale, and declared their innocence, and implored mercy.

The reply was brief.

"Secure them," said the leader, "and bind them hand and foot."

Some would have taken summary vengeance, but it was finally arranged they should be hanged.

They were then put under a beam that reached across the cave, which had evidently been placed there for the purpose of hanging those whom they had taken from wrecked vessels and robbed, and then destroyed.

Indeed there remained dangling at least a dozen pieces of rope, by which many such innocent porsons had undoubtly been strangled.

Several wreckers then threw a rope over the beams, and when the noose was placed round Ned's neck, others were ready to haul their victims up, when one of the girls before alluded to rushed upon the hangman.

CHAPTER LX.
VENGEANCE.

THE fisherman's son, like a spirit of evil, was ever ready at his merciless master's side to urge him onwards to fresh deeds of crime.

But these acts were confined to the desperadoes who served under Red Hand's banner.

"I GIB 'EM SÓMET'ING HOT, MASSA TOM, BY JINGO!"

One by one the crew were hanged or shot by Red Hand's orders orders, and Peter's subtile revenge commenced.

It was a deep-laid plan for one of Peter's years, and it required more than ordinary care to work it out.

The boy, in his keen desire to avenge his father's foul murder, had resolved on adopting one terrible course.

It was to destroy the band of desperadoes and their chief.

For this purpose he was now on the watch. His instincts were changed, and the least word or sign of disatisfaction was reported to the bandit, Red hand.

Since the open attempt at mutiny by Duhouse Red Hand's lieutenant, and his companions, the pirate's ferocity seemed to be increasing daily.

The plot worked bravely.

The wholesale execution of the crew that took place soon left the vessel short-handed.

Peter watched the success of his deeply-laid scheme with exultation, and every fresh victim to the pirate's rage, made him an enemy the less.

One day, when the ruffian crew had been deprived of their grog by their leader, the boy's quick brain saw an opportunity of working further mischief.

He was silently exulting over the success of his scheme, when a terrible uproar on deck caused Red Hand, who was in his cabin, to shout—

"What's that, Giffard?"

The boy smiled pitilessly as he thought—

"More of my handiwork. I purposely dropped the key of the spirit-room; it has been found, and the ruffians, now influenced by drink, are murdering each other."

He was again startled by the voice of Red Hand calling—

"Giffard! Giffard!"

The boy went to the outer cabin, for his savage master was in his cot.

"What is that noise?" he asked when Peter entered. "Go and see."

Peter ascended the companion ladder, and for several minutes he gazed on the wild scene going on among the crew.

His words were true.

The key had been found, and several kegs of rum had been brought from the spirit room.

The heads they had stove in, and the ruffians, rendered more savage by the effects of the spirit, were now fighting like angry beasts.

The knife and pistol were doing their work when the boy stood in the hatchway.

Red Hand sprang from his cot, and, hastily dressing himself, seized his sword and pistols, rushed to the deck.

The sight of their savage leader sent the crew cowering to their berths.

Those who were too intoxicated to move remained upon the deck.

These Red Hand ordered to be placed in irons.

The vessel was at this time in sight of land, and those who were fit for duty were ordered to see the vessel kept clear from the rocks.

"Sail, oh!" said the man on the look-out.

"Ay, ay," was the only response, as they began to take in the top-gallant sail.

Towards evening the breeze had freshened up, and the strange sail steered in towards the land.

And when twilight's dubious gloom began to spread over the waters, Red Hand, giving peremptory instructions to the man at the wheel as to the course to keep, went below.

But an hour later there came a terrible crash followed by the hurried rush of many feet.

Red Hand, followed by Giffard, rushed to the deck, and, to the pirate's rage, and Giffard's joy, they found the vessel upon a sunken rock.

The land lay within ten fathoms where the ship struck.

The hissing of the foam-crested waters evinced that the place abounded in hidden reefs.

Red Hand's face became diabolical in expression, and with dire expressions of ferocity threatened his crew with barbarous vengeanc

But for the time at least he was compelled to forego his design, for to save his vessel required all his attention.

She was shipping such heavy seas, that the men had arduous work to keep the pumps going.

Then the water, like an angry demon, began to rush through an aperture in the vessel's side with terrible force, threatening the Black Snake's early foundering.

It was clear also, that the rock upon which she had first struck had driven a hole clean through the vessel's bottom, and every fresh wave that washed over her so increased the danger, that even Red Hand himself felt a nervous apprehension that his wicked career was fast drawing to a close.

The scene that ensued baffles all attempts at a perfect description of it.

With blasphemous expressions against those who had caused the disaster, he ordered the pirates to keep at the pumps.

"Now," said Giffard to himself—"now is the moment of my escape. Quick through that port I have lowered a boat. This knife, and cut the painter; then away."

Red Hand was standing on the poop, his arms folded, and his cruel, cold, glaring eyes fixed upon the men working at the pumps.

Giffard touched his arm. The fierce pirate turned round quickly. Then Giffard, in a hissing tone, said—

"Monster! behold my work!—the work of Peter, the murdered fisherman's son."

Red Hand drew from his breast a pistol, and levelling it at Peter, pulled the trigger.

"Ha! Ha!" laughed Peter, "they are empty."

Then he sprang upon the nettings, and continued—

"It was I who caused the crew to muting; it was I who dropped the key in the spirit-room, as I told you; the purpose for which I did it is now manifest. Behold the result! Fast upon a rock; either to perish by hunger or by the waters, or to survive until I send a sloop-of-war to capture and hang you, dog! miscreant! murderer!"

Red Hand foamed at the mouth while these words were being uttered; and, drawing a cutlass, made a rush at the daring and rescentful boy.

With a laugh of defiance, Peter made for the boat; cut the painter, and was soon pulling towards the shore.

CHAPTER LXI.

THE COMBAT IN THE WRECKER'S CAVE.

PETER's words and actions had been so swift—so unexpected, that, before the crew could understand what had taken place, the boy was free of the vessel.

"Follow him! follow him! curse him! Kill him!" shouted Red Hand.

A dozen muskets were fired; but in the crazy state of the vessel, their aim was uncertain and their shots useless.

And with another laugh of ringing defiance, Peter pulled swiftly from the vessel until his boat grounded.

Without hesitation, he plunged boldly into the sea, and like an expert swimmer, as he was, dashed away through the billows, reached the shore in safety, and made for an adjoining forest, among the trees in which he soon disappeared.

＊　　＊　　＊　　＊　　＊　　＊　　＊

The young girl, regardless of her own safety, turned upon the brutal wreckers as she clung to the detective's arm.

"Demons!" she said, "have you not shed blood enough to day? Release this man, he is innocent of any crime! Back, or I will slay the first man who attemps to touch the cord."

She snatched a loaded pistol from the belt of a wrecker who stood near, and they saw, by the glitter in her eyes, she would use it.

A deed so nobly attempted, caused a momentary discomfiture to the gang.

That moment was a precious one, for suddenly

and furiously the door was thrown back, and a figure entered, robed in a long cloak.

All suddenly started back as though a spectre stood before them.

"Hold! cowardly wretches!" said a thrilling voice, too well recognised as that of the gallant outlaw, Tom wilson.

The reply was—

"Secure the intruder!"

The stranger gave a low laugh, which made the men feel anything but comfortable.

They made a rush towards him. The stranger made a slight signal with his fingers placed behind him.

Then came a rush of feet. A crew of jolly-looking tars ran forward; at the head was a gigantic African.

"Fools, you have sealed your fate by entering this cave!" said the leader of the band. "Forward men! Secure every one of them!"

The stranger gave another unpleasant mocking laugh.

One of the wreckers, savage at being thus laughed at, plucked a knife from his belt, and was about to lead his men to attack the intruders.

At this juncture the stranger threw off his cloak and revealed himself.

"Midshipman Tom!" gasped the leader of the wreckers as he fell back into the arms of one of his comrades.

Snowball began to finger the bone handle of his scalping knife.

He had an idea: it was—

"Dat somebody lose dere scalp, anyhow!"

The wrecker knew there was no escape now, save oy defeating the few men Tom had brought with him.

The outlaw had sworn to destroy the crew of demons should he ever catch them pursuing their infamous work.

He had sufficient evidence now, and was about to order his men to wreak a summary punishment upon the gang.

Before he could utter one word, the leader of the ruffians roared—

"Shoot the whelp! Down with him and his band!"

The outlaw drew his sword, and he stepped back, a smile of cool defiance upon his handsome lips, and an expression in his eyes that looked perfectly tiger-like in the gloomy light of the cave.

The African saw his leader's danger, and whistled to those who were behind them.

The hoarse command of the ruffian to shoot down Midshipman Tom was followed by the wreckers levelling their pieces at him.

Snowball threw himself before his handsome young master, and presenting a pistol at the wrecker, said—

"You rascal—take dat!"

He pulled the trigger as he spoke.

There was a flash and a report, followed by a howl of pain, and the brute uttered an oath and fell to the ground, with a bullet in his shoulder.

A hoarse cry of rage drowned the fall of their leader, and the wreckers, grasping their weapons, threw themselves upon the outlaws.

In numbers they were six to one, and soon a close, deadly conflict ensued.

"Got dat," Snowball muttered, as he felled a heavy fellow who was creeping behind the young leader, "By gar, you let him alone."

The dog seemed imbued with the fury of a demon.

His white teeth became reddened with blood as he stood savagely watching over his master.

Several wreckers had tried to strike a deadly blow at the young outlaw.

But those who made the attempt were either borne to the earth by the outlaws, or crushed beneath Snowball's battle-axe.

Thus defended, he held his ground against all who opposed him.

One by one his foes fell beneath his scimitar.

Around the cave various groups of outlaws were engaged hand to hand with the wreckers.

In the background stood Ned Hughes and Fred Baylis, the detectives.

Senseless upon a pile of rich merchandise lay the young girl the ruffians had brought from the wreck.

This strange, wild scene was lit by several torches, the flickering red glare lending a wild and not ungraceful charm to the scene.

Thus, when the fight was at its fiercest point, the clash of swords, the report of pistols, and the angry shouts of the combatants were all mingled in one dread sound.

To this another was added.

A sound so unexpected that the combatants paused involuntarily and looked at each other.

The entrance to the wrecker's cave was filled with the king's soldiers.

Outlaws and wreckers by mutual understanding turned their weapons away from each other's breasts, and faced the common foe.

The officer in command of the troops was brave as well as humane, and lowering the point of his sword, he said—

"Can we not spare the sacrifice of human life which this encounter must occasion? My men are disciplined and well armed, and as my orders are to arrest but one man in this assembly, let him surrender; and I will depart. Refuse to do so, and I give the word to fire."

He pointed to Midshipman Tom as he spoke.

Tom gave no answer, nor did he display any intention of yielding to the officer's threats. On the contrary, he wiped his ensanguined blade upon the jacket of a fallen foe, and said—

"You want me. You will have to take me. Midshipman Tom and his band never surrender."

"Be it so," said the officer.

Then turning to his men he gave the command—

"Make ready—present—fi "——

The words did not pass—his lips closed.

Snowball's savage eyes had been watching him, and with the uncompleted command on his lips Snowball slew him.

His pistols were both unloaded, but, like all savages, he understood the art of throwing the knife, and he made use of his skill.

A close volley followed from the soldiers when they beheld their officer fall.

Then with the bayonet, and giving one wild hurrah, they rushed upon their opponents. But the cutlasses and tomahawks of their foes overpowered them, and hemmed in on all sides, they had not time to reload.

Further fighting proving equally unavailing, the young officer in command ordered his men to—

"Trail arms! Right about turn! At a double! Forward!"

The men obeyed orders with great celerity, and started off at a run.

The young outlaw stood leaning on his trusty blade; and the leader of the wreckers, supported by two of his men, was immediately opposite.

The fighting thus over, outlaws and the wreckers mutually agreed to separate, each to pursue his calling, the only condition being, that Ned Hughes and Fred Baylis were to be declared free of the wreckers.

To the joy of the detectives, they were set free, and conducted to the cavern's mouth.

'Forget what you have this night seen," was the lowly spoken caution they received from their conductor.

The detectives bowed; and with lighter hearts than it had been their lots to possess since the moment Lady Mountsteven had locked them in the dungeon, they left the vicinity of the cave.

"A lucky escape," said Ned Hughes. "I shall remember that young fellow in my prayers when I say them."

No doubt," was Baylis' reply. "You looked as though you were about to say them for the last time a half hour since."

"And your appearance was not very cheerful," retorted his comrade.

"A weekness of mine, that's all, to look grave in any delicate position.

"Exactly," said Ned, drily.

"Yes, I —— Hullo! hullo! What the deuce is that? Look out there, upon the water!"

Hughes followed the direction of his companion's outstretched finger, and beheld the form of a young girl floating on the sea.

"Dead!" said the officer after a further scrutiny, "dead!"

"She seems so, at any rate," said Baylis, going swiftly towards the shore; "but there may be life eft;" and he was about plunging into the water, but his companion's voice stopped him.

"Nonsense," he said. "Come out of this. She has been dead, I dare say, some time—possibly one of the victims of this night's work."

Hughes silently acquiesced, and the pair went towards their lodgings in the village.

CHAPTER LXII.
A FEARFUL FATE.

WHEN the detectives had gone the young outlaw ordered his men to take charge of the two girls who with the young fellow had been brought into the cave.

The wrecker's eyes blazed with passion as he found himself thus deprived of his prey.

Tom smiled at him, and said—

"Your prisoners released will save you from further crime."

The wrecker muttered a savage oath of revenge.

"Now to prevent a recurrence of to-night's terrible scene. I have a few words to say."

Black Bob's eyes shone with a deadly glow as he glared upon the speaker.

"Mark me" said Tom, firmly, "this part of the coast must be rid of that terrible token, the death light. You know me, Black Bob, and know I keep my word. The next time its gleam shines from yonder cliff it will be the signal for your destruction."

The wrecker clenched his hands until the nails went deeply into the flesh.

"Now," the bold Tom continued, turning to his men, "away! Let us spread the War Cloud's white wings."

The men gave a joyous shout, and followed their leader from the cave.

They had not gone many yards therefrom, when the sharp crack of a rifle caused the whole party to turn.

A moment after, a fierce shout arose, and they rushed towards their chief, who was seen to stagger backwards.

The shot had been fired from the cavern at the outlaw and wounded him.

Snowball, like a startled panther, gave a strange cry, and sprung towards his beloved chief.

He wound his arms around the youth's waist, and said—

"You hurt Massa Tom?—you hurt?"

The young outlaw passed his hand over his forehead, and sinking into Snowball's arms, said faintly—

"Not much, Snowball. The ball has only grazed my forehead."

Tom roused himself as the men began to crowd around him, brandishing their weapons, and uttering savage cries.

"Hold your noise!" cried Snowball. "We go back in a minute."

By going back in a minute, he meant they would return to the wrecker's cave.

The outlaw chief gazed for a moment upon the excited faces of his band, and a proud smile illumined his face when he beheld the glittering array of weapons that were so ready to avenge his hurt.

He partook himself of the indignant rage which caused his followers to cry out for vengeance, for the base attempt upon his life.

Unsheathing his sword, the blade of which was of the purest Damascus steel, and the hilt one mass of priceless gems, he pointed towards the wrecker's cave, and said—

"Forward!"

Like a pack of hounds suddenly loosed, they rushed to the attack.

Before they reached the entrance, the young sailor altered his mind, and he vociferated—

"Halt!"

The men, who were thirsting for the wreckers' blood, quickly came to a standstill.

Midshipman Tom, sheathing his sword, said to them—

"Remain where you are. I will go in alone, and bring forth the fellow who fired that shot."

A gripping of their weapons, accompanied by fierce looks, told the fate of him who should fall into their hands.

Snowball followed his commander.

Tom entered the cave, and gazed sternly at the ruffian band.

The wrecker was bathing his wounds in the distant corner of the rocky cave, and when he beheld the outlaw chief, and saw his band crowding around the entrance, his face paled.

"Where is the man that fired the shot?" inquired Tom.

No one answered.

"Am I to repeat my question?" said Tom, hi eyes flashing fire; "if I do, it will be followed by s an instant order for my men to advance."

The wrecker knew the unflinching character of his questioner, and knew that should the outlaw make another attempt, it would totally destroy both himself and his band.

Driven, as it were, into a corner, he pointed to a swarthy-looking wrecker, and said, sullenly—

"There he stands."

The words had hardly left his lips, before Snowball, with a spring like a tiger, seized the wrecker by the throat, and dragged him outside the cave.

Another moment and the wrecker would have been cut to pieces; but before the keen steel could descend, Snowball threw himself before the trembling wretch.

"Stop!" said the African, "that too easy a way of killin' him; I tink of anoder."

What is it?" asked some of the outlaws.

It am dis—if Massa Tom say yes?"

Tom said—

"I leave his fate in your hands."

"Berry well."

Snowball dragged the wrecker away, followed by the angry outlaws, to the sea-shore.

"Dig a hole dere."

"Well, Old Snowflake, what then?"

"What den? Why, him put in de sand right up to him neck. Den de tide come in and him howl. Den de tide come closer, and him howl agin. But no use for him to howl, for de tide come over him head. Yah."

Snowball gave the "Yah!" It was the culminating point of joy when he thought of the lingering death the victim would be exposed to.

The outlaws soon dug a hole six feet in the sand.

Cold dops of perspiration oozed out from the doomed wretch's forehead, and, falling on his knees, he cried for mercy.

Snowball gave him a kick with his heavy boot, and growled—

"Shut up your ugly mouth!"

The hole was soon ready, and, despite the wrecker's shrieks and struggles, he was thrust, feet foremost, into it.

The sand was piled up around until nothing but his head was visible.

In this horrible position he was left to die.

The outlaws waited until Snowball's intentions thus to destroy his victim had been effected, and then followed Tom and Snowball to the beach where their boats were in waiting to take them on board the War Cloud.

CHAPTER LXIII.
RED HAND'S DOOM.

THE pirate soon gave up all idea of pursuing the gallant boy who had so well avenged a foul and cowardly murder.

The Black Snake occupied all the ruffian's strength and energy, and he had to keep his overworked men at the pumps by threatening to blow out the brains of the first who desisted from work.

It was a laborious task to keep the water under, but at last the villainous crew were able to take a brief repose.

The seething waters slowly subsided, and by sunset the tide had run out, and left the damaged hull high and dry upon the reef.

"By my patron, the Prince of Darkness!" laughed Red Hand, "we are saved now. To work all hands and repair damages!"

The men scrambled over the side, and gave all the aid that was needed by the carpenter to repair the damaged planking, and, by the time the tide began to rise, a hoarse shout of triumph proclaimed the pirates' success in making their vessel seaworthy again.

Their lives had been at stake, and they had struggled hard against the overwhelming seas, and before morning had dawned, they were once more in full sail upon the bounding waters of the deep—once more able to pillage and destroy.

Fortune seemed to favour the miscreant crew, for the vessel's prow had not long parted the billows before a heavily-laden, full-rigged ship hove in sight.

The dark sails of the pirate bark bellied out by the wind and the bow-chasers were loaded chain-shot to cripple the defenceless merchant-men.

The sun was tipping the waves with golden effulgence when the chase began.

But in spite of the sailing qualities of the Black Snake the merchantman still held her distance.

And, as though in defiance, she ran up the metan flag of old England.

Proudly the battle-worn banner shone under the sun's glow, mocking every effort of the pursuing pirates to overtake her.

All that long day the British ship kept the pirates in a state of rage and suspense.

Night began to close over the ocean, and Will-o'-the-Wisp-like, the merchant vessel's lights shone tantalizingly before the savage crew.

Red Hand ground his teeth with fury at being thus baffled, and, in the hope of bringing the gallant ship to, he ordered the guns to open fire.

Gun after gun was discharged.

Still the merchantman rode on in safety through the mighty waters, and, as though mocking the foemen's attempts to overtake her, red lights were displayed at the masthead.

Enraged at being again baffled, Red Hand sullenly looked at the heavens.

He saw enough therein to convince him that any further attempt to capture the swift bark would be useless.

The weather now gave unmistakable signs of an approaching storm.

And Red Hand sullenly ordered the officer of the watch to make all snug for the night.

He then descended to his cabin, there to solace himself with drink for the disappointment he had endured.

From a state of semi-intoxication he was suddenly aroused by the fearful cry of—

" Breakers ahead ! "

Simultaneously with the cry, the officer on deck had called all hands, and the ship was soon put about, and then commenced the eager inquiries of the whereabouts of the breakers.

As it had by this time closed in very dark they could only just see what appeared to be the white tops of the breakers.

No sound reached them, however, from that direction.

This gave them some hope, as they thought it must be a considerable distance from where their roar could not be heard.

After getting the ship on the opposite tack, the captain went below.

They had scarcely effected this, when the cry of " breakers ahead " was again repeated.

Once more everything was in confusion.

Men rushing here and there, and the officer in charge himself appearing confounded.

The captain's arrival upon deck soon brough matters right, and in a short time they had tacked the ship, leaving the danger, as he fancied, astern

By this time they had got considerably neare the breakers than they had been before.

Yet they could not hear the noise that such breakers would be supposed to make.

After a thorough examination of the charts and the vessel's supposed position regarding them they could not make out anything in the way o reefs or land that could create such breakers a they were witnessing.

It was evident they had certainly got into dan gerous quarters, but where, they could not tell and the charts did not enlighten them.

As the wind had been gradually freshening until it was blowing half a gale, they were now under a close reefed-topsail, and fore-staysail, and as the reefs were shown to be so alarmingly near it appeared that the current must have carried them.

In this way only could they account for being thus sorrounded by the reefs, and to get clear of them in the existing darkness, was almost an impossibility.

The only thing they could do, was to go about again, and get more sail on the timbers.

To do this, as the wind was, was a matter in itself of considerable difficulty and danger.

But it was the only resource.

All the sail possible was put upon her, their only hope being, that the spars would hold on till daylight, for if the Black Snake struck a reef with such a sea as was then running, it would be certain destruction both to vessel and crew.

By dint of labour and good seamanship, they soon had the bark rushing through the water at such a speed as she had never gone before, the bulwarks lay, for the greater part of the time, under, and it had become almost an impossibility to move about the deck.

The lee-boats were soon torn from their davits and carried away, and it was impossible to get the weather ones on deck, and they, in all probability, would be carried away when the ship went on the other tack.

The spars were now making that peculiar peeking and morning noise, what to sailors seems as though they were endowed with life; but still they held on.

Sails and rigging were parting at every moment, and they could not be replaced.

On the masts holding on, depended the further existence of the vessel.

On they ran, but only for a short time, here the breakers again loomed up ahead.

About the ship went again.

Then their hopes depended on holding on the same tack until daylight.

But hark! There goes the remaining boat, swept away before a monster sea that flooded the deck fore and aft.

HE STRUCK WITH ALL HIS FORCE AT THE HEAD OF THE HIDEOUS MONSTER.

The first fair signs of the coming day at length appeared, and the wearied and almost worn-out crew hailed it with no inconsiderable joy.

It was evident that the vessel could at least hold her own until the coming light would at least show the whole danger, and, possibly it might be, a way out of it.

Still on, making the last tack, it was plainly to be seen they were getting nearer to the seeming reef at every fathom.

Not another yard of canvas dared they stretch, as the old ship was labouring very heavily, and could not continue under such press of sail much longer.

But daylight had come, and the breakers now could be distinctly seen.

The Black Snake appeared to be completely surrounded by them, as not an opening could be seen in the terrible circle.

How had the ship got into such a place, Red Hand himself was unable to comprehend.

11

"There must be a channel," he thought, although neither with the naked eye nor the glass could they perceive any.

The ship could only be put about again, although it was plainly to be seen by the blanched faces of all hands that they cherished but a faint hope of its releasing them out of the mysterious circle.

The stern of the ship was now but twenty yards off the reef, and the next time they tacked, unless the wind changed, to a certainty the vessel would be driven on the rocks.

Red Hand had assured his crew of this—he was not mistaken.

The next tack, all hands were preparing for the final crash that was to send them to eternity, when—oh! glad surprise!—the ship was full in among the foaming and surging breakers, and instead of struck rocks and parting timbers, she was sailing smoothly over and among the boiling spray.

It was a strange sight to see the wonder and delight depicted on the faces of the crew.

Then it transpired that they had been beating all night from a tide rip; that is two tides meeting together, and throwing the water to a height of fifteen or twenty feet.

The escape from this appalling danger was the signal for a grand orgie among the pirate crew.

Casks of rum were brought on deck, and the heads staved in, and before morning dawned again the ship was scudding rapidly before the breeze without even a man to steer her.

While the pirate crew were thus in a helpless state of intoxication, a swift sail hove-to under her quarter.

The blood red flag floated proudly at the little vessel's stern. It was the silken banner of Midshipman Tom.

Followed by his hardy crew, he leapt over the vessel's side, and burning to avenge the treatment he had received, he sprang upon Red Hand before he could offer the least resistance.

The young leader's commands were brief and stern.

Before the ruffian could well understand what had happened, he was fastened to a mast and several of the War Cloud's crew breaking into the powder magazine, piled heaps of loose powder around the conquered pirate.

On the top of the heap, a lighted candle was placed, and Red Hand, bound hand and foot, within a few yards of the flickering flame, was left to watch it burn.

Vainly he called upon his ruffianly drunken crew to come to his assistance.

Stupified by drink, they were unaware of the awful fate which awaited them.

Another five minutes, then the light would reach the powder.

Red Hand yelled aloud in his agony, and the ghastly shades of his murdered victims seemed to troop before him in terrible array as he pictured the Black Snake and her vicious crew blown up together in infinitesimal fragments.

CHAPTER LXIV.

THE WARRANT TO ARREST MIDSHIPMAN TOM.

THE saucy War Cloud was soon dashing the white spray from under her graceful prow, and when the sun rose the young commander endeavoured to stand in towards the coast of France.

He saw the Channel Fleet moving under the command of the rear-admiral, and prudence told him that there was no possibility of getting past while the men were at their quarters.

"We must wait," said Tom to his dusky officer, "until the fleet anchors for the night. Meanwhile, as the wind is fresh, we will take a cruise on the German Ocean."

"Dat good, Massa Tom, for de boys want some exumcise wid de sails; not had much lately. But, Massa Tom, don't you tink it am a shame de English fleet stop about here to exumcise dem men? Why de debbil dey not go somewhere else?"

Tom laughingly replied—

"Well, Snowball, I have no doubt the admiral would go elsewhere if he knew we required the entire length and breadth of the English Channel."

"Um," muttered Snowball, "Massa Tom poke fun at Snowy."

The day was splendid, and the wind soon became a half gale; and Tom, who loved to have his saucy vessel under full sail, and to test her speed under any circumstances, forgot for a time the miserable sprig of royalty he had in the state room.

"Hurrah!" he said to Snowball. "This is a glorious change from the land and the dull rocks."

"It am, Massa Tom; but when we go, dis not de way to France, for we just passed Salt-fleet. We in the Nor' Sea now."

"Never mind, let her go, Snowy. She lies like a duck upon the billows. Look to your steering there at the wheel."

"Ay, ay, sir!"

"Massa Tom," thought Snowball, "forget eberyting when he on land. Dis chile understand where he go now. He sure to get in some scrape. Glad I with him, anyhow."

They did not get in any—that was reserved for Red Hand's miscreant crew, whose vessel, as related in the last chapter, they came across at a most opportune moment.

When retiring from their just retribution, the young outlaw thought there would be a possibility of placing his passenger on board the French ship.

For this purpose he bore up to the North Foreland, and while looking through the glass at the shore, the man in the foremost crosstree sang out—

"A sail astern—a line of battle ship!"

Tom was up the rigging in a moment, and be

held his old acquaintance, the Hercules, under a gigantic pyramid of canvas, giving chase.

Tom looked ahead, and saw another man-of-war tacking direct across his bows.

"That's a frigate," he thought, "and unless I am mistaken, the one that overhauled us when we were in the mouth of the Thames."

The young sailor's quick perception realised the danger he was in, and he summed it up thus—

"The Hercules is in chase, ahead is a frigate, and to leeward is the French boat I want to reach; to reach her I must pass under the guns of the fort, or else deceive the frigate. The latter will be the better plan."

In sailing qualities, the man-of-war stood no chance with Midshipman Tom's swift vessel; but in order to reach the French privateer they would have not only to pass the guns of the frigate and the Hercules, but the double-shotted batteries of the forts which guarded the harbour.

Once clear of these impediments, the Prince would be safe.

Midshipman Tom's first thoughts, when he beheld the Hercules, were to make sail and run the gauntlet of both vessel and forts.

But a moment's reflection convinced him of the folly of such a procedure. In this dilemma Midshipman Tom's ready wits were at work.

Calling the outlaw, Ben, to the quarter-deck, he said, "Ben, you must personate the captain of this vessel, for if I mistake not, this man-of-war is the same that overhauled us on the Thames."

"What am I to do, sir, if it should be the same?"

"Whatever your judgment may suggest, according to the exigencies of the occasion for exercising it," replied Midshipman Tom.

Boom! came the sound of a gun across the waters, and a shot whistled across the schooner's bows.

The outlaw looked towards the frigate, and beheld a cloud of smoke curling up from her bows.

"An order to lay-to," said Tom, quietly. "Now, Ben, take in your sails."

The War Cloud was now stationary on the waters.

Much to the surprise of all, the Hercules did the same, her snowy canvas being furled as if by magic.

Tom left the deck, leaving Ben in charge.

"Let's have a drink for the sake of luck!" cried Ben, bringing on deck a bottle of whisky and two glasses. "Here's to the frigate and her crew. May Old Nick keep them busy while I do the parley," said Ben; "should they overhaul us, and they will——"

He had barely said so, ere the mate reported a boat alongside.

"A boat!" said Ben. "Where did she come from?"

"Been waiting under the counter of that vessel. Just shot out and in no time."

Ben looked over the rail; there sat an English lieutenant in the stern of the boat, while for the crew he had half a dozen police officers, beside a magistrate. The latter short, fat, red-faced, and wheezy—the effect of ale and pudding.

When Ben glanced over the rail, the lieutenant, whom he had cheated before, was looking up and saw him.

It was the same lieutenant who had overhauled the War Cloud when she threw her guns overboard.

They recognised each other.

"To what are we indebted for the honour of this visit?" inquired Ben.

"We have a warrant for the arrest of Midshipman Tom and all on board his vessel," replied the lieutenant, "and I will come on board with the magistrate and read the document."

"Don't trouble yourself. We can hear from the boat all you have to say."

"But I must come, nevertheless, sir."

At this the lieutenant made a motion to take hold of the man ropes and pass up the side, but Ben had formed some outlines of a plot in his mind, and he hauled the ropes in to delay time.

The lieutenant, at this slight being paid to his authority, angrily exclaimed—

"Do you then intend to resist the law? Should I but make one signal to the frigate or the forts they would sink you and your craft at a twinkling."

At this time they were about a mile and a half from the ship and a mile from the forts, and Ben did not believe that either could harm the ship at that distance; but fearing to try the experiment, he made a signal to the outlaws to stand by the sails.

Tom now came out of the cabin to "know the row," as he expressed it, when catching sight of the lieutenant, he invited him very cordially to come on deck.

"Ah! I thought some one would listen to reason," said the lieutenant; and with a haughty glance at Ben he took hold of the manropes and was soon on deck, followed by the fat and fussy magistrate, whose wind was not improved by the climb.

"And now, Mr. Gross," said the lieutenant, "you can read your warrant."

Mr. Gross hid his eyes in a pair of blue spectacles, wiped his face with a bit of white cambric, and then unfolded the paper.

"Ahem!" he began.

"To the officers commanding His Majesty's ships of war,—You are required, by virtue of this warrant, to assist the bearer, a Justice of the Peace, in effecting the capture of the notorious deserter—and outlaw—Thomas Wilson, late of our navy; and you are further charged to seize his vessels, should he be at sea at the time this warrant is put in execution. Futher, this warrant will be sufficient to detain any vessel that may seem suspicious enough for the bearer to have searched before leaving the sight of land.

"Whitehall.   "GEO., REX."

CHAPTER LXV.

THE MAGISTRATE ASTONISHED.

THE fussy little gentleman, at the conclusion of his reading the special power he had obtained to capture the outlaws, looked around, as much as to say—

"There, what do you think of that?"

He was rather taken aback when he observed a grin upon the faces of the seamen who stood near.

"Well, mister," said Ben, "I am not the party you want; so the sooner you clear out of my ship the better."

"Clear out, sir!" was the indignant reply. "I shall arrest you; then we will, as you term it, clear out together!"

Here the naval lieutenant came forward and said—

"Now, sir, let us do our duty."

"Yes, most decidedly we must do our duty. Do you hear that, my fine fellow?"

"What's all this?" said Ben. "What! arrest me on board my own vessel? Do I hear aright?"

"Your ears have not deceived you," said the pompous little magistrate. "We are here to detain you as you have heard said; and we wish to do our duty gently. Will you step into the boat and save us further trouble?"

Ben grasped one of the stanchions on the rail to support himself, so overcome did he appear to be by the announcement.

"As for this man," said the fussy little magistrate, pointing to Ben, "he appears to be reasonable and sensible. Be the first to step into the boat."

Ben made no answer, but glanced at the forts and the Hercules, and then quietly gave the signal to the sail-trimmers.

It was understood.

The War Cloud was two miles from the ship-of-war and the forts.

The visitors did not appear to notice this fact; if they did, they paid no attention to the matter, and for the simple reason that they supposed the outlaws would now turn their vessels head and make for the harbour.

Mr. Gross, finding he was deceived in this respect, said, consequentially—

"Shall I be compelled to order the officers from the boat to assist me? If I am to, and I grieve to say so, my duty will compel me to resort to violence—thus your lives as well as your liberty will be in peril."

Ben halloed to one of the outlaws—

"Look in my state-room and you will find a pistol case. Bring it to me."

"If you mean violence," said the magistrate,

"I shall return to the boat and send the officers on board."

But Ben had neither desire nor intention that he should do either.

By this time the outlaw returned and place the pistol in Ben's hand. It was a single barr and Ben threw it over the windlass carelessly, it slid towards the feet of the lieutenant.

It was a dangerous style of handling weapons certainly.

The pistol struck the deck, hammer downwards, and a sharp explosion followed, the bullet going through the bulwarks and striking the water some ten fathoms from the ship.

The effect upon the nerves of Mr. Gross was most remarkable. He gave a leap upwards when the pistol discharged itself, and then uttering a terrific yell, all colour left his fat and highly suggestive face.

"Murder!" he shouted. "Help — officers— help! The rascals seek my blood!"

Still calling for help, and evidently quaking with fear, the little magistrate managed to scramble to the rail, and crawling over it he tumbled, in somewhat unofficial fashion, still keeping up his eternal cry of—

"Help — help me, officers! The miscreants would have my blood!"

The sight was so ridiculous, and altogether burlesquing the majesty of the law, that the crew could not help laughing; and Ben roared and clung to the rail for support.

"Cast off! cast off!" cried the magistrate when he found himself in the stern sheets of his own boat. "Cast off, I tell you, or we shall all be murdered by those villains!—they are bloodthirsty wretches, and not worth our notice."

But the outlaw's crew were not disposed to do so. If they had cast off the painter the War Cloud would have had the lieutenant on board, and they considered his presence a bore of the first magnitude.

"Will you be kind enough to leave us?" Ben remarked to the officer. "Your company is no longer agreeable to us. We wish to be alone."

"You mean, then," said the lieutenant, "to defy our laws, and not return."

"Such is our intention."

The officer sprang to the poop-deck and hastily unrolled a red-and-white flag, which he had carried in his bosom.

He waved it over his head to the right and to the left and several times up and down.

The outlaws knew what he meant, but did not interfere with his little amusement.

He was signalling the forts and the Hercules; but the game was played a little too late, for the War Cloud was then some three miles from either ship or batteries, and sailing at the rate of ten knots an hour, with the prospect of obtaining a higher rate of speed as soon as the vessel was well under way.

"If you had taken the pains to inform the batteries that it was desirable we should remain in the harbour, you would have exhibited a little more shrewdness," Ben remarked to the lieutenant, who was still waving his flag.

"I would have done so if I had supposed you would have proved the lawless characters you have done," was the snappish reply.

"You see we don't care for such justice as you would administer. We prefer that which is familiar to us."

"Outlaws' law," sneered the officer, still waving his flag, and looking unutterable things.

"Well, that is better than some of the laws of King George. But we will not discuss that point at this time. And now you will please to decide to take your departure for the shore, unless you wish to make a trip to France, that is if we do not sicken of your company before we reach there, and send you adrift in our boat, or throw you overboard as food for the fishes."

"No, sir; I would rather rely on the chances of taking you back to our harbour. See, the signal is answered from both ship and shore. Now, sir, surrender while it is time."

"Bah!" said Ben, laughing as he spoke. "You hav'n't a gun that will carry half the distance."

He was in a good humour now, and had forgotten all about the duel which he had intended to propose to the lieutenant when he sent for the pistol—the cause of the magistrate's fright.

Just as the outlaw spoke, the dull report of a gun from one of the shore batteries warned them the garrison were waking up to the fact that the ship all the time had been escaping.

It might have been five seconds—not more than that—when a hissing noise was heard in the air.

And then a mass of iron struck the water within ten fathoms of the War Cloud's starboard-beam, and threw jets of spray over the deck and those in the boat, who all this time had been unable to get on board the vessel for want of the man-rope.

A yell of terror was heard from the little magistrate, and, to the outlaw's surprise and infinite amazement, he commenced swearing at the guns and gunners of his Majesty with extraordinary ability, energy, and vehemence.

"Mr. Ripple!" he yelled, "tell them to stop that! They are endangering my life, and I won't stand it! I won't stand it, sir! I'll complain to the crown!"

Boom! came the sound of another gun, and this time the bolt struck the water just astern of the vessel.

"Cut the painter!" roared the terrified magistrate. "Do you hear? I shall be killed for nothing, just to gratify some few people!"

The garrison evidently had guns of extraordinary range, and that they were not to be trifled with was equally clear.

"Mr. Lieutenant," Ben said, "I'll give you a last chance. Leave the ship, or I'll throw y into the boat."

He saw that Ben was in earnest, and over th side he went.

He shook his fist as the painter was being freed from the vessel, halloing out—

"Another trick! It's the last one you'll play me!"

"Shove off!" yelled the magistrate.

And away went the boat astern in the wake of the flying ship.

The lieutenant glared savagely when he saw the whole outlaw band appear on deck to give him a parting salute, which they did, shouting "Hurrah for the War Cloud and Midshipman Tom, the King of the Outlaws!"

The magistrate looked blankly at the lieutenant as the boat rocked alone on the swell caused by the War Cloud.

"The villains!" he gasped. "They are a set of impudent scoundrels!"

The naval officer laughed at the fussy little man.

"You laugh, Mr. Ripple!" the fat magistrate said; "but my dignity and His Majesty's commission are not to be thus insulted!"

"What are we to do?"

"Do, sir?—do? Why, follow them, sir; follow them! Yes, as a Justice of the Peace, when we catch them they shall all go to prison—yes, sir, to prison!"

"No doubt, sir," said the lieutenant. drily, "no doubt, sir. But are we to give chase in this boat?"

"This boat?" gasped the magistrate, horrified at the idea, "this boat? Hang it! no, sir!" was the frightened response. "Do you think I am going to risk my life? No, sir; my commission distinctly states "——

"Never mind your commission, Mr. Gross," said the lieutenant curtly. "Let us rejoin my ship and report proceedings."

"Of course, a most excellent plan—a sensible one. Follow in this boat! indeed, such an idea would be madness."

They pulled quickly to the frigate; and much as the little functionary wished to detail the outrage on his commission, he had not pluck enough to mount the ship's side.

The man-ropes were too much for him. When asked by the junior lieutenant to follow, he shrank back into the stern-sheets and exclaimed—

"Up them? No sir, indeed I shall not. If you will have the goodness to lower a flight of stairs, I will come; but that monkey-fashion ill becomes a person holding His Majesty's commission as Justice of the Peace."

One half of the little man's speech was lost upon the naval officer, who, by the time Mr. Gross had ceased speaking, was reporting the ill-success he had met with to the captain of the frigate.

CHAPTER LXVI.

A DISAPPOINTMENT.

"THE commander of the vessel," said the lieutenant, "was as much unlike the young outlaw as two people could possibly be, yet he absolutely refused to come on board; but that, I think, was partly due to the officiousness of the magistrate."

"How is that, Mr. Ripple?"

"Well, he read the warrant he holds, to search all vessels passing here, and began at once to arrest the captain of yon light-hulled craft; insisting right or wrong, that he must be the deserter, Tom Wilson. Nevertheless, it was strange they would not submit to a search."

"It is strange," said the captain, to Lieutenant Ripple, "very strange. Did you act up to my instructions!"

"I did sir, in every particular."

"Have the goodness to recapitulate your proceedings."

The first luff bowed.

"I pulled alongside," he said, "then boarded the brigantine, taking with me the magistrate who holds the warrant to arrest any ship that leaves this point."

"Yes."

"The result you know."

"H'm. Yes. But do you think they properly understood that the detention would be but for a few hours?"

The officer coloured slightly.

He had quite forgotten to mention this to the magistrate or the outlaws.

"I am," he began, "truly grieved to say"—

"Yes, yes, I know, Mr. Ripple," said the captain kindly. "A little oversight. A mistake many would have made, acting under our peculiar orders."

"They are indeed peculiar."

"Don't mind, Mr. Ripple, should we overhaul y more vessels, be more explicit."

"I will, sir, but I must confess, I scarcely understood how to act."

The captain looked puzzled, and laughingly said,—

"Neither do I. But let us refer to the admiral's orders."

They read the document.

"Plain enough," said the lieutenant; "but with the exception of this most slippery customer, I have not seen any vessel that would warrant a suspicion that the rebel, Stuart, was on board."

"You say none except the brigantine?"

"I do."

The captain of the man-of-war became very attentive.

"Then," he asked, "you suspect the brigantine?"

"I have every reason to do so."

"Have the goodness to state your grounds of suspicion."

"I have many. When I boarded the schooner I felt sure that the fellow who so unceremoniously sent myself and the magistrate adrift, was not the captain. Again, the vessel, for her size, was very heavily armed: doubtless her crew was well disciplined. The few we saw were. Again, she was not a trader, but in my humble opinion nothing less than a privateer, and had I a boat's crew with me to justify my doing so, I doubt not but on making a search, I should have found the fugitive rebel in the cabin."

"Good heavens! Why did you not tell me this before? We must give the fellow chase."

The lieutenant smiled.

"Chase!" he said, we might as well try to overtake the whirlwind, as that fellow!"

"What's to be done, then?"

"Nothing can be done at present."

"That's consoling, and if he is, as I now suspect he may be," said the lieutenant, "on board that schooner, then one hundred thousand has just slipped through our fingers."

"True; but here is the despatch boat coming alongside. What's the order now?"

A light clipper-built cutter dashed close to the quarter.

Grasping one of the rattlins, a midshipman stood ready to hail the man-of-war.

The cutter's jib and mainsail came down with a run, and the little craft rubbed her sides against the large ship.

The captain of the frigate called over the side.

"Well, Mr. Tickle, any fresh orders?"

"Yes, sir."

"What are they?"

"Well, sir," the middy went on, "you are to keep a sharp look out for a brigantine with a white streak below her ports."

"A what?" ejaculated the captain.

"A brigantine, sir."

"Yes, yes. Why it—here, Mr. Ripple."

The first lieutenant touched his cap and approached the captain.

"Mr. Ripple."

"Yes, sir."

"Had that fellow a white streak?"

"Yes, sir."

"Then, by Jove, that vessel was the one, as she is confidently reported to have left England with the rebel, Stuart."

Then addressing the young middy, he said—

"Did you know that vessel?"

"Yes," replied the middy.

"And what she was?"

"Yes. I should think so," he replied, "it was Tom Wilson the outlaw, and his daring crew."

"And the name of the vessel?"

"Was the War Cloud."

The captain and first luff looked into each other's face aghast.

LEVELLING HIS PISTOL HE FIRED AT THE DARK FIGURES IN THE ADVANCING BOAT.

" Well," the captain said after a pause, " you've made a pretty mess of it, Mr. Ripple."

" I have, sir ; but I don't think one officer and a boatload of shore-going swabs could take such a trim craft as the War Cloud. Had you given me twenty marines, and as many blue-jackets, I might have felt inclined to try it."

" Forgive me, Mr. Ripple ; I meant not to offend."

The captain and the first luff talked the matter over, and the latter, addressing the middy, said—

" Is that all ? "

" That's all, sir," responded the middy, " I will be off. Stand by there you fellows, to hoist sail."

Then, after a pause.

" All ready ? "

" All ready, sir ! "

" Run them up ! Heave-ho ! Steady. Now then, you at the wheel, hard-a-port. Dang you, to want to foul the frigate."

The wind filled the despatch-boat's sails, and away she went like a gull before the storm.

Young Tickle gave a parting glance at the massive frigate, and laughed.

" Well," he muttered, " I'd as soon set a snail to catch a butterfly, as send the frigate to overhaul my friend Midshipman Tom's craft."

Those on board of the man-of-war were not of the same opinion, for the blue jackets were swarming up the yards, and shaking out the massive folds of canvas.

The despatch-boat was nearly hull down before the frigate, and like a leviathan bird, began to move through the water in pursuit of the War Cloud.

CHAPTER LXVII.
A CLEVER RUSE.

WHEN Ben Bight sent the magistrate, his men and his officers, together with the frigate's lieutenant, adrift, Tom came on deck.

Ben and the crew were grinning at the magistrate's discomfiture.

" You managed that very well, Ben," said the young chief. " I hope we shall get as clean over our next scrape."

" Sure to, sir," said Ben touching his cap, " if you makes me captain."

" Sail ho ! " sang out the man at the mast head.

The young sailor sprang into the mizen rigging, and opening his glass, he asked—

"Where away?"

"On the starboard beam, sir."

"What do you make of her?"

"A full-rigged craft. Should say she was a line-of-battle ship."

"Then we have no time to lose," said Tom. "Snowball!"

"Yes, Massa Tom."

"Alter the War Cloud's trim, or we shall be eaten up by this fire-eater."

"All right, Massa Tom. By Gar, we take in de debbil hisself! Yah! yah! yah!"

Snowball went forward, laughing at the idea of doing a man-of-war.

Everything was now confusion on board the little vessel.

Snowball's voice, like a brazen trumpet, sounded above the chirp of the blocks, and the trampling of feet.

Midshipman Tom and Charles Stuart were upon the quarter-deck, watching the transformation of the beautiful vessel into a lumbering-looking trader.

The snow-white sails were taken down, and in their place dusky patched canvas bellied out.

Empty barrels, spare sails, coils of rope, and a few bales of merchandise were heaped about the deck.

The ports were closed, and tarpaulins thrown carelessly over the guns.

Amidships was piled a heap of lumber.

Beneath it was hidden a long brass swivel-gun.

"What do you tink ob de War Cloud now, Massa Tom?" asked the African, when the transformation was complete. "By Gar, I not know the little beauty!"

The outlaw smiled as he gazed upwards at the clumsily set sails, and the untidy decks.

"You have managed admirably, Snowball," he replied; "but one thing is wanting to complete the concealment."

"What am dat, Massa Tom?"

"To lessen her speed through the water, for in spite of this gear she slips on too fast for a crawling merchantman."

Snowball answered—

"I spoil dat. I take the anchor, and drop him over the stern, dat make the little beauty drag."

"Capital! let it be done."

"It ar' d'rectly. Now, den, for'ard all of you —loosen the anchor, and carry 'em aft!"

Thirty stalwart fellows rushed forward to obey the order, and the anchor was dropped astern about two fathoms deep.

The stranger had by this time rapidly neared the disfigured War Cloud, and came through the waters, throwing up the spray until it resembled a cloud of snow.

When within pistol shot, an officer could be seen standing in the rigging.

Midshipman Tom followed his example, trumpet in hand. The officer suddenly hailed.

"What schooner is that?"

"The Mary of Leith," answered Tom.

"Where from?"

"London."

"Where bound for?"

"Gibraltar."

"By Gar, Massa Tom, we all right; hab dem, Massa Tom!"

The outlaw put the trumpet to his lips, and was about to hail when the officer shouted—

"Heave-to! we will send a boat."

Although every preparation, even to dressing the fugitive as one of the crew, had been made on board the War Cloud, still the outlaw knew that prevention was better than cure.

Before the boat could be lowered from the man-of-war, Tom shouted—

"What ship is that?"

"His Majesty's ship Fury."

"You need not," replied Tom, "lower a boat. I will come on board."

The response came—

"All right. Come at once."

A grim laugh from the outlaws showed how they enjoyed the success of their chieftain's manœuvre.

Tom disappeared for a few minutes below to change his costume.

His handsome dress, scimitar, and pistols were replaced by a quiet suit of clothes, such as worn by officers in the merchant service.

The boat's crew were attired as merchant seamen, and as they began to pull towards the man-of-war, the young chief said—

"The glasses of the ship are upon us; pull less regularly."

"Ay, ay, sir; we understand."

It appeared so, for the usual smart boat's crew now pulled as though they were trying who should first dip the oars in the water and who take them out last.

This clumsy advance was seen by the man-of-war's men; and the captain, closing his glass, said—

"If I had those fellows for a few weeks I would make them pull better, or they should have a round dozen every morning."

A group of officers, who were standing upon the quarter-deck, echoed the captain's opinion, and by the time they had finished their comments, the War Cloud's pinnace was bumping against the huge vessel's side.

Midshipman Tom was met on the gangway by a middy, and conducted to the admiral's presence.

The veteran surveyed the young chieftain for some moments in silence, then said—

"Your readiness to come on board has dispelled the suspicions I had as to the character of your vessel. Now, what are you?"

The young outlaw bowed, as he replied—

" Captain and part owner of that little craft."

" She seems to have a very clear run. Was she always a trader ?"

" I believe not, sir."

" So I thought. More like a private trader, eh ?"

" Correct, sir; she was built for that purpose, and abandoned by the owner, and sold to a friend and myself for the safer and better paying purposes of trading."

The admiral was highly delighted to find his penetration so quick, and, turning to his lieutenant, he rubbed his hands, and said—

" Hear that, Mr. Hart ? I told you so; you see it's no use trying to deceive the old admiral, eh ?"

The lieutenant touched his cap, and replied.

" No, sir, they would not get many points of you."

" I should think not. Ha! ha!"

Tom laughed quietly at the old fellow's self-conceit.

" Now," said the admiral, to our hero, " you can go; but, for goodness sake! try to make those fellows of yours pull a little more together."

" I will, sir; but I fear I shall not succeed, for the rascals are more fond of skulking than working."

" Like all you merchantmen. But here."

" Sir ? "

" Send them on board here for a week; I'll take it out of them."

" Will you ?" muttered Tom, as he went over the side. " I do not think you will have the chance of putting your theory into practice."

Returning to the War Cloud, Ben, who was pulling the bow oar, caught two or three crabs, and went head-over heels.

The accident was seen from the man-of-war, and greeted with shouts of laughter.

Tom's face reddened, and he said angrily—

" Stop this nonsense ! Now, pull together, and let the fellows see that you can pull."

Ben was stroke oarsman.

Turning his head towards his companions, he said grimly—

" Give way, you beggars ! Stroke !"

The outlaws gripped their oars firmly, and reaching well forward, pulled like one.

The light boat was fairly lifted out of the water by the strong-armed men.

A full splash, then she shot forward like an arrow, dashing the spray aside like curling snow-drifts.

The man-of-war's men soon changed their derisive laughter into a spontaneous cheer of admiration.

The admiral turned sharply, and inquired the cause of the uproar.

The first lieutenant pointed towards the War Cloud's pinnace.

" The deuce !" said the old martinet. " Look, Mr. Hart ! Why, they pull nearly as well as my cutter's crew."

" Ah ! undeniable fact, sir."

" Well, but I cannot understand it—eh ! a lot of fellows to pull like that."

" May I venture to give utterance to my thoughts ?"

" Of course—certainly."

" Then I should say sir, that the idea of pulling from such a ship as this must have put new life into those fellows."

" Well, perhaps it has. But about the intelligence concerning the Stuart; what think you of it ? I cannot but say that on reflection, I have some misgiving concerning it."

" I think sir, you are quite right, sir. May I be permitted to say my opinion entirely coincides with your own ?"

" Well, sir, just have a couple of guns cast loose forward."

The lieutenant turned to a middy and said—

" Pass the word forward to cast loose a couple of guns."

" Ay, ay, sir."

The middy had not taken two turns forward before he met a petty officer. To him he repeated the first luff's orders.

The petty officer, in his turn, met the chief boatswain, and repeated the middy's words.

By means of this human telegraph the admiral's orders were executed. Of course, the saving of time was no object : method was everything.

" All ready ?" asked the admiral.

" All ready, Sir William."

" Fire them at intervals ; then hoist the signal for the cruisers to come up with us."

The signals were soon answered by the cruisers, much to the satisfaction of Snowball.

The African, when he beheld the smaller vessels following in the track of the Fury, gave a yell of delight, and said—

" By Gar ! dere dey go, Massa Tom, like a lot of little chickens arter de ole hen."

The young chief smiled at his dark friend's simile ; and, raising the ship's glass to his eye, watched the majestic line-of-battle ship and her attendants glide through the water.

Snowball was gazing intently on the chieftain's face when Tom suddenly closed the glass.

" Golly ! what yer see, Massa Tom, to make you look so ?"

The young chief pointed to what, by the naked eye, appeared a mere speck, and said—

" There is a cutter overhauling the line-of-battle ship hand-over-hand."

CHAPTER LXVIII.

A HOT CHASE.

"Is dere?" said Snowball. "Den I tink we had better be cutters too."

"As I think, Snowball. Ah! I thought so—signalling."

Boom! came the dull report of a heavy gun, and a large shot fell half a fathom astern of the War Cloud.

"A signal to lie-to," said Tom, quickly.

"Snowball!"

"Yes, Massa Tom."

"Let go the drag astern, or we shall be over-hauled in a short time."

That something had gone wrong with respect to themselves the outlaws could plainly see, for the cutter had ranged up alongside the huge man-of-war.

A minute afterwards the lightly armed and fast-sailing cruisers could be seen making sail from the huge consort.

Again the Fury fired at the War Cloud; this time the shot carried a splinter from the gilding of the vessel's stern.

"Is the drag cast away?"

"Yes, Massa Tom."

"It is well. Put on every inch of canvas the masts will carry and beat to quarters."

The quick roll of the drum beat sharply out, and the boarders, grim and stern, stood silently at their posts.

The Stuart came to the young sailor's side, and placing his white hand upon Tom's shoulder said—

"Surely you will not engage those vessels?"

Midshipman Tom, true to the character he had earned, smiled and answered—

"If overtaken, I will."

"Brave, but reckless friend!"

"It may seem so; but while a timber of the War Cloud will hold together, the maxim of her commander is, she shall never yield. "Besides," added Tom. "men who sleep with their hands upon their sword blades are not apt to see danger until it faces them."

Ben approached his young leader at this moment, and, touching his cap, said—

"Beg pardon, sir, but there's a devil of a corvette coming fast on us."

Tom looked steadily at the approaching vessel, and his cheek reddened as he glanced from the corvette to the hatches and dingy sails that had been rigged to disguise the War Cloud.

"Curse them!" he muttered, "they will be here in an hour's time."

So it seemed, for the corvette was darting through the water at a tremendous speed.

Snowball was watching the advancing vessel with the deepest attention.

Suddenly he uttered a joyful cry, and said—

"By gar! Massa Tom, if dat fellow's foremast won't come down I know not'in about a ship."

Tom glanced at the mast of the corvette.

It was bending like a reed under the enormous pressure of canvas.

"You are right, Snowball," he said? "unless they take in sail, we shall slip away."

"Yar, dere it goes."

The outlaws, who had been anxiously watching the large vessel, gave a shout of joy, then relapsed into silence again.

The man-of-war, though for a time rendered incapable of further pursuit, now began to rig a jurymast; and while this was being done her bow chaser went to work with a right good will.

Luckily for the War Cloud she began to move through the water, and soon got beyond reach of the corvette's guns.

"Bang away ye debbils!" muttered Snowball. "ebery gun make you go farder back."

The man-of-war, finding her guns did not carry far enough to disable the schooner, wisely desisted from wasting powder and shot, and went to work at the broken mast with renewed vigour.

Another chance now opened itself to facilitate Midshipman Tom's escape from the pursuers.

The night had now begun to close in, and one by one the pursuing ships grew less distinct.

"Put out every light," was Tom's command to to his sable lieutenant, "and double the watches."

"De men am at dere quarters, Massa Tom."

"True; beat the retreat, we are safe from pursuit."

In the murky light they could just discern the gleam of the men-of-war's battle-lanterns, dancing upon the sea as the vessels rose and fell upon the waves.

Gradually they became less distinct, and at length disappeared altogether.

"We have slipped away from them," said Charles Stuart: "I cannot see one light."

Tom smiled.

"You think so," he responded; "but ten chances to one they are closer upon us than ever."

"Indeed; yet there are no lights to be seen."

"An oversight the enemies have but now corrected; they have smoked the battle-lanterns, and put out the remainder of their lights."

"Yes, yes, of course. Why did I not think of that before."

The young chieftain's conjecture was correct. The pursuing vessels had hidden their lights, and like silent sharks were coursing through the mighty waste of waters.

CHAPTER LXIX.

THE ADMIRAL LOSES HIS TEMPER.

A FEW words will explain the sudden change in he Fury, and her commander's intention towards the War Cloud.

The cutter seen by Midshipman Tom was the

same as had stood with the vessels, and much to the surprise of the admiral and his first officer, Lieutenant Hart, young Tickle, the midshipman in charge of the despatch boat, after hailing the Fury, said—

"Have you seen a vessel with a white streak round her hull?"

"Yes," said Mr. Hart, "and her captain has been on board."

"He has?"

"Yes—why?"

": Nothing much; only"——

"Only; go on sir."

"Only that schooner was the War Cloud, and the captain Midshipman Tom, and it is reported, I believe, that he had the Pretender on board."

The admiral and the lieutenant looked blankly at each other for a few moments.

"What!" yelled the former. "I thought so."

This was not quite true on Sir William's part, and the lieutenant knew it; but as his promotion depended on keeping in the good graces of his superior officer, he said—

"You did, Sir William, and mentioned it to me."

"Certainly, certainly. I knew I said so."

The admiral's hair stood bolt upright with rage, and he repeated, as though in a dream—

"The prince on board!"

"Yes," sang out the middy; "and there is a reward of £100,000 for those who capture him."

"One hundred thousand pounds!" said Sir William, gasping for breath. "Trouble light on him," added the admiral; "what can it mean?"

" A clear case of false intelligence, concocted to take your attention from the 'private trader,' Sir William."

"I said so; did I not, Mr. Hart?"

"You did Sir William."

"What a brace of falsehoods," thought the middy.

The admiral became in a very excited state.

He was a poor man, though a titled admiral, yet the lion's share of one hundred thousand pounds was not to be despised.

"I'd hang him to the yard-arm," he began, furiously; "and hang me if I won't yet."

Young Tickle overheard these words, and thought—

"When you catch him."

But he kept his thoughts to himself, and sat on the windlass, evidently enjoying his superior officer's chagrin.

"Open fire from the port side!" the admiral went on. "Confound it! don't stand there, Mr. Hart. Hoist the signal for the fleet to disperse and catch that fellow. By heaven, I'll hang him yet!"

Young Tickle looked up comically, and muttered—

"That's twice you've said that."

The Fury's guns began to blaze away; but be-

yond making a noise, and dashing up the spray, it did no damage to Tom or his gallant little vessel.

The admiral, having sent the lighter vessels in pursuit, began to pace the quarter-deck, a golden vision of the lost £100,000 tormenting him awfully.

He cursed the large ship because it would not go more quickly through the waters, and he cursed the sailors because they could not make her do so.

Then he cursed the officers, one and all, for being fools, and blamed himself for being the greatest, and not having overhauled the " private trader."

In the midst of this confusion of ideas, his eyes fell upon the despatch boat, which, like a dolphin, kept sailing round the line-of-battle ship.

And then, as though in mockery of her speed, would shoot ahead, and then lay-to until the Fury overtook her.

Whether the middy did this for mischief it is hard to say; but from its frequent recurrence the admiral became awfully enraged.

Seizing the trumpet he bawled out—

" What the deuce are you doing, sir?"

" Nothing, sir, only attending upon you."

"You young rascal! I'll have you reprimanded, I will. Follow in my wake."

The cutter dropped astern.

"Go down from that windlass; that it is not a proper position for an officer of his majesty's navy, and join the most advanced vessel."

"Ay, ay, Sir William."

The reply was scarcely uttered before the cutter dashed ahead of the cruiser like a bird suddenly released from a trap.

"I'm in for it," thought young Tickle. "It's a good job for me, perhaps, that I do not carry any heavy guns, or old Spiteful would have sent me to pitch into Midshipman Tom. If I had," he added, "I should have received a warming."

The boy's words were partly true; for the enraged admiral would have gone any length to have annoyed the bearer of the provoking intelligence Mr. Tickle had delivered to him. And, like a Dervish in his enthusiasm, he danced about the deck, enraged at his want of forethought.

He did not permit them to remain long in ignorance; for, recalling young Tickle, he sent him to every vessel with an angry message, a nd a promise of being severely reprimanded when the fleet returned to harbour.

A stern chase is invariably a long chase.

The proverb held good in this instance; for midnight came, and the chase could neither be seen nor heard.

He had just finished signalling the most advanced of the ships when, to his delight, the little despatch boat sent up three lights.

The admiral almost yelled with joy; and, rubbing his hands together, he chuckled—

"Lucky! lucky!—I have them at last."

So he thought.

While he is laying this flattering unction to his soul, let us return to the brave midshipman and his craft.

———

CHAPTER LXX.

MIDSHIPMAN TOM KEEPS HIS WORD.

"WHAT lights are those shown?" asked the young chief, pointing to some gleams that seemed to play, Will-o'-the-Wisp like, over the War Cloud's bows. "Are we too close to land!"

The question he directed to Prince Charles, who replied—

"Indeed, I know not, unless it is the coast of France."

"It must be that, said Tom. "Yet I am at at a loss to know what part. Do you know, Snowball?"

"I, Massa Tom? Golly, no! Dis chile only dere once, and dey shut him up in prison."

"Not a pleasant reflection—eh?"

"No, Massa Tom, me will tell yer. But I forgot Ben, he know all about dese parts."

The word was passed for Ben to be called.

But that estimable individual was not forthcoming.

At length a voice said—

"Ben's asleep under the fore-hatch."

Snowball filled a bucket with sea-water.

"I wake him up," said he; "dam rascal—him am eider asleep, or telling yarns, and all ob dem lies. I give him suffink."

Creeping down the fore-hatchway, he found the unconscious Ben crouched up among a heap of old sails.

Snowball raised the bucket, and away went its contents over Ben's peaceful visage.

The recipient of this cooling shower gave a yell, and sprang to his feet.

He at first made sure the War Cloud was sinking, but finding it not to be so, he seized his cutlass, and rushed on deck.

Snowball had quietly hidden himself, and waited until Ben had reached the deck before he emerged.

Ben stopped suddenly, and looked amazed.

"Ben," said Tom, scarcely able to repress a laugh at his appearance, "I want you."

"Yes, my lord," said Ben, shaking the salt water from his hair, and looking scared, like a mermaid out for a holiday. "I am coming."

"Cap in hand, he stood upon the quarter-deck, awaiting his commander's orders.

"Do you know those lights?" inquired Tom, pointing to the flickering lights ahead.

Ben looked steadily at them for a few moments,

"I do, sir."

"Where are they?"

"It is the lighthouse at St. Malo, and if I might be so bold, sir, I should advise you to lay-to until the morning."

"What, and a whole fleet at our heels!"

"Well, sir, they can't get near you; neither would you be here, were it not that the War Cloud draws but very little water."

"Ha! how is that?"

"Because this is one of the most dangerous parts of the French coast, and if you go twenty fathoms further, nothing can save you from being forced upon some of the sunken rocks; there are heaps of them about here. Look, sir, you can see the surf curling over them."

"By heaven, you are right! Sail-trimmers, stand by to take in sail."

"Ay, ay, sir!"

"All ready forward?"

"All ready, sir."

"All ready aft?"

"Ay, ay, sir!"

"Up, then, on the main-yards, a dozen of you."

A score of hardy outlaws ran up the rigging at the words.

"Haul up!"

The boatswain's shrill whistle sounded.

Then came the measured tramp of feet, and in in less than five minutes, the War Cloud was lying like a sea-bird at rest on the water.

"Only just in time, sir," said Ben, touching his cap, and pointing to a white streak of foam; "there's a big lugger ahead. Now you'll have lots o' work when it's light, either to fight or run."

"The former, if necessary," said Midshipman Tom; "if you will stand by me."

"That will we," was the hearty response of some thirty or forty of the crew who stood by.

Prince Charles now came upon the quarter-deck, enveloped in a long cloak.

"We are," he said, "within sight of St. ——, and I have to bid you farewell."

"You cannot reach the shore from here," replied Tom, in surprise; "a light boat would not live in the heavy sea that is now running."

Charles Stuart sighed mournfully.

"I had not thought of that," he said, taking hold of Tom's hand, and grasping it frankly. "I thought but of the danger to which I have so long, and am now exposing you."

"Name it not," said the young chieftain, kindly; "but tell me if there is a means of securing your safety."

"Brave and true friend," said the prince. "Would that in my highland home, I could have had twenty such staunch companions as yourself; I should now be on a throne, instead of being an outlaw."

Tom was moved by the speaker's sad tones, and said—

"I wish you were. But come, let me see

" MIDSHIPMAN TOM AND HIM BAND NEBBER SURRENDER!" CRIED SNOWBALL.

you safe; then I must look out for the means of escape for myself."

"There is," said Charles, "a vessel waiting for me close by the lighthouse; could I but reach that, I should be safe."

"It shall be done. Snowball, get the cutter ready, and let my men be well armed."

"Yes, Massa Tom, and dis chile go with you."

"No, I will go alone. You remain here in charge. Should I require assistance, I will send up a rocket."

"Berry well, Massa Tom; I keep good look out for you. Lower away dere! Don't let de cutter make noise in de water, case dem wretches be close to us."

Scarcely causing a ripple upon the water, the cutter was lowered, and Midshipman Tom and the Stuart went over the side.

Then the men, with muffled oars, pulled silently towards the moving lights.

In the dim mist they could see, about a mile ahead, the shadowy outlines of a French brigantine.

The unhappy fugitive was evidently expected, for they heard a lowly uttered—

"*Qui vive ?*"

Not a word was spoken by the French crew as Charles Stuart went up the side of the ladder.

Midshipman Tom had fulfilled his promise now. The fugitive was placed beyond the reach of the English ships.

CHAPTER LXXI.

IN PERIL.

WHEN he had gained the deck he stood as long as there was any chance of seeing the War Cloud's cutter and its noble young commander, leaning over the side, with his dark truthful eyes fixed upon the returning boat.

They had not gone more than half-way towards the War Cloud, when the steady stroke of a man-of-war's boat could be heard.

At a signal from Tom, the men ceased rowing, and in silence prepared their weapons for the anticipated conflict.

"Steady," whispered Tom, to his followers; "there must be no noise. When they come near enough, fire a volley in and pull for the War Cloud."

Nearer came the Fury's boat, and the sailors were even visible.

"Now," said Tom, "make ready—present—fire !"

A sharp report, a sheet of flame, and loud cries from the battle-ship's boat followed, showing that the volley had taken effect.

The cutter then shot ahead and escaped from the volley of marines who were in the Fury's launch.

A mocking laugh fell from Tom's lips.

But ere it had well died away another boat, crammed with armed men, shot across his bows.

Ben sprang to his feet, grasping his long ashen oar, ready to repel the attack, face their enemies, and save his young chief.

As he did so, the young chief sprang to his feet.

That act nearly cost him his life; for the boats meeting caused a violent concussion, and, had it not been for one of the rowers catching him as he reeled backward, Midshipman Tom's career must have come to a premature end.

"Stern all," the outlaws heard a deep voice utter in the boat which they had so unfortunately ran into. "Steady! Boat ahoy! What boat is that?"

Owing to the darkness, they were not recognised by the man-of-war's boats.

There was no time to be lost.

The Fury's boat was gaining fast upon them.

To successfully battle with both the boats Midshipman Tom knew would be impossible.

These thoughts ran through his brain while the officer in the other boat was speaking.

Tom ordered the outlaws to bend forward with a will; but they had not got more than two boats' length from the enemy before the Fury's boat sent up a blue light.

The flames burnt long and steadily, rendering surrounding objects as bright as the noon-day sun.

"Lay to! lay to!" he yelled. "By George! there they are. Pull, men, for your lives !"

The same light that revealed Tom to his foes also revealed the enemy to the young outlaw.

To his surprise, he saw three boats pitching about upon the waters, and when they beheld him, their crews raised a shout, and each turned its bow towards the War Cloud's boat.

Had the matter only rested with distancing his pursuers, Tom could easily have accomplished that.

But unfortunately, the nearer he approached the War Cloud, the nearer his pursuers also came to the little vessel, which, to crown the young chief's misfortunes, had settled upon a sunken reef.

Tom felt his pursuers were bent upon accomplishing their task—that of capturing him.

The blue lights had burnt out, but he could hear the regular jerking of their oars in the row-locks.

A sudden thought crossed the young chieftain's brain.

Were they going to attack his vessel ?

No—the War Cloud has escaped their observation.

"Ben," said Tom, "we must pull away from the ship, or we shall be boarded on all sides."

"Sure to," was Ben's reply. "Suppose we pull another way, and fire a pistol or two—it will draw them off the ship."

"It is our only plan. Discharge your pistols, two or three of you."

They did so, and the pursuing boats immediately turned their bows in the direction of the flashes of fire.

"Now," said the young chieftain, "we are safe for a time, unless we——"

Boom! Bang! bang!

The frigate commenced fire upon the corvette—a compliment which the smaller vessel more pluckily returned.

And not until several men had been knocked over on either side was the mistake discovered.

It was certain now, in the darkness of the night, they had mistaken each other for the outlaws.

The admiral, to prevent a recurrence of this, signalled for the vessels to hoist their lights.

This arrangement was most pleasing to Midshipman Tom; he had ample time to observe the motions of his foes as the light of their battle-lanterns fell upon the waters.

The War Cloud he knew was still enveloped in darkness, and owing to her light draught, she was safe from the vessels.

His principal difficulty lay in discovering the

whereabout of the heavily-armed boats, which he felt assured were still in hot pursuit.

As the boat was skimming through the water, the young chief, with his head averted, was trying to make out their locality.

Suddenly a shock was experienced; they had fouled a vessel, and immediately a boyish voice called out—

"Hallo! boat ahoy! Do you want to be run down?"

"Stern all, and keep silent," was Tom's lowly whispered order to his men. "Steady and quiet, or a cold shot will stove us in."

They had run foul of the despatch boat, which unlike the other vessels, had her light shaded.

Young Tickle, finding no response to his hail, repeated—

"Boat ahoy! Answer, or we'll drop a shot into you!"

The cutter was going before the wind at the time, therefore to back water was no easy task, so as to keep free of the despatch boat.

"Steady!" he whispered to his men; back on the bowside, and pull the stroke. Now, for your lives pull, and let us clear this horrid ship."

The boat yielded to the fresh impulse given her, when the bow oarsman's oar snapped short with a report like a pistol.

"Malediction!" muttered the young chief; "out with a fresh oar, or we shall be carried back by the swell."

The noise of the fracture was plainly heard by those on board the despatch cutter, and a voice startled the outlaws by saying—

"Heave-to, whoever you are, or we fire."

"Pull, pull," whispered Tom. "They cannot depress a gun to reach us."

"Where are they?" young Tickle was heard asking. "Cast loose a gun for'ard."

"Half a fathom ahead, sir," said a man who was evidently leaning over the cutter's bows.

Then came an order that caused the outlaws to hold their breath.

"That gun ready?" asked the middy.

"All ready, sir."

"Depress the muzzle and fire in the direction of the sound."

"Steady."

"As you were."

The gunner withdrew the lighted port fire from the touch hole.

"What are you loaded with?"

"Round shot, sir?"

"Well, draw the charge, and load with grape."

The outlaws' hearts stood still.

Tom felt the hazardous position they were in, and he only saw one chance of escape.

That was by a manœuvre, and a desperate one it was; but his courage rose with the occasion.

"Stern all!" he said, in a low voice. "Stern, and get under her bows.

A few back strokes, and the cutter falling off before the wind, left the outlaws' boat near her stern.

Then came the sullen sound—

"Fire!"

And the gun belched forth a sheet of flame, and the balls flew into the water, casting it up in angry jets.

The outlaws breathed freely.

At least for a time they were saved.

The young chieftain, however, knew the peril they were in, and, although fear was a stranger to his soul, and in moments like this, the qualities that made him what he was were shown to advantage, he said—

"Then we are surrounded. It would be wanton sacrifice of life to stand the hazard of this encounter. We are greatly encumbered; let us retreat."

Like an arrow the light boat shot ahead.

The pursuers immediately gave chase, and kept up a continual fire of musketry.

One of the pursuing boats, propelled by sixteen long oars, soon surpassed its fellows, and was rapidly gaining on the outlaws.

Under the brawny strokes of sixteen vigorous sailors the boat appeared fairly to leap out of the water.

It was evident the boat was fast gaining upon them, and they pulled with the energy that despair alone could give.

But the outlaws' efforts were futile. The long-boat was now alongside.

"Surrender!"

The young chief's reply was the swift levelling of a pistol, and the officer fell into the sea, the bullet having entered his skull.

A yell from the sailors announced their rage at their leader's fall, and, the boats closing, a deadly fight ensued.

The outlaws fought desperately, and with a heroism that would have befitted a better cause.

But overmatched as they were in numbers, the issue seemed very doubtful.

Each party had ceased using firearms in consequence of the difficulty in reloading their guns.

With cutlas and pike therefore they battled in sullen savage contest, the only sounds being the half-suppressed death cry as the combatants fell stricken to death.

By this time the other boats had arrived, and all hope of escape seemed passed for the still desperately fighting outlaws.

There seemed nothing left now but to surrender or be cut into pieces.

Midshipman Tom and his followers knew the fate that awaited them should they be captured a short trial, and an exit from this world at the yardarms of the different vessels.

To die gloriously, with their hands grasping a trusty blade, was preferable to such a death.

Setting their teeth firmly, they determined to die.

A defiant answer had just been given by Tom to an order to surrender when the combatants were startled by a loud war-whoop, followed by a sudden shower of bullets.

It was Snowball, who, with two boats fully manned, had come to his shipmates' rescue.

The half-naked African struck terror into the hearts of the seamen, as he stood on the bow of the boat, wielding a keen, glittering, long-handled axe.

Dashing into the midst of the enemy, he mowed them down like grass, the outlaws' boats keeping up an incessant fire of musketry.

The second boat from the War Cloud, led on by Hal, attacked the enemy upon the other side.

Then the assailants' attention was disconcerted by the withering, deadly volleys from each side.

The young chieftain seized the momentary respite from fighting to have all their fire-arms reloaded.

The men poured in a volley that shook their enemy's firmness, who, sending up several rockets for reinforcements, plied their oars and withdrew from the contest.

Snowball gave a savage yell of exultation and cried out to the young chief—

"This way, Massa Tom! pull for de War Cloud. Ebery gun am loaded with grape. By Gar, dey get suffink if dey foller us."

There was not a moment to be lost.

The signals were answered by the man-of-war, and several boats were being manned and lowered, and it appeared not unlikely the whole fleet would be down upon them.

Midshipman Tom determined, the weather being a dead calm, to tow the War Cloud from the place.

The African walked forward to see that everything was prepared for the boats, should they come, leaving the young chief standing with folded arms and moody brow.

The moon's disk now rose above the heaving bosom of the dark waters, covering the heavens with a resplendent gleam.

Streaming across in one long line of light from a point over the verge of the horizon, it extended until it came to the War Cloud.

What a glorious object looked the trim vessel as she rose and fell upon the undulating waters!

The young chief was struck by the spectacle; the man at the wheel looked like a shadowy phantom gleaming out from the effulgent beauty of the silvery light.

The rakish masts tapering to a fine point stood out in bold relief, and the ship herself seemed like a spectre rising out of the ocean, as one without life or motion.

The lazy creaking of the masts and the rattle of the tiller-ropes, which came at distant intervals, were the only sounds, that seemed to reveal more distinctly, rather than to break, the stillness of the hour.

From the contemplation of this, to a sailor, glorious scene, Midshipman Tom was startled by the rough voice of the look-out saying—

"Six boats making for the ship, sir!"

"Where away?"

"Right ahead!"

The African came swiftly towards his chief, and shouting to the advancing line of boats, said—

"Dey come, Massa Tom. Eberyting ready—eberyting."

Tom pointed to the long brass gun amidships, saying—

"Try the range with her."

His words were overheard by the men standing near, and a dozen rushed forward to load the gun.

An occupation that filled up a very few minutes.

Outlaw Ben was about to apply the port fire, but the young chief placed his hand upon the outlaw's arm, saying—

"I will fire this gun, Ben."

The outlaw drew back, and handed his chief the port fire.

Tom singled out the leading boat, and taking careful aim, fired.

The heavy shot went hissing through the air, and striking the boat at the bows, smashed the stout beams as though they were glass.

A cheer rose from the outlaws when they saw the crew struggling in the water.

A frown for a moment darkened the young chieftain's brow.

"Silence, all of you," he said, sternly. "The sacrifice of human life is not an exhibition to be applauded; were it not for our imminent peril, I would avoid this carnage."

The men were silent, and fell back abashed by their leader's words.

Again and again was that terrible engine of destruction fired.

And each time by the masterly hand of the young chief.

Some of the boats were staved in ere they could reach the ship.

Those remaining dashed forward to the attack.

Tom's eager eyes were fixed upon them, and waiting until they came within range of the carronades, he said, in a hushed and determined voice—

"Fire!"

A sheet of flame belched from the brigantine's side.

The contents of four guns, that had been crammed to the muzzle with grape, went hurtling among the devoted seamen.

This fearful shower of fire was kept up until only one boat was uninjured, which was now being pulled out of range as far as possible.

"Dey ab enough for dis time," muttered Snowball. "By Gar! some ob dem swim like ducks."

For several fathoms round the ship, the water was dotted with the dark forms of the sailors as they clung to the pieces of the boats to keep themselves from sinking.

"They will keep up the fire," said Tom, "until assistance comes from the fleet."

Then, turning towards the crew, he said in a loud voice—

"Stand by to lower your boats."

The order was promptly obeyed. The boats dropped from their davits into the sea with scarcely a ripple on the water from their contact.

A dozen sailors descended over the bows, made fast a couple of hauling ropes from the War Cloud.

The boats took their respective stations, each man grasped his oar; and, in a few minutes, in obedience to the chief's order, "Now—give way with a will"—the War Cloud began to move slowly through the water, the crew standing by their guns ready for immediate action.

From the line of battle-ship a night signal was seen to flash upwards. It was to renew the attack.

Fortunately for the outlaws they had but two vessels—a brig and a sloop—to pass, whose guns could reach them, the largest of the fleet being incapable of moving, in consequence of the dead calm that prevailed.

The latter had been distanced by the War Cloud, but the brig and the sloop showed excellent gunnery, for in less than ten minutes the War Cloud had lost her foremast and a portion of her bulwarks, besides several of the crew being frightfully mangled.

At last another shot deals greater destruction, and Tom's fortitude all but fails him as he beholds a large fragment of the remaining bulwarks torn away, and the splinters sweep into eternity a group of his beloved band who were standing round a gun.

Still Tom poured in his incessant fire upon the boats, one of which was cut in twain, another losing two of her crew by an explosion from a shell.

At length there is a cessation. The terrible and continuous fire drops to an occasional shot from the brig's bow-chasers, and the War Cloud's long brass guns. Then the strife is discontinued altogether, and a favourable wind blows the War Cloud clear out of the reach of further injury.

A smile of the proudest exultation curled the outlawed boy's lips, as he thought of his daring and providential escape.

A smile that soon changed to a look of despondency when he saw his wounded followers being taken below one by one.

"Terrible work, Snowball," he said. "We are free, but at a tremendous sacrifice."

"True, Massa Tom, but dey hab died better dea habing a rope round deir necks."

"True. Ah! here it comes!"

"What? Massa Tom."

"The wind. I felt it across my face."

"Jest so."

"Bring me a lighted candle."

Snowball brought the candle, and Tom, springing upon the bulwark, held it aloof.

But the wind was so low that the glare burnt some time steadily, and it flickered for several moments before it finally went out.

The injuries done to the vessel being temporarily repaired, she, favoured by an increase of the wind, made her way towards the cave.

Tom turned and took a long survey of the moonlit sea, and to his satisfaction, not a spar of the men-of-war was to be seen.

Tom, knowing the crew must be worn out with the terrible exertions in effecting their escape, piped all hands down except the watch.

Then, leaving the vessel in charge of Snowball, he went to his state room, where, worn out in mind and body, he threw himself on the couch and was soon asleep.

From a heavy slumber he was aroused by the noise of the anchor being lowered, and with a sigh of thankfulness, he was about to compose himself for sleep, when the rush of feet upon deck, mingled with angry voices, pistol shots, and the clash of steel, caused him to snatch up his sabre and rush on deck.

He hewed his way to the side of Snowball, who, like a lion, was keeping at bay Black Bob and a score of his followers.

The wreckers, in overwhelming numbers, had boarded the War Cloud, judging probably from her dismantled condition, to obtain an easy victory over their sworn foes.

Taken by surprise, the outlaws fought at a disadvantage, and were fast falling before the crowd of savages.

CHAPTER LXXII.

RED HAND'S ESCAPE.

"THAT villain's career is ended, Snowball."

"It am, massa, and no mistake, dis time—yah!"

These words were used by Tom and his lieutenant, when the young outlaw left Red Hand, bound hand and foot, within a few feet of the powder. Like a scotched snake he writhed in agony.

Slowly the candle burned downward, the flickering flame approaching nearer every moment to the powder.

The pirate uttered maddened cries of agony; but no help came to him.

With whitened cheeks, and his eyes starting from his head, he struggled—struggled as though he had some chance of escape.

But fainter every moment became his chance. The light was now within a hair's breadth of the powder.

Red hand, closing his eyes, gave one terrific yell. His head dropped on his breast, and he gave himself up for lost.

Expecting every moment to hear the report of the ignited powder, he was suddenly overjoyed to hear a gruff, drunken voice saying—

"What the deuce is up? Where's the key of the spirit-room, captain?"

Red Hand opened his eyes.

It was one of the drunken crew staggering about the cabin.

"Help! help!" the pirate leader shouted frantically; "put out that light."

The man's faculties were deadened by drink, and he looked vaguely at his leader.

Noticing for the first time that he was bound, he reeled forward, saying—

"Hallo! what are you bound there for?"

"Ho!" yelled Red Hand. "Look, you fool. There is a light burning upon that powder. Quick, or we shall all be blown into"——

The pirate gave one glance at the candle: it sobered him instantly. With a cry of terror he snatched a leathern bucket of water up and threw it upon the flame.

Another second and it would have been too late.

As it was the peril was over; the pirate leader breathed freely.

As his follower cut the lashings that bound him to the mast, he swore a terrible and blasphemous vow of revenge against the young outlaw. Like an angry demon he went on deck.

There he beheld his crew lying about in a state of helpless intoxication, and his face became black with passion.

Clutching a loaded pistol, he seemed as though about to sacrifice one or more of the sleepers in his mad fury.

The pirate who had released him from the jaws of death stood by his side and interceded for them.

Red Hand replaced the pistol and said significantly—

"Bring the hose."

The man brought the hose and pipe of the fire-engine, and Red Hand, with a malicious grin, clutched it savagely.

"Man the pump," he said, "and keep to it."

The pirate sullenly obeyed, and soon the hose began to swell out.

It was a strange sight. The ship running swiftly before the wind; the tiller-ropes creaking and giving as the ship obeyed the impulse of the sails; the huddled forms of the swarthy crew as they laid about the deck in drunken slumber; the man silently working the pump, and the fierce, pitiless pirate leader standing upon a carronade grasping the copper tube from which the water began slowly to fall.

A few more jerks at the pumps, and the water began to gush out in a dense volume.

Then Red Hand, with a grim smile of exultation, began to drench the drunken sleepers.

The effect of the overwhelming volume of water acted like magic. The pirates sprang to their feet with angry oaths, many of them to receive the dense body of water upon their face or back.

In less than twenty minutes the whole of them were up and at their stations, their clothes saturated with brine, and the cold piercing their very bones.

"Curse you!" said the pirate leader, turning the metal tube upon the deck. "You infernal drunken hounds, you deserve to be tied up and have your backs tickled. Wear ship and be smart."

The men silently obeyed, while Red Hand, with folded arms and lowering brows, paced the quarter-deck.

The crew had not long been at their stations before a vessel hove in sight.

A fiend-like expression passed over Red Hand's face when he heard the cry; and muttering between his set teeth, he brought his glass to bear upon the coming ship.

"Curse him," he growled, "the horrid whelp! Should it be him, I'll blow his vessel and crew to the regions below."

An hour brought the vessels within musket shot of each other; and, to Red Hand's rage, he found the stranger, in place of being the outlaw vessel, was a West Indiaman.

"Fire a gun across her bows," he said, savagely. "Then if she does not hoist her colours, send a shot into her hull."

The iron messenger went upon its errand.

But no notice was taken of it by the stranger.

A second shot was fired; and so near had the vessels came to each other, that the pirate could see a number of splinters fly upwards from her bulwarks where the shot had taken effect.

"Cease firing," said Red Hand; "her decks are empty."

The crew made a rush forward, and to their surprise, beheld the stranger bearing down rapidly upon them.

Her sails were set, yet not a human being was visible on any part of her decks or spars.

The pirates were awed for some time by the strange sight, for the vessel came with terrific speed through the water; silent, untenanted, and terrible it looked.

A murmur began to be whispered among them, that the moving vessel was manned by a crew of invisible fiends, and many of the pirates began to cower at the sight.

Red Hand alone stood unmoved.

With his glass, he kept watch on the strange ship, and he saw by the manner in which she turned from side to side that her rudder was loose.

AT THE MERCY OF THE WAVES.

Taking the glass from his eye, he looked at his swarthy fellows, whose faces were now white with superstitious fear.

The fiery liquid they had so freely partaken of was now dying away, and tended to weaken their faculties.

"Fools!' he said, savagely, "what are you slinking from? Are you afraid of an empty ship? Ready there with the grappling irons to catch her as she passes!"

Red Hand's words awoke the men from the stupor into which they had partly fallen, and some of them sprang into the mizzen rigging to obey his orders.

Red Hand saw, as the vessel came nearer, that it would require a masterly stroke to prevent collision in the attempt to capture the heavy Indiaman.

Standing trumpet in hand, he stood giving his orders in such quick succession, that the whole of the crew were employed in carrying them out, except those who were at the shrouds.

Like lightning the following commands were given:

"All hands wear ship!"

"Put the helm up."

"Let go the after bowlines."

"Run in the after braces."

He waited until the after-yards were squared, then he continued—

"Rise foretack."

"Ease off foresheet."

"Steady—let go bowlines."

"Shift over the jib-sheet."

Red Hand had the wind right aft, and every moment the danger of a collision became more imminent.

But sooner than lose the prize, for such he considered it, he determined to risk the lives of every man on board.

Finding the Black Snake still made too much way through the water, he sang out—

"'Way aloft."

Twenty of the crew ran nimbly up the rigging, and when the topsail braces were hauled in, the orders were given.

"Let go topgallant sails.

"Lower away topsail."

"Steady with the lee braces."

"Seamen aloft."

There was not time to finish reefing the topsails before the strange ship was upon them.

Red Hand gave the man at the helm a warning look, then sprang upon the bulwarks.

A dread silence reigned among the crew at this fearful moment; even the hardened ruffian who commanded them was not without a sensation of fear.

There was something so awful in the appearance of this deserted ship meeting them in mid ocean, that the closer it came the chill feeling of superstitious dread became stronger in the crew.

Luckily for the Black Snake, the wind shifted as the huge vessel came within a few feet of her bows, and caused her to fall off a little.

The favourable moment was not lost for seizing the prize.

One dexterous throw fixed the iron in the rigging.

Then, while the Black Snake's sails were being furled, the line affixed to the grappling hooks was permitted to run out a couple of fathoms.

The pirate ship being motionless, checked the mad career of the deserted Indiamen.

Then, as she again began to move through the water, the vessels' sides touched, and Red Hand, followed by a horde of ruffians, sprang upon the deck.

No time was to be lost by the pirates in lowering her sails.

While this was being done, Red Hand, with a dozen of his followers, went below.

Crime-stained, and hardened to every sight that could make the soul callous to all feeling, they were awed by the terrible spectacle that met their gaze between decks.

In every conceivable attitude that agonizing pain could suggest, the luckless crew and passengers were lying livid and ghastly where they had fallen.

Hardy, bronzed sailors were to be seen side by side with young and beautiful women.

It needed no words to tell the intruders the cause of this fearful sight; the blackened and swollen bodies proved but too plainly that one and all had fallen victims to some contagious disorder.

The very air was pestiferous with the exhalations from the rapidly festering dead, and to breathe it made many of the strong men shiver.

Avoiding contact with the dead, the pirates smashed open the windows with the hilts of their cutlasses.

The fresh breeze revived them, and, following their captain, they continued, not only to pillage the state-room, but the very persons of the stricken dead.

The work of plunder was soon completed, and the floating charnel-house was fired by the pirate crew.

A fearful price the cupidity of the pirates had cost them.

Little did they suspect, as they stood in the twilight watching the death-ship and its festering burden being consumed by the fiery element, that they were gazing upon the last of a plague-stricken ship.

With the incoming darkness the ill-fated Indiamen blew up into the air, and all was over.

The greater portion of that night and the succeeding day was passed by the ruffianly crew in quarrelling over the booty they had stripped from the plague-stricken dead.

Red Hand, with a savage glance, settled the dispute by threatening to shoot the next man he found quarrelling, and, ordering them to prepare their arms for an encounter with the outlaws, he went aft.

Taking with him his glass, he stood gazing upon the faint outlines of the cliff under which the outlaws' cave was situated.

Towards the close of the second day the Black Snake rode upon a single anchor in the bay.

And, under cover of the semi-darkness, the pirate leader and his crew effected a landing.

Burning to wreak his vengeance upon the young chief, he left his band among the broken rocks, and, pulling his slouched hat over his eyes, crept cautiously towards the cave.

Everything was silent.

Red Hand, with gleaming eyes, stood peering out from behind a huge mass of fallen rock.

"Not returned yet," he muttered. "Curse him! I would give ten years of my life to have his throat under my knife."

Whilst these savage words were being uttered, a light footfall near where he stood caused him to start and draw back.

The next moment the graceful form of Laura Grey walked slowly past.

The pirate suppressed his heavy breathing, and like a tiger ready for a spring, he crouched behind his hiding-place.

The young girl, unsuspicious of the danger that lurked so near, slowly ascended a small elevation, and gazed doubtfully at the gleaming lights of the Black Snake.

"Is he returned?" she said, half aloud; "or is that some vessel seeking safe anchorage for the night."

The quietude which reigned around, and the anxiety for her lover's safety, caused the gentle maiden to wander to the shore, there, as she imagined, to greet the boat that would bring her lover to shore, and her arms.

Like a panther, Red Hand stole out from his place of concealment with a pitiless purpose in his head, and dogged her footsteps.

"Now," he hissed, savagely, "once on board, I'll partly revenge that whelp's last attempt upon my life."

He drew back suddenly, for Laura paused; feeling afraid at the loneliness of the place, she was about to turn back to the cave.

Red Hand divined her purpose, and springing

out like a leopard or wild cat, he clutched her white throat savagely.

The cry that rose to her lips was choked back, and she reeled with terror.

The pitiless scoundrel rudely dragged her towards him, and tightening his grasp, held her until her face became black and swollen, her eyes started from their sockets, and her tongue protruded from her mouth.

Then, with a fiend-like cry, he released his fingers, and the helpless, senseless girl fell in a huddled heap at his feet.

The ruffian's strong grasp had nearly crushed out her young life, and when they reached the ship, Laura looked like a corpse.

Alarmed lest she might not rally, the pirate sent for the surgeon, who was advising as to the remedy to be adopted, when one of the crew approached him.

The man was looking ghastly pale, and was evidently suffering extreme pain.

"Sir," said he, "I am in awful agony—pray do something for my pain."

The surgeon looked fixedly at the speaker, and a deathly paleness came over him.

Turning his head to Red Hand, "that man is plague-stricken," he said.

The words had scarcely passed his lips ere the man staggered, and the next instant, fell to the deck.

"He is dead," said the surgeon.

"Dead?"

"Yes; and if you wish to save life, you will quit the ship at once."

"What—what the deuce do you mean?"

"I mean," continued the doctor, "that the plague was brought on board your ship from the Indiaman; that it has broken out amongst those who came in contact with the dead bodies, and that, unless you leave this vessel in less than twenty-four hours, it will be a charnel house."

Red Hand turned pale.

"Malediction!" he said, "will nothing stop it?"

"No human skill can arrest its progress."

"And the girl?"

"Will fall a victim unless taken away. Her life, even now, hangs upon a thread."

Red Hand left the quarter deck, and summoning his crew, ordered them to lower the boat, and be ready to leave the ship at nightfall.

By that time the doctor's words were being verified.

More than half the crew were stricken with the plague.

In the midst of this terrible scourge, Red Hand, the surgeon, and as many more of the crew as were able, left the ship under cover of the night.

The merciless wretch left the fair girl in the little cabin he had set aside for her use.

She seemed nearly dead when brought on board the vessel, and from this state had not rallied.

"Let her rot with those plague-stricken wretches," was Red Hand's reply, when the surgeon asked about the girl; "if she is not dead now, she will be so before morning."

"She cannot live longer," said the doctor, "so perhaps it is as well we left her in the vessel."

"Quite as well! and all I hope is, that the whelp Tom Wilson, will find his way on board the ship."

The miscreant little knew his words were prophetic.

CHAPTER LXXIII.

LADY MOUNTSTEVEN AGAIN PLOTS AGAINST THE
YOUNG OUTLAW.

LADY MOUNTSTEVEN soon had cause to regret the death of Pierre, for without his aid she was unable to proceed with her villainous schemes against our hero.

She was not long before she found another tool to aid her in her black design—an unscrupulous adventurer, called Ralph Ranger, and after a long conversation with her accomplice, she said—

"You understand me, Ranger—he must be got out of the way."

"Perfectly, my lady."

"Have you any plan for carrying out my wish?"

"None; but I expect a band here soon, the captain of which will assist me and you too, my lady."

"I care not what that plan may be. But hark, what noise was that?"

Ralph listened for a moment, then suddenly seizing the light, rushed to the door.

Lady Mountsteven rose from her seat, exclaiming—

"Back! there is danger."

Ralph returned.

Her words frightened him.

He closed the door and placed the light upon a table.

"That staircase," said the lady, pointing to a door, "leads to the north wing, a place of evil repute, and said to be haunted."

Ranger smiled.

"You do not believe it?" she asked.

"I have no faith or belief in the supernatural," he said. "In this case especially."

"Why?"

"Because the sound that disturbed us was a woman's footfall."

"You think so."

"I am sure of it."

"Then," said Lady Mountsteven, "our conference has been overheard. Some one has been listening."

"Listening?" Ralph replied; "a domestic perhaps."

"Whoever it was," said the lady, "will find it better to have closed their ears."

"Surely, madam, you would not"—

"would do anything," was the significant answer, "to prevent that boy from being the inheritor of these estates."

"And I will assist your ladyship."

"I know it? Do you not think there is a probability of getting him captured by the men-of-war?"

"No, madam. The officers like the boy for his daring; and another thing, he does the country some service in making war against the wreckers and pirates. Therefore, I should not be surprised to hear that private instructions have been issued by the government not to interfere with him."

"You think so?"

"I do, madam."

"Then why not put yourself in communication with the pirates and wreckers? they will be sure to assist you."

"The wreckers have already tried and failed."

"Let them try again."

"Madam, I will act upon this suggestion. The chief of the wreckers—a ruffian, called by his accomplices, Black Bob—has been desperately wounded by Tom Wilson, and would, I know, do anything to be revenged."

"The very man. Seek him at once, and make your own terms."

Ralph Ranger left the castle, and went to the wrecker's cave.

Lady Mountsteven, as she watched him cross the court-yard, muttered—

"When you have served my purpose, it will be my next task to remove you from my path. Dead men tell no tales. You will know too much to live."

The terrible woman's face bore a demoniacal expression as she said these words; then glancing round the richly furnished room, she muttered—

"It is worth a sea of blood to retain this proud castle, and as much shall be shed before I give it to this boy."

She paced to and fro for a few moments; then taking a taper from a side-table, went below to the dungeon where she had confined Fred Baylis and his companion.

"Gone!" she exclaimed, "and through the old entrance to the subterranean way. I must be careful and track these men. Yet they do not know everything. The door closing I can attribute to an accident—that is, if they become troublesome, and my word is better than theirs. There is my husband—ah! he must die; then I can work in future safety."

CHAPTER LXXIV.

A FIERCE CONTEST.

THE presence of their youthful leader inspired the outlaws with additional courage, and they were enabled to check the advance of their cowardly foes.

Those who had been so unexpectedly roused from their hammocks now hastened on deck, sword in hand.

Without asking or noticing who their foes were, they formed around their leader, and fought like lions. Black Bob was savage at meeting with this unexpected resistance where he had counted upon the certainty of obtaining an easy victory, and facing Tom he said, savagely—

"Accursed young dog! this for the wound you gave me in the cave."

He made a terrible stroke at the young sailor's head as he spoke; but the descending blade was met by the sabre our hero knew so well how to use.

The combatants instantly fell back, and the two chiefs met, hand to hand, in single combat.

Both were renowned for the use of their weapon, and both braced every nerve to sustain them in the coming fight, and each believed that one or the other must fall.

Their blades emitted a thousand sparks in defending and parrying the fierce and rapid cuts and lunges; but Tom fought coolly and resolutely.

At length, when both were nearly exhausted with the desperate fight, Black Bob, in preparing for a fearful downward stroke, exposed his right side.

The young outlaw saw the opportunity, and quick as lightning his blade descended with a crash, and the ruffian fell to the deck nearly cut in twain.

Then, like a tiger, Tom rushed to the head of his followers, and waving his sword, shouted—

"Clear the deck of these scoundrels. Forward! Hurrah!"

That cry was repeated; and with one irresistible charge, the wreckers were driven over the side.

"The cowardly wretches," said Tom, "to attack us in this disabled state."

He was about to walk aft, when he had said this, but turning, he looked at Snowball, and exclaimed—

"Lower a boat! By heaven, they may have attacked the cave!"

The same thought came into the African's head; but he said nothing. He could see by his chief's face that he was suffering a world of agony for Laura's sake.

The boat was soon skimming through the water; and the wreckers, who had reached the shore as the boat put off from the ship, scrambled up the bank, and took flight towards their rocky home.

When they reached this stronghold, they found Jack Ranger awaiting their return.

He swore bitterly at this defeat, and held a council with them as to the best means of putting our hero out of the way.

"You see," said the crafty villain in conclusion, "if he is once safely disposed of, the untold wealth of this cave may be yours."

The passion for riches thus excited, they sullenly agreed to join in a plan he had proposed.

Meanwhile Tom and Snowball had reached the cave, and like a thunderbolt came the news that Laura had disappeared.

Tom repressed all show of outward emotion; and disguising himself, left the band in charge of Snowball, and went in search of information that would aid him in the discovery of his lost love.

All that day was consumed in feretting out little by little, and when night came he had learned enough to discover that Laura had been carried on board a vessel that answered to the description of the Black Snake, Red Hand's ship— a vessel that he had imagined was blown into atoms long since.

Leaving him to promote his search, we will follow the miscreants of Ralph Ranger and his ruffianly companions.

With six of the wreckers to assist him, he laid in wait for the young chief, and while in his hiding place one of his emissaries came to him with the news that Red Hand's vessel had been at anchor in the bay.

The men knew the deadly enmity existing between the outlaw chief and Red Hand, and at once he started to his ship.

Ralph and his companions stealthily left their hiding places, and went down to the beach. Here he was brought to a stand-still for a few minutes, as they had no boat to pull off to sea in.

The vessel was anchored too far off to hear his hail.

He looked about, and soon succeeded in loosing a small fishing boat, which its owner was tying up for the night, and in this the seven took their seats, and the owner seized the oars.

CHAPTER LXXV.

THE ABDUCTION OF MIDSHIPMAN TOM.

"WHAT vessel do you wish to visit?" asked the boatman.

"I wish to overtake the Black Snake that left to-day. Can you not recommend a vessel?"

"They are all loaded down," returned the man dubiously, "there is only one lying here that is at all swift, and that a suspicious character; she came in here yesterday, and fitted up to day, so I suppose she is ready for instant departure; that is she lying yonder."

He pointed to a long dark vessel near them.

"Row us alongside of her," said Ranger.

Before he could mount her side, a dark-visaged man looked over, and demanded their business.

"That I will communicate to the captain," responded Ranger. "I wish to see him."

The captain, a sinister-looking man, was called, and came to the side and looked down upon them.

"I want to see you on private business," said Ranger, addressing him, " and in your cabin."

"Come aboard then." was the reply. "Your men can stay where they are."

The villain clambered up, and was conducted by the captain to the cabin.

"The Black Snake left here to-day," began Ranger, plunging directly into his business, "and I wish to pursue her. I will pay you liberally if you will run her down."

The captain shook his head.

"The Black Snake has hours the start, and a good breeze to carry her along," he said. "We couldn't catch up with her."

"I would pay any amount."

"No use. I can't do it. I would try if there was any chance."

Ranger bowed, and was about to take his departure, when his fertile brain invented another villainous plan, and he said—

"I hear, captain, that your vessel has a suspicious character. By that, I suppose, is meant that you are one of the pirates who have taken to the seas to plunder unarmed vessels."

He had taken a keen glance round the cabin, and noticed that it was half filled with weapons, and had made a sudden guess at the character of the vessel from those indications.

The captain's face paled and flushed.

"Pirate!" he ejaculated.

"Yes, pirate. Your manner confirms my suspicions; but you need have no fear for my discovery. I won't betray you. In fact, I'm one of your sort of men."

The captain brightened, but regarded his visitor suspiciously.

"I suppose you'll be leaving port soon?" went on Ranger.

"This very night."

"Good!" exclaimed Ranger, in a tone of complete satisfaction. "I have an enemy on shore —a fellow whom I am anxious to rid myself of. If I bring him aboard to-night, will you take him with you?"

"What would you want done with him?" asked the captain.

"Oh, anything," laughed the rascal; "anything but letting him come on shore. Sew him up in a blanket and drop him into the sea. Take him to the Algerines, or put him to work."

"I am a little short of men," mused the captain, "and one reason I ran in here was to get more. Yes, I'll take him, and be glad to, if he is young and active. I'll take twenty more just like him."

Ranger smiled, and took pains to express some of his private sentiments upon pirates and their trade in such a manner as to convince the captain he had nothing to fear from him; and he then admitted he belonged to that fraternity."

"I knew it," returned Ranger, quietly. "People don't carry cannons and so many weapons for nothing. I'll bring the fellow aboard some time in the night. He is somewhere near."

This being agreed to, they separated, Ranger re-entering his boat, and going ashore with his men.

He paid the boatman liberally, and engaged him to remain on the same spot until his return—even if it were not until the morning. And then he said—

"I believe the fellow has not gone back to his cave. It's almost bedtime, and he won't be likely to be out late. We'll go there. Have your rope ready to bind him."

They went towards the outlaws' retreat, and were about to conceal themselves, when Tom was seen coming towards the cave.

Ranger stepped out, and touched the young sailor on the arm.

Tom turned suddenly. Grasping him by the throat, he hurled Ranger aside.

Ranger paled with rage, and made a sign to the men. The latter understood, and Tom was instantly seized and pinioned before he had perceived Ralph's companions.

A scarf was tied over his mouth to prevent him calling for help, and the watchful villain then looked about him to see if his operations had attracted attention.

"We'll take him to the vessel," he said in a tone of jubilance.

Two of the men supported Tom, and the remainder of the party closed in around them, and in this manner they gained the boat.

They were quickly rowed to the pirate ship, and Tom was carried into the cabin, and then ungagged.

"Here he is, captain," said Ranger, pointing to the young chief. "Make a sailor of him, or convert him into food for fishes, just as you like; but never let him step on shore again."

The Captain consented with ill-concealed satisfaction as his dark eyes marked the noble form and the lithe, slight figure and keen eyes of Tom, and it was easy to see he was delighted with the acquisition to the crew.

"And now, young man," said Ranger, in a tone that was inaudible to the captain, but distinct to the hearing of Tom, "let me tell you that from this moment you can bid adieu to your country. Well, captain," he said aloud, as he turned to that officer, "I suppose you'll be off soon?"

"Immediately—the moment you go ashore."

"I would add one word to what I have said to you," remarked Ranger. "This fellow is high-spirited, and you will have to break him in. Be harsh with him—don't stand any nonsense."

"Never fear that," said the captain, smiling. "I know how to manage refactory seamen. I'll venture to say that I'll break his spirit."

"And here is a parting gift from me," said Ranger, drawing out a full purse. "It is to recompense you for any violence you may do to your own feelings by breaking him in."

The captain leered and took the bribe.

Ranger made a mocking adieu to Tom; but he quailed before the stern look he encountered.

With a jarring laugh he left the cabin and returned to his men, and went ashore.

Dismissing the boatman, they stood upon the beach; and the villain watched with gleaming eyes the sudden activity which reigned upon the vessel.

The anchor was lifted, the sails set, and the ship started on her way to the sea.

"He is gone," said Ranger, in a tone of gratification, "gone, and for ever! He has a living death before him!"

The captive remained for a long time bound and helpless in the cabin. Not one thought did he waste upon his ill fortune, but rather regarded it as otherwise.

His own vessel was disabled and not fit to put out to sea, as he thought. Should there be any truth in the rumour that Red Hand's ship had sailed that day, the vessel he was now in would most likely soon overhaul her.

His heart leapt with joy at the thought; then his dark eyes flashed as he thought of a plan whereby he could become master of the very craft that now held him prisoner.

But when the captain came to the cabin, his face was as calm and quiet as though no torturing fears were racking his heart.

"Sulky—eh!" was the officer's greeting. "We've left the land behind us, and we are now out upon the open sea, so you may as well make the best of your situation. I need hands here, and if you've a mind to obey orders and do your duty, why you may have your liberty. What do you say?"

The temptation was strong within the young chief's soul to utterly refuse doing anything about the vessel; but he reflected that he might be kept confined or killed if he refused, on the other hand he might have a chance to work out some plan for escape.

"You may unbind me," he said, briefly.

"You are sensible," responded the captain, taking a knife from the table and cutting Tom's bonds. "Tell me your name."

"Lupus Wilson."

"And I am Captain Dragon, your master," said the officer. "You will find me a hard one if you you are not particularly careful."

Tom's eyes flashed; but he controlled his spirit, and said nothing.

"And now sit down," said Captain Dragon. "This has been a rather singular occurrence, your arrival here. It seems strange that a gentleman like the one who brought you here should be so interested in a low fellow as he says you are. Not that I believe that, though," he added speaking more to himself. "I'd like to hear your story."

DEATH OF THE AMERICAN CAPTAIN.

Tom saw that the man was actuated only by curiosity, and that nothing would tempt him to restore him to liberty, so he replied coolly—

"I have no story, Captain Dragon, to relate."

"No story? and brought aboard bound! I understand you. You do not wish to tell me. Do as you choose; but remember that your refusal will only make your own case harder."

Tom took refuge in silence.

"Since you are so disagreeable," continued Captain Dragon, "you may as well go on deck and see about going to work. Report yourself to my lieutenant."

Tom bowed coldly and left the cabin, going on deck. There were plenty of seamen attending to their duties; and the lieutenant stood gazing over the side of the vessel into the water.

Tom felt a choking sensation in the throat as he glanced upwards at the glorious sky and downwards at the shining water, which seemed another sky with the reflections of the stars upon its surface.

He inquired of one of the seamen, and discovered the whereabouts and identity of the lieutenant in question, and then advanced to his side, saying—

"Captain Dragon wished me to report to you."

"Oh! you're the new sailor," exclaimed the lieutenant, regarding him with a look of curiosity. "We've heard of your advent on board. You want work. I'll give you work, and plenty of it; but not to-night. You can keep your eyes about you till it's time to turn in; and whatever you learn to-night may save you trouble."

The officer was deceived by Tom's disguise, and mistook him for a landsman, a mistake which the young chief did not wish to rectify.

CHAPTER LXXVI.
THE PLAGUE SHIP.

THE next day brought with it work; but Tom's quickness and activity disarmed the lieutenant of all impatience, and he declared to the captain that never had such a ready hand been seen on board the Triton.

On the fourth day out, when Tom had begun to gain more consideration from the officers on account of his quietness and reticence, they came in sight of a ship that lay at anchor.

They headed directly for it, thinking that they had found prey.

This ship Tom recognised with joy as the Black Snake.

She was strangely silent; not a form on her deck; her sails furled, and she looked lifeless and deserted.

Captain Dragon and his officers gathered on deck to look at her, and the former asked—

"Can this be a trap for us?"

"I think not," replied his lieutenant. "Don't you remember seeing her in port and remarking upon her? This is the same vessel."

"I remember," said the captain, with more animation; "it's the same ship that mysterious gentleman wanted us to chase. We shall have a chance now of overhauling her. I wonder," he added, "why she lies so still and seemingly deserted. We will see."

They came nearer and nearer to the anchored vessel, until they lay alongside.

The grappling irons were thrown.

Captain Dragon, his lieutenant, half-a-dozen men, and Tom went on board.

What a sight met their gaze!

The dead and dying lay about the decks, some just heaving their last sigh.

Some were already decomposing in the sunlight and heat.

The intruders paused in amazement.

"What is the matter?" asked Captain Dragon of a dying man, whom Tom recognised as Red Hand's lieutenant.

"The plague! the plague!" he gasped. "We were stricken on the very first day. The ship had been visited by the plague on her way out, and the infection lingered. Help! help!"

Tom looked wildly round the deck, but he saw nothing of Laura.

What if she were already dead! He reeled with the thought.

Some of the pirate crew began to demand their departure, fearing infection.

But the glitter of a necklace upon the throat of a dead maiden tempted the captain to remain, and Tom seized the opportunity of crossing the deck and descending to the cabin.

Although the small windows were open, the air was laden with a foul odour that almost stifled him.

On entering, he saw that the floor was covered with blankets, on which the sick reposed, and that the hue of death was on nearly every face he beheld.

"Laura!" he called out, with irrepressible anguish—"Laura! are you here?"

As his voice rang sharply through the cabin, a state-room door opened, and Laura, pale and wan, appeared.

He sprang forward, and she fell fainting in his arms.

"Thank God!" he articulated. "I feared— oh, I feared"——

Without completing the sentence, he carried her on deck, and from thence to the pirate vessel.

Captain Dragon stepped forward, and uttered a cry of admiration as he beheld the lovely girl.

He would have spoken, but the deadly glitter in Tom's eye warned him to keep a respectful distance from the glittering weapon in the young sailor's hand.

Captain Dragon was not the class of man to let pass any opportunity of making his calling profitable, and he imagined that a female, young and beautiful as Laura, in the possession of, as he had been led to believe, a humble personage like Tom, at least bore a very suspicious appearance.

And he concluded in his own mind that Tom's possession of her could be accounted for only by one of two ways.

He had forcibly seized her for wealth at her own control, or, being of wealthy family, he expected considerable pecuniary advantages as the price of her liberty.

Captain Dragon's first object was, therefore, to ascertain whether either of his surmises were correct; and if so, the ship being his own, to transfer Laura from Tom's to his own keeping.

Scarcely had Tom, therefore, descended with Laura into a cabin, when he was summoned into the captain's state room.

"You have a very young and lovely creature there," said the captain. "May I ask what is the nature of the interest you so evidently take in her?"

"My interest, captain," replied Tom, "is a trust I have to fulfil. I have months agone pledged myself to protect her in good or in evil times; and, by this good sword"—touching the handle of one he was wearing in lieu of his own— "will I keep my pledge."

"Of course, regardless," said the captain decisively, "of the wishes or intentions of others, if I understand you aright?"

"Yes," was the laconic reply.

Although awed for a moment by the young chief's commanding gesture, he soon recovered himself; and, placing his hand on the butt of a pistol, glared fiercely at Tom.

"What do you mean—eh?" ejaculated the captain. "What do you mean, you young lubber?"

Tom paid no attention to his words, but continued his tender attention upon Laura.

Captain Dragon was rather astonished at Tom's defiant words and actions, and coming closer to the young chief, he literally roared—

"Did you hear what I said?"

Midshipman Tom turned angrily upon him and replied—

"I did."

The dark fire that lurked in his eyes—the compressed lip, and resolute bearing, were not without their effect upon the pirate captain.

He drew back a pace as he saw the boy's hand wandering to the hilt of his cutlass, and repeated—

"You did? Then leave that girl alone."

Midshipman Tom smiled—but it was a demoniac smile—as he said—

"Leave her alone—why?"

"Why, you infernal lubberly powder monkey? I'll teach you why with a rope's-end."

Tom's face reddened with passion; and, gripping the hilt of his cutlass, he said, fiercely—

"Dare to threaten me once more, and I'll cleave you to the deck."

Captain Dragon, of the pirate ship, the Triton, was completely dumbfounded. The term "taken aback" would not be half expressive enough to describe his feelings on hearing such a rejoinder.

He stood silent for several minutes, then his rage found words.

"You'll cleave me to the deck!" he roared. "Why you—you bragging hound you! I'll flog every inch of flesh off your back! I "——

He stopped suddenly, and went back with his mouth streaming with blood.

The fiery young chieftain's spirit was aroused, and he dashed his clenched fist in the speaker's face.

Then, drawing his cutlass, he stood calm and daringly awaiting the result of his defiant blow.

Tom knew that he had openly aroused the hostility of the corsair captain, yet he quailed not, although any moment might bring down the whole horde of desperadoes upon him.

One arm encircled Laura's waist, and he stood with the courage and bearing of a lion.

The pirate captain evidently thought the young chieftain too mean an antagonist to require any assistance in punishing him, and, drawing his sword, he strode quickly across the deck, saying—

"You infernal mutinous young brute! I'll cut you into pieces."

Captain Dragon was no mean swordsman, and he thought he could easily fulfil his promise if he wished.

But he had calculated wrongly—he had mistaken his young assailant, and before he had made a third thrust he discovered it.

Tom parried them as easily as though Captain Dragon had been a child with a cane in his hand.

He saw he required caution, and became more careful, keeping well under his guard.

Again he crossed swords.

"So you can fence, can you? And, hang me! if I don't believe you know more about a ship than you pretend. Take that!"

He aimed a fierce lunge at Tom's heart as he spoke.

To his dismay, the point of his weapon glided smoothly over his adversary's.

"Curse you!" he muttered, savagely. "Surrender your weapon."

Tom, thinking it was time to end the fray, now began to act on the offensive; and pressing upon the captain, forced him to the deck, and kept him well employed in keeping a sound body.

"Captain Dragon," he said, as that officer began to fall back before his sword, "in two minutes I shall disarm you, and I could kill you as easily as I could strike that button on you jacket."

And, to the pirate captain's astonishment, Tom's weapon struck sharply upon a gilded button on his breast; and, before he had time to utter a word, or return the blow, his sword was wrenched from his hand, and sent flying up into the rigging.

Then, as it came whirling down, Tom struck it sharply with his blade, and sent it flying into the sea.

The second feat dumbfounded the corsair, and falling back, he asked—

"Who and what are you? By heaven? I never before met with so skilful a swordsman."

"Your men," said the young midshipman, pointing to the crew, who were now closing round him, "are too near. Send them to the forecastle, then you shall hear who I am."

"Fall back!" said the corsair; "further yet. Go forward, all of you."

The pirates fell back sullenly.

CHAPTER LXXVII.

AN EXPLANATION.

WHEN they were out of hearing, and before the young chief could speak, Laura raised her head from his shoulder, and said, feebly—

"Where are your men? Where's Snowball? This is not your ship."

Captain Dragon heard her lowly-spoken words, and replied in astonishment—

"Your men—your ship?"

"Yes," said the young chieftain, "my men and my ship. Does that astonish you?

"It does. Who and what are you?"

Tom drew his lithe, graceful form up, and said, proudly—

"Midshipman Tom, the outlaw!"

"Midshipman Tom!" gasped Captain Dragon. "And I have"——

"You are blameless," said the young chief. "I should have earlier proclaimed myself, but I had an object in view in not doing so."

"But your disguise?"

"That," said Tom, "I am not responsible for."

Captain Dragon fixed his eyes on the young chieftain. He could not understand him.

Then he looked at the young maiden.

Tom saw his look, and defined its meaning.

"This lady," he said, "is my—my betrothed. You can now perhaps understand why I consented so tamely to remain on board your vessel."

Captain Dragon looked more stupefied than ever.

"By some means," continued Tom, "this lady was forced on board the Black Snake. I had scarcely gained that knowledge, when I was seized and brought to you. My vessel being rather roughly handled by an encounter with several cruisers, I could not put to sea in pursuit of the Black Snake, or you would not have had me here. When I came on board this vessel I saw everything was ready for a start. Now do you understand?"

"Partly. But surely you would not have attempted a rescue in the very face of your foe, and that foe Red Hand?"

"I would."

The quiet tone in which these words were uttered surprised Captain Dragon. His respect increased every moment for his young and daring companion.

"You would?" he said. "Then I fear your band would have lost a leader."

Tom smiled.

"At any rate," he said, "that miscreant should have finished his career had we met."

Captain Dragon held out his hand, saying—

"Can I hope you will accept my hand as a token of friendship after what has passed?"

The young chief grasped his late antagonist's hand, saying—

"Willingly. Let us be friends henceforth."

"We will. I have a favour to ask."

"Which," said Tom, "I will grant, if possible."

"I am glad to hear it. You will honour me by accepting the use of my cabin for that lady; she seems ill and weak yet."

"Thanks for the offer, captain, for she must need repose after passing through such a scene of horror as that plague-stricken ship presented."

Captain Dragon led the way to his cabin, and Tom followed, supporting Laura.

"I have an old negress on board," said the corsair, "she will attend upon this lady while we take a turn on deck; I have a few questions to ask you."

Tom placed his pale, beautiful loved-one upon a couch, while the captain went in search of the negress.

He soon returned, bringing a middle-aged woman of colour to the cabin.

"She is not," he said, laughingly, "very handsome, but as faithful as a hound to me."

The black woman placed her hand upon her head, and made a slight obeisance.

"Poor devil!" said the pirate captain, "I saved her from being roasted alive; from that time she has been with me, and I believe would die to save my life."

The woman again bowed her head, and folded her arms meekly upon her breast.

The corsair pointed to Laura.

"Obey her," he said, "as you would me; attend upon her every wish."

The negress kissed his hand, and placed it upon her head, this act implying her head should answer for it.

The outlaw chief and Captain Dragon then went on deck, and as they went towards the poop, the former could not help asking mentally, whether this sudden desire, upon the corsair's part to befriend him, was not the crafty workings of a subtle mind.

Yet when he looked into his face, every suspicious thought vanished, and as though to clear away any lingering doubt, the pirate captain asked, as they stood leaning against the rail—

"Do you know anything of that fellow who brought you on board?"

Tom pondered a moment, then said—

"No. I never saw his face before."

"Are you sure of that?"

"Quite."

"Strange!" said the pirate captain, musingly, "very strange!"

"It is," said the young chief; "but stranger still when I begin to reflect upon the whole affair."

"Indeed!"

"This," continued the young chief, "is the third time I have been captured, and, strange to say, Red Hand's vessel has, on each occasion, been at anchor in sight of the coast."

"Once, his band carried you off after you were wounded, or was the rumour incorrect?"

"No, more truthful than rumour generally speaks. I was taken once by him; but this last clever capture seems even more incomprehensible. He had sailed some hours before my return."

Captain Dragon was not without a shrewd amount of cunning; his lawless life caused him to view matters in a different light to that in which the young outlaw regarded the affair.

After a silence of several minutes, he stopped suddenly in his walk, and said—

"Unless I am much mistaken, you have a powerful enemy somewhere."

The young chief's thoughts recurred to his incarceration in the dungeon at Mountsteven Castle, and he replied—

"I have."

"An unseen one," continued Captain Dragon, "but powerful; and if my penetration is not at fault, one who employs such tools as the fellow who brought you on board to do work that they fear to do themselves."

"You know him, then?"

"I do. Thinking over the matter here, brought the fellow's face more vividly to my mind. We met once before."

"Should I meet him again," thought Tom, "he will remember it."

The captain lit a cigar, then handed the case to the young chief.

"No," he said.

"What! not indulge in a weed?"

"No, not yet."

"So much the better. Well, let me see—where did I leave off?"

"You were saying that you had met the fellow that so cleverly trapped me."

"True, it was at Havannah."

"Havannah?"

"Yes, I used to do a little in the slave trade then, but the English cruisers were too sharp for me; and to prevent them from having the trouble of mustering the ship's company, and having a dislike to being run up to the yardarm of the flagship, I—I"——

"You gave it up."

"Well no, not exactly. I had made a capital run, and had just dropped anchor when a corvette, carrying the Union Jack, dropped anchor within a cable's length of me."

"Well?"

"Well, much to my annoyance, she opened her ports and placed me right under her batteries."

"I saw the game was up, and, as an armed boat put off to board me, I thought it time to retreat, which I did through the cabin window and swam ashore."

"Were you not seen?"

"No, it was growing late, and I daresay you know darkness comes on very suddenly in those latitudes."

"I have heard so."

"It was fortunate for me that it did so, for by the time I reached the shore, I heard the sound of firing on board my vessel; but it was over, for the blue jackets, few in number as they were, soon overcame my cowardly crew—but I am wandering from my story.

"You must know, when I made my exit through the cabin window, I tied several bags of gold round my waist, knowing I should want money to bribe some honest innkeeper to hide me until the search was over.

"They are used," he added, with a chuckle, "to that sort of thing in Havannah; for I don't suppose there is a house of entertainment in the city but has its secret chambers.

"I found one, at any rate, but was not permitted to have it to myself long, for that sallow-faced gentleman who brought you on board, came in—curse him!

"Well, from his yarn it appeared he was flying from the gallows, having, in a quarrel with a naval officer, shot some one who interfered.

"At least such was his yarn.

"Well, we turned in for the night, and when I woke up next morning, my companion had gone, and so had my money."

The young outlaw laughed.

"I should have thought," he said, "that you would have known him again."

The pirate captain puffed a cloud of smoke up to the sky, and replied, quietly—

"I thought the fellow's face was familiar; but this affair happening so long ago, I had nearly forgotten it. But," he added, savagely "the remembrance will not do him good."

"He is most sure to be near where I dropped anchor. If he is, there will be an unpleasant meeting."

The negress glided towards her master at this moment.

Making a profound salaam, she stood motionless; with bowed head, she waited for permission to speak.

"Well," he asked, "what would you?"

"The lady sleeps," said the African woman; "it is the sleep of peace."

The captain inclined his head, and was about to resume his watch with the young chief, when the woman gave a furtive, startled look towards the fore part of the vessel, and whispered—

"Master, be on your guard, there is treachery—black treachery—intended. Do not look towards the crew; they are watching you."

Captain Dragon was a man of wondrous nerve, and he knew the ruffianly, treacherous crew with whom he had to deal.

He knew also that the woman's words could signify but one thing—that the most terrible!

"Mutiny!"

Dreadful word! A hundred lawless ruffians ready to be pitted against one man!

Yet he kept his feelings so entirely under control, that for the moment the young chieftain almost doubted whether he had heard the slave's warning words.

Still puffing his cigar, he watched the smoke ascend, and in a low voice said to the young outlaw—

"The struggle will soon commence; this has been hatching for some time. I am sorry for you and the fair young girl in the cabin; but I will blow the ship and these mutinous vagabonds into the air before I give in."

"Do not," said the brave Tom; "bestow a second thought upon us."

"Pardon me, my young friend, but you do not know the fiends with whom I have to deal. My death is as certain as that we stand here together. See, they are coming towards us."

"Let them," said Midshipman Tom; "I am with you to the death."

"Thanks. I love a bold spirit like yours. Now down to the cabin, and load every firearm there. I will follow."

There was no time for more words, and the young chieftain passed to the aft hatch as the crew, with sullen, savage faces, came in a body towards their captain.

CHAPTER LXXVIII.

MIDSHIPMAN TOM AWES THE MUTINEERS.

WITH one hand resting carelessly upon the butt of a pistol, Captain Dragon stood and faced the mutineers, who came in a body and formed a semi-circle round him.

The captain's fiery eyes were fixed on a muscular mulatto, the boatswain's mate of the ship as he calmly said—

"So, Williams, is that true which I have heard—that you aspire to the command of this vessel?"

The mulatto looked around at the crew, as though to seek encouragement, as he said—

"Suppose it is?"

"If," said Captain Dragon, "such is your opinion, you will be disappointed, that's all."

"We shall see."

"We shall. Now return to your duty all of you, and come to my cabin in one hour's time; perhaps by then your minds will have undergone some change."

Not knowing what to make of their commander's strange manner, and thinking the rising would be equally effectual one hour hence as at that moment, the men left the quarter-deck and went forward.

No sooner was the captain relieved of their presence than he rushed down to the cabin.

And approaching our hero, said—

"What is to be done? Those scoundrels mean mischief."

The outlaw smiled.

"Will you leave me," he said, "to quell this mutiny? I pledge my word that every man shall obey you like a whipped cur."

"And how will you manage that?" inquired the captain.

"You shall see," was the quiet reply, and as the young chief spoke, he drew a chalk line over the centre of the cabin floor.

"Have you any powder here?"

The pirate captain opened a small door, inside of which stood two casks of powder, one small one and one large.

"Good," said Tom, "trundle them in."

That being done he stove in the head of the largest one, and emptied its contents upon the table and floor.

Then, seating himself on the remaining barrel, he took a pistol in each hand.

"Now, captain," he cried, "summon the crew."

The men readily obeyed the summons, and on entering the cabin, they appeared struck with sudden fear at the preparations they beheld.

Midshipman Tom surveyed them for a few seconds, then pointing to the chalk line across the floor with the muzzle of one of his pistols, he said—

"You all see that chalk line?"

The men were silent.

"The first man," cried Tom, "who places his foot upon it, or attempts to pass the landing, dies"

The mutineers looked blankly at each other; but the mulatto who appeared to be their leader, said, insultingly—

"What do you mean? And who are you who thus ventures to give us orders?"

"Listen," said Tom, and he spoke with fierce resolution, "you shall know who I am. I command this ship for a short time, in place of your captain. I am not afraid of a turbulent crew, therefore I order you to obey me."

The crew however made no manifestation of doing so.

"Do you deny my power?" said Tom, "Yet you shall obey it; ay, even as you have never before obeyed—like slaves, like crouching dogs. Yes; raise but one finger against me or your captain and look," Tom lowered his pistol, and pointed as he spoke to the heap of loose powder at his feet. "I'll pull this trigger and blow you, the ship, and ourselves to eternity."

Tom's manner was certainly resolute enough to carry unpleasant apprehension with it, and with only one exception the crew seemed paralyzed and fear-stricken at his words.

That one exception was the mulatto, who, bursting into a mocking laugh, exclaimed—

"You'll do no such thing. Who are you thus to bully and ——"

A bullet cut short his speech.

His feet had touched the chalk line, and the young chieftain fired and shot him through the head.

"So much for your leader!" said Tom. "Thus I have kept my word—thus will I ever keep it."

"And that you may not misunderstand me, I repeat that on the first appearance of any act of disobedience in you, that heap of powder I will fire."

The blanched faces of the crew proved to him that he had for a time, at least, succeeded in quieting them.

RED HAND SIGHTS A SAIL.

"And now," he continued, "pay particular attention to what I am about to say. Captain Dragon and myself will take it in turns to command the ship; and while one watches the deck, the other will sit here with a pistol ready to fire the train. And mark me, one act of disobedience committed by any one of you will be accepted by the captain and me as the act of the whole crew."

One of the men was about to speak.

"Don't interrupt me," said Tom; "we can anticipate what you would say—our lives would be nothing in your hands. We know, and admit it; but therefore is the sternness of our resolve now fixed. When we die, every soul of you dies with us. Now go, and take the body of that scoundrel with you."

The utterance of this extraordinary speech, coupled with the death of their leader, had its effect upon the crew, and with blanched cheeks and downcast heads, they left the cabin, dragging the corpse of the mulatto with them.

The captain primed his pistols and went on deck.

Tom, pistol in hand, remained seated over the heap of loose powder, ready, if needed, to send the ship into a thousand pieces.

Morning at last came, and Captain Dragon came below. He found the young outlaw in the same attitude as he had left him.

"What a fearful night!" said Tom. "I have been waiting to hear the report of your pistol from the moment you left me."

"I too," said Captain Dragon, "have passed a fearful night. With the deathlike silence, the subdued and cowed bearing of the men, they appear like so many spectres."

"This is terrible."

"Yes, but necessary."

"How long," asked the captain, "do you think it necessary for this fearful state of things to last?"

"Until," said the young chief, "the men are thoroughly cowed by the constant fear of death hanging over them."

Leaving the captain to take charge of the powder, Tom took his pistols and went on deck.

He had not been long there when one of the crew came towards him.

Tom levelled the pistol at the man's head.

"Don't fire," said the mutineer, "I am unarmed."

"What do you want?"

"To tell you that we will return to our duty without having to work the ship in this terrible silence and this fearful knowledge that an awful fate threatens our lives."

The young sailor made no reply, but kept the tube of his pistol pointed upon the speaker's face.

The man waited a long time to receive a reply; but finding the young chief inexorable, he went away moaning like one who felt himself doomed under the hangman's grasp.

In deadly silence the operations necessary to work the ship continued to be carried out, the silence only occasionally broken by the cold commands of either the young chief or the captain.

The courses at this time were set, and the Thunderer running before the wind.

The crew were collected in small groups about the vessel, looking fearfully into each other's faces, none daring to speak even in the lowest tones.

With the full knowledge of the instant destruction that would follow the least violation of their orders, they now felt like men accursed—doomed to endless torment—as they went moaning about that silent ship.

The young outlaw felt keenly the misery he was inflicting, but he stifled every feeling of humanity as he weighed the fierce and lawless character of the crew.

CHAPTER LXXIX.
THE END OF THE MUTINY.

THE day was fine, and the wind which blew steadily promised a continuance of fine weather, and Midshipman Tom, thinking it necessary to take some repose, was descending the steps that led from the poop, when one of the unhappy wretches, whose over-wrought feelings had overcome his fears, stepped forward.

Putting his hands up in a supplicating manner, he said—

"For heaven's sake, sir, have pity on us!"

"Pity!"

"Yes. This awful suspense is worse than being doomed to endless torment."

"You brought it on yourselves."

"We know it, sir; but we were misled by the mulatto."

"What would you have?"

"Yours and the captain's acceptance of our submission."

"No, it is impossible; you are not to be trusted. Go, leave this part of the ship."

He turned haughtily from them, and began to descend the hatchway, when a sudden moan of most intense and anguished suffering reached his ear.

It was the moaning of the overawed crew.

Captain Dragon looked up as the young chief entered the cabin.

"They must suffer," said the latter, meaning the crew. "But the struggle will soon be over."

"Would to God it were! The constant dread of being obliged to send so many souls into eternity seems to have shrivelled up my brains. Great heaven! it is fearful."

The young outlaw had not particularly noticed the face of the speaker; but when he did so, he started back with a cry of dismay.

The overtaxed tension of his nerves had worked a terrible alteration; and from being a fine-looking, hale man, bronzed with the sun of many lands, he appeared pale and haggard, shivering like a leaf, and his hair had changed to a snowy white.

"Great heaven, captain!" exclaimed Tom, "you must have suffered."

"Yes. I have been waiting your signal every moment since you left. So terrible has been my dread that it seemed as though the roof of my skull had been lifted off, and molten lead poured into the quivering membranes. Look at me; my skin is like dried parchment—my tongue hot and swollen."

Tom did look at the speaker, and all he described was true.

"Captain Dragon," he said, "you must take an hour's sleep."

The captain shook his head, and replied—

"No, my friend, here is my post, and here will I remain until those miscreants shall be so quelled that, like dogs, they will grovel in the dust at our feet."

Another and another day passed in this fearful state.

Human endurance could endure this state of things no longer, and the mutineers held a whispered consultation, rather to risk the blowing up of the vessel than continue in their present state.

One was deputed to convey their sentiments to the young outlaw.

He slowly approached the quarter-deck.

This in itself was a breach of the rules; but the men had evidently reached beyond the fear of death.

He paused not in his walk until the young chief's long deadly barrel caused him to stop. The seaman's features were wrung with anguish. He said—

"We are now willing to plead for forgiveness at our captain's feet."

"It is useless," said Midshipman Tom.

"Plead for us, sir," he replied—"plead for us. Another twenty-four hours of this infernal silence will drive me mad."

The young chieftain remained silent.

The man sprang upon the bulwarks, and was beneath the ocean's surface in a second.

"Let him perish," was his first thought; but a moment's reflection caused more humane feelings to prevail.

Making a gesture to a group of pirates, two of them sprang to the rescue of their desperate shipmate.

While they were drawing their companion out of the water the young chief went below; and, addressing Captain Dragon, said—

"I would now accept their allegiance; depend upon it they have suffered enough for their crime."

Without heeding Tom's words, the captain suddenly asked—

"How far are we from the land?"

"I sighted the white cliffs two bells since," said Tom.

"Know you where we are?"

"I do—well. We shall soon be near the place where you were when I was brought on board."

"Bring the vessel to an anchor when we are near enough; I will then put an end to this."

Giving the necessary orders, the anchor was dropped.

The clank of the chain passing through the hawse-hole had hardly subsided when Captain Dragon rushed on deck, exclaiming—

"Overboard with you all! I have fired a slow match, and the ship will blow up."

There was a mad rush to the vessel's side as the crew realized the fearful truth.

As the last man plunged into the water, the captain turned to Tom, saying—

"Thank God! it is over."

The young sailor started with surprise.

"Over!" he repeated; "and we"—

"Are safe," said Captain Dragon. "That was but a ruse of mine to get rid of those vagabonds."

"And left your vessel without hands."

"True, but not for long."

"You are sanguine, captain."

"I am. In less than twenty-four hours I will have the Thunderer manned and ready for sea. But what are these boats coming towards us? Not my rascally crew, I hope."

"No," said Tom, "it is my band. They have seen my signal."

"Your signal," said the pirate, looking up at the masts, "where?"

The outlaw drew him to the vessel's side, and pointed to a small flag.

"This," said the young chief, "has been affixed here from the moment we sighted those bluff headlands."

"Its meaning?"

"Simply," answered Tom, "to let them know I am on board and require their aid."

"Pleasant," said Captain Dragon, smiling, "had I detained you here a prisoner. But pardon me for asking,—why did you permit yourself to be carried off, when the exhibition of that signal would have saved you."

"In the first place," said Tom, "it was dark; secondly, my hands were bound; and thirdly, I wished to overtake the Black Snake."

"Three very good and sufficient reasons. Here come your men."

Several boats, filled with the members of Tom's band, now shot alongside of the ship.

And when the young chief showed himself to his men, a shout of joy came from their lips.

Snowball was the first to make his appearance on the deck, and rushing towards the chieftain, he embraced him.

"Nebber tought to see you again, Massa Tom," he said.

"How was that, Snowball?"

"Tought red-coats hab yer."

"Ha! Have they been here?"

"Dey hab, Massa Tom, and surrounded de cave. By Gar! though, we soon show 'em the way to go back."

"You beat them off, Snowball."

"Yes, Massa Tom; but I s'pect dey come back, stronger than ebber soon."

The outlaw bit his lip.

"I should not care so much," he muttered, "if the War Cloud was not in such a crippled state, because we shall be compelled to keep under cover, instead of refitting."

"Dat am it, Massa Tom."

"When were the troopers here, Snowball?"

"About ten days ago."

"You think they will return?"

"Sure ob it, Massa Tom—quite sure."

"We have no time to lose then?"

"Not a minute, Massa Tom. What we do now?"

"Leave half a dozen hands to look after the ship until Captain Dragon picks up some."

To Captain Dragon's satisfaction, this order was followed by the appearance of several broad-shouldered brawny outlaws, who at a gesture from their leader, went forward, and began to put the ship in order.

Captain Dragon began to express his thanks to Tom for the aid, but the latter cut him short by saying—

"No thanks are due to me, the danger has been equally shared; and now, any assistance I can give you is but a small return for all you have done for me."

"The debt is on my side," said the captain; "but have your own way, my friend."

Tom laughed, and went to the state-room.

CHAPTER LXXX.
SNOWBALL'S FORTIFICATION.

LAURA was sitting by the open port, her chin supported by her hand.

She turned her head when Tom entered, and a smile of welcome lit up her features.

"Of what were you thinking, Laura?" he asked, going to her side. "Were your thoughts of the past or the present?"

"Of both, Tom."

He sat by her side, and drawing her fairy-like, fragile form towards him until her head rested upon his shoulder, he said—

"May I become the possessor of those thoughts, Laura?"

"You may," she answered, "if you deem them worthy of listening to."

"Anything from your lips"—

"Hush!"

"Why hush?"

"Because you have often said that before, and yet you—you"—

"Proceed, Laura."

"Always refuse a request I make."

"I? Never. Have I done so?"

"Never mind. Will you grant me one now?"

"I will—I swear."

"You have sworn, and must not break your word."

"I will not, Laura."

"Well, this is it." She placed her two hands upon his shoulders as she spoke, and looked into his eyes. "You must, for my sake and your own, give up this lawless life."

The outlaw started back with astonishment, he had not expected this. For a few moments he was silent.

When he spoke, there was a cloud upon his brow, and a twitching of the lip, which showed but too plainly the effect his companion's words had taken upon his mind.

"The only request," he said; "the only one I cannot grant you."

Her face became saddened at this answer, and her head drooped.

"You are sad," he said; "sad that you have plighted your vows to a nameless outlaw—a desperado—whose hand is against every man's, and every man's against him. Is it not so, Laura?"

He raised her blushing face until their eyes met. Clinging fondly to his neck, she answered—

"Oh no, Tom. I never for one moment had such a thought upon my mind. Nameless outlaw

as you appear, you are, to me, all and everything in the world."

"True-hearted girl!"

"Yes—all—everything. The very light of day even the sun's glorious brilliance is without its charm when I am away from you."

"Why, then, do you wish me to change my mode of life?"

"The danger that ever menaces you, that makes me anxious and unhappy."

"Danger! 'Tis the charm of my life, Laura."

"Your charm, Tom, and my misery."

The young outlaw began to feel the influence of her mournful looks and pleading eyes.

And to prevent himself from making a promise he knew it would be impossible to keep, he took her hand, saying—

"Come, Laura, let me conduct you to the boat which awaits you."

She rose from her seat, and silently followed him to the deck.

He conducted her over the side, and from thence into the boat.

And while the light craft was cleaving through the ocean's glassy surface, the young outlaw looked into Laura's face and said—

"When you reach the cave, remain there until I return."

"I will, Tom; do not stay."

Tom went on board the Thunderer when the young girl had gone, and, taking Captain Dragon by the arm, they went aft.

"Prevention," he said, to the pirate captain, "is better than cure."

"An old axiom," was the reply, "that has lost nothing of its truth from age."

"Exactly so, Captain Dragon. Now, in all probability, I shall be attacked in a few hours by a detachment of troops; I want your assistance."

"Mine!" laughed the pirate—"mine! Why, how is it possible I can be of any use to you?"

"I'll explain."

"Thanks, do; for I'm in the dark."

"I will leave, if you will allow me, a couple o dozen men on board your vessel."

"Thanks! you are too"——

"Steady, captain. These men will be a guard for you, in the event of those rascals returning."

"A capital thought. They may return, seeing the vessel is not yet blown up."

"That is what I thought. Now for my request."

"It is granted before you ask it."

"I may as well tell you its nature."

Captain Dragon laughed.

"Yes," he said, "it may be necessary."

"Well, I wish you to lend me your guns."

"My guns—certainly. Guns and vessel are at your service."

"Thanks! that's all I wanted. I'll leave the

necessary directions with my men. Now I shall turn in for a few hours; you had better do the same."

Ben Bight was the man appointed in charge of the party that were left on board the Thunderer, and to him Tom said—

"Should the cave be attacked, Ben, you had best send one half the men on the tops to pick off the officers."

"Very well, sir."

"Then bring the vessel's head round, and let her broadside lay to land. You know what to do then."

"Yes, sir; serve out plenty of grape-shot to the beggars."

"Yes, that will be your best plan."

Having given these orders, he was soon in his boat, and in close conference with Snowball.

"Do you think," he said, "that it would be possible to plant a few guns to command the entrance of the cave?"

"Yes, Massa Tom, plenty of places for 'em! but it take all de boys to put our guns in position."

"Now, I had not thought of that, Snowball."

"Dere am anoder plan," said the African, "which I tink, Massa Tom, we can do without losing one man."

"Let me hear it, Snowball; your fertile brain is invaluable on the art of war."

The African drew himself proudly up, and said—

"Snowball chief in him own country, Massa Tom, and ebery chief dat wear de war feather hab to know all about de fighting."

"You do justice to your instructor, Snowball."

The black showed his teeth as he smiled proudly at his leader's compliment.

"Dere," he said, pointing to a sharp projecting piece of rock which overhung the sea—"dere, Massa Tom, am de place for de gun."

The spot chosen by Snowball was admirably suited to the emergency. A gun placed there would sweep the front of the cave at one discharge.

"A capital plan," said the young chief. "But how are we to get over the old difficulty about the man to serve the gun?"

"By habbing none dere."

"By having none there? You puzzle me."

"Just dis, Massa Tom. We load guns to de muzzle with grape, and den put slow match, dat will burn long time on de touch-hole."

"Put it on, should we see the troops coming."

"Zactly, Massa Tom. Dey sure to want to come into de cave, and while dey are halting de gun go off. Yah! yah! yah! By Gar, dey tink de debbil hab 'em."

"Perhaps he will have some. Now, Snowball, we are ashore. you go with the men to the cave and bring out a gun; I'll go and examine the spot."

With the nimbleness of a mountain goat, the young chief clambered up the almost perpendicular rock, and stood out at the extreme edge looking at the magnificent expanse of water which lay out before him.

From this view, so pleasing to a sailor's heart, he turned his gaze inward.

Suddenly he gave a start.

His fine face became crimson as his eyes were fastened upon a bright moving object some three miles away.

Could it be fancy?

No; it was his foes marching upon his stronghold, the last rays of the setting sun dancing upon their burnished weapons and glittering accoutrements.

If this was not sufficient to convince him, there came, borne upon the gentle breeze, the distant sound of drums, and the melodious swell of martial music.

The outlaw turned to unfasten a silver whistle that he wore.

One call upon that would give the alarm to his band.

It was lucky for him that the golden cord which suspended it from his neck had become entangled in his sword-hilt.

As, with an impatient exclamation, he turned his head to disengage it, he caught sight of a skulking form which was crawling upon him.

He freed the whistle, and gave three sharp calls upon it.

As the echoes went from rock until they died away, the young outlaw took measures to meet his foe.

Had he betrayed his knowledge of the assassin's presence there would have been a struggle upon the rock.

He waited calmly until he thought the would-be murderer was near enough to strike; then, stepping suddenly aside, he turned and faced his foe.

Matters had turned out just as Tom wished.

The villain was within two feet of him, and in the act of raising his murderous knife, when he found himself confronted by the outlaw.

Midshipman Tom's blood was aroused; and, without giving the skulking wretch time to defend himself, he seized him by the throat, and bore him to the edge of the rock.

One thrust, and the traitor went headlong down the abyss.

Tom then swiftly descended the rocks, in order to reach the cave before the troops.

To his dismay, he found the task impossible, for ere he could reach the open space which led to the cave, the advanced guard began to descend the rocky defile before him.

With an angry flush upon his cheek, he withdrew behind a fallen piece of rock.

CHAPTER LXXXI.

A TIMELY SHOT.

THE first attack upon the cave had, as the reader will have gathered from Snowball's report to his chief, been very unsuccessful.

So vigorous had been the African's defence, that the soldiery, after four hours' obstinate fighting, were compelled to withdraw from the conflict.

Their defeat rankled deeply in the heart of their veteran commander, who, after burying his dead and collecting his wounded, went back to their cantonments.

Increasing his party to treble their former strength, and despatching a messenger to the nearest artillery station, the officer waited the arrival of the guns before he returned to destroy the outlaws.

From the position he had taken, Tom watched the manœuvres of the foe with intense interest.

It was evident to him that the officer was well skilled in the art of war, and that he had profited by his late defeat.

The entrance to the cave, when the tide was low, was, as the reader will remember, reached by a long stone staircase.

And it was from its summit that the outlaws were enabled to pour destruction upon their foes.

The leader of the soldiery had found the impossibility of forcing their position.

Strong by nature, Tom had rendered it by art inaccessible, and for the easier destruction of their foes, a couple of guns had been so placed by the troops, that they could sweep the top of this staircase.

Behind each gun was a strong party of men whose duty, in the event of a sortie by the besieged, would be to drag the field pieces out of danger.

The main body of the troops were drawn up four deep between the guns.

Tom watched these preparations, and loaded his pistols ready in event of an occasion for his active services.

Everything being ready, the officer drew his sword, and walking boldly to the foot of the steps, cried out—

"In the name of His Most Gracious Majesty, King George of England, your lawful sovereign, I call upon you all to surrender, and promise to each and all of you, except your leader, a youth called Midshipman Tom, his majesty's royal pardon if you will surrender the aforesaid Midshipman Tom into our hands!"

The officer waited a few minutes for a reply, and finding no reply came to his proclamation, he looked up and repeated his words.

Another silence, but no reply.

He was on the point of calling upon them for the third and last time, when the gigantic African appeared on the topmost of the rocky steps.

Looking down upon the scarlet and gold-bedizened officer, he said, curtly—

"Midshipman Tom and him band nebber surrender. You want 'em, you come and take em."

"You rascal!" said the officer; "do you thus dare defy the mighty powers of the laws you have outraged?"

"We," said Snowball, "defy eberyting, and no care one dam for you or your king. You hab de answer—so, go."

With these words Snowball closed the entrance to the cave and passed quickly round to the circular gallery, which commanded a view of the beach.

This gallery has been before referred to in these pages as a position from which the outlaws were able to fire through a number of loopholes, and yet remain unseen.

Since the last attack, upwards of thirty additional holes had been bored, thus increasing their defences wonderfully.

When the leader of the soldiers emerged from the entrance, he beckoned a young officer towards him.

"Look here, lieutenant," he said, "you had better take charge of one gun, and keep it in constant use against the upper part of the cave."

The lieutenant looked up in surprise.

"The upper part of the cave?" he repeated. "Why, captain, there is nothing but the hard face of the rock."

"You think so."

"I scarcely judge from external appearances."

Captain Lucas pointed above the entrance to the cave, saying—

"Every yard of that seeming solid rock is loop-holed in such an ingenious manner that it is impossible to pick off the fellows that man it."

"Yet I am to use one of the guns against it?"

"Exactly; load it with grape—it will be sure to spread, and perhaps find its way inside."

"The other gun, captain?"

"That, for the present, keep loaded and pointed towards the entrance. It may prevent their making a sortie."

"Very well, sir."

The young officer fell back and went to his post, and gave the order for the gun to be raised and fired.

A deafening roar followed the explosion, and the death hail rattled against the hard rock.

The lieutenant soon discovered the truth of his superior's words.

When the smoke of the field-piece had rolled away, the sharp cracking of musketry was heard above their heads.

Officers and men looked upward, and, to their surprise, beheld between twenty and thirty little jets of smoke curling up from the face of the rock

BLACK BILL ADMINISTERS THE CAT.

And as the gun belched forth again its hurtling mass of destruction, so was it followed by the discharge of musketry from above, and with even more fatal results.

Again and again similar attacks were made by the soldiers, and again defeated by the besieged.

The young lieutenant, who had been directing the field-pieces, now addressed the captain.

"It is useless, Captain Lucas," he said, "for this to continue. Twice has my detachment been renewed; the third is now falling fast."

The officer's words were too correct. Upwards of thirty stalwart men lay upon the wet sands in death's icy embrace.

Nothing was now left but to attempt an assault a proceeding the veteran Lucas knew would be attended with immense slaughter.

He was about to head his men, and lead them up the rocky steps, when a wild hurrah from the besieged caused them to halt. Snowball was leading the outlaws down the steps. Captain Lucas smiled grimly. He thought of the trap they had fallen into. The second field-piece loaded with grape would blow them to eternity, he knew

And as they began to rush down the steps, he roared—"Subdivisions, backward! wheel! ready there with that gun."

The closely packed column of troops fell back in two divisions by the centre, and halted when opposite each other, thus making a passage for the contents of the gun to pass through.

The gunner's hand was half-way to the vent—an instant more, and the contents of the gun would have been poured into the advancing mass of outlaws.

Snowball now saw the error he had fallen into in exposing the band to the close and deadly re of the long gun.

The words rose to his lips to command a retreat; but before they could be spoken, or the gunner apply the match, there was a report of a pistol among the rocks.

The shot told. The gunner fell across the field-piece, dead.

Snowball knew the hand that fired it, and called out—

"Bravo, Massa Tom! he got dat!"

At the same moment, the lieutenant caught sight of the young chief, and cried—

"There is the assassin—there he goes up the rocks."

"It is Midshipman Tom," roared the captain. "Take some men with you, and capture or shoot him down."

Seeing the movement, the outlaw suspected their object, and Snowball and others of the band rushed forward to intercept them.

A sanguinary conflict ensued, although of short duration; for while the fray was at its height the sudden report of several guns, followed by a close volley of grape and canister, suddenly swept away the troops by sections.

CHAPTER LXXXII.
THE PLOTTER'S DISMAY.

WHEN the pirate vessel was out of sight, Ralph Ranger gleefully hurried to Mountsteven Castle, and obtained an interview with her ladyship.

"You have soon returned," she said. "Is it to bring me news of another failure?"

"Quite the reverse, madam."

"Ah! you have succeeded, then?"

"Beyond expectation. Shall I relate to you?"

"Yes, yes," she said, with eager joy; "let me hear all, every detail that has anything to do th your success."

Ralph told her how he had placed Tom Wilson on board the vessel; and the lady, with blazing eyes and quivering lips, listened to the story.

"You are sure," she asked, "quite sure the boy will never return?"

"I will pledge my life upon that, madam. England has seen the last of Tom Wilson th outlaw."

"The news seems too good to be realised," she said. "There cannot be any certainty that we have seen the last of the brat."

"Madam, this is a certainty; and I can give you a dozen reasons in support of my statement."

"One or two will be sufficient."

"Very well, madam. I will confine myself to two. The first is, the lawless nature of the ship Tom Wilson is on board. The captain is not used to have his authority questioned by any of his followers, and this Tom Wilson, being used to command his numerous band, will naturally chafe at being treated as a common sailor. The result of this will be mutinous conduct on the lad's part, and a pistol-shot, or a swing at the yard-arm, for those gentry keep a strict hand over their crew."

"You have told me sufficient," said the lady. "Now for your reward."

She gave her accomplice a roll of bank notes, and, as he placed them in his breast pocket, he said—

"Now, madam, if there is anything in which I can serve you, pray command me."

"There is one thing," said the lady, "in which you can serve me."

"I shall only be too happy, madam."

"Since your residence here," she said, "I have no doubt you have seen a gipsy woman"——

"Sybil, as she is called, madam."

"The same."

"Yes, I have seen her, and often thought it strange she should seem so interested in the affairs of this castle."

"Ah! what do you mean?"

"Well, madam, I have seen the old woman loitering about the gates and watching all who pass in and out, and one day when his lordship emerged she hastily fled and hid behind a tree."

"Fearing to meet my husband's anger, I suppose."

Lady Mountsteven tried to ask this question in a steady voice, but her faltering tones belied her.

"Possibly, madam; but at the time I had a different opinion."

"What was that?"

"I fancied it was to avoid being seen by his lordship."

Lady Mountsteven clenched her hands firmly as she muttered—

"The fellow has keen perception, and this act but confirms my suspicion as to the identity of the woman. Should it be her!" Here the lady's face wore a demoniacal expression as she added—"She dies, if I have to use a knife myself!"

"Of course, madam," the man went on, "I do not make this statement as a truth—I may have been mistaken."

"You may," she said. "Now, I want you spend the next few days in finding out all you can about this woman. Should you obtain speech with her, note carefully the lustre of her eyes and the difference in age apparent in her features, and the iron-grey locks that fall upon her shoulders."

"Madam, I understand you. The woman is not what she seems—I have thought so more than once."

"How? Speak!"

"Well, madam, I was passing through the wood in the rear of the castle, and in front of me walked the gipsy, but so different to her usual gait that I failed to recognise her at first. In place of being bent almost double with age, her form was erect and her gait easy in comparison to that which I had heretofore seen her use."

"Enough," Lady Mountsteven curtly said. "Lose no time in doing all I have asked you."

"I shall not, madam."

He left the room, and the proud woman sank upon a couch, and pressing her hands to her forehead, said—"That woman is Mountsteven's first wife, and I am"——

She started to her feet, and passionately added, "No, she must be removed by death. Good heavens! no sooner do I succeed in putting one stumbling-block out of my way, than another springs up."

She paced to and fro like an angry tigress, and after her passion began to cool there came a hope that after all she had been mistaken—that the identity of the gipsy and Midshipman Tom's mother being one and the same existed but in her imagination.

Days passed, and her emissary failed to discover even the whereabouts of the gipsy.

The villagers said she must have fallen from the cliffs into the sea, for there were no signs, judging by the condition of the hut, to lead them to the belief that its strange owner had premeditated leaving.

This intelligence calmed the plotting woman's mind, and she had already begun to look upon the vast possessions as her own, when her myrmidon rushed into her presence with news that caused her cheeks to pale with dismay—

"He has returned, madam "

"Who has returned? Not—not—the whelp you sent out of the way?"

"Midshipman Tom has returned, madam."

"Fool!" she began, fiercely, "you"——

"Madam, I am blameless; that you will say when I tell you the cause of his return."

"You must"——

"Madam, we have no time to lose in recrimination; with your assistance he can yet be removed, and for ever."

"How? what is your plan?"

"There is a number of troops encamped a mile from here. Could you not invite the commanding officer to the castle, and urge him to capture the outlaw?"

"A good thought. I will write to him at once—you can take the letter. What is his name and rank?"

"Captain Lucas."

The veteran came to the castle, highly flattered by the honour, and the crafty woman, by working upon his vanity, gained her point.

He objected at first, by saying—

"Our men have attacked the band before, and failed; and, in place of the people at headquarters being angry at the failure, they have issued secret orders for us not to molest the outlaws so long as they do not break the laws."

"Why is this?"

"The service they do the country by keeping the wreckers in check, and hunting the pirates from the coast."

Lady Mountsteven laughed, as she said—

"There is a pirate ship within sight of these windows, and the outlaw is on board."

"Ha! that is sufficient cause for me to avenge our former defeat. I will destroy the band before another sun has set."

"Do," she said, "and the influence I indirectly possess shall be used to obtain your promotion."

The soldier kept his word by attacking the cave; whether he will keep his promise by destroying the outlaws, remains to be seen.

CHAPTER LXXXIII.
THE PURSUIT.

ONE glance towards the sea explained to Captain Lucas the cause of the havoc amongst his men.

A vessel lay in the Roads, her broadside to the shore, and a number of men stripped to the waist actively working the guns.

The vessel was the Thunderer—the men working the guns, the outlaws.

An event so unlooked-for baffled the captain, and although a braver soldier was not in his Majesty's service, he considered it would be wantonly exposing the lives of his men if the terrible cannonade from the sea opened upon him; so before he could receive any damage from the loop-holes and the Thunderer's guns, he gave the order to the bugler to sound a retreat.

An order which the troops gladly obeyed, and, at a double, followed their captain.

He, with his sword raised above his head, to point out the rallying point, began to fall back upon the lieutenant's party, who, having been wounded in the previous conflict, had followed our hero.

Perched upon the highest peak of the huge cliff, and hidden from their view by a number of zigzag pieces of rock, he sat, pistol in one hand, watching every movement of those who sought his life.

There was but one way of reaching the place where Tom sat.

It was by crossing a chasm two yards wide.

The young chieftain, in his loose dress, had sprung up like an antelope.

But the cross-belted, stiff, leather-stocked soldiers could not accomplish it, and while they were divesting themselves of these trappings the deadly weapons of Midshipman Tom wounded them one by one.

Such was the state of things when Captain Lucas and his men joined the young officer, who explained that for a party to scale the cliff, at least twenty men would be required to cover their advance.

"Let it be done, and at once," said the captain; "for I see that vessel which gave us the broadside of grape is now trying to work her way closer in shore to give us a similar dose."

"By heavens, yes! and we shall have it too! Down men! flat on your faces! Here it comes!"

The order came not a moment too soon; for with the officer's last word the simultaneous roar of four guns was heard, and an iron storm came tearing up the sand and beating against the rocks where they were clustered.

"We shall have another as soon as they can load.   Jump up, men, and follow me."

He led them at a double to a place of shelter where they would be safe from the ship's guns.

When the scaling party and those who were to cover their advance were told off, the covering party drew back, and took up a position which would command a good view of the summit

Those who had to make the dangerous ascent threw off their cross-belts and their huge bear skins, and slinging their loaded firelocks over their backs began the steep incline.

These preparations were watched by Tom from his hiding-place, and by Snowball from one of the loopholes in the rock, who determined, much against the wishes of his comrades, upon going alone to the assistance of the young chieftain.

The men stepped back to let the African pass, and when he arrived at the bottom of the steps the huge mastiff bounded after him.

"Do not follow," said Captain Lucas to the men who were about to pursue the black.   "We can shoot him down from the cliff as he ascends."

But to the surprise of the men who stood awaiting his appearance, he was not seen until he reached the summit—every defile and pass being so well known had enabled him to scramble up without being observed.

Following the course taken by Snowball, however, after having passed under an overhanging piece of rock, they beheld the serpentine path by which he had ascended.

It was wide, and capable of permitting from three to four men to ascend abreast.

"We shall have the pair of them now," muttered the captain.   "There are no means of escape except by the path, which you must be careful to place under a cross fire."

It did not take the officer long to make the necessary preparations; then, with twenty men, he ascended the cliff.

Midshipman Tom and Snowball both looked anxiously down, and the knowledge of their coming peril caused them to draw a deep breath.

A tremor passed over the African's frame when the heads of the first three soldiers came above the level, and the leading files began to scramble to the top.

"Come," said Tom, seeing that his friend was working himself into an ungovernable wrath.

"We cannot contend against so many.   There are plenty of stones here—let us take shelter."

"Here, den, Massa Tom; dis de best."

A piece of rock, breast high, gave them safety from the muskets of the soldiery, and enabled the hunted pair to use their pistols against the foe.

The soldiers were kept at bay as long as the outlaw's ammunition lasted; when that was expended, Captain Lucas formed them in double rank, and, with their bayonets at the charge, they ran forward to impale the gallant pair.

The soldiers were within ten yards of the outlaws, for whom there seemed no mode of escape.

Then came an act of desperation which held the soldiers for some minutes breathless.

Snowball knew it was either impalement upon the soldiers' weapons, or being taken captive, and, without a word of warning, seized his young chief in his powerful arms, and, uttering one defiant cry, sprang with him from the cliff.

The soldiers rushed to the edge, and gazed, silent and overawed, as they beheld the two figures whirling over and over, and finally disappearing beneath the water's surface.

Down—cleaving the water's depth like an arrow—went the African and the boy he had so desperately saved from the soldiery—down, down to the ocean's stilly bed, scaring the denizens of the watery world by their swift passage.

It was a leap for liberty that would have cost many their lives.   But the African was equally at home in the briny deep as on the land.

When he disappeared beneath the ocean he closed his mouth firmly and suspended his breathing; his eyes he kept open.

Thus was he enabled, in some measure, to guide himself out of the sunken reefs that lay so thickly near him.

Midshipman Tom by this time had swooned. No time was to be lost.

A few minutes more his charge would be suffocated.

With this terrible knowledge, causing him to feel as though a cold hand was laid upon his heart, he looked wildly about him.

A few yards from him he discerned some rocks.

To go forward among the breakers to reach them was his only chance.

Collecting his energies s the last venture for

safe, he swept boldly forward among the troubled waters.

For a moment or two he seemed to be overpowered. He was too near the surface.

Dropping his arm by his side, and lowering both legs, he descended.

The water became calmer the lower he went.

One despairing look he gave to the pallid face of the senseless Tom.

Rendered desperate, he paddled towards the face of the rock, determined to rise when he reached it.

He succeeded; and clinging more firmly to his leader, and feeling the wet slippery surface of the rock, he ascended.

Both their heads were now above water, and he felt the sharp sea breeze playing upon his face.

But the joyful feeling was dashed away the next moment by the arrival of a huge white-tipped wave, as it came with fearful violence against them.

It seemed to the African that his very body was reft asunder by the horrible shock, and a groan of agony fell from his lips.

Still he struggled desperately, and looked fearfully around for a resting place from his peril.

He saw it, and heathen as he was, prayed to the idol he worshipped, and to the white man's God, to be able to reach it.

Temptingly, tauntingly, above his head, was a place of safety, a forked projection protruding from the cliff.

But how was it to be reached? The hand that could have saved them both grasped the form of his beloved chieftain.

What was to be done? Another huge wave was coming rapidly upon them. Snowball shrieked like a maddened beast. It was the wild cry of an overcharged agony; he was about to let go his hold and sink beneath the surging waters.

But before he did so, that fearful yell escaped him; a last hope had flashed across his mind.

To put it into execution was the work of a moment.

He fixed his sharp teeth in Midshipman Tom's shoulder, gripped firmly both clothing and flesh until the edges of his long white teeth met.

Thus the African had power to use both his hands, and he grasped the projection of the rock.

Secure on the rock he let go his grip, the young chief's shoulder streaming with blood.

"Massa Tom!—Massa Tom!" cried Snowball, "you wake up; you look like dead. Oh! wake up Massa Tom. We safe, but I hurt you drefful!"

He began to chafe the cold hands and forehead of the young chieftain, and at length his lips unclosed, and he faintly asked—

'Where are we?"

Their resting-place was a short, fantastic projection, left as a proof of what the waters can do.

Tom put his hand to his shoulder, saying—

"Save, Snowball, this stinging pain, nothing would have told me that my frame was yet earthly. I am wounded."

Snowball's voice faltered with emotion as he said—

"No, Massa Tom, you not wounded. I hurt you, bite you; but it saved your life;" and Snowball related to him the whole of the dreadful sufferings they had passed through.

Tom took the black's hand between his white, small palms, saying—

"Snowball, my brave, noble fellow, a monarch would be proud of such devotion."

Suddenly Tom looked at his follower, and asked—

"Is there no way of escape from this place See, Snowball, the water has now risen until our feet are reached."

Fortunately the water came no higher, and hour after hour they sat, their wet garments chilling them to the very bones.

At length, by wading up to their knees, they could have passed from their place of captivity; but as they were thus consoling themselves, the report of several muskets was heard.

The soldiers were like so many red specks placed all along the beach.

"Cuss 'em!" said Snowball. "Me tell you what, Massa Tom, if they don't go we shall hab to stop here till dey do."

"An undeniable fact, Snowball."

"Unless," the African went on, "I go to de cave and see how "——

"Go to the cave?"

"Yes, Massa Tom."

"What, with a company of sharpshooters waiting outside for you? You must pass between the cliff."

"Not me, Massa Tom, me go anoder way."

"Another—through the solid rock?"

"Not at all—under water; dat do for 'em, I tink."

"Yes, and for you too, Snowball, I should say."

Tom was about entering into further details as to his intended trip, when they heard the sound of voices apparently above them.

They looked up and saw Captain Lucas and several of his men descending the rocks, who was wondering, however, who the two figures could be, for he did not imagine it to be possible, after the fearful leap, that either of the outlaws could be alive.

"I feel confident," said the captain, addressing the lieutenant, "that leap settled both the miscreants. Where's the bugler?"

"Here, sir," another voice said.

"Sound the recall; we will go back to the cave and finish the remainder of the rascally band."

The bugler's clear notes reverberated among the rocks.

Soon the military were on their way to renew the attack upon the cave.

While this was going on by the soldiery Snowball had been determining with the young chief to take his projected journey to the cave under water.

"Had I not better accompany you, Snowball?" quired Tom.

"Not for de world, Massa Tom. You stop here; it not safe yet for you to go, and you not able to keep under de water like dis chile."

"I cannot stay here while my fellows are in such danger. And what will you do," said Tom, "when you get there? Have you laid a mine?"

"No, Massa Tom; but when dey retreat from de fire ob de ship—for, in course, de ship be den on de look-out for mischief—I give orders for de boys to put down two guns in a masked battery. Golly! dey get it."

The young chief would have risked his life to have accompanied the gallant black; but Snowball would not have it, and he was obliged to yield.

"You stop here," Snowball said, as he prepared for a plunge beneath the water; "I come to you soon."

Tom regretfully promised to do so.

Left alone in that dismal place, the minutes seemed lengthened into hours, and hours into days.

The young chief stayed until his patience was exhausted.

Then he stole carefully out, and began to scale the face of the rock.

Once out in the open air, he regretted his folly.

He was seen and recognised by a party of soldiers, who had been left by Captain Lucas to watch the cliff.

Below him lay the exterior of the cavern; and, from the sound of musketry and the boom of guns, it was evident a sharp conflict was taking place.

He would have given ten years of his life to have stood once more at the head of his gallant band.

But to reach them was impossible—utterly impossible, for the detachment of men stood between him and the cave—and worse, they were now, with their muskets at the trail, running towards him.

There was danger in one moment's delay, though he could easily escape them by hiding among the rocks.

The question was, how could he escape the shot from their muskets.

He bounded forward like a startled deer, and, to their chagrin, suddenly disappeared, as though the rocks had opened to receive him.

CHAPTER LXXXIV.

ABRAHAM LEVY, THE MAN CATCHER.

THE pirate captain could do no more than place his ship at the disposal of the gallant chief, to whom he owed so much, without being destitute of a proper feeling of gratitude for the great and efficient services rendered him.

Yet with that feeling there was a little prudence.

Of course, as long as the outlaws were triumphant, prudence was not a visitor to Captain Dragon's astute brain.

But when he saw the strong party of troops returning from their unsuccessful pursuit of Midshipman Tom, prudence began to whisper a word or two in his ear.

"Captain Dragon," said the little inspired voice, "suppose the troops should be victorious, you will certainly lose your vessel, perhaps your life."

There was no questioning the truth of this, and Captain Dragon began to turn matters over in his mind.

The Thunderer had an immense booty between her low decks, and the worthy captain had a strong desire to keep it to himself.

He stood reflectively smoking a cigar upon the quarter-deck, watching the efforts of the outlaws, as they endeavoured to bring the guns to bear upon the soldiers, who were again marching to the assault. In this they failed.

Captain Lucas had learned a little better than to bring his men into any exposed position.

The detachment had suffered by the guns of the Thunderer twice; and twice was quite enough for Captain Lucas, of his Majesty's —th Regiment of Foot.

He now crept quietly back to the outlaw's retreat, by a route that led to the rear instead of the front.

Ben and his companions stood by the loaded guns, blessing himself for his safe manoeuvre.

"I will tell you what," said Ben, savagely, to his companion, "we shall get another chance of picking off a few of those shilling a day beggars."

"How is that?" asked one of his young companions.

"How is that? Use your eyes."

"I am."

"It don't seem like it, or you would not hav asked such a question."

"Why not? They must come round the face of the cliff to get at the retreat."

"Not at all."

"Why?"

"You see that hollow sharp head?"

"I does."

MIDSHIPMAN TOM BOARDS THE FRENCHMAN.

"Well, they can come round by that, and take up a position behind those rocks."

"So they can. I never thought of that."

"You never think of anything except sleep."

"You can do your share of that."

"Well, what's the best to be done? These guns are useless to us now. I have a plan."

"Out with it, then."

"Let us run the vessel down to Beachy Head and drop anchor."

"Well."

"Then we get ashore and take them beggars in the flank."

Captain Dragon, who had been listening to their colloquy, now stepped forward and said—

"The best thing, my lads, I think you can do is to assist your comrades. A determination like that may do them immense service."

Ben touched his cap, and answered—

"That's my opinion, captain, if you won't mind us leaving you alone on board."

"I shall drop anchor in deep water, and I shall be safe enough."

He might have added—that he would be very glad when they left.

But Captain Dragon was a prudent as well as an

astute gentleman, and knew the wisdom contained in the old adage which sayeth—"Let thy teeth be a dungeon for thy tongue."

Captain Dragon's teeth were so in that instance, and he stood secretly chuckling as the outlaws began to trim the vessel to go about.

Beachy Head was not more than a mile by water from where the vessel then floated, less by land, owing to the manner in which the cliffs wound in and out.

The Thunderer was soon on her way to the place where the smugglers intended to disembark.

Captain Dragon went below for a few moments; when he reappeared, he had a small red ball in his hand. This he handed to Ben, saying—

"Run this up to the masthead for me."

Ben did so.

And when the small ball was swiftly flying upwards, it unrolled and became a long pointed signal of a deep red colour, save for two stars that were upon it, embroidered with silver lace.

The outlaw looked curiously at the fluttering signal, then at Captain Dragon.

"No treachery, Ben," said the captain; "it's merely a signal for that old sinner Abraham Levy.'

"The old varmint," said Ben, "I know him. You want some hands, then?"

"Well, yes, Ben. I do not aspire to become captain, mate, cook, and crew all in one."

"He will do it for you, captain. I wonder at times where the deuce he gets so many hands from."

"Do you?"

"I do; for no matter how large the bark may be, he can always fill the vacancies.''

"Ben," said the captain, lighting a cigar, "are there such things as men-of-war put in here?"

"Yes, confound 'em "

"Do you see how it is?"

"I can give a good guess, I think."

"Let me hear it."

"Why, the hands desert the ships."

"Exactly—but why desert here more than at any other station?"

Ben scratched his head, and confessed he did not know.

"I thought not," said Captain Dragon, smiling. "Well, I may as well enlighten you; the man-catching old sinner draws them off."

"Yes, but how? I"——

"How does he manage it?"

"Yes, sir."

"You have seen those lace-bedizened girls he calls his daughter   Well, those young ladies are the decoy birds that lure poor Jack away rom his ship."

"What! his own daughters?"

"His own fiddlesticks! They are no more his daughters than they are mine.   The Lord help me!' he added, "how I—— But here we are. There's the old villain as I'm a sinner."

Ben looked towards the shore, and then beheld the respectable Abraham Levy, *alias* the man-catcher.''

This gentleman, whose vocation Captain Dragon had pretty accurately described, was between forty and fifty years of age, tall, and weather-beaten, to judge by what little could be seen of his face.

He had been a purser, and since he had given up the sea had grown a pair of thick bushy whiskers and beard, which, for certain private reasons he deemed necessary.

"Yes, there he is," said Ben. "Why, the old beggar carries a pistol in his jacket pocket!"

Captain Dragon laughed quietly; he knew more of Mr. Levy than did our friend Ben.

The butt of the pistol, which could be seen protruding from the right-hand pocket of the old man-catcher's jacket, was no mystery to Captain Dragon.

Before he could enlighten Ben upon the subject, the latter sang out for his companions to go ashore.

Captain Dragon accompanied the outlaws ashore, and, but for the friendship he felt for Tom Wilson, he would have urged the stalwart scullers to serve on board the Thunderer.

CHAPTER LXXXV.
PROFESSOR QUINTON QUERBY MAKES A DISCOVERY.

WHEN Midshipman Tom disappeared so suddenly from his pursuers they began, like so many hounds when losing the scent, to run about the cliff.

Their search was fruitless.

So when they had tired themselves, the non-commissioned officer in charge of the party ordered them back to the regiment.

"Curse him!" he muttered—meaning our hero—"he must be in league with the Fiend of Darkness.''

The corporal little knew as he muttered these words that his head was within ten yards of Midshipman Tom's pistol.

Brought up from infancy among the wild and rugged cliffs, there was not a hole where even a bird could build its nest without his knowledge.

It is not surprising then, being thus well acquainted with the—to the soldiers—unknown parts of the wilds, he would be able to elude them.

He did so, and so successfully that he could not even ascertain the means by which he had done so.

Had they looked behind a cluster of wild-looking vegetation, that grew near the brow of the cliff, they would have beheld the subject of their search sitting, with cocked weapons in his hands, in a hole beneath the straggling leaves of the huge plant.

Tom waited until they had left the spot; then,

peering cautiously up from between the stalks of his leafy cover, he watched them return to their former station.

The firing at the cave still continued with undiminished fierceness.

How ardently Midshipman Tom wished himself once more at the head of his gallant band!

Painfully he listened to every boom of the guns—every roll of the muskets, as they belched forth death, with every faculty strained to catch a sound that would tell him whether his followers were yet masters of their position.

Snowball, too, had he reached the cave in safety? or had he been met by the enraged soldiers, and fallen beneath their bullets?

In this state of mind hour after hour passed.

Evening came on; still the sullen roar of firearms continued.

When the darkness came he quitted the hole he had been in for so many hours, and went back to the aperture beneath the cliffs.

Cautiously he approached the weird-looking place.

"Snowball," he said, in a low, hushed voice, "Snowball, are you here?"

No reply came to the summons, except the echo of his voice.

That echo went among the rocks, increasing in sound until it sank away in a mournful wail.

"Not here!" he said, "not here! Then he has either fallen or not been able to leave the cave."

Hoping against hope, and determined to make an effort to reach the retreat should Snowball not appear, he seated himself upon the sands, and began to form many plans in his mind to regain his band.

The most sensible seemed to be that of making an effort to pass the sentries after midnight.

"I will wait another hour," he thought, "if he does not come, then for the attempt."

Long before the glass of Time marked the flight of the hour, the gallant Tom was senseless to the position in which he was placed.

Determined to watch and wait, his head had fallen upon his breast, and worn out with fatigue, he was soon overcome with sleep.

The drowsy god had been a stranger to him for some time, and now that it gained an ascendancy over his faculties, he slept like one never more to be wakened.

Hour after hour passed; the storm-king began to rouse the billows, and fill the cave with a subdued roar.

Still he slept on, unconscious of the stormy elements, or the danger of human foes.

When he awoke the storm had passed away, and the morning's red effulgent sun shone upon the mighty waste of waters.

It was daylight—broad daylight, long before the tired youth awoke.

Like one just startled from a dream, he sprang to his feet, and looked wildly upon the smiling ocean.

He was dazed for a few moments, for he had awakened with a sudden start, caused by the sound of something or some one rapping against the rocks above his head.

The first thought was for his weapons.

But a chill ran through his heart, as he felt for his pistols, and found his belt empty.

His sabre yet hung at his hip.

But that, as he was now placed, was useless.

One hurried glance he gave around the cavern.

Joy! there, with the sun's bright beams glittering upon the golden ornaments of his pistol-butt, he beheld them.

Like a mother clutching her lost child, he clasped the trusty weapons, and examined them.

The flints were in their places—the powder dry.

He placed one in his belt, the other was grasped in his right hand, as he crept cautiously out, to discover the cause of the rapping on the rocks.

That it was caused by one of his own species Tom felt assured, for, mingled with the strange noise, he heard every now and then an exclamation of delight.

A wild thought crossed his mind, and sent a shudder over his frame.

"Had they discovered his hiding-place, and were boring a hole in the rocks to blow him into fragments?"

Such was his first thought.

But that passed away. He knew, were the soldiers seeking to blast the rock, there would be more noise.

What could it be, then? The question was soon solved.

For Tom, upon peering out from the opening of the cave, beheld a little, old-fashioned gentleman, dressed in a suit of seedy black, hammering at the hard rock.

That it was a labour of love, was very evident from the old fellow's disjointed sentences.

Tom stood for several minutes listening to the old enthusiast—for enthusiast he undoubtedly was; one of those strange beings whom the world styles a geologist.

A man whose soul was devoted to picking up little pieces of stone, or breaking them from quiet corners of the rocks, then carrying them home in triumph as specimens of geology.

"Bless me!—ha!" the little fellow kept jerking out at intervals. "Dear me! I never saw such a beautiful specimen of stone."

Then he bent lower over it, rubbed his hands in ecstasy for a few seconds; then the hammer was heard, and the rap, rap, rap continued zealously.

The young outlaw stood silently regarding the strange old fellow, and he became so interested in his movements that for a time his own desperate condition was forgotten.

Suddenly the geologist ceased hammering; the small piece of stone had broken off, and he clutched it as though a nugget had fallen suddenly within his grasp.

A small bag had lain by his side during the preceding operations, and Tom, judging from its size, saw it contained several specimens from the beach, or the surrounding rocks.

"There," the little man said, " will be a glorious addition to the valuable specimens I received from my learned brother, Theodolite Polypus—a rare one, indeed. I will prosecute my search a little further, and then return with my treasure —rare treasure, indeed—for the English Auriferous Gossan Manufacturing Company,

He turned to leave the place, and in so doing his eyes encountered the wild, picturesque figure of the young sailor.

"Bless me!" said the learned professor, "a native of these parts. How seafaringly he is dressed! Oh, Lord! Oh!"

The exclamations of fear was caused by the sudden report of a musket, and the whizzing of a bullet close to the learned professor's head.

The young chief looked up to where the report came from, and to his astonishment saw the brow of the cliff lined with soldiers.

There was not a moment to be lost.

Bullet after bullet came whistling down near them, and a sudden thought caught the young sailor's mind. He saw means of escape from his foes, and determined to profit by it.

In a quick manner he said to the geologist—

"In here. Quick—for your life!"

The professor needed no second bidding. Whatever desire he had to become acquainted with rocks and gold, he had none for lead, especially in the form of bullet .

Two long strides took him   , and, crossing to the side of Midshipman Tom, he said—

"Dear me! that was an escape—truly miraculous. Verily we live in a world of wonders. Tell me, friend, why do those men send down their bullets of lead in such a manner ?"

"Know you not," said Tom, gravely, "that it is certain death to be seen chipping these rocks, violating as it does the sanctity of an old legend of this place ?"

The hammer and bag fell from the professor's hands, and he stood the picture of mute amazement and terror.

"You were seen," continued Tom, with the gravity of a judge in his tone and manner, "and your life will pay the forfeit, unless you can make your escape."

"Canst thou assist me, young friend ?"

"I can."

"And thou wiltst?"

"I will, though by doing so I risk my own life."

"That would be a pity; but you are young and better able to escape from them than I. What do you advise ?"

"Shall I be rewarded for my trouble ?"

"Of a surety, yes. The secretary for the English Auriferous Gossan Manufacturing Company will amply repay you for the risk. I am his secretary, Professor Quinton Querby."

"Enough. I will do it. Now take off your clothes, and exchange with me. You will then be able to pass those men, who are even now descending the rocks."

Too much terrified to know exactly what he was doing, the secretary of the high-sounding company did as he was desired.

A few minutes completed the changing of apparel.

Tom donned the seedy suit of black, and placing his pistols in the pockets, left Professor Querby to complete his toilet, and departed from the caves.

————

CHAPTER LXXXVI.

A DANGEROUS CONFESSION.

WITH the assistance of the respectable Mr. Levy, Captain Dragon brought the boat he had used back to the ship.

Of their class, Captain Dragon and the man-catcher was gifted with a certain acuteness, which gave them a decided superiority over their followers.

For the first time for many years they now met, and each felt however easy it might be to deceive others, they had in each other met their match.

There was a striking difference however in these two men, as they stood upon the Thunderer's quarter deck.

Both were above the middle height, Captain Dragon of the two the taller, and as he stood with his hands in his coat pockets, a sneer played upon his thin lips.

Abraham Levy was trying to make the captain believe his statement respecting the scarcity of hands just then. He certainly went to a great amount of trouble for no purpose.

For, at the conclusion of his speech, Captain Dragon said, coolly—

"That will do for us, Abraham; you have wasted your words, my friend."

"Why, do you not believe me ?"

"No, I do not."

"What interest would it be for me to tell you a lie ?"

"Not much to me, certainly, but to others who have not the pleasure of being thoroughly acquainted with you."

"Who are you ?" he asked, looking at the other's face. "I do not know you."

"You may not remember me ?"

"I do not believe I ever saw you before in my life."

"Try again."

"It is no use trying. I tell you I don't know you; it's only waste of time for me to stand here."

"Not at all, Mr. Abraham Levy. I want men, you find them for me; I shall ay you a fair price."

"Find them for you ?" began the old villain. 'Find them ? Why, man, any one would think I had a ship's company in my house."

"Nothing likelier."

"What could I do with them, if even the hands were here ?"

"Kidnap and sell them to the first vessel that puts in short of hands. Is not that right ?"

"What do you mean ? Who told you I did such things ? You must be either mad or—or"——

"Drunk. Neither, so you can let the butt of that pistol alone. I want what I have told you; two dozen good hands at least, to work this ship to another port."

"How can I assist you ?"

"Come—still suspicious ?"

"No."

"Can you get the men ?"

"No," was the sullen answer.

"Then," said Captain Dragon, looking the other straight in the eyes; "I shall have to work the vessel myself, unless I set those fellows at liberty."

"What fellows ?"

"Ha! that is my secret, but I will tell you, Levy,"—and his look became more piercing as he spoke. "I have here—don't start—I have two hundred niggers, all fastened to the anchor chains. I don't suppose they are all dead, at least I hope not. Do you know why I had them lashed to the anchor chain ?—of course you don't. I'll tell you Hallo! what's the matter ?"

Something certainly was the matter with Mr. Levy.

Something, too, that came over him when Captain Dragon mentioned the niggers being fastened to the anchor chain.

What could it be ?

Captain Dragon seemed quite puzzled in the change in his companion's features, for he repeated—

"Hallo! what's the matter ?"

Levy made no reply, but stood pale and trembling against a carronade, his eyes dilating with horror.

Captain Dragon smiled slightly as the thought came to his mind—

"I shall not have much trouble now in getting a crew."

At last Levy spoke; but in such subdued, horrified tones, that showed the shock he had received was of more than ordinary import.

"Who," he gasped—"who are you, in the fiend's name, that comes to tell me this !"

"What was I then, you mean, my friend."

"Speak !" gasped the other—"speak ! I thought all who knew this were dead."

"They are all dead but one," said Captain Dragon. "The poison did its work with all but one; that one was Charles Dragon, captain of the slave ship, Light-o'-wing. He, you remember, was a passenger on board the Bacchus."

The blanched cheeks of Abraham Levy began to look less livid, and his breathing became less painful, as he asked—

"Are you the Charles Dragon that escaped ?"

"I am."

In a moment Levy's hand was on the butt of his pistol, and the wolf-like glare of his eyes told of murderous intent.

Charles Daagon saw and guessed the intention of the discomfited rascal; and, before the weapon could be withdrawn, his hands were suddenly taken from his pockets.

In an instant a brace of chastely-worked pistols were presented full at the head of Levy, and the pirate captain's stern voice rang out—

"Leave that weapon alone; your secret is safe with me. Take it from your pocket, and I'll send these bullets through your skull."

Abraham Levy's hand quitted the weapon. He felt, rather than saw, the deadly glitter of the other's eyes. They had met before, and the ex-slaver knew Charles Dragon was as pitiless as he was determined—a foe rather to be accepted as a friend than one to war against.

"I meant not to use it," he said, deprecatingly. "The recollections you brought before me by those words were so sudden, so unlooked for, that I knew not what I said or did."

Captain Dragon lowered his weapons, saying—

"I'll believe you. Now to business. You know who I am. Can you do what I require ? Although we are old friends,"—he smiled strangely as he said this—"I shall be most willing to do business fairly with you."

"I want no money, Charles."

"Nonsense, man; I am rich, and am well able to pay. Suppose we say five pounds for each head. Will that do ?"

"It is more than I desire. How many shall I bring you ?"

"A hundred, if you can."

"I can't obtain half that number."

"Do your best."

"I will."

The pair of rascals parted. Levy rowed himself slowly ashore; Captain Dragon stood leaning over the ship's side, watching him closely.

He saw Levy draw the boat upon the beach, then he turned away and began to pace slowly to and fro the deck.

"So, Master Levy, you thought all were dead, did you, my worthy friend. Ha! ha! the change that took place in that gentleman was worth know-

ing a little to produce ; but," he mused, " I must
be careful. That fellow is as treacherous as a
black-headed viper. Curses ! Fool that I must
have been to have told him how those mutinous
dogs escaped !"

The captain of the Thunderer became very
thoughtful, and after a few long strides he paused
and looked towards the shore.

" I should not be," he muttered, " at all surprised if those hounds who left me had been picked
up by his decoy birds. Should that be the case he
will bring them on board to-night, and the result,"
musing again, " would be beneficial to him ; to me,
not so, unless having a slit throat is any benefit."

This thought gave Captain Dragon a good
cause for uneasiness.

After a few minutes' reflection, his face suddenly lighted up with savage joy.

" Yes, curse them !" he said, half aloud, " I
will prepare for their coming."

He did so.

Strange preparations they were, too—very
strange ; and towards evening the pirate captain
had placed a mighty heap of powder loose upon
the deck.

There was a deadly determination in the mode
in which he made these preparations that showed
the man to be of wondrous nerve.

The terrible heap of powder was above his waist
in height.

The deep glow on his bronzed cheeks became
more heightened as he loaded two carronades to
the muzzle with grape, and trained them in such
a manner that the fire would sweep the decks.

The task was difficult for one man to accomplish ; but he accomplished it, and seemingly to
his great satisfaction.

And then, seizing an axe, he knocked away
the steps which led to the quarter-deck.

" Never !" he muttered, as he strode among the
preparations to destroy his fellow-men. " Let
them come. Should it be as I anticipate, there
will be red work before the moon has long risen.
First these guns, then this powder. Although I
blow myself to perdition, they will accompany me."

He sat upon one of the carronades, a smouldering portfire in his hand, and, with a cigar between
his thin lips, looked calmly towards the shore.

Suddenly he threw his cigar into the sea, and
sprang to his feet.

Three boats, crowded with men, were approaching the vessel.

CHAPTER LXXXVII.

ON THE WATCH.

LADY MOUNTSTEVEN was furious when she heard
the ill-success that had attended the soldiers'
attempt to shoot down Midshipman Tom.

" Curse him !" she said, " he seems to bear a
charmed life."

Ralph entered the room as she spoke, and the
baffled demon attacked him with her angry tongue.

In vain he endeavoured to explain the matter
to his future mistress ; her only anwer was—

" Listen to me, knave ; I want his death, and
that alone. Return with some proof of that ;
nothing having been accomplished, return not
all."

" Lady," Ranger said, " have I not tried all
that man could do to do so ?"

" What of that ? You have miserably failed."

" A failure, lady, must be better than not
having made an attempt."

" Go and make another."

" One was made but yesterday."

" And failed, of course."

" Yes ; that youth seems to bear a charmed
life, or is in league with the Evil One, for he
turned when the knife was within a yard of his
back, and threw the man who attempted it
headlong into the sea."

" Such is the coward's report."

" No, madam, I saw it, and saw the body as
it lay festering in the sun."

" The fool should have made his blow more
cautiously. Go, obtain another. Though this
one has failed, another may succeed. I care not
what you do ; but he must die."

Ranger was about to speak, but she haughtily
motioned him from the room.

When he left the castle an angry contraction of
the brow showed how deeply the woman had
angered him.

" The fiend !" he muttered ; " may perdition
take her black soul !"

She in turn watched the form of her dupe disappear ; and, as a black cloud overshadowed
her brow, she muttered—

" This fool, lured by his passion and my
promises, will yet accomplish my will. When
done, he shall taste of the wondrous elixir, distilled for me by the woman in Bucharia.

" Yes, Ralph Ranger, you shall be rewarded—
well rewarded. Ha !"

The door opened, and a young girl entered the
room.

The girl's face was pale, and about the close and
adder-formed mouth there was a determined
expression that told that she would carry out the
purpose for which she came into the service of
Lady Mountsteven.

She had not been there for many days, waiting
and watching to find some clue to the murder of
the Frenchman, Pierre.

Little knew Lady Mountsteven that her pale,
quiet attendant followed her like an avenging
Nemesis ; that in her sleep she hung over the
guilty woman, listening with bated breath for the
least sound that would clear up the mystery that
had cast her brother a wanderer from his home—
for the girl was Charley Philip's sister.

" LOOK DERE, MASSA TOM, DAT ALL GOLD, AND —— "

Something she had discovered—some secret that Lady Mountsteven thought hidden in her heart alone.

Still she retained the same gentleness of manner, and Lady Mountseven soon began to feel more kindly disposed towards her than she usually was towards her waiting-women.

For the haughty patrician had hitherto looked upon those who ministered to her wants as beings fit only to be placed on a level with the hounds that fawned upon her when she visited the castle kennel.

She had certainly twice or thrice behaved haughtily to Ellen, but the innate dignity of the girl's manner, and her quiet retorts, had in a measure subdued one that even the stings of conscience failed to disturb.

" You here, Ellen !" she said. " What brings you to my chamber ?"

" A message from Lord Mountsteven."

" Ha ! how is he ?"

" Fading rapidly, my lady. The Physician can't minister to his disease."

" How do you know that ?"

"It is well known in the castle, my lady."

An angry scowl for a moment marred the lady's glorious beauty as she said—

"Do those who fatten at my table dare to speak of my private affairs?"

"No more, my lady, than servants usually speak."

"And what do they say?"

The girl looked her mistress in the face as she said—

"They marvel much, my lady, that your husband should be passing inch by inch from life without the skilled men who hold hourly consultations around his bed being able to ameliorate his sufferings."

Lady Blanche Mountsteven dropped her eyes; she could not withstand that steady, steadfast gaze.

It seemed to her as though the girl's eyes plainly said—

"There is some infernal mystery at the bottom of this—a mystery that you alone can solve."

The lady spoke after a few seconds.

"Is that all," she asked, "all they say?"

"All that I have heard, my lady."

Pointing to an article of attire that lay upon her couch, Lady Blanche said—

"You can remain and finish that. I will visit his lordship."

Ellen inclined her head, and sat for a few moments without motion, evidently in deep thought.

Suddenly her face flushed, and rising quickly from her chair, she went to the dressing-table, upon which stood an ebony box, embossed with gold.

Quick as thought she opened the lid, and stood silently gazing on two rows of crystal beads which lay in the velvet interior.

Strangely fashioned were these glass vessels, and the exteriors were covered with peculiar hieroglyphics.

The top row was equal in number to the bottom; but the latter were filled with delicately-tinted fluids.

The contents of the former were colourless.

The girl's eyes dilated at the sight.

Passing her hand over her head as though to recall something to her mind, she muttered, half aloud—

"Yes, that must be it; the top is the poison, the bottom row the antidote.

A slight exclamation escaped her when she found one of the places in the top row vacant.

In a second her mind was made up.

And, as quick as thought, she poured the contents of the bottle, under the empty space, into a phial, which she found in her pocket.

This done she seated herself and began to ply her needle.

It was not long before the lady returned; and Ellen, without raising her eyes, watched her open the ebony box and place something there.

A slight flush, succeeded by an intense paleness, came over Ellen's features as she thought—

"The missing bottle! Then I am right. She has been again at her foul work."

Lady Mountsteven turned to her attendant, and said—

"You look pale. What is the matter?"

"A violent headache, my lady."

"Poor child! Put your work down and go to your room for a few hours. It may do you good."

The girl's eyes shone with joy as her mistress spoke; and with a quiet smile upon her looks she left the room; but not as Lady Blanche imagined, to go to her bedroom. Strange to say, she flew rather than walked towards the baronet's sick chamber.

She gave a hurried glance inside; there was no one in save the dying man, and he had fallen into a slumber.

Cautiously she approached the bedside, and an exclamation of horror escaped her lips when she beheld a glass standing upon a table near the head of the bed—empty.

"Heaven guide me!" she said, as she poured a few drops of the precious contents into the empty glass.

The bottle was then returned to her pocket, and the glass filled with water.

Then she stooped over the stricken patient, and looked pityingly at the form now worn out by sickness and sorrow.

He seemed insensible, for he heard not the girl's voice as she frantically called upon him to awake.

All efforts to arouse him were fruitless; and Ellen, regardless of everything, inserted the rim of the glass between his teeth and forced the contents down his throat.

She quitted the chamber like one who had been guilty of some fearful act, and, pale and trembling, went to her own apartment.

Lady Mountsteven sat for some hours by the open widow of the luxuriantly furnished chamber.

The cooling sea breeze played upon her white throat, but brought no relief to her heated brow.

Upon her cheeks there lived a deep crimson spot which gave an additional charm to her olive skin, and large lustrous eyes.

It was a sad sight to behold that glorious specimen of Nature's chaste handiwork, and know that beneath that beauteous exterior there lived a soul so blackened with crime as to make its outer covering revolting and loathsome.

She sat there looking out upon the rippling waters, her white arm supporting the head.

And as she gazed, her eyes became fixed upon a tiny speck that danced upon the golden ripples.

It was not upon this that Lady Mountsteven's thoughts were fixed, for the gentle witchery of the scene, and the deep silence that reigned around had drawn her mind from earth and all mortality to that mystic land beyond the grave.

And as she sat thus, the red spot faded from her cheek.

The guilty woman, in the midst of her subtle plans and dark, murderous designs, had been suddenly stricken with the remembrance that beyond this life she would have to pay for the sins she was now committing.

With an angry cry at her own weakness, she sprang to her feet, and stamping upon the ground exclaimed—

"Accursed folly! Of what am I dreaming? Let those whose minds are like the deluded savage, let babbling priests and rabid sophists, pour their jargon into the ears of fools and shallow-brained women! I—I will proceed in my onward path."

Her white lips and blanched face gave the lie to these blasphemous words.

And reeling from the window she fell upon her couch in a swoon.

When she recovered consciousness, her attendant was bending over her, chafing her cold temples and hands.

"Where am I?" she feebly asked. "Oh! is that you, Ellen?"

"Yes, my lady. I have not long been in the chamber. Only just time enough to awaken you from your swoon."

"Swoon? Yes, I was overcome."

"So I thought, my lady," said the girl; "but your ladyship has muttered very strange things, nevertheless."

"Strange things! Why, what can I have said?"

"Much, my lady, that I do not understand."

The baroness trembled with excitement.

"Speak!" she gasped, hoarsely, "speak! Tell me what you have heard?"

Ellen's eyes met those of her mistress as she said—

"I can tell your ladyship one strange thing you raved about."

"And what was that?"

"It was about a boy who had suffered for some crime."

"Was that all," said the baroness, with tears of relief—"all you heard?"

"All, madam," the girl answered; "all I can impart to you."

———

CHAPTER LXXXVIII.

MIDSHIPMAN TOM A PRISONER.

OUR hero's stratagem was not put in force one moment too soon, for as he passed the turn in the rocks, he came face to face with the soldiers who had descended the cliff, and who were now running towards the place he had just left.

Pulling the black three-cornered hat over his eyes, the young chieftain imitated the gait of the old professor, and stooping, appeared to be deeply interested in the study of several stones which lay upon the sands.

His heart beat a little quicker than its wont when the nearest of the red-coats stopped opposite him, and asked—

"Old man, have you seen anyone hereabouts? —a young chap, in long boots, with a sword by his side?"

Without raising his head, the boy said in a querulous tone—

"A plague upon thee, for meddling fools! I had just discovered the exact date when this stone was left here by the Ancient Britons."

The soldiers laughed.

And one, by way of explanation to his fellows, said—

"This is the old chap we saw yesterday, hammering among the stones. He is mad."

Tom raised his voice to a high falsetto.

"Away, ye ribald scoffers! Know ye not that science is the mighty—"

"Shut up," said the fellow who had before spoken; "and tell me whether you have seen anyone hereabouts."

"Of course he has," said another, "I saw them standing together when I fired."

Tom stole a glance at the speaker. From that glance he felt that he should know him again; and should they renew their acquaintance, the soldier would get that shot repaid with interest.

He lowered his eyes instantly, and said—

"He whom thou seekest passed onwards when the report of those long tubes began to fill the air with——They are gone! Poor old man. They will not harm him. And now for my escape."

The soldiers did not stay for the completion of the young chieftain's speech, further than to tell them which way the fugitive had gone.

Like a hunted deer, Tom sped along the shore, nor did he cease running until he came to the village.

Feeling faint for want of food, he went to a house to ask for some, when, as he entered the garden gate, he was met by a stern looking old gentleman walking slowly to and fro reading a book.

Tom recognised him as a magistrate of the county; but he had gone too far to recede now without exciting suspicion.

The magistrate bowed politely to Tom, who returned his greeting, and was about asking for food when the scrutinizing gaze which the magistrate cast upon him gave his nerves a thrill.

"Have you travelled far?" said the old Dogberry, "You look tired."

"I have travelled far, and am tired," replied Tom, "being a lover of nature, and having ample time on my hands, I am making a tour of the coast."

"Indeed."

The utterance of this word jarred unpleasantly on our hero's ear.

But what followed caused him to stand for several seconds dumb with astonishment.

The magistrate placed the book he had been reading behind him, and gazing fixedly on the young chieftain, said—

"Your disguise does not hide you from me,—for you are Midshipman Tom."

Here was a moment of peril, for the young adventurer had no chance of escape; and he stood silent, and for a moment thrown off his guard.

Had a thunderbolt fallen at his feet, he could not have been more surprised than when these words which placed him in such jeopardy were spoken.

"I know you," he said, "and know that even now there are men sent out to kill or capture you, Midshipman Tom."

His first feeling of astonishment over, Tom thrust his hand into his coat pocket and grasped a pistol.

The magistrate perceived this, for he said to him, sternly—

"Let that weapon alone and surrender quietly."

"What if I don't?" asked Tom, with flashing eyes.

"I shall have to use force."

"Pshaw! You are alone and unarmed."

"I am, save for the power of the law."

"A power," said Tom, snapping his fingers, "for which I do not care that."

"Rash, misguided youth!"

Tom laughed.

"You must accompany me to my house," said the magistrate, "and as my prisoner."

"I shall do no such thing."

"Then I must use force."

He placed his hand upon the outlaw's shoulder, and tried to drag him away.

Tom's face reddened with anger, and he struck his would-be captor a heavy blow in the face.

The magistrate was too astonished for several moments to speak. When he had recovered sufficiently, he said, in a voice half choked with passion—

"You infernal young villain! I'll teach you to strike a man, and that man a justice of the peace!" and he made an attempt to clutch Tom's throat.

The latter drew back, and in a quiet, determined tone, said—

"Keep back, or I swear by the heavens above, if your hand again touches me I will scatter your ains out where you stand."

The magistrate, after this, prudently withdrew his reach.

[To]m turned to pursue his way, and in so doing [came] face to face with Ralph Ranger.

[The] ready tool of Lady Mountsteven recognised [the] outlaw at once.

Tom had never seen him except on that night when he was taken on board the Thunderer, and then it was dark.

Therefore he saw not the cowardly foe who was so close upon him.

Ranger saw the state of affairs at a glance, and as Tom was turning away he got behind him, and suddenly throwing both arms around his neck held him until the magistrate rushed to the spot.

There was a close and desperate struggle for some minutes betwen the two.

Tom thrust them from him time after time; but his attempt to reach his loaded pistol or his pocket was frustrated by the repeated attacks of his foes.

Finding that, even with the assistance of Ralph Ranger, he could never drag Tom into his house, he shouted at the top of his voice—

"Help! help!"

Two men rushed from the house at their master's call, and seeing him struggling with the young sailor, assisted their master at once.

The captive was overpowered and hurled to the ground, and his head striking against a stone, stunned him for several minutes.

In this state of unconsciousness he was carried to a room above the stables in the magistrate's house, and a constable was sent for.

Tom making a show of resistance when that worthy functionary appeared, further assistance was called in, and all the farm servants were collected and armed with stable-forks, reaping-hooks, and other agricultural implements to convey the young outlaw to his place of confinement.

The village lock-up was not far from the magistrate's house, and it was not long ere he was safely under its lock and key.

The place where our hero was taken after his examination before the magistrate, was an old tower, which stood about a quarter of a mile from the village.

This tower was all that remained of an ancient Norman castle, the residence of a fierce and war-like baron, who, no doubt, like his contemporaries, used to ride with full a score of stout men-at-arms at his back, and rob all who came in his way.

But they had long since passed away.

And so had the grim stronghold, except this tower, whose rugged ivy had reared itself proudly over a pair of massive gates, as though defying the destroying hand of time.

From the gates which had once given ingress to the castle, the old tower was now called by the somewhat strange name of Old Nick's Gate.

Conducted hither by the whole civil force and the servants, Tom keenly noticed the place as he approached.

At other times his mind would have been struck by the majestic remains of fallen grandeur; but now he was noting down in his mind the bearings of the country that surrounded the tower.

Here and there he beheld, amid the confusion of the moss-clad fragments that everywhere strewed the ground, a mouldering buttress; the broken stonework of a window; and the lonely tower lifting itself in melancholy grandeur.

Over all crept the ivy, that sweet emblem of

charity, binding up with its sturdy tendrils the ruined stonework, covering with its leaves the gaps that time had made, and weaving as it were garlands of lasting verdure about the dilapidated wall.

The gates were opened, and a flight of winged creatures came wheeling out, uttering shrill cries of affright.

The young outlaw's eyes followed them, and in his heart he envied them their freedom.

The constable saw the young chief's earnest gaze, and said—

"There'll be fine company for them when they return."

Tom took no notice of the man's remark; but, with head erect, and with as proud a step as ever, he passed within its walls.

The chamber in which our hero was confined stood over the massive gateway. Shorn of its furniture and hangings, it looked anything but cheering for the tired captive.

He threw himself upon the only seat in the chamber—a rough stool—and resting his head upon the table he became lost in thought.

An hour passed, and he moved not.

At the expiration of that time the constable entered, and asked if he needed any refreshment.

Tom answered he would gladly partake of some, and inquired of the constable whether he could procure it.

"I can," said the constable, "but you'll have to pay for it."

Tom smiled, and putting his hand in his breast, threw a gold piece on the ground, saying—

"Will that suffice?"

The rustic's eyes glistened, and picking it up, he answered—

"It will, sir. What can I get you?"

"Anything," was the curt answer.

The constable had reached the door when the young outlaw called him back.

"Come here," said Tom.

The constable stood before him.

"Are you rich?" said the young chief.

The man stared, but was silent.

Tom repeated the question.

"Rich?"

"Yes, rich."

"No, sir, unless being in the receipt of seventeen shillings a week would entitle me to be so called."

"Seventeen shillings?"

"Yes, sir, that is all I receive, and I have to keep a wife and family on that."

"Poor devil!" said Tom—"and is that all?"

"All I receive, sir."

"Would you like to become the possessor of a hundred pounds?"

The man's eyes sparkled, as he said—

"A hundred pounds?"

"Yes; or two?"

The constable gazed at the speaker in perfect wonderment.

"I mean it," said Tom. "One, two, or three hundred golden pieces shall be yours, if you but say the word."

"If that were all, sir, I would gladly say it; but I fear there is more than saying yes, before I shall become the happy possessor of that sum."

"Not much more," said the young chief. "You have but to leave the door unfastened, and the money shall be yours."

The constable looked at him.

The bait was tempting, and he showed he thought so.

"Leave the door unfastened?" he repeated. "Is that all?"

"All I would ask."

"In order that you may escape?"

"Exactly so."

The man remained for several minutes silent, as though thinking the matter over in his mind.

At length he said—

"Have you the money here?"

"I have not," said Tom; "but it shall be found you before to-morrow's sun shall rise."

The constable shook his head, and said—

"You promise too much, sir."

"How?"

"Because if all is true we heard to-day, your cave has been taken by the soldiers, and your band all killed or captured."

"Ha!"

The young outlaw's head fell upon his hands as he muttered—

"All killed or lost! Good heavens! then I am indeed lost."

The man overheard his words and said—

"You are, indeed, if the report is true; but it may not be."

"I care not," said the young chief, desperately. "Will you do as I wish you?"

"No," was the blunt answer. "I dare not."

The outlaw raised his head, saying—

"Leave me. Then purchase anything the money I gave you will fetch."

The man retired.

It was then the captive's head dropped upon his breast, and he moaned aloud.

"Thus then, appears to be the end of my career. My band killed or taken, and I a prisoner."

"No, Midshipman Tom," a voice said, that caused the young chief to spring to his feet, and look round in astonishment. "No, this is not the end."

Tom looked in vain for the speaker, but nothing was visible save the four bare walls of the turret chamber.

CHAPTER LXXXIX.

THE PROFESSOR OUT OF TROUBLE.

WHEN the soldiers entered the cave where the erudite professor, Quinton Querby, had been left by Midshipman Tom, they raised a shout of great joy.

Two of them presented their muskets at the professor and called out—

"Surrender, or we will blow your skull to atoms!"

Instead of the professor unsheathing the sabre that hung by his side, he, much to the astonishment of the soldiers, fell upon his knees and gasped—

"Mercy! mercy! mercy!

"If I have done aught that has given offence against the just laws of this magnanimous country, slay me not!

"If I have erred, it has been from a zeal to advance the cause of science, and discover the glorious deposits lost sight of in those dark ages ere companies for the manufacture of auriferous quartz (limited) were by act of Parliament established."

This was all Arabic to the soldiers, and with profound astonishment they listened until he had concluded.

The suppliant professor, however, had no occasion to tell them he was not the man they sought —that shrivelled form, around which Midshipman Tom's habiliments hung like a shirt on a marlinspike, while the exquisite jewelled scimitar, in place of adding to his appearance, getting between his legs, gave him the appearance of a fowl half trussed.

Indeed, the change altogether from the aspect of the fiery young outlaw to the ludicrous figure before them was so great that one and all burst into a hearty fit of laughter.

"By the great hornspoon!" said one of them bringing his musket to the ground with a jar that went all through the professor's nerves; "that must have been the young outlaw we passed on the road here."

"It must," said the sergeant, a rough Hibernian, "that's true. Get up, old man—get up, and tell us how it was you aided in the escape of a desperate outlaw."

The professor attempted to rise, but the weight of Tom's sword, which looked to be anywhere but in its proper place, prevented him rising as quickly as he otherwise would have done.

After much scrambling, for the scimitar frightfully interfered with the free action of Mr. Querby's legs, he succeeded in getting on one knee, and the sergeant compassionately giving him a lift by the jacket collar, brought him to the position men usually assume.

"And now," said the sergeant, "without any philandering, tell me all about it."

"All about it," repeated the professor "about the hapless chance which brought me hither?"

"Spake reasonably man if you can; its about the clothes and the escape of the young villain that we wants to know."

"Woulds't thou hear it in proper form, oh man of warlike propensities, or——"

"Go on wid yer," said the Sergeant, "it's the whole thing we'd like to have; and none of yer murderin' the king's English, ye orchadaun."

"Well then," resumed the professor, "the cause of science prompted me to explore these rocks here. I doubted not but a rich harvest of the precious metal would reward my diligent search. The result was, I——"

"Bad cess to yer," roared out the sergeant, "is it to listen to yer twaddling that twinty of the most dacent soldiers of the king are standing here? out wid it; or——"

"I," resumed the professor, "I was busy in my scientific calling, and my heart was filled with joy at my success, when a youth of comely appearance, yet somewhat warlike, approached me.

"We had scarce time to pass the customary forms of greeting, when pellets of lead came rattling thick and fast around us.

"It was then the youth drew me in here, and told me that chopping these rocks was an offence punishable by death."

A suppressed laugh came from the soldiers at the old fellow's credulity.

Quinton Querby paid no attention to it, but went on,—

"I was sorely troubled at this, and besought him to help me. He did. We exchanged garments, and while I was so doing you entered."

With this explanation the soldiers introduced the learned professor to the captain, to whom he related a similar story, who, satisfied of its truth, let him depart.

The professor made the best of his way home, where he was sadly rated by his wife for being such a fool.

Quinton Querby meekly bowed his head and went to his study, and soon forgot the wickedness of the comely youth who had so greatly deceived him.

———

CHAPTER XC.

A VILLAIN'S GRATITUDE.

IT will be remembered when Red Hand fled from the plague-stricken ship he took with him the crew in the boats.

Took in fact all the seamen who were not infected with the fearful epidemic, and so great was their terror and anxiety to leave the fatal ship that they neglected even to place a barrel of water in the boat.

They had not been many hours on mid-ocean exposed to the sun's burning rays before they began to regret their haste and want of prudence.

Of all earthly sufferings, that of thirst on the open sea may be fairly depicted as one of absolute torture.

So the remnants of the pirate crew found it; their tongues were hot and blistered, yet they dared not lave them in the mighty waste of water

KNIFE IN HAND HE LEAPED INTO THE SEA.

which rippled so pleasantly against the sides of the boats.

Almost maddened by the excruciating suffering he endured, Red Hand stood up in the boat, and surveyed the watery waste in the hope that some ship might be passing.

Vain hope! The sea was without a speck, and with a terrible oath he sank upon the seat and gave way to the torment he felt by invoking the heaviest curses upon the famished wretches who suffered equally with himself.

In the midst of this terrible pang a dark cloud was seen to glide over the sunlit heavens, and the pirates looking above gave a loud shout.

Red Hand looked up and growled fiercely,

"What are you yelling at?"

The bow oarsman pointed to the dark cloud and replied—

"There will be a storm directly, captain."

Red Hand made no reply, but kept his wolfish eye fixed upon the dark menacing cloud which increased every moment in density.

All became bustle and animation now in the boats, where a few minutes before nothing could be seen save the forms of the tired and suffering pirates as they lay across the thwarts.

Everything capable of holding water was now spread for the reception of the welcome rain.

And the pirates for a time forgot their misery in the precious help those dark clouds betokened.

For nearly an hour they rowed under the drifting rain—charged masses of dark vapour—and just when every hope had began to die within them, the clouds burst.

The rain did not last above five minutes; but in that time their garments, even to their shirts, were spread out to receive the water.

And when it had passed away the boats lay motionless upon the water as the rowers were employed sucking the moisture from their clothes.

The pangs of thirst thus for a time allayed, hunger began to be felt almost as keenly as the want of water had been felt that morning, and the previous day.

At length, about midnight, the crew were startled by the pirate leader springing on his feet and shouting,

"Ship, ahoy!" But no response came.

Red Hand placed his head as near the water as he could, and looked in the direction of the vessel.

"Curse you!" he growled as he raised his head, "for a pack of fools, the vessel is two or three miles from us. Pull you hounds! pull for your lives!"

The boats were lying side by side when he uttered these words, and the men as though moved by a spring all bent forward together.

After a time the boat in which Red Hand sat began to forge ahead, and the lights of a full-rigged ship could be plainly seen.

Then they bent forward to their task until they were stopped at the welcome sound of the look-out's voice on board the vessel.

"Boat ahoy!" he sang out. "Keep where you are, or we will fire into you."

"We are cast away upon the ocean without water or food."

"From what vessel?"

"The Ogre. Sprang a leak and foundered during the night."

"Very well, I will call the captain."

Ropes were speedily lowered for the crew, and a plausible story well recited by Red Hand induced the captain to invite him to his cabin.

Red Hand had not long been on board before he found out that the vessel which had rescued him was an American privateer, called the United States, a large one of her class, well armed, and a swift sailer, and no sooner had he discovered her excellent qualities than he coveted her.

And he determined if possible to become master of the United States with as little delay as possible.

Now, on board the United States was another spirit—an equally bloodthirsty villain as Red Hand—and he and the black pirate were not long in concocting a scheme by which Red Hand's wish should be accommodated.

They were sitting one day upon a brass cannonade upon the quarter-deck, conversing in low whispers.

The result of that conversation was that the pirate leader, discovering the doctor had on board certain poisons in his medicine chest, formed a plan for poisoning the crew, and it was to be instantly put in motion.

And as by the daily use of "a few grains," mixed in wine or food the object was to be effected, it was not very many days before the result of Red Hand's plot began to display itself.

The privateer captain and Red Hand were walking the deck when the former remarked:—

"There is something very singular in all this; I suppose I shall be next; it seems to affect the officers alone."

Red Hand replied: "It is strange, indeed. Were any of the crew to be affected I should attribute it to some pestilence. Have you stowed anything away in the steamer likely to produce such results!"

"No—nothing," answered the captain.

Three days rolled over, and Red Hand with the doctor passed their frequent mutual congratulations that as the officers dropped off, so the certainty of

becoming joint masters of the vessel became more assured.

The captain's fate was certain. As a stroke of policy they delayed his death, in the meantime Red Hand, ingratiated himself in his favour by assuming a temporary command of the ship, and by cheering him up amid the desolation spreading around him.

Red Hand and the doctor's demoniac policy being so far played out, the captain's time approached: he was stricken by the invisible malady, and, as he described it, "felt a sensation about his head and chest, as though hot irons were being passed through him."

Feeling his death near at hand, he addressed Red Hand :—

"Come below with me," he said, "while I have life enough left to give you my instructions. You will take the ship into port for me."

"I will if the crew will obey me."

"A good thought. Will you summon them here?"

The seamen were soon gathered aft, and while the privateer leant upon Red Hand's arm he bade them obey the miscreant as they would himself.

He was then assisted to his cabin, and in less than two hours he was a corpse.

Red Hand was now master of the ship in all but one instance.

He had to gain over the crew to join him in his piracies.

Another master-piece of policy—and he would soon effect that.

The first act was to fill up the vacancies from among his own men.

Several of the ship's crew grumbling at this as an unfair proceeding were soon settled.

They followed their comrades over the side, and by similar means.

At length the poison had done its work, and so far Red Hand and the doctor had been successful in their designs.

CHAPTER XCI.

A MYSTERIOUS VISITOR

OUR hero listened for some time for the strange voice, but as all remained silent, he was compelled reluctantly to admit that it was nothing but a creation of his brain, and passing his hand across his brow he murmured,

"Am I dreaming?"

"You are not," responded the mysterious voice again, "I tell you this is not the end."

He listened intently to find the direction from whence the sound proceeded, and said,

"Mystic or invisible being, are you a spirit come from the other world to mock me in my hour of misery?"

"I am mortal like yourself, *Midshipman Tom.* Behold!"

The young chief sprang sharply round, and beheld to his amazement the form of a woman, old and nearly bent double, standing in the further corner of the room.

He knew the mummy-like form, and exclaimed—

"The witch of Mountsteven Nullum."

"Yes, Midshipman Tom, Sybil the sorceress has come to befriend you."

He scarcely noticed the words. His mind was too much mystified by the strangeness of her appearance.

She seemed to know what was passing in his mind, for she said—

"You seem confounded by my appearance?"

"I am."

"Know you not that Sybil has command over the spirits of the air?"

"Cease this mockery, woman, and tell me how you came here?"

"Ay—ay," she muttered, more to herself than in reply to his words. "Like the old stock from which you sprung, ever hasty and incredulous, but——"

"Woman," cried the young chieftain, "what words are these? Know you the secret of my birth?"

"I do."

He rushed forward with a startled cry.

But she waved him back with a crooked staff, saying—

"Begone, mad impetuous boy."

Her act and words were explained by the opening of the chamber door, and the entry of the constable.

The man placed the food he had brought upon the table, and, without speaking, retired.

The young chief looked again for the crooked form of old Sybil, but she too had gone.

The youth stood for a few moments gazing upon the place where she had stood, and a thought passed through his brain, that caused his proud lips to curl with scorn.

"Absurd," he muttered. "Witchcraft and magic for fools. She came here by some hidden means of egress, not by any black art. Ha!"

Then his faith was for a moment shaken.

The sorceress suddenly appeared in precisely the same spot where he had last seen her.

"*Sybil*," said the undaunted Tom, "what juggling is this? How came you here, you crone?"

The crone looked into his bold, handsome face, and said in a mysterious manner—

"How came I here—ha! ha! Know ye not that cells, doors, or walls cannot stay the progress of Sybil?"

A look of quiet scorn gleamed in the young chief's face as he answered—

"A truce to this folly, woman; take your mysteries and its charms to those who are ready to believe in them."

"Presumptuous boy!"

"Silence, woman! I would learn more of that matter you but hinted at when my jailor entered."

"The secret of your birth?"

"Even so—tell me that, and gold, aye, heaps of the shining metal, shall be yours."

"I want not your dross" said the witch; "know, you, boy, in the vaults where repose the bones of your ancestors, I have gold, aye, even more than your cave contains."

"My ancestors!" he said, his brain dazed by her words, "my ancestors! Speak—explain those strange words."

She seemed to take a keen delight in watching his surprise, and repeated—

"Your ancestors, proud boy—"

She had disappeared from him so weird-like before, that the bewildered young chief, burning to learn more of her strange secret, sprang upon her, and clutched her by her wrist with a grip so strong, that a vice could not have held her with greater certainty.

"You leave not this place until I know the meaning of those words."

She looked full into his flushed face, and replied, calmly—

"Unhand me, Thomas Wilson, or I swear not another word shall escape my lips."

There was no mistaking the old crone's determination, and much against his will, the young chief was compelled to release his grasp.

He stood before her with folded arms, and said with as much coolness as he could muster—

"You are free; speak on."

"What would you know?"

He started, and replied angrily—

"Know, woman! I would ascertain from whence I sprang—know the name of those who gave me birth. I would know this, that the secret yearning of my life should be fulfilled; then I care not what happens."

"I can tell you but little, Midshipman Tom," she answered, with more feeling in her tone than she had hitherto shown. "And that little will give thee more pain than pleasure."

"You know not; therefore speak."

"It is of your parents."

"My parents! yes, great heavens, ! have I parents, and living."

"You have both."

He started for a moment, as though a sudden flash of blinding light had passed before his eyes; then, taking his hands from his brow, he cried—

"I have both! oh Sybil do you mock me, or is it the sacred truth?"

"Yes, yes boy, both; but, hist, what is that?"

They both listened, and distinctly heard the measured tramp of men approaching the tower.

The witch grasped his wrist, "hasten and follow me," she said; "the bloodhounds are upon your track. Hush, not a word."

Led onward by an unaccountable impulse, he suffered his strange conductress to lead him forward, and to his surprise, he beheld her press the end of her crooked staff against one of the massive stones that formed the side of his chamber.

CHAPTER XCII.

LADY MOUNTSTEVEN ATTAINS ANOTHER ALLY.

HAVING resolved to put Ralph out of the way, Lady Mountsteven occupied her mind with the details of the newly-formed plan.

She had also to carry out the slow process of murdering her husband by a poison so subtle that its working defied the skill of the cleverest men in the medical profession.

"Lord Mountsteven removed," she thought, "and the boy shot or hanged, there will be none to bar my way to the possession of these estates; as for the gipsy woman, it was easy enough to imagine she resembled the woman she put out of the way to become lady of the castle; she was gone—not that her presence would have mattered, for had she been the Lady Alicia she would have long ago asserted her claims."

She pondered for a few minutes, then muttered—

"Yes, Ralph removed, there will be none in possession of my secret, and ——."

A footman entered at this moment, and handed the lady a slip of paper bearing these words, *Margerie Walsingham.*

Lady Mountsteven turned as white as a corpse, and crushing the paper in her hand, said mentally—

"One of my tools in ridding myself of Lady Alicia. I thought she died on her way to America."

She controlled her emotion sufficiently to tell the menial to admit the person, and when the man left the room she took a stiletto from a drawer and placed it in her bosom.

A woman closely veiled entered the room, and calmly seating herself said—

"I suppose you thought me dead—but I live, my lady, and have called to know what my secret is worth, for I want money."

Lady Mountsteven pondered for several seconds, and mentally repeated—

"What my secret is worth?"

She gazed at the dark expressive face, before she answered, and judging from the baleful gleam in her dark eyes that she was meditating mischief, the stranger broke in upon her reverie, by saying—

"I had forgotten, madam, to tell you, that ere I entered the castle I left a friend outside who will seek me if I am long absent."

Lady Mountsteven, bit her lips nervously, then said sarcastically—

"In fear, I presume, that your valuable life would be attempted?"

"Precisely the case."

"But woman, what benefit would your death be to me?"

The stranger shrugged her shoulders, and said—

"Much! to judge from the manner in which you clutch that knife in your bosom."

Lady Mountsteven's hand fell to her side.

"Now, continued Margerie, I should like an answer."

"To what?"

"My question."

Lady Mountsteven clenched her hands until the delicate pink nails were embedded in her flesh, and hissed—

"Your knowledge is valueless, fool!"

The others' lips relaxed into a strange smile, as she answered, quietly—

"Valueless to you, perhaps—but to others invaluable."

"Pshaw—of whom do you speak?"

"Of your husband, Lord Mountsteven?"

"Ha!"

"If report does not lie, he has spared neither time nor money to discover the boy."

"How know you this?"

"By being questioned by one of his agents."

"You were?"

"Yes," but here a sneer was perceptible. "I loved the companion of my early years too well to betray her."

Lady Mountsteven, made a courtsey of mock reverence, and said—

"Your generosity was overpowering."

"It was, when I knew sufficient to have made my fortune by disclosing it."

"Will you impart to me any of this knowledge?"

"Willingly, on conditions."

"Thanks—you are generous, very generous."

"I am, madam, to those I—I love."

The lady stamped her foot impatiently, and exclaimed—

"Let this foolery end. Tell me what you do know, then I may judge the value of your secret."

"The mother and the boy yet live."

"You have told me that," she said, fiercely, "once is quite sufficient."

Margerie inclined her head and resumed—

"I did not tell you, madam, that they were together."

Lady Mountsteven started, and from between her clenched teeth she hissed.

"And they know each other?"

"No—the woman may suspect, but she has no proofs."

"Ha!"

"My knowledge is becoming valuable."

"It is—go on."

"Should any beside myself learn this, Lord Mountsteven would pay them handsomely."

The lady's lip curled scornfully as she muttered.

"Lord Mountsteven will soon be among his fathers—the knowledge would not save him."

Margerie looked straight into the speaker's eyes, and shuddered; the woman's quick perception read the meaning of the other's words.

But she made no comment on the matter.

"It might," she continued. "Dying men often do strange things."

"Peace, fool! what interest is to you whether he live or die?"

"Only, should you refuse to purchase my secret I shall take it where my price will be paid."

"You have but told me part; let me hear all. Where are those two stumbling blocks?"

"Closer than you imagine."

"Ha, what, here?"

"Yes, within sight of the castle walls."

Lady Mountsteven looked at the speaker in amazement, and repeated—

"Within sight of the castle walls."

"Yes."

Margerie arose from her seat as she uttered these words, and beckoned Lady Mountsteven to follow her; she did, and when they both stood at the open window, Margerie pointed towards the rocks, and said—

"Know you that spot where that vessel rides a anchor?"

"I do; it is the outlaws' cave."

"Correct. Have you ever beheld a graceful youth whom the lawless band call their chief?"

"Yes, I have seen him."

"And could trace no resemblance between sire and son?"

Lady Mountsteven turned quickly, and gripping the stranger's arm, said—

"I have long known this."

Lady Mountsteven was silent for a time, and when she spoke there was such a pitiless expression on her face that it caused her companion instinctively to draw back.

"Margerie," she said, in a hushed voice, "I will purchase this secret and your aid?"

"For what purpose do you require my aid?"

"Can you ask, fool? To rid me of those that stand in the way of my rights. Can you aid me?"

"I will try."

The lady looked steadfastly at her companion, and said,—

"Margerie, remember both your neck and mine are placed in the halter by one deed. I would sooner be dead a thousand times, if it were possible, than live to see this outlawed brat within these walls. You can and must help me to rid the world of them."

"I have told you, my lady, I will do my best; everything except mur—murder!"

Lady Mountsteven passed her hand quickly across her brow, and exclaimed hesitatingly—

"Even that if it is necessary—but hush, some one approaches."

Two hours passed away, and these women sat by the window speaking in hushed voices, plotting a scheme so diabolical that it seemed a wonder that heaven, in its just wrath, did not hurl a thunderbolt upon their guilty, murderous heads.

When the moon was high in the heavens, they quitted their seats, each face looking fiend-like, and each heart filled with evil intent.

The lady to her luxurious chamber, her accomplice to a lone hut by the sea.

CHAPTER XCIII.

SNOWBALL DEFENDS THE CAVE.

WHEN Snowball left his chieftain in the cave beneath the cliffs, it was his intention to enter the outlaw's haunt, if possible, without being seen by the soldiery.

With his long deadly knife between his teeth, he dived below the ocean's surface, and swam unperceived past the enemy's outposts until he came opposite the cave.

The firing had ceased, and he beheld the soldiers' muskets piled a little distance from the cavern's mouth, and the men, out of range of the outlaw's rifles, busy round several fires.

The men had evidently used the whole of the ammunition their pouches had contained, and were now awaiting the arrival of an ammunition waggon from the cantonment.

Protected by a projection of the cliff from the defender's fire, two sentries were keeping watch over the entrance.

To get rid of these two men was the first matter of importance for Snowball to effect.

He crept forward upon his hands and knees until the water became too shallow to cover him.

Then he laid himself flat upon the sands, and snake-like, glided to the water's edge.

The sentinels then were standing with their backs turned towards Snowball, and clutching his long Indian knife firmly in his right hand, he crept towards the doomed men.

Arriving within a few feet of them, he rushed forward, and seized one by the throat, and choked back the cry of alarm that rose to his lips.

The other was quickly disposed of by Snowball, who now saw his road clear before him, dashed quickly on to the cave.

The outlaws raised a cheer when they beheld their sable lieutenant, and hastily removed the massive stone that blocked the entrance.

The outlaws crowded round the black, and eagerly demanded news from their chief.

"Him," said Snowball, "am alive and safe yet, if he but stay where I leave him."

They had been disheartened by the idea that their beloved young chief was either taken or dead, and that had weighed like an incubus upon their spirits, causing them to care little whether the cave was taken or not.

Now the good news had come of their chieftain's safety, and spontaneously they shouted—

"HURRAH! HURRAH! FOR MIDSHIPMAN TOM!"

A wild cheer broke from their lips again, and the troops, all of whom by this time had gathered around the cave, regarded each other in blank astonishment at the strange cry.

Looking like a fair visitant from the "land of shades," Laura Grey came from the inner cave, and stole timidly towards the burly African.

She had heard the glad shouts, and her fond heart beat with the hope that her love had returned.

Snowball saw the mute look of anguish she cast round for her lover. and he said to her—

"Him safe, Miss Laura—quite safe."

"Safe, Snowball, and not here; for pity's sake do not deceive me?"

"Miss Laura," answered the African solemnly, "I swear by the great spirit of my tribe what I say is true."

There was no mistaking the earnestness, with which these words were uttered—the look, the gesture both bore the impress of truth.

Poor girl, she had some strange misgivings, and she was about to express them to Snowball, when a loud cheer from the besiegers caused the outlaws to rush forward.

"It is the ammunition waggon," said one, "and we shall get it hot directly."

Snowball laughed, and said,

"You think so?"

"I do."

"Mee see," was the quiet answer. "Now, Miss Laura, you go in de uder cabe: dere will be sights here dat you must not see."

She shuddered and withdrew to the cave set apart for her use.

The mystic lady's kindly heart warmed towards the poor girl, and, rising from her seat, she embraced her kindly, and strove to wean her from her grief.

Basilisk-like shone the dark eyes of Bellinee, and in her heart she wished that the young chieftain had died ere this.

Anything, thought the passionate girl, rather than he should return to another while I so deeply love him.

The truth of the outlaw's words was soon verified, and the troops began again to batter at the walls, and pour volley after volley into the loopholes.

Sturdily the outlaws and Snowball defended the cave, but to the horror of the latter he beheld a portion of the rock begin to waver under the fearful cannonade.

Snowball saw it, and his face became demoniacal in its expression.

"Golly, once knock hole in here," he said savagely, " de place soon 'saulted, but before they come in I gib 'em suffing."

A cry arose from the smugglers at this moment that made Snowball fear it would not be long before the besiegers were led to the breach.

A massive piece of rocky wall began to totter under the terrific cannonade.

The united power of six heavy siege guns had been brought to bear upon this spot, hurling its mass of iron without intermission.

The African saw a few minutes would bring the fight to a crisis.

And opening a side door that led to a chamber on the left, he called out—

"Quick, out wid dem barrels."

A dozen men sprang inside to obey his commands, and a half-dozen barrels were tumbled into the battery.

"Pile dem up," he continued, "when de stone shakes."

This was also done; then came the order—

"Turn de bungs dis way; take dem out."

The points of half-a-dozen boarding-pikes quickly dislodged the bungs.

A few seconds after the piece of rock gave way, and the aperture was filled up by barrels of powder, placed by Snowball in a systematic manner to favour his future operations.

It did not take the troops long to rear the ladders against the exterior of the cave, and scarcely were they raised when a number of the excited soldiery rushed up them.

The first gleam of a bayonet between the chinks of the barrels caused Snowball to utter a cry like a wild beast.

It was the signal that the topmost barrel was to be toppled over, and the light applied as it fell.

It effects were appalling.

The daring expedient seemed to paralyze the besiegers, the gallant leader, Captain Lucas, being one of the first to perish.

The young ensign's cheek paled at the fearful carnage.

"Great heaven!" said he, "this is indeed shocking."

He had scarcely uttered the words, when a cry of—

"The ship! the ship!" excited fresh alarm in the minds of the troops, for the Thunderer had come swiftly round the promontory, and they were exposed point blank to the vessel's guns.

In their confusion they began to leave the spot.

"Steady men, steady," exclaimed the officer, "turn the guns round upon them."

With a lowly breathed voice of vengeance they began to turn the guns seaward.

Too late.

The Thunderer had swerved round.

Her batteries were double shotted, and before a shot could be fired from the shore her sides were enveloped in smoke and flames.

Hissing and hurtling through the air the stream of grape went sweeping away the devoted soldiers by sections.

The officer saw that it would be sheer madness to stay longer to expose his men against such tremendous odds, both in appliances and numbers.

"TELL YOU WHAT MASSA SAM, WE HAB TO FIGHT DIS FELLOW OR IT'S ALL UP WID US."

CHAPTER XCIV.

EVIL WORK.

UNKNOWN by Lord Mountsteven was the kindly hand which saved him from death, and the pale, gentle girl, true to her mission, still kept watch over the actions of Lady Mountsteven.

She found the task more difficult since the coming of Margerie to the castle.

The dark-skinned woman and Lady Mountsteven were inseparable, and often in the still hours of night had Ellen heard the pair stealing about the galleries like two unquiet spirits.

The girl's vigilance was redoubled: she felt assured that some dark plot was afloat, and she determined to watch more closely than ever.

Filled with this resolution, she one night hid herself in one of the recesses of the gallery that led to Lord Mountsteven's room.

Several hours passed, and she was about to give up her lonely vigil, when a light footfall at the far end of the gallery caused her heart to throb quicker than its wont.

Peering cautiously out, she beheld the forms of Margerie and Lady Mountsteven stealing down the gallery; both were in their nightdresses and shoeless.

The bright moonbeams streamed through the quaint old windows, and threw a prismatic light over their faces as they passed ; and Ellen trembled at the fell expression upon her mistress's face.

They passed her like two shadows, then Ellen, taking her shoes in her hand, quietly and cautiously followed.

The chamber door was closed when she reached it, and Ellen guided by the light which shone through the keyhole, stooped and took a survey of the room. By the sick man's bedside she beheld Margerie holding an empty glass, and at the foot of the bed stood her mistress, her face so changed by its fiendlike look, that the poor girl could scarcely repress a cry of horror at the sight. The nurse should of course have been awake and watching by the patient's bedside, but was lying on a sofa, asleep. She had been drugged by Margerie a few hours previous.

The girl beheld this at a glance, and before she had time to take a second, she beheld the guilty pair move towards the door.

She sprang from her knees, and fled swiftly back to her hiding place ; and scarcely had she reached it when the guilty pair softly emerged from his lordship's room.

When they had disappeared, and the closing of the door told her they had gained her ladyship's chamber, Ellen sped quickly to the room they had just left.

As on a former visit, she administered a portion of the antidote to him, then crept away back to her chamber with her legs trembling under her. She gave a faint cry as she reached her bed, and staggering forward, swooned.

Her ladyship and her accomplice were at the same moment sitting beside a bright fire in the former's luxurious bed-chamber.

Neither had spoken since they quitted the chamber where lay the broken-spirited man, and although the night was warm her ladyship sat close to the fire, shivering as though she had been exposed to a keen misty wind.

Her companion suddenly looked up in her face, and said in a low voice—

"You are cold."

"I am," was the answer. "The galleries here are exposed to the sea breeze, and are cold even in midsummer."

"Say rather," responded Margerie, "your frame shivers from the effect of an unknown fear. Come, shake it off ; the deed is done. What is he more than mortal that you sit and shiver thus over his death ? It is not the first we have sent to heaven by the same road."

Lady Mountsteven sprang from her chair, and clasping the speaker's wrist, said, in a low fierce voice—

"Silence ? Do you wish to drive me mad ?"

"No."

"Your words at this moment belie your answer."

"They may. I would not wish you to think so ; I do it merely to bring back a little of that wondrous nerve which you once possessed."

"Aye, once possessed," her ladyship answered, with a shudder ; "but now every passing shadow makes my soul shrivel up within me, and I tremble at meeting the look of any domestics who may chance to pass me."

"You must shake off such childish feelings."

"I have tried to do so," her ladyship answered, "and without avail ; each day they seem to grow stronger upon me ; aye, ten times stronger since the time I contemplated the death of my husband."

"Subdue them with a stronger will," replied Margerie.

"I cannot ; I would give, freely, one-half the wealth that will soon be mine to do so."

"You are unstrung to night. Seek your couch ; to-morrow you will be undisputed mistress of Mountsteven castle."

"Would the morrow were here : for since the last failure of the drug I have fearful doubts whether my poison will do its work upon him."

Margerie laughed lowly as she said—

"A nervous hand was yours when the draught was given. That poison never fails, I well know."

"My hand was firm—as firm as yours to night— and I saw each drop diffuse itself in the water, and saw him drink the cup to the very dregs."

Margerie rose from her seat, and said—

"Then another hand has administered the antidote. Where is the case ?"

"Here," answered Lady Mountsteven, handing her the inlaid box, with its double row of letters, and no one's hand but mine has ever opened it."

"We shall see," was the remark, as Margerie held the phail, the contents of which Ellen had changed, to the light."

A moment's survey told her all that had occured, and on unstopping the bottle she emptied it, and suffered the contents to drop on the floor.

Lady Mountsteven started up, and with eagerness demanded—

"Are you mad. What are you doing ?"

"It has been changed," was the startling reply. "This is water."

Lady Mountsteven fell back into her seat and gasped—

"Changed ! What mean you ?"

"Simply what I have said—the contents of this phial has been taken away, and water substituted in its place."

"Then," said Lady Mountsteven, as her eyes distended with passion, "Ellen has done this."

"Ellen !"

"Yes—my waiting woman."

"Then," exclaimed Margerie, "she must be silenced at once."

"What, more crime ?"

"Yes - more crime. To hide one it may be necessary to commit others."

"I will not consent to this," said her ladyship; " we have not the slightest proof."

"Is her chamber near?"

"It is."

"Come, then, we will seek the proof, and then stop this meddling fool's career, if necessary."

"You are right, Margerie," her ladyship exclaimed, suddenly.

"It must be Ellen who has foiled you."

"You recollect now?"

"I do."

"Malediction upon my stupidity. I left the case one night with the key in the lock."

"Come then, there is no time to be lost."

Placing a loose wrapper round her shivering form, Lady Mountsteven, left her chamber with her attendant.

As noiselessly as before, they traversed the long corridor, and went to Ellen's chamber.

The door was open.

Softly and like two shadows they glided inside.

Ellen was in the same position as she had fallen in her swoon, her face covered with her hands clutching the pillow.

With cat-like stealth, Margerie, crept about this apartment.

Every drawer—every cupboard, even the girl's small writing desk, were one by one opened.

No trace of the drug could be found.

CHAPTER XCV.

KEEL-HAULING A CRIMP.

MIDSHIPMAN TOM watched with a strange feeling of interest the movements of the peculiar being who had come so strangely to his side.

A small door yielded to the pressure of the gipsy's stick and disclosed a spiral staircase, the steps overgrown with moss and fungi.

"At the foot of these stairs," said the strange woman, " begins a vaulted subterranean passage which terminates within a mile from your cave. Leave me—go—your presence is needed by your men."

"But my —— "

"Some other time you shall know all; at present you are required elsewhere."

Tom Wilson could not dispute the woman's wish —he uttered a few words of thanks and hastened down the steps.

The passage was in total darkness, and Tom, after discovering the path by the light at the entrance, ran swiftly until he reached the end.

This was a small aperture at the base of the high cliffs, and as our hero leaped upon the sands he beheld a small boat containing a single rower about to quit the beach.

Midshipman Tom recognised the rower, and hastily running forward he called out—

"Boat, ahoy!"

The young sailor, for he was but a youth, paused in the act of pushing off, and in spite of our hero's disguise knew him.

"Midshipman Tom," he said, touching his cap, "my preserver, if I am not mistaken."

"You are Charley Phillips."

"I am, sir."

"I thought you were far away from here."

"We returned from our cruise a fortnight since, sir, but I am now on my way to engage with another captain."

"Is the ship here?"

"Just the other side of the promontory, sir."

"That must be," Tom exclaimed, " the Thunderer. Were you sent by that rascally knave, Abraham Levy?"

"I was, sir."

"I will go on board with you--give me an oar."

It seemed to our hero that it would be a matter of impossibility to reach the cave by land, and by going on board the Thunderer he could be of some service to his own men.

Captain Dragon met him at the gangway, and, much to our hero's surprise, he saw a number of his men on the privateer's deck.

"I will explain their presence," the privateer captain said, noting Tom's surprise, " your black giant sent them to work the ship, and aid him in repelling the soldiers' attack upon the cave; but," added the captain, laughing, " I had nearly given them a dose of grape, for I made sure when I saw the boats that they were sent by old Levy to seize the ship."

"But for the outlaws coming," said Charley Phillips, " the attempt would have been made by a score of desperadoes the old rascal had bribed to do it."

"Thanks for the information. I will hang the old villain before I leave here."

"Let him live," said Tom, " he has sent you one friend I know will be of service to you."

"I will spare him if you wish it, my friend. Now," turning to Charley, " what communication have you to make?"

"I come on behalf of the late crew of the Albion to make you an offer. They want a ship, and being tired of the merchant service and men-of-war, are willing to serve in a privateer under certain conditions."

"What are those conditions?"

Charley opened a paper and read—

"We, the late crew of the Albion, agree to serve on board the Thunderer under these conditions.

"First. Our pay to be two-thirds above that paid on board a man-of-war.

"Second. To have a third share in all the prizes.

"Third. All women taken to be disposed of according to the Captain's wish.

"Fourth. The vessel to be officered from amongst us; the Captain to make his selection, which we pledge ourselves to accept.

"Signed, on behalf of the crew,
"CHARLES PHILLIPS."

The captain took the paper and said—

"Very fair conditions; I accept them, and offer you, Mr. Phillips, the post of second in command of the privateer, the Thunderer."

Young Charley's face flushed with pride as he said—

"An offer which I proudly accept, sir."

The captain extended his hand, which Charley grasped.

"I am glad of it," said the former; "now, Mr Phillips—Lieutenant, I should say—when will the crew be here?"

"Send up a rocket, sir, they are waiting behind the hill—that is the signal agreed upon."

A rocket was fired, and before the sparks had quite died out, a crowd of seamen were seen descending the rock.

The Thunderer's boats were sent to shore.

It was not long before the blue-jackets came on board, and, cap in hand, they formed a group round their new captain, and with them came old Levy to receive his money.

Dragon surveyed the brave fellows with a proud look in his eyes, and whispered to the young lieutenant—

"This is a crew with which I would face a three-decker."

"You could, and stand a better chance of beating, than with an encounter with a brig, had you only your lately mixed crew of every nation under the sun."

Captain Dragon stood forward, and fixing his clear grey eyes upon the mass of upturned faces, said—

"Now, my lads, a few words before we start on our first cruise.

"I agree to all you wish, and as a commencement I have nominated your messmate, Charley Phillips, as my first officer."

A cheer broke from the men, young Phillips was their favourite.

"I have acted rightly, I find," continued Captain Dragon, "now I leave to you the nomination of the rest."

Cries of "No, no; you are the best judge," was heard from the seamen.

The captain waved his hand to command silence, and said—

"No, you are; come pick them out according to their qualifications."

This decision gave satisfaction to their crew, and the officers being appointed, the purser was ordered to give out a double allowance of grog to the crew.

"And now, gentlemen," said the captain, the double allowance having been done speedy justice to, "now let us put things in order. Station your men, for I shall beat to quarters at once."

A loud shout from several of the seamen put a stop to any further proceedings.

And to Captain Dragon's surprise, he beheld them dragging old Levy up to the yard-arm.

"Quick," he said to Charley, "and stop the men taking the old rascal's life."

The new lieutenant ran forward, and vociferated—

"Lower away there—what are you doing?"

There was a tone of command and confidence in the young lieutenant's voice that suggested the necessity for instant obedience, and the half-strangled old wretch was lowered with a jerk to the deck.

Charley then returned to his commander.

"I think, sir," he said, "you had better send the old crimp ashore, for his life would not be safe here long."

"Indeed; how is that?"

"He has, by the aid of those painted Jezebels he calls his daughters, robbed me and all of us since we came ashore."

"Has he? Oh, well, he deserves hanging for his rascality to me; but as to my only friend I promised to spare the wretch's life, why it must be spared."

"Very well, sir."

The young officer turned away to attend to his new duties.

"Lieutenant Phillips."

"Sir."

"Pass the word forward to the men to keel-haul him."

"Very well, sir."

"Stay—bring him here first."

A dozen ready hands brought him forward, and six times that number of faces were on the broad grin, waiting for the order to immerse the crimp into the sea.

"Now," said Captain Dragon to the trembling wretch; "I have but one question to ask you before I either hang you or send you ashore."

"I will tell you everything if you will spare my life."

"We shall see. You remember a young Spanish girl that was on board your vessel at Sierra Leone?"

"The Spanish girl, Meby?"

Captain Dragon's lip quivered as he said—

"Yes; where is she?"

"Dead," was the startling answer.

The corsair staggered backward and repeated—

"Dead; is she dead?"

"Yes," said Levy! "she perished by fire."

"What, miscreant! You—you——"

He sprang upon the unfortunate and would have strangled him, but for the young lieutenant who drew his hand away, saying—

"Let him finish his story."

"I had no hand in her death," said Abraham, as soon as he could speak. "She was on shore in a house at Del Centa, and it caught fire. One of the half-castes, at the risk of his own life, brought her from the blazing pile, but she died two hours after from fright."

Captain Dragon turned away to hide his emotion, and young Phillips, in his capacity of first lieutenant, gave the order to keel-haul him.

An order which was received with shouts, and in less than a minute a line was placed under his arms, and he was dangling over the ship's side.

One howl of agony he gave as he was lowered into the water, and dragged under the vessel. This operation was repeated three times. The crew then cast him into his boat and set it adrift.

When this act of justice had been executed, the men gathered round a huge tubful of their favourite liqour, not thin water-grog, but the real old pine-apple.

One old salt, when he had drained the tin pannikin, wiped the water from his eyes, and said—

"Dash my buttons, messmates, I'd fight like old Nick for a captain that loves such stuff as this."

And all who had partaken of the liquor fully agreed with the old 'un.

At this juncture a shout was raised.

"Boy overboard!" "Boy overboard!"—rang fore and aft, from mouth to mouth.

The boy was a good swimmer, nevertheless there was sufficient cause for the alarming cry, for, as a score of half-nude, powder grimed figures rushed to the bulwarks, they beheld the fin of a monstrous shark heading straight for the daring boy.

There was no time for reflection. In another minute the boy's tender limbs would be crunching between the monster's treble row of teeth.

The spectators shuddered. The very men who could have stood unflinchingly before the cannon's mouth—looked on in ghastly horror. By this time the old salt, who had been paying deep devotion to his grog, elbowed his way through the crowd.

"A tiger shark, by Jupiter," he exclaimed, as his eye took in the dimensions of the huge monster, and without another word, he snatched a bowie knife from his belt and leapt into the sea, close to the shark.

Both the man and the monster then disappeared.

When they rose to the surface the sea was all of a foam, the old tar was waging a deadly war with the shark. Streaks of blood began to crimson the water, and in a very few moments the bowie knife had done its work.

Cheer after cheer burst from the sailors, as they hauled the boy and his rescuer on board, and after the grog had been once more passed round, every man went cheerfully to his duty.

So well did the new officers perform their parts, that in less than an hour from the time of the men coming on board, they were all at their stations as though they had been for years in the vessel.

Everything was taut and trim, even the galley-fires were alight, and the cooks were preparing for the evening meal.

Captain Dragon looked proudly at his well-disciplined crew, and gave orders for the sails to be set.

It was done noiselessly, and in a few minutes the Thunderer was gliding towards the outlaw's cave.

The young lieutenant and his men were standing by the mainmast, when the cave suddenly burst upon their view; and to their profound rage they beheld the soldiers were actively engaged with heavy artillery trying to effect a breach in the rock.

Captain Dragon saw it, and at once gave the orders.

"Man the starboard battery, and disperse those red-coated devils. Come, my lads, be sharp."

At the same moment young Phillips ordered the sails to be furled, and the Thunderer to be ranged close in shore.

Captain Dragon's next order was—

"Stand by the quarters there, ready to lower the boats."

The order was instantly obeyed, and the crew armed with cutlass and pistol, stood ready to go ashore.

The troops saw the vessel's ports open and her guns run out, and, rendered savage by her second attack, turned their guns seaward.

Captain Dragon laughed, and said—

"Now, my lads, they are preparing to give us a return. Ready there?"

"Ay, ay sir, all ready."

"Fire!"

The vessel's timbers creaked at the mighty discharge, and her beautiful outlines were hidden in the smoke.

CHAPTER XCVI.

RED HAND CUNNINGLY ENTRAPS THE SEAMEN.

RED HAND's merciless plot had succeeded, and the ship and crew were his; the red-cross banner was supplanted by the ghastly emblem of piracy and rapine.

It was some days before he had complete mastery over the crew; for many, although they sullenly obeyed his commands, determined to quit the vessel the first opportunity that occurred.

The pirate leader knew this, for among the numerous hands on board the vessel, there were plenty ready to become spies upon their fellows.

It was from one of these that Red Hand learned the internal dissatisfaction among the crew, and the cunning villian determined to place them beyond the power of leaving his vessel, unless they went to the gallows.

"So," he muttered, as he paced the quarter-deck, "they will leave the ship and proclaim my character, will they? Curse them, I will soon place a noose round their necks that will keep them here, as my slaves—worse than slaves, the mutinous dogs!"

Early the next morning, the look-out signalled an approaching sail, and Red Hand, who seemed never to quit the quarter-deck, at once raised his glass.

"A gun-brig," he muttered, after a long survey "British, I think."

The entire crew were American, and cordially hated the English. This was sufficient to gain the pirate's purpose, for, without waiting to consider the truthfulness of his words, they began to clear the deck for action.

"Run up the Union Jack," said Red Hand, "or she will show us her heels." The stranger, when he spoke, was sufficiently near to make out her decks, and the crew beheld to their delight the men at quarters and the guns run out.

The little brig, when the flag of old England was seen floating in the breeze, fired a shot into the Black Squall.

The gun was well aimed, for the iron missile struck the wheel and shivered it into fragments.

The men were rendered savage by this, and thoroughly enraged by Red Hand's crafty words.

No sooner had the wheel been shattered, and two men who had been wounded by the splinters taken below, than Red Hand came on deck, and turning to the crew, said—

"We are now at her mercy, shall we surrender or fight?"

From every mouth came the hoarse response—

"Fight while a plank holds together."

"Be it so, my lads, and should we be victorious, the spoil shall be divided among you."

The men gave a cheer; the same moment another gun was fired from the brig.

A cry of rage came from the crew when they beheld the shot go through the mainsail.

Every stitch of canvas was set on board the brig, and soon after this shot had been fired she came within a cable's length of the Black Squall.

The crew of the latter were worked now to a terrible pitch of excitement, for Red Hand had craftily forbade a shot to be returned, or the ports to be opened.

A dozen of the crew were busy dragging up a spare wheel from below to supply the place of that which had been shattered by the gun from the brig.

The greater portion of those who had hitherto been at the guns were compelled to leave them, to work the sails, the loss of the wheel for the time having rendered her unmanageable, and it required all the pirate leader's skill to prevent the brig running into his vessel.

Disappointed in this, the brig suddenly ran across the bows of the disabled vessel, and an officer sprang into the shrouds and shouted through his trumpet—

"Haul down your flag and surrender, or we'll sink you."

A yell of derision followed this command from Red Hand's crew.

The officers sprang to the deck, and those on board the Black Squall could see the brig endeavouring to rake them fore and aft.

The excitement among the men became terrible, and one and all quitted the ropes and rushed to their guns.

"Steady," said Red Hand. "Down with that rag, and run up the black banner."

The Union Jack was in a moment supplanted by the black flag, then Red Hand said—

"Now, give it them."

The ports flew open as if by magic, and before the brig could clear herself she received the Black Squall's broadside.

The effect was terrible.

The iron storm stove in parts of her bulwarks, and smashed two boats into fragments.

The brig was evidently unprepared for this, for it threw her crew into a state of confusion that lasted several minutes.

"Give them another. Hurrah!" shouted Red Hand; "Hurrah for the black flag!"

The cry must have been heard on board the brig, and as though in defiant response they ran up their flag.

There was a moment's silence on board the Black Squall as the seamen saw the stars and stripes of America floating in the sun's glow.

Red Hand noted the change, and, with a face such as the arch fiend would wear when he obtains another soul, he said—

"It is an American brig; quick with your guns, or she will be foul of us! *Remember, those who are captured will swing at the yardarms!*"

Too late, the men saw the trap into which they had fallen; and, seeing only the hempen halter before their eyes, they redoubled their fire.

The brig by this time had recovered from the pirate's broadside, and her commander, seeing there was no hope of victory unless by boarding, endeavoured to range alongside.

Red Hand saw his intentions, and not knowing whether he could yet trust his crew to repel an attack of their own countrymen, strove all in his power to avoid the encounter.

In this he was baffled, for the loss of his wheel rendered the ship so unmanageable, that at the third broadside the brig had fastened herself to the pirate.

Amid the crash of the vessels as they met, the voice of the American commander could be heard shouting—

"Boarders, follow me! show the piratical dogs no mercy—kill or capture them!"

Red Hand drew his sword, and placing himself in front of his men, shouted—

"Follow me; remember, victory, or death at the, yard-arm!"

These words were not lost upon the men, and like so many demons, they repulsed the attack of the brig's crew.

Twice they gained a footing on the deck, and twice they were beaten back again.

A third attempt was made by the plucky commander, who sprang from the side of his ship into the midst of the pirates, and stood face to face with Red Hand.

SNOWBALL WARNS MID TOM OF HIS DANGER.

"Yield, miscreant!" said the captain of the brig.

Red Hand's reply was to level a pistol at him, and shoot him dead.

"Now," yelled the pirate, "clear the deck of these vermin."

His men answered with a shout, and hurling themselves against the man-of-war's men, drove them from the ship.

Red Hand led his men forward to attack the brig in his turn, but the close volley of musketry that blazed in their faces caused them to recoil with the loss of twenty men killed and wounded.

Red Hand, with a terrible oath, again dashed forward, but too late. The brig had cast off the grapplings, and with every sail bellying out in the wind, was forging ahead.

One parting broadside was all the pirates had time to give the gallant little brig before she was out of range.

This action, brief as it was, had made the crew all that Red Hand desired. They had fought under the black flag, and were beyond the pale of civilisation.

With deep cunning Red Hand ordered a plentiful supply of rum to be issued to the crew, and before they had time to reflect upon the cause in which they had just played the first act, one and all were in a hopeless state of intoxication.

The vessel, with scarcely sufficient men to work the sails, ran before the wind all that night, and not until the next day were the crew able to return to their duty.

To Red Hand's chagrin, several days passed without a sail appearing. He wished but for one thing: that was to fall in with a richly-laden merchant ship.

Fortune favoured the miscreant's evil wish.

CHAPTER XCVIV.
IN THE TOMBS.

WITH a disappointed look upon her dark face, she whispered the result to Lady Mountsteven.

At that moment, Ellen's hands relaxed their grasp upon the pillow, and a deep sob came from her lips.

"She wakes," hurriedly whispered her ladyship, "come."

They glided from the apartment.

As they closed the door, Ellen, recovering from her swoon, sat up and gazed wildly around her.

She passed her hands over her burning forehead, and murmured—

"Can it be fancy—or was there a shadow glided towards the door?"

Acting under the influence of some half-designed plan, she quickly arose and searched the room.

"Nothing," she mused. "It must have been fancy."

Yet she did not feel at ease.

The glimpse she had obtained of Margerie's form, as she went away from the chamber was too real to be easily dispelled or forgotten.

A sudden thought flashed through Ellen's brain, and sent a feeling of coldness rushing to her head.

Great heavens! she thought, can those fiends in woman's form have been here, if so my life is not safe.

This thought filled her with dread.

Yet, in spite of her fears, she sprang towards the door, and passing through said—

"I will know the worst."

She went swiftly to her mistress's chamber, and placing her ear to the key-hole, through which the light gleamed, listened to the words of those within.

Each word that fell from their lips added to the girl's terror, and her breath came short and quick as she strove to catch each lowly-spoken word.

"It can be no other," she heard Margerie say.

"She alone has access to your chamber."

"But we found nothing to support our suspicion."

These words convinced Ellen that her vision had been a reality, and in place of a shadow she had seen a form steal from her room.

Margerie's answer sent an icy shiver to her heart.

"Still," the woman said, "it is better to make everything safe. A few drops of this will send her out of the way."

Her ladyship was silent for some time, and Ellen, with bated breath, kept her ear pressed close to the key-hole to catch the answer that would seal her fate.

It came at length, and every word fell like molten lead upon the girl's heart.

"Do as you will, I leave it in your hands."

Ellen wanted to hear no more.

Terror took possession of her faculties, and she rushed from the door and flew, rather than ran, to her own chamber.

Without pausing a moment, she placed a few things in her bundle, and, putting on her cloak and hat, left the castle.

She did not feel safe even when the massive portal closed behind her.

Neither looking to the right nor left, she flew onwards until she reached a small cottage about two miles from the castle.

Here, in answer to her feeble summons, an upper window was raised, and an elderly female looked out and said—

"Who's there?—Ellen?"

"It is I, Kate; do not be afraid."

"Bless the child," muttered the old dame; "what can bring her here this time in the morning?"

The speaker was an old relation of Ellen, and as she hobbled down the stairs by the aid of her crutches, her mind was full of conjectures respecting her young relative's visit.

With a garrulity peculiar to age, she poured a flood of questions upon the agitated girl, to all of which Ellen replied—

"To-morrow, Kate; I am too unwell now to answer any questions."

She went to her little chamber, and threw herself upon the bed—but not to sleep.

The danger that filled her brain drove all thoughts of slumber far away.

Great was the consternation of Lady Mountsteven and her accomplice when they discovered the girl's flight, and for several days they were in hourly dread of the appearance of the officers of justice.

Another thing puzzled them.

It was the failure, for the second time, of the poison; and when a week had elapsed, and all thought of Ellen had passed from their minds, a consultation was held between the two.

"Do you think it possible," said Lady Mountsteven, "that some unseen power destroys the effect of the drugs, and scorns every attempt to destroy life?"

The woman's lips curled scornfully, as she replied—

"Pshaw! Are you mad enough to believe in such idle trash? What is he more than any other mortal that he should be watched over by an invisible guardian?"

"He is not."

"Very well. The drug has failed because its potency has evaporated. We must try another."

"There is but one, and that is a rare one."

"That will do if it is the ruby coloured."

"It is."

"That is all we require. Know you the peculiar properties of that drug?"

"Partly."

"Partly? Do you know it has the power of subduing every faculty for seven days; in fact, producing so near an appearance of death that even the body becomes stiffened?"

"Yet it does not kill."

"No. At the end of that period suspended animation returns. Not a nerve, not a muscle is injured by its action."

A few days after this conversation a grand funeral took place, and the last Lord of Mountsteven was borne to the vault of his ancestors.

Then the guilty woman breathed freely.

Her wishes were accomplished.

At last she was sole mistress of the title and domains, and she laughed to scorn the bare idea of the wronged wife and outlawed children ever claiming their rights.

Still listening to the crafty counsel of Margerie, she kept to her determination of either destroying or removing Lady Alicia and her son from her path.

Lord Mountsteven had died, she thought, without making a will; but there was one, who crept like a shadow about the whole place, who knew the secret, and where the parchment was hidden that would restore the rightful heir to his ancestral home.

Thus stood affairs at the castle, and Lady Mountsteven slept in fancied security, little suspecting the scene that had taken place in the vaults when the funeral *cortege* had returned.

From behind a stone monument of a Crusader, the founder of the name and fortune of Mountsteven, there emerged the bent form of the witch Sybil.

Looking vacantly around the tomb like one just awakened from a long sleep, she muttered angrily—

"Who disturbs my slumbers?"

A brief survey told her that the place was empty, and with a second angry expletive, she was about to crouch down behind the stone figure, when her eye beheld the glittering plate and armorial bearings upon Lord Mountsteven's coffin.

The woman stood motionless for several moments.

She hobbled towards the coffin, muttering—

"One of the old race dead, and I did not hear the death cry. Impossible; yet none others dare lay their bones in this vault."

She had reached the coffin by the time her mutterings ended, and leaning upon her stick she read the gleaming silver plate, which set forth the titles, honours, name and age of the dead.

"No, no," muttered the crone, "Lord of Mountsteven is not dead, there is some horrible work here; the death cry has not been heard yet, and until then none of them can die.

She stood for a length of time watching the coffin, as though the inanimate structure of wood and velvet could clear up the mystery.

The crone's brows were wrinkled deeper than ever, and a thousand wild schemes passed through her head.

Among them were that the coffin was filled with stones, and the body of Lord Mountsteven had been conveyed away by the instrumentality of his wicked wife to insure some sinister purpose.

What that purpose was she could not divine.

"He is not here," she muttered, tapping the coffin-lid with her stick, "the death cry has not sounded; none can pass away."

She was about to turn away as she finished her strange mutterings, when a sudden thought struck her.

Acting upon the impulse of the moment, she picked up a heavy iron bar, and raising it above her head, brought it down with crushing force upon the coffin-lid.

Thrice she repeated the blow before the stout elm plank showed any signs of giving way.

Excitement gave her strength when she beheld a slight crack in the hard wood, and blow after blow fell in rapid succession.

Pausing at length from her task, she saw a portion of the cover was beat under, and a small space visible of sufficient width to allow the admission of her hand.

Another moment and her fingers would have been inserted, but as she advanced a cry of half terror, half surprise escaped her lips.

Familiar as Sybil was with death, the sight she had beheld for a moment kept her spell-bound.

There, from the crevice in the coffin, a white wasted hand was seen to clutch nervously at the jagged opening, then a part of the arm became visible.

Sybil's terror soon passed away, and she sprang forward and clutched the hand, crying, "Not dead. I knew it."

"The death cry came not upon the night wind, speak, Lord Mountsteven, if you can."

Faintly from the interior of the ghastly receptacle, there came a sound as from a man suffering. She listened.

"Where am I? where am I?"

"Hush, my lord," said the crone; "you are among your fathers; lie still and you shall be free."

A feeble moan followed her words; then the hand was withdrawn.

The crone again seized the iron bar.

In nervous haste she wrenched off the lid.

Then the living occupant of the tomb arose, and with the witch's assistance, got out of the coffin.

In the dim and mystic light, in his white shroud, he stood looking around him.

One glance told the fearful story; he had been entombed alive, he thought, and with the thought he fell senseless.

The witch raised him in her strong arms, and passing beneath a small arch, after a short time disappeared with her burden.

CHAPTER XCVIII.
A STRANGE SCENE.

WHEN the breeze lifted the cloud of battle from the Thunderer's hull and rigging, a loud cheer came from the outlaw, and it was answered from the vessel.

Then followed a galling fire of musketry on the besiegers.

And now, amid the loud roar of the cannons, and the sharp report of musketry, the bugle's clear notes rose high, as the retreat was sounded.

The troops, at a quick pace, gladly obeyed the order, and, casting looks of compassion at the fallen forms of their companions, they soon hastened out of sight.

This retreat was seen on board the Thunderer, and another deafening cheer arose.

This, like the former, was answered by those in the cave.

The smoke had barely drifted away from the vessel when the young chief and his followers were seen to leave her side.

The boats were not long in bearing the outlaw through the blue waters, and once more he stood proudly free upon the beach.

And not another minute passed before Laura Grey came forward with open arms to receive her long absent lover.

"Laura," he murmured, "my own beautiful girl."

"Safe, safe, darling!" was all she could utter.

Then her head fell upon his shoulder, and she swooned from excess of joy.

The young chief took her light form in his arms and bore her to his cave, where he left her in the care of the mystic lady.

Then he returned and surveyed the damage done by the enemy's fire.

"Can't hab dis hole here, massa Tom," said Snowball, "cos we hab dem red-coats back agin."

The outlaw was silently looking at the gap in the wall, and revolving in his active brain a plan whereby he could turn the seeming misfortune to a good purpose.

He laughed at Snowball's puzzled face, and answered at length—

"We should always take the good things the gods provide us, Snowball; so the sooner we repair damages the better."

"Yes, massa Tom."

The outlaws, under Snowball's direction, soon converted the break into a battery, mounting two guns.

"Tink dis am sufficient, Massa Tom."

"It is, Snowball."

"Soldiers won't say so when dey come back."

"No," said Tom; "let us hope they will not."

Three days passed, and as there was no sign of their foes returning, Tom went on board the War Cloud to superintend the getting of stores on land.

When he returned to the cave he found a boy awaiting him.

In the torn lining of his cap he had a dirty piece of paper on which the following words were scrawled:—

"*The witch Sybil to the outlaw. Would you behold your sire, proud boy, follow the bearer of this.*"

Midshipman Tom's handsome face paled at the strange words, and following the irresistible impulse that filled his heart, he armed himself, and to guard against treachery he desired four of the band to follow him there. Following the boy, he left the cave.

The crescent moon shone brightly as they wended their way towards a solitary chapel that stood within the grounds of Mountsteven Castle.

At the side door of the solitary building the guide stopped, and, imitating the cry of an owl, beckoned the young chief to follow him.

Tom's followers would have entered, but the old crone opening the door turned them back, saying—

"You alone, boy, must enter here. Do so, and speak."

The outlaw paused.

"You are afraid of an old woman, MIDSHIPMAN TOM," she said, when she saw his hesitation, "or you would not pause thus and look around for those that follow you."

He blushed, and, motioning Snowball and his men back, he said, haughtily—

"Enough—I will enter alone."

He passed through the door. Keeping close to the old crone, they descended the steps that led to the vaults."

A chilly feeling of awe came over Midshipman Tom as he felt his way among the tombs, and treading upon the marble pavement he uncovered his head.

"Aye, boy, 'tis a proud race that lies here," Sybil muttered, when she saw his action. "Tread lightly, or the bones of mighty warriors may rattle in their leaden coverings at thy presence."

"Cease your idle words," he said, I came here not to listen to this."

She heeded not his words, but muttered on.

As though in answer to her own thoughts, she continued—

"The day will come when the wronged shall be righted, and the last of the race shall sit in the halls of his fathers."

Tom listened to her strange words, and mentally pondered over their meaning.

"Can it be," he thought, "in reference to myself, or is it she?"

He paused, and placed his hand upon his sword. The old crone turned and looked at her companion.

"What," she asked, "makes that heart quake which fears no mortal foe? We are alone, boy, alone with the dead."

A ray of bright moonlight here streamed in at one of the grated openings, throwing her radiant light upon the grotesque figures and carvings upon the tombs, giving them the appearance of life, and causing the kneeling figures to appear like armed men ready to spring upon the intruders.

Tom saw that the causes of his fear were but effigies carved in wood or stone, and his hand quitted his sword.

"It is nothing," he replied. "The moonbeams gave yonder figures the appearance of life."

"To you, boy!" she said; "not to Sybil, who lives among the dead."

"You live here?"

"Aye, what better place for the homeless wretch at whose appearance children run and shrink into their homes?

"At whose footsteps mothers, when they hear them, press their babes closer and closer, silently evoking heaven to guard them against contact with me."

"You have an ill repute among the villagers?"

"I have," she said bitterly. "There is not a cow dies but Sybil has cast her spell upon it. So say the ignorant, benighted fools. There is not a maiden strays from the right path, and brings shame upon herself and parents, but 'tis Sybil's evil spell has worked its shame upon."

"Yet ——," he began.

"But they are foul lies," she said fiercely. "Sybil has never harmed even a babe in her life."

"Yet you have this evil name."

"I have. Would you know why?"

"I would."

"It is because I dwell not as others do that I am pointed at, hunted and driven from place to place; aye, and thrown into the horse pond by the men of the village. To escape this I dwell among the dead. There the rats and myself hold our nightly revels. There the crowd who attack me by day dare not come. Ha, ha, ha! They are afraid; aye, afraid of even the quiet dead."

Sybil raised her arms, and her small grey eyes blazed fiercely.

In her tattered garb and almost fleshless limbs she looked a fit inmate for the ghastly place she dwelt in, and the young chief, in his mind, could not help likening her to a connecting link between the living and the dead.

They had now reached a small arched opening in the vault, and ySbil, with her hand upon the tattered curtain, which seemed to screen it from the vault, said in a solemn tone—

"Now for the fulfilment of my promise. Behold!"

She pulled back the curtain.

Tom stood like one petrified at the strange sight that met his gaze.

Upon a couch formed by a pair of trestles and two coffin lids, was laid the form of a man.

The sharp outlines standing out in bold relief as the moonbeams played upon a spotless white cover which was thrown over the body, enveloping it from head to foot.

One part alone was visible.

That was the right hand which had been brought from beneath the pall, and Tom noticed that upon one of the white fingers there gleamed a massive ring set with a large emerald.

He was about to spring forward, but, the Sybil motioned him back, saying solemnly—

"Move not nearer, boy, and listen to me."

He stood pale and motionless like a granite statue.

"There," she continued, "is shrouded the form of your father. Seek not to profane the sanctity of the pall, or live to dread its vengeance."

A mighty sob swelled up from the boy's yearning heart, and he faltered softly with quivering lips—

"My father—and dead!"

"Aye, aye, sent to the tomb by a wife's subtle hand."

Tom recoiled and gasped—

"Killed by my mother's hand?"

"I said not so."

"Yet—yet— yet you tell me my mother lives?"

"She does."

"And she did not kill him?"

"No, boy, an angel could not be more free from sin."

Every fibre in his frame trembled, and while the blood rushed from his heart, he said in low anguished accents—

"Miserable woman, am I—I a child of sin? Was my birth not in wedlock?"

"It was."

"Great heavens. What mean you?" he said wildly. "You tell me my parents live; tell me then that my father has been slain by his wife, and that wife not my mother—yet my mother lives, and I am legitimate."

She placed her hand upon the boy's shoulder, and looking into his dark eyes she drew him towards the lid, and said—

"Kneel boy."

He reverently knelt beside the body, and clasping the white cold hand between his palms sobbed—

"My father! my father! speak!—speak, if only one word, to your boy!"

Hot tears of bitter anguish fell upon the powerless hand, then it was carried to his dry, quivering lips.

Standing, silently watching the outpouring of a pent-up filial love, was the old woman, whose heart was hardened against humanity, marvelling at this display of feeling for one whose face the grief-stricken son had never yet seen.

"To him," she thought, "I will give the task of punishing the guilty. It will give a purpose to his life; and should he be able to work out the foul blot upon his name, then will I bring parents and child together."

"And then," she continued, exultingly, "shall the Lord of Mountsteven and his proud, handsome son sit in the home of their fathers."

The first transport of grief over, the young chief upturned his face and asked pleadingly—

"Uncover my father's head, that I may behold the lineaments for which my heart has so long yearned."

"I dare not," was her strange reply; "it is written in the future that you shall meet again, but at present you must be unknown."

"You will drive me mad. Can I not behold the face of my dead parent?"

"No."

"I will."

He sprang to his feet to pull the shroud aside; but before his hand could reach it the windows became darkened and the chamber was as black as though they had been buried in the bowels of the earth.

The young chief stood like one transfixed; there was so much of the supernatural in this, that he was for several moments spellbound.

From this state of feeling he was aroused by the voice of Sybil, and her words sounded weird-like and doubly solemn in the inky darkness of the charnel-vault, as she said—

"Now listen! Kneel, boy, and hear the strange story of the wrongs your mother has suffered."

With folded arms and compressed lips, he did as the old witch desired.

Half-an-hour passed, and still she spoke, and with her last words ringing in his ears, the hidden darkness passed away, and he again beheld the shrouded form of his father.

CHAPTER XCIX.

A CRUEL DEED.

WHEN Red Hand sighted a merchant ship, and gave orders for the guns to be run in and the vessel to assume a peaceful appearance, he was obeyed, and like vultures the pirates were ready to pounce upon the weak and helpless.

Twice they were chased by a British frigate, but owing to the sailing qualities of the Black Squall, they easily escaped the heavy pursuer.

Scarcely was the frigate hull down, when the outlines of another vessel became visible.

The pirate leader, after scanning her narrowly through his glass, turned to several of his men and said—

"A merchantman, by the cut of her sails."

All became bustle and confusion upon the deck at the intelligence; and crowding every inch of sail upon the Black Squall, they bore down upon the ill-fated ship.

The merchantman saw the destroyer, and made every effort in her power to escape.

Futile were their frantic cries and prayers to the Virgin, and when the black flag was run up to the pirate's masthead, there arose a scream of such utter hopelessness and despair, that the men who were as yet unused to lawless bloodshed shuddered at the cry.

There was no time given by the ferocious leader for reflection.

No sooner had the grappling-irons been thrown than Red Hand, unsheathing his sword, leapt on the stranger's deck.

There was no attempt at resistance save in one instance. This was an old merchant, who besides having a large amount of property on board, had a beautiful dark-eyed daughter.

She was standing by her father when the pirate crew poured over the side.

Red Hand's eyes blazed with passion when he beheld the young creature, and striding to her side, clutched her wrist.

Maddened at the sight, the old man raised the tomahawk which he had grasped when the pirate had first bore down on them, and made a down stroke at the pirate chief.

Quick as thought Red Hand stepped aside, and the next instant his blade was through the old man's body.

One convulsive throb the old man gave as the reeking weapon was withdrawn, and fixing his glassy eyes upon his horror-stricken child, he gasped feebly,

"Caroline, kill thyself, and hide my gold from them."

These words were his last, and the poor girl, without even staying to imprint a last kiss upon her only parent, was ruthlessly dragged away to the pirate ship.

The scene that now ensued beggars all description. The men who but a short time before would have at least scrupled at committing a cold-blooded crime, now equalled the most hardened of Red Hand's original crew.

Like demons they shot and destroyed the inoffensive crew.

The carnage, however, from its fearfully resolute character, was happily but of short duration, for in less than twenty minutes from the time when the pirates boarded the vessel the crew were slaughtered and thrown overboard.

Excepting the young girl, not a soul was spared.

Gloating over their prize, they rushed on board their own vessel, Red Hand retaining his hold of the beautiful captive.

By degrees, the heart-rending shrieks of the drowning and massacred passengers ceased, and the miscreant beat to quarters.

"Now, my lads," was Red Hand's address to the excited crew, "are all the valuables aboard?"

THE WAR CLOUD IN A STORM.

"All aboard, captain," responded the boatswain.

"Well, go ahead and settle that hulk."

A dozen men moved off in the direction of the side to execute the order, but Red Hand arrested them before they could quit the vessel by saying—

"Stay. Did you find any gold aboard ?"

"A few bars, captain."

"None in specie ?"

"None."

"There is some ?"

He turned to the young girl—

"Come, girl, tell me where the gold is hid of which your father spoke."

"Never, miscreant," was the girl's courageous reply.

Red Hand smiled.

"You hear that," he said to his crew, "can we make her tell us, do you think ?"

"Tie her to the mast," said a hoarse voice among the group.

This cruel proposition was repeated by many.

Red Hand stroked his silky moustache, and said—

"Upon an occasion like this, I always allow the men to take direction of affairs. Do with her as you will; the old man's gold is hidden somewhere, and she alone knows where it is concealed."

He stepped aside as he ceased speaking, and left the poor girl to the mercy of his savage crew.

Great mercy she received!

In a moment her hands were bound firmly to the mast, and a cry arose among the men for—

"Black Bill."

In answer to this a powerful negro made his appearance, a fellow whose countenance stamped him as belonging to the lowest order of his class.

"Here, Bill," said one, "touch her back with the cat; that'll make her answer."

"You better tell, or I'll scratch your back for you."

The girl, though deadly pale, turned her head and replied—

"Do with me as you will—I am bound by the will of my father. I shall never disclose the secret, not had I to suffer a thousand deaths."

One of the crew handed the cat to the brutal negro, who, tearing the girl's clothes off as far as the waist, passed his fingers through the thongs to separate them, and whirled the terrible instrument above his head.

"Tell 'em where de gold is," said the fellow.

Through the girl's clenched teeth came the single word—

"Never."

The negro looked towards Red Hand, who stood leaning upon his sword near the half nude girl, for the signal to commence.

The miscreant inclined his head, and said—

"One."

The rushing noise made by the terrible instrument as it clove the air followed the word—then with a dull thud the knotted thongs fell upon the girl's skin.

A shiver was seen to pass over the young creature's slender form as the knots were drawn across her flesh, but no sound escaped her lips.

"Two," said the pirate.

Again the rushing noise was heard—again the heavy thud, and when the blow had been given several black marks were visible upon the white shoulders.

"Three."

This time faint drops of blood began to flow slowly from the wounded flesh.

There was a pause as they listened for the girl's voice, but no sound came.

She stood like a beautiful statue—not even a muscle of her lacerated back moving under the terrible torture.

One by one the lashes were continued until they reached twenty.

By that time the poor girl's back was one mass ~ated flesh.

When the twentieth stroke was given the sufferer fell backwards, and one long scream of agony came from her lips.

With that cry her spirit had winged its flight; and the merciless wretch who had calmly witnessed her cruel murder turned upon his heel, saying coolly—

"Throw her carcase overboard. Curse her. She is the only woman I ever knew to keep her tongue quiet."

While the pirates were unfastening the body from the mast, one of them uttered a cry of delight—

"Look here! stuffed with shiners!" said he.

He raised the girl's long raven tresses as he spoke, and roll after roll of gold pieces were discovered.

And thus closed another scene of these audacious and remorseless men.

No design too daring for them to attempt, and no villainy too profoundly fiendish being wanting to carry that design into execution, Red Hand and his crew had achieved their victory; and they gloated over the result of their bloodshed and rapacity committed on board the merchantman, with no other feeling than as an easily-made addition to their ill-gotten booty.

In the rush for the fair division of the spoils, as Red Hand had promised them, and the confusion consequent upon the division, the swift approach of an armed vessel had been unnoticed by the pirates.

Suddenly, the deep voice of their leader aroused them, and to their dismay they beheld a corvette with the haughty flag of Spain floating at the stern.

A mad rush was made to cast loose the guns; but before this could be done a terrible broadside was fired from the Spaniard.

This was succeeded by another; then one of the pirates, who had been below at the magazines, rushed upon deck, his face as pale as death.

Springing upon the deck, he shouted—

"We are sinking! A ball has struck below the water-line!"

There was a terrible panic, and those who had been loading the guns left them and looked round in wild confusion.

The Spaniard had ceased firing, and was bringing the corvette alongside to board the sinking ship.

Amid this momentary silence, the wild roar of the ocean could be heard as the water poured in through a rent in the vessel's side.

The only man among that heaving mass of terror-stricken men who retained his self-possession, was the pirate leader, and when everything seemed lost, his voice, trumpet-like, was heard shouting—

"Back, back, all of you! are you fools or madmen? Arm yourselves! this vessel is sinking; there is another! We must take that or perish."

A wild cheer followed his words, and the pirates, forming a dense mass behind their leader, waited his command.

The vessel began to sway to and fro as the water filled her hold; the stern began to disappear rapidly.

This was seen from the corvette, and a cheer arose from the Spaniards who crowded her decks.

Red Hand, with compressed lips, and blazing eyes, was watching every movement of the Spanish ship.

Her commander, with more humanity than prudence, came close alongside the sinking vessel, and brought his vessel's stern, under the pirate's bows.

The corvette was the lower vessel of the two, but owing to the water having raised the other's bows, her prow was much higher than the Spaniard's stern.

Red Hand jumped upon the bowsprit, and waving his sword, sprang upon the astonished Spaniard's quarter-deck.

Too late the doomed crew came rushing forward to intercept the career of the fierce horde who came like a torrent upon the vessel.

"Form!" yelled the pirate, "Drive them into the sea!"

A fierce and bloody contest ensued; but piece by piece the Spaniards were driven towards the bows of their own vessel by the overwhelming numbers and desperation of their foes.

When the pirate-ship had disapppeared below the mystic ocean's surface, the Spaniards had been driven into the water, and Red Hand and his murderous horde had become masters of the vessel.

The shout of victory died away upon the conqueror's lips, for within ten miles of them an English frigate came sweeping towards their vessel.

CHAPTER C.

PREPARING FOR THE CRUISE.

WHEN the young chief returned to his followers, the morning sun was just gilding the tops of the trees, and the blithe song-birds were smoothing their plumage and carolling joyfully at the return of day.

Snowball gave a yell of delight when he beheld the chief emerge from the chapel, and, rushing towards him, he said gleefully,

"By gar, Massa Tom, I taught you had buried yourself in dare all dis time."

Tom heeded him not, but waving his followers back, walked slowly onwards, his mind filled with melancholy.

What passed at that strange interview was known only to Sybil and the young chief; but his followers whispered among themselves that from the hour he visited the chapel of the dead, he became strangely altered in his manner, silent, moody, and seldom speaking to those around him.

Yet in spite of the perilous life he led, and the heavy secret that now weighed upon his soul, he did not forget to execute a promise he had made to young Charley Phillips.

The boy had wished a letter to be conveyed to his sister when the Thunderer sailed, and Tom's messenger after many day's search found Ellen at the cottage of old Kate.

With the messenger came a stranger who desired to speak with Midshipman Tom, and when he saw him, his cheeks went pale and his limbs trembled.

There was nothing in the appearance of the stranger to cause the young chief to betray the emotion he did when that gloved hand was placed upon his shoulder—nothing to cause his face to flush and pale again almost at the same moment.

Nothing in all this, yet the boy felt a sharp delirious thrill enter his heart, and he could scarce refrain from seizing the stranger's hand and carrying it to his lips.

Midshipman Tom could not account for this strange feeling; he was ignorant there were natural ties between himself and the sable-clad stranger which might have caused it.

Moving as though under a spell, he followed the stranger until they stood out of earshot of the men.

Then his visitor partially raised his drooping hat, and revealed a pale, grief-stricken, yet handsome face.

That face the young chief thought he had seen before, yet when he knew not.

Then, thronging memories came quickly before him, and he remembered having often seen that sad face in his dreams.

The stranger spoke—

"I came," he said, "to bid you be careful of your life. A great danger menaces you, shun it as you would a pestilence, for your safety is dear to many, and, when the time comes, a bright and happy state awaits you. Farewell! we shall meet again; until then, remember!"

Tom's tongue was held mute with surprise.

When he could have answered, the stranger had disappeared behind a jutting piece of rock.

Acting upon an uncontrollable impulse, the young chief rushed forward, but fleet-footed as he was, the mystic being had disappeared.

He searched every crevice, but to no purpose, all trace of his visitor had passed away.

With a sad and moody brow, the young chief rejoined his followers; then they returned to the cave.

His mind pre-occupied by that strange warning, he sought the privacy of his own chamber, there to ponder and dwell upon every word and look uttered in that strange, rich voice, that had stirred the very depths of his soul.

In this self-communion he passed the greater part of the day.

The grim sentry, who paced outside the entrance of the chieftain's chamber, marvelled much at the strange orders he had received, and, leaning upon his weapon, he shook his head sagely, and muttered—

"He is not to be disturbed on any account. Well, I don't wonder at it;"

Although the young chief was thus moody, his band were not idle.

Tom's orders had been given to Snowball before he retired to the privacy of his own chamber.

Orders which the ebon lieutenant quickly carried out.

He had taken the greater portion of the band with him to the War Cloud, and all that day the din of hammers and the sound of preparations could be heard on board the vessel.

Among other improvements a long gun was placed amidships upon a pivot, which enabled it to be moved at pleasure.

Indeed, everything was in most perfect order—ropes neatly coiled, sails and deck white as snow, and every portion of the brass shone like burnished gold.

"I go fetch Massa Tom," he said. "He will tink sometink ob her now."

Midshipman Tom was soon on board, and Snowball's trouble was amply acknowledged by the words of praise which his chief bestowed upon the appearance of the ship.

His only care now was to lay in a necessary store of provisions, which Tom said should be for six months, in case of accident.

"Bery well, Massa Tom, it be on board in no time."

Tom soon after left the ship, and walked slowly under the beetling cliffs towards the cave.

A cry of agony arrested his steps, and as he looked around him to see whence it came, he beheld the stranger who had accosted him so mysteriously struggling to free himself from the grasp of one whom Tom recognised as one of the wreckers.

The swarthy scoundrel had the stranger by the throat with one hand, the other was raised, pointing a knife to his heart.

Tom saw the flash of the blade, but the wreathings and struggles of the two men prevented him from firing his pistol, and the stranger being stabbed by the wrecker, his body was thrown over into the deep.

Tom levelled his pistol at the wrecker in return, and missed the wrecker, who sprang back and gripped his knife.

But Midshipman Tom gave him no time to use it, and, with one straight lunge, he brought his foe disabled to the earth.

The young chief then dived in the water, but no trace of the murdered stranger could be discovered.

As he stood, pressing out the water from his clinging garments, he was overtaken by one of his mounted spies.

The young man drew rein, and bending low in the saddle, said, respectfully—

"I have news, sir."

"Affecting our interest?"

The spy bowed.

"Its import?" asked Tom.

"A great and terrible danger."

"Ha!"

The young chief thought of the stranger's mystic words, and could not repress this ejaculation of astonishment.

"You had the misfortune," the spy went on, "to deceive the Admiral of the fleet?"

"I did."

"He has reported the occurrence at headquarters, and in less than six hours a fleet will be in the bay.'

"More bloodshed!" muttered Tom.

"And," continued the spy, "simultaneously with the sailing of the vessels, a strong body of troops will come by land."

"To capture me, of course?"

"It would appear so, sir. for the troops will be accompanied by artillery and engineers, with powder, to undermine the stronghold and blow it into the air if you resist."

The young chief smiled.

"I will save them the trouble," he said. "How many hours?"

"Six, sir."

"Sufficient," said Tom, "quite, for my purpose, Bidder; you ride on to the cave, and rest, after your long journey."

The man bowed, gave his horse the rein, and was soon engaged in that very agreeable occupation of ministering to his own wants.

The young chief slowly followed his communicant, his brain busy with thought.

"They have been active," he muttered—"very active; but not active enough to capture Midshipman Tom, nevertheless!"

After he had arrived at the cave he found Snowball awaiting him. The black's face wore a look of troubled anxiety, and greeting his chief, said—

"I thought you got hurt, massa Tom. I heard de look-out say dat you had jump into de water. What de matter?"

"Nothing of particular moment, perhaps. Have you heard Bidder's report?"

"I hab, Massa Tom, and I tink de fight we shall hab will be a hard one for us."

"That's my opinion, too, if we do fight."

"Surely, Massa Tom, we no gib in?"

"Not exactly. I have no wish to dangle from the yardarm, have you?"

"I hab'nt, Massa Tom. No, anyting but dat."

"So I thought. Now, Snowball, we have much to do, and but little time to do it in."

"Yes, him all 'tention."

"Our first care must be Miss Laura."

"Xactly Massa Tom, dat am de first."

"I think that can be managed."

"How?"

"By removing her to the old house on the cliff."

"'Xactly; de bery plan. Nobody go dere, because they tink it haunted. Yah! Yah!"

The house mentioned by the young chief was a ruined mansion, one wing only being habitable.

This place an agent of Tom's had purchased some time before, the young chief foreseeing he would have to use another spot besides the cave in case of any formidable assault.

His anticipations had turned out correct—the hour had come for its use.

The ruined house and its wild grounds were the property of the young outlaw, although an old member of the band, together with his wife and family, were the supposed owners.

They had been put in there by Tom, to keep a number of rooms at all times ready in case of any emergency.

Nor was that all.

He had caused a long passage to be hewn from the cave to a cellar beneath the old building—a safe and speedy means of communication.

This explanation is recorded, that the events about to pass may be rendered clear to the reader.

"Summon the band," said Tom, to his dusky officer, "and let them remove the treasure to the vaults below the old house."

This operation was speedily commenced.

"Six hours," muttered Tom, when he was alone, "are already passed. I must be quick, or they will be here before I can get to the War Cloud."

He went into the chamber which was used by Laura Grey.

At the threshold he was met by the latter, whom he at once informed of his intended removal from the cave.

"Remove from here?" she said.

"Yes, and at once, Laura."

"Am I to accompany you," said Laura, "on board your vessel?"

"Not now, Laura. My expedition is one fraught with too much danger."

"Should you be wounded, who would watch and attend you as I would?" the anxious girl enquired.

"I must risk that, Laura. Ha! here comes the men to remove everything from your chamber. Come, dear one, follow me."

She was used to implicitly obey her young lover, and did so on the present occasion without a murmur.

When the men had completed their arrangements, he took Laura's hand and led her by the secret passage to the sea-gulls' tower, so named from its being built upon a rock, where those birds for centuries had congregated.

On their way several of the band passed laden with the treasures of the cave beneath.

The young girl marvelled much at the steep place they were ascending.

On arriving at the summit, to her surprise they were made to pass through a trap-door, when they were in a vast apartment, from the windows of which the sea was visible for many miles.

"I trust," said Tom, "you will find the place agreeable to you, after your long stay with—— Ha! by heaven, here they come!"

He broke off thus abruptly, as he beheld several vessels shaping their course towards the shore, mere tiny specks then, but to Tom's practised eye the faint outlines of several men-of-war.

Snowball was close by his chief. He had just ascended with a bale of silk upon his brawny shoulders.

The young chief thus addressed him.

"They are in sight, you see, Snowball."

"Nebber mind, Massa Tom, de cabe will be cleared out before dere hulls are up."

"I hope so," thought Tom, as he waved an adieu to Laura, and passed down the secret passage, followed by his lieutenant.

CHAPTER CI.

OVERTAKEN BY THE FRIGATE.

HERE and there floated pieces of the wreck, spars, bars, hencoops, and other loose *debris* of the sunken pirate ship.

With frantic eagerness, the Spaniards who had been driven overboard by Red Hand's crew, clung to these floating fragments, and prayed to the Virgin for strength to sustain them until the distant ship should arrive.

A gladsome spectacle to those poor wretches was the sight of that noble vessel as she came like an avenging spirit to chastise the evildoers.

But for the perilous position in which Red Hand was placed, their term of existence would have been short indeed.

The order to fire a volley of grape upon them had twice trembled on his lips.

His second officer read the meaning of those hateful looks, and as he passed the merciless savage, he said—

"Better leave them where they are, sir, because the frigate is sure to round to and take them aboard. It will give us a chance of getting away."

"Very well; but what are those fellows doing aloft?"

"Laying on extra canvass."

The lieutenant left the quarterdeck, and springing into the shrouds, gave a few hasty orders to the men aloft.

Like a baffled demon Red Hand stood on the quarterdeck, his eyes fixed upon the huge vessel, which every moment brought closer to them.

The corsair's eyes gleamed savagely at the white sails, and, with a fierce oath, he invoked a curse upon the luckless moment that brought him in contact with the Spaniard.

"Yardley!" he yelled to his first officer, "will the horrid tub carry any more sail?"

They were going through the water at nine knots, the frigate was making ten.

The officer looked at the already overcrowded masts, and shaking his head, answered—

"No, sir."

"Hang you all, for a set of lubbers, then that ship will be alongside in six hours."

"It will be dark by then, sir."

"Dark be hanged, send the carpenter on deck."

Red Hand knew there was but one expedient left. That, dangerous as it was, he had made up his mind to try.

He knew full well no mercy would be shown him by the man-of-war. Knew that, in all probability, his carcase would perhaps swing at the yardarm, should he be overtaken.

There remained but four hours between darkness. Could he keep out of range till then, there was a chance of escape. A remote one, certainly, but still a chance.

There was none as matters then stood, for the frigate's dark hull became higher every hour.

One short hour would bring her within range.

"Set your men to work," he said to the carpenter, "and cut the mast through."

The carpenter silently obeyed, inwardly wondering at the strange order.

Beneath the blows of the keen axe, the stout masts were nearly cut through, and only prevented from falling by the strength of the cordage.

There was a gleam of exultation upon the pirate's face as he beheld the success of his daring manœuvre.

The wind bellied out every inch of canvas the swaying masts carried, and the vessel plunged madly forward under this additional impulse to her sailing powers.

"We shall escape them now."

Scarcely had the words escaped his lips, before the boom of a gun came across the water.

The pirate chief laughed—a low, devilish laugh.

The shot tore up the water full twenty fathoms in the ship's wake.

"Fire away, you hounds!" said Red Hand, "you will soon see the last of this——Ten thousand furies, we are lost!"

In the midst of his exultation, the mainmast fell with a tremendous crash, slaying and crushing all who stood in the way.

The heavy weight of iron, wood, and canvas, crashed through the bulwarks, causing the vessel to careen over until her bright copper bottom gleamed in the setting sun.

Amid the shrieks and groans of the dying, the voice of Red Hand could be heard as he vociferated for those who stood spell-bound at the appalling sight, to cut away the wreck.

"Curse you all!" he roared, "for a set of white-livered curs. Cut it away, we shall still escape!"

He showed the example by hewing at the cordage with his sharp sword, and the men were soon at work beside him with axe and tomahawk.

"Bang!" came another gun from the frigate.

This time the heavy shot struck the vessel's quarters.

Red Hand turned savagely towards the coming vessel.

He saw, for the first time, that all hope of escape had gone.

Like a tiger at bay, he made up his mind not to yield tamely.

The guns were soon loaded to the muzzle with grape and canister, and the pirates stood with lighted matches, waiting the leader's orders to fire.

The frigate had ceased to fire, and with the glorious emblem of freedom floating in the sun-glow, she came hand over hand upon the captured ship.

Every eye was fixed upon the mighty vessel, and simultaneously a cry of joy came from the pirates' lips.

The frigate had suddenly paused in her headlong career, and rounded to, and those on board the pirate saw two boats drop like magic from her side, and glide swiftly towards the drowning Spaniards, who yet clung to all that floated of the wreck.

This cry of joy soon changed into one of dismay, for, contrary to their expectations, the frigate again came dashing forward, leaving her boats to follow when their work of mercy was completed.

Red Hand heard their half-suppressed cry, and stamping his foot fiercely upon the deck, he said, savagely—

"Stand by your guns, you shivering curs, and give it them close."

He had not time to say more, before the beautiful vessel was under his quarters, and a strong, manly voice cried out—

"Surrender, miscreant, or we'll fire into you!"

Red Hand's reply was to level a pistol at the speaker.

A flash—a report—and the frigate's officer fell on the deck—dead!

"Now," roared Red Hand, "fire! fire!"

From stem to stern the frigate's side was dotted with bronzed and manly faces, and this sudden hail of death-dealing missiles slew two thirds of those who had, but a few minutes before, been all life and ardour.

"Another like that!" roared Red Hand. "We can but swing, let us swing for something."

The misguided crew were soon busy at the guns; but, before they had time to load a thorough British "Hurrah!" burst upon their ears, the frigate yawed, and from her side twenty streams of fire belched forth.

Three-fourths of Red Hand's crew lay upon the deck after the terrible discharge, and the foremast fell by the board.

For several moments a white opaque mass of clouds hung over both vessels, and before it could roll away a hundred blue jackets poured upon the deck.

Resistance was useless.

THE MAST-HEAD MAN SIGHTS A SPANISH MAN-OF-WAR.

All who grasped a weapon were cut down by the angry sailors.

The remainder were at once secured, and placed in irons.

"Where is your villainous commander?" asked a grey-headed officer, who had led the boarders.

One of the captured crew pointed, silently, to Red Hand, who stood upon the quarterdeck, one hand grasping his sword, the other a loaded pistol.

The officer, with two seamen, went towards the savage miscreant.

"Deliver your sword," said the officer. "Surrender, "or I'll cut you down where you stand!"

Red Hand growled like a wild beast, and, dashing to the side of the vessel, made an effort to spring into the sea.

But a blow from the clubbed musket of a marine stretched him senseless.

Twenty glittering bayonets were raised to pin the miscreant to the deck; but the captain would not permit it.

A young midshipman came to Captain White, and saluting him, said—

"Let me be the first to congratulate you on the capture you have made, sir."

"How so, Mr. Rilcher?"

The midshipman pointed to Red Hand, lying senseless on the deck.

"There," he said, "lies the famous Derrick, the pirate!"

"Derrick!"

"Yes, sir. The miscreant! But we have paid dearly for it. The first and second mate of the frigate are slain by his hand, and altogether the loss she has sustained is forty-seven wounded and eleven killed."

"A bad day's work, Mr. Rilcher! Are the prisoners ready to be put in irons?"

"Quite, sir."

"Very well—then let the whole of them be placed below. And commanding the hatchway, do you have a couple of guns always loaded with grape, and two men over them with lighted matches."

"I will," said Mr. Rilcher; "and a dozen men will be sufficient for you to supply."

"Very well. Pass the word for the carpenters to come aboard, and rig jurymasts. You will never be able to get this craft in without."

CHAPTER CII.

THE WAR CLOUD AT SEA.

WHEN Snowball came to our hero with the intelligence that the cave was cleared, the masts of several ships of war could be seen sailing in a semi-circle towards the shore.

At the same moment, the sentry stationed upon the cliffs came running in with the news that a large cloud of dust was perceptible about two or three miles from his post.

"Did you," observed the young chief, "observe anything beside the dust?"

"I fancy I did, sir."

"What did it resemble?"

"Although it seems impossible, yet, sir, I could swear I saw the glitter of weapons when the sun shone across their march?"

The young outlaw bit his lips.

"It must," he said, "be the land force; therefore we have no time to lose. Yes," he added, as the bright colour flew to his cheeks, "I should like to give them battle—one shot, at least."

"Better not, Massa Tom," said Snowball, "case dey cut off our retreat."

"True. Let us get on board at once, then. Down, Rupert."

Rupert was the mastiff, which came bounding to his master's side, and stood gazing wistfully in his master's face.

The young outlaw stroked his glossy head, and calling Outlaw Ben, he said—

"Ben, go to the tower and stay there."

Ben's face became overcast with gloom at this order; he would have much sooner accompanied his chief in his expedition than have stayed behind.

"I wish you to stay behind," Tom added, "to protect Miss Laura—an honour I cannot confer so well upon any but you."

Ben's face brightened up at this remark.

The young chieftain extended his hand, which Ben eagerly grasped.

"May you be prosperous," he said, "and return safe from your journey!"

"Thanks, Ben."

He turned and left the spot, at once proceeding to the entrance of the cave.

"Are there any pickaxes ready?" he asked.

"Plenty," was the answer.

"Quick, then; fetch as many as you can here."

A dozen implements were soon brought to the spot.

Then Tom, pointing to a circular stone, said, "Remove that."

The stone was removed, and beneath it a large iron ring was perceptible.

The ring was attached to a plug, which being pressed, would admit the rushing waters of the ocean, and fill every part of the strange dwelling.

A stout rope was passed through the ring; then a dozen outlaws, after a few vigorous pulls, dislodged the plug, and the water with a subdued roar began to fill the rocky chambers.

"They will find it rather damp," said the young chief, laughing, as he stood outside, watching the eddying waters, "when they enter."

The outlaws smiled grimly at the young leader's coolness; but there were many angry looks, and many hands grasped their weapons as they passed from the cave to the vessel.

At this time the fleet was majestically rounding the point.

Tom fixed his dark eye intently upon them for a few minutes, and his face bespoke the wish at his heart.

"They have well timed their arrival," muttered Tom, partly to himself, "ten minutes later there would have been hard work upon the sands."

"Berry bad work," said Snowball, "and de War Cloud hab lost all her crew."

"I fear so, too," said Tom, "but to fly from a foe is gall to my spirits."

"So it am to mine, Massa Tom. Perhaps we catch 'em yet, when dey ain't all of a heap like dis."

"I trust so, Snowball. Is everything ready for a shot?"

"Ebery ting, Massa Tom.'

"Up with the anchor, then.

During the time the men were turning the windlass, Midshipman Tom took a mental survey of the great danger in which he was placed.

While he remained in the inlet he was safe, but emerging therefrom, even to half a cable's length, and her canvas spread, the War Cloud was full of danger.

The young chief calculated his chances of running the gauntlet, and at once made preparations for doing so.

Everything was made ready, and the guns double shotted.

Midshipman Tom sprang lightly to the deck, and walking quickly to the long gun amidships, said—

"I will fire the gun should it be necessary; set full every sail, Snowball; I long to be on the boundless deep."

The rattling of pullies and the clash of the ropes followed his words.

The sails hung idly for a few seconds, then as the wind caught them the craft glided out of the inlet.

Snowball was at the helm.

A deathlike stillness reigned aboard

Every face was turned towards the young commander, who stood calmly by the long gun amidships.

They had faith—these bearded men—great faith in their youthful commander, and although a double tier of guns grinned at them from the sides of the heavy man-of-war, they would have staked their lives upon the issue of the desperate manœuvre.

When the inlet was cleared the War Cloud s sails caught the freshening breeze, and like a thing of life she sped through the waters.

The moment the vessel became visible to the fleet a frigate manned her guns.

Tom found that a span of nearly two miles lay between them and his vessel.

In place of keeping close to land, and out of range of the enemy's artillery, the dauntless young leader had the prow of his vessel turned towards the last ship of the enemy's line.

This vessel was the frigate that had manned her guns, and yielding to the promptings of his nature he determined to give her a parting salute.

Those on board the frigate could not have been aware of his intention, for the crew remained idly looking over the side.

Suddenly a signal was sent up from Admiral Popham's ship.

A blue light.

Then the crew sprang to the guns.

Too late.

The War Cloud flew through the water, throwing up the spray under her bows like wreaths of smoke.

She was within range when the frigate's guns were manned, and the young chief sprang upon the long gun amidships, and shouted excitedly,

' Run up the banner. Stand by the larboard battery. Fire.''

The recoil of the guns shook the little vessel, and took the wind out of her sails. For several seconds she swayed to and fro, then the wind again caught her just as a double line of fire and smoke belched from the frigate's side.

"Give them another. Quick my lads," he shouted, as the iron storm came hurtling over his head. And that before they can get our range.''

For the second time the War Cloud's guns did their work.

Every shot told upon the large vessel. The hull being a fair and certain mark.

While the War Cloud, in consequence of lying so low in the water, had escaped scatheless.

Now was the time for action.

The bold young outlaw gave them no time to depress their guns, but running his vessel close beneath the frigate's stern he fired the contents of the long field piece through the state-room windows.

A smashing of wood and broken glass followed his well aimed shot, and the crew, in their enthusiasm, ran up the rigging and shouted defiantly,

"Hurrah for Midshipman Tom. Hurrah!"

Before the frigate could use her stern-chasers, and the enraged captain partly repay the audacious attack, the War Cloud, under every stitch of canvas her slender masts could bear, was out on the boundless waste of water, and soon beyond the reach of her pursuers.

———

CHAPTER CXIII.

THE SPANIARD.

IN one of the many small inlets which abound upon the shores of the western ocean, the War Cloud lay at anchor, every sail nearly furled.

It was a warm tropical night, and the hardy outlaws, overcome by the heat, were lying in all directions about the deck.

Snowball and the young chief seemed to be the only living beings on board, the former leaning upon his sword, and gazing wistfully at the crimson hued sun as it sank behind a low range of hills, he said—

"Even here, hundreds of miles away, I can see that pale face as it disappeared beneath the waters. Curses on that fell assassin for that blow which took away his life, and doubly curse my treacherous pistol for missing fire."

He became silent for a few seconds, and seemed lost in deep reverie, until his thoughts found vent in words.

"I would stake my life upon the truth of my conjecture," he said, "that that form I saw hurled into the sea, was the same that gave me that warning, pregnant with such mystic import? unmanning me by day, and rendering my nights nought else but torturing dreams and broken rest; and that, on the murdered man's finger, there glittered the very ring I saw upon my dead father's hand when he lay shrouded in the chapel of the dead.

He smote his forehead fiercely with his clenched hand, and began to hurriedly pace the narrow limits of the quarter-deck.

And well might the impulsive Tom chafe at the strange doubts and fears which beset him—uppermost at all times, the strange revelations Sybil had made.

She had left his mind dazed and filled with wonderment, and the inactivity he had endured for the last few days since he had left England, coupled with the enervating influence of a tropical climate, had added much to his mental disquiet.

He wanted activity—something to banish this awful *ennui*, and call other thoughts, other nerves, into play.

He would soon have all he desired.

A cry of an owl was heard among the rocks, announcing the return of the look-out, who had been watching the movements of a Spanish vessel, which Tom was anxious to encounter, but which had skulked in shore.

Tom and Snowball went towards the bow of the vessel to meet him.

His news was rather surprising, and told the young chief that he had no time to lose if he wished to capture the rich prize.

"Well, Alique," asked the young chief of the man as he stepped on board, "what have you seen?"

"Sufficient, sir," replied the man, "to cause m to believe that, unless we are pretty sharp, there is a Frenchman will be there before us."

The speaker was alluding to a French vessel, which had been seen from the War Cloud, and remarked upon by Snowbal¹ as being in search of the Spanish vessel.

"Ha!" said Tom.

"I was standing at the headland above," continued the look-out, "when I had a good view of both vessels. The Frenchmen I could see were busy at work muffling their oars and greasing the rowlocks of their boats."

"How did you see all this?"

"By the light of several battle lanterns, sir."

"Is the Spaniard keeping a good look out?"

"Yes, sir; and from what I can see, they were preparing for an attack."

"Well then," said Tom, "we must time our arrival at the Spaniard's side the same time, or perhaps a little latter than the Frenchman."

"Yes, massa Tom."

"It will be dark, and with muffled oars and without lights, we can easily approach the vessel.

"The Spaniards will be engaged with the Frenchmen on one side, we can get on board the other; and while they are fighting it will be an easy matter to secure the cargo, at least so much of it as we want."

"Yes by gar!" yelled Snowball; "dat will be de ting if we only do it."

"We can but try; there's only six boxes of gold dust that I want. If we cannot get them, we must fight—that's all."

"Both the French and the Dons, too?"

"Yes, and beat them, too—if possible."

The crew gave a suppresed murmur of approbation at this.

Tom waved his hand for them to be silent.

"Return," he said to Alique. "Watch the Frenchman well, and let me know every move."

The man touched his cap, and stepped nimbly over the bows; he slid down the anchor chain, and without scarcely leaving a ripple on the water, he swam noiselessly ashore.

CHAPTER CIV.

A MYSTERIOUS FOE.

.T was a magnificent day; a delicious breeze fanned the Don Jose's sails as the vessel lay becalmed upon the blue waters.

The Don Jose had parted company with the frigate two days previously, and, to the young midshipman's annoyance, he was now becalmed opposite the coast of Africa.

The pirates and their fierce leader were below in the orlop deck.

The hatches were open to permit what little air came on the stifling atmosphere to pass down to the crowd of seething humanity who lay half stifled with the heat and invoking the direst curses on their captors.

Young Mr. Rilcher was standing near the wheel, looking anxiously at the heavens, and silently praying for the wind to rise.

The pirates had twice attempted to surprise the little crew under him.

A bronzed, muscular sailor, about fifty years of age, came to the boy's side, and wiping his forehead, said—

"This is burning hot, and no mistake, sir."

"It is, Dick, certainly; stifling. But how must those fellows feel below?"

The old sailor started at the suddenness with which his name was pronounced by the young midshipman.

"Dick," repeated the boy, "I wish I had never undertaken this business."

"So do I, sir. Axing yer pardon for being so bold—to think that we should have lost four of our messmates in so strange a way; only think, sir."

"It is strange; two days on our passage—each day have we lost two of our number."

"Mortal strange, your honour."

They were both silent for several seconds.

And yet on examination of the prisoners' irons every day they were all found securely fastened.

What could it be?

What was the little band to think?

They had all seen the missing men turn in each night, and when the morning came, the hammocks were empty.

There was no trace of blood, no signs of a struggle, no noise had been heard!

Yet they had gone!

No wonder with this fearful mystery on board that the midshipman and the old sailor should stand gloomy and thoughtful.

"If I may be so bold," said the old seaman, the same evening, "would you mind me putting a little plan of my own into execution, to endeavour to find out this mystery."

"Anything you like, Dick," said the middy, with a sigh, "something must be done, or I shall go mad with this fearful fate hanging over us."

That night young Rilcher sat upon a coil of rope in a drowsy slumber. Three men out of the eight were on deck with him: two over the loaded guns, the other on the forecastle.

Old Dick was below watching.

Wearily the hours passed, twice the old tar had fallen asleep.

Three bells sounded. It wanted but one half-hour to daylight, and they were all yet safe.

The old seaman felt a weight taken off his head. The morrow would not tell the same dread tale; the little company would not again be thinned by the invisible hand.

While these thoughts were passing through his mind, there came upon the pent up air of the sleeping place a strange soothing perfume.

It was as though a million flowers had been distilled, and their perfume came under his very nostrils.

"Them flowers," he thought "smell very strong on the shore. I've heard they always do towards morning, but it's mighty pleasant in this reeking place to smell 'em."

Every moment the delicious aroma increased, and with it a sense of drowsines crept over the old seaman; his head fell forward and he slept a death-like sleep.

The bright sun was gliding the waters when he awoke.

Jumping to his feet, he rubbed his eyes and looked around.

Could it be so!

Impossible!

He stayed not, but rushed upon deck.

"Are they here?" he gasped to the young middy, "or has old Nick flown away with them?"

"Here, whom do you mean?"

"Ned Quilter and Bob Baker."

"No; are they not below?"

"No!" shrieked Dick, "their hammocks are empty. Great God, Mr. Rilcher, this is awful."

The old sailor's words brought the remainder of the watch to his side, and, with pale faces and blanched lips, the whole party went below.

There the terrible reality came with crushing force to their brains.

Five men had retired to rest that night, three only were found in the morning.

A chilling gloom fell upon them, and each looked into his messmate's face and wondered which two would be next.

When night came again, every nerve in old Dick's body relaxed, and his mind became a complete chaos.

Young Rilcher bade him cheer up.

"For," said he, "we shall yet find out that the ruffian who lately commanded these pirates is at the bottom of this mystery."

Old Dick shook his head thoughtfully.

"May be, sir," he said, "but I can't see how he can, when his hands have not been out of the irons since we had him on board. And yet, Mr. Rilcher."

"Well, Dick."

"Didn't I tell your honour of the strange smell that came into the ship when I was keeping watch over those poor fellows that are gone?"

"A smell, Dick?"

The young middy's face bore a troubled look.

"Dick," he said, at length, "I recollect you did tell me of it. I myself recognised it, but that was a perfume that can have nothing to do with our mystery."

"P'raps not, your honour."

"You were saying, Dick," continued Mr. Rilcher, "that in four days there would be none of us left, and those pirates would have the ship again."

"I was, your honour, and it must be so, if we continue to go off like this."

The young midshipman's face bore as brave a look, as ever shone upon a hero's face, as he asked,—

"Dick, are you afraid of death?"

"I, your honour? Lord bless you no! Man or boy I never feared it for six and thirty long years,— why should I now? But why ask me?"

"Well," said Mr. Rilcher, "call the crew up.'

Old Dick, with a wondering look upon his face, went for his companions, and when they stood round their gallant leader, the youth said—

"Now, my lads, I want your advice. I need not tell you that in spite of our vigilance, we are all doomed to die before our time."

"It seems so," said the men one and all.

Young Rilcher proceeded—

"Death would be far preferable to this suspense."

"It would, sir," said two of the men.

"Then let us meet it like men, not stay until we suffer an ignominious one by the hand of these pirate miscreants. Listen to me, my lads, let us this night baffle them. This vessel and all on board shall be far below the ocean's surface, they shall not cut us off and live. Are you willing?"

"We are, sir, we are."

"Very well, disperse, while I write an account of all that has passed; some vessel will fish up the bottle I shall put it in. They will say at home we died for our king and did our duty."

He went below to pen the dispatch.

By the feeble light of a small oil lamp, the devoted boy penned an account of the mystic fate that had befallen six of the crew under his charge.

He also gave in plain language the determination he and his crew had come to respecting the vessel and his prisoners.

Then he rolled the well filled sheets of paper into as small a compass as possible, and passed them down the neck of an empty bottle, which he securely corked and threw into the sea.

"'Tis done," he muttered, "and I feel more at rest."

Still there was a heavy dulness over him, and he could not prevent his mind wandering to a sweet little English cottage, where he knew his sad fate would throw its blight for once and for ever over a loving mother and sister.

The coming of old Dick broke the painful bias of such contemplation.

He was about to speak, but old Dick placed his fingers to his lips to enjoin silence.

"Mr. Rilcher," whispered the old tar, "it's too late."

"What is too late, Dick?"

"The scuttling of the ship.'

"What do you——"

"Hush, ah, the whole of these devils are getting the irons off; some are at liberty and soon will be on deck."

"Where have you been all this time? why not have scuttled the ship?"

"Prevented by the position the pirates had taken, your honour."

"Then there is another plan yet—I will fire the magazine."

"Too late again, sir; the pirates are guarding it."

The young middy smote his brow.

This was a turn of events he had not anticipated.

He soon became cool, and between his teeth he said—

"I will baulk them yet. You, Dick, take one of the guns, I will take the other, and we will at least send some of them to their last account before we surrender."

The old tar shook his head.

"It is no use, sir," said he, "King George would preserve valour such as yours for a much nobler purpose. To serve our God, our king, and our country is not to commit murder, which your act would be. No, sir, we must escape, everything is ready for us."

Even in spite of this honest reasoning of old Dick, the young midshipman declined leaving the ship in possession of the miscreant crew; so Dick, seeing his persuasive powers did not serve him, watched his opportunity, and catching young Rilcher in his arms, sprang into the sea with him.

Not a moment too soon.

For Red Hand by this time had released his hands and was rushing on deck.

"Run a gun out here, they are escaping," was his first and hurried order.

That order was too late. Old Dick and his charge were in the boat, which was cleaving the water like an arrow.

Red Hand was once more master of the vessel he had gained with so much bloodshed, and with an impious oath swore he would blow up vessel and crew should he be ever taken again.

CHAPTER CV.

AN UNEXPECTED MEETING.

WITH the agility of a mountain goat, Alique scaled the precipitous rock, and laid himself upon its summit.

He had not been long in this position, when his attention became rivetted upon the moving lights that were held over the Frenchman's side.

By their faint gleams he could discern a number of men going over the sides, the lights gleaming upon the skeans or cutlasses, and the bright laced hats of the officers.

He almost held his breath.

Presently the lights were put out as if by magic; and the spy, placing his ear to the sound, could faintly discern the ripple of the waters, as the boats glided away from the vessel's side.

"They are off," thought Alique, "I must out their strength."

By clinging to the tough vegetation that grew thickly over the face of the rock, he was enabled to reach the other side before the boats had left the inlet.

Prudently hiding behind a mass of thick underwood he was enabled, by the aid of the twinkling starlight, to make out the size of the boats, which, ghost-like, passed within a few yards of where he stood.

From their size, the experienced outlaw was enabled to make a near guess of the number of men on board.

He waited until the last boat had passed out into the open sea, then walking into the water, he struck out in their wake.

Alique's boldness nearly cost him his life, for he had not gone above twenty yards when a voice sang out sharply— "Qui vive!"

It was a French marine who had been stationed near the mouth of the inlet to prevent their vessel from being surprised.

Alique became stationary in the water, and listened attentively for what he supposed would be the next movement—the clicking of a pistol or a musket lock.

He was disappointed—perhaps agreeably so, for no sound, save his own breathing, disturbed the stillness.

Alique was not to be deceived. He thought, and thought rightly—that the man was listening for the noise made by a person swimming.

"Not this time, mounseer," muttered Alique, "you must eat more frogs before you can catch me so easily."

He waited for several moments, then thinking that his chieftain would be anxiously waiting his return, he again extended his arms, and began swimming forward.

He had not made more than two strokes when the same voice roared out—"Qui vive."

"Go to the devil," muttered the hardy outlaw, as he went swiftly forward, "who do you think can wait here like a log for you to fire at."

"Qui vive," again sounded from the shore.

Alique dived.

Well for him he did so, for the third challenge was immediately followed by a rushing sound through the air, and then something struck the waters within a few inches of the place where Alique had disappeared.

Too cunning to fire either musket or pistol, and thereby create an alarm, the Frenchman had skilfully hurled a sharp barbed harpoon in the direction of the unseen swimmer.

So close did the missile fly to its mark, that the handle touched Alique's fingers as it passed downwards.

"This won't do," was his reflection, as he rose to the surface, "he may have another or two left. I must settle him."

MIDSHIPMAN TOM STILL CONTINUED THE PERILOUS ASCENT.

He kept under the water until he reached near enough to feel the sand beneath his feet.

Then he stooped and crawled quietly upon his hands and knees toward the place he supposed the sentry would be standing.

A rustling among the leaves caused the stout-hearted fellow to pause.

The next instant the sentry came within six feet of him, and from what Alique could make out in the dim light, he seemed to be peering into the darkness.

Like a tiger preparing for a spring, Alique crouched, and as the man came slowly on he gave one bound and closed with him.

The outlaw's strong grip choked back the cry of alarm that rose to the Frenchman's throat.

A savagely muttered oath in the Saxon language, a slight scuffle, followed by a plunge in the quiet waters, then all became still.

The Frenchman had paid with his life for his vigilance in guarding the little islet.

Alique ran swiftly along the bank, and soon reached his chief's vessel.

He was about to gain the deck by climbing the cable, but ere he had gone a yard, a lowly-spoken challenge caused him to pause.

"Who comes there?"

With the words, Alique heard the ominous click of a pistol lock.

He knew the strict discipline carried on in the ship, and promptly answered—

"A friend."

"Stand, friend," was the stern response, "and give the countersign."

"Fourteen fathoms by the line."

"Advance, all's well."

Alique was soon upon the deck, and the look-out coming towards him, remarked—

"There's something afloat—the chief has given strict orders to-night."

"So it would appear. Where is he?"

"The chief?"

"Yes."

"At the side, waiting till the boats are lowered. You had better be sharp, or you will miss him."

Alique ran quickly towards the stern, and met the young chief coming from his cabin, when he saw Alique, he asked impatiently—

"Well, any fresh news?"

"Yes, sir, the Frenchman's boats are on the way."

"How long is it since they started?"

"Ten minutes as near as I can judge."

"Did they take any men?"

'Yes, sir—I should think nearly all they had on board."

"Send Snowball aft."

"Yes, sir."

He found the black lieutenant at the side, and communicated his chieftain's order.

"Want me," muttered Snowball, "what de debbil up now, I wonder?"

He went to ascertain, and was electrified by the bold scheme the daring boy had determined upon putting into execution.

"Snowball," the young buccaneer said, "I intend to cut the Frenchman's cable, and spike his guns before we visit the Spaniard."

"By gar," said Snowball, after a pause, "you take my breff away, Massa Tom, by gar you do."

"How is that?"

"How am dat? Why you tink we able to do both?"

"It must be done."

"Dat right, Massa Tom; you say it be done, and it will."

The young chief smiled.

He was in his heart secretly gratified at the wondrous power his words had over the lawless crew under him.

Snowball stood rubbing his woolly head, and weighing well the chances they had of having a cannon shot dropped into their boat from the man-o'-war.

"By gar," he thought, "Massa Tom am a perfect debbil. Him no stop at anything, fancy him no content with the chance ob getting the plunder, while de oder two fight, but he must go and do some mischief to the Frencher. Well, him know best— by gar, I stick to him anyhow.'

He was disturbed in his reflections by the young chief.

"Come, Snowball," he said, "we have no time to lose."

The black giant ran forward and accelerated the men's movements, by calling them

"A set of lazy debbils."

At which rebuke the outlaws smiled good-humouredly, and began to tumble into the boats.

The young chief was the last to seat himself; he took his place in the foremost craft, and with Alique at the helm, they started silently towards the huge man-of-war.

"Lucky I stopped that fellow's gab," thought Alique, as they pulled passed the place where he had thrown the Frenchman into the sea.

The remaining boats followed the swift gig quietly, and by low whispers, the chief's orders were circulated among them.

"Pull," he said, "close alongside the Frenchman, the gig and pinnace upon the larboard side, the cutter upon the starboard; creep into the ports, if they are open, and spike the lower deck guns, if they are not, open them, and be quick about it. Those who linger will be left behind, for I shall cut her cable and pull off at once."

The men took these peremptory orders as a matter of course, and knew full well that should they linger over their task, he would leave them behind as promised.

Like so many ghosts, the outlaws crept up the vessel's sides, and with the exception of gagging a drowsy marine, they effectually spiked the whole of the lower deck guns.

This done, they as quietly regained the boats, and awaited their chief's order to leave.

He was with Snowball in the gig, and while the men were spiking the guns he cut the cable.

Not content with this, his daring spirit prompted him to glide to the vessel's stern, and enter the cabin windows, one of which, unfortunately for the French captain, stood open.

He accomplished this feat by standing upon Snowball's huge shoulders. This brought his knees level with the window. To draw his lithe form up and spring inside was the work of a moment.

Snowball's heart sank when he saw the daring boy disappear; he felt sure some injury would befall him. It would had he been discovered.

Luckily, the cabin was untenanted, and the young chief, prompted by a mischievous spirit, upset the tables and placed the books and papers in the stove.

A handsome gold watch hung against the wall this, with the French captain's cocked hat, dress sword, and his commission, which Tom found in one of the table drawers, he transferred to his own keeping.

"They may be useful some day," he thought, "one never knows."

The gallant boy was correct. They stood him in good need, when he least expected it ; but more of that anon.

He handed the cocked hat and sword to Snowball, the medals and commission were placed in his jacket pocket.

Tom glanced round the cabin to see if he could do any further mischief, but he was called away by Snowball, who scrambled to the window and said energetically—

"Come, Massa Tom, you'll be cotched as safe as——"

"Here, catch," said the young chief, throwing a heavy mounted Damascus scimitar to Snowball.

The black clutched it eagerly, his eyes expressing the delight he felt at the receipt of his welcome present.

"It's a beauty, Massa Tom," he said, when they were gliding softly from the vessel's side, "and a big one, too. Where you get it ?"

"From a number that hung against the wall," the young chief replied, "I expect the Frenchman took it from some Algerine by it's make."

"Spect so too. By gar it not taken from dis chile while——"

"Hush, steady, there is the cutter. Rest on your oars ; they are not a fathom from us."

Every bearded face was lowered, until they came level with the boats gunnel, and in the gloomy light they could discern some large dark looking objects in front of them.

Tom placed his hand upon Snowball's shoulder and whispered—

"They cannot have finished this affair so quietly."

"S'pects not, Massa Tom."

"What can it mean, if——," he added, his dark eyes flashing fire, "they have despoiled the ship, I will wrest it from them, were they four times as strong."

"No 'casion for dat. I spect they hab lose dere way, Massa Tom, unless—but no, dat not it."

"Unless what ?"

"Well, unless they are going to try de War Cloud first, dat all."

The young chief laughed quietly and remarked, "Indeed."

The outlaw's boats were lying motionless upon the water, and the young leader, going to the bow of the boat, took a long survey of the French flotilla.

"They must have lost their way, "he said at length, "look, they are nearly out of sight."

"S'pected so, Massa Tom, what we do now ?"

"Follow them," was the boy's answer; "pull gently, my lads, we have plenty of time."

The oars dipped noiselessly into the water, and like silent phantoms the outlaws glided onward.

Onward, until the mouth of the inlet was gained ; then the rowers rested on their oars.

There were a few minutes of painful anxiety, as they waited for the sounds of conflict—a feeling that soon changed to one of feverish daring, as the loud boom of a gun, followed by the rattle of small arms, broke the stillness of the night.

The daring young chief's sword leapt from its scabbard, and standing up in the bow of the leading boat, he called out in a low voice—

"Pull—pull for your lives."

Like reeds, the stout blades bent in the water, and the boats gradually making way, were soon rushing through the water.

They needed no guide to show them the vessel— the fierce sounds of battle and the flashes of firearms pointed out, but too well, where the overmastered crew yet gallantly strove to beat off the armed body of men who sought to gain a footing on her deck.

The French boats had boarded on the larboard side. Tom, with his men pulled to the starboard.

It was evident to the outlaws' practiced ears, that the attacking party were getting the worst of it, and to their amazement, just as they had fastened their boats to the guess ropes which hung over the vessel's side, an unmistakeable British hurrar greeted their ears.

Snowball pricked up his ears, and remarked—

"Dat English shout, and no mistake."

Before Tom could reply, a voice on the deck above them cried out—

"Give it to the frog-eaters ! Pitch them overboard, there for'ard !"

"Captain Dragon's voice, by all that's good," said Tom, springing into the chains, "follow me, lads."

Tom was over the bulwarks before the words were out of his mouth.

It nearly cost him his life, for the captain of the Thunderer, thinking he was attacked upon the other side, sprung towards Tom, and levelled a pistol at him, at the same time shouting to his men—

"Slew a gun round here. I'll be —— if I give in to six times as many frog eaters."

The pistol ball whistled close by Tom's head, and before the redoubtable Captain Dragon had time to draw another, Tom was close to him.

They recognised each other simultaneously, and Captain Dragon said—

"Midshipman Tom, a better friend I could not meet at this moment. But how the devil did you get here ?"

"The same as yurself—tell you more anon— look out there for'ard—they are coming over the side ! Follow me ! Hurrah ! Midshipman Tom to the rescue ! "

His men repeated the cry, and like an irresistable avalanche, they threw themselves against the Frenchmen, who had gained a footing upon the Thunderer's deck.

The accession of Tom's band made the gallant crew of the Thunderer about equal in number to that of their opponent.

The fight did not last long.

The French captain, thinking he had pitched upon a ship manned with fiends, called his men from the conflict, and scrambled to his boat.

The darkness of the night prevented Captain Dragon from firing upon the fugitives, who, with many *sacres* at the mistake they had made, pulled with all possible speed away.

"To think," muttered the captain, as he bound up a wound in his left arm, "that I should have attacked those English dogs instead of the Spaniards. *Sacre*, but I'll be revenged!"

"Now," said Captain Dragon, when the Frenchmen had been driven from his vessel, "how in the name of all the imps in sulphurdom, did you come here?"

"A mistake, I expect," said Tom. "It was the Don I intended to visit."

"The Don?"

"Yes. You seem surprised, do you know her."

"Not yet," said Captain dragon. "I want to."

"What! you came here to—to——"

"To wait for the Spaniard. Did you?"

"I did. This seems strange that I should have mistaken your vessel for her."

"Not at all."

"You were disguised, then."

"I was," said Captain Dragon, "and effectually, it seems."

Snowball, who stood by his chief's side, burst into a fit of laughter.

The two captains turned towards him inquiringly.

"Yah! yah! yah!" Snowball went on, "I nebber heard better den dis."

"Than what, you black devil?"

"Why, dis: you come here wid de Spaniard's rig; Massa Tom take you for him, and you come to catch de berry vessel him take you for."

"Well?"

"Yah! yah! by gar, dat not all."

"Let's have the remainder," said Captain Dragon, pettishly, "or you will roll down your own throat."

"Just dis: de Frencher, he come here for same ting, and mistake you, too; but he get de wust ob it.

"Hang him," muttered Captain Dragon, "he didn't; he's disabled about a dozen of my crew."

"It strikes me," said Tom, laughing, "that we have made a pretty mess of it, amongst us."

"I'm of your opinion," said Captain Dragon: "and I would not give a yard of old rope for either of our chances of handling a doubloon belonging to the Don; it might have been different, had not that frog-eating gentleman brought his men here."

"How?" asked Tom, "the Spaniard has not yet arrived."

Captain Dragon laughed outright.

"My young friend," he said, "I must correct you, the Don by this time has safely landed his cargo, and is loading up with negroes instead."

"What, on this part of the coast. Surely there is no trade to be—"

"Stop—exactly four miles from this inlet there is a populous town, and the old rascal who governs it does quite a snug little business in black flesh."

Snowball's face bore a look, when he heard these words, that boded no good to the governor.

"It is there," continued Captain Dragon, "that our friend the Don lies moored, and it was my intention to have helped him unload to-night, had not the coming of that swarm of Frenchmen prevented me."

"Is it too late now?" asked the young chief, who felt more than ever a desire to possess the Spaniard's wealth.

"Too late—yes, by the time you reached there the cargo would be safe under lock and key."

"Where?"

"In one of the iron sheds near the wharf."

Tom drew Snowball aside, and held a whispered consultation with his black adviser. When it was over, he said to Captain Dragon—

"Would it be impossible to get at this store?"

"Not impossible, but useless."

"Why?"

"Because the doors are impregnable, and a strong guard of savages is always stationed there."

"You do not intend to make an attempt."

"No, Tom, once bit twice shy. I tried it some years ago, when my blood was a little hotter than it is now."

"The result?"

"Not encouraging, I can assure you; there were only two escaped, I was one, my coxswain the other. We managed to overcome the guard except one, he slipped away, and began to hammer a gong, and to this delightful music, no less than six hundred black devils surrounded us. You can guess the result."

"I can—but shall make the attempt to find my way inside."

Captain Dragon gazed at our hero as though he doubted his senses.

"I am serious," said Tom, "quite serious."

"Then," said Captain Dragon, grasping him by the hands, "I shall bid you farewell for ever."

"Nonsense, my career is not over yet."

"You know not the danger of the——."

"Danger," laughed Tom, "danger, I would not care a straw for an expedition unless well seasoned with danger."

"You will have plenty, more I fear, than will be well for you if you undertake this rash design."

"I shall do so."

"I am sorry to hear it. I feel it will be useless for me to try and dissuade you, so farewell, and a safe issue out of the hornet's nest."

"Can you give me any directions for reaching this delightful spot?"

"Yes. The nearest and safest is by land."

"By land?"

"Yes. Captain Dragon pointed towards a towering rock that flanked the inlet. "From the point of that rock to the bay is one straight line; you cannot miss it. Keep through the jungle for a mile, and you will see the lights hanging from the mastheads of the vessels—slavers, by their build—that are in the bay."

"Thanks. Will you do me a service?"

"A thousand, my dear boy."

"One will do."

"Name it."

"Look after the War Cloud until I return."

"I will. If—if—"

"I do not, you would say."

"Yes, I fear it will be so."

"Well, should such be the case, take the men home in your vessel, and burn the War Cloud to the water's edge."

"I will; but it will grieve me to destroy the little beauty."

"You must. No other than myself shall ever tread her deck. In friendship's name, should I fall, I ask you to do it."

Captain Dragon grasped his hand, and replied—

"In friendship's name, it shall be done. I would accompany you, but I have this little account to settle with that French gentleman."

"You will not find it difficult."

"How so? He has a large vessel and active crew."

"Correct; but, unless I am mistaken, the man-of-war is adrift and unmanageable by this time."

"Captain Dragon's face gleamed with pleasure, as he asked—

"How know you this?"

"I cut her cable," said Tom, "and disabled the steering gear before visiting you."

"You have done me a great service," said Captain Dragon; then, turning to his first officer he resumed—

"Man the boats, Mr. Phillips—we have no time to lose!"

Young Charley sprang to the deck and passed the word, and while the boatswain's shrill whistle sounded, he buckled on his sword, muttering—

"I'll pay that black-looking Frenchman for knocking me down with a hand-pike, or my name is not Charley."

"Ax your pardon, sir," said one of the men, accosting him as he walked aft, "are we going to pay out that Frencher?"

"Yes, Thompson, I am glad to say we are."

"Thankee, sir; cuss 'em, the lubbers; they'll get it now, leastways, if we can get at 'em."

Thompson went back to his messmates with the good news.

Harry went aft to his superiors, who stood by the side bidding Tom farewell.

There was a something glistening in the rough seaman's eyes as he bid the gallant boy good bye.

Something which brought no discredit to his manhood; for he loved the dark-eyed manly young chief, as only a brave man can love a congenial spirit.

"Good bye," said Tom, returning the pressure of his friend's hand. "One more question before we part."

The other's voice was husky as he asked—

"What is it, my dear boy?"

"What ever made you," said Tom, "show me your heels when I gave you chase?"

"Before I entered the inlet?"

"Yes."

"Well, I'll tell you it was not fear."

"I know that."

"I thought had I stopped to give you battle, the sound of our guns would have put those gentlemen at yonder port on the *qui vive*."

"You had no suspicion of my identity?"

"Not the least, although I thought the rakish look of your vessel familiar; but I put you down for one of the swift slavers that abound in these waters."

"Swift, are they?"

"Yes, I doubt if even your light-heeled beauty could catch one of them."

Tom smiled as he answered—

"Well, if I escape this affair, I'll try and overhaul a few of them."

They parted, Tom, Snowball, and six of the band, upon the enterprise.

Captain Dragon and boats to repay the Frenchman for their visit.

CHAPTER CVI.

SAVED.

THE boat which contained the remains of the prize crew soon pulled out of reach of the Don Jose's guns.

Once safe from that danger, the brave old tar succeeded in calming the young midshipman's excitement.

Reflection—cool reflection—followed, and he was compelled to grasp Old Dick's hand, and thank him for saving his life.

Without a compass, except the pale stars, they felt it would be useless to wear out their strength in pulling the heavy boat through an unknown sea.

This course was decided upon after a short conversation between Old Dick and his young officer.

"You are right, Dick," said the middy, "it is useless to wear ourselves out by rowing in the dark; let the boat drift, perhaps chance may befriend us."

"I hope it may, sir; anyhow, we are safe for some time, unless a storm should arise."

"Safe, Dick."

"Safe from starvation, sir; I have taken care to have the boat well stocked with provisions, and in case we should run short, there is half a dozen muskets and plenty of powder and shot to bring down as many sea birds as we shall want for the next month."

With a greater feeling of security than they had felt when on board the Don Jose, the little crew arranged themselves for a good night's rest, Old Dick taking the first turn at watching and his place at the rudder.

That night passed away, and the next day came, and the man-of-war's men still allowing the boat to drift, looked out very anxiously for land, or a passing ship.

But evening came and neither had been seen.

With hopeful hearts for the morrow, they passed the second night.

The morrow came, and about day-break Old Dick was standing in the bow of the boat, anxiously scanning the horizon, suddenly he exclaimed—

"A ship!"

This gladsome cry awoke the sleepers, and in a dreary manner they repeated—

"A ship—where?"

"Listen," said old Dick, placing his ear as near as possible to the water without touching it, "listen, mates, and you will hear."

Every living soul suspended their breath, and listened for several minutes.

But all was silent.

"Well, messmates," said the old sailor, "though everything is quiet now, I can swear I heard the bos'in's whistle of some ship, and that ship not far away."

But old Dick was rather in advance of the fact when he stated he heard the bo's'n's whistle, for suddenly a rushing sound caused them all to start in the boat, and an exclamation of joy escaped their lips.

It was the sullen roar of the sea as it surged against the bow of a huge ship.

"Out oars!" shouted the middy, "it is the back wash of the waves—pull—pull."

The boat had now shot twice its length ahead, when a huge mass passed within this distance of them.

It was hull of some mighty vessel, looking still larger in the mist which surrounded every object.

And as the boat rocked to and fro they could hear the wind rushing among her sails and cordage.

Not a moment was to be lost.

Impelled by the wind she would soon be out of reach or hearing.

"Rest on your oars," said the middy. "Now, together."

Then in one voice came the cry—

"Ship ahoy!—ship ahoy!"

An interval of a moment; then came the response, "Ahoy!—where are you?"

"Lay to," shouted young Rilcher, "you are leaving us behind."

They could hear the rattle of the blocks and creak of the ropes as the huge vessel rounded to.

At the same instant the vapours, as though by magic, rolled away, and the sun burst forth with glorious brilliancy.

And what a joyous shout broke out from these grateful wayfarers, as they beheld the vessel lying motionless a cable's length from them.

It was the glorious old frigate, the Avenger, and they beheld a score of well-known faces over the side.

A few strokes brought them alongside, and with beating hearts they soon stood on the gallant old frigate's deck.

The explanations given by young Rilcher were listened to gravely by the kind-hearted captain, and when old Dick mentioned the desperate resolve the young middy had formed, he shook his head and said—

"I am glad, Mr. Rilcher, you did not carry that project into execution. England cannot afford to lose her men in that manner. You have done all that became you as an officer. You shall receive thanks—perhaps more—from the proper quarter."

The proud boy retired with a flushed face and happy heart, and was soon among his young companions in the gun-room recounting his adventures since he left them.

The captain repeated the story; and among the group of officers who stood upon the quarter-deck there was not one but felt eager to grapple with the swarthy miscreant, Red Hand.

The captain of the Avenger pondered for a few minutes when he had finished the narration, then addressing his officers, he said—

"Gentlemen, we must forego our intention of finding the French frigate; for I swear never to unbuckle the sword from my waist, or drop anchor until I meet this barbarous villain again. When I do," he added, "he will not escape my vengeance. Gentlemen, are you with me?"

"We are!" was the general response; "we swear not to rest until our men are avenged!"

The Avenger was soon upon the track of the ruthless pirate, whose total destruction would satisfy the angry officers and crew.

CHAPTER CVII.

THE TORNADO.

WITH fearless hearts and bared weapons, Midshipman Tom and his companions took their path through the thick jungle.

The night, in place of growing brighter, increased in darkness, and every instant a startled beast of prey, disturbed in its lair, would give out its monotonous growl, and slink farther into the wilderness.

Regardless of the presence of these troublesome and fierce animals, Tom and his party went

MIDSHIPMAN TOM AND SNOWBALL MENACED BY A NEW DANGER.

resolutely on, frequently having to cut a passage with their sharp broad-bladed weapons.

They had gone nearly a mile without catching sight of the lights Captain Dragon had mentioned.

Tom halted his party under a huge tree.

"Snowball," he said, "what are we to do now?"

Wait a little, Massa Tom, and I will tell you."

The African sheathed his knife; then, by a vigorous spring, he seized the end of a long branch of the mighty tree under which they stood.

The limb bent nearly double under his iron grasp, and seating himself astride, as near the end as possible, said—

"Dis de way um go up tree in my country."

He gave himself an upward jerk as he spoke, and the supple branch sprung back to its place.

In its swift rebound Snowball was thrown sharply upward, which he took advantage of by springing on to a higher branch.

This he repeated several times, until he reached the top, when he gave a yell which astonished his companions.

Then they could distinguish the words—

"Right, Massa Tom—two, three, four lights 'bout two points to nor'ard from dis."

Before Tom could answer, he heard his trusty friend descending the tree.

He was not halfway down when the wind, which had hitherto been as gentle as the zephyr, increased.

Then a terrible clap of thunder seemed to shake the earth beneath their feet; closely following came a flash of lightning that, at the moment resembled a livid sheet of fire.

Following this came the rain in huge drops.

High among the noise of these warning elements, Snowball's voice could be just heard.

"Down, ebery one ob you!" he was shouting. "Tis the tornado coming. Down, for your life; but not near dis tree."

This was several times repeated before the outlaws could well comprehend the dangerous position they were in.

Snowball sprang down from the tree, and taking the young chief in his arms, cried out to the others—

"Follow me, quick, ebery one ob you. See de

tornado coming. Keep away from de tree, dey come down like noting, sometimes."

Barely had the words left his lips when the wind came rushing across the mighty wilderness, tearing up trees that had stood for hundreds of years.

Hurling three of the outlaws who had disregarded Snowball's warning to the ground, they disappeared with the oversweeping element.

Then arose a peculiar rushing noise, which Snowball apprised his companions bore a significant meaning.

It did, and in a second they would have the full force of the storm upon them.

He did not wait to pass words with his chief, but springing forward threw himself upon the thick vegetation, his burly form uppermost, as a shield against his leader.

He had barely done this, ere the huge tree from which he had seen the lights, was uprooted by the remorseless wind, and as it fell, one strong limb smote two of the outlaws to the earth,

They died instantly.

Spreading devastatation in his track, the storm king went madly onward, and as the roaring noise died to a feeble moan in the distance, the rain ceased, the wind lulled, and the twinkling stars shone out brilliantly.

It was now as peaceful in the wilderness as before it had been wild and fearful.

The seamen arose, and by the bright starlight beheld the mutilated forms of their companions.

Midshipman Tom's face wore a gloomy aspect as he gazed at the stalwart forms that had but a few minutes before been his hopeful helpmates.

"Bury them," said he, "that the beasts of prey may not tear their forms into piecemeal; I would have wished them a death in the smoke of battle. But it was their fate."

"It was, Massa Tom," said the African solemnly, "be tankful all ob us dat are here, for the great spirit came on de winds to night."

Tom felt the truth of his companion's words and thoughts, and there was a chill feeling at the hearts of the little band of men as they made a hole in the earth to protect their dead companions from the fanged wolf, the prowling tiger, or the hungry leopard.

Their arms were strong and the blades of their weapons good, and soon the bodies were laid in their final home, and the men whose rugged hearts had witnessed the butcheries of hundreds in their time without feeling a pang, leant upon their earth-stained weapons weeping over what they considered to be the untimely deaths of their comrades.

The chief, not less touched than his companions, was the first to break the silence.

He pointed to the weapons which had been worn by his dead followers, and said—

"Place their blades by their sides, in their graves."

Cutlasses, pistols and knives were placed as they had been worn during life; then the loose earth was pushed in by the outlaws' naked hands.

When the mound had been erected a weight seemed taken from the hearts of those who had witnessed the sad scene.

Under the guidance of Snowball they pursued their journey.

The lights seen by the African suddenly became visible to the outlaws as they reached the summit of a steep hill.

"Ship lanterns," said Tom; "then our way is to the left, amid the small lights."

"Right, Massa Tom, come on! we had better look out, dere am plenty ob people down here."

He pointed to a cluster of white-looking houses, which comprised the town.

Captain Dragon had given our hero much sound advice respecting the locality of the slave dealer's hiding-place, which contained his ill-gotten wealth.

He had told him also that a number of paid blacks were constantly on the watch and would lose their lives in its defence.

Thus cautioned our hero went carefully to work.

When they came in sight of the building which contained the treasure, Snowball divested himself of his clothes, and with only a white cloth round his loins, grasped a long Indian knife and went forth to reconnoitre.

CHAPTER CVIII

THE STRANGER WHO CAME TO THE TOWER.

WITH longing eyes, Ben Bight from the window of the tower beheld the War Cloud sail upon her distant voyage.

Fain would the gallant outlaw have accompanied his young chief, and when the War Cloud's white sails grew less and less, he soliloquised—

"Well Ben, my boy, you've come to something at last—looking after a woman whilst your mates are fighting. Never mind, perhaps you will have something to do before they come back. Ha! here comes them beggars."

The concluding remark was caused by the arrival of a number of soldiers, who were marching towards the outlaw's stronghold.

"Guns too," muttered Ben, as the artillery made their appearance close behind the red-coated infantry; I s'pose they think they've nabbed us this time."

He rubbed his hands with glee when he beheld the troops form up in front of the cave, and the gunners began to fire at the casement over the entrance.

Gun after gun was discharged, and when the roar ceased he peeped out of the tower window and saw the officers in close consultation.

"They can't make it out," said he; "our silence appears to have astonished them. They had evidently made up their minds to dislodge us. I suppose they'll go now and see whether we are at the cave or not."

Ben's surmise turned out to be quite correct, for shortly after a company of soldiers marched quickly towards the entrance.

They retreated in a few minutes, and Ben did a grin of satisfaction, for by their actions he knew they had opened the key door and let the flood of water loose.

"Them chaps," muttered Ben, "don't like salt water, that's clear, or else they'd never run back so quickly."

Ben was quite right. The heavy rush of water was too much for them, and after several useless attempts to enter the cave, the signal was given them to withdraw.

From the peculiar manner in which Midshipman Tom had caused the water to be admitted to the cave, it defied all attempts of those not acquainted with the secret to stop it.

The flood, as the reader will remember has been explained, came through a circular orifice on the ground, and being brought there through a tunnel bored below low-water mark it would be certain to flow as long as might be wished.

The military officers were sorely perplexed to account for the water's entry, and after waiting several hours to see whether it would stop, they went back the way they came, fully impressed that the water had broken into the cave and drowned the outlaws.

Ben chuckled when he saw the red sun shining upon their glittering weapons, and muttered—

"When you're gone shipmates, I'll go and put the plug in again. It might make the cave damp to have too much wet just now."

Stopping the water and shooting a few seagulls passed the remainder of that day away.

But as day succeeded day, three quiet months of looking out from the tower window began to tell upon Ben, and he heartily wished to behold the banner of his young chief again, for, as Ben expressed it—

"Looking arter wimmen didn't suit him."

On one calm and lovely eve, Laura was sitting by the tower window anxiously looking over the ocean for the return of him she loved so well.

Weary of watching, she was about to turn away when the sky suddenly became black and heavy, gusts of wind, followed by a drenching downfall of rain, caused her to stay.

The sea, too, began to rise, and huge white-topped waves could be seen rolling landwards.

Ben stood near her, viewing the stormy waters through a night-glass, and to Laura's timid inquiry he said—

"No, Miss, the War Cloud is not in sight, and I hope she will not be this night, for the storm which is now but coming would carry a larger vessel than the War Cloud upon the rocks. God help those who are near this part of the coast to-night!"

The timid girl shuddered at the outlaw's words, and fastened the windows.

The storm, as Ben had predicted, increased in violence every moment, and amid the howling of the wind, and the raging of the angry waters, could be heard the sullen boom of several guns from the passing ships at sea.

In this roar of the elements a loud summons from the gate of the old tower came.

There was nothing of superstition in Ben's character; but, for a few seconds, this hasty summons sent a thrill through his frame.

"It can't be anyone," muttered Ben; "the wind would blow any one into the sea—unless, indeed, it is the ghost of the old exciseman, who was found murdered down here last winter."

Ben's conjectures were cut short by a second summons, louder than the first, and, amid a momentary lull in the storm, a voice called out—

"Open the door. In the name of Christianity, let me in!"

Midshipman Tom's black mastiff was lying at Laura's feet.

He sprang towards the door and began growling.

"It's a stranger, anyhow," thought Ben, as he drew his cutlass, and went to open the door, "the dog knows all the band."

Ben was jealous of his trust, and did not feel much inclined to admit a stranger to the solitary tower.

He was just making up his mind, indeed, to send the benighted traveller away, when Laura's sweet voice broke upon his ear and pleaded for his admittance.

Ben immediately complied, and removing the heavy fastenings, cried out—

"Come in, whoever you are."

A man strode through the doorway, and shaking the rain from his cloak, said—

"Thanks for your kindness. Another such a gust as the last would have blown me into the sea."

Ushered into the outer chamber, where a bright coal fire was blazing, and Laura was sitting.

"Your servant," said he, with an air of much gallantry.

Seeing that the stranger was drenched with rain, Laura placed a seat for him near the fire.

"You are welcome sir," she said, "to such hospitality as our home affords."

"Thanks, dear lady, I sorely need it."

"Have you travelled far to night?" inquired Laura.

"I have. I started with a view of reaching the village to night, but, overtaken by the storm, I found the roads impassable; leaving my carriage in the valley below, therefore, I am continuing my journey on foot."

"And are your servants provided with shelter?"

"They are. They have taken refuge in a fisherman's hut, but I, seeing the light from your window, struggled on in the hopes of meeting that protection and shelter you have so very courteously afforded me."

He looked steadily at the face of Laura and her companion for a few minutes, then said—

"Pardon my boldness, but is there another habitation near this?"

"None nearer than Mountsteven Castle," replied Laura, "that is at least two miles from here."

"It must have been there, then, I was directed."

Ben turned away, and while busy arranging supper he thought many things concerning their guest, but nothing good of him.

A small room where Ben slept was prepared for the stranger.

He was conducted thither by Ben, who muttered to himself as he left him—

"I don't overlike them soft-spoken oily-tongued sharks; they seem to me as though like a snake—they licks you over first and swallows you afterwards."

The stranger upon whom Ben was thus expending his philosophy was at the moment thinking of Ben.

"A pretty sort of guardian for such a beauteous charge," he said, as he threw himself into a softly-cushioned chair. "Well, I begin to think my old father is right when he says chance on many occasions turns out the best thing to trust to."

While thus soliloquising, the stranger was removing his glossy beard and moustaches.

Placing them on his pillow, he continued—

"To think that I should have thus stumbled upon the very spot where Laura is hidden; her fiery lover away, and his cutthroat band away with him."

Neville Wirely retired to rest full of emotion.

The next morning in descending from his sleeping apartment he fell down the narrow winding staircase, doing himself, as he alleged, considerable personal injury.

This gave him a pretext for delaying his stay at the tower for a few days, and skilled as he was in the art of ingratiating himself into the good graces of all with whom he came in contact, he thus found means of making himself agreeable to Laura.

In the meantime also he took the opportunity of conferring with his companions, whom he had left in the fisherman's hut.

Laura, one calm eve, when the red sun was sinking to its rest, took a walk on the cliff, Ben and the mastiff following at a distance.

Seated beneath a clump of trees they watched the distant ships as they passed, Laura improving the occasion by reading from an interesting book until the shades of evening had begun to fall before either appeared to notice it.

On their return home, in consequence of a heavy shower suddenly overtaking them, they entered a small cottage, Ben being dispatched for suitable covering.

With an awkward attempt at courtesy, the owner offered her a seat and left the room.

Immediately after the sound of voices could be heard.

Laura arose from her chair and went to the window.

Then the door of communication opened and the nearest ruffian, with a muttered oath, tore her from her grasp of a creeping plant, that grew outside the door, and dashed towards a beaten path in the cliff.

Her frantic cry was heard by Ben, who was hastening back to the cottage with a cloak.

Drawing his cutlass, he flew to the door of the hut.

Too late!

Before he could ascertain the road by which the abductor had gone, the second ruffian levelled a pistol at Ben's head and he fell senseless, the mastiff with his nose to the ground speeding to the trail of Laura and her abductor.

CHAPTER CIX.

SNOWBALL HAS A PLAN OF HIS OWN.

TOM and his companions seated themselves behind a low wall, and anxiously awaited the officer's return.

Half an hour passed, and they began to feel uneasy; an hour more, and still Snowball had not returned.

Tom felt saddened yet from the catastrophe in the forest, and his mind naturally bent itself to the most gloomy forebodings.

A feeling haunted him that his faithful follower had been detected and killed, and he and his companions were discussing the policy of proceeding in search of him, when they beheld a sight which puzzled and yet assured them.

Three figures were coming towards them; one, by his towering height, was Snowball, his companions, like himself, were black, and attired in the same primitive fashion.

The outlaws peered over the wall, and saw that they who were in company with Snowball were drunk, by their staggering gait and the frequent clutches they made at Snowball to keep them from falling.

The African brought them close to the wall, and suddenly turning upon them, he caught each of their throats in his iron grasp.

"Quick," he cried to the astonished outlaws; "tie these two debbils togedder while I go and fetch more."

His words were quickly obeyed, and before the astounded darkies could well understand what had befallen them, they were both bound and gagged.

Tom emerged from his place of concealment, and said—

"I was about to come in search of you, Snowball. I feared something had happened."

"Not'ing, tanks, Massa Tom, I all right—been habing a leetle plan ob my own to get dem debbils away from de place."

"And succeeded, to judge by appearances," said Tom."

"Not quite, yet, Massa Tom, dere is too many ob dem dere for us six, at least dere are twenty dere, but it ain't dem as we care about, only de noise dey make fetch all de town out."

"How did you manage to get those two away so quietly?"

"Easy enuff, Massa Tom. Dese beggars are berry fond ob drop ob rum. Dis chile go 'mongst dem, you see. He look jist like dem in dress. He say—'I hab jist 'scape from master's clutches. I hab kill him, and got him rum a little way off. Dey come directly—at least, dem two did. I gib 'em rum till dey got so dey don't know de way back. Does you see, eh?"

"And how did you manage to obtain the rum, Snowball?"

"Easy enuff, Massa Tom. I go into a shop, and find it."

"Find it! But was'nt the door fastened at that hour of the night?"

Snowball chuckled at his leader's simplicity, and said—

"Fastened! Yes, Massa Tom, him fastened; but doors here am only bamboo, and it no take dis chile long to get him way in. But I mus'nt stay, or him 'spect something."

He was gone before Tom could make any comment, and in about twenty minutes he returned with three of the slave merchants' dusky guards.

He was leading them to where the outlaws lay, waiting to pounce upon them, by saying—

"Dis de place for the rum. I hab a big bottle behind dis wall. Come on. De oder two got drunk by dis time, I 'spect."

They confidingly followed him until near enough for the outlaws to rush out.

A momentary struggle took place, and they were safely deposited by the side of their companions.

Snowball repeated the manœuvre until he had secured fifteen out of the twenty; then he dressed himself, and they went cautiously to the building.

The dusky guardians were sitting before the door in a half sleepy state, and did not observe the outlaws until they were close upon them.

A sudden rush was made for the loaded muskets that stood within reach; but before they could be brought up the blacks were seized, and hurled to the ground.

Snowball's giant strength soon wrung off the fastenings of the slave-dealer's door, and, with a suppressed cry of exultation, the outlaws rushed inside.

To judge from the display of rare and costly treasures that were heaped around, the slave-dealer must have been very successful in his nefarious pursuits.

In gold and rich merchandise there was sufficient ransom for a dozen kings.

The men, under their young leader's direction, were not long in making their selection.

Each took as much as he could carry, and quietly leaving the store, they were about to make for the road they had come.

"Stop," said Snowball, suddenly; "dat not do, wait a minnit.'

He dashed inside the store, and when he returned, his arms were laden with striped cotton garments, such as those worn by the unhappy slaves.

These he deposited on the ground, and in an instant he was inside again.

When he came out he had four broad-brimmed palmetto hats and two bonnets.

Tom looked at him in surprise, and asked—

"Whatever are these things for, Snowball?"

"Dem, Massa Tom; dey might be useful, so I tought we ab them; dere is a suit apiece. I don't know if they all for men, some women's, I tink; but come on, see the light is coming; and if we found here, it be lucky if we get away wid our own lives, let alone de gold."

The morning light was just appearing as Snowball spoke; and the young chief, dividing the apparel among his followers, said—

"Keep them for the present. Now forward, we have not much chance if we linger."

The men shouldered their heavy burdens, and were about to proceed, but Snowball once more stayed them.

"Not dat way," he said; I think of a better plan."

"What is it?" asked Tom.

"Dis, Massa Tom," was the reply; "we get back to the ship sooner with this heavy load of gold if we go by the water."

"True; but we have no boats."

"Boats, by gar—dere must be plenty of them down dere. Come on. I see de water."

Shouldering a huge boxful of gold dust, Snowball started forward; the others, as well as they could, kept close in his wake.

Early morn was approaching, and every moment was now worth an hour.

A sharp run brought them to the beach, and, to Snowball's satisfaction, several long, narrow boats were drawn up on the sands.

The vessels were of very primitive shape, being very narrow, and having a prow at each end.

Two that were side by side had the broad-bladed paddles lying in their bottoms.

Snowball's choice fell upon these; but paddling was slow work, therefore the subtle black ran towards a cluster of bushes, and, after a few minutes search, he began to pluck several long, reddish-looking leaves from a tall plant.

These he brought to his companions and said—

"It light shortly, and we neber get all de way back without being seen. All ob you take one, dip him in water, den with the juice rub your face and hands—look sharp. Ha, by all de debbils dere go de gong!"

As he spoke the brazen instrument began to sound amid the trees.

One of the slaves had slipped his cord, and was now sounding the alarm.

This induced the outlaws to increase their movements, and before the gong had ceased sounding, they had stained their hands and faces as black as though they were all engaged to play the Moor that night.

Their rakish-looking red caps and golden tassels were placed in the boats, and in their stead the large brimmed palmetto hats were used.

Snowball and Tom were the last to disguise their European dress by drawing the striped cotton over it.

Then to the secret merriment of their companions, but much to their own disgust, they were compelled to adopt the looose cotton robe and the peculiarly ugly bonnets as worn by the negresses.

The young chieftain drew the dress on, but the bonnet was too much for him.

He gave it a look of eneffable disgust, and threw it into the sea; then, winding his white handkerchief round his head, followed Snowball into the boats.

Three of the smugglers were in one boat, Snowball and Tom, to support their assumed character, sat in the middle of the other, while the remaining outlaw, seated on the bow, was to use the paddle and follow the other boat.

They were about to push off when the distant sound of angry voices came upon their ears.

The loss of the spoil had been discovered, and the whole slave-dealing population were rushing in all directions in pursuit.

CHAPTER CX.

THE LAWYER AND THE LADY.

THE death of Lord Mountsteven placed Lady Blanche at the head of the immense estates; but cleverly as she had managed her bold task, her schemes had been for a time foiled by a will left by her murdered husband.

It was upon her return from the funeral of the Master of Mountsteven, that she became acquainted with the existence of that document which made her bitterly regret the oversight she had committed.

"So," she thought, "after all my toil and guilt, I am but to hold the estate in trust for the boy—a trust to be surrendered, should he ever be found."

Margerie came softly to her mistress's side.

"My mistress," she said to her, "you think too much of this unexpected discovery."

"Too much?"

"Yes, my lady. The words were 'should t boy yet live.'"

"Well?"

"What boy! Remember, Madame, we alone know the secret; none know but ourselves that this long lost heir is an outlaw, and ——"

A scream of rage stopped Margerie's speech.

"You know not, woman," said her ladyship passionately, "of what you speak!"

"My lady."

"I repeat it, you know—but then, why speak, I waste words in useless anger. Come here, Margerie."

The woman obeyed, and her ladyship resumed—"That document, which makes me but temporary heiress of Mountsteven, was witnessed by two men that you perhaps saw."

"I did, your ladyship."

"Such being the case, it is not improbable that Lord Mountsteven may have put these men upon the task of discovering this boy."

"Ha, Madame is right, there—"

"They know nothing more, and our task is clear."

"I understand your ladyship's meaning! You would say it is best they do never know any more."

"Precisely."

The will was in the possession of her late husband's legal adviser, and Lady Mountsteven, having sent for him, found no difficulty in obtaining the information she desired.

"Perfectly legal, my lady," was the old lawyer's reply to the question put by her ladyship. "The first witness, I presume, is not unknown to you."

"To me!"

"Even so, my lady; his name is Herbert Beale, an officer in the Royal Navy."

Her ladyship was astounded.

"Captain Beale," she repeated; "I was not aware my husband ever exchanged half-a-dozen words with him."

"Indeed," was the lawyer's curt reply.

The lawyer held the parchment towards her. It was truly enough his signature, and she felt dismayed, still she schooled her feelings, and in a calm voice said, "It is strange that Lord Mountsteven did not make me acquainted with the existence of this document."

"The will was drawn within a few hours of his death, my lady."

"Indeed! And were you with him at the time?"

"I was."

"Did he leave any clue by which the heir, as he has termed him, could be discovered?"

The lawyer's ferret-like eyes were fixed upon her ladship as he said—

"He did, my lady."

"With you?"

"No, with the naval officer; the will only was to be left in my keeping."

Lady Mountsteven paused a few moments; she had a very poor idea of human nature, and she was not long in showing it.

"MIDSHIPMAN TOM TO THE RESCUE."

"You say," she asked, "that the will is to be left in your keeping—for safety, of course?"

"Yes, my lady."

"And the nature of the payment you are to have for the great trouble you will have taken to preserve it"—

"Will be," interrupted the lawyer, "fifty pounds a year, should the document remain in my keeping so long; and should the young heir be found, I am to have five hundred pounds."

"You naturally wish this to take place."

"Certainly, your ladyship—and five hundred pounds is a consideration—much as I should grieve to see your ladyship no longer mistress of the estate.

"And supposing the will were lost or destroyed accidentally. A fire, for instance, might take place at your office in London and destroy your papers. What then?"

"A matter of frequent occurrence in London, my lady. Well then"—and the lawyer paused—

"Well then," her ladyship mused, "for such an unlooked for catastrophe I should have to make you amends. Say five hundred pounds, the bonus, and five hundred pounds in requital of your loss of fifty pounds annually."

Her ladyship looked at the lawyer with a condescending familiarity, and added, "what do you say, Mr. Quick?"

Mr. Quick understood her ladyship clearly, and bowing almost to the ground, answered—

"Your generosity, my lady, is as unbounded as

19

it is unlooked for. But I fear you have forgotten one thing—and a most important omission, it is——"

"And what is it ?"

"It's the witness," said Mr. Quick, "this captain——"

"He shall be removed where yellow fever and cholera may keep him from interesting himself with matters he has no business with."

"You can do this, my lady, certainly. The sooner the better."

He gave her his card as he spoke, then placing the parchment in his bag, shuffled from the apartment.

She watched him leave the castle, and a wicked smile played upon her lips as she muttered—

"I like not the cunning look which accompanied his words. What if he should fire the place and keep the will ? No, sir, there must be a safer means devised yet."

The confidante soon made her appearance.

"You sent for me, my lady."

"I did," said Lady Mountsteven, "come here."

They both stood in the deep recess of a window, and Lady Mountsteven with flushed cheeks related her interview with the crafty lawyer.

Her companion looked grieved for some time.

"My lady," she said, slowly, "you have made a great error. This man is not to be trusted."

"Is it too late to repair it ?"

"I cannot say, unless I know how long he may be in this place."

"Not an hour. He is now gone to wait the departure of the stage coach."

Margarie's swarthy face flushed, and going quickly from the room, said—

"There is but one chance. Await my return."

She sped swiftly from the castle, and taking a narrow path under the cliff, stopped at the door of a dirty hovel.

CHAPTER CXI.

OVERBOARD WITH THE GOLD.

HALF-CASTE boy gave the outlaws the first intimation of the slave dealers coming.

This young rascal seemed to enjoy the prospect of a fight, for he came close to the boat, and shouted—

"Here they comes. Me see you blackie me tell."

"You young varmint," said the outlaw as he grasped the coloured urchin by the hair of the head, "I'll put a clapper on your jaw."

"Sit dere," he said to the frightened child as he placed him on the stern of the boat; "If you move or speak, by gar I eat you up. Give way wid dat paddle, or we shall hab dem down on us."

The outlaw obeyed, and under the swift stroke he gave the light craft was soon skimming through the water in the wake of the other boat.

From the noise and shouts that could be heard from the direction of the slave-dealers' houses, it was evident that the alarmed inhabitants knew not what direction the spoilers had taken.

Ten out of the slaves that Snowball had lured away were sacrificed to the slave-dealer's wrath. The remainder, when they were liberated, made their way into the jungle.

Snowball, who knew the crafty nature of the dealers in human flesh, felt assured that the loss of the boats would soon be discovered, and when they were out of range of a chance musket, he relieved the man at the paddle.

In passing a thickly-wooded part of the shore, they beheld a square, flat bottomed boat moored to the trunk of a tree.

When the African saw this his fertile brain at once saw a fresh means of escape.

"Massa Tom," he said, "dat boat be a good friend to us; him carry a sail. What you tink if we all get in him and sink dese two ?"

"A capital plan; although I do not see that we require it."

"You berry much mistaken, Massa Tom, for no sooner do dey find dese boats hab gone down den de dam slave-dealers get dat little African sloop-of-war to follow us."

"Perhaps you are right. Hail the other boat and we will disembark."

The change was soon effected.

The outlaws and their spoil were soon transferred to the large boat.

The two narrow, canoe-like vessels were filled with stones and sent to the bottom of the ocean.

By this time the slave-dealers had put off in their canoes, and were paddling with all speed towards the outlaw's boat.

Midshipman Tom was equal to the emergency.

"Keep down below the gunwale," he said to his men, "and I'll just give those beggars a shot."

He was obeyed, and the shot had the effect desired; the slave-dealers, seeing one of their number fall, turned tail, and returned to the shore much quicker than they left it.

Well for the daring outlaws that Snowball's forethought had turned the boat into such good use.

They were sailing smoothly upon the sunlit ocean about two hours after when a sloop-of-war under a cloud of canvas, overtook their slow-sailing craft.

The commander ordered Snowball, who was at the sail, to haul it down.

He was obeyed, and as the sloop hauled up her canvas, the officer called out—

"Hi, you fellows, have you seen two narrow boats pass you this morning ?"

"No, massa, we hab seen notin' 'cept dat little boat out dere."

"Are you sure?"

"Yes, massa, me am."

"—— them, they cannot have come this way, then."

"Beg massa's pardon, but who am de talking about?"

The master of the sloop was in a towering passion, and he told Snowball to go to the devil.

After this polite reply, he put his vessel about, and to the joy of the outlaws, soon sailed away.

Had he seen the thumbs of each outlaw placed against their noses, he would not have been improved in temper.

"Now, my lads," said Tom, "if that fellow should discover the loss of this boat, he will be after us like the wind; so out with your swoops and pull for your lives."

They had not parted company with the sloop more than a hour before the white sails could be seen coming towards them again.

They were discovered; for no sooner did the African get within range, than he fired a gun within two yards of the boat.

"By gar," muttered Snowball, "it all up wid us."

The young chief's dark eyes kindled, and throwing off his disguise, he drew his sword and said fiercely—

"We are; but I will not yield to these fellows! Arm yourselves. Let us fight while we have life."

The gallant fellows seized their arms, and with compressed lips awaited the coming of their antagonists.

"Lower the sail," said Tom. "It is useless to try to escape. We will wait for him!"

The men answered with a cheer, and determined to stand by their intrepid young leader until one and all should be slain.

The sloop came hand over hand upon the gallant half-a-dozen outlaws who stood so bravely grasping their weapons, awaiting the enemies' attack.

"Massa Tom," said Snowball, savagely, "I wish this dam sloop was at de bottom ob de sea."

"Our wishes will avail us nothing in this matter, Snowball. We must use our blades while we have strength."

"Fraid we won't hab de chance, Massa Tom. Dey will drop a cold shot into us, dat's sartin."

"You are right, perhaps, Snowball—there is but one chance of saving ourselves."

"What am dat, Massa Tom?"

"We must conceal our weapons and surrender quietly, and then await the chance of events."

"Dat very good, Massa Tom; but if dey put de irons on us, we done for, anyhow."

"They will not do that."

"Massa Tom."

"Well."

"It griebe me very much to lose all the spoil in dis manner."

"Ha, a good thought! Quick Snowball. Overboard with the lot. Should we escape, there may be a chance of fishing it up again; if not, we can but lose it."

They had barely time to drop the valuables over the side when the sloop came up with them.

It was then seen how wise the young chief's precautions were, for no sooner did the sloop range up alongside the boat than a port flew open and a gun ran out.

At the same moment an officer sprang upon the side and shouted—

"Surrender, you thievish vagabonds, or I will blow all the lot of you into the water."

"We surrender," was the young leader's quiet reply.

"Well for you," said the captain. "Now come on board."

Tom led the way, and his followers sullenly stepped aboard after him.

"Now, my fine fellow," said the captain, maliciously, "where's the plunder you've so cleverly made away with?"

"Where you will not find it, my fine captain," said Tom, coolly.

"What," he yelled, "have you had the assurance to make away with it?"

"We have had such assurance," answered Tom.

"Then," said the captain, "your carcases will grease the gallows in front of the houses you have robbed."

"We are not at that most pleasant place yet, most amiable captain, most brave officer, with pluck enough to abuse unarmed prisoners."

"You had better take care. Go forward with your thievish companions."

Under an easy press of canvass the sloop sped swiftly back to the harbour.

They had proceeded not more than seven miles when the captain was much astonished to behold four boats rowing towards him; and from the glitter that could be seen, it was evident they were all armed.

This was not all. The steady, long pull showed the rowers had attained something like a man-of-war's proficiency in the art.

He could not make it out.

His ship was the only armed vessel, he felt sure, near the place.

He was not long in forming a pretty good conjecture.

"Malediction," he muttered, "these fellows must have their vessels at hand, and sacre, these are her boats coming."

He yelled out to his crew to clap on more sail and to load the whole of the guns.

Both these commands would have been obeyed but for a little incident which most effectually stayed their execution.

Whatever doubts the captain had respecting the boat's true character, our friends, the outlaws, did not share them.

No sooner had the boats made their appearance than the outlaws recognised in the two leading ones the War Cloud's gig and pinnace.

The others, when they came a little nearer, he saw, were belonging to the Thunderer.

Tom did not waste time in speculating whether they were coming to the sloop or not, but stepping quickly to the bow he held a red ball as far as possible out of sight of the captain.

By opening his fingers the ball became suddenly lengthened to a red and blue flag.

Its folds had not fluttered long in the breeze when a similar sign was made in the bow of the gig.

The young chief turned quickly away, and whispered to his sable lieutenant—

"The danger signal is seen. Now to prevent the sloop escaping."

This was at the same moment the captain's orders were bellowed forth.

"You hear," said Tom, "upon them, or they will show the boats nothing but their stern."

Like six flashes of light the outlaw's blades were drawn from their concealment, and with a hearty cheer, they dashed upon the crew.

In such moments as these, men's hearts being steeled to effect an object or die in its attempt, a half-dozen men can overawe thrice the number.

So the crew of the sloop soon discovered, for before they could loosen a sail, the cords were cut in twain by the outlaws' bright blades, and the sails released from their fastenings, fluttered idly against the masts.

Shoulder to shoulder the gallant little band went from one end of the vessel to the other, hewing at all the ropes that came in their way.

The work of destruction was completed before the astounded captain and crew of the sloop knew what had occurred.

The first surprise over, the enraged officer yelled out to his men to shoot down the daring captives.

The last words had barely fallen from his lips, when he found himself seized in a grasp that forbade all idea of being easily loosened.

Snowball held him by the throat, and with angry, gleaming eyes, he placed the point of his weapon against the captain's breast, and said—

"You gib rope's end—eh, by gar ! De fust man ob you crew dat put him finger on a trigger dis blade go clean through him."

There was no mistaking the voice and manner of the angry African.

The man at the wheel had been promptly cut down by the young chief, who now held the spokes' end to keep the sloop from falling off before the wind.

The three officers who had been upon the quarter-deck with the captain, were also disarmed and in the hands of the outlaws.

Thus they were complete masters of the quarter-deck, and for a time of the vessel.

It was not to be expected that this state of affair could last long, for the crew numbered upwards of a hundred and fifty men and boys.

With a rush, the greater part of the crew went to the gun-room, and began to load both muskets and pistols, but before they could do any damage, a British hurrah announced the arrival of the boats, and Captain Dragon rushed upon the deck.

Young Peter, the fisherman's son, now midshipman on the Thunderer, followed closely upon the heels of his commander.

"Forward my lads !" shouted the captain, cutting his way to the quarter-deck, "do not give them time to rally."

A cheer from his own men and the outlaws answered his words, and dashing forward, they engaged the Africans hand to hand.

When the men who had so opportunely come to his rescue began to pour over the sides, Tom released the wheel, and clutching his trusty blade in his hand, he called out to Snowball—

"Release that fellow, let him head his men."

The clash of steel and the quick flash of pistol and musket, set our young hero's blood on fire.

He could not tamely stand there in safety, while so deadly a struggle was taking place.

CHAPTER CXII.

MARGERIE'S ERRAND.

MARGERIE'S summons was answered by a ruffianly looking fellow, half smuggler, half fisherman, who when he beheld his visitor, surlily asked her to step inside.

"I have no time to waste," replied Margerie; "come with me at once."

Placing something in his breast, he followed her up the cliff, until they reached an eminence that overlooked the sands.

Margerie was busy with her instructions. Pointing downward, she said quickly—

"A man will pass by the beaten path towards the village in a few moments. He has some apers, which you will find in a small blue bag There is no time to linger here ; you must obtain them at once and at any price."

The ruffian smiled grimly, and began to descend the cliff.

Margerie returned to her mistress.

She fancied murder might result from her mission, and had not the courage to stand by and see it committed.

The reader will, by referring to a former chapter, readily understand what followed the wrecker's cowardly attack upon the wrong person, and the assassin's death by Tom's hand.

Crouching behind a huge fragment of rock, the assassin awaited his victim.

Not more than three minutes elapsed when a footfall upon the sands caused him to peer cautiously out.

He saw a man's form slowly passing towards the village, and unsheathing his knife, sprang upon him.

There was a short struggle; the assassin's knife tered the stranger's heart; but before he could rifle the stricken man, he heard the click of a rifle; looking round, he beheld to his dismay Midshipman Tom close upon him.

How he threw the stricken form into the sea, and met his own death by the hands of the outlaw king, is already known.

When Margerie saw the wrecker conceal himself behind the layer of rock, she came to a standstill and mused.

"If the fellow" — so ran her thoughts — "succeeds in his object, he will be close upon my heels; that will not do. I will await his return."

She seated herself to carry out this intention; but the loneliness of the place, and the knowledge that a terrible murder would soon, perhaps, be going forward, caused her resolution to waver, and springing from the little grassy knoll where she had been sitting, she walked quickly towards the castle.

Lady Mountsteven was anxiously awaiting her return.

With a nervous and impatient gesture she met her and said—

"Have you succeeded?"

"I know not yet, my lady."

"Have you any hope?"

Margerie told her mistress what had occurred since she had left the castle.

"You have done well; he is sure to be a time," she answered; "the road is long by the shore."

They waited upwards of an hour, watching for the wrecker.

But without avail.

Lady Mountsteven's patience could brook no delay, and with her accomplice in crime she left the castle, to discover whether Margerie's plan had been successful.

"Consider, madam," the woman said, in a tone of remonstrance, "it is daylight, and we may be observed."

"Absurd supposition, Margerie! Surely we can walk past the place without being suspected as accomplices."

"Perhaps your ladyship is right."

They came to the fragments of rock, and peered anxiously about.

Suddenly a low startled cry from Margerie caused her ladyship to turn and ask—

"What is the matter, Margerie?"

"Look! look!—there are blood-stains on the sands—it is done."

She followed the direction of Margerie's outstretched finger, and beheld the crimson marks, which led from the rocks to the sea.

"There has been blood spilt here," said her adyship, "See! there are the prints of a man's feet in the small pools."

"The sea tells no tales, madam."

"What mean you by that, Margerie?"

"The lawyer is below the ocean's surface; he has done his work well."

"The papers, Margerie."

"We must to the cottage of Pike, the wrecker, for them. Ha! the Virgin protect me!"

They were about to move forward, when this exclamation came from Margerie.

But she had not taken more than two steps, when the form of Pike, the wrecker, was seen amongst some tangled seaweed.

Lady Mountsteven boldly approached, and turning the body over with her foot, said—

"The lawyer has been too much for him. See! a sword has been driven through his heart."

Margerie clutched the speaker's arm, and whispered in low frightened accents—

"No, no, the lawyer was an old and feeble man, whom Pike could have crushed; there has been some foul work here."

"But the red foot-prints, Margerie?"

The woman was about to answer, when a low malicious chuckle of delight sounded upon the ears of the guilty couple.

"Ha! ha! ha!"

They both looked upwards, and perched upon the projecting peak of rock, stood Sybil, the gipsy.

"Ha! ha!" she laughed again, "ha! ha! ha! what does these fine ladies among the rocks, and among blood — fresh drawn blood? Ha! ha! ha!"

They were paralysed by the witch's sudden appearance.

Even Lady Bianca's haughty cheeks paled, and her tongue clove to the roof of her mouth.

Margerie stood as though a sheeted spectre had suddenly risen from the tomb and confronted her.

The old hag seemed to relish their fears, and in a high mocking tone, resumed—

"Ha! ha! ha! This blood scents the air, but it is not the blood of him whom yonder carrion was meant to slay. No, he has been slain instead, and the old man,—ha! ha! ha! No, no; he is on his way to London to kindle a fire."

With these words, delivered in a shrill tone, she disappeared, and left her fear-stricken hearers dumb with apprehension.

They stood for some time, not daring to lift their eyes from each other's guilty faces.

When they did so the old beldame had gone.

"Margerie," gasped the lady, "heard you those words?"

"Too well, my lady."

"She knows all."

"She does; but come, let us return; were the old beldame in league with the arch-fiend, I would thwart him.

She had to support the baroness to her chamber so blighting had been the effect of old Sybil's words upon her guilty mind.

The blow came with crushing force upon the pair, striking them with more than customary dread.

Neither had scrupled about the shedding of blood to obtain the fancied fulfilment of their wishes, and now when the hapless lord had been placed in the tomb of his ancestral home a dozen new phases of danger had sprung up, as it were, from his death.

The discovery of the will, Lady Bramar's schemes to obtain it from the lawyer, the mysterious death of the wrecker, and old Sybil's words when she confronted the gulity pair upon the rocks.

The suddenness of these discoveries threw Lady Mountsteven upon a sick bed, and for several days she lay between life and death.

And while in that state she raved incessantly of the dark doings of her sinful life.

That night there arose a report among the servants that the ghost of Lord Mountsteven had been seen crossing the corridor from her ladyship's room.

CHAPTER CXIII.

A DESPERATE COMBAT.

LIKE an antelope Tom bounded to the deck, and shouting his well-known battle-cry, he placed himself in front of his men.

"Hurrah !" they shouted. "Midshipman Tom to the rescue !"

In vain did the crew try to beat back the daring invaders.

The captain no sooner found his throat released from Snowball's grasp than he rushed to his men and shouted—

"Beat them off the deck—they are not half your number."

He seconded his words with many a well-aimed stroke that sent several of the gallant little band to their last resting-place.

A man of gigantic stature, he hewed down and slew all that came before him.

Actuated by their leader's example, his crew rallied.

Twice the outlaws and their gallant young leader were driven to the quarter-deck.

Now they drove the African's crew back amidships, and the fierce struggle was again renewed.

Like three Paladins of old, Midshipman Tom Snowball, and Captain Dragon fought bravely side by side.

Several times had the gigantic African hurled himself against the three, only to be repulsed by the splendid swordsmanship of our hero.

So the struggle continued until the deck was slippery with blood.

At length, and by degrees, the shouts of the combatants became less, and the African captain with a despairing look at the decimated crew, waved his red sword above his head, and shouted to those who were falling back—

"Forward ! one charge, and let's drive them into the water !"

A fierce shout of anger came from their lips as the voice of their resolute leader was heard above the din.

"Forward !" he shouted again. "Hurrah !"

Taking up his fierce cry, they hurled themselves upon the outlaws.

Prepared even as the latter were for the onslaught, they wavered, and the line was for the moment in danger of being broken.

It was a critical position.

The gallant band recoiled.

Another step or two backward Tom saw would be fatal.

Equal to the emergency, he sprang to the front, and, clarion-like, his voice could be heard crying—

"Follow me ! the outlaw's banner forward !"

The gallant band battled bravely to gain the young chieftain's side, but the effort was futile.

A number of the sloop's crew placed themselves between the young chieftain and his band, another portion, armed with long, deadly-looking pikes, opposite them.

Snowball and Captain Dragon nobly vaulted forward to the rescue, but in vain, and all encompassed as he was by the foe, the hope of saving him was leaving their breasts, when seeing his dusky follower's towering form hewing a path to his side, a thought nerved him, and with his keen scimitar drinking deep of the blood of those who barred his progress, he cleared a path through the surging crowd.

But he had a deadlier foe to contend with yet—the enraged giant, who commanded the sloop placed his bulky form in the way, and, as though, by magic, the conflict ceased in the vicinity of the two leaders.

Tom did not share the dread that entered the hearts of his men, for although he saw himself so fearfully overmatched—mere stripling as he was when compared with the powerful limbs and giant strength of his opponent—he gripped his blade fiercely, and with compressed lips stood like a young gladiator awaiting the attack.

There was a scornful curl on the young chief's proud lip when his opponent threw off his jacket to give his sword arm more play.

Those who stood round—friend and foe alike—forgot the raging strife around.

Twice since the fray began their blades had crossed.

Each time the officer had been foiled in wounding his young adversary.

Now, for the third time, their blades crossed, and they stood for a moment as though seeking more surely each other's weak point.

SNOWBALL HAILS THE CUTTER.

Then the duel began.

The officer's heavy weapon was constantly engaged in forming guards to protect his heart; for our hero gave him no time to return a single thrust, and his light blade seemed like a serpent entwining itself round the heavy cutlass.

Suddenly there came a pause in the deadly fray —the young chief had locked the point of his weapon in his opponent's hilt.

A savage laugh broke from the commander of the sloop and his anxious crew.

The advantage, he saw, was his; brute strength would now befriend him.

There was a struggle for a few minutes, as he tried to wrest Tom's weapon away.

Still the supple wrist and lithe form of the young chieftain prevented it.

Suddenly, however, there was heard the snapping of steel, and Midshipman Tom fell upon the slippery deck, his weapon shivered to the hilt.

His adversary uttered a shout of triumph, and whirled his heavy blade upward to make its finishing stroke.

Snowball, dashing aside all who opposed him, rushed forward, quick as thought, levelled a pistol, and sent a bullet through the enemy's brain.

The huge form rolled to the deck beside the gallant boy whose life he had so nearly taken.

"Massa Tom, you hurt?" said Snowball, as he assisted his chieftain to rise. "By gar, dat fellar nearly do for you for life!"

"Narrow escape, that," said Captain Dragon as his young friend passed him with a swarthy sailor.

The fray was now ended.

The fall of their leader and the dogged resolution of the outlaws cowed the crew, and throwing down their arms, they sued for quarter.

And to say the truth, Midshipman Tom and his companions were not disinclined the carnage should cease.

The elements during the fierce battle had been in a state of repose.

The hot wind had lulled, and the sea's glittering surface had been without a ripple.

But to the weather-wise this was but the premonition of a violent tempest—one of the sudden changes common in tropical latitudes.

The conquerors were busy securing the arms of the vanquished, and Snowball, with a small number of men, was placing the prisoners in security.

Midshipman Tom and Captain Dragon were

standing upon deck conversing on the late fight, the latter examining his sword, which bore many a gap from frequent contact with a foeman's steel.

Tom was watching steadfastly a small black cloud that rolled swiftly towards the ship, and before he could hazard any opinion of it, Captain Dragon said—

"The forerunner of the storm, by all that's good!"

"That small cloud?"

"Yes. You gentlemen of the English Channel are unacquainted with the almost magical change in the elements here."

"The storm will burst soon, then?"

"In less than half-an-hour we shall be in the midst of it."

Tom uttered an exclamation of annoyance, and, in reply to Captain Dragon's question, he said—

"Shall we, think you, be enabled to weather it?"

"Why?"

The young chief pointed to the severed ropes.

"There," he said, "is the cause of my foreboding!"

"Ten thousand fiends!" said Captain Dragon, in alarm; "how did that happen?"

"We cut them when you made your appearance, to prevent the sloop running under the batteries."

"If you wish to see England again," said the corsair, "there is not a moment to be lost! Ha! here it comes!"

As he spoke, a sudden gust of wind swept through the damaged rigging, and carried away the topsail.

A moment after, everything seemed in a state of confusion aboard.

The sloop's rigging was covered with men, in eager haste to repair the damage done but a short time before by their own weapons.

Every effort was made to weather out the approaching storm, but to no purpose.

Every gust of wind came with greater force, and the sails, deprived of their stays, were either blown away or torn into strips, and, borne upon the crest of huge waves, the vessel sped onwards—none could tell whither.

The darkness set in, and for nearly an hour the vessel urged forward.

Suddenly the distant gleam of a hundred lights became visible.

The young chief still kept his feet, holding on by a stanchion to keep himself from being washed overboard.

"Are we near the shore?" he called out to Captain Dragon, when the lights first appeared.

"Yes; those are the lights from the Fort San Jose."

"Fort San Jose! We are lost, then—totally lost!"

"We are, Massa Tom," said Snowball; "for de ship's sides go to pieces 'gin the rocks, or they sink us from the fort."

Those words were too true.

Ten minutes after, there was a terrible crash, as the vessel's prow came in contact with the rock.

All who stood up on the deck were hurled from their feet—some to go overboard amid the seething waters, others to be mangled by the loose guns and other heavy articles which had broke from their places.

Some few saved themselves by clinging to the ringbolts, stanchions, or rigging, and amid that wild scene of destruction a dozen jets of flame came from the embrasure of the fort.

The savage soldiery were firing upon the storm-ridden vessel for not answering their private signal.

CHAPTER CXIV.

A TRAITOR'S CONFESSION.

FROM the Thunderer, the traitor Ralph Ranger (the reader will remember) was conveyed by young Charley Phillips to the island.

It may perhaps be thought that Captain Dragon was rather too severe in thus punishing his old associate, but taking the facts of the case into consideration, the corsair captain was more merciful than Ralph Ranger would have been had they changed places.

Perhaps Captain Dragon would have overlooked the injury sustained by himself, but the cowardly attack upon Midshipman Tom's life called for retribution.

As may be seen, the corsair captain and the young outlaw had become fast friends, and the former looked upon Ranger's baseness with as much wrath as though the attempt had been made upon himself.

When the Thunderer sighted the island, Ranger was brought on deck, and confronted by the angry captain.

The culprit's heart quailed at the sight of the other's stern face.

"The time has come," said the captain quietly, "for me to repay the little obligation I am under to you."

Ranger made no reply, but his eyes were wandering warily to a rope which dangled at the yardarm.

Captain Dragon saw the look, and interpreted its meaning.

"You need not look there," he said "I have too much respect for my vessel—outlaw as I am—to suspend your foul carcase to one of its spars."

Ranger breathed freely, and asked in a dogged voice—

"What do you intend to do with me, then?"

"That you will know soon enough."

Ranger's heart throbbed again.

He thought the corsair intended to hurl him overboard.

"You would not drown me," he said, imploringly; and as he said so his face grew white, and the blood run colder in his veins.

The man feared death—assassin as he was—as cowards do when they feel it approach, and he stood before the captain like one grovelling at his feet for forgiveness.

Captain Dragon, spite of the wild and lawless life he followed, was not without the possession of many good qualities.

He had taken a liking to the daring young outlaw from the time their blades had crossed upon his own deck; and ruminating since upon the abduction of our hero, his quick perception told him that the removal of the handsome youth was prompted by others than Ralph Ranger.

To get at the truth he sent for Ranger on deck.

"You have no wish to die yet, I suppose, though to do my duty I should hang or drown you like a dog that you are," said he to Ralph.

"Wish to die, Sir! I—I do not understand you."

"I expect not; but you soon will, unless you answer a question I have to put to you properly and truthfully."

Captain Dragon looked strangely at the speaker; whose imperturbable manner had occasioned him more alarm than had he shown the worst signs of passion.

"What would you have of me?" he asked. "I am in your power. Do as you will; but spare my life."

"I have not yet threatened that," rejoined the captain. "Be frank in your answer to me, you shall save it. Attempt to deceive me, and a cold shot will be fastened to your leg, and overboard you go."

"I swear faithfully to answer every question you may put."

"Well, then, my questions will be few and long."

"1st. Who paid you to place the outlaw chief on board my ship?"

"No one; it was from a motive of—of—"

"A lie," said Captain Dragon.

"I'm telling—"

"Lies, Ranger. Here, Williams, bring a couple of large shots here."

The seaman hastened to obey; and Ranger, fearing he had placed his life in jeopardy, said, in a voice tremulous with fear—

"I will answer truly. Recall your order."

"Proceed, then. Who employed you to kidnap Midshipman Tom?"

"The lady of the castle which overlooks the bay."

"Her name?"

"Lady Mountsteven."

"What was her motive?"

"I know not, unless she feared the boy might supplant the place of her daughter."

"How?"

Ranger related that portion of Midshipman Tom's history which is already known to the reader. At its end he beckoned Lieutenant Shopland to lower a boat, place in it a bag of biscuits, some pork, a musket, and some ammunition.

These orders were carried into effect, and young David Shopland, with a well armed crew, took Ranger ashore.

When he struck into the forest he had no knowledge whether the island was inhabited or not.

He had not gone far when the noise of the conflict between the boat's crew caused him to pause and listen intently.

He heard the yell of the natives, and the lusty hurrah of the seamen, mingled with the report of fire-arms and the clash of steel.

Ranger was not overloaded with courage, therefore when the sounds of fighting came he at once resolved to start off in another quarter.

And upon the margin of a winding brook, the silver stream of which was not a hundred feet wide, Ranger paused, and held a silent conversation with himself.

CHAPTER CXV.

SNOWBALL'S HEROISM.

IN the whole course of our gallant young adventurer's life he had never been placed in such peril as when Captain Dragon's vessel struck against the rocky base of the fort.

Beneath and round that ill-fated bark the waters seethed and boiled, and her strong timbers were being crushed by the sharp rocks.

Above them, the heavy guns of the fort were firing a continual hail of iron shot.

And the murderous shot fell within a few feet of where he stood, and struck down numbers of his hardy followers.

Flash after flash the guns belched forth their sheets of deadly smoke and flame.

"The cowards," said Tom, angrily, to Captain Dragon; "would that I had the War Cloud within gun shot of their accursed fort."

"I wish you had," responded the captain; "but what are we to do?"

"We can do nothing; the ship must break up in a few minutes, and we shall be engulphed in the ocean."

The proud-spirited young chief shook the deck with his feet as he spoke.

"Curse them," said Captain Dragon, "can we not get a gun in position?"

"We will! though it's the last shot we fire, and at my command," enthusiastically replied Tom in response to his friend's words.

He instantly gave orders to have a gun run out.

In a minute all was bustle and activity.

A gun was quickly got into position.

But at that instant a bomb struck the quarter-deck, upon which our hero was standing.

Snowball, his frame quivering with a thousand emotions, rushed madly on to the quarter-deck, grasped the deadly missile in his brawny hands, and, quick as thought, away in the seething waters hurled it.

Captain Dragon grasped him firmly by the hand, and, in a voice husky with emotion, said—

"Noble Snowball. A deed of bravery, the like of that I never saw; you have saved all our lives. Please Providence it may be some day in my power to befriend you."

"Dat nottink," replied Snowball, as he calmly proceeded to assist in loading and covering the gun.

The young chief applied the match and the iron missile fulfilled its mission, the battery losing a gun and seven of its blue-coated artillerymen being killed and wounded by the sudden overturning of the piece they were loading.

Captain Dragon gave a cheer, and exclaimed—

"Fire another, Tom!"

"It is impossible—ah—by Heaven, there she goes!—cling to that spar."

His warning came but in time, for the vessel, rising upon a mountainous wave, came down with such crushing force that her timbers parted at the waist.

A subdued cry of terror came from the hapless captives who were confined between decks; a moment after friends and foes were battling for life in the roaring waters.

Some struggled in the breakers, the receding waves of which left many upon the shore; others clung to the ship's severed timbers, and their feet touching the shingle, battled through the blinding spray, and scrambled to the beach.

Two of the first to land were Captain Dragon and the young chieftain.

They had collected their men together, and were conversing as to their future action, when suddenly there came a sheet of flame above their heads, coming from the ranks of a company of sharpshooters drawn up on the tower of the fort.

Captain Dragon and Tom both said that the destruction of their whole body was inevitable, and the former proposed that he, speaking the Spanish language familiarly, should negotiate with the soldiery.

After much persuasion, Tom consented to this course being taken, and Captain Dragon crawling forward upon his hands and knees to escape the calamity of being riddled, should another discharge of guns take place, got safely within reach of the sharpshooters.

"Cease your firing—we are unarmed. Tell the officer in charge that his wanton act of cruelty in firing upon a shipwrecked crew, is a disgrace to civilization," cried Captain Dragon.

"You disregarded our signal," was the curt answer.

"I have traded many years on these waters," said Captain Dragon, "and thus I know your language. Why, our ship came so close to your batteries was the fault of the storm, not of us."

The great dignity of Captain Dragon as he made his reply had its effect upon the young officer, who, up to that moment, had been under the impression that the same vessel which had broken to pieces upon the rocks was a Spanish frigate, whose arrival the garrison had been some days looking for.

"You must see the governor," said the officer.

Upon the assurance of the young officer that he should leave the fortress free, he consented to be led bandaged into the presence of that personage.

The governor of Sin Coup was busy looking over some papers when the young lieutenant entered with Captain Dragon.

"A prisoner, lieutenant?"

"No, general," was the reply; "the commander I believe, of a trading vessel which the guns of our fort have sunk."

"Eh! remove the bandage."

The Captain's eyes being uncovered, the governor went on.

"So we have sunk your vessel instead of the Hansard. Have you lost crew and vessel?"

"Not all the crew, general; those who have escaped are now on the rocks."

"And need assistance?"

"Yes; without shelter they die!"

"Lieutenant, bring them in and rest them in the western tower."

The officer bowed, and left the apartment with Captain Dragon.

Arrived at the postern gate, the young soldier handed the corsair captain a lantern, desiring him to collect his men.

"Well," asked the young chief, "how have you succeeded?"

"Admirably; I have made the old fellow in command our friend. But follow me."

They soon arrived at the fort, and the governor as though to make amends for the misfortune which he imagined he had inflicted on the vessel ordered every attention to be bestowed upon the crew, and invited the corsair and Midshipman Tom to sup with him.

An offer which our adventurers were not slow in accepting, though the end was by no means as agreeable as anticipated.

Supper was scarcely over when an orderly made his appearance, saying he had something of great importance for the ear of the governor.

The governor begged to be excused for a short time; when he returned his face was flushed, and an angry frown was visible on his forehead.

Looking straight at his guests, he said—

"There is roguery here. What ho, without!
g in the ——"

efore he ended the summoning of the soldiers
daring corsair drew a pistol from his belt, and
ing it point blank at the governor's forehead,
said in a quiet, stern voice—

Finish that word and you die !"

The old officer turned pale, for the dark unflinching eye that was kept upon him showed that
ne had but small mercy to expect.

Thus, with a score of men within a few feet of
him the governor of the fort was a helpless captive
in his stronghold.

Still with the forefinger upon the trigger, he said
to the young chieftain—

"We are lost if the guard enters here. This
old rascal has found out the capture of the sloop
through one of the men escaping, and unless I can
frighten him into an agreement to let us go, we
shall soon be in one of those unapproachable
chambers near the sea. You be ready for any
emergency."

Tom's reply was the unsheathing of the bright
blade that hung at his side.

"Now," said Captain Dragon speaking, addressing the commandant. "A few words with you ;"
placing at the same time a long shining barrel
before his face.

The governor was evidently ill at ease, and made
a movement as though edging away from the table.

"Sit still, governor," said the captain, "I wish
you to listen carefully to what I am about to say—
carefully, because if you should make any outcry,
or attempt to move when you hear any part of it
that will excite you, this pistol is sure to go off."

The young chief, while his companion was speaking, went quietly to the door and fastened it by
placing a heavy wooden bar across ; the shuffling
of feet indicating a number of men being on the
outside.

Captain Dragon placed his elbows upon the table,
an resting the muzzle of the pistol upon the top of
a decanter, he went on with mock levity.

"We require you to pledge your word as an
officer and a gentleman to allow the pirate captain
and his friend to leave the port unmolested, the
condition being, that on your refusal this bullet
shall scatter your brains against yonder wall."

The old officer was too much astonished to
answer at first ; but when he felt the icy cold ring
of the pistol pressed hard against his temple, he
gasped out—

"You do not intend to murder me in cold blood,
surely ?"

"No," answered the corsair, "but I will shoot
you if those men break open the door."

At this time the men, acting under the lieutenant's order, were doing their best to burst open
the door with the butts of their muskets.

The governor, finding the assailants obdurate,
and not caring for the posthumous fame of having
been slaughtered under such circumstances, said—

"Take away your pistol ; I promise my word to
allow you to go free."

Captain Dragon took a small wooden crucifix
from the wall, and handing to the governor,
saying—

"Swear !"

He placed the symbol of the Catholic faith to his
lips, and said after the captain's dictation—

"By the blessed Virgin, I swear that my word
shall be kept sacred."

Scarcely was this ceremony over when the top
of the panel of the door gave way under the heavy
blows of the soldiers muskets, and through the
splintered aperture a dozen shining barrels were
thrust.

The young chief stood with his naked weapon
beating up the muskets as fast as they made their
appearance.

"You can take that bar away," said Captain
Dragon ; "the governor will give us safe guard
from the fort."

But no sooner was the heavy bar removed than
the soldiers, with the young lieutenant at their
head, dashed into the chamber, and secured our
adventurers.

They were evidently ignorant of what had taken
place, for they levelled their muskets at the young
chief and Captain Dragon.

CHAPTER CXVI.

A PAIR OF RASCALS.

THE man who carried Laura Grey away in his
stong arms, sped down a side path that led to the
beach.

At its termination he was met by the stranger
whom Laura had so hospitably treated in the
lonely tower.

Muffled in a large cloak and with a large drooping hat over his brow, the stranger stood beneath
the shadow of a large tree.

"Have you got her ?" he asked as the man,
breathless with his long run, entered the narrow
end of the path.

"Yes," was the reply. "Quiet, there is some one
on the track."

The stranger relieved the man of his senseless
burden, and turning sharply amon a clump of trees,
ran towards a carriage and pair in waiting.

He had barely time to place Laura within it
before the deep bay of a dog was heard.

"The mastiff," he said to the man, who had
brought Laura from the cottage, "your life is in
your own hands, now shoot him or you will be torn
to pieces."

Then to the driver he added, "Speed on and
don't spare horseflesh."

But mingled with the noise of the swift wheels
there came a cry of anger.

The mastiff had seized Laura's abductor in his
long, terrible fangs.

A long and fierce struggle ensued between man and beast, but the former was overpowered and killed by the enraged animal.

Seemingly satisfied with his work the dog placed his blood-stained nose to the earth and started in pursuit of the carriage.

Overtaking it the stranger drew a pistol and fired, and the faithful dog dropped on the road, and lay a dark, huddled, bleeding mass.

The report of the pistol aroused Laura from her stupor, and throwing back the sunny hair from her forehead, she looked wildly round and asked—

"Where am I?"

"Quite safe, Miss," was the reply; "and in good hands."

"Where is Ben," she asked, "why am I in this carriage?"

"Ben," said her companion, "is at home, no doubt, drunk by this time, and why you are in this carriage is because we are going to London together."

"To London?"

"Yes, little one, when we get there I mean to make you my wife."

"Who are you that dare speak to me thus?"

The stranger took off his mask as he said—

"Neville Wirely."

"Wirely, I thought Snowball had rid the world of you."

"No, curse him, he scalped but did not kill me, so—"

Laura fell back in the carriage and remained in a semi-unconscious state till they reached London, then Neville went to his father's to relate the success of his venture.

"You were indeed merciful this time," said old Neville to his son; "and now let us profit by the last adventure, and keep or make away with our little captive."

"She must be removed," said Neville, "and at once. The splendid estate and twelve thousand a-year is not to be lost now we have gone so far."

"Lost!"

"Entirely so, while Cecil Grey's daughter is alive."

"I really can't see how she can interfere with our success."

"Because she does not know her father has left this property—eh, Neville!"

"Exactly; she does not know that she was left heiress to the old man's property, and as far as I can hear she might remain in ignorance among those outlaws for ever."

Mr. Wirely senior stroked his chin reflectively, and said—

"Such is your opinion."

"It is."

"Listen to me, Neville. **Your theory** would do very well, but for one fact."

"What is that?"

"There is a trustee for the property, and by some infernal means he has found out that Laura was not carried off by the pirates when the old man was slain."

"Well?"

"'Pon my word, Neville, you take it remarkably cool with your 'wells?'"

"Go on, father," said young Wirely; "I am almost tired of hearing about this."

"The trustee having found out, as I said before, that the girl was alive, and to be found somewhere about the coast, has sent detectives all over England for means to be taken to discover her."

"Curse him!"

"I echo your words. Now you see our plan is easy. We have Laura, and by quickly removing her beyond a chance of discovery we must, in the order of events, become masters of a fine estate and its rent roll."

"Perhaps not!"

"Why perhaps not?"

"This trustee is no friend of yours, I believe?"

A dark cloud came over old Wirely's face as he answered—

"He is not; but that has no reference to this affair."

"I should say it had!"

"How?"

"Because he will hold the property until he is certain of her death; or in the event of his not being certain, keep it until he dies himself."

"That he cannot do, because there is a clause in the will that prevents the estate from being without an owner for four years."

"Two of that has expired—why not let it run the other two?"

"Simply because she may be found before as many weeks by the trustee's emissaries."

"But suppose I marry the Laura Grey," interrupted Neville."

Old Wirely jumped up in his chair, and roared—

"You must be a fool or a madman!"

"Why?"

"Don't ask why. Have I not told you before that the trustee has such power that he can alter the disposal of his trust, that beyond a small annuity, while she lives not a penny would reach you."

"The deuce he has! Well, I must forego my honourable intentions, then—although, really, I seem to love that girl—so I will go and see her."

He left the room as old Wirely was about making a suggestion he had been plotting, which in all probability, if adopted, had cost the amiable Laura her life, when a terrible scuffle was heard on the stairs.

Wirely rushed from the room, and immediately afterwards shrieks were heard, so terrible, that old Wirely thought murder had taken place.

Already he had begun his descent.

MIDSHIPMAN TOM PREPARES TO RECEIVE THE "SAN JOSE."

The noise of a yet severer scuffle followed—then heavy fall ensued, which shook the house.

Old Wirely's hair bristled with terror.

He rushed to the room from whence the sound came, and he stopped spell-bound at the threshold.

The fearful scene that met his eyes harrowed up his very soul, and froze the blood in his veins.

One cry of horror escaped his lips, then he fell in a confused heap.

Almost powerless—as though stricken by the hand of death.

20

CHAPTER CXVI.

THE CAPTURE OF MIDSHIPMAN TOM.

THOUGH our hero and Captain Dragon were menaced by forty bristling bayonets, they shrank not.

But with drawn weapons and shoulder to shoulder, they stood waiting the governor's order for the men to be withdrawn.

The treacherous old officer, however, finding he had the adventurers in his power, came forward, and with a malicious chuckle, said—

"Ha! ha! ha! outwitted after all. Piratical rascals. Secure them, and march them to separate cells. As for my oath, it was a forced one, and vows made in pain are void."

Thus, without the remotest chance of resistance being successfully made, Midshipman Tom and Captain Dragon were seized and led under an escort to their respective cells.

"Halt," said the young officer to his men. "Here is your apartment."

This was to Tom, who shook hands with his companion, and said—

"Good bye, old fellow. I suppose we shall meet again."

"Yes," was the reply; "either at the place of execution, or upon the deck of my vessel. Good-bye"

Tom went inside his cell, and the escort passed on to the next and placed Captain Dragon inside.

No sooner had the sound of the soldiers' steps died away, than the corsair began a survey of his cell.

Gifted with a full flow of animal spirits, he treated his incarceration very philosophically, mentally saying—

"Well, I'm in, and as I don't like being shut up, I shall do my best to get out."

The walls he gave up at once: they were nine feet high, but the window was a matter of consideration.

"First," he said, suiting the action to the word, "I'll draw this table under the window and this stool placed on the top will, I think, bring my handsome face in a stone frame."

He mounted the stool and peered out into the murky light.

His survey barely lasted two minutes for the grating of a key in the lock bespoke the propriety of making a speedy descent.

A much speedier one befel him than he intended for in his haste to get down and remove the table and stool before the turnkey entered, he upset the stool and came backwards tumbling on the head of the intruder.

In a minute, a dozen men entered, and, as though well up to the business, they placed a set of leg irons upon the captive before he had time either to recover his senses or his perpendicular.

Captain Dragon indulged in a few sea-faring oaths at the proceeding, but as the gentlemen who had made the addition to his costume did not understand a word, he might have saved himself the trouble.

The Corsair watched them leave the cell, and as the sound of a bolt being drawn across the door, fell upon his ears, he growled.

"Well if this is not adding on the elegant person of Captain Dragon insult to injury I don't know what is."

He rubbed his aching-head, as well as the manacles would permit and broke out again—

"I'll be —— if they should have put these ornaments on these precious legs if I had been up with the stool in my hand. Curse that stool for slipping, serves me right. I recollect when a boy, scrambling upon a table after a dish of secreted baked apples in a high cupboard. Then I had my fill though a broken head followed it. Now I've had my fill and a broken head too without any satisfaction."

"Let me see, here I am, to say nothing more about my head, with all the skin rubbed off my back-bone against the edges of that official table, shut up in this filthy room, the door locked, the window to look out from, and my legs encircled in iron ringlets."

"Well—but poor Tom; I wonder if they've put these confounded ornaments upon his legs? He's a splendid fellow that, one of the true lion-hearts, and I like him. I wish I now stood on the saucy Thunderer's deck, he should not be here long. But there, what's the use talking and bragging here to myself? I can't do what I wish, and so I'll turn in and make the best of a sleep."

Thus saying he walked to the corner of the cell and contemptuously turning over a heap of straw with his foot, resumed—

"I suppose they call this the bed, the vagabonds, well, it's a down bed, at any rate, and down I go into it."

He rolled a dirty looking blanket round him and was soon fast asleep, indifferent to his hard couch, his captivity, or its consequences.

Leaving Captain Dragon to enjoy his repose, we will proceed to the next cell, and see how our young hero bore his captivity.

Like his friend he was ironed soon after entering the cells, but the matter was not so easily accomplished with the high spirited boy.

When the men entered his cell he was pacing to and fro like a chafed lion, and upon one of the fellows approaching him with the manacles, he, in no measured language threatened his instant annihilation.

Though not comprehending one word of the captive's language his gestures were too significant to be misunderstood, and at a call, a simultaneous rush of a dozen men was made, and by whom he was borne to the ground by their sheer weight.

While down his hands and legs were secured, and the galling manacles locked upon his ankles.

Satisfied with this they left him alone to solitude and misery.

The young chief's hot blood boiled at this indignity, and seating himself on an empty powder-barrel, the only seat in his prison, he began to reflect upon his perilous position, and fell a prey to such bitter heart-anguish as in all his chequered career he had never yet experienced.

As for the treacherous old governor, his wish was to rid himself as soon as possible of his distinguished prisoners and their band, and he accordingly sent a well armed sloop to the republican head quarters with a long dispatch reporting our hero and his followers as a set of determined foes to the government which he had the honour to represent.

The captain of the sloop had orders also to bring the old officer's daughter, the dark-eyed Narcisse, from Lima with him on his return voyage.

The sloop had the wind in her favour, and in a day or two she was upon her errand home having the young maiden on board, and a death warrant for the prisoners in his possession.

The captain of the sloop, a dark-bearded Peruvian, in the picturesque costume of the Republican navy, was pacing the quarter-deck and conversing with the old general's pretty daughter.

The young girl, who had been to Lima on a visit, learnt from him the cause of the voyage, and with the curiosity natural to her sex, had made many inquiries respecting the poor fellows whose death-warrant her companion carried in his breast.

And that she felt a lively interest spring up in her breast in regard to one of them soon became manifest, the description of Tom's handsome face and lithe and manly form had woven a charm around her guileless and impassioned heart.

Intense was the governor's delight when he reviewed the death-warrant signed by the President of the Republican State; and a malicious twinkling shone in his cold grey eyes when he closed the official paper, and sent for the officer of the guard.

"Have the garrison paraded on the ramparts," he said to the officer, "and bring the prisoners from their cells."

The officer saluted and withdrew.

Soon after the drum beat the assembly, and the troops were marched to the ramparts.

The general attended in cocked hat and scarlet plumes, to read the fatal orders to the gallant little band, who, under charge of a company of sharpshooters, stood in the centre of the troops.

Unintelligible to them all were the words rendered by the general; and when he had ceased reading, Captain Dragon obtained permission from the general to translate it to them.

Turning to his companions he said—

"Comrades, the meaning of that paper from which yonder vinegar-faced old scarecrow has been reading is an order for us all to be shot to-morrow morning at sunrise."

"So soon!" said Tom.

"Yes; not a pleasant thought, is it? But as we are not consulted upon the matter, I think the sooner it is over the better."

The governor saw the two leaders conversing, and in an impatient tone demanded—

"Have you finished?"

"Yes."

The order was given to take the captives back to their cells, and the troops marched back to headquarters.

Midshipman Tom and the corsair captain walked side by side.

Taking advantage of the opportunity they conversed eagerly together in a low, earnest tone.

"Do you expect to turn up your toes to-morrow, Tom?" inquired the Captain.

"There's nothing left but to do so," answered the young sailor; "still, ere the curtain drops I would I could send a parting message to one in England."

A wish, half-sorrowfully expressed as it was, touched the old captain's heart, and his voice trembled as he said—

"Would to heaven you could, Tom."

He could say no more.

The strong man's voice became husky, and he turned his head aside until he felt assured no evidence of weakness could be traced in his manly countenance.

"I don't wish," he resumed, as they neared the prison door, "for these fellows to see me unmanned. They may think it is fear. Good bye. I would give much to save you, Tom; it is hard for one so young to die thus."

"I have no fear, Dragon," he replied, "and have no regret, beyond the inability to fulfil that one wish; and to-morrow, on the ramparts, you will see me meet my fate like a son of old Albion and a true British sailor."

"I know you will, my boy. Good bye; God bless you."

They shook hands, and the followers of the gallant Tom, one by one, took a farewell of their beloved leader.

"Good bye," said a brawny, bearded old outlaw, taking the chief's small hand in his rough palms. "I wish we could have slipped our cable on board the saucy little War Cloud, with our flag flying above our heads."

Others came forward, and were content to kiss the outstretched hand of their gallant chief.

The stern orders of the escort separated them at last, and they were locked up for the last time in Fort San Jose.

CHAPTER CXVIII.

NARCISSE.

FROM one of the windows in the grim fortress, Narcisse saw the death-warrant read by her father.

She heard not his words; she saw not the glittering pageant drawn out upon the ramparts.

Her eyes saw but the form of one of the doomed captives—that one the graceful form of the daring young chief.

Born in a land where every soft emotion of love is fanned into a flame by a warm, voluptuous climate, the romantic, impulsive girl became in her mind enamoured of the princely youth.

She watched his every look, his every act; and when he was marched from the scene, her gaze followed his every forward step until a door that led to the prison hid him from view.

Narcisse was fresh from school, and her mind filled with the warm, glowing romance of the sunny land of her country, and she had read of men whose bravery and valour had made her love, and wish it had been her fate to have lived in the days of chivalry.

And in these soul-stirring thoughts and longings she had pictured to herself a face and form corresponding with the brave deeds of those knights whose hands were ever at the service of a damsel in distress, and in the young chieftain she saw the perfection of her ideal hero, and the impulsive girl shed bitter tears at the harrowing thought that on the morrow he would cease to exist.

She sat by the open window, the sea air playing among her glossy curls until the twilight's gentle shades began to hover about the glorious expanse of water.

Then she arose, and, drying her eyes, went to her own chamber to plan a means of deliverance for the handsome young Englishman.

"He must not die," she thought. "I will save him!"

Midnight came and the young chief sat in his lonely cell thinking of that fair girl who mourned his absence in that lonely tower upon the cliff.

He was striding to and fro in short, angry steps, as this thought crossed his mind.

Could it be fancy that caused him to pause and listen? or was it the wind sighing past the grating of his cell?

No!

Again he listens; this time more intently, and plainly he hears a light step pause at the massive door.

The grating lock was turned quickly back, and to our hero's astonishment, a fair girl enters his cell.

Her cheek was pale and her frame trembled slightly as she looked upon our hero, and in a low, faltering voice, she said—

"Stranger, I come to save you."

The lowly spoken accents fell sweetly upon his ear, but he understood not their meaning.

Seeing that the Spanish was incomprehensible to him, in fluent French she asked—

"Can you speak this language?"

Midshipman Tom was perfectly master of this tongue, so he readily replied—

"I can."

"The Virgin be praised," she said.

She then approached our hero, and in a subdued tone added, "You wonder who I am, and what brought me here?"

The young chief bowed.

"I am," she continued, "Christina, the daughter of the commandant of this fort, and hearing you were to die at sunrise, have resolved to save you."

"Save me?"

"Do you mistrust my words? Your prison door is open, and this passage leads to the ramparts, beneath which a boat awaits you."

The young outlaw could scarcely believe his ears, and once or twice passed his hand over his forehead. Meanwhile Christina continued—

"It wants but three hours to dawn; say, do you accept your freedom?"

The young chief gazed at the handsome girl whose fair bosom was heaving with excitement and said—

"You ask me will I accept my freedom? Can I refuse? when in a few hours I shall be led from this cell to certain death."

"You will come then?"

The young chief paused. He knew the impulsive natures of the dark-eyed daughters of that sunny clime. "May I ask why you, a stranger, should take such a wondrous interest in my fate?" he said.

"Were I to tell you, young sir, born of a colder clime and haughty nature, you would think but ill of me, who would thus risk her fame and life for a stranger."

The words touched our hero's sensitive soul, and moving forward, he took the girl's hands between his own, and said—

"To think ill of one so beautiful and good would but barely grace my manhood or my chivalry; but let me, lady, repeat my inquiry why you thus interest yourself in my fate?"

Christina tried to speak several times, but a husky sob choked her utterance. At length, resisting these emotions, she said—

"Senor, on my passage from Peru, the officer in charge, in his description of your person and the jeopardy in which your life was placed, strongly prepossessed me in your favour. I have since seen you when your death-warrant was being read. I marked your proud look, your unflinching features —and in my admiration I saw in you the ideal of a brave and chivalrous spirit, such as my impulsive heart, under the influence of a sunny clime, has ever yearned to meet. To see you was to love you; to love you was to do as I have done." The lady held down her head as though abashed at her position, and falteringly concluded, "Senor, may I share your fate."

The young chieftain stood as one perfectly amazed, but said—

"And my followers. Lady, what of them?"

"They," she said, "I am powerless to serve. They must stay and meet their doom, while we— that is, you, escape from the fort."

"On such conditions, lady," said Midshipman Tom, releasing the olive-tinted hand he had held, "your gentle mercy, though it has come like a sunbeam to gladden the last hours of my life, I cannot but reject. Chide me not! I cannot leave this fort without my faithful friends, who came within it with me."

The maiden gazed at him in silent astonishment

—she was totally unprepared for this refusal. Not even in the many romantic old books it had been her delight to ponder over had she met with such a noble and chivalrous speech.

After a pause, the unbidden tears rolling down her face, she sobbed—

"Senor, your answer has filled me alike with admiration and sorrow. You will not accept your life without theirs. I will try, upon my knees, for my father to delay the execution for one day; can I but give you a respite you may yet be saved."

"Impossible."

"No, it is not; there are English vessels of war on the coast. I have influence, and will endeavour secretly to inform the commander of your danger —but what is that?"

"The signal for our execution," said Tom, as the drums rolled out the reveille.

"Farewell." she said, sadly, "I must not linger but I may yet serve you. Adieu, and it may be for ever."

The young chief pressed her hand to his lips as she passed from the cell.

CHAPTER CXIX.

ANOTHER FRIEND.

WHEN she left the cell the young chief stood for a few moments like one suddenly aroused from a dream.

For a time he could scarcely realise the truth of so sweet a face visiting his lonely cell, and as he remembered her words and looks a bright spot reddened his handsome face.

"A romantic temperament," he thought " has caused this unsophisticated maiden to conceive a fancy for me, and she would have left her home and linked her life with mine if——"

The drums ceased beating at this moment, and the warlike bugles rang out a stormy call.

He seated himself upon the empty bench that stood near the table and his thoughts flew to the lonely tower, where he had left his heart's idol.

He knew the narrow limits of his cell, and his eye sought the grated aperture to discover the signs of the coming dawn that would end his brief career.

As he did so, he fancied he heard a tapping on the wall beneath his window.

Listening, it was repeated, and his mind turned to Christina as herself being the cause of it.

He was deceived, for "Massa Tom" fell on his ear, and he knew it was Snowball.

The young chief stood appalled.

Had the dark sea which washed his prison-house sent up the voice from its mystic depths? were the words but a chimera of his brain?

"Snowball?" he called out.

He turned and beheld the welcome face of his African lieutenant at the window.

"Snowball!" he exclaimed, joyfully, "Snowball alive?"

"Alibe, Massa Tom, tank de Lord. What you do wid dem dere irons on your legs."

"I am a prisoner, my old friend, and when the first streak of day shines through yonder dark mass of clouds, I am to be led forth and shot."

"You die, Massa Tom, and like a dog. No, no! Here one of your Damasus sabres, and your long-handles pistols—at least, Massa Tom, die like a hero, and Snowball die wid him."

While Snowball was thus speaking, he was wrenching at one of the bars, when suddenly one gave way under his iron grasp.

"By gar, I got 'em yet," he said, "and we die as we libbed—together, fighting for each oder. Dis I swear by de Great Spirit ob my tribe."

"Snowball, noble-hearted fellow, I would rather you acted upon my advice. Seek out the War Cloud, take her back to England, with news of my fate."

"De War Cloud, Massa Tom, am under dis fort, wid de Black Squall 'longside her. Come, help me wid dis bar—dat's it—push—pull—dare it goes—gib your hand. I'm in. Off wid de irons, and we go de way I come. Dare are plenty left to save the boys from being killed. Come on, Massa Tom."

Our hero was too much astonished at Snowball's words and the easy manner in which he wrenched the iron bars from the windows to clearly understand his meaning.

But while the African was busy breaking his chieftain's fetters, he saw the practicability of the scheme.

The plan was soon arranged, and Snowball, seeing his young chieftain's limbs free, and his hands once more grasping a trusty blade, departed the way he had come to bring the united crews of the War Cloud and the Black Squall to the cell.

The strange appearance of Snowball at the young chief's cell, may be a matter of surprise to the reader, but taking up the African's adventures from the time the vessel struck, the reason will be easily understood.

When the Peruvian Sloop went to pieces, Snowball was standing by the foremast, which, as the vessel parted, snapped off close to the deck, and before the African could spring out of the way, he was struck by one of the crosstrees and hurled into the boiling surf.

Though partly stunned, he had the presence of mind to thrust his arms through the broken shrouds, and in this half conscious state he was carried out to sea by the broken mast.

The night was intensely dark, and, tossed upon the crest of huge waves, Snowball's heart began to fall.

He saw at intervals the lights of Fort San Jose gradually lessen, and at length become indistinct.

Then he knew he was being carried out to sea, and nothing short of a miracle could save him.

Long before the darkness was broken by the coming light of day, the sea began to subside, and the howling winds to abate their fury.

Snowball's position began to improve, and by merely touching the broken mast he was enabled to keep himself afloat.

Daylight found him lying on his back in the now quiet waters, and as the misty veil began to dissolve under the sun's rays a cry of delight came from the African's lips.

Between the fringe of misty vapour and the water he saw the hulls of two vessels coming slowly towards him.

And as he recognised the hull of one his joy found expression in a gladsome shout.

"De War Cloud!" he cried. "I saved; tank de great Gorramighty!"

Yes; it was the War Cloud, and her consort the Thunderer, who were sailing in obedience to an order left by Captain Dragon before he left with the boats to rescue his rash young friend from his peril.

"If I do not return in twelve hours," the Corsair said to his lieutenant, young Phillips, "sail towards those mountain tops, and you will find me either dead or a prisoner at their base."

The stipulated time passed, and the Thunderer's anxious crew began to grow impatient at their commander's absence.

Young Phillips signalled to the War Cloud to accompany him in his search for the two leaders, and spreading their sails the vessels went in quest of their chiefs.

For several hours they cruised about the place where Captain Dragon had indicated, but to no purpose.

They could obtain no tidings of those they sought, except the War Cloud's empty pinnace, which had floated from the Peruvian's sloop when her crew rushed on board.

With heavy hearts the crews of each vessel held a council as to their best mode of proceeding.

Young Phillips was at their head, and, after many schemes had been devised, he said—

"There is but one thing left for us—if they are prisoners, to find out where they are, and, if possible, liberate them; if dead, to wreak a terrible vengeance."

His words found a ready echo in the hearts of all present, and they sailed to the place where our hero had performed his daring exploit.

The young lieutenant would have bombarded the place, had not the principal inhabitants voluntarily came forward and offered themselves as hostages, for they truly said—

"Your chieftain is not here, he has been and carried off a considerable amount of wealth, and to prove our words, we would remain in your hands until he is found. Should he be found in this town, we will suffer by any death you may inflict."

There was no doubt in their truthfulness,

and the young officer with a sigh bade them depart.

The merchants were evidently impressed with the youth's generosity in setting them free, and, as though to make a return for it, told David Shopland that a sloop of war had passed.

Young Shopland's face bore a joyful expression. This clue was sufficient.

The next step was to discover the course taken by the sloop, and by cross-questioning the lieutenant of the Black Squall learned enough to cause him to spread all the sails the vessels could carry and leave the town.

Scarcely had the shore faded from their sight when the storm, which had been so destructive to the sloop, burst upon the Black Squall and her companions.

Both were good sea boats and well handled by their veteran crews and rode out the hurricane in safety and at the time they were seen by Snowball, young David was cruising in the South American waters, watching for the sloop that he supposed held his commander a prisoner.

Side by side the vessels gracefully skimmed the waters and when they were within two cables' length of the overjoyed Snowball, he gave a mighty shout that was heard on both vessels.

Those on board the War Cloud instantly recognised the well-known voice of their sable lieutenant, and the vessel was speedily rounded to and a boat lowered before those on board the vessel could well understand that mighty voice, which seemed to come from the depths of old Naptune's domain.

Snowball floating about at the mercy of the ocean and Snowball on board his ship were two different beings.

His former sadness soon passed away as he trod the deck, and instead of seeking that repose which his frame so much needed, he gave the instant orders for the vessel's head to be turned towards Fort San Jose.

The lieutenant, though not aware of Snowball's reasons for altering the course of the outlaw's craft, trimmed her sails, and kept her company so close, that every word spoken by Snowball could be plainly heard on board the Black Squall.

Young David's mind was in a state of suspense until he knew whether his commander was alive or dead.

For, like too many, he looked at the dark side of everything first, and naturally concluded, when he saw Snowball hurled from the broken mast, that some terrible misfortune had overtaken them on board the sloop, and all except the African had perished.

He determined to know the worst at once, and, jumping upon a gun, he called out to Snowball—

"What has occurred, are you only left?"

"Nebber say die, David. I hope not, but tink it berry likely dere are but you ob dem alive now.'

THE ENGAGEMENT.

"Why ? has the ship foundered ?"

"It am a long story, but I will tell you some oder time, at present, all I know was dat de sloop go to pieces on de rock just under dam fort, and I was taken out to sea, dat all I know, now."

"On the rocks, you say ?"

"Yes."

"Then there was a chance that our messmates may have escaped last night's storm."

"Yes 'scaped de storm, but dere was de guns ob de fort firing 'pon de vessel afore we smash, so dat if dey are on de rocks de dam red coats ab dem."

"Take them prisoners you mean ?"

"Yes."

"Let us hope it is so," said David, "if we cannot rescue them we will go down under the batteries."

"Dat am it, Charley, clap on de sail my boy for we hab a long way to go."

There was a chance that their friends were yet alive should Snowball's surmise be correct.

In spite of the speed of the vessel, it was nightfall when they came in sight of the frowning walls of Fort San Jose.

Both Snowball and Charley Phillips were too well acquainted with the treacherous nature of the garrison to permit their vessel to be seen.

A sheltered spot was found for an anchorage, and both vessels remained stationary for the night.

Though the vessels were at anchor, their commanders were not wasting time.

Snowball, Charley Phillips, and a well-armed crew put off from the War Cloud, and with muffled oars rowed beneath the batteries.

Everything was as silent as the tomb, and save for the lights which gleamed from the fort seemed deserted.

The little band of determined men in the small boat were not deceived by the quietude which reigned above them.

They knew that the slightest sound would cause a dozen guns to belch forth fire and destruction upon them.

"We not find out much dis way, anyhow," whispered Snowball to David ; "s'pose we pull to de place where de sloop went down, and see if we can learn a little more."

"It will be the best plan," was the whispered reply ; "pull softly lads, remember there are fifty guns above you."

The men needed no reminding of their peril, they knew one false move would cause them to be blotted out from the world for ever.

The boat was taken as near the shore as possible without the keel grating upon the sands.

Then Snowball and David Shopland went ashore.

Creeping forward upon their hands and knees, they neared the rampart where Captain Dragon had first spoken to the Peruvian officer.

Here they paused, and held a whispered consultation.

While they were holding council to consider the next move, a footstep caused both to start and turn.

Emerging from the shadow of the rampart, they beheld a man's form.

Snowball drew his long deadly knife from its sheath and awaited, ready to slay the intruder should he pass them.

Whoever the man was, he had no knowledge of the presence of Snowball and his companion.

CHAPTER CXXI.

SNOWBALL LISTENS TO A YARN.

He stepped lighly on the uneven ground, and at times stopped and listened intently.

"Stay here," whispered Snowball to his companion, "I'll go de trail."

As noiselessly as a panther, the African, knife in hand, followed the stranger.

Swift as the eagle's swoop, the black giant, when within a few feet of his prey, sprang forward and seized his throat.

"The debbil," he muttered, as he did so, untwining his sinewy fingers from the prisoner's throat, " dat you, Jack? Where de young Chief?"

"Along with the rest in the fort."

"Hab you been dere, too?"

"No. I saw them all go inside, and should have gone too, but the figger head of that furrin wash tub was laid-to athwart my timbers, and I was too far for them to hear me by shouting."

"Hab you seen de chief since he go inside?"

"Yes, once. This morning I was able to get loose from the lump of wood which tumbled on top of me, and, thinks I, well, the boys are inside enjoying themselves, suppose I go too."

"Just as I was a going to hail the fellow on that tower to let me in, I hears the drums going like mad inside. I stopped short and listens, and precious lucky I did, or I should have been one for cold lead to-morrow."

"What—de—debbil—but go on."

"Heave to a minute, have you got a morsel of baccer, I've been behind that good looking stone without tasting the weed for nigh two days."

Snowball threw a roll of pigtail to Jack, and grumbled—

"Now, go on."

"Well, as I says before, the drums were going like mad."

"You say dat before—go on."

"So when I hears them at it I stops short, jist as I was about to hail and, thinks—"

"Yes, go on."

"I thinks there's something up, and mounts up behind that lump of stone; all the way up to where the drums was agoing was like steps."

"Cut out of a rock you mean?"

"Yes, so up I gets and peeps over, and sees all our messmates with irons on."

"What, de chief and all? Go on."

"Yes; and a little fellow in a big hat reading something in a lingo I couldn't overhaul."

"Yes, but go on."

"So I waits until he'd spun his yarn; then the Captain of the Thunderer tells our boys that they has all to be shot to-morrow morning at sunrise.'

"Gorramighty—you—but go on."

"Then, of course I was going to get down as quiet as I could, but the soldiers takes away the prisoners, and I had to be quiet until they passed."

"Yes, yes, go on."

"When they had gone by, I began to get down as quick as I could, and in swinging off from the mouth of a gun, I put my foot on a window; of course the next step brings my face to the window, and I saw—"

"You saw de—go on."

"I saw the chief sitting on an old powder barrel."

"What, by gar! Where dis window?"

"You see that light?"

"Dere?"

"Yes. Well, a little to the right of that is some iron bars, and that's where it is."

Snowball waited to hear no more.

A few steps brought him to young Phillip's side, to whom he related the particulars of Jack's rather longwinded account.

Charley Phillips was silent for a few seconds; then he asked—

"So you think you can climb the face of that rocky fort?"

"Climb," said Snowball, "sartingly."

"He is, you say, to be shot with the others at sunrise."

"Yes; dat's his words."

"Well, there is plenty of time: but before you make an attempt to see him, you let the garrison go to rest."

"You tink that the best?"

"Certainly; let us go back to the ship and bring all the men we can muster here, also a sabre and pistols for the young chief."

Charley's advice was acted upon.

The crews were silently disembarked under the ramparts, and Snowball ascended the rocky face of the fort.

How he found the young chief the reader is already aware.

When Snowball made his perilous ascent, he took the precaution to carry a coil of rope round his body, one end of which he fastened to the iron bars to facilitate his descent and enable the men below to ascend.

The young chief's face bore a proud look as he walked to and fro in his cell, one hand grasping his bright weapon, the other a loaded pistol.

"Let them come now," he thought, "I will meet them, not as a manacled felon, but as a foe, ready with my good blade to contest my life."

The regular tramp of armed men interrupted his reverie; they were in the corridor.

"Halt," said the officer commanding.

Then the door was flung open, and a non-commissioned officer with a dozen men entered the cell.

A sign was given for the young chief to follow him.

Midshipman Tom gave an anxious look at the grating.

The sign was repeated.

The young chief gave another look for the expected assistance, then threw himself in an attitude of defence.

For a moment the soldiers stood astounded, but at a word from their officer they brought their bayonets to the charge and rushed upon the gallant fellow who had determined to sell his life so dearly.

CHAPTER CXXI.

A VILLAIN PUNISHED.

Had Neville Wirely been wise, he would have been warned by the glisten in Laura's grey eyes when he entered the room.

The flash of indignation, the look of scorn with which she regarded his order to the housekeeper to leave the room, were either unobserved or unheeded by him.

"Laura," he said in a thick voice, "do you think I have risked so much in bringing you here without some motive?"

His question remained unanswered.

"You do not answer, my fair Laura," he said, drawing towards her; "and I would not insult so lovely a charmer's delicate mind, but we must understand each other. That becomes a necessity. Yes, Laura, you must be mine—willingly I would much prefer—and whatever wealth can bestow upon you, and an adoring husband grant you, shall be yours; but refuse, and—"

She listened to him with suppressed breathing and dilated nostrils, but before the coming threat could escape his lips, the poor girl's indignation broke forth.

"Monster!" she iterated, "for man you are not, with all your sophistry, with all your cunning—I know you. I hate you; and ere those foul lips of yours shall sully my cheek, this hand shall wrest you with a giant's strength."

"This is your final answer?" said Neville.

"It is."

Wirely made a movement towards her, his teeth close set and his face distorted with unbridled passion.

"Fool!" he hissed, "do you—"

Before he could complete his sentence the brave-hearted girl stepped aside, and, snatching a marble figure from the mantel-piece, held it aloft.

"Stand off!" she exclaimed, "or by heaven for you or me the last hour has come."

A mocking laugh came from Neville Wirely's lips, and he clutched her disengaged hand, at the same time, struggling to wrest the marble figure from her spasmodic grasp.

"Heaven will help me, and I despair not."

As she gave utterance to this exclamation, she raised she instrument of defence above her head and brought it with the force of an athlete upon the miscreant's temple, and he fell bleeding and senseless at her feet.

It was this appalling sight that Neville's father beheld when he opened the chamber door. The half frantic maiden, with the shattered figure besmeared with blood in her hand, and his hopeful son apparently dead, the crimson fluid weltering from a deep gash on his forehead.

Laura saw the old man fall, and she stood for a few minutes dazed and powerless by the deed she had thus, in her own defence, committed.

The feeling having passed away, she sprang to the door to escape from the house, but before she could step over the elder Wirely's prostrate form, the housekeeper and several servants, male and female, came rushing up the stairs.

To secure Laura was their first object.

Laura reeled backwards, and two strong men-servants quickly had her in their grasp, and fastened her small wrists together.

This done, they raised Neville Wirely from the floor, and carried him to his bed, the father being assisted—stricken down with horror and fear—to follow him.

Neville was not so much injured as at first was conjectured, and old Wirely, leaving his son, went below to confer with a person who desired to see him upon most important matters.

In the same chamber where Neville and his father had talked over and plotted against the unfortunate Laura, a stranger was awaiting the arrival of the elder Wirely.

A glance at his weather-beaten face at once proclaimed him to be a seafaring man.

He was the captain of the vessel called the Psyche, a craft renowned for her speed as well as her beauty.

It seemed strange to those who knew the captain that so small a vessel as his should carry merchandise to the East, and realise the immense profits that he was wont to boast about.

Many who had seen the Psyche were probably aware there was no storage room between decks, and had the crew been asked, they would have said that the trim little craft carried as neat an armament as any vessel afloat.

Twelve long polished brass guns were wont to gleam from her sides when she cut her way through the sunny seas.

The captain was jealous of his worthy freight, and in those waters well-manned Adriatic proas were in the habit of attacking merchantmen.

The Psyche herself had been once attacked, but the reception they met engendered so much respect for the little rakish craft, that she could now pass in safety through the whole piratical fleet.

At the time when her captain visited old Wirely, his vessel was snugly moored in the mouth of the Thames, and dozens of the king's vessels passed and repassed her without more than a slight notice.

She was small they had remarked for a merchantman, and they wondered how she managed to escape the many dangers that existed by the swarms of freebooters infesting the seas.

But these king's officers knew not that hidden between her decks were the long brass guns that enabled the Psyche to cope with an enemy in size much her superior.

They knew not that besides the half-dozen seamen who were hanging about her deck, that below nearly a hundred brawny fellows were hidden.

CHAPTER CXXI.

A WOLF IN SHEEP'S CLOTHING.

THE captain of the Psyche was a man from forty to fifty years of age; a bland, smoothed tongued gentleman, with oily words that forced their way to the listener's heart, and invariably gained any point that his worthy self wished to accomplish.

When the elder Wirely entered the room the captain of the Psyche rose, and, with a courteous bow, said—

"I trust, my dear sir, I have not disturbed you."

"No, I wish you had come before," was the reply.

"Had I known that, nothing would have given me greater pleasure to have earlier sought you."

Old Wirely stayed his visitor's flow of words by a wave of the hand-

"Now, Captain Glitter, let us proceed to business."

"Oh, with the liveliest pleasure. I am quite ready."

"You, perhaps, understand partly from my letter, the business I wish you to undertake."

"Certainly—partly yes, but not exactly thoroughly."

"Very well, then I will enlighten you; but first you must inform me whether there will be any chance of the person I shall hand over to you ever returning to England."

"Is it a lady?"

"Yes."

Captain Glitter of the Psyche smiled blandly as he asked—

"Is she pretty?"

"As beautiful as Venus."

"You interest me, Mr. Wirely—very much interest me; young and beautiful you said, dark, I suppose, as the ra—"

"No," Wirely interrupted, "a blonde, hair of a sunny hue, eyes blue and melting."

"You are quite poetical, Mr. Wirely, 'pon my soul you are. Well, should the original be but half as beautiful as you have described her, I can safely say, when she leaves England it will be for ever."

"You can assert this without fear of contradiction."

"My dear sir, Paulus Glitter, of the Psyche, never asserts more than he can fulfil."

Old Neville's face wore a self-satisfied expression as he listened to the other's words, then he arose, and motioning his visitor to follow him, they left the apartment and went to Laura's chamber.

The hapless girl was lying on a sofa in a state of the greatest despondency, and the housekeeper was seated near her couch, soothing the weeping maiden.

The entrance of Captain Glitter and the elder Wirely caused the weeping girl to look up, and, seeing that neither of the intruders was her persecutors she sprang from the couch, and rushing towards them, said—

"Have you come to save me, to release me from this fearful place?"

Captain Glitter took the cue, and answered—

"I will save you, young lady, if you are in peril."

Laura burst into tears; the kindly voice and deceptive look caused tears of joy to spring from her heart.

"In peril," she answered piteously; "oh sir I am indeed in the greatest peril—as great as ever a poor defenceless girl was placed in. Will you protect me?"

"You can go now, Mrs. Maberly. This is the doctor; he will take our patient away with him and take Miss Laura under his special care."

The woman curtsied and left the room, thoroughly blinded by the cunning of old Wirely.

When the door had closed, old Wirely stood aside, and listened intently to Laura and the captain of the Psyche.

"The game is in his own hands," thought the old rascal, "if he has sense enough to seize the chance, she can be taken from here as easily as I could have arranged had I planned it for months."

Old Wirely need not have been under the least apprehension respecting his associate; Captain Glitter always had his eyes and ears open.

With one of his blandest smiles, he took Laura's trembling hand and said—

"If you will command me, my dear young lady, I will do anything you wish. I am but a rough sailor, and unused to make courtly speeches, but before any harm shall come to you, I will be your champion."

The word sailor fell upon the young girl's heart with a joyful sound, and she replied—

"Take me from here is all I ask! You are a sailor and will help me."

"I will; and woe be to those who dare bar our passage."

Old Neville accompanied them to the door and left the

Poor ill-fated girl. She clung to the treacherous scoundrel; and when he asked her name, and how she came in the power of Wirely and his son, she told him the story, not only of her abduction, but of her life, beseeching him to take her back to her youthful lover.

He listened to her words with well-assumed interest, and when she had concluded he said—

"Fortune has been, under all your afflictions, kind in bringing you to that home. My ship will weigh anchor upon my return, and sail to the very nearest port to the cave of the famous outlaw chief. Can you feel safe under my charge?"

"Oh, sir, I could indeed, feel safe with you. Your kindness has already made me feel towards you as a child to her father."

The captain of the Psyche called a coach, and placed his young charge inside.

He took a seat beside her, and, with paternal kindness, wrapped his boat cloak around her thinly-clad form.

"The night air is cold," he said, "for one so delicate as yourself."

She thanked him in a low sweet voice, and for the first time since her abduction from the tower, a ray of hope brought relief to her heart.

A hackney coach conveyed them to a piece of waste ground on the banks of the Thames, and Captain Glitter handed the young maiden from the vehicle, paying the driver; the coach rolled away, and they were alone.

Laura, full in the confidence of her conductor's honest intentions, nestled closely to his side.

They walked slowly towards the turgid water, and when near the edge of the river the Captain took a boatswain's whistle from his pocket, and blew a shrill call.

It was answered apparently from the middle of the stream, and Paulus Glitter, in reply to Laura's question, said—

"My boat is here awaiting me."

In confirmation of his words, the long steady jerk of a practised boat's crew could be heard, and in a few seconds an eight-oared boat grounded at their feet.

With courtier-like grace, Captain Glitter handed the deluded girl to the stern sheets, and when they were seated the boat was pushed off and, impelled by eight muscular rowers, shot down the stream towards a vessel whose lights were barely discernible.

In five minutes more Laura Grey was on board the Psyche, and cut off from all hope of ever again beholding those she loved.

CHAPTER CXXIII.

A GALLANT DEFENCE.

WITH a haughty look of defiance the gallant boy met the line of steel that was levelled at his body.

Swift as the vivid's lightning flash, his bright blade beat off the bayonets and sent two of the foremost of his foes to the ground.

One never to rise more.

The sudden change in our hero's position had imbued him with a reckless disregard for life.

He had been doomed to death, but ere the sentence could be carried into effect, he found himself with a trusty blade in his grasp, and, lion-like, he determined to perish rather than submit to capture.

With an impetus that the soldiers were unprepared for, he bore down upon them and cut and hewed without mercy.

The doorway was narrow and prevented them from using their bayonets with effect, and not daring to load, they were fain to beat a hasty retreat, leaving four of their companions dead and two wounded in the cell.

Flushed with his victory, the young chief stood leaning upon his reeking blade and waiting for the door to re-open and the contest to be resumed.

While standing thus, a noise at the side of his cell caused him to start, and turning towards the sound, he beheld one of the stones vibrating.

Before he could form any idea of the cause of this strange phenomenon, a husky voice as though the speaker's head was muffled in a blanket, rung out with a—

"Are you alive, Tom?"

"Captain Dragon," exclaimed our hero, "what are you doing?"

"Picking away the rotten mortar from the old stones; bear a hand, and I will come and see you."

The young chief snatched a bayonet from the ground, and began to loosen the dried mortar.

His aid soon enabled the corsair captain to push the stone from its place, and squeezing through the narrow aperture, he rolled into the cell.

"Hallo!" was his exclamation when he beheld

the fallen men and Tom's weapon, "what the deuce—how did you manage this?"

"Snowball has been here."

"Snowball—hurrah! then we have a chance of cheating the devil and the governor."

"I fear not; but here lies the first of the messengers; but here——"

"What is the matter?"

"Your legs are free?"

"Oh, is that all? Well, yes, Tom, two clumsy fools gave me a pair of leg-irons big enough for Fin McCaul the Irish giant."

"You were fortunate."

"Yes, and more so when I found this old piece of iron,"

"You dare, Massa Tom?"

The friends looked up and beheld Snowball's shining face at the window.

"Yes, Snowball; come down or we shall be overmatched. I hear the tramp of the soldiers coming down the corridor.'

"Dey be dam, Massa Tom. The boys are behind me on the rock—look out!"

With this caution, the African scrambled through the window, and was soon followed by the crew of the War Cloud.

Captain Dragon had provided himself with a musket and bayonet of one of the fallen men.

The soldiers' tramp was coming nearer and nearer, and to judge by the sound it was evident that there were a great number of soldiers on their way to the daring young chieftain's cell.

"Hush," said Captain Dragon, "get back all of you to the cell; quick, the door will be opened directly and if these vagabonds see all our cheerful faces, they will most likely close it again, and trap us like so many rats."

"We can get out of the window," suggested one of the outlaws.

"Yes," said the captain, "and they can shoot your messmates while we are sneaking away like so many monkeys down a rope."

The man fell back; he felt sorry he had spoken.

The quiet rebuke in Captain's Dragon's answer took more effect than a loudly spoken reprimand.

Squeezing themselves as closely as possible against the darkest side of the cell, the followers of Midshipman Tom and Captain Dragon awaited a word from their leader.

The prison door was slowly opened, and the young officer waved his followers back and advanced a few steps inside.

"Why senor," said he to Captain Dragon, "I thought you were in the next cell."

"Well, you see I am here," replied the Captain.

The officer continued "you will probably guess my errand, it is, I regret to say, to lead your friend and yourself to the place of execution, or shoot you in your cells."

"Then," said Captain Dragon, "you have made a mistake; neither myself nor my friend mean you to do either in cold blood at any rate."

"Senor must listen to reason. I have fifty men outside with loaded weapons."

"And I," said Captain Dragon, "have twenty thorough British bull-dogs that are able to lick four times your number of scarecrows that you have at your back." Then he added in English, "Come out and show yourselves."

The sight of Banquo's ghost had not a quarter the effect upon Macbeth that the appearance of this score of sturdy Englishmen had upon the Peruvian officer.

He fell back and called upon his men to fire.

But before he could cause a trigger to be pulled, a soul-stirring British hurrah rang through the vaulted passages of the Fort San Jose, and cutlass in hand the hardy Englishmen rushed like an avalanche upon the foe.

Tom, Snowball, and Captain Dragon were in the rear, and, despite the close volley of the musketry that was poured in upon them, they bore back the foremost of the soldiers.

Fighting in such close quarters, the cutlass and pistol told with deadly effect upon the men armed with the long unwieldy muskets and bayonets.

The last was the only weapon they could use, for the sturdy Britons pressed them so close that they had no opportunity of reloading.

Long and deadly was the contest in that narrow passage, until the fallen bodies of the dark clad sharpshooters formed a rampart between the foes.

Inch by inch the troops fell back until they gained the ramparts, then forming lines they tried to repel the further advance of the seamen.

The effort was useless.

The gallant young chieftain waved his red sword above his head, and in a ringing voice, shouted—

"Forward, charge—charge!"

He led them at a splendid pace, and hurling themselves against the soldiers a fierce struggle ensued. A struggle that was worthy of England's tars, for the men were used only to fight behind stone walls, and they could not resist the onset, and after trying for a few seconds to keep their position, they turned and fled towards a body of men that were being brought down by the old commander in person.

"There goes the invincibles," laughed Captain Dragon, "and here comes some more."

"Massa Dragon," said Snowball, "dere is two guns dere; shall we take dem for our own use?"

"A good thought, Snowball. Forward, a dozen of you; and swing those guns round upon the head of that column."

Twenty men sprang forward to execute the order, and to the surprise of the adventurers, the old commander ordered his men to halt.

"See," said Captain Dragon, "the old scarecrow and his invincibles do not like our position; and they will hold a parley soon if we stand firm."

In halting his men the old officer had shown a little discretion, for the outlaws had clustered

"STAND TO YOUR GUNS, MY MEN!" SAID MIDSHIPMAN TOM.

upon a part of the ramparts considerably above where the troops had been advancing.

And to gain this spot the old fellow would be compelled to ascend a narrow pathway sufficient only for two men to pass at a time.

This part was now covered by the guns Captain Dragon had caused to be swung round.

"There will be no fighting," said the captain to Tom, "for another hour at least; the old beggar will shell us out."

"Not at all impossible. Had we not better cut our way through at once?"

"It would be best had we the fellows released from the cages."

"Ah! I had nearly forgotten them. Promise me you will not begin the fight until I return, and I will see and liberate them; they will be a welcome addition to the ranks."

"I promise you, Tom. Away, my lad."

The young chief sprang quickly towards the long corridor, and speedily unfastened the door of the chamber where the men were confined.

They gave a glad shout at beholding their young leader alive and well, and picking up some weapons that had fallen from the hands of the dead and dying, they followed Tom to the ramparts.

"Now, my lads," said Captain Dragon, "hurrah for the red cross banner. Follow me."

"Follow!" said Tom. "Down with the foe!"

The men answered their leaders' appeal by the Briton's war cry, and like a resistless flood, they bore down upon the soldiery.

There was another hand-to-hand struggle for a short time, but the men who had been condemned to death pressed to the front and soon hewed a passage through the foe.

The little governor would have been cut piecemeal had not Snowball placed his hand under his arm as they fought their way to the gates of the fortress. The African growled—

"By gar! you want to shoot the chief! I gib you suffink when we get on board."

The capture of their commander soon ended the affray, although one or two attempts were made to rescue him from the black giant; those who attempted it felt the weight of the African's weapon, which struck such a terror into the hearts of those who beheld their comrades' fate that they readily made way for the victorious seamen.

When they reached the open ground, the crews of both vessels were assembled to count the missing.

In the midst of this proceeding a howl of rage came from Snowball.

All turned to ascertain the cause, and on appealing to the African they found that their beloved young leader was absent.

They would have returned to the fortress to search, but a glance at the batteries told them that another moment's delay would bring a storm of grape upon them.

With cries of vengeance loud and deep, the sailors went towards their vessels, and the soldiery in impotent rage fired a dozen shotted guns upon them.

Captain Dragon turned and shook his clenched hand at the fortress, and said, fiercely—

"Well, my invincible friends, I'll rattle your old place about your ears. Poor Tom; if there's any hurt comes to him I'll put them all to the sword."

"By gar! dey better not," said Snowball, "or I'll cut dis little governor, who am de cause of it all, into little pieces. Poor Massa Tom. I wonder when him taken. I thought he came out wid us."

"I saw him," said Captain Dragon, "cut down two fellows who were trying to stop his way."

"When was dat?"

"Not a minute before we passed through the gates."

"Well where the debbil is he, then?"

Snowball shook his head; he could not answer that query, and he felt sure that something very strange had occurred.

With the sad uncertainty of their chief's fate hanging over them, the men longed to begin the bombardment of Fort San Jose.

CHAPTER CXXIV.

RED HAND'S STRATAGEM.

AMONG the many marauders who formerly infested the seas, Derrick, alias Red Hand, ranks as the most merciless of his class.

Jones, Ilian, Larrent, and other pirate leaders have been distinguishable in no way from cannibals, except that they abstained from eating each other's flesh.

But these men, savage as they were, were never known to act unmercifully to their hapless prisoners—a redeeming trait that was never found in the barbarities exercised by Red Hand.

He seemed at all times like a hungry panther, who had just tasted blood, and went prowling about to finish his meal.

His doctrine was ever to kill all who came in his way.

The captain of the Hercules well knew the difficult task he had assigned himself when he vowed to track Red Hand, and not put into port until he had accomplished the miscreant's destruction.

The gallant officers, down to the youngest midshipman, followed the example, and slept with their swords at their sides, determined to keep them there until they had rid the world of a monster.

A week had elapsed since the day when young Rilcher and old Dick had brought the hapless captain of the merchant ship and his wife and child aboard.

A week which had passed heavily on board the stout old frigate—a week of anxious watching for the hardy crew, and one of ceaseless vigilance on the part of one of the officers.

It was now mid-day, and the bright sun rode high in the heavens, throwing its resplendent rays on the pathless waters.

The Hercules, with every sail set, was gliding through the golden-tipped waters with a swiftness that seemed to please her bronzed commander, for he would pause in his monotonous walk and look upward at the spars with a pleased expression upon his weather-beaten face.

The middy was standing near the captain, in obedience to the latter's command.

The young middy had risen high in his commander's estimation, in consequence of the clever manner in which he had escaped from Red Hand's clutches, and the brave way in which he had stood at the open hatchway, daring the whole pirate horde to ascend and face him—a mere boy.

The captain of the Hercules had heard this from

the mouth of old Dick, who loved to sing the praises of his young favourite.

The commander's eyes were now fixed upon the young midshipman as he resumed his walk to and fro the quarter-deck, and as he came near the side where Sydney was standing, he said—

"There's a week gone, Mr. Rilcher, and I do not even see a speck of that scoundrel's vessel. I wonder whether I shall have to say the same this day week."

"I hope not, sir."

"I hope not too, my boy, for to tell you the truth, I begin to feel I made rather a rash vow."

The midshipman was silent.

He didn't care about telling the captain his own opinion of the matter, and he was too manly to utter a falsehood.

What was passing in the young officer's mind was easily guessed by the commander, for he said laughingly—

"Rather Quixotic, was it not, my young friend? But, anyway, it is rather unpleasant to remain so long in these calm latitudes, without unfastening a belt or a button."

"It is, sir, but I—and I think I can say every officer and man in the vessel—will remain in their garments until the pirate either goes to the bottom, or your wishes are accomplished. No matter when that may be."

"Then, Mr. Rilcher, I'm afraid it will be some time before we change our rig."

"Why, sir, one broadside from us would send pirates and ship beneath the water."

"True, my boy. In a fair fight that would be child's play to us; but the subtle dodgery that scoundrel is master of will give us some trouble yet to grapple with him."

The midshipman was about to answer, when his eyes detected a faint speck on the distant horizon.

"What do you see, Mr. Rilcher?" asked the captain, when he saw the boy straining his eyes towards the distant object.

"A sail, sir."

"A sail!"—taking the glass from the rack as he spoke—"why so it is. It's coming towards us too. Take the glass; you will make her out better than I can."

Sydney placed the glass to his eye, and soon after an expression of great joy came from his lips.

"Why, sir," said the delighted boy, "it's the Don Jose herself—Red Hand's craft."

"Sure?"

"Certain. I know her. I could tell the peculiar cut of her bows among a thousand."

This little parley had scarcely taken place ere the man at the masthead sang out:

"A sail on the starboard bow!"

The men sprang from the booms and from behind the guns where they had been lying out of the sun's rays, and ran to his side.

Then to their joy Captain White sang out—

"The pirate is in sight now, my boys, hurrah!"

"Hurrah!" came speedily from two hundred lusty throats, and the drum rattled out the well-known signal that caused every heart to beat in anticipation of a great victory.

"The pirate in sight," went round like magic, though the crew and every man and boy was on the deck, eagerly waiting to grapple with the foe.

Old Dick who partook of the share of the excitement by jumping about the forecastle, shouting—

"Remember, messmates, six of us was poisoned by the cutthroat gang. Give 'em no quarter."

This suggestion coming in the shape pretty much of a command, met a willing acceptation from the seamen; and it was clear enough that but scant mercy might be expected for Red Hand from the blue-jackets crew on board the Hercules.

There was but little noise and no confusion, as the Hercules was being prepared to meet the enemy.

About the same time the Hercules' glasses were busy making out the strange sail; the pirates' captain, in a state of half-drunk fury, came on deck, having been aroused from his sleep by his first officer, reporting a sail in sight rapidly nearing them.

The Don Jose at the time was under but little canvas, cruising about in hopes of meeting a small fleet of traders bound to Genvenala.

These vessels were single masted, and not larger than a modern yacht, but then trading was prosperous not only in rich merchandise but in wrought gold and silver.

It was the apprehension that he might have to relinguish the capture of the rich booty that caused Red Hand's outburst of temper.

Glaring savagely at the spectral outlines of the Hercules and turning to his first officer he said—

"That is the infernal frigate that overhauled us. Put on all the sail she will carry."

The Don Jose soon increased her speed but to add to Red Hand's rage, the frigate still hung upon his track.

"Curse them," he hissed, "we shall not only have to slip away from these waters during the night, but that English hound will hunt the Red Indian Fleet, and convoy them to port."

"I don't think we can escape her anyhow," said the first officer. "See, her white line is now distinctly visible."

Red Hand gnashed his teeth in a complete frenzy.

The huge vessel's hull was still bearing more and more towards them.

"More sail!" he roared. "Splice an extra topmast for'ard, or you'll find your ugly carcasses dangling at the frigate's yardarm before long."

The men swarmed up the shrouds, and speedily executed the corsair's orders.

Another hour passed, and by this time the evening shadows began to creep over the blue waters:

but, though he at first thought the darkness might favour his escape, to his dismay the Hercules came hand over hand upon him, and he saw that before morning he must be overtaken.

Thus finding his escape impossible his subtle mind engaged itself in devising some crafty means for eluding his mighty foe.

Ten minutes' thought occupied him.

"Send the carpenter here and his crew," he called out.

The word was passed, when he made his appearance he was astounded by the captain saying—

"Bring aft the spare masts on deck, quick, don't stand staring there. If you want enlivening I will order a rope's end for you."

A number of the crew were sent below to assist the carpenter, and in an incredibly short space of time the deck was strewn with spars.

"All saws and axes now upon deck, and cut these spars into pieces as long as your ugly carcase," was the next order.

Mutely wondering at the strange orders, the men set to work and cut up the spars.

"Now," said Red Hand, "fasten them in an upright position on the deck, some near the guns, some there," pointing to the quarter-deck, "and above a dozen on the fo'castle."

The pieces of wood thus arranged, he further startled his men by saying.

"Down below all of you, and bring your kits an deck, every hat, every jacket, and cap or glazed hat, and look sharp about it."

The meaning of the pirate's strange orders now began to flash upon the crew, as he ordered every block of wood to be rigged out in a jacket or cap, or glazed hat, while those on the quarter-deck were dressed from the chests of the officers and himself.

The effect of those dummies was most strange.

At a short distance they gave the vessel an appearance of being armed with men.

"Now," said Red Hand, "put the helm down, and lower the boats. Ha! ha! ha! They shall capture Red Hand and his ship—of course they shall!"

Darkness had now set in, and the crew of pirates were ordered to leave the Don Jose, and the more thoroughly to deceive the Hercules, a couple of lights were suspended from the stern of the abandoned vessel.

Safely out of the imminent danger of getting into the boats and being swamped, as they were pulling away from the Don Jose, the lines that held the boats on were cut, the back wash of the water, as the vessel surged on, threatening every moment to upset them.

"Pull for your lives!" Red Hand screamed out.

Though the pirates were resting upon their oars, awaiting the command, they had not taken two strokes when the huge hull swung round, and forced the boats down to the gunwale under her side.

A cry of alarm came from the unfortunate wretches, who made sure their last hour was come.

This cry was followed by one of rage from their leader, who, drawing a pistol from his belt, stamped and roared—

"The next one that opens his lips dies! Pull you hounds!—pull for your lives! The rudder has broken loose! Pull, or this minute we are swamped!"

His savage words saved them from death.

By the assistance of their oars being pressed against the sides, they escaped being drawn beneath the huge hull of the deserted vessel.

Calling upon the other boats to follow him, he led the way to Peru; but the darkness increased the sea began to rise with fearful augury, the wind howled and shrieked above their heads and vivid flashes of light started from the murky heavens.

What chance had these miserable crews out in such a night in open boats, without compass?

None!

And every crime-stained miscreant sank sullen and savage in their boats, crouching to escape the heavy seas they shipped, and waiting for the moment that would swamp their frail boats sending them, their wicked occupants, to eternity.

———

CHAPTER CXXV.

THE STRATAGEM SUCCEEDS.

"Well, Mr. Rilcher, do you think we shall overtake the Don Jose before dark?"

The midshipman looked long and attentively at the vessel before he answered.

"I think not, sir," he said; "see, they are putting on extra canvas."

"We will follow the example," said the captain.

This conversation took place between the captain of the Hercules and his young middy at the time Red Hand ordered an extra sail to be jury rigged.

The Hercules increasing her canvas at the same time, caused her to sail in equal speed with her foe.

Captain White stood upon the quarter-deck holding the night glass to his eyes.

Suddenly he closed it with a loud snap, and exclaimed—

"Portway, Rilcher! that fellow has the impudence to show a pair of lanterns for his stern."

This daring challenge caused the greatest excitement on board the man-of-war, and being thus as it were, mocked by their antagonist, the officer's cheek reddened with indignation.

There was one thing that astonished the captain of the frigate—that was, the manner in which the pirate craft seemed to sail before the wind.

To follow that strangely-handled craft kept the crew at the sails the whole night.

Once, for an hour, she disappeared altogether, then they beheld the tantalising lights suddenly appear in quite a contrary direction.

Towards daylight, however, they had the joy of beholding the troublesome Don within reach of the bow-chasers.

The vessel looked as though the deck was covered with men, so skilfully had the corsair placed the dummies; and in the distance it seemed, by the ship rolling to and fro, that the figures were in motion.

The black flag was flying at the Don's stern, and that emblem of piracy caused the red-crossed banner of St. George to be hoisted on board the frigate.

They were now within speaking distance, and Captain White, placing the speaking trumpet to his lips, shouted—

"Lower your flag, you scoundrel, or I'll fire!"

No response came, and the command was repeated.

Again the same death-like silence prevailed.

"Captain Biddles," said the commander of the Hercules to the officer of marines, "give those fellows a volley of musketry."

The rattle of fifty muskets was soon heard: but, to the surprise of all, the pirates still remained in their positions.

"What can the fellows mean?" said Captain White, angrily. "Surely they do not intend to cope with us by reserving their fire until we get alongside?"

"Such seems to be their intention," was the marine officer's reply. "Shall I give them another volley, captain?"

"No, thanks. Steady there with the helm. Now jam it down. Away there, boarders—follow me!"

The Don Jose was in the grip of the old frigate, and the gallant captain, at the head of his boarders, sprang upon her decks.

Every blue-jacket not wishing to be far behind his superiors reached the deck of the pirate ship about the same time as their captain.

The latter, averse to useless bloodshed, was calling upon the supposed leader in gold epaulettes and blue coat to surrender; but the seamen, not actuated by such considerations, began to lay about them with their cutlasses.

The first blow caused a roar of laughter, as the hats were knocked off the dummies, and in the place of men they found they had been chasing blocks of wood the whole night.

Captain White's face reddened with anger, and fully believing that the pirates were yet below he called upon them to follow, and dashed down the open hatchway.

Before he reached the bottom, a warning cry came from his lips, and he sprang up again, saying—

"Back! back, all of you! The villains have deserted the ship, and laid a mine! Back at once!"

The men fled hastily from the dangerous spot, and Captain White again descended, but this time with slow and cautious steps.

Luckily for the gallant fellows, their leader saw as he rushed down the steps another mine, the entire length of the lower deck.

The least touch from a foot even would have been sufficient to displace the other end, which was attached to a smouldering slow match, and so placed, that upon the wire being trodden upon, the match would fall into an open barrel of powder butts.

Thus the design of the villain was frustrated, and Captain White withdrew the open barrel of powder from the vicinity of the lurking fire, then crushed it until every spark had become extinct.

When he came upon deck, he was met by the gallant young middy.

"You here, Mr. Rilcher?"

"Yes; I thought I perhaps might be of service, as I am so well acquainted with the vessel."

"Thanks. I have removed the mine. There are no boats left to the vessel, are there, Mr. Rilcher?"

"None that I see, sir. They must have escaped soon after nightfall, and before this must have perished in the gale."

"I should think so, though we scarcely felt it. An open boat could not have lived an hour."

The young midshipman looked thoughtful as he said—

"No, sir; I do not think Red Hand would have put out to sea in those frail boats without having some place near at hand to shelter him."

"You think then——"

"That he is upon some island near here; certainly I do so."

"So much the better—remain on board the vessel and keep in my wake. I will scour these waters until I find some trace of the miscreant, dead or alive."

A clue was found sooner than they expected.

Two hours after this, a small, single-masted vessel shot alongside the frigate, and from the men on board Captain White learnt that Red Hand had fallen in with the little flotilla at daybreak, and butchered the crews of four vessels, his cutter alone having escaped the ruthless destroyer.

CHAPTER CXXVI.

TOM IN THE LION'S DEN.

CUTTING down all who opposed him, the gallant Tom fought his way to the gates of the fort.

Here his progress was stopped by the sudden rush of his companions, and he became separated from them, although it was but for an instant that he was borne back by the swaying combatants.

In that short space of time his little band had cut their way through the soldiery and passed outside the fort.

The gates were immediately closed by the troops, and they ventured to turn their guns upon the gallant little band.

Midshipman Tom saw at a glance the fearful peril in which he stood, and hastily stepping back he concealed himself behind a buttress, determined to wait until the soldiery left the vicinity of the only means of egress from Fort San Jose.

Even now his position was anything but a safe one.

He knew it, and prepared for danger, one hand grasping his trusty blade, the other a loaded pistol.

Then he stood and listened to the wild shouts of the men as they worked the battery over the gates.

Afar he heard the well known British hurrah, which came responsive to the yells of the Peruvian troops.

In the midst of these cries, he heard a low voice above him utter—

"Senor, you are in great danger! Quick, in at that gate."

He looked up and beheld the sweet young face of Narcisse, the governor's daughter, looking out upon him from a small casement.

His danger was of too great a magnitude for him to linger long after this friendly offer, and entering the open door which the maiden had referred to, he passed unseen into it.

The young girl met him upon the step, and, putting her fingers to her lips to enjoin silence, beckoned him to follow.

He was soon by her side, and then silently passed along a wide gallery, which, from the piles of arms that were fastened upon the walls, the young chief had no difficulty in recognising as the armoury.

At the end of this Narcisse opened a small door, and led him into the apartments used by her father.

"You can speak now, senor," she said, in a low sweet voice; "you are safe here."

The young chief bowed, and answered—

"Thanks, sweet lady, for your kindness. How can I sufficiently repay you?"

"By not mentioning it," she replied, artlessly. "I have seen you before. I would not allow you to be mercilessly butchered by those savage men. You are safe here. This is my father's chamber; none enter it but himself."

As though to contradict her words, the door opened, and an officer of the Peruvian artillery entered the room.

Narcisse turned aside, and held by the back of a chair to support her trembling frame.

Our hero laid his hand upon the butt of his pistol, and regarded the artillery officer with a bold, haughty look.

The latter seemed much surprised to find our hero in the commander's chamber, and bowing coldly to Narcisse, he said—

"Well may the arms of the invincible army be useless, when you, signora, act a traitor's part towards us."

The young leader's eyes flashed fire at the haughty manner of the artillery officer, and his fingers began to play nervously with the hilt of his jewelled scimitar.

The officer observing this, said, in a contemptuous manner—

"You are my prisoner—as such I seize you!"

And walking swiftly towards the young chief, endeavoured to seize him by the collar, which being resented, he drew his long sabre, and rushed madly upon Midshipman Tom.

The young chief met the onslaught with the most perfect coolness; his easy style of defence now made the officer understand that he whom he had before him was not to be despised.

Making a sudden feint, he sent the point of his blade through the fleshy part of the officer's arm.

The sabre fell from the latter's grasp, and with a yell of rage and pain, he rushed past his antagonist, shouting—

"Here!—beware!—bring up the guard!—treachery!—treachery! Here is one of the villains in our midst!"

The young chief had not noticed that during the fray the door had been swung partly open, and left sufficient room for a person to pass.

He only noticed it when he heard the other's voice, and would have followed him had not Narcisse cried out—

"You will be slain, senor! This way—come to my chamber!"

She led the way quickly through the guard rooms, and opening the door of her own room, motioned our hero to pass through.

No sooner had he done so than the angry voices of several men could be heard, and the hurried sound of many feet, as they dashed after the fugitive, headed by the wounded officer.

To close and bar the door with a cross piece of iron, was the work of a moment, and scarcely had she done so when the troopers rushed to the spot, and began beating in the panels with the butt ends of their muskets.

Unfortunatly for our hero, there were no secret doors or sliding panels in the stone-built fortress of Fort San Jose.

Thus, when he took refuge in the boudoir of the fair Narcisse, and his pursuers were trying to batter the door in, he felt that, unless some unexpected aid should arrive, he had but a short time to live.

But the dire peril his life was placed in did not dismay him; and when the splinters began to fly

A LEAP FOR LIFE.

out from the upper panels, his features possessed an expression of unyielding resolve.

Narcisse stood near the window, watching the gallant Tom with horrible feelings of apprehension.

A ringing blow upon the stout oaken door made her cower inwardly, and she saw the necessity for prompt action.

"Here, senor, quick!" she said. "Tear down the curtains—you can get on the ramparts by their aid."

Down the silk hangings speedily came, and quickly knotting them, Tom threw one end out of the window, the other end being fastened to the framework of the window.

"Thanks, lady," he said, as he sprang upon the window-sill, just as the door fell inside, and his foes, with a shout, rushed into the room.

Whilst the officers were searching the room, Tom was upon the rear of the rampart.

Now he was fired at, and having to battle to prevent his foes effecting a landing, he became weak and worn out with exertions and long fasting.

"Yield!" cried the officer.

Tom saw the blue waves a hundred feet below him—he saw his vessel standing out for the port—and determined to escape or die.

"Never!" said Tom, "behold death before surrender!"

Springing upon a gun, he gave a defiant cry, sprang upon the battlements, and went through the air until the ocean's mystic bosom hid him from his foes.

CHAPTER CXXVII.

ON BOARD THE PSYCHE.

REJOICING at her fancied escape from the hands of her foes, Laura Grey hailed with delight the fresh morning breeze that filled the sails of the Psyche.

Cleaving the water like a seabird, the low-hulled vessel soon left the crowd of shipping that filled the entrance to the Thames.

The white cliffs of England she saw recede from her sight with the pleasing thought that they would soon reappear, and she would be at her lonely home upon the crest of the rocks, filled her mind.

But when the days wore on and she saw no sign of land, a vague feeling of uneasiness began to steal over her.

Captain Glitter, though yet kind in his manner to her, she saw a change in him that was unexplainable.

Several times she had essayed to speak with him as he walked the small deck of his vessel.

But each time her words had been checked by a cold, haughty answer, and he had turned away as though her presence was distasteful to him.

Laura began to feel that all was not right on board the Psyche, and no sooner had this feeling taken possession of her mind, than a thousand little circumstances happened to strengthen her conviction.

A great change had taken place in the appearance of the Psyche since she had left England.

Fifty stout determined looking fellows composed her crew, she found, whereas in port, it appeared to consist of only a dozen hands.

Formidable weapons were bristling about the deck, which had been hitherto kept clear and as snow-white as a gentleman's yacht.

Around the masts were a number of long bladed formidable pikes, which were fitted into iron sockets to keep them in their places.

From stem to stern, muskets, pistols, and cutlasses hung from hooks beneath the sides, ready at any time for use.

Nor was this all.

Six brightly polished brass guns of formidable calibre, and great length of bore, had been placed at each side.

Upon the forecastle, too, there was a long heavy brass gun upon a moveable platform, and upon the quarterdeck a similar engine of destruction.

No wonder, therefore, that Laura Grey possessed sad forebodings.

"Surely," the poor girl communed with herself, "surely he cannot be a pirate, or he would not permit so many vessels to pass him unmolested. What can he be?"

This question put so often to herself as it had been, became at length more than she could endure to be in longer doubt concerning, and one day when Captain Glitter was standing amidships, Laura with flashing eyes and flushed cheeks approached his side, and in a tone of mingled despair and resolution, said—

"Captain Glitter, we have now been at sea nearly a week; surely it would not take a swift vessel like this to accomplish the passage to that portion of the coast where I——"

He turned sharply towards her with a look upon his face that plainly said—

"You have sought information, which I would have avoided. You must have it."

Then, in a freezing tone of voice, he said—

"A week. Yes. We have been that time, I believe, and it will be many yet before you leave this vessel; therefore, my dear young lady, do not trouble me with any further questioning, or your mind with conjectures. You have heard all you will know for the present."

He gave her no time for reply, but walked quickly to the poop, leaving the poor girl dazed and bewildered by a thousand terrible fears.

Laura went to her own little cabin to ponder over her terrible fate.

She had scarcely begun doing so, when a sudden roar shook the vessel from stem to stern.

It was the discharge of the huge gun at the Pysche's stern.

A beam of joy and hope sprang up into Laura's face, and starting up, she exclaimed—

"There is a vessel in pursuit—we may yet be saved!"

Again the fearful roar was heard above them; again the vessel shook with the concussion.

Then followed the rapid discharge of a number of guns on the lee side.

The face of the helpless girl blanched with fear at the terrible sound, and when a shot came crashing through the Psyche's side she crouched in the farthest corner of the little cabin.

When Captain Glitter went aft, after the beautiful maiden had left the deck, the officer of the watch reported a vessel coming rapidly towards them.

The captain took up his glass and greeted the stranger with a long scrutiny.

As he finished his observations he placed the glass gently on the rack, and remarked—

"A brig of war, and in full chase. Load the big guns. Beat to quarters! It is the Magpie; she sails as if the devil pushed her on."

Used to every emergency, his crew, long before the drummer could be found, took their position at the guns, and were selecting arms from the number always placed ready for use.

The captain of the Pysche paid no heed to the brig.

Not an inch of canvas was spread to urge the vessel forward, but when the brig-of-war came within reach of his long stern-chaser, he turned to the men at the gun and said—

"Now fire and hit her if you can!"

The huge gun belched forth fire and smoke, and those who watched the flight of the ball towards the brig uttered a cry of disappointment as they beheld the missile drop into the sea within a cable's length of the advancing ship.

"Wait a little, the range is bad," he said, calmly.

Then, after a pause of nearly five minutes, "Now try."

The second shot was evidently not true to its mark, for the brig's bow chasers opened fire upon the Pysche, and one of the iron misiles came plunging through her side.

"We are too close," remarked Captain Glitter. "Stretch out a sail on the mizzenmast."

The Pysche was sailing smoothly under single-reefed topsail courses, topgallant sails, jib, and spanker.

Five minutes after the commander's quiet order she was skirmishing through the water under a perfect cloud of white canvas.

The brig was not idle.

She was a splendid ship, and well handled, and before the Pysche could let out her sails, her plucky pursuers had gained considerably upon them.

"Give that fellow a broadside," said the captain. "Quick my lads, before we lose a few sticks."

Six of the long brass guns sent forth their messages of destruction, and when the smoke had cleared away, the Psyche beheld the brig reeling upon the waters, her jib and foremast gone.

A hard cruel smile played upon the captain's lips as he found the brig disabled, and glancing complacently at his bellying canvas, he remarked to his chief officer—

"This is the second time the Magpie commander has tried to meddle with affairs that do not concern him."

The object of his remark, though hopelessly and helplessly crippled, kept up a continual discharge from her bow chasers.

"He hopes to pull up, and try his boats. We will not wait to give them so much unnecessary trouble."

The shots all fell far short of their mark, and the Psyche left the dismasted brig to sink or get into port the best way she could.

With the black ensign flying at her fore, the Psyche sailed up the famous Straits, where the gilded summits and spires of Algiers could be seen glittering in the glorious effulgence of the Eastern sun.

Captain Glitter bore up for Algiers, and dropped anchor beneath the guns of a small fort.

Laura Grey was on deck.

Though sad at heart with her wretchedness, she could not help admiring the brilliant prospect which spread before her.

She was leisurely watching the small boats as they flitted past the vessel, and eagerly looking for a face among the crowd of boatmen that bespoke a kindness of heart sufficient to rescue her should she drop overboard.

But the stolid, apathetic faces so common in the East alone met her eye, and she turned from the waters to ascertain the cause of an exclamation from the captain, who was giving orders from the head of the aft-hatch.

"Bring them to the state-room by force if they will not go peaceably," was his command.

The words recalled her to the horrors of her position, and with a cry of affright she sprung upon the bulwarks.

Before her intention could be carried out, a strong hand grasped her dress, and she was pulled forcibly backward.

"Not this time, my beauty," said a rough voice; "you are wanted below."

In the strong grasp of one of the crew, she had no alternative but to submit, and she was carried down to the state-room.

There to behold an unexpected sight.

Between twenty and thirty young girls, all more or less gifted with extreme beauty, sitting around the Psyche's saloon.

Some were clustered in groups clinging to each other in agony; others were giving vent to their sorrows in sobs and tears; while others seemingly indifferent to their fate, were silently watching their unfortunate companions.

This was Captain Glitter's slave-market—the place where he every year sold a bevy of England's fairest daughters to the highest bidder.

Within an hour of the vessel's coming to anchor, several gaily decorated boats, came alongside, and their richly-attired occupants with a grave greeting stepped on board.

Many were evidently persons of rank and had kindly-looking countenances, but the greater portion were men whose hair had a silvery tinge, betokening they had seen more than one-half of their allotted time on earth.

Others again there were who merged upon a second childhood, and who had to be helped on board by their slaves.

And this motley group came to the cabin of the Psyche to gaze upon Captain Glitter's fresh importation of English loveliness.

Exclamations of surprise and delight were at once manifest—surprise at the matchless beauty of the victims; delight that such a lovely array of charms were so easy to obtain possession of.

"Allah be good to us," said one old Bey, as he fixed his eyes upon Laura's exquisite face and graceful person. "This maiden is fair."

Captain Glitter was near the speaker, and instantly said in the same language—

"She is a maiden fairer even than the houris that dwell in paradise." The old fellow seemed to devour her with his lack-lustre eyes, and gravely assenting, by an inclination of the head, to the captain, he asked—

"What, O son of an infidel, is the price of this maiden?"

"Ten bags of gold, mighty governor, will purchase the ecstatic privilege of calling that maiden yours."

"Ten bags!—and you sold me two last year for that sum. Too much."

"Too much! On my head be it, most potent bey, but I can get twenty bags from the Governor of Lepro, whose harem but requires a maiden so fair as she to make it an earthly paradise."

"The Governor of Lepro?"

The hoary old fellow repeated the words.

The governor was his foe, and sooner would the bey have spent his last piastre than the fair girl should have gone to stock his harem.

"Fair as the moon she is; but the price is high. Still I will pay. There, captain, the maiden is mine."

"Your condescension is too great, most potent signor. Send the bags, and I will complete the transfer."

The old man tottered off to the boat, and while being rowed back, flattered himself at the prospect of possessing so much beauty at so large a price.

Other girls were, in a similar manner, sold off before the evening, none reaching more than two hundred pounds English money.

The bargaining was carried on by Captain Glitter and the Algerines in their own language, and many of the helpless victims remained uncertain of their fate until the next day.

Then came the dark-skinned emissaries of the bey with the price of each victim, and as the money was placed in the coffers, the poor girls were torn asunder, and carried to the homes of their future eastern masters.

Poor Laura!

She was among the last who left the vessel.

She had swooned from the terrible ordeal she had gone through, and was carried in the arms of a gigantic negro to the harem.

CHAPTER CXXVIII.

THE WAR CLOUD ENGAGES THE FORT.

THE soldiers discharged their muskets at Tom when he took that fearful leap from the ramparts into the sea beneath.

One of the balls struck him on the shoulder grazing the skin, then taking a downward flight again wounded him severely.

Our hero felt the sharp cut as the ball struck him, but beyond a firmer compression of the lips, he took no notice of the pain stinging him.

A bold swimmer, he soon rose to the surface, and struck out for the hulls of two vessels that were standing in near the fort.

In one he recognised his own swift craft, the gallant War Cloud; the other of nobler proportions and higher build he knew was the Thunderer.

A new danger awaited him when he began to swim towards the vessels.

The soldiers, infuriated by the death of their officer, no sooner saw Tom rise to the surface, than a quick fusilade was poured down upon him.

Our hero dived and kept under water until he was compelled to rise for fresh air.

Getting weak from the loss of blood he despaired of ever reaching even the nearest ship, the guns of the War Cloud having opened fire upon the lower part of the fort, and the huge iron balls flying about his head.

Still his stout brave heart bore him onward until a ray of bright hope shot through his heart.

Rising upon the summit of the billows, he saw beneath the dense curtains of smoke that rose between the vessels, and the port, a hencoop floating towards the shore.

He scrambled to the lucky waif, and holding on with one hand, he paddled himself with the other, and safely reached his vessel.

Midshipman Tom's life would have been ended had the War Cloud been under sail—for it is impossible for the fastest swimmer to overtake a ship moving through the water.

Luckily for our hero, his ship had become stationary preparatory to opening fire upon the fort.

Once alongside, the young leader grasped the main ropes that hung over the side, and in the smoke of the guns, made his appearance upon the bulwarks of the War Cloud.

Snowball was the first to behold him, and here he thought was the apparition of his young chief, and springing forward he cried.

"By gar dere am de chief's ghost, he hab been murdered, and come to tell us."

Men left their guns and ran amidships—this unexpected apparition had appalled them.

The delusion was soon over, for the gallant leader quickly comprehending the cause of their fear, called out in a cheering voice—

"Stand to your guns, my men, Midshipman Tom is still in the flesh."

A joyous shout came from his band, and Snowball, running forward, seized the boy's soft white hand and wept for joy.

"Tought it all ober with yer, Massa Tom," sobbed the African; "how you get away?"

"By springing from the ramparts, Snowball, when menaced with a score of deadly weapons."

With the exception of the flesh wound in the shoulder, and one in the lower part of his body, Tom had received no injury in his flying exit from the fort; these Snowball took under his special treatment, and by the aid of a rude lotion, distilled from dried herbs, he was speedily recovering.

The roar of the War Cloud's guns had not ceased since he came on board, and the young chief, as he listened to the hurried tramp of the gunners, and the loud commands of Snowball, felt his heart beat with excitement.

At every fresh discharge his ardour became more aroused, until, at length, no longer able to endure the promptings of his fiery soul, he snatched a sabre from the table, and, with throbbing heart, buckled it round his waist.

The pain of his wound prevented him from wearing a jacket; so, with his white shirt bedaubed with blood, he stepped on deck.

Snowball received his patient with a look of much surprise, and said—

"How berry wrong, Massa Tom—dat wound ob yours want plenty ob rest. You nebber get rite widout it."

"I cannot help it," replied Tom. "It would be certain death were I compelled to remain below while the noise of battle roared above my head."

The young chief now took charge of the vessel, and ordering the men to cease firing, made a long survey of the fort.

A smile played upon his lips, and turning to Snowball, he said—

"Signal to Captain Dragon to cease firing."

A small black and blue flag was run up to the masthead.

In a few minutes the Thunderer's guns became silent.

Tom looked towards his friend's vessel, and when the smoke had cleared away, he saw Captain Dragon, speaking trumpet in hand, standing upon the bows.

He started when he saw our hero, and shouted through his trumpet—

"Glad to see you, my boy; what have you ceased firing for?"

"To save powder and shot. We have knocked two batteries over."

"I can see that by the glass. Their guns are nearly silent, too. How is that?"

"A good reason. They have not a dozen serviceable pieces mounted, and I expect we have silenced two-thirds of them."

"Come on board, will you?"

"Yes."

The guns from the fort had now ceased firing altogether; in fact, the grand invincible fortress, as the old governor deigned to style it, had totally exhausted her ammunition.

Captain Dragon's cutter was soon alongside the War Cloud, and when he had congratulated our hero upon his providential escape, he asked—

"And now, is there any way I can serve you?"

"You can," replied Tom, "and greatly I would like you to be interpreter of my wishes to the commandant."

"Send for him, I know he will be overjoyed to meet us again."

"No doubt. Go below two of you, and bring the prisoner on deck."

Two men hurried away to fulfil their chief's orders.

The old general, boiling with indignation as he was at his capture, was pacing the little cabin when the seamen entered.

"The chief wants yer on deck," said one, "so tumble up."

The old fellow made a reply in his own language,

"What does he say, Jack?"

"Blest if I know," said Jack. "He don't understand our lingo—we don't understand his'n. Hoist a signal, Bill."

Bill did so.

He pointed first to the angry old officer than upward to the hatch.

The old fellow drew himself up erect and shook his head in sign of refusal.

The sailors were in a fix until Jack said—

"It ain't no use signalling to the old beggarbow, let's clap all hands on him, and hoist the old lubber on deck."

Much to the gentleman's horror, the sailors seized him by the neck and heels, and despite his struggles, carried him to the deck.

CHAPTER CXXIX.

CAPTAIN DRAGON AND THE GOVERNOR OF FORT SAN JOSE COME TO AN UNDERSTANDING.

WHEN they came within a few paces of their chief, they hoisted the old fellow upwards, then dropped him with a jerk upon his feet.

Captain Dragon turned his face to hide his mirth, and the young chief, controlling his inclination to laugh outright, asked—

"What is the meaning of this violence?"

Jack hitched up his trowsers and pulled his forelock, and answered—

"We couldn't help it, sir. When we tells him you wants him on deck, he screws up his figure and speaks double-Dutch to us; then we makes a signal, and the old lubber wouldn't come—so we fetched him."

During the seaman's speech, the little general had been chattering and gesticulating in a most ludicrous manner.

"What does he say?" asked Tom when he had sent the men to their quarters.

"Oh, something about the honour of the invincible flag being violated. But what are the wishes you would have me interpret?"

"Well," said Tom, "I wish you to inform the governer that, as he has given us a great deal of trouble, and we have had hard work and no pay, we require a compensation in gold at his hands—and that a handsome one."

"Leave him to me. I'll drain his mouldy money-bags of every dollar, or my name is not Captain Dragon!"

He turned towards the governor and raised his cap courteously.

"Monsieur," he said, "we have the pleasure of meeting once more."

"Pleasure," retored the little fellow, angrily, "pleasure indeed. The flag of my country has been outraged by you English dogs, and when my brave gunners have rested, they shall destroy your vessels."

"Will they," said Captain Dragon, complacently. "Be good enough, general, to look at the spars of these vessels, they are perfect and free from damage. Take this glass, look at your fort, and see what has befallen your invincible defence."

He clutched at the glass and took a long survey at the grey old ramparts, and began to threaten the unfortunate gunners with dire punishment for allowing the old walls to be knocked about their ears.

Captain Dragon stopped him by saying—

"They cannot hear you, my brave general, perhaps never will."

The prisoner looked up, and an expression of wonder passed over his features.

"Never will," he repeated.

"That will entirely depend on Monsieur's answers to a proposition I am about to make to him."

He beckoned a sailor to him, and said in English—

"Run a noose up to the yard arm."

The order was quickly obeyed.

"That, general," said the captain, pointing to the noose, "is for your neck."

"Never," said he. "The English are a brave nation, and never murder their prisoners."

"No gammon, old gentleman; they were dogs but a few moments since. How much money have you in the fort?"

"Money!"

"Yes; golden coins in hard cash—or anything you may please to call it. How much have you?"

"Will forty—no fifty golden pieces do?"

The governor jumped back a full pace at the yell Captain Dragon gave.

"Forty—fifty! You miserable old sinner—no. Four hundred or five even will be of no use—hang your impudence."

"Then mercy—I have no more. I-I—"

"Then," shouted the corsair, "take him away and put the noose round his neck."

The governor was instantly seized, and to his horror was carried beneath the rope.

"Fifty pieces," he shouted, as they placed the hempen halter round his neck, "sixty—seventy," the rope was getting tighter every second, "eighty—ninety."

No response from Captain Dragon.

He was directing the men at the rope to tight the rope by degrees.

"Hundred!" shrieked the terrified old fello' "two, three, four, five, six, se-v-en, oh! ei—"

At a sign from the captain he was lowered again, and the rope loosened a little.

"A thousand," said the corsair, "or by every saint in your calendar, up you go."

The general saw the men preparing for a run with the slack end of the rope, and in a frenzied tone, he yelled out—

"You shall have it, though it will take all my earnings, and leave my daughter a beggar."

"Talk no nonsense, tell no lies," said the corsair; "you got more than that from one unlucky vessel. Five thousand doubloons were in her cabin when she ran aground a mile beneath fort San Jose."

The governor reeled backwards as though suddenly confronted with a snake.

"Yes, amid the howling of the storm," continued Captain Dragon, "the governor of the fort had the shipwrecked wretches butchered in cold blood, and before morning came, the treasure chest was taken to his room by four soldiers."

The governor shook like a leaf.

"Aye, well mayest thou whine, thou befouled hypocrite, for when the whole four were found dead on the ramparts two days after, that same governor spread the report that they had died of eating poisoned fruit. Dost thou remember it?"

The trembling wretch fell upon his knees.

"Spare me!" he shrieked; "kill me if you will, but, oh! speak not more of that terrible night."

"I have done," said Captain Dragon; "it matters not to me how the governor of fort San Jose increases his revenues—such cold-blooded slaughter is his to contemplate—but lie he shall not!"

The governor stood mute and conscience-stricken in front of his daring accuser—he had thought none knew but himself that damning secret—how that with a subtle poison his four accomplices had perished by his hands.

Yet, in the midst of his abject terror his thoughts were not idle—the dreaded consequence of that great crime lent intensity to his imagination, and felt that a master-stroke might yet put Captain Dragon in his power, and thus free himself of a man who would ever have the means of bringing him to the scaffold.

"Monsieur has me to an advantage," said the governor, as his thoughts encouraged him to dis-

"YONDER ROLLS THE BLUE WAVES," SHE SAID.

play a little more nervous energy; "he can make whatever terms he pleases."

The corsair's answer was short and to the purpose—

"General," he said, sternly, "your words bear their full significance. I understand you, but my secresy no ill-gotten gold can purchase. Pay the ransom, and we part for ever, I and my followers —refuse, and I will cause the world—"

The old man did not require the corsair to finish his speech, but cried out—

"Enough. The ransom shall be paid. Monsieur will accompany me—he shall secure it."

"Be it so! I will accompany you; but be assured any attempt at treachery will be followed by an immediate attack upon the fort. You know our strength and your own weakness.

"Monsieur will be as safe as on the deck of his own vessel. Of what use would treachery be with the fort at the mercy of your guns?"

There certainly was no disputing this feasible argument, and Captain Dragon turned to the

22

~~ng chief and made him acquainted with the ~sult of his negotiations.

"Don't go," said Tom, "the fellow may mean treachery."

"But it would avail him nothing. I shall take a boat's crew of my fellows, who are a match for six times their number of invincibles. Ah! ah! he dares not act treacherously; but it may be as well to understand that if you should not behold my splendid form emerge from the fortress at the expiration of an hour, something has occurred to prevent me—the rest I leave in your hands. To the rescue be the word!"

"Understood," Tom answered; "and if you are not safely on board again, I swear I will never leave this place while one stone remains upon another. If I cannot save you, my friend, you shall have a glorious tomb."

The boat which had brought Tom to the Thunderer soon bore him back to his own vessel.

The old governor and Captain Dragon went to the Fort, and Tom watched them as the Thunderer's cutter sped through the water, a white flag flying at her stern, with a vague feeling of uneasiness at his heart.

"I suspect that treacherous old rascal," thought Tom, "Heaven help him if my suspicions should turn out correct."

When the boat touched the shore the young chief ordered the anchors of both vessels to be weighed for the purpose of taking up a closer position to the fort.

An hour passed, the cutter was yet lying on the sands, the white flag was still flying, but no Captain Dragon's face could be seen among his crew.

The order to man the boats was then given.

Before he could speak further the look-out above cried—

"A strange sail rounding the entrance to the harbour, sir."

Tom looked and beheld the towering masts and huge hull of a frigate coming steadily towards the fort.

"A heavy armed man-of-war," he muttered, "there will be blood shed before long."

The frigate showed the Republican flag, and our hero ordered the red cross of Albion to be displayed.

The frigate dipped her ensign in acknowledgement and fired six guns as a salute.

Then bringing up close beneath the batteries of the fort her anchor was dropped, the sails furled, and soon after a boat was seen to glide towards the shore.

Tom stood and pondered over this unexpected incident.

"Terrible odds," he thought; "should the governor proclaim us corsairs. I care not for the vessel were Dragon safe. The old rascal can now boldly keep him a prisoner. Too hasty, my friend. But what's best to be done."

He paced the deck slowly, and revolved a hundred plans in his brain.

One, at length, seemed to please him, for he ordered the cutter to be lowered and the crew armed.

When they were ready he seated him If in the cutter, and ordered the men to pull alongside the Thunderer's boat.

This young chief knew, unless he could place himself between the officers of the frigate before they could return to their vessel every chance of saving Captain Dragon would be gone.

His intentions were to join his men with those of the Thunderer, march boldly to the fort and demand Captain Dragon.

And he not being delivered up immediately, to quickly return and wait until the officers belonging to the frigate returned to their vessel.

Then, by a bold stroke, he meant to capture them beneath their own guns, and keep them as hostages for Captain Dragon.

To Snowball was left the task of watching the frigate, and the African made preparations for any emergency.

The War Cloud's guns were double shotted, as also were the Thunderer's, and carefully sighted at the most vulnerable part of the frigate's hull.

The Peruvian seamen, who were lounging over the side criticising the graceful War Cloud, little knew that the double tier of guns that were so skilfully levelled, wanted but a word to vomit forth death and destruction upon them.

"We 'stonish dem," said Snowball, "if we wanted; but, by gar, I'd give much if Massa Tom was safe on board ag'in."

The African saw his graceful young leader step ashore, and place himself at the head of his men; and he anxiously watched them until an angle of the fort hid them from his sight.

CHAPTER CXXX.

A BATTLE WITH THE INDIANS.

How the gallant Captain of the Hercules and his boarders escaped the snare set for them by Red Hand, has been related.

To resume the broken events connecting Red Hand and the pursuing frigate, we must return to the night when Red Hand and his ruffianly crew were fearfully awaiting the surging waves to engulph their frail boat.

There seemed not the least possibility of one of them beholding the coming morn.

Their boat were tossed about at the mercy of the waves, and one and all were too much weakened to use their oars.

The boats in which Red Hand sat still kept the lead, and the fierce leader, his passion subdued by the dire peril in which he found himself, used every effort to keep up the drooping energy of his men.

"Keep to the oars my boys," he said, as a heavy wave washed the cutter from stem to stern. "There must be land within a few fathoms of us."

A sheet of vivid lightning lit up for a moment the surrounding darkness as he ceased speaking.

Red Hand uttered a joyous shout, for in that flittering second he saw by the lightning gleam, a dark mass of rocks right ahead.

"Pull!" he yelled, "pull—there it is right ahead. Pull, and we shall be saved."

Saved! There was magic in the word that gave each hopeless wretch a giant's strength, and under the exciting spell of the moment, they gave a gladsome and unanimous shout, that was heard above the roar of the angry waters.

That cry was taken up by the boats in the cutter's wake, and those who had begun to look for death as a grim certainty, nerved themselves for a fierce struggle for life.

The bright flashes of light that continually broke the murky gloom, served the struggling pirates as a guide to the haven of safety, and within a few seconds of each other the three boats' keels grated upon the shore.

The men eagerly sprang ashore, and would have abandoned the boats to the mercy of the foaming billows, had not the harsh loud tone of their leader been heard as he called out—

"Pull the boats up high and dry, we shall want them when the storm subsides."

He had been saved from a watery grave by a miracle, and scarcely had his foot touched the firm ground, when his mind reverted to the single purpose of his life—rapine and bloodshed.

Such was the meaning of those few words, for he thought of the richly laden little vessels that would, within a very few days, be on their homeward voyage.

His orders were obeyed, and the boats were drawn up far away from the reach of the troubled waters.

There was no shelter or food upon the narrow strip of coast.

So they sat crouching from the pitiless rain, until exhausted nature caused them to fall fast asleep.

Even the look-out that was posted a little in advance of the spot they had selected, was too much exhausted to keep his eyes open.

A heavy lethergy fell upon him, and forgetful of the safety of his companions, he threw himself upon the wet sand, and despite the drenching fall of water, and the roar of the elements, he sank into a state of happy forgetfulness. That sleep cost the luckless wretch his life.

The morn broke bright and beautiful, and the pirate leader soon awoke by the sun's rays pouring upon his face.

Starting from the ground he sprang to his feet and looked out upon the glorious expanse of water now glittering like a vast lake beneath the rising sun.

Then he turned his face inland, and a cry of rage passed his lips as he saw, emerging from a grove of tall trees, a number of semi-nude forms.

Red Hand knew them, and the purpose that brought the forest children so far from their wigwams.

The hope that during the night some luckless vessel had gone to pieces, had lured them to the shore to glean any spoil that the waters had left upon the beach.

Red Hand saw their shining axes and flint-headed spears—weapons they had brought to terminate the life of any helpless castaway.

In numbers they appeared to be tenfold to Red Hand; and grinding his teeth, he looked round for the man whose duty it had been to warn them of their danger.

The tired sentinel was still enjoying his long-required sleep, when Red Hand unsheathed his sword, and the red stream rolled out from the sleeper's side upon the sparkling sands.

Then jumping amidst his men, he began to kick them with the toe of his heavy boot until they were thoroughly awakened.

"To the boats!" he said, as the men rose to their feet, "if you wish to see the sea again."

His outstretched finger pointed to the dusky forms which had by this time emerged from the trees, and the pirates in a second comprehending their danger, ran towards the stranded boats.

The boats were just putting off from the beach when the natives caught sight of them, and incited by a thirst for plunder, they gave a terrible war whoop, and spreading out like a fan, they dashed towards the fugitives.

Destitute of fire-arms, save a few pistols which the rain and saltwater had rendered useless, the pirates made the best of their time to get into deep water.

The savages saw their intention, and strove to prevent its accomplishment.

Strong of limb, and equally active in the water as on land, those who had reached the sea plunged in and swam towards the receding boats.

The water was alive with their black forms, and even to the tried nerves of the hardy pirates, there was a terrible significance in their angry eyes, and the white gleaming teeth which gripped spear or hatchet, as the savages cleaved their passage in the wake of the pirate's boat.

Those who were not rowing drew their cutlasses and stood on the stern of the boat awaiting the onslaught.

Though every stout oar was bent nearly double by the sturdy rowers, and the speed of the boats caused the water to seethe as the sharp prows cut their way onward, the swift Indians gained perceptibly upon them.

Red Hand, the muscles of his swarthy face writhing with passion, stood on the cutter's stern, watching the efforts of two stout limbed Indians who were in advance of the rest.

They were so close upon the boat that he could plainly hear their heavy respiration.

They reached it together, and the two dusky hands grasped the rudder.

Red Hand's heavy sword severed one arm off close to the shoulder.

The second native sunk to the bottom by a blow on the head with a hand-spike.

Maddened at the sight of this, the Indians swarmed round the cutter, and in a moment the progress of the boat was stopped, and a hundred yelling devils tried to scramble on board.

The pirates are brave, though ruthless wretches, and they battle with a heroism worthy of the country which gave them birth.

The other boats heave to, and the crews, seeing their messmates' peril, back water and come to the rescue.

There is no time now for words of command from their leader—each one acts and thinks for himself.

The Indians, though so greatly preponderating in numbers over the pirate, soon find that it will be no easy work to overpower the fugitives.

Around the boats the sea became tinged with blood, and at every yard there floated either a dead dusky form, or those wading about disfigured by frightful wounds.

Twice had the natives scrambled over the cutter's bow while the defenders were battling with the swarm at her stern.

Each time they were stabbed or swept into the sea by a thrust from an oar.

And so the fierce fight raged until every arm began to grow weak and feeble with the sickening work.

Many of the pirates had fallen, and Red Hand saw with dismay that it would be impossible to hold out much longer.

Even had the task been to slay the red skins without any resistance on their part, he felt his men, so tired and weakened were they by exertion and want of food, could not accomplish it.

In fact, fighting their way through the dusky legion was hopeless to think of.

In this moment of dire extremity there came a deliverer as welcome to one party as it was terrible to the other.

Ahead of their boats, where the ocean's surface looked like a mist reflecting the sun's effulgence, the dorsal fin of a huge shark shone above the water like the sail of a small boat.

The sea monster, attracted, no doubt, by the plentiful feast that awaited him, came rushing along through the water.

Every now and then the huge forked tail was seen to send the spray upwards as though a volcano had suddenly burst in the ocean's bed.

With wild yells the savages beheld the dreaded creature approach, and giving way to the panic the visitor caused, they made off from the boats as fast as possible.

Many in their terror at the coming monster tried to scramble on board the boats—in this they failed—and many a yet warm body found its way to the shark's mouth.

Red Hand's first act was to order all those who had fallen to be thrown into the sea.

Then the tired oarsmen began to row silently away.

CHAPTER CXXXI.

LORD MOUNTSTEVEN'S GHOST APPEARS BEFORE THE LADY BLANCHE.

LADY MOUNTSTEVEN, though so far steeped in crime, had never felt the enormity of her sin until her husband fell, as she supposed, by her hands.

A portion of this feeling was also entertained by her confidante Margarie, who, though less educated than her ladyship, did not share the latter's apprehension respecting the shadow of Lord Mountsteven suddenly appearing in the castle.

That a figure had been seen much resembling the late master of the Norman castle, was a truth which neither could dispute.

Every domestic who crossed the corridor after nightfall were ready to swear by candle and book that the buried lord had glided towards the north wing before their very eyes.

It was in the evening after the report had been circulated, that Lady Mountsteven and Margarie were seated in the chamber where Lord Mountsteven had died.

They had gone there to empty an inlaid jewel-box of its priceless treasure, preparatory to their flight from the scene of murder.

Margarie had all that day been using her influence to dissuade her mistress from carrying out her resolution to quit the castle.

"My best friend," said Lady Mountsteven, "it is useless to urge me. I cannot stay any longer in this hateful spot."

"My Lady, it is for the best that you should do so."

"Why, Margarie, do you think so?"

"Because, my lady, your enemies will seize the opportunity to spread the evil reports that already begin to find their way beyond the castle walls."

Her ladyship laughed with a harsh satanic sound, that grated upon her listener's ears and caused her to shiver.

"My enemies," said the haughty woman, "I care not for them—it is this."

She struck her forehead as she spoke.

"Yes," she repeated, clutching Margarie by the arm, "know you that there is not a moment sleeping or waking but I can hear Lord Mountsteven crying for help as he lies in his living tomb."

"A phantom of the brain, nevertheless, your ladyship."

"Just so, Margerie, and one that will ere long make me a raving maniac, at least so I feel it, unless I quit the scene of my crimes."

Her ladyship's voice sank to a whisper.

"How long could he have lived, Margerie?" she said, "when the effects of the drug wore off?"

"Not many hours; suffocation must have speedily ensued; the coffin was air-tight."

"But was it not possible he could have wrenched his tomb open, and now walk about the castle?"

"Impossible—utterly impossible; reject such impression I conjure you. This idle talk will soon be over, and you can remain and enjoy that for which you have so toiled and sinned for."

"I dare not, Margerie; like the ignorant domestics, as you call them, I see a white spectre in every chamber in the castle."

A mocking sneer played upon Margarie's lips, and she asked—

"Is your determination unalterable?"

"It is."

"And when do you intend to leave?"

"Would it were now. I shall never know peace until I am once more in Italy's sunny land."

"One thing I would ask you then, my lady—have you arranged about the estate?"

"Yes, Margerie, I have. And now, if you like, we will examine the great heirlooms of this proud family."

She unlocked the inlaid ebony box as she uttered these words, and a cry of admiration broke from her ladyship.

The inside of the quaint old casket was filled with the priceless jewels of an ancient and noble line.

In a velvet lined case was the identical chain of the purest gold which the first of the old family was wont to wear over his armour as a proof of his knighthood.

The women's eyes glistened as they beheld these precious gems, and Lady Mountsteven proceeded to lay them out one by one and place them in a small iron box.

The last article had been placed inside, and she was about to turn the key in the lock, when a sound proceeding from the head of the massive bed caused them both to turn.

There could be no fancy in the terrible vision, there was no phantasy of the brain.

There as he often stood in life, was Lord Mountsteven, his pale, sad face turned towards the plunderesses of the family relics.

Menacingly, his finger was pointed towards his guilty wife, and in a tone hollow and unnatural, the spectre said—

"Defame not the heritage of the wronged with your accursed hands, or a doom as swift as the scathing lightning will fall upon your guilty heads."

The women were rooted to their seats.

Their terror was too great to find utterance in a cry of alarm.

Palsied and horror-stricken they gazed with startling eyeballs and parched tongues at the appalling visitor.

The spectre now began gradually to fade before their eyes as though it had melted in the thin air; the heavy hangings of the bed closed, and they were alone in their terror.

Neither spoke, but actuated mainly by one impulse, arose from their seats and staggered from the room.

Once clear of the heavy atmosphere that seemed to chill their faculties, terror gave them strength, and they fled along the dim corridor as though followed by a legion of fiends.

Then the heavy curtain that screened the great bedstead opened, and Lord Mountsteven emerged therefrom.

He replaced the jewels in the casket, and locking the box, took the key away and silently left the chamber.

Lady Mountsteven, more dead than alive, entered her boudoir, and sank upon an elegant couch.

Margarie, still with the terrible vision before her eyes, fled to her room, and in agony of fear and remorse, sank upon her knees and would have made her prayers heard for forgiveness, for the share she had taken in the murder of Lord Mountsteven.

Her ladyship, in a stupor of fear, still lay upon the couch when the door opened and old Sybil entered the room.

The old witch stood for some time upon the threshold, and gazed at the recumbent form of Lady Mounsteven.

A deadly look of concentrated hate dwelt on the crone's countenance, and the muscles of her throat worked in a strange convulsive manner.

With the silent tread and wary gait of a panther, she stole forward, placed her thin hands upon her ladyship's shoulders, and a single word came hissing from her lips.

The haughty woman sprang from her couch as though a serpent had stung her.

She turned and eyed the intruder, and in somewhat her old tone of voice demanded—

"Sybil, here! How dare you enter this chamber?"

The weird-woman laughed wildly, and shrieked in her ear—

"How darest thou question my right?"

Her ladyship stepped back and clutched the bell-pull.

"Leave," she cried, "or you shall be thrust forth as a vagrant from my castle."

Again the wild, provoking laugh came from old Sybil's lips, and she cried—

"You dare not!"

Her ladyship's hot blood suffused her white face

and neck, and jerking the heavy cord, a sharp summons rang out.

"Let them come," said Sybil, "and there shall be such a story or the winds as shall make the country ring. Hear that, ye murderess!"

Lady Mountsteven's face went whiter than the sheeted dead, and with a low cry of pain she sank upon the rich velvet couch, and hid her face in the cushion.

"Let them place but one finger upon me," Sybil continued, in that cold, weird manner that sent a chill to her hearer's soul, "and I will tell them I have come for my husband."

Lady Mountsteven sprang from her seat, and pushing back her long, black tresses, looked wildly into the speaker's face.

She uttered no sound; some strange fear held her mute and spell-bound, and while she stood thus a domestic entered the room.

He stood and looked at his mistress, then at her strange visitor.

"Did you ring, my lady?" he inquired.

Lady Mounsteven neither saw nor heard the man, and Sybil answered—

"No; your lady was taken unwell, and caught at the bell-pull to save herself from falling. You can go."

The servant looked towards his mistress for a confirmation of the strange woman's words—then withdrew, closing the door after him.

That sound recalled the lady to a perception of the strange sight she must have presented before her liveried lacquey, and with an effort of calmness she said—

"Your ready lie, Sybil, has saved you."

"And yet you," said the gipsy, "proud woman as you are—dare—dare not recall that man to thrust me from this room."

"Woman, devil—or whatever else thou art—what mean you?"

Sybil's thin fingers worked convulsively, and she answered—

"You shall know. The time draws nigh when the borrowed plumes you wear shall be torn from you. When, like a detected and detested thing, you shall be driven from these stately walls to face the world emblazoned with the story of your crimes; and she whom you so wantonly wronged shall reassert her heritage, and the heir of Mountsteven's proud house shall sit in his father's halls!"

Lady Mountsteven's white teeth clenched, and upon her lips a streak of white foam gave mute but terrible evidence of the fearful passions that were at work within her breast.

"Grind your teeth, she wolf," Sybil said, with bitter, taunting gesture. "You have run the length of your chain, Lady Mountsteven. Across the seas I have tracked you. Like your shadow, I have never left your side. Listen—when your message went forth to slay that noble boy which the waves preserved, I heard it. I saw the hand

that sent Lord Mountsteven to the tomb; and when I knew that your unholy fingers sought to grasp another's right, I called the silent dead from the tomb to stay your guilty hand."

Sybil paused, and her cold, glittering eyes were fixed upon the blanched face of her listener to note the effect her words produced.

Great heavens! Could these blazing eyes, now shot prominently forward, have ever beamed with love's gentle tenderness, for there was expression in them that might have warned Sybil that a deadly intent lurked, and was fast gathering strength, in her heart.

But Sybil heeded it not.

She saw before her a foe at whose hands she had suffered a terrible injury, and now the time had come for vengeance.

And she determined to apply the bitter torture of laying vividly before the guilty woman her long list of crimes, then to inflict a fitting punishment.

"Now," resumed Sybil, her eyes lighting up with a strange light, "I come to your first, and to me, the most terrible of your crimes. How I can have been so near to you and not have slain you I should have wonder were it not that I have waited for this hour to proclaim myself to you."

Sybil threw the hood from her head, and with the long, elf-like, grey, lank masses of hair that were wont to hang in unkempt confusion round her neck.

"Ha! you know me," she said, as her ladyship recoiled. "Now devil in woman's form, I ask you for the husband you have slain, and for the noble boy, his and my son!"

Lady Mountsteven had, during the time Sybil was speaking, gradually crawled towards her, and when the last words left her lips, the crouching tiger-like form bent lower.

Then, with a wild, half-suppressed cry, she sprang upon the daring speaker, grasping her firmly by the throat with one hand, while from the other there gleamed, in the mellow light of the waxen tapers, a long, keen stiletto.

Sybil seized the upraised hand with a strength not less than her antagonist exerted to carry out her intent.

For several moments their bodies swayed to and fro in the fearful death-struggle, and with the hot breath that came upon Sybil's hand, her ladyship hissed—

"This time my blow shall be sure. You shall perish!"

She threw herself upon Sybil, and bore her by sheer strength to the ground.

There was a crash of shattered glass as the table was overturned.

Then the lady arose, her face fiendish and exultant, the long-bladed weapon crimsoned with blood.

Sybil lay motionless at her feet, and the beautiful fiend cried—

"So much for my—"

KNEELING BESIDE HIS YOUNG CHIEF, HE RAISED HIS BLOODSTAINED FACE.

The knife fell from her grasp as the form of rd Mountsteven glided into the room, and ntly confronted the guilty woman.

CHAPTER CXXXII.

CAPTAIN DRAGON IN THE FORT

HEN the boat which conveyed Captain Dragon d the governor ashore grounded, the prisoner ked—

"Will Monsieur take some of his men to the fort with him?"

"No," answered the corsair, "I alone will accompany you."

Perhaps an inkling that all was not so fair as the governor's courteous speech would suggest, had crept into Captain Dragon's mind, for in his parting instructions to his boy officer, Charley Phillips, he said—

"The best advice that I can give you is, that you pull back to the ship if I do not soon make my reappearance, for these Peruvians are as treacherous as they are cowardly."

"Why not take us with you?" inquired Charley.

"No, simply remember my orders now, back to the ship if I do not return."

"Captain," said Charley, "you may command me in all things but this. Unless you are safe, I will not return. Good-bye."

The sight of the commander was sufficient for the gates of the fortress to be opened, and the old general led his way to his private room.

Captain Dragon with a feeling of pride looked at the battered walls which the soldiers were repairing with sandbags, paying no attention to a few whispered words which the governor exchanged with an officer who stood near the gate, at the same time motioning to several men to come after him.

Following the little governor they soon reached his private room.

"Now, senor," he said, "pray be seated, I will go and fetch the money."

He would have slipped from the room had not the captain placed himself before the door and said—

"Does not your excellency keep the money here?"

He pointed to a large chest as he spoke.

"Yes, but not mine, but that which I receive from the republic to pay the troops."

"It matters not," said the corsair, "pay me from that, and when I am gone you can replace it."

The governor was not prepared for this; he shifted uneasily from one foot to the other, and strove to peer over the captain's shoulder.

The latter saw the act and his suspicions became aroused.

"Why that look towards the door?" said he to governor.

"Merely,—"

"Halt!" said a stern voice outside the door, "ground arms!"

The rattle of a dozen muskets rang out as their ironclad butts struck the stone passage.

Captain Dragon comprehended his position, and drawing his sword he levelled the point at the governor's breast, and said fiercely—

"Betrayed, and by you!"

He seized the governor by the throat, as he spoke, and brought the keen point of the weapon to the old rascal's breast.

"Send those fellows away," he said.

The governor's ghastly face betrayed him, and he fell down upon his knees and pleaded for his life.

The captain urged him to the door, and compelled him to order the guard away.

"And, now the ransom," he said.

The heavy chest was reluctantly opened by the governor, and he began sullenly to count out the sum agreed upon in hard gold pieces.

He had not gone more than half way through his task, when the door was suddenly opened, and the officers from the frigate entered the room.

"Your arrival is most opportune, gentlemen," said the governor, "here is the leader of these ships yonder, whose heavy guns have so much damaged our fort. He is now here to levy a ransom upon the Republic."

There were five strong men who now drew their weapons, and formed a circle round the corsair.

The captain of the frigate replied—

"Monsieur must give up his sword and his ships."

"My sword," said the corsair, "will never leave my hand until death claps hands on me. As for my ships, as you term them, they are yours when you take them."

This coolness and daring won even the admiration of his foes, and, as though unwilling to kill him, they hemmed him on all sides, and strove to knock the weapon from his grasp.

But they very soon found that it would be as much as they could do to defend themselves.

Two of the officers' thin cut and thrust rapiers had already broken beneath the heavy sabre which the corsair knew so well how to use.

Two of the remainder were quickly disposed of —one with a flesh wound in the shoulder, the other with a slash across the face.

Captain Dragon's blood became aroused: he was bleeding from several wounds, when the sharp clink of the steel and the tramping of the combatants' feet were suddenly stayed by an officer of the garrison rushing into the room.

Turning to the governor he said—

"General, the English pirate boy is at the gate, and he swears unless this captain is set free, he will bombard the fort, and we have not a charge of powder left."

"Let him," said the governor, "there is the frigate below which is more than a match for twenty such craft as theirs. Go tell him to begin and send up a guard of soldiers here; let them load as they come. This English dog, I swear, shall not leave here alive."

As though by mutual consent during this colloquy between this young officer and his superior the combatants had discontinued their strife.

But when the former heard the order given by the governor respecting the soldiers, he said—

"Your men will not be required; this is our affair, not the governor's."

The officer saluted and withdrew.

"Now," said the captain to the corsair, "you have done all a brave man can do; but were you to continue the contest you could not escape certain death.

"Hark! there is the tramp of armed men on the stairs. Yield yourself my prisoner; I will give you parole, and you shall wear the sword you know so well how to use. On board my ship we can arrange any further matters ; here among these troops you are not safe."

"Be it so," said Captain Dragon after some reflection. "I sheathe my sword and yield upon parole."

A short conference then took place between the officer and the governor.

"I'm in a pretty scrape now," thought the corsair. "The arrival of that confounded frigate has nicely upset my little programme. Tom is at the gate and threatens to bombard the fort ; but he will try a little stratagem, I suspect, before coming to blows for my release."

"You must accompany me on board the frigate," said the captain to his prisoner, whose eyes lit up with a glad sparkle as he thought of his staunch friends outside.

The officer soon undeceived the corsair as to an early chance of rescue by saying—

"We must leave the fort by a secret entrance. Your friends are at the gate."

Captain Dragon bowed, and trusting to the many chances that might yet facilitate his escape, he silently followed the officers from the room.

In doing so he pressed close enough to the old governor to whisper—

"I'll have your money yet, you infernally treacherous old scoundrel."

The old gentleman replied with an exulting rant, and said—

"You will soon grace the yard-arm of the frigate."

Captain Dragon stalked haughtily from the room, and began the descent of the winding stone staircase that led to the secret door in the fort.

When the young chief found his demand for the release of his friend treated with defiance, he strode moodily from the gate, followed by his trusty crew.

Near the boats he came to a stand, and called young Philips to his side.

"Lieutenant," said the young chief, "I shall feel it a favour if you will accompany me on board my vessel."

CHAPTER CXXXIII.

RED HAND CAPTURES THE MERCHANTMAN.

FEELING assured that the Hercules would be hovering about the spot where they had deserted the Don Jose, Red Hand kept his boats as near the shore as possible, also kept a good look out for the India traders.

About ten in the morning the pirates forgot their past dangers and the death of their messmates by the welcome sight of six little vessels gliding smoothly along close to the land.

The pirate pointed to the peaceful traders, and said to his dauntless band—

"There is food and drink in those vessels—shall we take them ?"

There was no answer save a tightened clutch at the oars, and the boats hand to hand shot away to intercept the small vessels.

The traders saw the boats coming towards them and tried to escape.

The attempt was futile : their single sail was no match for the eight-oared boats that came with a rush upon the leading vessel.

Gallantly the little crew, consisting of only three men and a boy, tried to beat off the boarders with their handspikes. As well might they have tried to put their little crafts against a line of battle ship.

All save one of the little fleet fell into the pirate's hands.

Their crews were mercilessly slain, and tossed into the sea, and the hungry pirates without staying to pursue the escaping craft, began to devour the food on board.

Their rioting was soon changed to flight when they saw the beautiful outlines of their old enemy looming in the distance, and following in its wake the little vessel they had allowed to escape.

"Ten thousand devils !" roared Red Hand, "there is that infernal frigate after us again. Come on board all of you !"

There was a rush to get on board the craft, and Red Hand, with a fearful oath, turned the vessel's prow towards the shore, hoping to run aground and escape into the interior of the country.

Before they could reach the shore, Red Hand beheld a canoe containing two men, who were trying all they possibly could to run their craft aground before the pirates could reach them.

Fortunately for the gallant blue jackets who had so persistently followed the murderous pirates, the canoe was tenanted by men whose presence there seemed inexplicable—for they were Europeans.

One was the traitor, Ralph Ranger, who had been left on the island by Captain Dragon's orders ; the other was an Irishman who had come from the mainland to hunt the wild animals.

The canoe, though well handled, was soon overtaken by the schooner, and Red Hand ordered its occupants to come on deck.

They complied, and the pirate turning to Ralph savagely asked—

"How the devil did you come here ?"

"I was left on that island by mistake," was the reply.

"Your companion ?"

"He dwells on the mainland and comes here at the fall of the year to obtain the skins of the forest animals."

Red Hand made no reply, but stood a few moments in deep thought, his eyes fixed upon the frigate's boats, which were flying through the water.

Red Hand's first impulse was to have Ralph

and his companion hurled back into the water, but a second reflection told how useful they might be in acting as guides when they reached the land.

Ranger and his friend little knew how near a sudden death they might be when they tumbled on board the little vessel commanded by the ruthless pirate, nor did they dream of danger until Red Hand put a pistol to the Irishman's head.

When he felt the cold rim of the pistol placed against his temple, and heard the stern words which accompanied this act, something like a chill passed through his frame.

It was gone in a moment, his constitutional pluck was not easily overcome.

"If yer will be kind enough to take that little shooting iron from me head," said he, "may be I'll take yer."

Red Hand lowered the pistol and growled—

"Quick, lead on. If those boats touch the shore before you find a place of concealment for us, I'll shatter your skull without remorse. Remember, Red Hand, the pirate, never breaks his vow."

Pat pricked up his ears.

"It's Red Hand ye are, is it?" he thought; "then, by the blessed eleven, I'll be kilt ten times over before I'll show yer a place to hide in."

"Quick," said the pirate, raising his pistol, "the boats are within their length of the shore."

"It's thinking I am," said Pat, "of the best place, bedad, I could hide yer. Just tell yer boys to go on towards those big trees."

He sank his voice to a whisper, and putting his mouth close to the pirate's ear, continued—

"There's only a place for one, so send them on, and I'll put you in it."

Red Hand swallowed the bait easily.

He cared not what became of his men if he were safe.

Pat's eyes glistened mischievously as he heard Red Hand order the band to disperse in the adjacent wood, and he could have given a yell when they rushed forward and disappeared among the trees and he was left alone with the dreaded pirate chief.

The frigate's boat was grounded, and a fresh young voice could be heard saying—

"Forward, men, there he is."

Red Hand turned savagely.

He knew the voice to be that of the gallant young midshipman, Sydney Rilcher, and forgetful for the moment of his own safety, he levelled the pistol at the boy's head, and hissed—

"Die! meddling fool!"

Before he could press the trigger, Pat struck the weapon from his grasp, and seizing the pirate, said—

"It's stopped ye are, Misther Red Hand. Come on, me boys, I've got him!"

The pirate reddened with passion, and tried to wrest himself from the iron grasp.

He failed.

The hardy Irishman held him until the young middy and his blue jackets came to his assistance and bound the ruffian strongly with cords.

CHAPTER CXXXIV.

SNOWBALL'S ADVICE.

WHEN our hero asked young Philips to go on board the War Cloud, the lad answered—

"My captain is within those walls a prisoner, and I have sworn not to leave here until I have released him at the risk of my life."

"A commendable idea," said Tom, "but at present powerless of execution."

"Why?"

"Come aboard and we will take Snowball into our counsel; he is far seeing on these occasions, and may very probably suggest some plan by which he may be enabled to release the captain."

"And if he should not be able to, what then?"

"What then," replied Tom, calmly, "there would be but one alternative, we should have to do battle with the port and the frigate."

They entered their respective boats and were soon on their way to the War Cloud, which by this time had swung her broadside across the frigate's bows, a position from which her guns would rake the larger vessel, should the order be given to fire.

And but little doubt there seemed that such would not be the case, the present calm was but the precursor of a coming storm.

Midshipman Tom, Snowball, and Charley Philips went to the War Cloud's luxurious cabin, there to take measures for the release of the gallant Captain Dragon.

Every plan which promised the faintest hope of success was discussed, but the case only appeared to be hopeless when they came to the disposal of the frigate.

It was indeed there the real difficulty lay, for she was guarding the shore.

"There is but one way," said the young chief, "we must draw the frigates out to sea. I will engage her in a fight while you, Philips, must attack the fort."

"That will I do," replied the Thunderer's officer, "and, desperate as the resolve may appear, I will release him or my bones, and it may be those of my comrades, shall be left to whiten on the sands."

Snowball had not as yet been asked for his opinion. He had been looking out on the sea with his hand clasped behind him, which the young chief knew to be his usual position when any plan requiring the exercise of more than ordinary subtlety in execution was passing through his fertile brain.

The young chieftain therefore did not distu

him, but at this point in the conversation, he asked—

"May I give an opinion, Massa Tom?"

"You may," replied Tom, "we have been waiting to hear it."

"I hab been thinking it all ober, Massa Tom," he said, "an dere are many tings dat make it a debil of a job wid de frigate as you say. You see dat no sooner dem officers go on board dan dey show us fight."

"How do you know that, Snowball?"

"Simply enough, Massa Tom: because de old gubnor tell them how we knock the dam old fort about, and dey want to get revenge."

"They shall have it!"

"Sartinly dey shall, Massa Tom, dat for sartin. I tink de sooner dey come de better, but stop, you no hear my plan yet."

"We have not."

"You know dat lubly daughter dat be such good friends wid you?"

"The governor's daughter, you mean."

"Yes; dat same. You speak to her in French."

"Yes."

"Well, dis my plan: you know, Massa Tom, it will be dark soon, I tink; den you go shore and go under window. Pr'aps she come if she do wake tell you where Captain Dragon am,—don't you see?"

"Yes, partly."

"Partly, Massa Tom! it clear what you do den."

"No,—what?"

"Ask her to get you rope; well you no feard ob a lady, Massa Tom, make lub to her and get into de room of Massa Dragon, and both ob you cut as fast as you can."

"Through the lady's window?"

"Zactly, nothing else; you no break her neck doing that."

"No, but suppose I might be successful in all this, how is the frigate to be kept silent till then?"

"Quiet be dam. Massa Tom—scuse my little swear I know—we no want him quiet. If he no fire into me, I fire into him directly you go ashore."

"By that means, Snowball, I shall not be able to get on board again."

"Oh, won't you. I take de frigate out ob de harbour, him sure to fellow. Tink he smash me and den come back."

"Why?"

"Come back to smash Thunderer, which, ob course, will wait for you. You go on board, make sail, come on de frigate's track and help me smash him, den we both go back and play de debbil wid de fort."

"A good plan if successful, Snowball. We shall save our powder and outwit our foe."

"Sartin, Massa Tom, dat's my idea. You nor me not able to fight de big ships an' de fort at de same time."

"No."

"By driving de ship off, I take care we no come close enuff to hurt de War Cloud, den when you and Massa Dragon join me, by gar, he got it hot."

"It will not be an easy fight, Snowball."

"Easy enuff, Massa Tom. I know dem Peruvians, dey not worth noting at close quarters; bery well, and long as we can keep de length ob dere guns from us."

"What think you of Snowball's plan?" asked Tom of the young lieutenant.

"Admirable, sir, but one that will require great foresight to prevent a calamity."

"How?"

"Should the frigate not take the bait and follow the War Cloud, we shall have some difficulty in getting away from the fort."

"You will aid me greatly, Phillips," said Tom, "if you'll bring a boat's crew with you, and wait near the place where I disembark at."

"I will, sir; and you may rely upon my brave fellows as though they were your own men."

"I know it," said Tom, "and next to my faithful lieutenant, I could seek no better companion than yourself in any dangerous enterprise."

The young officer's cheek reddened at the chief's words, and he would have followed the princely young outlaw to the cannon's mouth.

In that part of the plan which related to their staying until darkness set in, the young chief had miscalculated the impetuosity of his own fiery nature.

"Snowball," said Tom, "I see no movement on board the frigate; I cannot brook this impatience much longer. I must—ah! what's the meaning of that?"

The sharp report of a pistol came from the frigate's deck, and those on the War Cloud could plainly see the white puff of smoke as it rose upwards and became lost in the air.

"Dat sumfing," remarked Snowball, "perhaps a signal for dem in the fort, and may mean mischief to us, Massa Tom. Stand by dere near de windlass."

Snowball's acute hearing had detected the tramp of men upon the frigate's deck as they began to weigh anchor.

This movement was followed by a similar one from the War Cloud.

"Come, Mr. Philips," said Tom, "the first move is taken; the fellow thinks to get down upon us unawares—let us enter the boat before the War Cloud spreads her wings to the sea."

With this they left the War Cloud, and rowed towards the Thunderer.

Before they had progressed three lengths the frigate showed her intentions.

She fired a shot within two yards of the boat.

"Come back, Massa Tom," shouted Snowball from the War Cloud, "or dem debbil's sartin to sink yer."

"We shall have to swim for it then," said the

dauntless young hero, laughing; "pull away, men."

Presently came another shot, and so near, that it shattered an oar of one of the rowers.

The African watched it, and turning savagely towards the excited outlaws, who stood grimly by their guns, and said—

"Gib 'em a broadside, boys."

Six white puffs of smoke travelled from the little vessel's ports, and the iron messengers went with unerring precision against the frigate's side.

An attack so sudden and unexpected drew the gunners' attention from the boat, and with a loud cry of rage they opened their double tier of guns to crush the daring little craft whose well-aimed shots had torn away part of their bulwarks, and killed a dozen men.

Snowball saw the ports fly open, and in a second the War Cloud's white sails began to be shaken out.

The Peruvian seamen, in their haste to hurl on a deadly volley, waited not to level their guns, but fired as fast as they loaded; every shot thus went wide of the mark.

The outlaws gave another well-aimed salvo, which shook the War Cloud from stem to stern.

Then, as the breeze began to fill her sails, the War Cloud was turned towards the sea, and the outlaws manning the yards, gave a long defiant hurrah.

The enemy, thoroughly enraged at this bravado took up the gage of battle; and as soon as their frigate's heavy sails caught the wind, the huge vessel went slowly after her saucy antagonist.

The Thunderer and the boat were forgotten by the angry Peruvians, and Midshipman Tom reached the corsair ship in safety.

CHAPTER CXXXV.

THE CAUSE OF THE PISTOL SHOT.

WHEN Midshipman Tom saw the success of Snowball's plan to draw his adversary from the fort, he could not help joining in the cheer his gallant fellows gave as the War Cloud sailed swiftly away.

The cheer was taken up by the War Cloud's crew which crowded the privateer's decks, and their lusty voices were heard on board the frigate as she went slowly astern of the War Cloud.

The Peruvian captain was upon the quarter deck when the deep toned hurrah from the Thunderer pealed across the water.

He turned and shook his clenched hand and savagely muttered,

"When I have crushed this wasp, I'll come back and settle you."

Confident, therefore, as he appeared to be, of an easy victory he sent half his crew below tell- ing them that their services would not be required.

Calling one of the officers who had accompanied them to the fort, he asked—

"Is our prisoner much hurt?"

"No," was the answer, "merely a flesh wound."

"Let him come on deck and behold the vessels taken then. That will repay me for the blow I received at his hands."

The captain's left arm was in a sling, and an ugly gash, red and scarcely dry from the blood that had flown from it was visible across his face.

These wounds had been received from the hands of his hardy captive the corsair, Captain Dragon.

He had accompanied them quietly on board the frigate's boat, when the captian neglectful of the promise he had made, sent a seaman to deprive Captain Dragon of his sword.

He turned like a lion at bay.

The sword they would have wrested from him leapt from its scabbard, and the man who had been sent to wrest it from him fell wounded at the corsair's feet.

"Behold!" shouted the enraged corsair, as he pointed to the fallen man. "That is the fate of all who dare to place a finger upon me while my arm has strength to use this blade."

A number of men, who had rushed to their captain's rescue, paused; they quailed beneath the glare of that fiery eye and upraised weapon.

The captain saw this hesitation, and his sinister face was stirred with anger.

"Cowards!" he roared. "Advance upon him!"

Captain Dragon threw himself into an easy posture of defence, and replied—

"The first that comes within reach of my arm meets, at least, a similar fate."

He looked over the frigate's bow, and beheld the symmetrical outlines of the outlaw's vessel.

The sight fired his blood, and he determined to make an attempt to regain his freedom or perish.

Moving all who stood in his path by flourishing his blade, he dashed towards the bulwarks, and sprang upon a gun.

In another moment he would have leapt into the sea, but the captain of the frigate, with an oath, drew a pistol from his belt, and fired at the daring captive.

The bullet sped true to its mark.

Captain Dragon's weapon was shattered, and the ball glancing off, took an oblique direction, and struck him on the temple.

The corsair fell stunned to the deck, and was carried below by his foes.

"Now," said the Republican officer to his subordinates, "get the ship under weigh, and we will destroy those vessels, one by one."

While speaking, he saw the boat which contained

RED HAND BROUGHT BEFORE THE CAPTAIN OF THE HERCULES.

our hero and the corsair's boy officer pushed off from the War Cloud.

"Here," he shouted to a gunner, "send a ball through that boat."

The shot fell short.

He ordered another to be sent.

That, as the reader is aware, shivered one of the oars of the rowers.

It was at this point that the well-aimed broadside came from the War Cloud, the shots crushing through the frigate's side, and slaying the men as they stood at their guns.

"By the heathen gods," shouted the enraged officer, "everyone of those fellows shall be hung at the yardarm. By heavens, they are spreading their canvas to escape. Fire!"

The double tier of guns poured forth their deadly contents—and to the captain's rage he saw, when the smoke had blown away, the War Cloud with her sails bellying out before the wind, and her crew perched upon the yards shouting defiant hurrahs.

"Spread the sails!" he yelled; "by the Virgin she shall not escape."

23

Had Snowball wished it, he could have disappeared on the distant horizon long before the heavy frigate had well cleared the harbour, afforded by the jutting of Fort San Jose.

But such a course would have spoiled his plans, and caused the frigate to turn back and fall upon the Thunderer.

The African, therefore, kept a tantalising distance between himself and the pursuer.

Sometimes he let the frigate gain upon him—then, when they felt assured of overhauling the daring fellows, the War Cloud would bear off in another direction.

Thus tantalised, regardless of any other duty, the Peruvian captain followed the War Cloud out to sea.

Darkness began to creep over the ocean before the captain of the frigate began to suspect a trick had been played upon him.

The captain could see nothing of the little vessel, and a sudden thought relieved his anxious mind that she had doubled back and joined her consort which remained near the said fortress.

No sooner was this idea conceived than the vessel was put about, and, guided by the far off glimmering lights which shone from the casemates, they bore up for their old station.

Before reaching the place the captain changed his mind; he determined upon sailing towards a small inlet about a quarter of a mile below the fort.

Every light had been extinguished, and in darkness and silence they reached the inlet, the captain overjoyed to think how he was overreaching his cunning foes.

Twenty men were sent ashore, immediately the vessel anchored, to reconnoitre.

The frigate was soon missed by Snowball; and he began to tack about in hopes of finding his huge foe.

Unsuccessful in this, he doubted whether, after all, the frigate would not return and spoil the plan of Captain Dragon's release.

It never occurred—for the very sufficient reason that the fact was unknown to either Midshipman Tom or his sable officer—that the very man they wanted was all the time on board the huge vessel.

"By gar," grumbled Snowball, "here's one too many for dis chile. We shall have to go back, my boys, or him swallow up the Thunderer and Massa Tom as well."

He went back, but not in time to prevent a most unlooked for calamity.

When it became sufficiently dark for his purpose, our hero went ashore accompanied by young Phillips and a picked boat's crew.

The latter he left at the beach, ready to push off at a moment's notice should he be discovered and pursued.

Taking with him a guitar he found in Captain Dragon's cabin, he crept close along under the sombre walls until he reached the small window where the governor's daughter slept.

Our hero's rich full voice was well adapted for singing a plaintive love song, and accompanying himself on the guitar, he sung two verses, and the window was cautiously raised, and Narcisse's lovely face appeared.

A look of wild delight played upon her exquisite features when the twinkling starlight revealed the singer's statuesque form, and a joyous thrill went to her heart as she thought—

"My prayers are heard, he loves me—oh joy! and has come to bear me from this dull old castle to his own beautiful ship."

She had imbibed deeply of romance from reading the old legends of Spain, but these all faded away before the entrancing ideal she had formed and realised.

Here at last her wildest fancies could be indulged in, and her best hopes realised.

"Hush, senor, I am here."

Tom ceased his song and looked upwards, and for a moment he began to regret the plan he had adopted for the rescue of his friend.

"This warm, impulsive creature," he thought, "will construe my visit—if she has not done so already—into one of love. How can I undeceive her, and yet gain the intelligence I require?"

The reflections were broken by the girl's low tones, in which passion and joy were blended.

"Ah, senor, you run a great risk for one so unworthy."

"Unworthy, lady! you wrong yourself. Love, which in my country is said to laugh at bars and bolts, will surely not fear the chance of a stray bullet. It surely ought not."

"You love me then, senor?"

"Lady, could those lovely features be seen without kindling the sacred flame in the beholder's breast?"

Narcisse clasped her hands joyfully, and said—

"For me you have risked your life, what can I —oh, merciful father, he is slain!"

She tottered and fell back from the window as two forms sprung out from the darkness and seized our hero.

The guitar was hurled to the ground, and he drew a pistol from his belt.

Before he could raise it, it was knocked from his hand, and he found himself in the grasp of two officers belonging to the frigate, and a dozen men with drawn weapons were coming to their aid.

Resistance was out of the question, and the young chief, folding his arms, stood and gazed calmly at the group of armed men who surrounded him.

One of the officers snatched the remaining pistol from Midshipman Tom's belt, and before he could take one step the indignant youth with one blow of his white clenched hand struck him to the earth.

Twenty weapons gleamed above his head, and he would have been immolated by the irate crew, had not the second officer struck up their blades and said—

"Secure your prisoner, and take him to the boat."

The influence of the officer who had saved our hero from the seamen's cutlasses again stood him in need, or the angry man whom Tom struck down would have slain the defenceless boy.

"He is unarmed," said the first lieutenant, "do not disgrace yourself by a coward's act."

The other sheathed his weapon.

So quietly had our hero's capture been effected, that young Phillips, who was within twenty yards of the spot, knew nothing of it until he found the guitar and one of Tom's pistols on the ground.

The search he made was useless, for Tom was a close prisoner in the frigate's hold, manacled wrist to wrist with Captain Dragon.

CHAPTER CXXXVI.

A PROPOSITION.

WHEN the young lieutenant of the Thunderer had recovered from the first feelings of surprise at finding the pistol and guitar dropped by the outlaw chief, he turned to his followers, and said—

"Some misfortune has befallen Midshipman Tom. Can any one among you see any traces of his captors?"

The fisherman's son, Red Hand's inveterate foe, was standing by the young officer's side.

"If you will allow me, sir," he said, "I'll go round that rock, and find the cause of that strange noise which I heard but a few minutes since."

"A noise?"

"Yes, sir; a sort of a scuffling sound. Hark!"

They all listened, and distinctly heard the chafe of oars propelling a boat forward.

The boy glided quickly away from the group, and ran to the water's edge; that which he saw caused him to hasten back to his companions.

"There's a boat," he said, "going quickly towards that frigate that went in chase of the War Cloud this morning."

"Impossible," said Charley; "the frigate cannot be there."

"It is, sir; she has evidently doubled back on the War Cloud."

The Corsair lieutenant went to the place where the boy had seen the boat, and by the glimmering starlight he saw the frigate's hull looming out against the sky.

"The outlaw chief," he said, "has been taken aboard. Into the boats all of you; we must go in search of the War Cloud."

The men pulled a long and strong oar, and soon reached the Thunderer.

Then Charley had the anchor weighed, and the vessel began to glide through the water.

Their search was not of long duration, for the War Cloud was coming towards the fort with the speed of a sea bird.

Charley Philips bore up within speaking distance, and shouted through his trumpet—

"Your chief is a prisoner on board the frigate."

An angry yell came from the outlaws, and Snowball asked—

"Sartin ob it, are yer—Massa Tom on board?"

"Quite. We found a pistol within a few yards of where he last was seen. That pistol belonged to Midshipman Tom."

"Then, by gar," said Snowball, "we hab him out ob dat, or lose both our ships and lives."

"I am quite ready to aid you, Snowball. What's your plan?"

"Wait a minute, den, I tell you. Anyhow, get the boats ready in case we should have to cut de frigates out before morning."

"Let us attack them," said the impetuous young lieutenant; "I hate that cowardly plan of coming upon our foe unawares."

"No, Massa Philips, why dey might hurt de chief, p'raps one ob our own shot go through the side and kill him. Tink ob dat, sir."

The young lieutenant had not thought of this possibility. Snowball's words induced him to reflect, and he saw that it would be quite possible to do the outlaw chief a deadly harm by his rash mode of attack.

"I have a plan," said Snowball, suddenly, "come closer and I will tell you."

The ships neared each other until their yards touched. Then Snowball resumed:

"Dere am danger enough in it, Massa Charley, so if you like you may go."

"Will you trust me in place of yourself?"

"Yes, dat I will."

"Then I'll do it, unless a shot stops me."

"Plenty ob chance of getting one. Dis is de idea: you take some of your men in a boat, and haul up under the frigate's stern."

"Yes."

"When you get dere, find you some way to get aboard."

"Never fear, I'll get on board if there is a chance."

"Dat's all you hab to do. You get inside the ship, find Massa Tom, den help him to knock de irons off."

"Well, after that?"

"By gar," said Snowball, and he gave a good laugh; "by de time dat is done, I shall not be far away from you. Yah! yah! yah! You hear de little War Cloud talking to dat gentleman."

"If you bring the vessels together," said Charley, "by the time I have freed the young chief's hands, I think I shall alter my plan."

"What dat, Charley?"

"Simply," said Charley, "in place of going to the boats I think we will go on deck."

"Among de enemy?"

"Yes."

"By gar! you plucky, dam if you ain't."

"Thank you, Snowball."

"Nebber mind tanking me—be off. I take charge of your vessel."

Charley's boat was soon noiselessly dropped from the side, and with muffled oars they pulled cautiously towards the frigate.

Six of his best men were on the little craft—men who knew not the meaning of the word fear, yet, as they pulled towards the huge black hull that stood out like a dusky giant above the sea, they felt that a few minutes would decide their fate.

When the young chief was forced down the frigate's hold, manacled to the corsair's wrist, he gave an exclamation of surprise when he recognised his friend.

Captain Dragon returned the cry, and said carelessly—

"Come to keep me company, Tom?"

"Unfortunately, yes. I never expected to meet you here."

"No."

"I thought you were safely ensconced in the fort?"

"I was, until the captain of the vessel kindly helped me on board. How were you captured?"

The young chief told him.

"Serenading, Tom?"

"No, Dragon, you wrong me if you suspect it. It was solely on your account I came."

"Your pardon, my gallant boy, I meant not to wound your feelings."

"I know it. Now, Charles, how are we to get out of this mess?"

"Faith, I hardly know. What is your notion?"

"Mine," said the young chieftain, "is a decided preference to liberty to being here."

"And mine, too."

"About the plan?"

"Have you none, Tom?"

"Had I this confounded manacle off my wrist I should be more comfortable, and able to talk better."

"I don't know but I should myself."

"Let's remove them. You can stand pain?"

"A little."

"Raise your hands with mine, and we'll smash this bracelet against the iron rim of this barrel."

In spite of the excruciating pain, the hardy fellows brought their wrists down upon the iron rim of the barrel, and shivered the manacle into twenty pieces.

"Free, so far," said Tom, binding up his bleeding hand. "Are you much hurt, Charles?"

"Only broken a finger or two of my left hand. What's the next move?"

"Make a jump through the open port and swim for it."

Captain Dragon shook his head.

"Why not?" asked Tom.

"There is a man stationed above whose especial duty it is to watch that port which stands so temptingly open."

"What are we to do, then?"

"I'll be hanged if I know; yet perhaps chance may do something for us."

"Chance brought me here," said Tom, savagely. "I will not trust to it again."

"Don't, unless you can make it benefit you."

Captain Dragon began whistling softly, and placed his wrist close to Midshipman Tom.

Our hero saw this sudden action was caused by something more than chance.

Before he had time to ask its meaning the first lieutenant and several sailors came into the hold.

"Something up," growled Dragon. "I hope I shall not forget that my hand is supposed to be manacled."

The first lieutenant came to the corsair's side.

"Senor Capitani, the commander of this vessel has sent me to make a proposal to you."

"Has he; and what is it?"

"You shall hear, senor. The commander of this invincible ship——"

"What did you say, invincible?"

"Yes, senor—invincible ship of the great Republic."

"Old tubs, belonging to a set of duffers. Good."

"As you please, senor; we will not quarrel about a name."

"Whether we quarrel about a name or do not is of very little importance to me. What have you come here for?"

"You shall hear, senor. The noble captain, under whose instructions I am now acting, desires me to tell you that he will give you your liberty if you will act according to his orders."

"What are they?"

"In the first place, you will go on board your vessel, and while the men are asleep, let others sent by us——"

"Go on."

"When the crew has been transferred to the fort, you will bring the small ship, the War Cloud, I think, is her name, along with your vessel."

"Yes."

"Our men will then be able to leap on board and capture the crew of the War Cloud."

"What is this treachery required for?"

"Because, senor, my captain is averse to shedding blood, and would rather take your vessels by stratagem."

"Is this all?"

"All, senor; do you agree?"

"You shall hear my opinion of the matter, first."

"I am all attention, senor."

"Well, then, a more rascally scheme," said Captain Dragon, his eyes in a blaze with indignation, "I never heard."

"Stratagem is quite fair in war, senor."

"Stratagem may be—nay, undoubtedly is, but treachery is not only cowardly, but the consummation of the direst villainy. And now what do you think my answer will be?"

"You refuse."

"I do."

"Then I am grieved to say, senor, that you will be hung at the yard-arm."

"Go tell your noble captain this, then, from me," said the corsair, dashing his clenched fist in the officer's face; "tell him I would sooner die a hundred deaths, if he could will it, than betray one of my men."

The officer recoiled from the heavy blow, and glaring upon the corsair, his face white with passion, he hissed—

"Then die you shall, and that before long."

Saying this he rushed from the hold followed by his men.

"I suppose," said Dragon, "they will put a hempen collar on my neck for that."

"Not while the sea can drown you," said Tom, pointing to the open port.

"Right, my boy. Hark! what is that?"

They listened and heard a man utter in a low tone—

"I wish I knew which part of the ship the captain is confined in."

"Charley Philip's voice," said Dragon, "by all that's holy!"

CHAPTER CXXXVII.

A DESPERATE ENCOUNTER.

THE young chief ran to the port and peered out. There he beheld the young lieutenant beneath, and the men resting on their oars.

Tom silently extended his hand, which the young officer seized, and he was drawn quickly inside.

Captain Dragon grasped his hand eagerly and said—

"By George! only just in time; another hour would have seen me strung up."

"They perhaps won't have the chance now. Here, quick, take these weapons; see, the War Cloud is at work!"

Bang came the report of a gun above them; and the sound was repeated over and over again on both sides of the frigate.

Tom and Captain Dragon looked at Charley for an explanation.

They soon had it.

"It is," said young Philips, "the War Cloud and the Thunderer; they are engaging the frigate on both sides."

"Into the boat then," said Tom, "let us be among them."

The War Cloud and the Thunderer had by this time got within a short distance of the frigate, and were using their guns as only British tars can use them.

It was pretty evident from the incessant shouts of the officers and the trampling of feet on the deck that the battle was becoming rather exciting.

Captain Dragon would have rushed up, but Charley explained Snowball's intention to be that "when the vessels all come to close quarters we were to rush upon deck to create a confusion the better to enable him to get his boarders over the side."

"A good plan!" said the young chief, "and the sooner they close the better."

"My opinion," said Dragon. "that last shot came through the side and whistled too close to my ear to be pleasant."

Tom laughed, "It has done us a service at any rate," he said, "for it has made us a hole sufficiently large to look through.

The corsair applied his eye to the orifice when a foot above him came a chance shot which tore away the tough wood and cast the splinters in all directions about the hold.

"So, so," muttered the corsair, laughing and blinking his eyes, "might have spoilt my beauty a bit. One of the splinters fell across my nose, and made me feel as though I saw a feast of Chinese lanterns—the lights I saw were a caution "

Tom and the sailors burst into a fit of laughter at Captain Dragon's soliloquy.

The young chief stood now upon an empty barrel and by the red flashes of the guns above head and those fired from the War Cloud, he witnessed the unequal fight between his little vessel and the frigate's double tier of guns.

He also saw that the frigate had suffered considerable damage among her spars and rigging, and that every flash that came from the War Cloud's guns proved they remained intact.

"Bravo, Hal," he remarked, as he saw that individual nail his banner to the broken stump of the foremast. "Well done, my gallant fellow. I'll reward that act should I ever put my foot upon the saucy War Cloud's deck."

Captain Dragon looked about when he heard this soliloquy. "You are having a cheerful contemplation, Tom." he said, "I wish I could see how my fellows are getting on the other side, only your spars are damaged I see."

"Don't depress their guns enough."

"Then drawing an inference from that," went on the corsair, "I suppose him standing much higher out of the water is getting, as the Yankees say, 'pretty tarnation well hulled.'"

"No doubt, look out; isn't she coming? Yes, ready there."

As he sprang from the barrel, a mighty shock caused the frigate to tremble in every beam.

The War Cloud and her companion had closed with their big opponent, and from the cries that could be heard above, it was evident an attempt at boarding was being made by the devil-may-care crews.

Midshipman Tom, Captain Dragon, Charley, and the sailors, made a crush up the hatchway, and unnoticed by the officers of the frigate, reached the deck.

Captain Dragon, mindful of past favours he had received from the captain of the frigate, sought him out.

"Follow me!" on approaching him, shouted the corsair, levelling his pistol at the captain.

As he spoke his arm was struck suddenly aside, and the bullet was sent whistling among the rigging, bringing down a marine on the foretop, who was busy firing on the outlaws.

Captain Dragon let fall the empty pistol, and drew his sword, just in time to parry a lunge made by the enraged captain.

In a twinkling, a cool scientific duel was taking place between them, much to the enjoyment of the governor of the fort, who it was that had struck up Dragon's hand.

Midshipman Tom with young Philips and the men pressed forward to effect a junction with their messmates, who were climbing the frigate's sides.

In the melée they had not noticed Captain Dragon, who still continued his fight with the officer.

Inspired by the young chief, the men cut their way through the circle of foes and leapt upon the quarter-deck.

"Quick!" said he, "slew round those guns; we will make a lane for our friends to come on deck."

Snowball and the crew of the War Cloud saw their young chief, and gave a shout, that for a moment staggered the Peruvians.

Tom waved his hat in return, then seizing a rammer, assisted in loading a gun.

Another second, and he would have sent a shower of grape along the crowded deck; but when his hand was within an inch of the gun he paused.

It was the sight of his gallant friend, Captain Dragon, who was at this moment struggling with a number of the crew, who had seized upon his hands as he fought with their captain.

He saw our hero's hand was stayed by a regard for his safety, and called out—

"Fire away, Tom! Never mind me. If I fall there will be plenty of those dogs fall with me."

Tom's face flushed; he was prouder than ever of his friend.

But he had lost the opportunity he had of gaining a victory without more bloodshed.

The boy's hawk eyes swept the sea of faces, which was now turned towards him.

He saw by the captain's gestures that he was urging the men to drive him and his party from the quarter-deck.

With a significant glance at his men, he pointed towards the loaded gun.

The seamen noticed, and there was an evident disinclination among them to face the deadly showers which they knew would sweep down the whole length of the ship, should any attempt be made to dislodge Tom and his companions.

Thus Tom continued in command of the quarter-deck.

The attacking crew saw his position, and fought like demons to effect a passage through the boarding-nettings, and the points of weapons that met them upon every inch of the frigate's bulwarks.

Tom would have fired among them, but the chief officer had ordered Captain Dragon to be lashed to the foot of the after-mast.

Leaving thus a clear space between the bound captain and the possessors of the quarter-deck, the frigate's crew now concentrated all their efforts in repelling the attacks from their two enemies.

Yet, although Tom remained nominally in possession of the vessel, he was compelled to stand behind the guns and behold his men slaughtered in their attempts to scramble over the frigate's side.

In vain did the devoted corsair call upon the young chief to fire.

Tom's reply was invariably the same.

"I shall not, Charles," he said. "I'll cheat the cunning devils yet. Should they destroy our men I'll blow them and ourselves into the air in their moment of victory."

"Fire, Tom!" again repeated the corsair.

Tom only shook his head.

Young Philip's fond affection for the captain was more like a son's, and with a soul full with rage, he had listened to the oft repeated words that fell from the corsair's lips.

He saw, too, the courage among the boarders, and with a devotion that would have stamped him as a hero had he been sailing under the king's flag, he stepped beside Tom, and said—

"This position is useless to us, sir, under these conditions; we'll alter it, or die in the attempt."

"There are no means of altering matters," said Tom, "unless our men can effect a lodgment on the deck, and then we can join them."

"With all deference to you, sir, there is."

"How?"

"By liberating my captain."

"The attempt would be certain death to both."

"It is worth trying."

Tom was silent.

He was mentally calculating the chance of Charley being able to render the assistance before Dragon could be shot down.

While his mind was thus engaged, a sharp cry of anger from young Philips caused him to turn.

CHARLEY PHILIPS AVENGES THE TREACHERY TO MIDSHIPMAN TOM.

Following the direction of Charley's angry glance, he saw one of the Peruvian officers deliberately prick the corsair with the point of his sword.

"Swift, Charley, and encounter the villain," cried Tom.

Charley grasped his sword and bounded towards the cowardly officer, but he fled and joined his men.

The chance then was for him to return to his captain and set him free; his knife blade had severed Captain Dragon's cords, and they were running towards the quarter-deck, when Tom cried out—

"Down on your faces, both of you."

They both fell flat to the deck, and the sailors in pursuit were swept into eternity by the unexpected discharge of the gun which Tom had so long been unable to use.

The deadly shower of grape spread like a fan, mowing down the men with a fearful certainty.

Captain Dragon and his gallant boy-officer sprang to their feet, and were soon beside their friends.

Charley registered a vow that should he escape the ensuing slaughter, he would, foot to foot and steel to steel, revenge the indignity his leader had suffered.

The cordial greeting over, Captain Dragon, who, although faint from the wounds received from the dastard officers, picked a cutlass up from the deck and cried—

"Fire ! fire ! Tom, then let us charge the lubbers."

Then he waved his hat, and cheered lustily to his crew.

A returning huzza was lost in the deafening noise of the two guns, which belched forth their murderous contents.

The horrible sight presentable along the frigate's upper deck was sickening, as the odour of blood mingled with the sulphurous smoke.

The Peruvians were aroused from the stupor which the fearful slaughter had spread among them by the captain's jumping on a gun, and pointing to the little band who were upon the quarter-deck, preparing for a repetition of the deadly work.

"Men," he said, "there are two ways of dying —one is to pass from life like sheep in a pen, the other is to die like heroes for your country and your flag. You are fulfilling the first."

He saw that the crew cowered beneath the reproach.

"Well, then," he proceeded, "follow me. Let us drive them from our ship. Some may fall, but those who remain will avenge them and be amply rewarded by their country."

Regardless of the hardy boarders, who had been time after time hunted back from the nettings, and who were again preparing for an attack, they followed their spirited captain towards the death-spreading guns.

"Steady," said Tom, who was noticing their every movement ; "give them a close volley, then to work with your steel. We have but one chance left—that is, the coming of your messmates, who I see are preparing for another attack."

His words were hardly delivered when the enemy came rushing towards the steps that led to the quarter-deck.

On ! until they advanced within two yards of the guns.

A dead silence prevailed amongst the dark surging mass, it was a stillness unbroken by the sound of but one deep word.

That word came from the young chief.

"Fire !"

There was a pause in the second rush—twenty of the foremost and bravest fell.

"Fire !"

The second gun was discharged, and the advancing mass recoiled as they were bespattered with the blood of their closely mingled companions.

Then followed a yell which told how highly strained their nerves had been, and they rushed towards the steps.

"Fire !"

The blazing sheet of flame that shot forth was so close, that it charred the faces of the crew and made a perfect gap among them.

There was a moment of awful pause ; then the remnant of six hundred men, thinned by death to one half that number, uttered a loud whoop, and threw themselves upon the little band.

No time existed to fire the two guns they had re-loaded ; so, abandoning them, the men drew their cutlasses, and ranging themselves in a line they hacked and stabbed at the hooting swarm who were climbing up the steps.

Another five minutes and Midshipman Tom and his men would have been slain ; but before that time had passed and their brave arms had begun to grow weary with slaughtering their fellow mortals a loud huzza in rear of the Peruvians told them that aid was near.

The well-known cry of the British sea-dog—so often heard in the din and smoke of battle—was followed by a close volley of small arms ; and the Peruvians to save themselves from being annihilated had no alternative but to face the courageous heroes from the two little vessels which had so long and obstinately fought their huge frigate.

CHAPTER CXXXVIII.

A DUEL.

TOWERING high above the boarders could be seen the huge form of the African lieutenant.

His chief in danger, he cleaved his way through the densely packed mass of men to reach the quarter-deck.

Disdaining to use the ordinary weapon usually found in a ship's armament, Snowball had a tremendous axe in his grip.

Using it with both hands he committed fearful havoc among the foe, and when he had fought his way to his commander's side, blood was springing from more than one mighty gash in his nude body.

He had only time to catch his young chief's hand and convey it to his lips, when a furious charge made by the invaders, drove the enemy like scattered sheep upon the quarter-deck.

This sudden rush, caused by the determination of their foes, placed Tom in imminent peril. He became totally isolated from his friends.

But neither eye nor hand lost their wonted power.

His keen pliant blade, wielded with that extraordinary skill which had carried him through so many dangers, he now employed solely on the defensive.

Baffled by his skill and forestalled in every

attempt to get below the young chief's guard, his foes plied their blows thick and fast.

One, to terminate the conflict, withdrew a few paces, and carefully loaded his pistol, and before the young chief could prepare for this new danger the trigger was pulled, and the ball ploughed a deep furrow across his temple.

The shot, striking him thus, was followed by a stream of warm blood, so blinding him, that his sword played at random around the heads of his foes.

But the god of battles had not yet forsaken the young outlaw, for at that moment, when his brain became dizzy, and he in his imagination felt death's revengeful steel seeking his heart, help came—came in the huge form of Snowball, who cleaving right and left with his fearful weapon of slaughter, smashed in the skulls of those of his young leader s foes, and leaping to the boy's side, he faced those who yet stood their ground.

"Nebber mind, Massa Tom," he said, "Snowball is here now, and by gar, only just in time."

The boy heard the friendly voice; then his head fell forward, and he dropped to the deck.

"You hab kill him!" he shouted, "kill de chief, den by gar, and by de Great Spirit of my tribe you all die—take dat! and dat man here—'twas you killed de chief."

The spirit of a demon seemed to take possession of the dusky giant; he laughed at the efforts to slay him, and each blow that fell from his axe levelled an antagonist to the deck.

Five of Midshipman Tom's foes lay upon the deck; the others, however, horror-stricken, turned and fled from the terrible unearthly being, who seemed to them to bear a charmed life.

Now the quarter-deck was deserted, and the contest raged only amidships.

Like the storm when about to pass away, the struggle had been more desperate as it reached its termination.

His foes, he saw, soon found their companions, and became lost in the surging shouting crowd.

Kneeling beside the young chief, he raised the blood-stained face, smoothed the dark masses of wavy hair, now clotted together by the warm life stream, burst into tears.

He thought he was dead.

In the midst of his anguish there came a mighty shout, and looking towards the mast-head, he saw their banner floated above the gaudy ensign of the republic.

The frigate was theirs, and a crowd of blood-stained men flushed with victory, came rushing to the quarter-deck, shouting for their young leader.

There was a sudden pause when they beheld the dusky lieutenant stooping over the beloved form of the chief, and every voice became hushed and every head bowed at the sight of the sad spectacle.

"The chief has fallen!"

Ran in a husky whisper from one to the other

until it reached Captain Dragon, who wa ing the captain's sword in token of the sut. of the frigate's screw.

He looked round and his eyes fell upon the st ing group upon the quarter-deck.

Snowball, like an ebony statue, supporting his young chief's head, and a group of men standing round.

The crosair sprang forward, and taking Tom's hand, said in a low, hushed voice—

"Is he dead?"

"He am," was the brief reply; "killed by a dozen ob dem."

A man placed his hand inside the young chief's jacket, and called out in a loud tone—

"There is hope yet—he is not dead—his heart beats!"

Snowball was silent with joy. He was afraid to speak lest it should undo the charm these words had produced.

"Fetch the surgeon," said Captain Dragon to a man who stood near.

The surgeon was soon on the spot.

Captain Dragon loosened the gold fastenings of our hero's jacket, and then his white undershirt, when an expression of alarm came from the corsair's lips.

The soft, white material, which was wet with blood that had flowed from a deep gash just above the boy's heart.

"Another inch," said the surgeon, "and he would have died; but as it is, a few day's quiet under my remedies may restore him."

Under the advice of the surgeon, the patient was carried to his own ship.

The doctor had not much time to render his services—scores and scores of maimed and wounded wretches were fearfully awaiting his coming in the cock-pit of the frigate.

Arms, hands, and legs were amputated, and so great was the number of wounded that these ghastly emblems of the carnage were thrown on a heap near the centre of the stifling place.

They all left the War Cloud, except Snowball, for there was much to do yet on board the frigate.

The African remained seated by the couch of his wounded chief watching every twitch and convulsion that heaved over the sufferer's face.

From that post nothing could move him, and when, after several days' care, the young outlaw opened his eyes, there was joy in his heart; but there was greater joy when, on the next day, Tom gazed wildly and murmured—

"I am getting faint—they are too many for me. See, there is blood before my eyes! Snowball—Dragon—help!—help!"

The last impression of the terrible fight was still strong upon him.

He knew not that he had been saved; in fancy he was still battling with the circle of angry forms.

Snowball drank in every word.

He heard his name mentioned, and that was music to his ears.

"You better now, Massa Tom?"

"Snowball, what has happened? Surely this is the War Cloud?"

"It am, Massa Tom. You keep quiet and you soon be well."

"Who saved me, Snowball?"

"I stop dem from killing you, dat all, Massa Tom; but I thought you gone when I see you all of a heap on deck."

The young chief extended his hand, which the devoted fellow carried to his lips with more sincerity than ever monarch's hand was kissed by fawning courtiers.

The boy fell asleep, and Snowball, with a sob, caused by his great joy, fell upon his knees, and thanked the Good Spirit of his tribe for saving the young leader's life.

On board the frigate Captain Dragon was busy with his friends.

The fight was now over, and the men's angry passions had subsided.

Much as the captain of the frigate felt his defeat, he could not but admire Captain Dragon's generous conduct.

He gave the officers back their swords, and offered them their ship upon payment of an easy ransom.

The offer was gladly accepted, and many a goodly bag of treasures was transferred from the coffers of the frigate to the Thunderer.

The old governor he had taken on board, intending to repay him for his treachery at a future period.

When the officers had again filled their empty scabbards, young Philips stepped forward, and walking up to the officer who had behaved so barbarously to Midshipman Tom, challenged him to mortal combat.

He would have refused, but when the frigate's captain heard the facts of the charge against him he was as indignant at the cowardly action as was the actual sufferer himself.

A place of meeting was therefore appointed—the entrance to a thick forest close beneath the fort.

At daylight young Philips, with his second, went ashore in a small boat.

The officer, with a companion, followed.

Their combat was brief.

The cowardly nature that prompted the outrage was not equal to sustain him through a hand-to-hand encounter.

Here the Peruvian's treachery was again displayed.

Feeling himself unequal to cope with the gallant youth single handed, he made a signal to his second, who immediately drew his knife and crept silently behind young Philips, with the intention of burying it between his shoulders.

"Back!" thundered Charley's friend, springing forward, and thrusting a pistol in the fellow's face. "Cowards, I have a mind to send a bullet through the skulls of both of you!"

The cur-like ruffian shrank from the deadly tube, and casting a despairing glance at his companion, urged him to try his best.

Seeing there was no way of escape, and fearing that the Englishman would keep his threat, he clutched his weapon, and, with a fearful oath, prepared for the duel with his young antagonist.

Five minutes after he had crossed blades with the English lad, he lay upon the greensward pierced through the heart.

"He has met the fate of a coward," said Charley, as he stooped over the outstretched body.

Charley stood for a moment, then wiping his stained weapon, he returned it to its scabbard and went slowly towards the boat.

CHAPTER CXXXIX.

THE RANSOM.

WHEN Charley Philips reached the Thunderer's quarter-deck, the frigate had disengaged herself from her companions, and from deck to truck her crew were busy repairing the damage she had sustained.

The same activity was going forward on board the War Cloud and the Black Squall, and when David Shopland reached the quarter-deck he was met by his captain.

"I have been anxiously looking for you," said Captain Dragon, "and felt uneasy until I saw you step into the boat. Have you heard any news of the young chieftain's determination?"

"No, sir, what is it?"

"Why," he said, thoughtfully, "he has come to the determination of sailing for England as soon as we have refitted."

"What has caused this sudden change—do you know?"

"A dream, I imagine, to see his fair Laura, and some matters relating to his birth; for if all we hear is true, our young friend will one day become a peer of England."

"Unless," said Charley, "the law of outlawry may compel him to forfeit his birthright."

"I have thought the same. However, he can but make the attempt. Should he fail, the wide sea will continue to find him riches."

"A far preferable proceeding," said Charley, "to sitting at home living upon the luxuries which others have created. By the way, what about the treasure you were obliged to drop overboard?"

"Snowball has taken a boat, and gone to fish it up, if such be possible."

"Well, he may find it, certainly—I hope he

may. There is not much fear of his returning without it. That fellow can live under water like a fish. Now, Charley, I want you to go to the fort."

"Alone?"

"Yes; but as a protection against treachery, you will take the old governor in the boat. Leave him in charge of one of the crew, with orders to shoot the old rascal should the fellows inside betray any inclination to keep you."

"And what would be the object of my going, may I inquire?"

"This," the captain said, giving him a paper. "This is an order, written by the governor, commanding his captain to convey to your boat an iron-bound chest, which stands in his apartment."

"Containing money, I suppose?"

"Yes, his ransom."

"Should they refuse to deliver it?"

"Bring your prisoner back, and I'll hang him by the heels to the yardarm."

Charley, with an armed crew, went ashore, and placing the governor in the bow of the boat, and one of the seamen with a loaded pistol close to the old fellow's ear, he gave him fully to understand that any resistance to the fulfilment of the order would be followed by immediate death.

The governor's face showed fear was within his heart.

He had, as he surmised, overreached the corsair, but when he found himself placed in this unenviable position, a dire foreboding that he might not have been quite shrewd enough came into his brain.

Owing to Captain Dragon's knowledge of the Peruvian language, the governor had been compelled to write out a peremptory order for the delivery of the chest.

The old governor, on the other hand, equally alive to securing his ends, had mentally contrived it, that when the money was brought to the boat, he would give his men a signal to fire upon the English seamen.

"And then," thought the wily old fellow, "before their vessel can send aid sufficient to repel the attack, I will be safely inside the fort, and my treasure-chest saved."

The arrangement, therefore, respecting the pistol being kept close to his temple was as unexpected as disagreeable, and inwardly cursing the unlucky hour that brought the corsair to Fort San Jose, he sat gazing at a number of his own men, who had crossed their muskets to bear the money-chest to the boat.

The old fellow's eyes suddenly gleamed with joy as he saw the chest in course of being delivered, his little dodge, he thought, ripened for speedy execution.

Then he made a sign to the sailor intimating that now the ransom was coming, he might be permitted to walk ashore.

Bob understood his gestures, and, to the old double-faced officer's rage, he shook his head and replied—

"No yer don't, not if I know it, yer old sarpent. I'm up to yer nigger tricks afore to-day."

"What's the matter, Bob?" asked a messmate.

"Why, this old beggar," Bob replied, "keeps a-signalling a summat to them there lubbers as is bringing the box. He says to me I oughter let him go now."

"Well, why don't you? He can't do you no harm, nohow."

"You ain't so sure o' that," Bob went on, "and I'll tell yer how it 'ud happen. No sooner had I let the old yellow sarpent depart than he'd make sail for them lubbers as is conveying that box. Do you see that now?" said Bob, exultingly.

"Well, I does, as far as you says."

"And then what would he do next, eh? Why, he'd give the word, and one on 'em would shove his bayonet into our young luff, then off they'd go, like the Old Nick himself arter a sinner."

"What should we be doing to let 'em"

The speaker gave utterance to this with the air of a man who had put forth something that had completely taken the wind out of his opponent.

"What should we be doing to let 'em?" Bob repeated; "why, we should be glad enough to step it with our karkisses complete."

"P'raps."

"There's no p'raps in it. Dick, look there."

The old sailor extended his left hand towards the dark embrasures of the fort.

Dick followed his gesture, and beheld the ramparts swarming with armed men.

"You was right, Bob," said another of the crew, who had been listening to a part of the conversation; "you are perfectly right. Stick to the old varmint; they is as treacherous as a adder, all on 'em."

"Balay there, messmates, here comes the first luff and the swag," said Bob.

Charley Philips and the party of soldiers who carried the treasure chest came towards the boat at this juncture.

The old governor was writhing in the sailor's strong grasp.

"Look here," growled Bob, "I shall shake the life out of yer old karkiss if yer ain't quiet."

The men were sullenly placing the chest on the boat, when the old fellow roared out—

"Soldiers, rescue me! I will give you——"

Old Bob saw by the sudden manner in which the box was tumbled over the side, that his words had acted on the soldiers' minds.

Without waiting for orders, the old tar brought his hard fist in contact with the governor's physiognomy, and laid him kicking at the bottom of the boat.

The old governor's sudden fall in the world created temporary merriment among the observers, but Charley, looking around him, saw there was no time to be lost.

One spring took him to the boat, and standing on the bow, with a loaded pistol in each hand, he said—

"Give way, my lads."

Eight tough oar-blades bent like reeds as they sent the boat spanking through the water.

"Now," said Charley, "to business. Bob, just pitch the old gentleman overboard."

Away went the governor, head first, into the sea, and the soldiers, fearing to shoot him, abandoned the idea of firing, and ran to the beach to help the frightened rascal ashore.

CHAPTER CXL.

RED HAND'S REVENGE.

WHEN the pirates and their ferocious leader were drawn up in line before the stern captain of the Hercules, Red Hand felt that he had but little mercy to expect.

"Again, Derrick," said Captain White, "fate has thrown you into my power."

The pirate, with folded arms and head erect, looked defiantly at the speaker, and answered, doggedly—

"It has; but I care not for the unlucky chance. I shall yet tread the deck of a vessel. When I do, Captain White, this debt shall be paid."

"Do not deceive yourself, Derrick; from this ship you will pass into a prison, and there meet the fate you have so long deserved."

The pirate's reply was a mocking laugh.

"Send them below," said the captain; "confine them in couples in the lower hold, and bind each of them together in such a manner that they will have one hand at liberty."

He turned from the group and went to the quarter-deck, where young Kilcher was standing relating the capture of the pirates to an admiring crew of his fellow-midshipmen.

The captain's orders were carried into effect respecting the pirates.

Red Hand and his lieutenant—a half caste—were taken to the after part of the hold.

Red Hand's left hand was manacled to his companion's right, and in darkness and silence they were left to their own reflections.

A long time elapsed before Red Hand spoke; when he did so his words were blasphemous curses upon his captors.

"Swear away, captain," growled the half-caste; "if swearing could get us free you can do it. But is there nothing to be done? Are we to dangle at the gallows after all?"

Red Hand was silent. His mind was busy forming wild plans to regain his liberty.

There seemed to be no hope.

Manacled in the lower hold of a huge vessel, where was it to come from?

Such might have been the reflections of most people.

Not so with Red Hand.

He crouched like a sullen tiger, ready to spring on the first of his captors who should enter his place of confinement.

But hour after hour passed, and nothing save a hollow ripple of the waters from some passing ship broke upon the monotony of the ocean.

And then his brain seemed on fire, and he felt he could have strangled his companion, whose heavy breathing indicated he was slumbering by his side.

"Leno," he said, savagely, "awake."

He accompanied the words by jerking the sleeper's wrist.

The pain caused the half-caste to start, and rubbing his eyes with his unfettered hand, he strained them in search of some small aperture to realize the surrounding darkness.

"Did you speak, captain?"

"I did," said Red Hand. "Have you forgotten where you are that you thus soundly sleep?"

"No, captain; but we shall swing for it, I suppose, and until the time comes I don't see any necessity to trouble about the matter."

"Then you would die like a rat taken in a trap."

"There is no help for it."

"There is—feel this?"

The half-caste extended his hand, and his fingers came in contact with a piece of sharp-pointed twisted iron.

"It's a drill," he said, in a tone of wonderment. "Where and how did you get it?"

"Groping about in the darkness my hand clutched it," replied Red Hand.

"Well—captain?"

"Can you not guess its use?"

"Yes; it is for the purpose of boring holes through wood."

"Right, Leno; and by using it we shall be able to revenge our death upon our captors."

"You would not——?"

"Listen! Do you hear the waters rippling beneath us?"

"I do."

"In a few hours more the sea shall find its way through a dozen holes," and in a voice of fierce hate, he added, "the ship shall go to the bottom. Ha! ha! ha! there's a revenge for you; that fellow shall die before Red Hand's career is ended."

The half-caste went cold to his fingers, such a diabolical revenge, for a moment, chilled even his nature.

"Captain," he said, "we may escape yet; this is——"

"Curse you, for a chicken hearted fool. They must all die. Ha! ha! The story of Red Hand's revenge, shall in future days, blanch the cheeks of those who have read it."

"THE SHIP IS FILLING!" CRIED SYDNEY BELCHER.

Leno recoiled from his miscreant companion. His soul, blackened as it was by the perpetration of many foul crimes, was not sufficiently hardened to listen calmly to this projected murder.

"Now to begin," said the miscreant, "we must make use of our hands."

"Have you a knife, with which to cut the cord?" asked the half-caste.

"No, your teeth are sharp, use them, and gnaw them through."

There ensued a long silence, during which the half-caste's sharp teeth were occupied gnawing the thin rope.

Presently the teeth had done their appointed duty.

Red Hand's hand became liberated, and he gave a shout of savage joy as he grasped the drill, and began to drive it slowly through the tough oak.

Leno sat in moody silence.

He evidently was praying that some of the crew might descend and stop the monster's work.

His prayer seemed answered, for a couple of men came below.

One carried a lantern, the other food for the prisoners.

Red Hand desisted, and placing the drill under him, waited the departure of the men.

Then he set to work more vigorously with his task.

Twice the words came to Leno's lips.

He would have told the sailors Red Hand's fell purpose, but Red Hand had made him like one spell-bound, and his throat became parched and choking as his companion's eyes were fixed upon him.

Already had he noticed Leno's quivering lip, and he whispered in his ear.

"The white face and trembling muscles betray your cowardice. You would have disclosed the danger there to these bloodhounds. Had you done so, I would have driven this pointed iron into your heart.'

The half-castle made no reply, but sat near the side, listening with a sinking sensation at his heart to the sound of the sharp-pointed tool, as it ground through the tough wood.

"One—three will be enough. Leno!"

"Here, Captain.'

"Quick! bring something—anything—and hold over the hole, ready to plug it when I draw this tool out!"

Leno complied by untwisting a silken scarf from his waist, and tearing it into three, he began to roll one of the pieces into a hard ball.

The rush of water for a moment appalled him, and caused his hand to shake so violently, that it was some minutes before he could plug the hole.

"Keep your hand upon it, fool!" said Red Hand with savage glee; there will be another very soon, They have sent me some grease to make it work easy."

He alluded to a piece of pork, which had been brought to them with some biscuits by the two seamen.

Leno shuddered, but was silent; he was revolving a plan of another nature—it was how he might save his own life, and the lives of the crew.

The silence continued until the second hole was drilled, and stopped in the same manner as the first.

Before the morning light began to peer through the dark-vaulted canopy of the ocean his task was completed.

"They are all asleep except the watch Leno," he said "Ha! ha! ha! I should like to see them when they wake, and hear their yells when the water comes rushing up—ha! ha!"

Then he thought of his companion.

"Here Leno, Leno! Where the devil is the fellow? Sneaked into a corner, I expect. Come out you fool, the water will find you if I don't.'

There was no answer, and Red Hand groping about in the dark in search of his companion began to utter the most frightful imprecations that could be cast from human lips.

Suddenly he sprang to his feet, a suspicion that the half-castle had fled in order to betray him flashed to his mind.

Seizing the log iron he crept cautiously up the hatch, his eyes blazing with fury.

He reached the upper deck when a voice caused him to creep behind a gun, and clutching the dangerous weapon he waited until a group of men who were evidently struggling should pass his place of concealment.

Red Hand's suspicion respecting Leno's purpose was correct,

He had stolen from the hold, and, unperceived in the darkness, had silently reached the quarter-deck.

It was the first lieutenant's watch, and the half-caste, creeping silently towards the officer, suddenly stood by his side.

There was sufficient light from a lamp to render the pirate's features and dress distinguishable, and the lieutenant, imagining that the prisoners had broken loose, and were about to attempt a surprise drew his sword, at the same time calling.

"Help! the pirates are loose!'

Those of the watch who were within hearing rushed to his assistance, and before Leno could utter a word he was seized.

"Lieutenant," he screamed, "hear me, I come to save you and your crew——"

"Take him below," were the words which stopped the completion of his sentence, "and see that his hands and feet are well fastened. Are there any others at liberty besides?"

"No, sir, everything is quiet below and there is none on 'em on deck.'

The half-caste struggled madly and longed to free himself, and again broke out.

"Lieutenant, I swear by the eternals, that I came to warn you of a death which is fast approaching."

"Take him below. This trick will not serve you; take him away, men.'

The delinquent was thrust into his prison, and when he was left ironed hand and foot, Red Hand stood over him exulting.

"So, dog, you would have sold me to those bloodmakers would you?"

The half-caste cowered at his companion's feet.

No word escaped his lips—no prayer for mercy; he could see he was doomed.

"And now for your reward, good senor," said Red Hand.

In an instant he thrust the drill into Leno's chest, saying—

"Thus do I purge thee of thy treachery. Now for the remainder."

He drew the plugs one by one, and the water came through the holes like fountain jets.

Red Hand stood listening to the gurgling sound and the plash made by the water as it struck against the top of the deck.

He waited until he felt the lower part of his

legs immersed in the cold ; then, with a laugh of satanic glee, he crept towards the hatchway.

The man who had so demoniacally doomed five hundred of his fellow-creatures to death, now thought of his own life.

He knew not how this was to be accomplished—to obtain a boat was an impossibility.

To remain on the deck would be certain death, he would be drawn in the vortex of the sinking ship, and drowned with its victims.

Another hour and the terrific doom that awaited the sleeping crew would be discovered.

There was no time for the man to reflect on the means of escape, and death was certain if he remained where he was.

Another foot of water had entered the hold and Red Hand was driven up another step.

In taking this step he heard the hoarse cry of the boatswain calling the watch.

Should they come down to where he stood death was certain.

Groping and creeping about occupied his next few moments.

An open port was near.

He reached it and a heavy piece of timber that had been placed there to repair damages lay in the stream.

Another moment he had crept through.

He was afloat on the log.

Setting astride the spar in mid-ocean, he first drifted to leeward of the noble ship.

He became callous of the fate that appeared to await him. He would behold the ship, go to the bottom, and gratify his ears by the death-shrieks of the crew.

"I shall not get far on this stick," he muttered, as the spar he sat upon sank nearly level with the waters ; "but I should have died had I stayed, and I shall only die now, what matters."

Farther from his gaze went the ship, until the lights only glimmered out at intervals.

Between the time which elapsed before the rising of the vessel upon a wave, he watched with fiendish hope to discover the huge ship was sinking.

But the sign came not.

At last there arose the hoarse shout of men ; then the boom of a cannon, the furious glare shot upward to the sky, as a rocket was fired from the deck.

Then all was still, and Red Hand, with his eyes shot prominently forward, as he looked and listened for a sound from the ill-fated ship, yelled with mad delight.

"There they go, that's Red Hand's revenge. A frigate and five hundred foes gone to perdition by his hand.

Again he listened, but no sound. The ship must have gone and he was alone upon the boundless waters.

A few hours more, he thought, without food, without drink, and on this spot that scarcely sustains me, death is certain. But he was helpless.

And yet he cared not, he had glutted his revenge and could die.

He felt contented, and, demon-like, he laughed aloud with his reeking breath.

CHAPTER CXLI.

THE PARTING.

ALL through the long sickness that followed the young chieftain's wound, Snowball paid him unremitting care.

It had become necessary, when the treasure which had been accumulated by this dashing enterprise had been equally shared among the crews that the War Cloud and the Thunderer should part company.

Captain Dragon, in compliance with the wishes of his crew, had taken this step, and the young chieftain was desirous of returning to England.

"Well," was Captain Dragon's parting salute, "I cannot blame you, Tom, you have a treasure at home worth beholding."

"It is not that object alone that takes me to England," replied Tom.

"No ?"

"There are matters that effect the whole of my lifetime. I want," he added, sadly, "to know the secret of my parentage—in fact, to know who I am."

"The world knows you, Tom. It is true there is many a story told by the fishermen about the deeds of a boy whose courage has earned for him the by no means to be despised title of Midshipman Tom."

A flush of pride came to Tom's pale face when Dragon spoke.

"Whether I merit such praise or not," he said, "is to me a matter of second thought. I want to repair a great wrong that has been done to me and mine ; clear my name from dishonour."

"Meet your enemy, Tom ; place your foot to his foot, and your steel to his heart."

"Would it were possible."

"Why not possible ?"

"It is not a man with whom I have to deal."

"What then, a woman ?"

"Yes, a woman. A merciless, cold, calculating woman ; one who has enamoured my parents, that my father dare not openly behold me as his child."

"But your mother, Tom, what of her ?"

"Alas ! I know not, whether dead or living, or whether murdered by this fiend, who has cursed my life, remains a mystery."

"Go, Tom," the captain said ; "even now, can I be of service to you? the Thunderer shall stand bow to bow and yard to yard with your saucy little ship."

"Thanks, my friend, for your offer, but I shall not require bold hearts and strong hands in this matter. Guile must be met with guile, trickery by trickery. Those who have the most cunning will be master of the fight."

"Bad weapons, Tom. A good sword and a supple wrist are more in my line."

"I know they are; still you will not be a stranger to me?"

"I hope not. I shall go to one of the West Indian islands, and let my fellows spend their money ashore; have my old ship refitted, and be in England a few weeks after you."

"I am glad to hear it—perhaps, though, I may be going out to sea before you come; a family misadventure would be sure to cause it, and I really see no great harbinger of good before me in that respect."

The young chief's words were prophetic.

Terrible news awaited him.

Well for him in his then state of health he did not know it.

They parted as brothers would, and Captain Dragon, as he held his young friend's hand in his lingering grasp, said—

"I hate uncertainties, Tom. I shall be in sight of the Home Rock twelve days after you."

"Where, if you do not see me, go to the old tower on the cliff; you will there learn my whereabouts."

So they parted, to meet again under the skies of another clime, and under widely different circumstances.

Upon leaving the ship the captain shook hands with Snowball.

"Look after your chief, Snowball, and these are my parting words with you. He may need all your vigilance; he has more foes there than he can cope with single-handed."

"He hab, Massa Dragon, and Snowball know some ob dem, too; and by de Great Spirit dey yet feel de grip ob dis chile's fingers."

Captain Dragon glanced at Snowball's sinewy hand as he took it in his grip; then he shook it heartily, saying—

"But for Midshipman Tom, I could wish you were Captain Dragon's lieutenant."

There was a hearty cheer exchanged between the crews as the vessels parted company.

The War Cloud with her prow towards old England.

The Thunderer for the West Indies.

CHAPTER CXLII.

THE WAR CLOUD IN DANGER.

THE golden sun had just burst upon the deep blue waves as the look-out ahead gave the signal that land was in sight.

There was a rush to the forecastle by the crew to gaze on the welcome sight, and Midshipman Tom, with his dark lieutenant, peered through their glasses at the small hazy line in the distant horizon.

"It am de ole shore again, Massa Tom. Golly, dare am ebery ting just as we left it."

Tom was silent; he was thinking of the fair girl who he supposed was at that moment sleeping in the tower on the cliff.

At length he gave attention to Snowball's remark, and again betook himself to the examination of the coast.

The voice of the look-out interrupted his congratulations, which was taken up by those on the forecastle.

"A sail on the weather bow!"

"What do you make of her?"

"She's as much like the Preventive brig, sir, as anything I can remember."

The young chief's face flushed, and his glass was brought to bear upon the stranger.

"It is," he said. "Snowball, our old foe is the first to welcome us."

"Dam," growled the officer, "so it am. What we do, run or fight?"

"Fight. That fellow has boasted he will take us and sink the ship. The time has come, it seems, for him to carry out his boast."

"P'raps. Wake up dare, you lubbers! Clear de decks for action!"

There was a moment's noise—a slight hum of low conversation - and the hardy crew stood to their guns.

They knew the enemy they had to meet—knew it was a fight no longer between British pluck and Peruvian swagger; knew, in fact, they had to encounter an enemy stronger in guns than themselves, and men made of the same prowess.

And a feeling of awe ran through the hearts of the crew on either side, as they were preparing to slay their fellow men—both in sight of the land that gave them birth.

Still, the first drop of blood spilled, that awe would be extinguished, and their minds bent upon each other's destruction.

"Now, my boys," said Tom, as he himself levelled the first gun, "remember the enemy we have to deal with; remember there will be hard work for whoever wins the fight. Are you well nerved for the fray?"

There was a general huzza, and the words "We are," swelling as they passed from man to man into a soul-inspiring cry, brought the rich blood to our hero's cheeks, and made him seem prouder than before that fate had placed him in command of such a daring band.

"Lead us on! Hurrah for Midshipman Tom!" was the cry.

"I will lead you. Thus do I command."

His words were followed by a stream of smoke and fire from the open gun port, and the first messenger of death went onwards to its mission.

Every eye on board followed the shot as it bounded from wave to wave, and when it struck the brig a shout came from the outlaw's crew.

"Well done, Massa Tom," said Snowball, as he jumped from a gun, "dat shot carry away him maintopmast."

"Not quite," said Tom, as he levelled his glass at the brig, "it's only the maintopsail-yard which I have cut in the slings. Try your hand, Snowball."

As these words left the young chieftain's lips, away went the iron contents of the gun that Snowball had fired.

The shot went skimming from sea to sea, and finally lodged in the hull of the advancing brig.

"Dam!" said Snowball, savagely, "dat am all de fault of de War Cloud going down between de waves when I fired."

"Try again, Snowball. If we can only damage a few of her spars we may avoid a bloody engagement."

Snowball and several of the best gunners did their best and rarely was a gun fired but it struck some part of the gallant revenue brig.

Midshipman Tom stood watching this duel, for the brig was not long in replying with her long guns; but owing to the War Cloud lying so low in the water, there was not much damage done.

"That fellow is worth fighting," the boy muttered. "Ha! there they go again!"

The reason of this remark being made, was the wondrous quickness with which the sails that were injured by the outlaw's guns, were replaced —an activity that could not but call forth the admiration of a skilful sailor like our gallant hero.

Hour succeeded hour, and day began to merge into night, still the resolute captain of the brig sought to close with the War Cloud.

The reader will easily understand that this was a thing the young chieftain particularly wished to avoid, and while, therefore, some of the crew were kept at the guns, the remainder were standing by the ropes, shifting sails in obedience to a gesture of the young chief's hand.

And so well was the War Cloud handled, that when darkness had set in both vessels were about the same distance from each other as when the fight commenced.

Still the outlaws kept up an incessant fire from the two long guns on the quarter-deck, guided only by the light from the brig's fighting lanterns.

Every light in the War Cloud was extinguished, and the only guide the brig had to aim her guns, was the red flash of her enemy's guns.

Well did the gunners use the slight mark, and to the dismay of all on board the War Cloud, the brig kept so close to the little vessel that she was enabled to pour in a volley from her starboard broadside.

The iron storm came rushing through the War Cloud's rigging, and high above the noise of the guns that replied to it could be heard the cry—

"Out of the way! the mast is falling!"

The young chief had scarcely time to spring backwards when the tall mast, sails, and cordage, came down with a crash that shook the vessel from stem to stern.

Mingled with the shrieks and cries of those who had been struck down by the falling mast, was the young chief's voice—

"Steady there," he said; his tone as calm as though he had been giving an order when the ship was sailing safely upon a summer sea; "steady; to work with your axes and pitch the useless wood overboard."

The confusion the falling of the mast had occasioned soon passed, and while the blow of the axe was being used in executing the chieftain's order, he again spoke.

"Cease firing until the brig is within musket shot."

Every gun became silent.

"Now," continued Tom, "load to the muzzle with grape. This fellow has caged me like a bear."

While he was speaking the shot came fast and thick from the brig.

Splinters from the wounded spars were falling around him.

Still he moved not, his mind intent upon watching every movement of his tenacious foe.

The men's nerves were strung to the highest pitch by being compelled to stand beside their guns and not allowed to return the iron hail which was diminishing their messmates.

Nearer came the brig; so near that the young chief could see the half-naked groups of men working at their guns.

A few yards more and he would give the word to loosen the terrible mass of destruction that lurked in his guns.

The command trembled upon his lips.

Another moment and the War Cloud's battery would have been discharged, but ere he could give the command a sudden change of his enemy caused him to pause.

The guns were now silent and the vessel which had been running before the wind was suddenly seen to swing round and place her broadside parallel with the War Cloud.

"We get it now," said Snowball, "gib de word, Massa Tom."

"They have made a mistake, Snowball, wait a little."

"Mistake, Massa Tom?"

"They must have imagined the fall of our mainmast has caused us to give in. Ha! I thought so."

By the glare of a dozen battle lanterns they were enabled to see an officer spring to the side speaking trumpet in hand.

"Listen," said Tom, "here comes a message."

CHAPTER CXLIII.

THE MESSAGE.

WHILE he spoke, there came faintly across the intervening space that separated the vessels, the sound of a human voice.

"We have ceased firing," were the words, "seeing you are crippled. Let the commander of the War Cloud come aboard and surrender; refuse, and we open fire upon you. Quick with your answer, or we'll send you to the bottom.

"You shall have my answer," muttered Tom, then aloud: "you hear the terms of yonder fellow, my men?"

"We do, sir—we do."

"Which shall it be—surrender or fight?"

The reply came from nigh one hundred determined men—

"Fight!"

"Be wise unto death," replied Tom.

At this moment the same voice that had before hailed the War Cloud, sang out—

"Your answer?"

"This!" shouted Tom. "Fire!"

Six guns sent forth their hellish discharge point-blank at the hapless brig.

Among the first who fell was the officer who had stood upon a gun to hail the daring outlaw.

The crew had crowded round the side while the young chieftain was deciding on the answer he should give; they were mowed down by the death-dealing missiles.

"Quick!" called the captain to his men, "bear down upon them, spikes and cutlass must do their work."

Before he could range up beside the War Cloud another iron tornado swept his vessel from stem to stern.

Another broadside was intended, but before it could be launched the brig had grappled with her foe, and her boarders began to swarm over the side.

But met by men who had come from the same fighting-stock, not one had reached the War Cloud's deck.

No matter where he hurled his boarders the result was the same.

There was no attempt now upon the outlaw's part to avoid the fight; another rigging was filled with battle-lanterns.

The captain of the brig saw our hero with Snowball by his side, cutting down all who attempted to pass over that part of the vessel.

And then it was that his true English pluck inspired him to single out and fight his daring foe.

He darted at our young hero.

There was a smile of defiance upon Tom's lips, and stepping forward, he met his foe with a swift lunge from his blood-red scimitar.

"Surrender or die!" said the officer.

Midshipman Tom made no reply, but pressed hard upon the angry captain.

His ardour nearly proved fatal.

He now followed his enemy to the deck of his ship, and in a moment he was surrounded by a dozen of the crew.

The War Cloud at the same time swung away from the brig, leaving a chasm between the two vessels that was too wide to be leaped.

A dozen cutlasses were opposed to his single blade, and before he had well comprehended what had occurred, he found himself standing in the midst of a crowd of angry foes, his weapon broken off short near the hilt.

Dashing the useless brand in the face of the captain, he stepped back and drew his pistols.

His case appeared lost, when Snowball sprung to his rescue, who, with his heavy scimitar, was the terror of all who opposed him.

Madly, savagely, the two fought, until a rush was made by a number of Tom's followers to relieve their chief.

The captain of the brig had also given orders to bring all the men that could be mustered, but the sudden accession of strength to Tom's force totally changed the aspect of affairs, and the brig in turn became the scene of terrible slaughter.

But it terminated to the advantage of the young chief, who, followed by his band, regained the deck of his own vessel.

The revenue men cast off the grappling irons at the same moment, and the brig slowly forged ahead of her plucky little antagonist.

Midshipman Tom made no effort to stay her departure; both vessels had had sufficient of the fight, and neither had lost her prestige.

As Snowball expressed it—

"De brig tried to beat dem and dey tried to perwent it. But we lose some ob our best men by it, and dam hard for dem too, when dey fought in sight ob Ole England. What we do now, Massa Tom?"

"Have the vessel cleared."

The word was passed to cleanse the decks, and in less than an hour the dead were cast into the sea, the wounded taken below, and the vessel turned her stem towards the shore.

CHAPTER CXLIV.

TOM AT THE CASTLE GATES.

BRINGING the vessel sharply before the wind was followed by the fall of the injured mainmast, and to the horror of the crew, Midshipman Tom was swept into the sea.

The distance from the ship to the shore was considerable, but Tom dashed out boldly and swam to the beach.

It was a hard struggle, and his devoted crew,

THE WAR CLOUD ON THE ROCKS.

when they saw their leader on the beach, crowded to the side and gave a hearty cheer, to which Tom replied by raising his cap and waving it in the air.

Keeping close under the cliff, the young chieftain reached what he remembered as the beaten path that led to the Parrot's beak.

The arduous ascent of the rugged cliffs had rendered him foot-sore and weary, and fain would he have rested his aching limbs had there been even a stone to have sat upon.

There was nothing; the flat-lying country was as level for miles as a well-kept lawn.

The tired wayfarer found a staff upon the ground, and by its aid he continued his journey.

Every moment becoming fainter, he looked about for a place of shelter, and his eyes encountered the grey walls of Mountsteven Castle, towering above the sea in melancholy grandeur.

There was a stone he remembered outside the castle gate, which served as a protection against the carriage wheels coming in contact with the masonry of the grand old gateway.

"It will serve me as a place of rest," he thought.

"At this early hour none of the servants are likely to be astir."

Scarcely had this thought passed through his brain when the gates were thrown open.

Midshipman Tom paused, and to his surprise, he beheld the stately carriage belonging to the noble family passing through.

It was drawn by four horses, and near one of the windows rode a stranger dressed in a brilliant military costume.

The young chief walked onward until he reached the gate, then seating himself watched the carriage until it had passed out of the broad road turned towards the sign-post marked "to London."

There was something in this occurrence, trivial as it seemed, that caused the boy much thought, and he mentally wondered who the occupants of the carriage could be.

Could it be the dark beautiful woman who had been such a bane to his young life?

From this subject his mind reverted to his own strange life, and he upturned his eyes to the stately pile, and mused—

"Whenever I gaze on these walls, I think of

that mysterious meeting in the vaults and the wild woman's words. They say I am the rightful heir to this proud place, and yet it seems impossible it should be so, yet——"

The gates again opened, and Tom, moving quickly from his seat, passed round the wall in order to watch the person he saw about to issue forth.

There was a strange tumult of feeling in his breast when he beheld the tall form of the mystic stranger leave the gates and walk towards the cliff.

There could be no mistake; there glittered the costly ring upon the stranger's finger—the jewel that the young chief had noted when he grasped the cold clammy hand in the chapel of the dead.

Carried away by a sudden rush of feeling he sprang forward and exclaimed—

"Father, I am here."

The stranger turned and to our hero's astonishment he beheld the kind genial features of a man considerably younger than his lordship.

The first feeling of surprise over, the young chief bowed and said apologetically.

"A thousand pardons, sir, I—"

"No apologies, I beg," said the gentleman, kindly, "in the great human family there must be many alike."

"A truth which has been illustrated in my case at any rate, sir," said Tom.

The young chief had, during the few moments he had been exchanging words with the stranger, felt himself sensibly drawn towards that genial look and kindly word which seemed the emanations of a benevolent nature.

He was less embarrassed by the stranger's questions than he would have been under ordinary circumstances, and with the ingenuousness of youth he freely answered this query.

"And whom, may I ask," the stranger said, "have I been mistaken for?"

"One, sir," the young chief said, "though I called by the sacred name of father, that I know but so little that I do not feel justified in giving a name."

A look of more than ordinary interest came over the gentleman's face, and surveying our hero's elegant form which his ungraceful garb failed to conceal, he muttered—

"It must be; there is the likeness, the same high brow, dark eyes, and aquiline nose. Poor boy, he has a hard, bitter battle before him to even get his pardon, much less his birthright."

"I must not," he said, "pry into your secrets, but the strangeness of your reply leaves me open to make a guess respecting the identity of this nameless personage."

Tom was silent, he knew not what to say to these words.

"Come," the stranger continued, "were I to say that Lord Mountsteven would be the father you sought would I be wrong?"

"You would not, but—but—you astound me."

"One moment; you were rightfully or wrongfully called Thomas Wilson in your infancy since the disappearance of your reputed parent, and since your alliance with certain men you have been known as Midshipman Tom."

Tom began to entertain the vague suspicion that, in spite of the favourable impression the stranger had made upon him, he should perhaps, by admitting the truth, place himself in the power of his foes."

Grasping his stick, he answered—

"I know not who it is that speaks to me thus."

"Be under no apprehension from me," said the gentleman, "I am Thomas Mordan."

"Thomas Mordan!"

"Yes; does the name seem familiar to you?"

"I have heard it before," said Tom, as though trying to recall some nigh forgotten countenance to his memory, "but where I cannot now remember."

"Suffer me to refresh your memory."

Tom lowered his head in silent acquiescence.

"One dear to you," said Mr. Mordan, "if report speaks truly. Laura has mentioned the name of her father's oldest and most attached friend."

"Laura Grey!" exclaimed our hero in surprise.

"Yes, it was from her lips I once heard your name."

Mr. Mordan smiled as he said—

"Perhaps before we enter into the reason of my journey down here it may be as well that I may tell you how I became acquainted with so much respecting yourself."

"A favour," Tom said, "for which I cannot feel too grateful."

"You may remember," the stranger said, "the unprincipled scoundrel who carried off Miss Grey?"

"Neville Wirely?"

"Yes; a great pity it is that you did not kill him in your altercation with him in London. Had you done so much misery would have been averted."

Tom's heart began to quicken its pulsation.

"Did he not die then?"

"No," said Mordan, "he did not, and with his returning health he began to plot anew for the orphan's inheritance."

Tom had not the least knowledge that Laura was the heiress to the rich lands left by her father, and Mr. Mordan's words sorely puzzled him.

"I perceive," said that gentleman, "by your face that you are ignorant of Miss Grey's true position.

"Her father, you must understand—whom you were not in time to save from the pirate's steel—was a man of immense wealth, and the whole of his property fell to his daughter.

"This fact was well known to the Wirelys,

father and son, who by the way are related to the young lady.

"When they became acquainted with the attack upon the vessel that Mr. Grey was coming to England in, and heard that he was dead, and his daughter carried into slavery they conceived the idea of taking possession of his property.

"I shall not trouble you with the details of their plotting and scheming, but pass on to the time when they imagined they had succeeded in their object, and were about to apply for the title deeds.

"Before this could be done they discovered that the young lady was alive, and Neville, as you may remember, succeeded in carrying her forcibly to London. What followed you were an actor in."

"I was," said Tom, "and have often since wondered at the weakness I showed in not putting a bullet through the scoundrel's head."

"You would have saved the hangman his task," said Mr. Mordan, "that's a more fitting end to such a subtle villain's career."

"Perhaps so. Pray proceed, Mr. Mordan. I am anxious to learn the end of this strange business."

"At the time of this occurrence," Mr. Mordan resumed, "I was not aware of Miss Grey being in existence. When I became acquainted with this fact, I was still in ignorance of her whereabouts, and did not succeed in finding it until I had sent messengers to all the seaports in the kingdom.

"I found it at last and sent an express messenger—in fact my own foster brother, with a letter to you and one to the young lady."

"Which I never received," said Tom.

"I am aware of that, you were absent at the time. Had you been here you would not have received the communication."

"Indeed!"

"Thanks to that precious pair of scoundrels, the Wirelys, my messenger was stopped before he could reach his destination."

"Stopped?"

"Yes, one of their vile emissaries shot the poor fellow in the lungs as he was dismounting from his horse and left him for dead."

"Did he recover?"

"He did; and to prevent a recurrence of their assassin work I came down here myself."

"It was a hazardous venture," said Tom; "they are quite capable of employing the same means to slay you."

Mr. Mordan smiled at the thought of danger to himself.

"They dare not," he said, "I know that which would place them in the felon's dock to-morrow."

"So much the worse, Mr. Mordan."

"Why?"

"Dead men tell no tales."

"True, I thought of that, and took my measures accordingly."

"Indeed! How?"

"I told the pair of miscreants of my intended journey, and also that I had left a sealed packet in the hands of the officers of justice, the seal to be broken should they not hear from me within a certain time."

"The packet, of course, related to them."

"It did; and had anything befallen me, the estimable pair would by this time be inside the walls of Newgate."

"A wise precaution, Mr. Mordan, and a power singularly well made use of. Have you seen Miss Gray yet?"

"I have not. Several times I have been to the tower, but the place seems left to the owls and bats."

"Why?"

"Because I have not succeeded in gaining admittance."

Tom smiled at this, and inwardly commending the prudence of outlawed Ben not admitting strangers to the lonely tower.

"You will be more fortunate now, Mr. Mordan," Tom said; "that silence on the part of those I left behind in the tower was but a necessary means of safety for their young charge."

"I am glad to hear of it. When shall I have the happiness of seeing my old friend's child?"

"We will go there at once if you wish."

"The sooner the better. I was going when you accosted me."

They turned towards the road that led to the Parrot's Beak, and Tom said—

"And I may ask you, Mr. Mordan, how you came in possession of so many facts relating to my life."

"Tom, admit you're the same."

"I am, since concealment would be useless with you."

"It is a strange story," began the stranger, "I came here, as you are aware, to make myself known to the young lady of whom we have been speaking, and not being able to obtain access to her, I called upon my friend Lord Mountsteven."

Tom changed colour and said—

"Hush!" he stopped abruptly and said, "Lord Mountsteven is dead, or supposed to be so."

"So, to my surprise, I heard, when I came to the castle."

"Indeed! from whom did you hear the sad tidings?"

"From a young naval officer."

"His name?"

"Walter Freeland."

"Walter Freeland! Is he here?"

"No; he was called away yesterday to join his vessel."

"I am sorry," said Tom, "for this; Walter above all men, I should like to see."

"You are friends then?"

"We are friends and attached friends; but pray proceed."

"The castle, I must tell you, was in a state of great confusion, on account of a most terrible charge against the Lady Mountsteven."

"A charge against Lady Mountsteven!"

"Even so, and one of the most terrible ; murder, in fact."

Tom started.

"Has her husband," he thought, " put a stop to her guilty career by proclaiming her villany to the world ? "

Mr. Mordan's next words relieved him.

"It appears," he said, "that an old woman, called, I believe, Sibyl, was found with Lady Mountsteven's dagger in her breast."

"Dead?" said Tom, horrified at the strangely terrible woman's misdeeds.

"Truly so," was the reply ; but she had sufficient strength to make some strange charges against the lady."

"Do you know what they were ?"

"Yes, but I, of course, cannot give them credit."

"Why so ?"

"Simply of their extreme audacity."

"Indeed ! what may they be ?"

"The old woman," said the gentleman, "told some ridiculous statement to the crowd of servants, which, if true, must indeed be terrible to the honour of an ancient family."

"Lady Mountsteven," said Tom, impetuously, "is the incarnation of evil, and I can credit now old Sybil's statement, whatever it may be."

"You will alter your opinion when you hear the accusation."

"I shall not."

"We shall see. The gipsy, or whatever she may be termed, charged the lady with the crime of poisoning her husband."

"A solemn truth," said Tom, faintly, and Mr. Mordan looked surprised.

CHAPTER CXLV.

MIDSHIPMAN TOM'S DESPAIR.

By the time our hero and his companion's conversation came to a close they had reached the tower, and Tom placed his hand upon the latch.

The door yielded to his hand, and with a beating heart he rushed inside the gloomy building.

All was silent and deserted.

From chamber to chamber he bounded.

Still the same terrible stillness, and when the truth flashed to his mind he sank upon a seat and groaned with anguish.

"Gone !" said Mr. Mordan, " and no clue left ?"

Tom raised his head, and said sadly—

"Yes, there has been a clue left, unless some foul play has been resorted to."

He arose, and silently followed by Mr. Mordan, went to the room occupied by outlaw Ben.

An old sea chest stood in the corner, and the young chief. opening the heavy lid by means of a spring, took a small open box from among its contents.

"This," he said, in answer to a question from Mr. Mordan, " is a means of communication agreed upon between myself and the faithful follower I left behind."

While speaking he opened the oaken box, and took from it three papers.

One was from outlaw Ben, and the young chief, tearing it open, read its contents.

A deep groan came from his lips as he finished its perusal.

It contained the account of Laura's abduction by Neville Wirely.

It gave no clue to the abduction, as Ben was unacquainted with him, so successfully had Neville disguised himself.

"Cursed mischance," said our hero suddenly, "my vessel struck on a rock this morning, and it will take hours to get her off, and every moment increases the poor girl's danger."

"She will be safe from danger," said Mr. Mordan, hopefully, " if the writer of that letter reaches there before she is sold."

"If not ?"

"We must not imagine so terrible a fate for one we love so. Be of good heart—all may yet be well."

Mr. Mordan felt for the poor boy whose anguished face told him how deeply the blow had fallen upon him.

There was not much time lost in idle words.

Both went forth on their separate paths of vengeance—the young chief to his vessel, Mr. Mordan to London, a deep purpose in his heart and a determination to carry that purpose out.

Old Wirely and his son were much in need of an angel of mercy to plead their cause with the stern Mr. Mordan, the friend of Laura Grey's father.

CHAPTER CXLVI.

THE WAR CLOUD ON THE ROCK.

The loss of the mainmast caused the outlaw's vessel to strike upon a rock, and when the waves gradually sank, the vessel was left high above the placid ocean.

In the absence of his young commander, Snowball ordered all the boats out, and a stout cable being fastened to the capstan, the end was taken ashore by the boats.

It was Snowball's intention to fasten the shore end around a huge piece of fallen granite, then by placing a strain upon the capstan to wrench the vessel off the rock.

The shore end had just been fastened when our hero, pale and haggard, rushed to the waterside. He noticed not the work his men were engaged in, but with a gesture of his hand, signified his intention of being taken on board.

Half a dozen men sprang into the pinnace, and he was quickly rowed to the ship.

A cry of disappointment came to his lips when he saw the hull left upon the rocks by the receding tide.

Snowball saw that something unusual had happened by the wild look of his young chief, and meeting him at the gangway, he asked—

"What de matter, Massa Tom?'

The young chief silently handed him the letter he had found in the tower.

"Miss Laura gone to be sold for a slave," he said fiercely. "Dam, who de commander ob de Psyche?"

"I do not know either the vessel or its commander yet, Snowball. When I do——'

"Yes, Massa Tom, when we do he have suffing to not forget in a hurry. He gone to Algiers. Wait a bit, Massa Tom. Perhaps we find out dat boat; come here, Mat."

The outlaw came aft.

"Where dat man who joined us last?"

"Allen, sir?"

"Yes, Allen; whar are he?"

"Below, sir," said Mat, "sharpening cutlasses."

"Go fetch him d'rectly."

Allen soon made his appearance, and stood before his chief.

"You eber hear ob de Psyche?" asked Snowball.

"Yes, sir."

"Where?"

"At Algiers, sir."

"Ha, dam. Go on—tell what you know about her."

"I know the craft very well; before I took French leave of the king's service, we had many a smart chase after the Psyche."

"Dam the king's service, we want to know 'bout de ship."

Allan touched his cap and resumed,

"The Psyche, sir, is one of the fastest and best armed vessels of her size afloat."

"Well, what she do?"

"She pays a visit every year to the east with a cargo of young girls that her captain picks up and sells at the slave market."

"What de rascal's name?"

"Glitter—Captain Glitter—and a slippery customer he is."

"Why am he a slip'ery customer?"

"Because he has carried on the business for the last ten years, in spite of a dozen cruisers."

"Indeed, how am dat?"

"The Psyche you see, sir, has two sets of spars and sails, as well as a false figure-head."

"Well, sir, besides that, he always takes a merchant vessel that leaves England at the same time as he does."

"Well, and what den?"

"Well, sir, when it suits him he sinks her, and uses the papers to pass the cruisers should he be boarded by any of them."

"De debil; but how you know all dis?"

"A messmate of mine, sir, shipped on the Psyche, and one night, when he was ashore at Algiers, he got drunk, and told me how they used to dodge the cruisers if they were overhauled, which wasn't very often, for she was too fast a craft."

"You know this fellow—the captain?" asked Tom.

"I do, sir. I could swear to him or his vessel, no matter how he puts the disguise on."

"Do you think he can sail fast enough to escape from me?"

"Well, sir, I don't think even the War Cloud, fast as she is, could overtake him had he much of a start."

"Very well, Allen; that will do for the present, I shall want you when we sail."

The outlaw touched his cap, and went below to resume his occupation of sharpening cutlasses.

The young chief then said to Snowball—

"Have you tried to move the vessel yet?"

"Just going to hab a try, Massa Tom."

"What is your plan?"

Snowball explained it, and to his surprise, the young chief shook his head doubtfully.

"Not do, Massa Tom?'

"I am afraid not."

"Why?"

"There will be too much strain upon the rope, for one thing."

"P'raps not. What the debbil we do den?"

"Call the men on board with the shore rope. I'll show you."

When the boats came alongside, the young chief had his two best anchors carried out into deep water right ahead of the ship.

Snowball opened his eyes with admiration at the plan for getting the ship into deep water, and muttered—

"Coorse, why de debil I not tink ob dat?"

The anchor was soon firmly fixed in the sand, then the capstan bars were placed ready to tighten the cables.

At a signal from our hero a powerful strain was put on the strong ropes.

"That will do now," he said to the men, "we must wait until the tide is high enough to float us. If the cables do not break we will draw her off. Snowball!"

"Yes, Massa Tom."

"Have the carpenters ready below to ship a plank over the hole when she goes into deep water."

"Yes, Massa Tom; dey sarten to be done."

"Should the water be too much for them, what is our best plan, Snowball?"

The black giant scratched his head reflectively.

"Best plan, Massa Tom?"

"Yes."

The wool was again agitated, and he exclaimed—

"Dam if I know, unless——"

"Unless. Why do you pause, Snowball?"

"Cos Massa Tom, I afraid you tink me a fool for giving such a speech."

"Go on."

"Well, if de water too much for dem, if I won't shove one ob dem darkies in de hole—dat all."

"A lively idea, certainly, Snowball; but I think we must find another, and one more humane."

"Have you thought ob anything, Massa Tom?"

"We can but try mine; if it does not succeed, we——"

"It succeed, Massa Tom. Sartin to, if you tink it."

"I hope it will."

"Sartin, I say, Massa Tom. Let dis chile know."

"Have a dozen of the heaviest shot fixed in a wooden frame, and should the water come in, clap it over the leak."

"Dad de idea, Massa Tom. Now I go and stir the carpenters up a little."

Snowball went to stir the carpenters up, and the young chief, left to wretched thoughts, began to pace the deck.

Between the danger which menaced Laura Grey and the strange tidings he had gleaned from Mr. Morden concerning the inmates of Mountsteven Castle, his mind was well nigh distracted.

He would have given the whole of his wealth had Laura been at the tower. Then he could have been near and heard the revelation that he felt sure would be made at the coming trial of Sybil.

One circumstance sorely puzzled him : it was the words used by Sybil when they were dragging her away faint and bleeding from the castle.

"Three witnesses!" he pondered. "The gipsy woman had some strange meaning in those words —three witnesses! Accursed mystery!"

He looked around at the calm ocean and resumed—

"Better far had I never listened to the delusive yearnings of my heart!

"Why should I seek for a parent's caressing hand, or hope to share a name which will never make me one half so great as I am now."

The white jewelled hand was extended towards the sea unconsciously.

"Here," he went on, "I am king—aye, more a monarch than half the puppets men place—"

"Stirred 'em up, Massa Tom, eberyting's ready."

The young chief turned sharply at the welcome voice.

"Thanks, Snowball," he said, "I am glad you have come."

"Berry glad to hear you say so, Massa Tom, out why you glad now more dan anoder time?"

"I am always glad when you are near, Snowball, by now I am especially so ; my own thoughts are a torture—ha! by heaven, look yonder!"

"Dere?"

"Yes."

"I see, Massa Tom, it am—eh—no—yes it am, a fishing boat. I tink."

"Give me the glass," said Tom.

Snowball handed the glass to his chief, who, after a few seconds closed it with a sudden snap and exclaimed—

"A man-of-war ! look Snowball !"

Snowball took the glass handed to him, and pointing at the object replied.

"Yes it am as you say, a man-ob-war. By the Great Spirit, den, we in a nice mess to meet dat fellow."

"See," said Tom, "the water is rising, and were King George's fleet drawn up to bar my progress, I would leave this place and start in pursuit of the Psyche."

"Bravo, Massa Tom, dat right! A good fight 'fore we go will—"

"Send us to the bottom in this crippled state."

"P'raps so, but what we do den?"

"Escape."

"How, Massa Tom? It trouble my tinking berry much to know how we 'escape."

"Ask me not how," was the excited reply, "but get clear of this fellow we must."

"Berry well, you say so, Massa Tom, den we do."

"We may have to sustain a running fight. If we can plug the hole this accursed rock has made. Man the capstan ! There is water enough to make an effort."

The word of command rang out in clear, decisive tones, and a score of strong men gripped the capstan bars,

"Now," said Tom, "give way men with a will."

CHAPTER CXLVII.

IN CHASE OF THE PSYCHE.

"Snowball, get the long gun forward ready for action. That fellow's spars must be brought down before he gets near enough to grab us."

This order was more in Snowball's way of doing business, and he rushed gladly forward to see the guns aboard.

At the same moment the men were struggling hard to wrench the vessel off the rock.

This attempt was unsuccessful.

That the young chief had been caught in a trap

THE PANIC ON BOARD THE HERCULES.

was evident to him, and he bit his lip and his face paled with suppressed anger.

The hull of the approaching man-of-war was preceptible.

Another hour and he would be within pistol shot.

There was not a moment to be lost, and driven to desperation the young chief called out.

"Fix a double rope upon the cable and carry them aft."

This order being obeyed, the ropes were then passed through the blocks at the mainyard, and the ends drawn through ring bolts on the deck.

A man was placed to each rope ready to pull in concert with these who manned the capstan.

The pressure upon the cable would necessarily pull the vessel from the reef, Tom thought, but he feared a sudden rush of water in the hold might ensue.

"If I can but manage to stop that," he thought, "I am safe."

He cast a haughty defiant look at the fast approaching ship and shouted loudly—

"Now my lads, pull with all your might."

The muscles of fifty pair of strong arms stood

out like cords as the ropes were tightened and the capstan turned.

This was succeeded by a crushing noise, followed by a shock that caused the vessel to totter from stem to stern.

Like a hound released from the leash she shot into deep water and escaped.

The outlaw from whom Tom had gleaned the information respecting Captain Glitter was the envy of his messmates as he walked the deck beside the young chief.

But the most displeased among the lot was Mat Smithers.

As the War Cloud left the reef he was sitting on a boom, with a number of his companions near him.

And as he saw the lately joined outlaw continuing in conversation with the young chief, he made no scruple in expressing loudly his indignation.

"Well," he growled, "see that swab with the chief?"

"Allen?" said the discontents.

"Yes, the longshore ape. What has he done to merit such distinction?"

"Better go and ask him," suggested a tall fellow, who was busily engaged putting a new flint to his pistol.

The reply was taken up by a general laugh.

Mat turned savagely.

"What the deuce are you laughing at? Puts me in mind of grinning through a horse's collar, and that ain't very sensible, anyhow."

This time there was a general roar at the manner in which Mat had compared their merriment.

Mat became more and more angered, and a little more chaff being indulged in, he stepped down from the boom and saluted the shins of his nearest messmate with a heavy kick.

The recipient of this favour soon had his jacket off, and the group formed a ring in pleasing anticipation that a fight was coming off.

Mat was not long in putting in an appearance, and four clenched hands had just began a preliminary spar, when a voice above sang out—

"Sail ahead!"

The young chief and Snowball levelled their glasses, and took a long survey of the stranger, who was crossing their bows when the signal was given.

"A smart, rakish-looking craft," murmured Tom, as he gave the glass to Allen.

Snowball lowered his glass and answered—

"Berry, tink him a fast gentleman."

Allen looked long and earnestly at the stranger's outline. A smile played upon his lips as he said—

"He's at it, sir."

Tom took the glass, and when the vessel became perceptible he uttered an exclamation of surprise.

At the same moment Snowball uttered a most emphatic—

"Dam!"

"It is the Psyche, Allen?" said the young chief, interrogatively.

"I could almost swear it is, sir."

"By gar!" said Snowball, "when I look a minnit ago dere was a debblish small craft, now I look and dere I see a clumsy-looking ship with dirty sails."

"A false figure-head, sir," said Allen, "and a spare set of Dutch sails."

"De debbil!"

"And no doubt," the man continued, "by this time she has shipped the name of the last vessel he overhauled for the sake of her papers. As I have told you—his customary habit."

Additional sail was spread upon the War Cloud's yards, and her speed became tremendous.

"Strange," said the young chief, "that he did not make an effort to escape, he must have seen us about the same time we sighted him."

"Not at all, sir," said the outlaw who knew too much of Captain Glitter for that clever gentleman's good, "he has evidently found a good cargo on his way."

"I understand you. As you before remarked, he takes the vessel only for the sake of her papers."

"Beg pardon, sir; not exactly 'only,' the captain of the Psyche is not the man to scuttle the ship and let the good cargo go to the bottom with her."

Snowball who had been listening to the colloquy with deep interest asked—

"What him do with crew?"

"They go down with the vessel sir. Captain Glitter boasts he never shed blood in his life."

"Dam rascal. Clap on de sail dere; we gib him suffink; if we go to the bottom he hab to swim for it, I think; aye, Massa Tom?"

"Right, Snowball," replied Tom, "keep all the ports closed, and do not show too many on deck. I should wish to avoid coming to a cannonading with the fellow."

"Why, Massa Tom?"

"He has probably a number of poor girls on board, and the shot from our guns may slay some of the poor creatures."

"Nebber tought ob dat. What you doing dere?"

This was to a party of men who were busily loading the brass gun.

They desisted when Snowball spoke, and walked away quickly from the place.

In proportion as the War Cloud increased her velocity through the water, the heavy looking ship decreased her speed, as though anxious to meet the coming vessel.

Captain Glitter had not of course the least idea that any tie existed between the beauteous girl he had sold to the Bey and the commander of the swift vessel that was bearing down upon him.

Had he known it, Midshipman Tom's feet would

not have touched the pirate's deck while a charge of powder was left in the magazine.

When the ships came within hail, the young chief sprang upon a gun and shouted through his speaking trumpet—

"What ship are you?"

"The Pelican," was the reply.

"Where from?"

"Liverpool."

"Where to?"

"Algiers."

"I thought so," muttered the young chief, his eyes kindling with anger. "What's your cargo?"

"Silks and wool."

"Lay to, and I'll send a boat aboard."

The Union Jack was flying at the War Cloud's stern.

The captain of the Psyche chuckled over the prospect of hoodwinking a British ship, and remained patiently watching the boat as it skimmed the water.

Absorbed in this reflection, he did not notice the vessel creeping slowly towards him, or his suspicions would have been aroused.

CHAPTER CXLVIII.

A JUST RETRIBUTION.

MIDSHIPMAN TOM, in the neat undress of a naval officer, mounted the Psyche's side, followed by Allen and a dozen of his men, all wearing the dresses of seamen in the Royal Navy.

When Tom stood upon the Psyche's deck, Captain Glitter came towards him.

"A young 'luff,'" he thought, "to mount the epaulette; some bombastic old lord's son, I expect."

"You are the commander of this ship?" said Tom.

"Yes, lieutenant."

"Your name?"

"Reginald Spicer."

Tom looked the white slaver straight in the face as he said—

"Well, Captain Spicer, I am sorry to detain you, but I wish to ask you a few questions concerning a vessel that passed you about the time we came in sight of each other."

Captain Glitter was used to this interrogation, and bore it without a muscle of his face moving.

"A vessel that passed me?"

"Yes; a long, rakish craft, which went hull down as we made you out."

"I think I saw her, lieutenant."

"You do?"

"Yes."

"Can you give me any explanation about her?"

"No; she sailed too quickly."

"Indeed! Well, I may as well tell you to be careful. It is the Pysche, commanded by a rascal for whose neck we have a noose ready at our yard-arm."

Captain Glitter winced.

The pair of dark eyes, searching as it were, his innermost thoughts, he did not seem to fancy.

"Indeed!" he said, forcing a smile, "may I ask what he has done to merit such a promised fate?"

"Piracy on the high seas and carrying off young girls to sell as slaves."

"The rascal," said Captain Glitter.

"I suppose your papers are quite regular," said Tom, turning as though about to leave the ship.

"Quite, lieutenant, you can see them."

"Thank you, I will."

The Pelican's papers were produced.

When Tom had seen them, he gave Captain Glitter a turn by looking up at his masts.

"This cursed fellow," he thought, "does his business better than the generality of the English asses."

"A pleasant voyage," said Tom, walking towards the gangway. "Good-bye Captain."

Captain Glitter began to inwardly chuckle over his success.

It was premature.

Tom turned suddenly, and made a gesture to his followers.

At the time the young chief went aboard there were a dozen men visible on the Psyche's deck.

But by the time the interview had reached this point the number had dwindled down to six.

The sudden act which followed the young chief's word took Captain Glitter by surprise.

The outlaws ran to the hatches and fastened them down, thus keeping the whole crew out of mischief.

Captain Glitter felt he was discovered, and thrust his hand inside his breast for a loaded pistol.

He had, however, no sooner touched the stock of the concealed weapon with his fingers, than our hero drew his sword, and placing the point against the slaver's throat, said quietly—

"Attempt to move your hand, and I will pin you to the mast!"

The quiet determination of the threatening voice, his angry eye, and naked weapon, quelled even the spirit of the captain of the Psyche.

"You are my prisoner, Captain Glitter," said the young chief; "resistance is useless. Behold! your vessel is under my guns."

The slaver looked towards the War Cloud, and beheld the guns run out, and the men at quarters.

Captain Glitter gnashed his teeth with fury.

"Upon what charge," he asked, "do you arrest the captain of a merchant vessel?"

"A merchantman?"

"Yes."

"Knock off that bulkhead now," said the young chief, "and one of you remove the Pelican's name from the stern of the vessel?"

The men obeyed.

"Now," said Tom, "Captain Glitter, I think the Psyche and this vessel are much alike, except the sails, those we will bring from below."

The outwitted captain of the Psyche saw the game was up, but no sound escaped his lips.

He allowed his arms to be bound by Tom's followers without breaking silence.

"I think," said the young chieftain, "the gallows that we prepared will not be long without its owner."

"I shall never swing there," said Captain Glitter, savagely.

Before he could be stayed he sprang past his captors, and bound even as he was, rolled into the sea.

Tom watched him sink beneath the ocean's surface, and with a cold smile upon his lips, he hissed—

"Laura is avenged! The arms were pinioned, and no mortal power could save him."

The splash of the falling body as it struck the wave was heard by the boat's crew, who were coming from the War Cloud to the assistance of their messmates.

They watched the spot where the eddying circles showed the surface had been broken, but nothing appeared.

The miscreant must have soon perished by his own act.

The coming of the boats crammed with men enabled the young chief to have the hatches opened with safety, and as the crew came sullenly up they were bound with cords, and placed upon the fo'castle under a strong guard.

"Now," said Tom to his sable lieutenant, who had come on board, "we will descend to the cabin and release the hapless girls."

"By gar, yes, Massa Tom. Poor tings, dey must be berry tired ob bein' down in that suffescating 'ole."

Around the cabin was a soft couch and innumerable cushions.

Here, in every attitude that continued terror could assume, were grouped together upwards of fifty young girls.

A shriek of amazement and fear came from their lips when they beheld Snowball's shining face at the cabin door.

"Don't be frightened, marmzelles," said the African, "by gar, you hab more cause to be frightened ob de white face ob de cap'n ob dis ship dan my black one."

The poor girls had come to the conclusion, by the sound of the scuffle that had been taking place above, that they had fallen into the hands of a gang of pirates.

Snowball's face appearing at the cabin door confirmed this idea.

The looks of dismay soon passed away quickly as our handsome young hero entered the state room.

"Ladies," he said, gallantly doffing his cap, "be under no apprehension. You will be as safe with my men as though you were under your own roof."

The manner of his voice carried truthfulness with his words, and many of the beautiful women who had been torn from their homes by Captain Glitter, came to the handsome boy and poured forth their thanks.

"The same hands that tore you from your homes," said Midshipman Tom, "bereft me of all I love. Fate has given me the power to stay the villain's career, and restore you to the aching hearts which yearn for you.

"Under the protection of my crew," continued our hero, "a portion of which will man this vessel, you will be taken back from where you came free and unmolested."

The joy—the outpourings of gratitude from the kidnapped maidens filled our hero's heart with the liveliest emotion and the most supreme satisfaction.

He left them with the joyful hope in their hearts of soon beholding again their country and their homes.

Then he took his position before the ruffianly crew like an avenging demon.

The softness had passed from his heart, and pitiless in his purpose, he ordered two of the boats to be lowered.

"Down in those boats," he said sternly to the miscreant crew; "if you are not out of range of my guns in twenty minutes I will fire. Remember, Midshipman Tom never breaks his word."

Too glad of the opportunity of escaping, the men rushed to the boats and pulled like demons from the ship.

Ten men took charge of the prize, with orders that when they had landed the poor girls in England to crowd all sail after the War Cloud.

Snowball and Tom watched the vessel as she went on her errand of mercy, until she became a mere speck on the ocean.

"I feel," said the young chief, "better, and more sure of recovering my beloved Laura, since doing this good action."

CHAPTER CXLIX.

THE CHIEF OF THE DERVISHES.

"Poor tings," said Snowball, "dey seems bery glad when you tell 'em to go home."

"Spread the canvas, my lads," said Tom; "before the sun is set to-night I must be in sight of the golden minarets of the Arab city."

The vessel, like a thing of life, bounded forward as though partaking of the feeling that actuated the young and brave commander.

His wish was fulfilled: the second sunset from the hour he met Captain Glitter, beheld the War Cloud at anchor near the fort of Algiers.

Grand as was the spectacle to European eyes, Tom scarcely glanced at the gilded minarets or the marble domes of the mosques.

His mind was racked by the danger that menaced his beloved Laura.

His dark eyes blazed with passion as he gazed towards the shore, and he prayed that fortune would aid him in discovering the spot where dwelt the beauteous idol of his boyhood.

"If the profaned hand of an infidel," he muttered, fiercely, "has been placed upon her, the wretch had better never to have been born. The fangs of a tiger fixed upon his throat will be more merciful than my grasp."

Snowball came to his side and handed him a heavy boat cloak.

"De boat ready, Massa Tom," said Snowball. "Am you?"

"Quite."

"Hope you got sword. We may want it, Massa Tom."

Tom tapped the golden hilt of his scimitar significantly.

"I have my Damascus blade, Snowball," he said, "and should not my arm fail me, it will be death to those who try to bar my way."

"And I," said Snowball, grimly, "hab my little axe. By gar! dat no plaything for some lubber's head."

The weapon Snowball referred to was as much as an ordinary man could lift; yet in the black's grasp it seemed little more than a toy.

The young chief and his sable officer stepped into the boat, making their way through the many vessels that lay at anchor until they reached the shore.

Passing through the narrow streets, the outlaw chief and Snowball found themselves in a curious throng.

There were Armenians, with black sugar-loaf hats and long robes; Greeks in their picturesque costume, Moslems in turbans and baggy trousers, burly Europeans from every civilised part of the world.

The pair of adventurers walked unnoticed amid this motley throng, except when Snowball pushed a stately mussulman off the narrow pathway into the dirty mud.

The fellow took no notice of the insult, but meekly passed on his way.

"Snowball," said Tom, suddenly, "where are we to find the chief of the dervishes?"

"At de Mosque, I s'pose, Massa Tom."

"Where are they?"

"De Dervishes?"

"Yes."

"Dey de priests, and de chief ob dem is a great man."

"The next thing is to find this great man."

"Dat easy enuff."

"How?"

"We ask somebody."

"I do not know a single word of the language."

"Dat no matter. Snowball do. Him knew ebery word. You stay dere a minnit."

He left the young chief and crossed the road to meet a stately, venerable, old man, who, with downcast eyes, was coming towards them.

Tom saw his follower and the old man in conversation. Then Snowball saluted in true Moslem fashion, and rejoined his chief.

"Have you succeeded, Snowball?"

"Dat I hab indeed. De chief ob dem at de mosque."

"The mosque—which one?"

"Dat one ober dare. You see that top shining, eh, Massa Tom?"

"I do."

"Well, dat's him. Come den, we only in time to catch him."

They hastened towards the sacred building, and reached the door as the believers were about to leave.

Snowball and Tom stood aside until the multitude had passed out. They then took up their station in a doorway.

"Him must come dis way, Massa Tom; it better dan going inside."

"Why?"

"'Cos dey not let us in—dey tink you infidel, and cut off your head in a minnit."

"Under such circumstances we must wait."

They did until the chief priest or Dervish arrived from the mosque, attended by his assistants.

Tom glanced at the high priest's face, and felt strangely attracted by his personal appearance.

His was a face full of kingly majesty, and far elevated beyond the pale, sickly countenances of the attendant Dervishes.

He cast one look towards the young chief and his follower, and paused; then, turning to the attendant Dervishes, he waved them back, and approached the adventurers.

Then, to Tom's astonishment, he said in English—

"A ship came across the sea in search o' a lost dove."

The young chief turned and said—

"Did the ship find that which she sought?"

There was a mournful cadence in the stately Dervish's voice as he answered—

"Yes, my son, but only to lose the timid bird again."

A deathly faintness came over the boy as he gasped—

"Great heavens . Has she then fallen into the hands of——"

"Fitting time and place, my son," said the Dervish, kindly, "I will reveal all to you. Until then be of good heart."

"When, holy father, shall my—"

"Come to me when the sun has set behind the hills. Now there are so many eyes upon us," the Dervish answered.

"Where?" asked Tom.

The kingly old fellow pointed to a handsome building.

"There," he said, "you shall learn all—now depart in peace."

It wanted but an hour of sunset, and Tom, whose mind was racked by a thousand conflicting thoughts, wandered about the city of spires.

"By gar," muttered Snowball; "dat beats de debil's fury, dat old feller speaking English."

At the time appointed, the adventurers posted themselves at the gates of the marble palace.

They had no occasion to demand admittance, as they passed up the steps the door swung back, and two slaves, clad in white, ushered them to a high vaulted bed chamber.

The Dervish was seated upon an ottoman, and smiling at the surprise visible upon the faces of his visitors, he motioned them to a seat.

"You are no doubt," he began, "much surprised at the knowledge I possess of the English language."

Tom bowed.

"I am," he continued, "as much an Englishman as yourself."

Tom looked in surprise.

"It would be a very long story," the Dervish said, "too long for me to relate now. This much I may tell you—I came to this country many years since, and by good fortune attained the position I now hold."

The young chief was all in a dream.

"I expected you," the venerable man went on, "I had been warned of your coming, one glance at your features told me that he that—at least I knew you directly.

"Now respecting the lady; my news is but meagre at best—listen.

"When the night," he continued, "shed her dark coverlet over yon stately Minaret, the dove was safely in the cage. The golden sun was scarcely seen in the horizon on the following morn when the dove had departed."

"Heavens!" ejaculated Tom; "do you suspect under what devilish influence? To what unholy place has she been carried?"

The Dervish replied—

"It were well my speech be limited. See yon tower?"

"I do."

"And yonder patrol?"

"I do."

The answer had scarcely escaped Tom's lips ere the Dervish bowed his salaam, and suddenly departed.

Mystified as they were by this unlooked-for proceeding, Tom and Snowball pondered not long, nor spake they much over the event.

Their opinion was the same, their determination also.

Laura had been taken to the harem. By force they would have her released.

Conversing on their way, they reached the harem into which they felt Laura had been betrayed.

Not a light was visible of any kind from within.

A monotonous silence reigned around.

"Knock," said Tom.

Snowball did knock.

It was the butt end of his battle axe that he struck the door with.

No answer to the summons.

Snowball repeated it louder this time.

All was silent.

"Massa Tom, me knock de door down in a minnit," said Snowball, savagely, "dare no mistake about dat."

"I shall wait two minutes only," said the outlaw chief, as he beat against the door with the pommel of his sword.

But the same unbroken silence reigned around.

"Dey no let us in, Massa Tom."

"Then we will let ourselves in," was the determined reply, "Midshipman Tom never brooks delay."

Then came a crash.

The mighty axe wielded by Snowball's powerful arm made a rapid circle in the air, gleaming like a flash of lightning; then with terrific force it descended upon the door, burying itself in the wood and splitting it to a considerable extent.

The dusky Hercules wrenched the destructive weapon from the wood.

Again it was whirled around, and again it sank deep in the massive door, this time with greater success.

The bold young outlaw looked on in grim silence, his scimitar bared and grasped in his hand of iron, ready for the foe.

"Follow me," said Snowball, as for the third time the axe descended.

The door fell in with a crash, and the gigantic African strode over its splintering fragments.

"Now for my beloved Laura and—revenge!" said Tom.

The last sound was fairly hissed from between his set teeth.

Snowball paused.

"Stop, Massa Tom, I will get a light," he said, taking a tinder box from his pocket, and striking the flint and steel together he kindled the calamed rag.

A torch was lighted, and by its dull red glare they were enabled to renew their search.

Every nook and corner they carefully scrutinised

THE SHIP ON FIRE.

in each room they entered, but without the least success.

Midshipman Tom was mad with disappointment, while Snowball strode from place to place with a look of dangerous ferocity playing about his ebony face.

At length they reached the door of Zaima, the chief eunuch.

"Dis am de last room."

"Then here rests my last hope," replied his youthful leader. "Open the door, Snowball."

Snowball did, and came to grief in consequence.

Thinking it, like the rest, was securely fastened, he placed his herculean shoulder against its panels, and gave a terrific push.

The door flew open, and in he went, head first.

The undignified nature of the flight of his huge lieutenant amused Tom.

Snowball regained his equilibrium as he best could, but with a most sedate air; it hurt his dignity to hear his young chief laugh.

"De cusses," he muttered, "um would like to know who left this door open, he might hab 'im headache."

By intimating the person that left the door open would have a headache Snowball meant that it was possible for his axe to ascend, and accidentally fall upon the offending individual's cranium.

Snowball picked up the torch which had fallen from his grasp, and stepped aside for Midshipman Tom to enter.

Tom did so.

His sable officer held the light up high that his young leader might reconnoitre the apartment.

A cry of baffled rage and despair escaped his lips.

"Curses, Snowball, we have been outwitted; the place is deserted."

"What am dat, Massa Tom?" said Snowball, indicating a piece of paper that lay upon the floor.

Tom sprang forward and snatched it up.

It was written upon in the eastern tongue.

"Read it," he said, handing it to Snowball.

It ran thus—

"The morning bloom of the harem is lost to the infidels for ever. Seek not to discover the place of concealment or the dogs of the unbelievers will die. "ZAIMA."

Snowball dashed the paper down with a cry of rage, and Tom clutched his sword menacingly.

"Fools, they think to foil us; they——"

"Hark Massa Tom—what dat noise? it's the sound of feet surely," said Snowball.

"Ah, so it is - so much the better. Follow, Snowball."

He strode towards the door.

An exclamation of rage broke from his lips.

With a loud click the door had closed.

They were shut in.

"Force it open, Snowball."

"Yes, pale-face dogs, force it open, Nah Rah."

It was Zaima who spoke.

"Aha, are we foiled?" cried the young chief, his sword leaping from its scabbard.

As he ceased speaking, a door at the further end of the harem flew open, and Zaima appeared with a dozen fierce bearded followers at his back.

Midshipman Tom sprang forward and faced the Oriental Guard.

"Stop, vile dog of the infidels," said Zaima, in a voice hoarse with savage hate; "thou hast dared the mighty sovereign of the harem, thou hast smote Zaima, and thou hast come into the lion's den. The pale face dogs shall die—cut them down," shouted he to the guards.

They had been inspired by the offer of a large reward if they could slay the daring intruders.

They bounded forward, their curved swords flashing in the air.

Then came a gasping sob—a groan—a sinking crash—a heavy fall.

One fell pierced by the scimitar of Midshipman Tom, another fell cloven from head to chine by Snowball's murderous axe.

The others shrank back appalled.

"Come on. Who's next?" cried the daring Tom.

"Yes, come on," roared Snowball as he stood with the reeking axe raised on high.

Zaima literally foamed with rage.

"At them, slaves," he yelled, "slay them—hack them to pieces—if one escape, by Allah thou shall die by the bowstring."

The guards advanced at a double.

Their weapons were pointed at the breasts of the daring outlaws.

Tom saw it; the danger was apparent.

A slight pressure upon the trigger, and he and his faithful lieutenant would be swept into eternity.

He leapt forward like an enraged tiger, and before the astonished guards could understand what had occurred, the outlaw chief had Zaima by the throat, and placing his red dripping scimitar's point against the Nubian's heart, he said in a voice of thunder—

"Now, brute, call off your men or I strike!"

CHAPTER CL.

THE FRIGATE IN DANGER.

WHEN the miscreant Red Hand was floating slowly away from the noble frigate the water was rushing in with relentless fury.

Four large holes had his murderous fingers bored in the stout vessel's planks, and like fountain jets the sea spouted upward, dashing against the decks with a dull heavy noise.

The malignant destroyer floated far away to leeward, his black heart cheering him in his loneliness with the thought of the fiendish revenge he had gratified.

The brave crew sleeping soundly were not aware of the peril that threatened them until the hoarse cries of the infuriated pirates gave the alarm.

It was young Rilcher's watch, and as he passed the main hatchway the shrieks of the drowning pirates smote upon his ear.

"There must be something wrong below," he said, saluting the lieutenant of the watch.

"Something wrong, Mr. Rilcher."

"Yes, sir; for the last half-hour there has been a continual shrieking from the prisoners."

"They are cutting each other's throats," said the officer, "just to keep their hands in."

"Shall I go below and ascertain the cause, sir?"

"Perhaps it will be as well. Take a file of marines with you."

The boy took a lantern from the deck and went below, followed by the marines.

Each step he took shouts and yells became louder.

Quickening his pace he reached the lower deck and beheld a sight that for a moment blanched his ruddy cheeks and caused his heart to sink within him.

The lower deck was half-filled with water, and the pirates who had been bound together were struggling to escape from drowning.

They were fastened together in gangs of eight to ten, and fought like so many demons to break the bands of steel which bound them.

Many were already dead, and as the survivors battled madly to get beyond the reach of the waves the lifeless bodies were dragged to and fro in the fierce struggle for life.

Young Rilcher placed the lantern upon the steps and rushed upon the deck.

The officer, observing his scared look, was prepared for some terrible catastrophe to be told him, but when the fearful words were uttered he could scarcely credit his senses.

"The ship is filling, sir!"

"You are mad, boy!"

"Would to Heaven the assertion were that of a madman! Give the alarm, sir, we have not a moment to lose."

The lieutenant, as pale as the young middy, rushed below to the captain's cabin.

Mr. Rilcher looked after him and exclaimed—

"Curse their routine! While he is going through all these forms the ship will go down. All hands this way."

The watch sprang to their feet in an instant.

"Here," shouted Rilcher. "Cast loose a gun." It was soon done.

"Quick, my lads, for your lives! Load with blank ammunition.

The men worked with a will, though some knew the dreadful state of affairs.

"Well done. Ready?"

"Aye, aye, sir."

"Fire!"

The starting report rang out like thunder, and in an instant the sleeping crew sprang from their hammocks and rushed on deck.

"Rig the pumps," shouted Sydney Rilcher. "Quick there, my men! We have sprung a leak and the water gathers on us fast."

"Shall I sound the depth, sir?" asked an old tar.

"Do," said Rilcher.

The man went below, but soon appeared above the hold.

All eyes were fixed upon him, and many a brave heart sank when he said—

"Five feet of water below, sir, and the prisoners are being all drowned."

"Great heavens!" said Rilcher, "this is dreadful. Master-at-arms! Master-at-arms!"

"Here, sir."

"Go below and knock off those poor devils' irons."

The master at arms went to execute the order and the captain at the same time came on deck.

When he heard the fearful story from the first lieutenant, who for the time had lost all self-control, he sent to young Rilcher and grasped the boy's hand warmly.

"Thanks, my brave boy," he said, "for your forethought; should we, with heaven's help, survive this calamity, I will take care that you are not forgotten."

"I have but done my duty, sir," said the gallant youth, "and—"

"Six feet of water in the hold," shouted the man at the hatch.

There was a frantic struggle by the dismayed crew to cast off the boats, and in their terror they would have defeated the object in view.

"Belay there!" shouted the captain, "the first among you that touches a rope belonging to the boats shall have two dozen!"

"Gentlemen!" this to the officers who were clustered upon the quarter deck, "draw your swords and cut down the first man who attempts to cast off a boat!"

The crew shrunk back, awed by the stern voice of the gallant captain of the Hercules.

"Now my lads," he said, "behave like British seamen! the boats shall be our last resource.

"To the pumps all of you! let us keep down the water for an hour, and all will be well."

The men dispersed; and strong sinewy arms worked the pumps with a vigour that kept the gallant ship from foundering.

But in spite of all their exertions, the water rose to seven feet.

The captain and his young favourite ran from group to group encouraging the men, and the officers with loaded weapons, stood silent and sedate by the boats.

Sydney Rilcher and his commander met near to the windlass, and both prompted by one impulse, stood and gazed in each other's faces.

"Mr. Rilcher," said the captain in a low voice, "this is not caused by the starting of a plank—what think you?"

"My conviction is," said the boy, "that it is the work of that pirate gang."

"And by heavens you may be right!—where is the captain of the marines?"

"Here said a voice."

"Go below, Captain Richardson, and drive the prisoners on deck—let your men load and fix bayonets."

The marines soon caught the suspicion that the present danger emanated from the gang of desperadoes who had been confined on the lower deck.

Loading their pieces as they ran below they came upon Red Hand's gang, who had gathered round the door of the spirit room and were striving to burst it open with a spar.

The heavy piece of wood was bound with iron at one end, which the miscreants were using as a battering ram.

A dozen of the band ran backward with the pole, and had not the marines come so suddenly upon the scene the door would have been smashed.

"Down with that spar," said the captain, firmly "put it down I say."

The captain's face flushed angrily, and turning to his men, he said—

"Prime."

The muskets were brought to the priming position and the hammers thrown back with an ominous click.

The pirates, with a yell of defiance, snatched up every article that could be used as a weapon of defence, and turned savagely upon the gallant fellows who had come so opportunely and stayed the orgie contemplated by the wretches.

This hostile movement was greeted by the marines with a grim defiant look, and as they closed shoulder to shoulder the officer's voice rang out.

"Ready! present! fire!"

A dozen barrels were emptied among the miscreants, and nine who were foremost in their efforts to rise upon the captors, fell lifeless upon the deck.

Such sudden punishment, it was evident, had been little expected by the ruffians.

Those who were not hit by the close volley dropped their weapons and cried for mercy.

"Drive them on deck," said the officer, "six of you bring up the dead and wounded."

The captain corrected himself immediately.

"As you were," he said, "make them fellows carry up the dead assassins on deck."

With a serried, gleaming line of steel closely following them, the pirates were forced on deck and ranged before the captain of the Hercules.

"You know these fellows," he said to Rilcher, "see if any are absent."

"Two," he said, "are absent."

"Two?"

"Yes, sir; the leader of the gang and his lieutenant."

The captain turned to the midshipmen in charge of the pumps and asked—

"Does the water gain upon us much?"

"No, sir, but the men cannot hold out much longer."

The hardy fellows' veins stood out like whipcords, and many had fallen exhausted at their work.

"Captain Richardson," said the commander of the Hercules, "relieve the men at the pumps with these pirates, and remember those who don't work, as my men have worked, shall have an ounce of lead in their bodies. Let your men keep guard over them."

The overworked seamen were quickly relieved by the pirates, who, much against their will, were compelled to labour at the pumps until big drops of perspiration fell from their foreheads.

Over every gang stood four stalwart marines, with fixed bayonets ready, and only too willing, to carry out the orders.

While the pumps were kept at work, the captain, Rilcher, and several seamen, went below to search for the missing pirates.

Floating on the surface of the bubbling water they found Red Hand's lieutenant.

There were many suggestions put forth as the body was drawn out of the water, but to all the captain shook his head.

"This fellow and his leader were ironed together," said Rilcher. "See here on his wrists. By heaven! he spoke the truth, then, when he came upon deck during my watch, and told me that Red Hand was drilling a hole in the ship's bottom."

"And you did not believe him?" said the captain.

"Well, I did not. I thought it was but a ruse to cover his appearance on deck, and I ordered him to be taken below immediately."

"The explanation is now easy," said Rilcher: "Red Hand must have found out his accomplice had betrayed him, and this death is the work of his hand."

"Quite right in your conclusions, Mr. Rilcher," said the captain; "now to discover the villain."

They sought far, but found no trace of Derrick, but on an explanation by the carpenter, they at once concluded that by means of the plank he had effected his escape, preferring to trust his life to even so frail a craft rather than the chance of a speedy and inglorious death at the yard arm.

"Water decreasing, sir," said a voice from the lower deck; "only four feet now."

"Continue at the pumps; serve out a double allowance of grog," shouted the captain in reply.

"Thank heaven!" he ejaculated, fervently; "now, carpenter, take your crew and try and stop the holes."

"Ay, ay, sir; I think we can do it in——"

"Water decreased to three feet, sir."

"Well done, lads—keep the lubbers at the pumps," again ejaculated the captain.

At last the water was pumped out, the holes plugged, and three cheers wafted in the air.

The frigate was saved.

CHAPTER CLI.

A WITNESS FROM THE TOMB.

WERE it possible for the fiend of darkness to send spirits of evil upon earth, the haughty Lady Mountsteven would be sure to realise such a being.

To the reader, who has followed her path in these pages, and marked that pathway red with blood—the blood of those that stood in the way of her ambition—they must have marvelled that such a being in woman's form could have ever been guilty of so many foul deeds.

Alas! that it should be so.

Her character is no creation of the brain, but a faithful record of one who, by her alliance with an English nobleman, plunged a proud family into everlasting disgrace, and caused those who escaped her blood-stained hands to leave their country in humiliation and despair.

The victims were the lady whom Lord Mountsteven had married, then the pitiless act of throwing the young babe into the sea from the lofty towers of Mountsteven Castle.

Then the willing instrument of her past crime, Philip Wilson, was her next.

Then the French steward died by a stroke of her keen poignard, and young Charley Philips was transported for the crime.

The several attempts she made upon our hero's life, when her suspicion pointed to him as the young heir whom she thought the sea had drowned.

The diabolical attempt to poison her husband and consign him to the tomb, completed the measure of her crimes.

Yet this woman, whose hands were red with blood, now appeared before a crowded court of justice, and without a muscle of her face changed, she kissed the sacred book, and swore to give evidence against the supposed gipsy woman, Sybil, of the Tombs.

Lady Mountsteven's dark eye and pale handsome face wore an expression so stony, so fixed, that many who had crowded to the court to hear the singular trial, felt an icy chill pass over their frame when gazing at the proud pitiless woman.

Then from her the curious gaze travelled to Sybil, the prisoner, whose dark grey angry eyes and firmly compressed lips spoke more of defiance than fear for the result of the trial.

She was now divested of the long elf-locks that had given her an appearance so weird and witch-like.

Her hood and crooked stick had also gone, and she stood before her judges and the assembled multitude dressed as a lady of rank.

Some dark rumours had gone abroad from the few words Sybil had uttered in the preliminary examination, and the morbid taste for mystery was highly excited at the revelations that were expected to appear at the trial.

Calmly defiant, Sybil bore the scrutiny of the mob, and so far relied upon the evidence she had to refute Lady Mountsteven's charge, that she was without counsel.

"I can defend myself," she said to the judge. "The innocent require none to defend their cause in a court of justice."

There was a breathless silence when the trial commenced, and every word uttered by the counsel for the prosecution went deep into the hearts of the hushed multitude.

He told his story.

"A noble lady," he said, "had been awakened by a stealthy form crossing her chamber. She watched the intruder, and saw the prisoner ransack a small cabinet that contained the priceless heirlooms of the Mountsteven family."

He paused, so that his words should have their proper weight upon the anxious listeners.

"Lady Mountsteven," he continued, "beheld the attempted robbery with feelings of terror, and trembling for her life, should she be discovered by the gipsy woman, the lady endeavoured to steal from the chamber to give an alarm.

"In this," he added, with emphasis, "she was frustrated, for the midnight thief, hearing the rustle of a dress, turned, and drawing a knife, attempted to add murder to her crimes.

"Providence," he said, in conclusion, "willed it otherwise. A struggle took place. The sharp point of the weapon was turned against the would-be murderess, and the lady was saved."

This speech, delivered with all the eloquence the counsel was capable of, evidently produced a deep impression upon all who were in that court-house.

Their glances of curiosity were now changed to looks of detestation, and Sybil was in the hearts of the crowd already convicted of a crime that would place her neck in a halter.

The counsel sat down, and Lady Mountsteven was called to give her evidence.

The judge, sternly addressing Sybil, said—

"Prisoner, you have heard the crime with which you are charged, and the evidence, which leaves not the slightest doubt of your guilt. Do you still adhere to your protest of innocence?"

"I do, my lord, and charge yonder woman with inventing this story to shield her guilt."

"Woman, you are mad."

"I am not, my lord. Here before the whole assembly, I charge that woman, falsely calling herself the Lady of Mountsteven with murder. You start, my lord. I repeat my words—cold, calculating assassination in several instances."

There was a buzzing and swaying too and fro of the densely packed crowd in the court, as those words left Sybil's lips, and all eyes were directed towards the cold marble-like face.

This dread accusation had been expected by the guilty woman, and she had steeled both her face and nerves to bear it.

Well had she succeeded.

Save for a slight trembling of the muscles of her throat, she remained calm and unmoved.

Again her counsel rose and spoke—

"My lord," he said,. "this is no answer to the charge perferred against the prisoner. Let her answer this; prove her innocence, then, my lord, the Lady Mountsteven will be able to refute her malicious calumny."

A murmur of approbation came from the spectators, so easily were the feelings of the multitude swayed by a powerful speaker.

The judge was evidently struck by the lawyer's words, and after pausing for a few minutes he said—

"Before entering upon the ridiculous charge against the noble lady, I must first behold you released from the crime for which you are placed in the felon's dock."

There was an awful pause, and the eyes that had been fastened upon Lady Mountsteven were now turned upon Sybil.

A smile of quiet scorn was upon the strange woman's lips, as she listened to the judge's words.

"True," she said, slowly, "I must first refute this crime, then, by Heaven's help, I will drag yonder murderess to the scaffold!"

Though outwardly unmoved by these words, the mental agony endured by Lady Mountsteven was enough to deprive a strong man of his reason.

The big drops of sweat oozed from her forehead, her brain felt hot and oppressed, her eye-balls felt as though about to start from their sockets.

Yet she stood immoveable, no figure of Parian marble could have excelled her calm strange appearance.

Now when Sybil began to speak, the firmly closed lips became slightly parted, and her white hand clutched the gold mounted perfume bottle she held with a grasp which threatened to crush the rich enamelled glass.

Sybil's words were delivered with slow measured pronunciation.

She told her judges of the encounter between herself and the Lady Mountsteven.

She paused, as though suddenly remembering some half-forgotten circumstance, then added with startling abruptness.

"My lord, where is the knife that was used?"

Lady Mountsteven's frame shivered, but she was reassured by the prompt action on the part of her lawyer.

"There it is, my lord," he said, holding up the richly jewelled stiletto, "you will observe it has her ladyship's initials, which proves that the prisoner must have snatched it from the dressing table where it was placed."

A red spot of passion came to Sybil's cheek, when this speech came from the lawyer's lips.

She saw that in contesting the charge with the wily man of law, she had no chance of producing anything further to her cause.

"I must summon the proofs," she muttered, "and end this farce."

"Have you anything else to say?" asked the judge, "as far as you have gone you have not altered the evidence that has been brought forward against you."

"You do not credit my statement respecting the true nature of our meeting?"

"I do not," was the stern answer, "your base attempts to traduce the lady before this assembly do not act favourably for you."

"I require no favour," said Sybil, proudly, "if you convict me of the crime for which I am now charged, death will be my sentence; but," she added, fiercely, "I tell you, my lord judge, peer of England, and judge of the realm, you dare not convict me upon the oath of a murderess."

A fearful sensation was caused by these words, and for a moment the Lady Mountsteven trembled.

She feared that Sybil, by adhering to her charge, had some witness that would come forth and wreak the woman's vengeance.

Once more her wily lawyer roused her.

"Again I say, my lord, this is not as it should be. Let the woman bring forth her witnesses in support of her vile charges; unless she can do so she should be at once sentenced."

The judge, enraged at thus being reproved before the court, said angrily—

"Woman, we have listened with patience to your bare accusations. Think you that such a charge can be entertained upon your words?"

"I do not, my lord."

"Ha! Then what do you charge this lady with?"

"I charge her," said Sybil, pointing towards the Lady Mountsteven; "with the murder of Alfred, Lord of Mountsteven."

A stifled shriek came from Lady Mountsteven. The spectators, many of them, grew sick and faint.

Even the wily lawyer stood for a moment dazed and horror-stricken at the hideous charge.

Alone in that vast assembly stood that pale woman who was accused of that terrible deed.

When the astonishment had subsided, the judge said—

"Are you aware of the nature of the charge you have made?"

"My lord," said Sybil, her eyes kindling, and drawing herself proudly up, "I can but repeat my words—I charge that woman with the murder of Lord Mountsteven."

The lawyer had by this time become sufficiently composed to take his client's part.

"My lord," he said, addressing the judge, "this woman's words cannot be taken until she has cleared herself of the charge that my client, Lady Mountsteven, has placed up——"

"Silence! babbling fool," cried Sybil, "that tongue of yours wants clipping. I tell you this charge shall and must be taken."

The lawyer was in the act of opening his mouth, when Sybil's words rang upon his ears.

Surprise, anger, insulted dignity, and wonder, held him for a moment spellbound.

When he had recovered his self-possession he turned round to the judge, and said—

"My lord, in the whole course of my career—I I——"

"We will listen to you hereafter," said the judge, "now we will investigate this woman's extraordinary statement."

The high functionary had begun to entertain a suspicion that all was not so clear against the prisoner as the counsel for the prosecution had by his sophistry attempted to make apparent.

"This is a grave charge," he said; "remember, woman, that more than a feeling of revenge should actuate you in this matter."

"I have been driven to speak, my Lord," answered Sybil, "my life has been placed in jeopardy by this woman, and my lips, which would have held their secret until the proper hour have been unclosed."

"Enough. Before I can arrest that lady I must have a proof of her alleged crime."

"Proof," cried Sybil, "proof! look at that white face and trembling form! Seek you more proof than is to be found there?"

Every eye was bent upon Lady Mountsteven, whose whole face trembled as though stricken by ague, and her cheeks wore such a pallor that it seemed as though death had already fastened upon her heart.

She felt the eyes of the assemblage were fixed upon her, and by a mighty effort she recovered her self-control.

She silently arose.

Coming forward to the edge of the witness-box,

A TRANSFORMATION.

she looked towards the judge, and said in a firm clear voice—

"My lord, is this the justice of England? Is it legal for a prisoner, an attempted murderess, to harrow the feelings of those whose duty compels them to appear as a witness? I most solemnly deny these charges, and demand a thorough investigation of that woman's words."

"You shall have what you require, lady," said the judge; "be under no apprehension that you will leave this court with any stigma upon your character from what that woman may assert."

Lady Mountsteven reseated herself.

The wondrous nerve which had sustained her during this extraordinary scene was by this time exhausted, and with a proud, half scornful look at the gaping crowd, she waited for the judge to cross-examine Sybil.

"You have heard my lady's words, and unless you can bring forth evidence to prove your assertion, I must pass sentence upon you for the crime with which you stand charged."

"I have," said Sybil, "and I hurl back the lie she has uttered. There, my lord, stands a witness who will prove most of my assertions."

She motioned, as she spoke, to a tall figure

who stood among the closely packed mass of spectators.

Little could be seen of that stranger's form.

He was wrapped from head to foot in a large Spanish cloak, and the lower part of his face was hidden by a mass of beard.

"Let the witness stand forth."

The crowd made the way to pass to the witness box.

As his tall form passed slowly forward, Lady Mountsteven bit her lips and clung to the front of the box.

That gait and form could belong but to one, and he she knew was long since in the tomb.

The stranger gravely took the oath, and in answer to a question from the judge he suffered his cloak to fall to the ground, and removing a false beard, there stood before that silent assembly the form of Lord Mountsteven.

An electric shock could not have produced a greater effect upon the spectators than did this sudden apparition.

From the judges on the bench to the crowd in the area below, the name passed from mouth to mouth, and swelling into a chorus, it rang upon Lady Mountsteven's ears.

"Lord Mountsteven—it is he!"

Her eyes were starting from their sockets, and gasping for breath, she murmured—

"Can the grave bring back its dead?"

It was some time before silence could be restored.

When at length the usher's voice had ceased, a quietude reigned in that vast hall that equalled the silence of the tomb.

Then upon the startled senses of all present Sybil's voice rang out.

"There, my lord, is my witness. Ask him whether I speak falsely, when I accuse yon trembling woman of murder?"

CHAPTER CLII.

TOM MORDEN MAKES INQUIRIES.

WHEN Tom Morden parted from our hero he went towards London as fast as four powerful horses could gallop.

"So," he muttered, his fine eyes kindling with anger, "the miscreant has placed me at defiance, and my threat has been treated with scorn."

He lay back in the carriage in deep thought; the vile natures of the two Wirelys were an enigma to the frank, open-hearted fellow, and aroused all the bitterest fierceness of his nature.

Clenching his hands, he murmured, angrily—

"Twice they have escaped my vengeance. Mark! they shall feel the power that I possess, when my fangs are fixed upon their villainous throats."

And while these thoughts passed through his brain, the carriage wheeled onward.

Past quiet villages, whose inhabitants ran to the doors, and gazed after the flying vehicle as it sped upon its path of fierce vengeance.

Twice they stopped to change the weary horses!

Then whip and spur did their work, and as though pursued by a legion of fiends, the high-mettled steeds, goaded to madness, rushed through peaceful hamlets, and passed grim, old roadside mansions.

The dark mantle of night had fallen upon the earth when the postchaise drove up at the Bell Inn, Aldgate.

The reeking steeds and fired post-boys needed rest and Tom, leaving them to the care of the host, stalked away, Nemesis-like, upon the track of those he had sworn to hunt down.

Unarmed, save for the light rapier which hung by his side, he went to the sombre old house where dwelt the Wirelys—father and son.

Looking up at the darkened windows a misgiving stole into his heart; the place seemed empty.

Tom Mordan's summons rang with a hollow sound through the old place, and for some time received no answer.

At length, to the avenger's joy, a faint gleam of light appeared at one of the upper windows, and descending slowly, at length threw its feeble glimmer through the window above Tom's head.

There was much fumbling at the bolts and locks, then the door was opened to the length of a small chain.

Tom beheld a brown shrivelled hand shade the guttering candle, and above it an aged female's face.

"Mr. Wirely," he asked, imperatively, "is he at home?"

The old woman shook her head.

"His son, then?"

The same reply.

"Where are they?"

"I don't know, sir," said a croaking voice, "maybe the gentleman that bought the house can tell you."

"Bought the house! What do you mean?" he asked.

"What I say. I say I don't know nothing about Mr. Wirely; Mr. Watchorn may know, I don't."

The last words were delivered in a falsetto, and had not Tom's strong hand held the door, it would have been shut in his face.

"My good woman," he said, slipping a crown piece into the greasy candlestick, "don't be angry, I want to ask you a few questions."

A pair of sharp, grey eyes were twinkling at the bright silver coin, and the voice that answered was much softer.

"I am not angry, sir, but I didn't think you were a gentleman."

Tom dexterously dropped another coin beside the one over which the hot tallow was congealing.

The measured chink of the two pieces caused a smile to pass over the lady's face, and making an involuntary curtsey, she asked—

"Would your honour like to step inside?—it is cold standing here."

A sudden thought crossed Tom's mind, and he answered in the affirmative.

The chain was unfastened, and he passed through the portal, which was carefully closed after him.

One glance at the interior showed that everything remained in the house as he had last beheld it, and the hope that had prompted him to bribe the old woman grew much stronger in his breast.

"Now, my good woman," he began, "pray explain the cause of Mr. Watchorn's buying this house."

"I don't know the cause, sir. All that I know is that he did so, and sent me here in charge, and though I say it myself, there ain't a more respectable wom——"

"Yes, yes, I can see that. So the gentleman you have named bought the place from Mr. Wirely?"

"Yes, sir, and though I——"

"How long is it since the Wirely's left?"

"Not long, sir—may be three or four days, not more."

"Indeed! And don't you think you could, if you were to try, remember where they went to?"

"Sure, I couldn't, sir. It was some place abroad."

"Ha!"

"Somewhere in the West Indies, I think."

"Ah, indeed, was it Cuba, think you?"

"No."

"Jamaica?"

"No."

"Martinique?"

"No, not one of them; the name was nothing at all like either of them."

"Foiled," thought Tom; "they have been warned of my visit, and fearing I should see the letter, have made off. There is only one chance left to put me on the track. I'll try."

Aloud to the old woman—

"Of course the furniture remains in the rooms as they were occupied by the last owner?"

"Most the same, sir; in fact, the rooms is just as they left 'em."

"Did the gentlemen take any luggage with them?"

"Lots, sir, a coach full of boxes."

The old lady meant, no doubt, it was the roof of the coach that was filled.

"These boxes, I suppose, were packed in one of the rooms?"

"Yes, sir; master's."

"Could I see the room?"

The old party was silent.

She was thinking there was a possibility of making a trio of the coins that looked so tempting beneath the flaming candle.

"Well, sir," she began, "you see I'm not allowed to have anybody in the house, so——"

The clink of a third piece of money sounded upon her ears as Tom placed it beside its fellows.

She had gained her object; the trio was made, and her objection vanished.

"So you see, sir," she continued, "I am obliged to be so very careful as to who I let upstairs."

"Has there been any one up here before then?"

"No, sir; but you see there's no knowing how soon there might be; they say it never rains but it pours."

The old dame looked longingly at the crown pieces.

Whether she used the old axiom with respect to them was uncertain.

"I understand; you are afraid that if it be known you have shown the rooms to any one, others may seek the same indulgence?"

"That's just it, sir; but if you won't say a word, I can't refuse such a gentleman as you."

"Not a word, my good woman."

"Very well; this way, sir."

Preceded by the old dame, Tom went to the study lately occupied by his foe — the elder Wirely.

He saw at a glance that the room showed the hasty escape of the vile pair.

Pieces of rope which had been used to fasten the luggage were thrown about, mingled with scraps of paper, evidently portions of letters which had been torn hastily into shreds.

The old woman, by Tom's direction, held the candle high above her head, and, to her great astonishment, her visitor examined the scraps line by line.

With a patient diligence he read every word that could be distinguished, and when they had all passed through his hands a cry of rage and disappointment came from his lips.

"Not the faintest clue," he thought, "not a sign. Had I but found one torn diminutive label, I could have followed their track perhaps."

He arose, and after opening a few doors, turned to leave the room.

The astonished dame hobbled forward to open the door, and as it swung back a piece of crumpled paper attracted Tom's notice.

It was crushed, and still retained the form in which a strong hand had clutched it.

Mechanically Tom picked it up, but despairing of any chance now affording the information he was in search of.

Still, he opened the paper, crumpled up as it was.

The first line that met his eyes drew a cry of joy from his lips.

There was a vengeful fire in those kindling orbs as he deciphered these words:—

"Shipping-office, Commercial-road.
"July 25th, 17—.

"SIR,—The ship you mentioned in your letter of to-day will sail to-morrow morning at sunrise—wind and weather permitting.

"I have placed two berths at your service as you requested, and wish to inform you that passengers and luggage must be on board to-night.

"I am, Sir,
"Your obedient servant,
"George R. Cloudsley.
"To Messrs. Wirely and Son."

The joy of old Tom's heart was too great for utterance.

This letter, at the last moment, when every chance had seemed gone, appeared as though the hand of fate had thrown it into his possession.

So strange were his actions, that the old party, after opening the street door, stood and watched him down the street.

When he had turned the corner she went inside muttering—

"Mad, mad. Clear gone, poor man. Well-a-day, he is a generous gentleman after all."

Clutching the letter tightly in his hand. Tom called a Hackney coach, and drove to the shipping office, Commercial-road, East.

To his chagrin, the office was closed, and in spite of his frantic inquiries none could tell him where the clerk dwelt who had written to old Wirely.

Baffled but not dispirited, he drove to the docks.

Hours of fruitless research he spent there.

The sleepy officials either could not or would not assist him, and he was compelled to abandon his pursuit until next day.

The dawn was just approaching, when tired and dispirited he alighted at his mansion in the fashionable quarter of Bartholomew Close.

The few hours that intervened between then and the opening of the shipping office were passed in preparing to follow the runaway.

Strong excitement kept his frame from succumbing to fatigue, and when the industrious maidens were cleaning the doorsteps he departed from his house.

CHAPTER CLIII.

MIDSHIPMAN TOM GAINS AN EASY VICTORY.

IT was a terrible moment for Tom and Zaima.

He saw by the look in the young outlaw's brilliant eye that his fate was sealed, should he not call off his men.

The guards stood resolute.

That Zaima would be impaled on the young chieftain's sword, should they stir, was obvious.

Snowball's fine colossal figure was shown off to advantage, as he stood at bay—his mighty weapon poised above his head.

One word—a look—or the slightest movement on the part of his beloved leader would have set the gigantic African to work.

But the noble leader wished to avoid needless bloodshed.

He was not sanguinary by nature, but when ordered to it, he had the the courage and power of a lion.

Then he spared none.

"Call off your men," he cried again!

Zaima was silent; his crafty brain was at work.

Midshipman Tom watched him closely—his hand tightened upon the hilt of his sword,

The point entered Zaima's dusky skin.

The point of Tom's sword was sharp—the sensation was not pleasant.

A red streak of blood could be seen upon the man's breast.

That was quite sufficient to make him feel miserable and dreadfully sick.

"Call off your men, I shall not repeat the order," said Tom.

Zaima did not want him to, especially should it be accompanied by another dig.

The lank slave, with an inward groan of pain, motioned the soldiers back.

They retreated, and Zaima tried to wriggle from the powerful grasp of his youthful captor.

"Not yet, my copper-coloured friend," said the gallant boy, "it is not my intention to let you go quite so soon."

Zaima's face fell.

He had indulged in the momentary anticipation of outwitting his young opponent.

The young outlaw seemed to read his thoughts.

A smile played around his handsome mouth, as he said—

"Firstly, I wish to save bloodshed; and secondly, to leave the place without any noise; and knowing you are troublesome, I intend spoiling your playful arrangements, and unless you do what I tell you, I shall run you through."

Zaima began to shrink.

Suppose they did intend to kill him.

His teeth began to chatter at the fearful thought.

Snowball looked on with a grin upon his face.

"Now," said Tom, "order your men to stack their arms in the centre of the room. Come—quick!"

The last word was followed by a shove.

Zaima bit his tongue; his eyes began to water.

"Got some dirt on um eye," yelled Snowball, with a groan.

"Do as I bid you," cried the young outlaw, restraining his laughter with the greatest difficulty.

Zaima could not speak for the moment.

"Has he bit a piece ob tongue off? and I get in any way, den Snowball cut it off—that make um speak."

It did make um speak.

Zaima, fearing Snowball would put his threat into execution, gave the necessary order to the men.

One by one they very reluctantly stacked their fire-arms in the centre.

Snowball shouldered his axe, and looked on in grim satisfaction.

"Now," said Tom, as the last soldier placed his musket with the others, "give me your sword."

Zaima did so.

"Look after the arms, Snowball."

"Dey all right, Massa Tom."

"Stand in front of these, Snowball, with gun ready to fire in your hand."

"Yes, Massa, um understand," replied the faithful fellow, following the young chieftain's orders.

Midshipman Tom then stepped forward, and throwing open a small door, that seemed built on the wall, he took his place by the side of Snowball.

Leading from the door just opened was a narrow dark passage, which led to a small loathsome chamber, the use of which was best known to Zaima.

But when he heard the outlaw king's next order his dusky cheek went grey.

Taking a musket from the stack, Tom pointed the muzzle in a line with Zaima's head.

"Enter," he said, sternly, "enter; if any one of you is not out of my sight in twenty seconds I fire."

"Yah! dam yer black lubbers; off wid you, or by gar I fire."

He meant it, too.

The Mussulmen, terror-stricken, stood staring upon the daring outlaws.

Zaima was trembling with fear.

"The time has expired," said the young chief, cocking his piece.

"Sheer off um dam wretches," chimed in Snowball, following his leader's example.

The guards seemed to comprehend what was required of them.

The click as the hammers were drawn back upon the muskets filled their hearts with terror.

Leaving the door open, they fled through the narrow passage.

Zaima lingered behind.

Snowball brought his piece to bear upon the slave's dark form.

He uttered a yell and followed his men.

Snowball gave a whoop as he fired.

The report was succeeded by a scream.

"Somebody was hit," he said; "call again."

Somebody was hit.

The bullet lodged in a tender part of Zaima's person, causing that individual a deal of pain, without doing much harm.

Midshipman Tom securely fastened the door through which the affrighted soldiers had fled.

A loud scream of agony or fear assailed his ears.

"In heaven's name, what can that be?" exclaimed the brave boy, pausing before the door.

"Never mind, Msssa Tom. Yah! Um daresay they see more p'raps den Zaima wish 'em to."

Tom took the hint.

"Where go you now, Massa Tom?"

"Anywhere from this place."

And he strode from the room.

"Snowball foller in a moment, Massa Tom," said his trusty officer.

Tom looked back to see what his lieutenant was doing.

"What do you intend doing with those, Snowball?"

"Take 'em to de War Cloud, to keep 'em dare fellows from mischief."

While this little dialogue was going on, Snowball had been very carefully binding the firearms together with his belt, and then throwing them upon his shoulder, he strode after his young chief.

"Snowball," said Tom, as they retraced their steps to the War Cloud, "what is to be done—accursed wretches, are they ever to foil me."

"No, Massa Tom; dey no foil you any longer."

"Have you a plan?" asked the princely boy, eagerly.

"I ab been thinking, sar."

"Speak, Snowball; I will not rest until I have found Laura."

"Dare is only one way, Massa Tom."

"And that?"

"Am to enter the harem again."

Tom made an impatient gesture.

"Such a thing would be madness," he said.

"It am easy enuff, Massa Tom," replied Snowball, not at all put out by his young chief's angry reply.

"Perhaps you will explain, I am not used to solving riddles."

"Dis den am my plan, sar, s'posing a young English lady, who am very lubly am sold in de market; and de Pasha find it out, come and buy her."

"Well," said Tom, wonderingly.

"Why den he take her to 'um harem, de young lady cry and make 'um fuss 'cos she am alone wit no one to speak to, den if Miss Laura am dere the Bey will carry her to de other for company."

"I am at a loss to understand you yet," said Tom, growing more perplexed.

"He, he!" grinned Snowball, who seemed delighted at the plan he had formed. "He, he! Why den, Massa Tom, de young lady cry, and say she be ebery ting de Bey want if he grant one wish. Den he say what dat? De lady say she hab a black servant she berry fond of. De Bey buy her slave, and—he, he!—don't you see, Massa Tom, now?"

Massa Tom saw then, or thought he did, through the other's plot.

A faint glimmering of what his dusky officer meant passed through the young outlaw's mind.

But he was determined to be certain and he asked.

"And who, may I ask, is this young lady supposed to be?"

"De same one as Miss Montague was—yah!"

And Snowball chuckled with delight.

Tom paused and grasped his faithful officer's hand.

"Thanks, my noble Snowball; thanks for the idea. It shall be done, and at once."

"It am awful dangerous though, Massa Tom, should you be discovered."

"Midshipman Tom knows no danger. I would do ten times as much to save my adored Laura."

"We ab better make haste, sar."

"Yes, Snowball, we have much to do and no time to lose," replied the daring boy, accelerating his speed.

"Give the signal," said Tom, as they approached the arch.

"Here it am, sar."

Snowball handed a small white roll of something hard to his youthful leader—in shape it resembled a wax candle.

Kindling a light, Midshipman Tom applied it to the article in question.

A loud hissing noise followed, and a blue flame shot high in the air.

Again all was darkness.

Midshipman Tom and his powerful lieutenant remained for a moment motionless, gazing through the gloom in the direction of the War Cloud.

Then came a red, lurid flash; in an instant it had disappeared and died away in the darkness.

It was an answer to their signal.

"All's well," said the boy, as he stepped to the water's edge.

The sound of oars came upon the still night air.

A moment later a boat's keel grated upon the rocky shore.

Midshipman Tom leaped in, followed by the huge African, and seating himself in the stern sheets gave the order to return.

Simultaneously the oars were dipped in the water, a few long powerful sweeps, and Midshipman Tom was again climbing the side of his gallant craft.

CHAPTER CLIV.

ADRIFT ON THE OCEAN.

CLINGING to the frail plank, Red Hand drifted far away from the gallant old frigate, the echoes of his devilish glee still ringing in the breeze.

After the sudden flash and loud report of the frigate's gun reached him, and a huge wave leaped over his frail bark, proclaiming to his fevered imagination that the sinking of the ship had taken place, he gave a loud "Ha! ha! ha!" and cried—"Red Hand's revenge is accomplished."

But when the joyous sun broke the leaden sky and lit up the ocean's surface, with no affected wrongs to avenge and no fresh deaths to lust for, his feelings underwent a total change, and he became giddy with the reflection, whether or no it was possible to save his own life.

While his mind was being racked by these thoughts, he beheld the hazy outlines of a ship bearing close towards him.

With compressed lips and starting eyeballs he shrieked for help, but the sound of his voice was either lost in the breeze or purposely unheeded, for with every sail set and her double tier of guns run out, she went majestically on her way.

Red Hand clutched at the plank which floated between him and eternity, and gazed at the heaving ship.

"Curses," he muttered, fiercely, "she has escaped me after all. It is the Hercules, and I am left to perish."

Surely enough it was the gallant vessel he had sought to destroy whose white sails he now beheld gleaming in the sunshine.

Down—down until his face touched the water the miscreant crouched, until the salt spray dashed over him, and the uplifting of the plank caused by the swell of the water told him the frigate had passed.

When he raised his head, the sunbeams shining out with wondrous splendour, caused the golden letters upon the frigate's stern to stand out in bold relief against her timbers—THE HERCULES.

He followed the ominous name until the vessel passed his vision, then he cursed himself for allowing the ship to pass without an effort to attract their attention.

He was now alone upon the waters.

Alone beneath the blazing sun, his tongue swollen and his mouth parched for want of water.

A speedy death was preferable to the horrible torments he now endured; and cursing wildly, he uttered a shriek of dire agony.

From that hour until the sun had reached the meridian, he fell into a state of stupor.

His head was bowed upon his breast, and his swollen tongue protruded from his parched mouth.

It was a strange and horrible sight—the crime-stained miscreant left to perish in the midst of the wide ocean.

ALONE ON THE ISLAND.

Left to die a lingering and horrible death, and those he had doomed he beheld sail past him scatheless.

While he continued in this state his brain was filled with delicious dreams of clear running waters.

He saw a rippling brook flowing through a beautiful little village, and the sight caused him to cry out with joy.

In his vision he knelt upon the grassy bank and was about to drink.

But at the moment his lips touched the cool stream the limpid waters became changed to the hue of blood, and he beheld a thousand demons dancing around him mocking his agony.

With a horrible curse he regained his senses, and looked around.

Then the horrors of his position came with tenfold force to his mind.

"Better," he thought, "to end my life than suffer these tortures any longer. I would sooner be torn piecemeal with red-hot pincers than endure another hour like this.'

It wanted but one swerve and he could have rolled off the plank and ended his misery.

Twice he was upon the point of precipitating himself in the ocean's mystic depths.

Each time he paused—all hope had not yet died within him.

So through the long sunny day the miscreant's sufferings continued, and more than one sin was expiated by the terrible agony he endured.

Night began to throw her mantle upon the wide waste of ocean, and Red Hand, more dead than alive, prayed that death would come and take him from his agony.

That death he could so easily find he feared to meet.

The long frightful catalogue of crimes which stained his soul came vividly before him, and he found that it was impossible to die until he had made some expiation for his sins.

Many a vow he registered to alter his evil life, should he be spared to again mingle with his fellow men.

But in spite of both prayers and curses, darkness set in, and he was alone.

Towards midnight a quick cry came from his lips, and he yelled—

"Ship—ship ahoy!"

It was a strange spectacle that caused this cry to come from his lips.

A sight that, to the uninitiated, would have been of the most terrible kind.

But to the now overjoyed miscreant it showed hope of salvation from the grim grisly tyrant who was striding slowly but surely towards the villainous castaway.

Within a fathom's length of the plank which for twenty-four hours had been Red Hand's home, a brilliant sheet of flame lit up the ocean's sombre expanse.

Beyond this strange light Red Hand beheld the outlines of a ship.

The vessel appeared to have taken fire, but her crew, instead of rushing violently about under the influence of fear, he saw the men moving about quietly in front of the flame.

What could it be?

Was it a reflection of the mocking vision of the rippling hull, or was it a spectre ship manned by a legion of fiends whose elements were flames of sulphur?

Red Hand paused not to ask himself these questions, but with all the strength he had left he yelled—

"Ship ahoy! ahoy there! help!"

No notice was taken of his frantic cries, and with a chilled feeling of despair creeping over his heart, he watched the bright sheets of flame that sprang up in front of the vessel's foremast, the forked tongues of which served to lick her lower spars.

Using his hands as paddles, Red Hand went slowly towards the strange ship, and when within a few yards of her side, he shrieked out—

"Help—help!—ahoy! ship ahoy!"

This time his cries were heard, and several of the figures which, demon-like had been moving apparently among the flames, came to the side.

"Help, help!" shrieked Red Hand. "Help! for the name of heaven, help!"

The elf-like forms stood silently gazing upon the strange spectacle of a swarthy man upon the ocean; and not until Red Hand repeated his cry did they cast off the gripes, and lower a boat to his assistance.

When they dragged him aboard he was senseless. Hunger, thirst, fear, and the pangs of a guilty mind, had done their work.

The supernatural outlines of the strange vessel may need explanation.

She was a whaler, and the huge sheet of flames came from the furnace in which the whaler's men were casting from time to time pieces of blubber from a newly caught whale.

When the flames from her furnace had burst upon Red Hand's sight, the whaler's men were engaged in extracting the precious sperm oil from a huge monster they had harpooned on the very day that Red Hand beheld the frigate pass him upon the ocean.

A few hours' rest sufficed to revive the dormant faculties of the wretch who had suffered so terribly for his unparalleled crime.

The captain of the whaler, as soon as Red Hand became able to appear on deck, expressed his anxiety to learn the strange circumstances which placed the pirate in such a strange position.

All Red Hand's vows of amendment and expiation for his crimes were soon forgotten, and with returning strength his villainous brain began to hatch a plan whereby he could obtain the rich whaler for himself.

He coveted the stores of sperm oil which filled her hold, and saw already a mode by which he could buy and equip another vessel for his old career of crime.

In answer to the captain, he said, craftily—

"I have to thank Providence for guiding my frail craft to your ship."

"You have, indeed. In another hour you would have died from exhaustion, as it was I had much difficulty in bringing you round."

"I have given myself up for lost several times."

"Not without cause. Are you all that is left of the ship's company?"

"All," answered Red Hand, "my vessel was destroyed by fire."

"And the crew."

"They put off in boats, and perished to a man."

"Poor fellows! How did you escape?"

"I was the last to leave the ship, and just before she blew up, I sprang into the sea with this plank you found me on."

"Terrible! How long have you been drifting alone?"

"Three days."

"And not tasted food or water?"

"Neither has passed my lips until you gave them to me."

"I am glad I found you. Now, Captain, I presume that is your rank?"

"It is, and my name's Johnson."

"Very well, Captain Johnson, you are at liberty to stay with me until we reach a port where you can obtain a passage home. In fact, make yourself as comfortable as though the ship were under your command."

"Thanks; you are too kind."

"Not so; we never know what may happen to us."

"That is true, but I hope you may never suffer as I have."

"I hope not."

The conversation ceased, and Red Hand went below to his cot.

Before he closed his eyes, he lay for some time plotting and planning a dozen schemes for the realization of his wishes.

"There is sure to be," he thought, "a portion of this whaler's crew ready to rise and seize this valuable cargo. I must find them out. This done, I shall soon be the commander of the vessel that will recruit my empty coffers.

A week had not passed before he found all he wanted.

Among the crew were a dozen ruffians, who had been picked up at various foreign sea-ports.

Men, whose wayward habits and disinclination to submit to discipline had led them to desert their former vessel.

Red Hand soon singled them out, and began to pave the way for the realization of his infernal purpose.

CHAPTER CLV.

THE CASTAWAY.

TOM MORDAN had determined not to return until he had arranged the abduction of Laura.

Commercial-road was in the bustle of business when he alighted from the coach.

Entering the shipping office the heavy door swung back to its place, as a sharp, active, little man descended from his stool, and bowed to the early visitor.

"Your name is Cook, I presume?" said Tom Mordan.

"It is, sir."

Mordan held the letter open in his hand, and said—

"You are the writer of this?"

"I am."

"Will you have the goodness to tell me the name of the vessel here mentioned?"

"With pleasure; the 'Reculver.'"

"Her destination?"

"Canada."

"Thanks. When does the next vessel leave?"

"Let me see, this is the sixth?"

"Yes."

"The next mail will sail on the twentieth."

"None before that day?"

"None, sir."

"Fourteen days," thought Tom Mordan; "the chase will be useless with that time between us."

The clerk was mentally valuing the ornamental pistols that were thrust in Tom Mordan's waist belt.

He was aroused from that occupation by the visitor's voice.

"It is," said Tom, "a matter of life and death that I should overtake that vessel. Is it possible to be effected?"

"Not by waiting until the next ship sails."

"I am aware of that. Can you suggest nothing to aid me?"

"I can, sir."

"My purse and service are ready at your command if you but will it."

"It can be done, then. We have several fast schooners that are always in readiness."

"And are they for sale?"

"They are, and I could almost venture to assert that you could by chartering one of those small vessels overtake the vessel before she can sight the West Indies."

Tom Mordan lost no time in coming to terms with the respectable shipowner's clerk, who, seeing the eagerness with which Tom grasped the idea, took especial care to make him pay four times the value for the hire of the craft.

But money was as dirt compared to the object before Tom Mordan.

So, towards evening, by a plentiful disbursement of the yellow boys, he stood upon the Raven's deck, and with strange interest, watched the anchor as it was being drawn slowly from the muddy bed of the old river.

Taking advantage of the wind, the small vessel spread her sails, and before morning she was dancing upon the billows.

Tom Mordan was following the trail of those whom he had sworn to destroy.

Behind the office where the shipping business was carried on was a small dingy parlour.

Here the respectable Mr. Cook entered, when he had seen Tom Mordan safely on board the Raven.

Mr. Cook was the shipping agent's clerk.

Softly closing the door, and locking it to prevent entrance, he stepped briskly to the table where two gentlemen were seated laughing gaily as they discussed the merits of a bottle of port of which they were partaking.

"Trapped," said Mr. Cook, helping themselves to a glass, "caught, and without a word on my part."

"Ha! ha! ha!" laughed Wirely senior, in the little back parlour of the shipping office, "caught, caught! capital, capital! excellent, excellent."

"Ha! ha!" remarked Wirely junior, as he likewise sat in the back office of the shipping agent's, "ho! ho! ho! he thinks we are on the way to Canada does he? Capital! ah, Mr. Cook!"

"Excellent, sir. I may say, supreme. Do you know, Wirely, such a stroke as that would immortalise you, if you were a public man?"

Old Wirely smiled grimly.

"Not bad; ah Mr. Wirely?"

"Bad! no; it was, to use our friend's word, supreme."

"Yes. He! he! he! after all, you see, sending that letter to the outlaw has been the means of doing us good."

"It has. Let me see: in addition to the girl's fortune we shall have Tom's."

"After a time, after a time, we shall most certainly; but we must first be sure that Mr. Cook has succeeded in his part with the men on board the Raven."

"Be under no apprehension, sir. The gentleman will be drugged and taken ashore. When he awakes from his stupor, the ship will be far away. and he will be alone with the savages."

"Most excellent; ha! ha! ha! The old woman played her part well. Little did our friend Tom Mordan imagine that we were watching him when he picked up the pieces of paper."

The trio laughed long and loud.

Their plan was both ingenious and successful. When the worthy Wirely left the office, Mr. Cook the respectable agent, mounted his stool, and soliloquised.

"Should he ever return, which is very unlikely, I am quite safe. He came here and said he wished to overtake the Reculver, and did not ask me whether the parties he wanted were on board."

"Quite safe for me ; quite safe."

*   *   *   *   *

The little vessel, which Tom Mordan had chartered, skimmed the waters like a thing of life, but day after day passed, and still the Reculver, of which she was in pursuit, remained invisible.

Unsuspicious of the well-laid plan for him, Tom Mordan was continually upon the schooner's deck.

Every hour that passed he expected to behold the Reculver.

So the days went on until they merged into weeks.

Then a fear crossed his mind that he would be, after all his trouble, too late to overtake the runaways.

He spoke of this to the captain of the little vessel.

"The Reculver," he replied, "is a fast craft, but she will be far away from Canada when we come in sight."

"You think so ?"

"I am sure of it."

Tom Mordan felt more at ease.

"Perhaps, after all," he thought, "it would be better that I should meet them when they disembark, and crush their fancied safety as they touch the soil of a foreign clime."

The Raven, one brilliant morn, was gliding slowly within sight of land.

Visible to the naked eye were the drooping palms and thick tropical foliage of as fair a scene as the vision of man ever beheld.

Tom Mordan for the first time beheld the rich beauties of the favoured spot ; and when the vessel rounded to, and the captain signified his intention of sending a boat ashore for water, he expressed a wish to accompany the men.

The captain's eyes lit with joy.

"You will find," he said to Mordan, "the paradise very dangerous."

"Indeed !"

"Fever and ague are among the blessings bestowed upon the natives."

"Yet you send a boat's crew there."

"True ; but before they start each man fortifies himself against infection."

"How ?"

"By a drink which we always keep on board for such occurrences."

Tom Mordan smiled.

"If," he said, "it would not be asking too great a favour, may I be permitted to share in the draught ?"

"With pleasure. I would have asked you, but the generality of my passengers scorn the simple remedy, and, as a natural consequence, fall victims to the pestilential vapour which the sun draws from the earth."

"I have too important a mission to accomplish," said Tom, " to endanger my life."

The captain gave orders for the boat, which was on the point of leaving, to remain by the vessel's side.

Going below, he returned with a bottle and glass in his hand.

"This," he said to Tom, as he filled the glass with a bright liquid, "is as precious as the famous elixir of the ancients."

"More so," said Tom, draining the glass, "it saves that which the elixir cannot prolong."

The captain of the Raven watched him over the side, and a triumphant leer came over his face.

"Fallen into it," he muttered, "trapped like a fox, and my fortune is made."

Before the boat reached the shore Tom Mordan had fallen forward and his senses forsaken him.

The potent drug had taken effect, and the strong man was rendered as powerless as an infant.

The boat's keel grated harshly upon the beach, and the boatswain's mate, who had charge, pointed to the unconscious form, and said—

"Bear a hand, my lads; the Raven must be away before he revives."

To carry Tom ashore was the work of a moment.

Placing the inanimate form above the high water mark, his companions stripped him of his sword and pistols, and he would have been left without the power of defending his life against the howling beasts or the equally fierce redskins, had not one of the men, with more compassion than his companions, left a bowie-knife where the prone form lay.

As the Raven bore away from the spot, the captain, with a grim smile, beheld how well his task had been accomplished.

With his face upturned, the castaway lay beneath the vertical sun's scorching rays, his senses numbed and his limbs rigid from the effects of the subtle fluid which the captain had given him.

When Tom Mordan awoke from his deathlike sleep, the red sun was sinking behind the western hills.

He looked round the strange place with a feeling of wonderment.

When he found himself alone a dim foreshadowing of evil crept into his heart.

Regaining his feet he walked swiftly towards the sea.

Then a cry came from his lips as he beheld the broad sheet of water gleaming beneath the sun's glow.

His empty belt and the loosened buckles of his sword added to the conviction that he had been the victim of a foul conspiracy.

Tom's brave heart did not, however, sink beneath the terrible weight of his crushing blow.

Walking back to the place where he had been left to perish, he looked eagerly about for some food.

Bad as the men are who have abandoned me to this fate, he thought, they would surely have not left me without food and water in a desolate land.

But his search was fruitless, and with a cry wrung from his strong heart, he seated himself upon the trunk of a fallen tree.

The glitter of the bowie knife left by the kindly sailor caught his eye, and springing towards it, he placed the friendly weapon in his belt.

While withdrawing his hand, a folded paper fell to the ground.

Tom stooping to pick it up, saw his name in the corner, the writing being that of the villanous old Wirely.

Biting his lips until the blood came, he read the strangely found letter.

It read as follows:—

"Tricked and by me. When you receive this you will be cast away upon a strange land, and I shall not only be in the enjoyment of the girl's property, but yours also; and enjoy it I shall, for the red-skins will never allow you to remain long alive. "Your foe,
"NEVILLE WIRELY."

CHAPTER CLVI.

TOM IN THE HAREM.

"SNOWBALL?" cried our hero, when he stepped on board the War Cloud.

"Here, Massa Tom."

"You had better get under weigh at once."

"Yes, sar."

"I will go and prepare, therefore. The management of the War Cloud I shall leave entirely in your hands."

"Me understand, Massa Tom."

"Lose no time, Snowball, and be careful."

"Never fear, sar," replied Snowball, saluting his gallant young chief, who went below.

And while Tom was closeted in the cabin, holding a long conference with Ben, the War Cloud underwent a startling change.

"Ben. Me want you," said Snowball, addressing the outlaw.

Ben approached the gigantic officer.

"Yes, sir. Me, sir?"

Snowball took him by the arm and strode slowly up and down the deck.

For some minutes they remained thus conversing in an undertone.

At length they ceased.

"You will hab to be careful, and we trick um, dam pirates!" said Snowball.

"Never fear, sir," replied Ben, with a chuckle.

"Have all hands piped up. Ay, go to work quickly," said Snowball.

The boatswain's whistle sounded the shrill call.

In an instant the deck was crowded with the daring outlaws.

"Now, my lads, alter the beauty's trim—remove her figure head; with a will, my lads, and quickly."

"Aye! aye!" came merrily from the brave fellows.

They were in expectation of some fun.

"Half-a-dozen idlers away there! Over the stern nail a thin plank over her name. Do you hear there?"

"Aye! aye! sir;" responded half a dozen of them as they rigged Jacob's ladders, and began the task allotted them.

"What name shall we paint on her?" asked Ben, of Snowball.

"De Giaour," replied the African, "nearly all ready?"

"Yes, it does not take us a long time to undress the beauty," said Ben, laughing.

Snowball gave one more look at the work going on and then went below.

"Weigh the anchor," sang out Ben.

His order was immediately obeyed.

* * * * *

Morn. The heavy masses of clouds slowly rolled away from the eastern hemisphere, leaving a long, grey streak across the horizon, threw its faint light upon the face of the calm waters, and mantled the land with the first blush of the coming day.

Slowly, but gracefully, a low hulled schooner swims through the mighty waters.

Her crew were idling or lying about her snowy deck.

A young officer passed the quarter-deck.

The sails of the beautiful vessel were stretched to catch the coming breeze, and everything displayed good seamanship and discipline.

Still there was a rakish, saucy look about her that would make a merchantman alter his course, should he be coming in her wake.

Her hull was particularly low in the water; her prow was short, and cut through the sea like a knife, and upon her stern was painted in large gilt letters, The Giaour.

We will take a look in the chief cabin of this suspicious-looking craft.

Seated round the table were five or six persons.

One, evidently the captain, a fine, bold-looking fellow, sat with a cup of delicious coffee in his hand.

By his side sat an officer of gigantic proportions, and who kept laughing in high glee each time his eyes encountered those of a handsome young lady that sat nearly opposite him.

There was a merry twinkle in the flashing eye of the young lady, who indulged in most unladylike expressions now and then.

There were two others in the cabin—females—one evidently a Greek or Spaniard.

The herculean African rose, and glancing at her spotless, white linen garments, with a look of deep disgust, saluted the young lady with long, golden hair, and went upon deck.

Our readers no doubt recognise who these individuals are.

Presently the lady with long golden hair came upon deck.

"Weigh anchor soon, Miss Rosaline?" said Snowball, with a laugh.

"In ten minutes let go the anchor, and have everything prepared," said Miss Rosaline, in a very masculine voice.

"Snowball attend to it, sar. You better go below, Miss, de air am chilly; he! he! he!"

Miss Rosaline—alias Midshipman Tom—went below.

The vessel was anchored in the bay.

Outlaw Ben came up and took the command.

A boat was lowered and manned by six men, into which was placed Miss Rosaline, looking as beautiful as nature, adorned by the art of Snowball, could make her.

Snowball followed in his white linen suit.

It was with the greatest difficulty the men could restrain their laughter, but they knew their beloved young chief was playing a desperate game.

Nevertheless everyone was in a state of the greatest consternation.

They felt that should their leader be discovered a speedy and awful death would quickly follow.

"Pull my, lads—altogether," said Ben, taking his seat in the stern of the little craft.

The boat shot from the vessel's side with her wonted liveliness, and quickly landed the bold young outlaw chief into one of the most desperate undertakings—the most daring deed and the one presenting the greater risk of life than had ever been ventured upon even by Midshipman Tom.

The Bey, being in excellent spirits, had strolled out for a morning's walk.

By chance he went to the slave-market; he noticed an unusual bustle, and, upon inquiring, learnt there was a white maiden to be sold—from the christian lands. The Bey was delighted with the information.

He had a special weakness for the beauties of England.

But he had another object in wishing to purchase this one.

The idea had flashed across his mind that if he could but obtain a companion from her own native land, that he might, through her, cause Laura to become reconciled to the harem.

The hoary old sinner's heart jumped with delight as the thought entered his mind.

At once he set about seeing this Christian maiden.

The first sight was sufficient.

He was struck with the bold beauty and noble bearing of the young lady, and he made up his mind, at whatever cost, he would obtain her.

High had been the offers made for the pale faced beauty: but as yet to no purpose—all had been declined.

The dealer was vain of his christian prize, and the more the intended buyers fed his vanity, the more his appetite increased.

At length an almost fabulous amount was offered.

It was about being accepted, when the Bey turned to the captain who commanded the slaver, and who had brought over the white maiden.

A few words only passed between them.

The Bey had bought the beautiful prize, to the great envy and disgust of several other old connoisseurs in Christian beauty, who had promised themselves possession of the charming girl.

The same day saw Miss Rosaline in the Bey's harem.

She was waited upon by a dumb slave, and every description of refreshment and elegant attire brought to her.

But Miss Rosaline would not partake of her kind patron's hospitality.

A good part of her time she spent in looking over the apartment.

She was aroused by the Bey.

He entered the apartment with a most engaging smile playing about his wrinkled old face.

Miss Rosaline was just then reposing on a luxurious couch, her face hidden in her hands and sobbing as though her poor heart would break.

The old Bey looked confounded.

"Is the maiden not happy?" he said.

She made no reply, but sobbed all the more.

"Why does not the Rosebud speak? The Bey is great and will grant anything."

Rosebud rose at this.

Still she kept her handkerchief up to her face.

The Bey seated himself beside her.

One arm glided around her waist.

Perhaps had the Bey being aware of the eyes that were flashing upon him through those fingers that covered the Rosebud's face, and the inclina-

" THREE RINGING CHEERS FOR MIDSHIPMAN TOM!"

tion she had to knock the old sinner down and strangle him, he would not have been so loving.

But Rosaline continued her crying, and made a rather strong effort to free herself from the old wretch's grasp.

"Oh, why—why was I brought here?" she cried, feigning hoarseness, the better to disguise the fulness of her voice.

"Is not the daughter from the infidel's land happy?" inquired the Bey.

"No, no! oh, no! This strange place. Oh, where is Nino. Oh, Nino, I should be happy comparatively happy, if you were only left me."

The old gentleman pricked up his ears.

She spoke in his tongue.

"Whom does my Rosebud sigh for?"

"Oh, great and mighty Bey,' she said removing the hand from her face and looking beseechingly into her admirer's eyes; "oh, mighty Bey, grant me but one wish and I may be happy!"

"Speak, my child, speak. The Bey is great and will grant anything," replied the old barbarian, delighted in expecting she would turn out a willing slave.

"Grant then, oh light of the world, grant me the favour of having the only friend left me in the world to be my companion, when you, oh mighty Bey, are absent from me."

The old gentleman pricked up his ears again.

"Whom, oh daughter of the infidel, whom did you say you wished for? Tell the great Bey thy words, they shall be heeded."

"Oh, great and merciful Bey, it is the slave thou saw standing by the side of the wicked man that sold me. Oh, if he should be sold, I—I shall die!"

"Dry those sweet eyes, most beautiful perfection of animated nature, as thou art. Your wish shall be granted; the slave shall be sent for."

Rosaline could scarcely restrain a cry of joy.

"Would the Rosebud like to see the Blooming Flower who came from her native land?" inquired the Bey.

"Has the great Bey a young lady who speaks my language?" asked the Rosebud.

"She is in the next chamber."

"Does she love the mighty Bey?"

The old gentleman scowled.

"No, she is stubborn and shuts her ears to the words of the great Bey, who would teach her the language of his faith."

"Oh, mighty Bey, grant but thy slave her wish, and in return she will teach the Blooming Flower to answer you in her own tongue."

The old gentleman leapt with delight.

"The Rosebud shall have her wish," he said, as he strode for the harem.

In a few minutes he returned, leading in Laura by the hand.

Laura gave a cry of joy at seeing an English young lady.

"Oh! this is joy indeed!" she said, tearfully.

Rosaline did not speak, but drew the poor suffering girl to her breast.

The Bey retired to his own room, where he wrote out the necessary order for purchasing the Rosebud's slave.

Laura clung to her new-found friend as though she had at last a protector.

"And have you been stolen away from all that is dear to you?" she sobbed.

"No, Laura, I came to save you," replied Rosaline, in a low voice.

"You know me?" said Laura, looking up in surprise.

Their eyes met.

That one glance revealed all.

There was no time for explanation.

With a cry of wild joy Laura fell upon her friend's breast.

"Ah! heavens! it is you! Oh! Tom, dear, dear Tom!"

"Hush, darling, walls have ears!" replied the boy, holding his beloved Laura in a passionate embrace.

But joy had overflowed her heart.

She was in a flood of tears.

"Calm dearest, calm yourself,' said Tom, "I must have speak with you, and it will require all your strength and nerve, my darling, to leave this cursed place. So cheer up. Courage, girl, courage It never failed you yet in the hour of trouble Never!"

"Oh! dear Tom, what terrible danger have you come into?'

"Fear not, for my sake, dearest; I would have dared three times as much to have saved you. None darling, but Heaven and myself, know what I have suffered since you have been taken from me.'

Laura clung more fondly to her gallant young lover than ever.

Drying her tears, she glanced up into his handsome face, then at his strange attire.

In spite of herself she could not help smiling.

The very idea of the terrible young outlaw, Midshipman Tom, whose very name was a terror, being dressed in female attire, would have amused her heartily.

But fear for her lover's safety drew the smile from her face.

"Oh! but, dear Tom, should you be discovered?"

"Why, darling, then—"

The princely boy shrugged his shoulder.

"S'death, I have no weapon yet; but I expect Snowball here."

"Here! Snowball, here!" reiterated Laura, in astonished exclamation. "Here."

"Yes, darling, here," replied the young outlaw chief. He then led his beloved Laura to a couch, and related what had occurred.

Laura listened, with flushed face and flashing eye to the recital of her noble lover's deeds of daring; and when he ceased she told him of all the dreadful sufferings she had gone through.

Midshipman Tom knitted his brows, and the dangerous gleam came in his dark, brilliant eye.

Laura knew the meaning of that terrible look upon the outlaw's face.

It meant mischief.

Hours thus glided by, and the reunited lovers were undisturbed, save by a dark attendant, who brought in refreshments.

CHAPTER CLVII.

SYBIL'S OATH.

THE judge lost his gravity when Sybil's words rang out, and leaning forward he said in a voice of strong excitement—

"Speak, Lord Mountsteven, and say how it is you appear among us in life."

There was a terrible struggle going on in the nobleman's breast.

The words trembled on his tongue that would criminate his wife and stain the honour of a proud family.

With this feeling there was one of strong pride.

A pride of caste, so inherent in the hearts of the old aristocracy.

He looked from his wife to Sybil, and mentally pondered whether he should bring an everlasting stain upon his escutcheon, by proclaiming the truth to save his own name from disgrace, and sacrifice Sybil.

"I can," it quickly passed through his brain, "save my name and rescue Sybil. After her conviction she will be inadequately guarded in her cell."

He had no long time to consider.

The judge's voice rang upon his ear, conjuring him to clear up the fearful mystery of the day.

"My lord!" he responded, "my appearance here is well calculated to excite your astonishment. You all believed me dead and I was so for a time. A trance had fallen upon my faculties and in that state I was buried."

Every ear was strained to catch his words.

"The prisoner," he continued, "as you are aware, has for some time dwelt among the tombs in the lonely disused chapel on my estate. She heard me move, and broke open my coffin."

It would be impossible to pourtray the feelings excited by this explanation among the lookers-on.

It was one of awe not unmixed with dread.

With Lady Mountsteven and Sybil it was quite different.

The guilty wife listened painfully for the words that would consign her to the scaffold; but as he proceeded the truth gleamed upon her mind.

She saw the motives that dictated his speech, and began to breathe freely.

Sybil listened with bated breath; and when the last words had fallen upon her startled senses she felt crushed by the weight of his seeming ingratitude.

But no sound escaped her firmly closed lips.

She felt her cause was lost, and listened for the final act in this strange scene.

The judge broke the solemn stillness that succeeded Lord Mountsteven's words.

"I have no wish," he said, "to ask you, my Lord, any questions that may be painful to you. If you would tell me how it is that your wife was not aware of your merciful preservation from the tomb."

Sybil's face shone with hope.

She thought Lord Mountsteven would have the truth wrung from him by the keen dispenser of the law.

His lordship reflected for a moment.

He was well aware that a single word would bring to the ground the fabric he had raised for preserving the family honour.

At length he spoke, and Sybil's heart sunk within her.

"Your question, my lord, shall be answered. When I left the chapel to return to the castle, I, as you may be aware, was compelled to cross a narrow pathway in the rocks."

"I know the place well, Lord Mountsteven."

"It was night a night of more than ordinary darkness, and while I crossed the rocks I came suddenly upon a group of men who were bearing some heavy packages from a boat."

"Ha! outlaws?"

"One moment, my lord. They saw me by the glare of their torches, and probably mistaking me for a spy, seized and carried me off to their ship. When we were out at sea I found my captors were under the pay of the Young Pretender, and had been lending arms for the rebels. They carried me to sea, and I returned but yesterday.

"Thanks for your frankness, Lord Mountsteven, your explanation clear up everything."

"And," thought the baronet, "makes me a false perjurer. But the stake is worth the crime—the honour of an old family must be preserved."

The judge again addressed Lord Mountsteven—

"You of course, heard the charge made against your lady?"

"I did," was the calm response; "a charge I can easily account for by the relative positions they occupy here."

"Precisely. Now, woman, have you any more malignant charges to make, or has the utter refutation this one has received taken the venom from your tongue?"

Sybil stood for a moment, her grey eyes fixed upon Lord Mountsteven.

There was a world of reproach in that mute appeal, and the quivering of her lips showed but too plainly the silent agony within.

She heeded not the words of the dignitary of the law, but in a voice full of touching pathos, she said—

"You have nobly done your part, Lord Mountsteven—well has the hand that snatched you from the tomb been rewarded. But enough—this is the first act in the drama, that will soon close. I will keep your secret, peer of England; better that I should suffer than your honoured name become tarnished."

She turned then fixed her eyes upon the now triumphant face of Lady Mountsteven.

"With you," she said with bitter emphasis, "the triumph you have gained will be but short-lived. Beyond the seas there are witnesses that beheld your sacrilegious hands tear my babe from my grasp when I lay senseless from the coward stroke of your stiletto."

The judge made an impatient gesture for her to be silent.

"A few words, my lord, and you can do your duty. Lord Mountsteven," she added, "I tell thee the hour is nigh when my child shall come to the heart that so long has yearned for it—then, woman, remember! My words shall lay bare every black act in your past sinful life. There shall be witnesses that have no family honour to enthral them, whose tongues shall speak the truth, and you shall stand in the felon's dock, where I now stand, your heart and brain scorching by the hideous details of your vile guilt, while the populace shall tear you limb from limb, and cheat the gallows of its due. This shall be my task—then shall I be avenged. Grant it, thou blessed Virgin!"

Sybil seemed like one inspired, as this fearful speech came from her lips, and Lady Mountsteven stood cowed, shrinking and aghast at the fearful picture that was conjured before her vision.

"Now, my lord," said Sybil to the judge, "do your office."

Her whole appearance seemed to change as she thus addressed his lordship.

The mystic look passed away, and there was a quiet irony in her manner that puzzled the spellbound crowd.

"The law," began the judge, "must take its course in this matter. You will receive for your atrocious crime the penalty of death. Had not such malignity marked your conduct in trying to fix a fearful charge upon the lady who has appeared against you, I should have recommended you to mercy. As it is, you will hang by the neck until you are dead, and may the Lord have mercy on your soul!"

As the last word left the judge's lips, Sybil gave a defiant laugh, and hurling a bottle in the centre of the court, there arose a dense body of stifling vapour, and Sybil, in the confusion, escaped from the bar.

"What is that report?"

The question was put by several voices simultaneously in a group of persons who, not having been able to gain admission to the court during the trial, were waiting outside to hear the verdict.

In an instant a rush was made to the court.

And what a scene presented itself!

The screams of fainting women, and the shouts of terrified men, were gradually dying away, becoming powerless by the effects of the stupefying vapour, while those who had not been overcome by its influence, were in deadly encounter in their endeavours to reach the doors.

Suddenly they flew open, and every window was uplifted.

The sight paralyzed the beholders.

Strong men were there, grouped in huddled heaps, and deadly embraces, as they had fallen overcome by the powerful chemical.

Women, as they clung to their husbands, their brothers, and their lovers, in their frantic horror!

And then again, giving increasing woe to the sickening spectacle, the felon's dock was covered with lurid flame, the dry woodwork supplying ample food for the greedy destroyer.

To add to its mystery, the form of Sybil, the witch of the tomb, had disappeared.

The weird woman had escaped from her custodians, who, engaged in the laudable purpose of assisting to carry the senseless forms of the stricken crowd beyond the reach of the fire, had totally forgotten their prisoner.

Mingled with the glare of the red sunset, a vast column of smoke and sheets of flame shot beyond the sky.

The roof of the hall of justice had fallen in, and when the shadow of night came upon the earth, all that remained of the ruined piles were a few charred embers and the blackened walls.

Little marvel that all spoke of Sybil with panting breath and pale cheeks, and when they thought of her threats to the proud Lady of Mountsteven, the modest cottager would not have changed places with the rich and titled lady.

They felt she would return—a feeling that was the herald of the mystic woman's re-appearance in another guise among them.

She had sworn revenge, and that oath was to be kept.

CHAPTER CLVIII.

AN UNWELCOME VISITOR.

TOM MORDAN crushed the missive in his hand, and hurled it away among the thick undergrowth.

"Fate," he said, "gives that man the victory, but unless I err, even though he may procure the wealth, I shall live to conquer when success to him seems most certain.

"Yes! Yes! Then like a shadow from the grave will I cross his path, push the cup from his lips, and wreak such a vengeance, that he shall curse the mother that brought him into the world—ha!"

He turned as the exclamation fell from his lips.

A powerful, half-naked Indian was creeping slowly towards him.

Tom perceived the savage, knife in hand.

The redskin carried a rifle in his hand, and stuck through his belt was a keen-edged tomahawk.

Tom saw at a glance his inferiority in means of defence, and skipping lightly backward, waited for the redskin's approach.

The savage leant upon the muzzle of his rifle, and scanned Mordan from head to foot.

When his scrutiny had finished, he threw the piece over his shoulder, and uttered a loud—

"Waugh!"

Tom Mordan was not deceived by the Indian's amicable manner.

There was something in the furtive look which he cast around that led the castaway to believe the Indian suspected there were more of the brutal white men about the lonely spot.

Whatever were the Indian's thoughts, he turned abruptly away, and disappeared in the entangled brushwood.

Tom Mordan listened to the crackling of the bushes until he imagined the savage had passed far away from the shore; then replacing his knif in his belt, he turned, and walked swiftly in an opposite direction.

"My life," Tom Mordan thought, "will not be worth much should that fellow return. I must go further inland, and seek a better sheltering-place than this."

He walked until he came to a high range of hills.

"This," he said, half aloud, "seems better. Up there, among the clefts in the hills, I can find a secure resting-place, and the cocoanut trees will find me in food."

As he ascended the steep incline, the rushing sound of falling water fell upon his ears.

Tom paused.

The twilight was fast deepening, and he feared that an incautious step would hurl him into the foaming cataract which rushed between a mighty cleft beneath.

He crept on his hands and knees, and went slowly forward.

Soon he came to the edge of a deep abyss.

Beneath this the mountain torrent swept with a noise like distant thunder.

Long the castaway gazed at the sublime spectacle of nature's grandeur—gazed until the fall of a stone and a few pieces of earth caused him to turn his head.

That dislodgment of loose earth saved his life.

Twenty feet above the spot where he crouched, he beheld the dusky form of the redskin who came suddenly upon him near the sea shore.

Despite Tom Mordan's natural bravery, a cold shudder passed over him when he saw the savage peering over the edge, as though in search of something.

Tom's heart began to beat fiercely.

So long as he remained under the jutting piece of earth he was safe—no longer.

Never for a moment taking his eyes from the dusky form, he stepped quickly back and drew his knife.

That the redskin was on his trail, he felt certain.

He felt certain, also, that should his form become visible, a bullet from the long-barrelled rifle would place him beyond the hope of wreaking his revenge on Wirely.

It soon became evident that the twilight rendered the spot where he hid safe from the Indian's greedy eyes.

The savage looked long and searchingly for a trace of him, and then began to slowly descend.

Mordan nerved himself for what he felt would be a death struggle, and crouching like a panther, he waited for the moment that would bring his foe within his reach.

The time came.

The stealthy tread was visible to the anxious listener.

Then he could distinguish the rifle muzzle held forward ready, evidently, for slaying him whenever he might put in an appearance.

Compressing his lips, he waited until the redskin was within two feet of where he lay.

Then, with swift and deadly spring and fiery nerve, he seized the savage by the throat.

By this sudden act the rifle was rendered useless, and the foe fought long and desperately to grasp his tomahawk.

Silently and for a considerable time the death-embrace continued, but the Englishman's grasp of iron never relaxed its grip.

And vain were the efforts his enemy made to shake him off.

So with the mutual determination to slay in their hearts, they struggled on with murderous pertinacity.

At last they reached the edge of a precipice, whence the eye would daze and the heart quail to look from even in the hour of quiet and imagined security, but in this deadly hour of strife, the position was positively horrifying.

Each saw it plainly, a moment's advantage to one was certain death to his antagonist.

It is done.

Tom Mordan's knife is raised, and finds a sheath in his adversary's breast.

The Indian gave no cry, but the grasp which would have pushed Tom over the abyss relaxed, and he fell beside his panting conqueror.

Tom stooped over the bleeding form, and possessed himself of the rifle and tomahawk.

Then the leather bag which carried the powder and shot were taken from the Indian, which Mordan fastened to his own waist.

"And now," said Tom, "I am thus far released from the fate my enemy had consigned me to. That whelp there shall be left to his fate. This rifle will protect me in future, and shall procure me sustenance."

Tom left the Indian for dead, and quitted the scene of the deadly encounter with a flash in his dark eyes, and a step and mien that seemed to defy fate and the malignity of foes.

CHAPTER CLIX.
THE DISCOVERY.

THE hour seemed to fly like minutes to Midshipman Tom, as he sat in a wild transport of joy with his beloved Laura clasped to his heart.

They were in this attitude when the door was cautiously opened, and a woolly head was thrust in the aperture.

Midshipman Tom caught sight of the grinning face.

"Snowball," he exclaimed.

"Hush! Massa Tom," said the dusky lieutenant, gliding into the room.

An exclamation of intense surprise escaped the African's lips as he beheld Laura, and bowing, he said—

"Oh! Miss Laura, Snowball am glad to see em pretty face again."

Laura rose, and gave Snowball her hand.

He took it in his own sable palm, and kissed it with the ardent love a father would upon recovering a lost child.

"How came you here?" asked Tom, smiling.

Snowball securely fastened the door, then replied, in a lower tone—

"De Bey send for dis child, and he make haste here, but he hab no chance of seeing you here until de Bey am called away."

"He! he! den Snowball put de dam——beg em pardon, Miss Laura, us mean de copper-coloured retch out of window, den dis child take him place. Yah!"

And Snowball chuckled with delight.

"That is all very well, Snowball, but how are we to get from here?"

"Easy enuff, Massa Tom."

"Pray explain."

"Why, walk out, Massa Tom."

Massa Tom thought this very impracticable.

Laura smiled.

"You no do dat, sar."

"I think it almost impossible, Snowball."

"Why, Massa Tom?"

"Because walking out of this place is much more easily to be talked about than effected, especially when unarmed."

Snowball's ebony face relaxed into a broad grin.

"Wait a minute, sar—um come back soon."

With that the faithful fellow retired from the presence of the wondering pair.

In a few minutes he returned, bringing with him a small bundle, out of which he handed his beloved young chieftain a pair of pistols, beautifully mounted, and ready for use.

Then he handed the noble boy his terrible scimitar, and lastly, a gold-laced jacket to throw over his shoulders.

Midshipman Tom's joy knew no bounds.

He was enraptured.

"Where?—how can you possibly have obtained these?" inquired Tom.

Snowball grinned.

"Dis chile arrange all dat."

"Still, to me it remains a mystery."

"Why, sar, Ben am not far off—he bring me word if der is a row a blue-jacket will bring de boys to de rescue."

"Thanks! a thousand thanks to you, my brave and thoughtful Snowball," replied Tom, warmly, almost overcome by his thankfulness.

"You take dem tings off, Massa Tom."

"Yes, Snowball; and if you knew how I feel in them, you would know how glad I am to do so."

"Um don't wonder, sar," replied Snowball, arranging his pistols and knife, which were in his belt, beneath his white linen blouse.

"Now for it," said Tom, removing his curls, &c.

"Aha! wat dat, Massa Tom?" exclaimed the African, holding his head in the attitude of carefully listening.

Tom listened too.

Then arose suddenly a great noise and hubbub.

The shouts of men, rushing of feet, the clank of arms, and lastly and most important, the tramp of soldiers.

"We are discovered," muttered the dauntless boy, between his teeth. "Now, Snowball, for a resistance worthy the words emblazoned on our banner—No Surrender."

"Dat's so; but it am dat fellow I chucked out ob de winder ab kicked up all dis noise," said Snowball, as he grasped the handle of his terrible battle-axe.

He was right in his conjecture.

The guard he had unceremoniously thrown from one of the lattice windows had recovered his senses, and was about to rouse the guards, when Zaima came up, looking wild and haggard.

The fellow lost no time in acquainting him with what had occurred.

"Ah! ah! The infidels have come unto death. Curse them!" he hissed, his eyes fiercely blazing.

He instantly called the guards to arms, and sent for the Bey.

"What?" he thundered, "have the cursed dog dared to come here? By the Great Spirit, they shall be slain! Follow me."

The guards followed close to his heels.

And he dashed through the corridors, his scimitar bare and flashing in his hand.

He dashed open the doors of the room in which the supposed Rosaline was.

He started back with a cry of horror and fear.

Standing demoniac and terrible, his fearful instrument of death—the axe—raised, was Snowball waiting for them.

Midshipman Tom was by his side.

Not as Rosaline, but as chief of the daring outlaws.

His lithe, graceful form drawn to its full height, was encased in a most magnificent suit of silver-laid mail, showing off in all their splendour his broad expansive chest and sinewy limbs.

A small gold-laced jacket was thrown over his shoulders, and a silver sash encircled his waist, in which was placed a handsome pair of pistols.

His long glittering scimitar was gripped in his strong and delicate hand; his left arm encircled Laura's waist.

"Come on," he cried hotly, "come, hoary-headed old wretch! Lead on your men, ah, ah! I am prepared; ah, ah! and now, old scoundrel what do you think of your rosebud?"

The boy was mad with fury.

His guards shrank back appalled.

Tom and his trusty officer took a step forward.

The guards wavered.

They did not care to face the terrible young outlaw and his gigantic lieutenant a second time.

THE ENGAGEMENT.

A smile of scorn lighted up the young chieftain's face.

"Back!" he cried, "stop me who dares!" and he strode forward.

Snowball was at his side.

The soldiers began to give way.

The Bey saw it.

Stamping his foot in fury, he yelled like a madman, and shouted to his guards—

"Shoot him! shoot him through the head! move a step if you dare, and by Allah I ll cut you down!"

The oriental guards paused

A moment after they were rallying round their aged chief, bringing their long barrelled weapons to bear upon the dauntless boy.

"Cover the girl with your rifles! shoot her too. Through the heart if you are able, if the cursed infidels attempt to move!' was the murderous order given by the enraged Bey.

"Ah! ha!" he shouted in triumph. "Die dogs of the unbelievers!—Fire!'

Snowball sprang forward with a yell like a savage beast.

Then came the sharp ring of musketry.

A wild piercing shriek from Laura, as the noble African staggered forward and fell prone at the feet of Midshipman Tom.

CHAPTER CLX.

REVENGE.

MIDSHIPMAN TOM, the brave princely fellow, whose gallant unyielding nature knew no fear, and whose daring deeds had made his name a terror, was slightly unnerved by the fearful danger that menaced his beloved Laura when the merciless Bey gave orders to fire.

He leaped aside from the deadly range of the long barrelled weapons as they vomited forth a livid sheet of flame.

He saw the sable African bound like a tiger before the form of Laura, as the leaden missiles clattered against his armour.

He heard the sharp cry of agony, and beheld his faithful officer roll at his feet senseless and bleeding.

The bullet that was intended for the heart of Laura having struck Snowball upon the temple, causing him to fall like a piece of lead to the carpeted floor.

But the death-dealing missiles that were meant for the head of the invincible young chieftain did not reach the mark, through the gallant boy springing aside in time to get from the range.

A cry of heart-rending anguish escaped his lips as the noble African fell apparently dead, then clutching the now senseless form of Laura, he sprang like a young demon forward.

The guards advanced to cut him down. All the wild relentless blood in his unflinching nature became aroused.

Like one gifted with supernatural power he vaulted forth.

His terrible lion-heart swelled with the wild fury of a revenge his soul was burning to gratify.

Pitiless! Merciless!

Such was the outlaw chief.

"Curse them!" he hissed; "they wanted blood and carnage—they shall have it."

With eyes blazing like a hungry panther's, he put his scimitar between his teeth, and drawing a pistol, took steady aim and fired.

The foremost man fell with a cry—dead. The fierce young chieftain laughed like a fiend.

Another deadly weapon he drew forth.

Another guard fell, his brains blown out—head shattered.

"Slay him! Cut him down!" vociferated the Bey, himself rushing upon our hero.

A mocking laugh came from the infuriated boy.

Clutching his pistol by the muzzle, he dashed the butt-end against the brow of his antagonist.

The Bey gave a scream, and reeling back fell into the arms of one of his soldiers.

"Ah! ah!" cried Midshipman Tom, his staunch scimitar flashing in the air. "Ah! ah! Cut me down! Come on, ye cutthroat infidels! Death to him who bars my way!"

The guards stood aghast; Tom appeared to them as a demi-god, or an avenging angel.

No one ventured to approach his mail-clad figure.

But suddenly Zaima appeared amongst them, his sallow crafty face working convulsively with fierce revengeful passions, burning for revenge.

"Dogs!" he cried to the guards, "dogs, would ye fly from one man? Cut him down! Re-load your arms! Ah! ah! I will see if the pale-face dog of the infidels will escape Zaima."

He meant destruction.

Tom saw it.

He meant destruction too.

But as he stepped forward to cut the taunting Moslem to the ground, he found himself opposed by a bright gleaming scimitar.

It was that of the Bey, who stood before him, his face besmeared with blood, his eyes flashing in baffled fury upon the young outlaw king.

He made a terrible lunge at the noble boy's neck.

Tom parried his thrust with his own terrible blade, and would have clove the hoary old sinner in twain had not Zaima slashed at our hero with a long rapier.

Seeing the chief thus battling with the stalwart foe, the guards gathered up their courage and took part in the unequal strife.

The outlaw chief was then opposed by a score of thirsty blades.

Wildly he fought—bravely.

Like a meteor his well-tried sword leapt round, flashing lightning from side to side.

In its terrific sweep the foremost blades of his opponents were knocked down like reeds.

Two fell, their bodies headless and nearly in twain.

Still he could not hold out much longer.

Encumbered as he was by the inanimate form of Laura, he found it hard work to act upon the defensive.

And, but for the armour that shielded him in this he must have been hacked to pieces.

As it was, his head and neck required guarding. This he could have done easily enough, or he could have cut his way through his opponents as easily, but the senseless form of Laura Gray required his care and attention.

The Bey cut and slashed at him in wild frenzy, he foamed at the mouth with hate, rage, and pain, thus to see the bold young Englishman hold out against such sweeping odds.

Zaima, too, saw how uselessly they had combined to slay him.

But the crafty villain, Zaima, had sworn to have revenge—and it should be a fearful one.

A diabolical idea suddenly entered his head.

He would madden the gallant Tom's sight by slaying Laura in his arms—that would give his master an opportunity to slay the invincible outlaw chieftain.

But such an awful tragedy was not destined to come off, though something even more horrible and unexpected did.

Zaima dashed forward with the foul intent of running his cut-and-thrust through the suffering girl's heart.

The young chief was fast tiring. It was impossible to hold out much longer, he thought.

He was likely to drop from sheer exhaustion. Large beads of sweat stood upon his brow, his face was pale and rigid, save from the blood that trickled from a gash in his face; his eyes were becoming bloodshot, and their dark, dangerous glitter was truly horrifying; his mouth was closed like a vice, and his untiring arm still kept the thirsty blades from drinking his life stream.

Never had he taken part in such an unequal conflict—such a murderous fray.

"How much longer will this dreadful fight last?" he thought.

Not long.

It had nearly arrived at its culminating point.

Midshipman Tom got his back against the wall, there he obtained some slight support, and also kept the guards from creeping behind.

The Bey could have had him shot down like a dog, but he did not want to harm the Rosebud.

Midshipman Tom began to flag.

The guards saw it, and made a simultaneous rush upon him, beat down his guard, and dashed the reeking scimitar from his hold.

The Bey uttered a loud exultant cry, and dashing his guards away, with a wild savage laugh, pinned our hero by the throat, and placed a pistol at his head.

Zaima at the same moment, blood-thirsty and fiendish, snatched Laura from the gallant midshipman's arm.

Tearing her dress open, he gave an awful unearthly laugh, and placed the point of a long gleaming dagger against her snow-white bosom.

Her fate seemed obvious to all.

A loud scream of heart-broken agony broke from Midshipman Tom when he saw the act.

The Bey paused.

With his finger on the trigger of his pistol held to the chieftain's head.

The guards stood gazing on in horror; casting the points of their spears upon the boy's heaving breast.

Madly he struggled to get away.

One hand he got free, and dealt his captor a terrific blow.

Again the Bey placed the pistol to the boy's mouth!

Zaima still held the dagger to Laura's breast.

The horrible death of each seemed certain.

The Bey's finger was already pressing the trigger.

But the struggle was stayed.

Without a moment's warning a fearful interceptor arises.

Accompanied by a loud horrifying yell, the assassin's arm was stopped, and the knife that threatened the heart's blood of the unfortunate Laura was dashed to the ground.

Then came a loud whiz, something huge and terrible flashed around.

One swift rapid circle it took.

Horrible!

Then came a sickening crash.

A *trunkless head* was hurled past the guards, bespattering their faces with blood.

On it went—on, as though sent forth from the mouth of a cannon, and dashed full in the face of the bewildered Bey.

With an unearthly screech he let go his hold; his pistol dropped to the floor.

He caught a full view of the distorted features—he knew the head then.

It was Zaima's.

The horrible tragedy was too much even for him

He gave a cry of horror and consternation at what his bloodshot eyes beheld.

Standing, drawn to his full height, his eyes blazing like living coals, his nostrils expanded, his large white teeth showing like the fangs of a panther, was Snowball.

Leaning one hand upon the handle of his mighty axe, which ran with blood, the other was supporting the senseless form of Laura.

Zaima's headless trunk lay at his feet.

Was he invulnerable, or was he a fiend?

He appeared to the affrighted guards as the personification of Satan.

Had he not been dead?

But the bullet that struck him down had merely stunned him, with prolonged effects, and he ultimately recovered, as though by Heaven's mission, to prevent a foul and cowardly murder.

Midshipman Tom staggered forward, but he could scarcely comprehend what had occurred.

He saw his brave officer.

He saw his darling Laura was saved, and her would-be assassin slain.

Snowball caught the youg chieftain in his arms and placed him on the carpeted floor.

Then he turned his dark-skinned form towards the soldiers.

The Bey gave him a look of malignant hate.

" Surrender ! or, by Allah, I will cut thee down ! "

The blood-stained axe was again seized.

The Bey gave an order to his guards to reload.

Snowball saw all hope was lost.

They should all be sacrificed.

An impulsive thought took sudden possession of his brain.

With as much coolness as the circumstances would allow him to assume, the better to disembarrass the guards of any suspicion of his intention, he walked to their front and stood face to face with the Bey—probably, the guards thought, to speak a word in token of surrender.

The plan succeeded.

In an instant, with a precision and quickness of action our pen is totally unable to describe, the axe gave one sweep round and descended on the head of the Bey, levelling him to the earth, apparently lifeless.

The suddenness and boldness of the attack unmanned the guards altogether.

They were mute, dumbfounded, as though awe-stricken.

They had been before appalled at Snowball's reappearance among them when they believed him to be dead.

They were now convinced he was supernatural—a messenger from the GREAT SPIRIT to avenge the misdeeds of the Bey, their master.

Snowball divined their helplessness aright.

It was not the agency of a *natural* fear that pervaded the breasts of such an overwhelming force.

It was the will of the GREAT SPIRIT.

And the occasion was quickly profited by— Snowball assisting Tom with one hand, and folding Laura tightly in the arm at liberty, made good their retreat.

Five minutes later, three ringing cheers told the bold young outlaw that Snowball, the talisman preserver of his life, and his beloved Laura, was safely in a boat being rowed back to the WAR CLOUD.

CHAPTER CLXI.

HUSBAND AND WIFE.

THE indulgent reader will now accompany us to Mountsteven Castle and its inmates—the lovely but unpitying mistress, who is seated in a listless attitude of deep meditation.

The trial and sudden disappearance of Sybil, and the return of Lord Mountsteven, totally prostrated, for a time, the energies of the lady.

The web she had been so nicely weaving to ensnare her enemies had suddenly broken, and left her in its meshes, from which it would require all her native craft and obduracy to extricate herself.

Lord Mountsteven had returned to the castle, but strictly kept to his study.

He glided from room to room like a statue, his noble features calm and rigid.

None, not the keenest observer, could have seen from his outward appearance the mental agony, the terrible grief in his breast, that rankled to his heart's core, and slowly, but surely, was bringing him to his grave.

He carefully shunned the presence of his guilty wife; his time seemed taken up in writing. He had formed a resolution.

It was this ominous silence, the fearful uncertainty, that kept Lady Mountsteven in constant trepidation.

She knew not how it was likely to end.

She sat, now, muttering to herself.

"I must—I will know the worst," were the faintly spoken words that left her lips.

"Aha!" she continued, "I will consult Mira."

A knock at the door caused her to start.

A servant entered, and stood in a cringing attitude before the proud beauty.

"Your message," she said, haughtily.

"Lord Mountsteven, my lady, wishes an interview. He waits your ladyship in his study."

The haughty woman waved her hand.

The servant retired.

"At last!" she muttered, between her set teeth, and calming her excited features, she proceeded to Lord Mountsteven's chamber.

She found her deeply wronged husband sitting before a table covered with writing materials.

He glanced wearily up as her ladyship entered —a look of pain came upon his pale, wan face.

Not the slightest notice did he take of his guilty wife.

Motioning her to be seated, he continued his occupation.

Lady Mountsteven, with flashing eyes and compressed lips, declined the proffered seat. She stood bold and defiant, waiting for her husband to speak.

There was an embarrassing pause.

Lord Mountsteven's eyes were still bent on the documents before him, but he did not move.

He seemed like one in a sleep.

Perhaps it was to hide the convulsive twitching of his mouth, and the look of deep anguish that overspread his rigid features.

There was a terrible conflict going on in that strong man's heart.

He dared not trust himself to speak.

Lady Mounsteven stamped her tiny foot on the carpeted floor.

She was growing impatient—her husband's strange conduct unnerved her.

"Lord Mounsteven, you sent for me?" she said, unable to bear the suspense any longer.

"I did."

The reply came in a hollow, sepulchral tone.

Lady Mountsteven trembled.

Her cheeks paled—her bosom heaved and fell, and it was with difficulty she could still the beat of her guilty heart.

Bad, wicked as she was, she could not look upon that pale, sad face, her own evil work, without a shudder.

"Lady Mountsteven," began his lordship, and his voice, solemn and passionless, sounded ominously upon the cowering woman's ears, "I, as the master of this ancestral pile, sent for you; it was my duty so to do."

There was a slight pause.

Lady Mountsteven stood mute, wondering what was coming next.

"I have summoned you," he said, "that I might inform you of my final decision."

He paused as though expecting a reply, which he did not receive, so he resumed—

"I intend closing the castle, never again to return until the fearful stigma, the awful disgrace that hangs over a once proud family is forgotten. I cannot, dare not remain where I can be pointed out by the finger of scorn. You will return to your native land; I shall well provide for you. For myself, I shall seek forgetfulness and death in some distant clime, that I may pass from this world unknown."

Lady Mountsteven trembled with intense despair and disappointment.

She knew by the tone in which he spoke that he was determined.

The hot blood mounted to her olive cheek—all her natural passion returned.

Her look was one of fiendish hatred, and she replied—"Never!"

Lord Mountsteven rose from his chair, and strode rapidly across the room.

His sombre, quiet air vanished, and a look of stern determination sat upon his angered countenance.

He faced his crime-stained wife.

"Woman!" he faid, in fierce accents, "for I cannot again call you wife—I am Lord Mountsteven, master of this now disgraced edifice, and will have my own way!

"Henceforth there is but one master, and he is Lord Mountsteven."

He ceased speaking—his eyes flashed dangerously.

Lady Mountsteven shrank from his burning gaze.

She was dumb with amazement.

The alteration in her lord was as startling as unexpected.

"You," he continued, more fiercely than before, "you, vile traitress, are the cause of the disgrace and shame that has fallen upon me, and yet you dare think to remain here to pollute me with your presence. Ah! ah! ah! hear me."

Lord Mountsteven gave a horrible grating laugh.

His fingers worked nervously as though he could have strangled the beautiful demon, who stood with pale cheeks and quivering lips before the enraged nobleman.

"Where!" he cried, "is my poor innocent wife? Where is my boy? Cold pitiless, murderess. What have you done with them? Ah, you shrink back; your cheek pales at that, but I will find them. Yes find them, and place them in their defrauded rights. Yes, and you—you, ah! ah! shall no longer remain under the roof that is tainted with your crimes."

Lord Mountsteven seemed to have lost his senses.

There was an awful glare in his eyes, a crimson spot upon his cheek, and a foaming gathered around his mouth.

Lady Mountsteven trembled from head to foot, but all her evil passions were aroused. She saw how matters stood—the fearful abyss that was yawning at her feet.

She determined to throw off the mask and dare the worst.

"Listen, Lord Mountsteven; you dare not do hat you threaten."

"Dare not, madam! Ah! ah! I will do worse!"

"If I refuse to accede to your will?"

Lord Mountsteven's face became pale as marble, the look in his eye was deadly and menacing, as he hissed between his teeth—

"Then you die!"

The dusky cheek of the bold woman paled.

"Ah! ah! would Lord Mountsteven turn assassin?"

His lordship shivered.

"No; you should die a more disgraceful death. You should terminate your existence on a scaffold, surrounded by a scoffing crowd of brutal vagrants, who would grin at your death struggles, and laugh with glee as the last sigh escaped your lips. Such, vile woman, once the wife of a peer, should be your ignominious death. Dare you thwart me?"

Lady Mountsteven could scarcely stand, she reeled against the wall and clutched a chain for support.

The horrible death, pictured by her husband, rose vividly before her heated imagination.

The thought was torture to her proud nature.

Recovering herself, she replied, viciously—

"Lord Mountsteven forgets the disgrace that would follow."

"That I should not care for, I should have done my duty."

"You dare not, Lord Mountsteven, were you to give me over to the law, you would never leave this castle gate, and you would live a life of perpetual ignominy; you would become an object to be pointed at with loathsome disgust, and by the *plebeian*, who would rejoice in the downfall of a *once* noble race. Ah! ah! Lord Mountsteven, I defy you."

"You deceive yourself, madam. I should leave England, as I told you before, and pass the rest of my unhappy existence in some far off clime; and should there be no heir to claim the dishonoured property, it can go to the Crown. So you see, unscrupulous woman, it will depend upon yourself, whether you go from here to your native land or the scaffold."

"Such is your decision, Lord Mountsteven?" said her ladyship, with a terrible calmness, and her dark, brilliant orbs shone like a panther's.

"It is," was the laconic reply.

"Very well, my lord, do as you will. I trust you will give me time to consider."

"Until I have completed my arrangements," replied Lord Mountsteven, coldly.

Lady Mountsteven gave him a look of bitter hate.

"As you will, my lord," she responded, and retired.

Lady Mountsteven's aspect went through a complete transformation as she strode rapidly through the corridor.

There was a wicked glitter in her eyes; her hands were tightly clenched, and any one passing the crime-stained woman might have heard the grating of her teeth.

She made a deadly resolve.

Her pitiless nature was fully aroused.

Her crafty brain was plotting more red work.

Again she was thinking of murder.

Summoning Margerie, she returned to her boudoir, followed by her accomplice.

"Lock the door," she said, entering the room, and throwing herself upon a couch in rage and despair.

Margerie saw something unexpected had occurred.

"Madam is ill?" she said.

But Madam was not, only in ill-temper.

She told Margerie so.

"Has my lady seen his lordship?" interrogated Margerie.

Lady Mountsteven shot on angry glance at her serving woman, and said in the most vicious manner possible—

"I have."

Margerie felt satisfied.

"Madam does not seem pleased," she said, harshly.

Madam glared at her savagely.

"Quiet that noisy tongue of yours," she replied, pettishly.

"I thought my lady wished to speak with me. I ask madam's pardon," said Margerie, rising and going towards the door.

She could be very provoking when she liked.

She had a quick way of getting people out of temper.

It was an outward nonchalance, behind which lurked a subtle, deadly malice.

One to be feared.

Lady Mountsteven, with all her native craft, had a match in Margerie, though she did not know it.

"I did want you," she said, angered by the other's cool insolence.

Margerie returned and took a seat.

Lady Mountsteven sat tapping her tiny foot upon the floor.

She was meditating.

And what was she meditating?

One of the most awful crimes—murder.

Her husband was to be the victim.

"Margerie," she said, leaving her table and speaking with unpleasant calmness.

It meant mischief.

"Listen, Margerie, I have seen him. Ah! ah! and he has dared to threaten me!"

Margerie looked as though anyone threatening her mistress surprised her.

Lady Mountsteven continued—

"He has dared to say I must be turned out like a beggar, or he will——"

She paused, as though overcome with the audacity of the threat.

"Will what, my lady?" asked the woman.

"Have me HANGED!"

Margerie started.

This did somewhat surprise her.

The demoniacal look that came upon Lady Mountsteven's face showed the intensity of her passion.

"Can you not dissuade him from such a step?"

"I have tried."

"And the result?"

"He laughed in my face, and repeated his threat."

Margerie knitted her brows.

"He has given you time to consider?" she asked.

"No. I am to be prepared any moment he may take it in his mad brain to start me. I am to be thrust from the door like a dog, and return like a vagrant to my native land."

"And he?"

"And he," Lady Mountsteven iterated, "has an insane idea of closing the castle, leaving England, and searching after his lost brat, whom he will never find. Then he intends dying in some unknown land."

"But in the event of him not finding the heir?"

He will turn his immense property over to the Crown," hissed Lady Mountsteven through her clenched teeth. "But it must not be; it shall not," continued the beautiful demon."

"It would be a sin to allow such a thing to take place," said her companion, artfully.

Lady Mountsteven's lips curled in scorn.

"Why do you not say what you mean?" sneered Lady Mountsteven.

"Because it is not wise," thought Margerie.

But she said nothing.

She seemed thinking.

"Of course you do not intend this to take place?" she asked, breaking suddenly from her reverie.

"Why pretend such ignorance?" replied Lady Mountsteven, ironically. "You know I do not. And, Margerie, I want your aid and advice."

"I cannot advise," replied Margerie. "What are your ladyship's intentions?"

"Firstly," replied her ladyship, "he must not carry out his intentions. No! The estate shall be mine. Lord Mountsteven must die!"

Margerie's cheek paled, but she asked—

"Is he the only obstacle?"

"Ah! ah! Yes. Lady Sybil is dead. She will never stand in my path. Lord Mountsteven shall perish too——"

"But," interrupted Margerie, "the boy, the proofs."

"The boy is dead—all documents are destroyed. Ah! ah! There was a packet of papers, the only written records of my guilt, and proved the boy's identity, and they are——"

"HERE!" said a sepulchral voice.

Lady Mountsteven leaped around.

Margerie gave a scream.

Each looked in the direction of the window.

Both recoiled with a simultaneous cry of alarm.

There, quiet and motionless, with the pale moonbeams faintly shining upon its sable garments, stood in the recess a cloaked figure, and the utterer of those ominous words.

A chill fell upon the two guilty beings.

It seemed to have come like a dark and terrible warning.

Still and motionless the figure stood, as though carved from a solid stone.

The dark, glittering eyes were fastened with an awful look upon the would-be murderess of

MIDSHIPMAN TOM NAILS HIS COLOURS TO THE MAST.

Lord Mountsteven, and the women slowly left the room.

The cloaked figure followed them down the corridor, then turned and left the castle; a moment after the lady and her accomplice strolled forth, each armed with a keen stiletto, the light of murder in their eyes.

CHAPTER CLXII.
THE FATE OF RED HAND.

RED HAND, the Pirate, exulted in the possession of the ship whose captain had taken him from the raft.

The evil disposed of the crew were only too ready to join the miscreant, but, bad as they were, they would not seize the ship until Red Hand promised them that the captain and such of their shipmates who were not to be corrupted, should not be in any way molested.

The tiger was compelled to forego his desire for blood, and inwardly promising his future crew a life that would alter their sentiments, he said—

"Let it be so; we will put them and the captain ashore on the first island, then hurrah for the black flag."

That night the ship was seized, and the captain and his faithful seamen put in irons.

A couple of days' sail brought them to within gun-shot of an island, then the captain and about twenty men were put ashore.

The boat was about to leave the beach when a man emerged from the bushes, and accosting Red Hand, said—

"Will you take me aboard?"

The speaker was a strong built man, and the pirate, after scanning him for a few moments, asked—

"What is your name?"

"Tom Mordan."

"Well, look here, Mister Tom Mordan, if you like to come aboard I'll take you."

"But I am no seaman."

"You can use a musket or a knife, I suppose?"

"I can."

"You'll do then, jump in."

"Where are you bound for, captain?"

"England first," said Red Hand, "then where-ever the wind may take us."

"You are going to England. I am your man."

Tom Mordan took a seat in the boat, and as he passed to the ship he muttered—

"Messrs. Wirely and Son will not be pleased at the visitor they will soon behold."

Tom worked with a will, and before he had been many days aboard he disarmed the pirate leader's suspicions, for he looked upon the cast-away as a man who would soon be a useful member of the band.

It was Tom Mordan's watch on the foretop, and he had not been long at his post when a sail became visible in the distance.

He gave the signal to the captain, who at once brought his glass to bear upon the stranger.

"That whelp, Midshipman Tom," growled the pirate; "he has saved me a journey to England."

The order was given to the men to stand to their guns, and when the War Cloud was within range a broadside was poured into her.

"Nice way ob speaking to a friend, Massa Tom," said Snowball, "and dam if I not think dat de debbil Red Hand on de poop."

"It is. Bear up alongside and carry the ship by boarding."

Unused to the work, the whaler's crew were swept back by Tom's veterans, and in ten minutes the ship was theirs, except the poop; there Red Hand and half-a-dozen rascals stood at bay.

There would have been a struggle to have captured the pirates had not Tom Mordan suddenly turned upon his chief and levelled him to the deck with a handspike.

Our hero and Tom Mordan met on the whaler's deck, and in a few words their mutual explanations took place.

"Thank God!" said Tom, "you have found the daughter of my old friend; now there is but one mission of vengeance to fulfil."

"That, Mr. Mordan?"

"To wrest her property from the Wirelys, and hand them over to justice.

"It would," said Tom, "be a better plan to send them to the Island."

"True, my young friend, but of that anon. Now—pointing to Red Hand—what shall we do with this fellow?"

"Consign him to the gallows," our hero said. "Snowball! come this way."

"Yes, Massa Tom."

"Look to the safety of this miscreant."

"Tink," said Snowball, feeling the bone handle of his knife, "I better calp him, make sure of his hair den, any how."

"No, Midshipman Tom said, "we will place him in the hands of the law when we reach England."

"Berry well, Massa Tom, what you say is right. And tell you what, he not get away dis time."

He did not; and as our story is drawing to a close we have but to add, that our hero handed the miscreant over to the authorities, and the crew of the War Cloud were permitted to be present at the execution of Derrick, for the Lord High Admiral was very grateful to the men who had rid the ocean of such a monster. Furthermore, the merchants of England subscribed for and gave our hero a sword of honour, and the crew a handsome sum of money.

Not satisfied with this, the authorities and the merchants got up a petition to the King to pardon the noble boy, and the whole of England ringing with the exploit, which will be found in the next chapter, the petition was graciously received.

CHAPTER CLXIII

TOM NAILS HIS COLOURS TO THE MAST.

BEFORE the War Cloud reached their old anchorage off the coast of England, a large and newly armed corvette was seen, the tricolour of France flaunting at her stern.

Tom run up the Union Jack in defiance, and turning to Mr. Mordan and Snowball, said—

"There is a prize in view that will tax all our powers to capture, and if we succeed I think I may safely reckon upon receiving the royal pardon for my misdeeds."

"Then you propose giving up your wild life?"

"For the present, Mr. Mordan, there is one in the cabin below who demands my care, and I am also resolved to prosecute the search for my father, this done I shall offer my services to the Government."

"Who," Mr. Mordan said, "will accept if only for bringing the miscreant Red justice."

"This ship," said Tom, "is of more consequence than the pirate, for it is the celebrated French cruiser, L'Aigle, who has been for the last two years the terror of our merchant vessels, and so well is she commanded that none of our cruisers have as yet been able to cope with her single-handed."

"Yet you are rash enough to make the attempt."

"I must, she's bearing down upon me, and the War Cloud never yet declined the gauge of battle. Snowball."

"Here, Massa Tom."

"Get the men to quarters, then take the helm; we must work close in shore, for our only chance is to take the wind from this fellow."

It was a desperate manœuvre for the place abounded in sunken reefs, that the boldest mariner would have shunned, yet it must be made or the French Corvette would not only have an advantage in size, guns, and men, but the wind in her favour.

The Corvette saw the War Cloud's design, and tacked on every inch of canvas to prevent it being carried out.

Tom with compressed lips stood in the bows, giving directions to Snowball, whose muscular hands grasped the spokes of the wheel.

Several dangerous places had been passed, and the young chief's heart began to beat joyfully, but a sudden gust of wind struck the vessel out of her course, and she struck upon a reef.

Snowball gave a howl of despair, and rushed below to see what damage had been done.

here was a deep silence on board, and every eye was anxiously watching for the appearance of Snowball.

When his curly head re-appeared above the deck their anxiety ceased—the African's face heralded good news.

"Safe for de present, Massa Tom," he said. De piece of rock broke like a carrot, and now stick in the hole it make."

The welcome news was received by a lusty shout from the outlaws, and with one accord they ran to the guns to prepare for their foe.

The young chief's gallant heart, that had been sinking with a feeling of dread and anxiety, now filled with joy, and fixing his dark eagle eye upon the approaching war vessel, he said—

"Keep the carpenters below to watch the damage until we get clear from this fellow."

The order was passed, and now every face was turned towards the corvette.

The appearance of the vessel was well calculated to draw from the young chieftain's lips many an ejaculation of admiration.

A stiff breeze began to agitate the water, raising white crests upon the waves, and to those on the War Cloud's deck these signs were the precursors of a rough gale.

Scorning the danger that lurked beneath the white-topped wave, the corvette held her course direct upon the little vessel, which had by this time spread her sails to the wind.

The corvette held her head as close to the wind as the pyramid of white waves she carved would allow.

The young chief bit his lips.

"That fellow," he said to Snowball, "is determined we shall not out-do him."

"So it 'pears, Massa Tom, but I tink we shall, and berry easy too."

"Then you imagine he will run foul of those rocks."

"Sartain ob it, Look at de sail he hab, and in dis wind, too. Him caught."

The young chief did not answer, and his pale face bore an expression of deep sorrow.

He felt sad at the thought of that noble ship and her gallant crew perishing upon the sunken rocks.

"Here him come," Snowball suddenly exclaimed, "dat am number one."

A white puff of smoke was seen upon the corvett's bows, and a shot came skipping from wave to wave, then disappeared half a fathom from the War Cloud's stern

The men stood grimly at their guns, and looked eagerly at their young leader, as though trying to read his dark, inscrutable face.

He remained with close lips, gazing at the banner of France, which hung at the corvette's mizen peak.

Another shot came.

The distance rapidly lessening, for the iron missile soared through the rigging, cutting away several of the back-stays.

Still no word came from the chieftain's compressed lips.

A slight murmur came from his crew.

The next shot might hit them, and they liked not to stand idly by the guns when the foe was within range.

The outlaw turned his gaze from the corvette, and bending his dark orbs upon the crew, he said sternly—

"Silence, there! The next man that murmurs shall be punished."

Every eye was turned towards the sea, each felt the stern rebuke.

It was no idler's threat upon the young leader's part.

In spite of the character of his ship he upheld a strict discipline among his men.

The corvette was soon plainly visible, and her double tier of dark gun muzzles could be seen run out ready for action.

Tom watched every movement narrowly, and when he saw top-gallant sails added to the already dangerous press of canvas his lips parted, and smiling he said—

"Saved!"

The speed of the man-of-war was terrific.

The waves rising before her prow were broken

and scattered into curling masses of white feathery foam which marked a white trail as she tore through the waters.

By the rising colour upon the young chieftain's face, and the blaze in his dark eye, it became evident to those that watched that index of his mind, that he was bracing his nerves for a bold effort to master his heavily-armed and dangerous foe.

The War Cloud up to this time had not moved forward more than three times her length, owing to the manner in which our hero had had the sails worked.

He had not answered the man-of-war, only had his silken banner been displayed in defiance to the tricolour.

The corvette had ceased firing after the second gun.

Her commander was evidently paralysed at the strange behaviour of the War Cloud.

He knew by repute her wondrous power of sailing, and feeling assured that the bold young outlaw was contemplating a move, crowded all sail to overtake him before he could put his design into execution.

By doing this he fell into the trap our hero, with sorrow on his heart, had set for him.

The corvette was rushing onward.

Onward to her doom.

The crew and officers could be seen upon her deck, evidently watching the little vessel as she rolled to and fro on the rising waters.

At last the moment came

The young chief's words rang out clarion-like, causing the ready crew to spring from the guns and rush to the ropes.

"Now," he cried, "round with the yards! Jam the wheel down hard—hard!"

The effect of these words acted with almost magical power upon the little vessel.

The white sails bellied out before the gale.

Her sharp prow was turned seaward, then like a startled deer she plunged forward turning the water aside in derision of her baffled foe.

The corvette's captain saw the manœuvre, and saw too that after all the rich prize would slip through his fingers.

Vainly he roared for his men to—

"Veer ship!"

Before the evolution could be performed a mighty crash was heard, and the foremast shivered like a reed and fell over the side.

When the crash was heard, those who were standing were hurled to the deck, and from amid the confused mass of wood and cordage men could be seen struggling to regain their feet.

The well-ordered deck of the French man-of-war presented a scene of indescribable confusion, a scene that soon changed to one of dread import, as a hundred voices shrieked aloud in their terror the fearful words—

"She has struck! Help! help! We are upon the sunken reef!"

The gallant commander's face for a moment paled, then became scarlet with rage, as he beheld the War Cloud gliding safely through the waters, the banner of England floating defiantly at her stern.

He saw this, then glared at his terror-stricken crew, who in the first moments of their deadly fear, were running about the decks in all the frenzy caused by the fear of a sudden and unexpected death.

He saw all this, and knew how brave men are, when thus suddenly brought face to face with a terrible danger, apt to loose all power of self-control.

In such moments it is that a calmer, though not braver mind, can restore the temporary loss of reflection.

The captain saw his danger, heard the affrighted cries of the men, and seizing his trumpet, he shouted in a voice that could be heard high above the shouts of frenzy—

"Beat to quarters—beat to quarters!"

The drummer a lad scarcely fourteen years of age, stopped suddenly in a prayer for his mother, whom he never thought to behold again, and seizing the drum, struck out the well-known signal.

"Again," shouted the captain, "and those who are not at their stations before the last tap of the drum, by the eternal, I'll give them a dozen if the ship went to pieces at the time."

CHAPTER CLXIII.

THE LAST.

THESE words stayed the panic, and all who were not wounded or hurt by the fallen mast, were at their stations, as calm and statue-like as though their vessel had been in port.

Such is the effect of discipline.

Men who had been first in a frantic rush at the boats, now had time to reflect, and discovered that the danger was not so imminent as it at first appeared.

The vessel was stationary.

The waters were not sufficiently disturbed to move the massive hull.

The captain glanced at his now quiet deck, and pointing towards the War Cloud, said—

"Give that fellow a taste of the long gun for'ard."

"Ay, ay, sir, we will."

"That's right, my lads. Fire away. Where is the carpenter?"

"Here, sir."

"Go below, and see what damage is done."

The guns now began to belch forth fire and

smoke; and the captain, as calmly as though he were saluting another vessel, continued—

"Clear away that broken mast. Well, carpenter?"

That personage rushed up to the captain's side when he was giving the order for the broken spar to be cut away.

"A plank bulged in, sir."

"Well?"

"She is filling, sir."

"Nonsense."

"I——"

"Curse the fellow!" thought the officer, "his long face will spread another panic. Then aloud, "You what, eh?"

"I do not think we can stop the leak, sir."

"Go below again and do so. Are there any holes?"

"No, sir, only a beam splintered."

"Away with you, and patch it up."

"Lieutenant!"

This was to his first officer, who touched his hat in reply.

"Keep them fellows amused for'ard with the guns."

"Is she filling, sir?"

"Yes, but keep the hands from being confused, and all, I hope, will be well."

The first lieutenant went for'ard, and between each salvo from the guns kept up an imaginary bit of damage sustained by the War Cloud.

The officer affected to see this through his glass, and the men in their excitement forgot the perilous position of the noble vessel.

The War Cloud's masts and spars were shattered, but the vessel still came round, her guns vomiting their iron hail, and above the smoke could be seen Midshipman Tom nailing the Union Jack to a broken mast.

By the time he had done this the War Cloud closed and grappled her foe; then he appeared at the head of the hardy boarders, and in less than ten minutes the famous L'Aigle had struck to the gallant outlaw.

That evening Midshipman Tom went into port under the heavy guns of the English men-of-war with his prize in tow, and in the hold safely manacled was Red Hand, the pirate.

And the crews of the men-of--war, when they knew this, manned the yards, and gave the little War Cloud and her crew a round of hearty cheers.

"Massa Tom," said Snowball, when our hero was preparing to go ashore; "Ben gib me dese papers, me tink dey have suffing to do with you."

Tom took the packet, and began carelessly to read the first of the papers, and his face alternately paled and flushed as he became interested in their contents.

"Lower the boat!" he exclaimed suddenly, "and place a cloak in the stern."

"Yes, Massa Tom."

"Why this hurry?" Mr. Mordan asked. "Has anything unforeseen taken place?"

"I go," said Tom, "to pay my duty to my father, and place the proofs of my birth in his hand."

"The end has come sooner than I anticipated," said Mr. Mordan, "go my boy, and may success attend you; but may I ask where you are going?"

"To Mountsteven Castle."

Tom was quickly rowed ashore, and throwing his cloak over his uniform, made his way to the castle.

Stalking haughtily past the domestic he went towards the corridor, and before he had traversed its length the forms of Lady Mountsteven and Margarie caused him to take refuge in one of the rooms.

He heard their conversation, and when the beautiful demon said the papers were lost he startled her by the utterance of a single word—

"Here!"

Quick in action, he at one saw his safest plan would be to endeavour to lead the lady and her accomplice to the beach, and send them on board his vessel.

They followed him down the rugged path, intent upon his destruction; but the Nemesis had at last come upon them—a false step made in crossing the most dangerous part of the rock precipitated them in the surf below.

A wild shriek and the two guilty women passed from this world to answer for their crimes before a higher tribunal than man's.

* * * * *

There is little more to be told, and that little can be explained by a paragraph taken from a newspaper of the time; it was worded thus—

"A ROMANCE IN REAL LIFE.—The notorious outlaw and deserter known as Midshipman Tom has been pardoned for his past offences by the King, who, in consideration of his exploits, has been graciously pleased to give him the rank of Captain, and a herculean African the rank of Lieutenant in the Navy, the crew, of course, being rated as able seamen.

"The vessel, renowned for its speed, is to be employed in the Channel against the French privateers, and judging by the young commander's former deeds, we shall soon hear less of the mischief caused by these active gentry.

"A certain Captain Dragon and a vessel named the Thunderer, under letters of marque as a privateer, sails with the young Captain.

"The romantic portion of the story is this: the young Captain turns out to be the son and heir of the Lord of Mountsteven, and great preparations are being made at the Castle to celebrate the nuptials of the young Naval Lord with the wealthy young heiress, Miss Laura Grey.

"The next piece of startling intelligence we have to impart, and can vouch for the truth, is this :—A supposed gipsy woman, known to many of our readers as 'Sybil,' turns out to be the mother of the young lord, and the first wife of Lord Mountsteven, who, disguised as a gipsy, took up her abode near the Castle, of which she was in reality the mistress.

"What became of the second Lady Mountsteven the public are well aware—she fell by accident into the sea.

"Possibly it was for the best, for had she lived, it is said, a long lawsuit would have been the result before the young lord could have established his claim, or his lady mother hers.

"We may add that Lord Mountsteven is very proud of his gallant son, and intends to accompany him upon his first cruise against the enemy's privateers."

From a London paper we extract this paragraph :—

MYSTERIOUS DISAPPEARANCE.—The well-known firm of Messrs. Wirely and Son, ship brokers, has afforded matter for much comment in the commercial circles of London, in consequence of their sudden disappearance. A man, whose dress betokens him a mariner, came to our office, and said that Mr. Wirely and his son had been carried off and taken on board ship, to be placed on a lonely island in the South Pacific; but as the Messrs. Wirely were several thousands in debt when they so strangely disappeared, we are inclined to believe the sailor's story to be a yarn, and the facts of the matter are—the ship brokers, finding they could not meet their engagements, 'bolted' to evade their creditors."

The newspapers were wrong, the sailor's story ight, for Tom Mordan gave the estimable pair an opportunity of exploring the beauties of the island he had dwelt upon so much against his will.

One more extract and we prepare our readers for our future story :—

GRAND BALL ON BOARD THE FLAGSHIP.—Among the distinguished company we noticed Lord and Lady Mountsteven, Captain Mountsteven and his bride, Captain Dragon, the gallant commander of the famous Thunderer, Lieutenant Wilson-Wilson, the brave second officer of the War Cloud, who cut out and captured from under the guns of Brest the enemy's gun brig, La Vengeance.

Lieutenant Wilson-Wilson, kind reader, is your old friend, Snowball; this is how he came by the name.

"All berry well, Massa Tom—no, Captain Mountsteven, beg pardon—but what de debbil use ob de King giving me de rank ob lieutenant ?"

"Why not, Snowball ?"

"I tell you dat it not sound de ting to say Lieutenant Snowball, and as I hab no order name I—"

"Here's a name for you," said Tom, laughing, "I will give you mine. Suppose you call yourself Wilson-Wilson, that will sound well."

"De berry ting, but you sure you not want it."

"No," said our hero, "it was but a borrowed name, but very useful when I was simple Midshipman Tom."

"Three cheers for Captain Mountsteven," said Snowball, we beg pardon, Wilson-Wilson, "and six for Midshipman Tom. Dat right, boys ; again.

"Thanks," said our hero, "I am grateful to you, and wish you always to remember though fortune has given me my proper name, I shall always be to you the same, as when I was the outlaw, MIDSHIPMAN TOM."

[THE END.]

www.ingramcontent.com/pod-product-compliance
Lightning Source LLC
Chambersburg PA
CBHW080819020726
47501CB00009B/2340

9781535807401